The Shadow of an Ass

The Shadow of an Ass

PHILOSOPHICAL CHOICE
AND AESTHETIC EXPERIENCE
IN APULEIUS' *METAMORPHOSES*

Jeffrey P. Ulrich

UNIVERSITY OF MICHIGAN PRESS

ANN ARBOR

Copyright © 2024 by Jeffrey P. Ulrich
All rights reserved

For questions or permissions, please contact um.press.perms@umich.edu

Published in the United States of America by the
University of Michigan Press
Manufactured in the United States of America
Printed on acid-free paper
First published November 2024

A CIP catalog record for this book is available from the British Library.

Library of Congress Cataloging-in-Publication Data

Names: Ulrich, Jeffrey P., author.
Title: Shadow of an ass : philosophical choice and aesthetic experience in
Apuleius' Metamorphoses / Jeffrey Ulrich.
Description: Ann Arbor : University of Michigan Press, 2024. | Includes
bibliographical references and index.
Identifiers: LCCN 2024024820 (print) | LCCN 2024024821 (ebook) |
ISBN 9780472133567 (hardcover ; acid-free paper) | ISBN 9780472221929 (ebook)
Subjects: LCSH: Apuleius. Metamorphoses. | Apuleius—Appreciation—History—
To 1500. | Reader-response criticism. | LCGFT: Literary criticism.
Classification: LCC PA6217 .U47 2024 (print) | LCC PA6217 (ebook)
LC record available at https://lccn.loc.gov/2024024820
LC ebook record available at https://lccn.loc.gov/2024024821

Cover illustration: Lanuvium Actaeon, second century CE.
Photograph © Trustees of the British Museum, reproduced with permission.

To Allie,
animae dimidium meae,
my beloved wife and best friend for life

Contents

Acknowledgments		ix
List of Illustrations		xiii
Texts, Translations, and Abbreviations		xv
Introduction: Encountering the Silenic and Sirenic Socrates		1
ONE	Setting the Stage for Apuleius	43
TWO	Reading as a Choice in the Apuleian Corpus	85
THREE	Entranced by the Mirror of Myth	137
FOUR	Visualizing the Goddess	197
FIVE	Paradigms of Life	247
Epilogue: Asinine Priest, "Madauran" Reader		295
Appendix		309
Bibliography		311
Index Locorum		343
Subject Index		355

Digital materials related to this title can be found on
the Fulcrum platform via the following citable URL:
https://doi.org/10.3998/mpub.12867312

Acknowledgments

This book has had a very long period of gestation, starting with its conception as a dissertation project in 2013 and undergoing many phases and iterations from then until now. During this time, I have been quite fortunate to have had a great number of interlocutors and to be sure, I am very much indebted to more people than I can remember or enumerate here. First and foremost, I am extremely grateful to my adviser, Emily Wilson, and to my first readers, Cynthia Damon and Joe Farrell, all of whom supportively shepherded this project through its earliest stages and sharpened my thinking on every aspect of it. I could not have asked for a more nurturing and simultaneously, challenging and intellectually rigorous committee, and for their meticulous reading of my work I am extraordinarily thankful. I would also extend this gratitude to the whole Department of Classical Studies at the University of Pennsylvania, which is one of the most wonderful places to do graduate study out there. I single out, in particular, James Ker, Ralph Rosen, and Peter Struck, who have all generously given of their time to read and discuss issues with me even since I left the program. In addition to the wonderful professors who taught me at Penn, the graduate community there is unparalleled, and I learned a great deal from my fellow students, especially Bill Beck, Kyle Mahoney, Lydia Spielberg, Lara Fabian, Caitlin Gillespie, Charles Ham, Jennifer Gerrish, Marcie Persyn, Addie Adkins, Wesley Hanson, and Amy Lewis.

Beyond my community at Penn, I also had the benefit of a second intellectual home in graduate school, as I had the opportunity to spend a year during my dissertation-writing in Heidelberg, working and engaging with Jonas Grethlein's ERC-group on "Experience and Teleology in Ancient Narrative."

Jonas has been an extremely kind, thoughtful, and generous reader in the long process of writing this book, and I am deeply indebted to him as well to the members of that group, Luuk Huitink, Jakob Lenz, Annika Domainko, and Aldo Tagliabue, for their kind welcome and graciousness as well as their support over the years.

Since my time at Penn and Heidelberg, this book has continued to evolve and develop in different intellectual climates, seeded and reseeded in different soils: first at Haverford College, then at Wellesley College, and finally, at Rutgers University. I am very grateful to all my colleagues from these institutions for their support and intellectual guidance through my time as an itinerant academic and through the tenure process, especially Robert Germany, Bret Mulligan, Deborah Roberts, Radcliffe Edmonds III, Asya Sigelman, Bryan Burns, Carol Dougherty, Ray Starr, Joseph Williams, Emily Allen-Hornblower, T. Corey Brennan, Serena Connolly, Tim Power, Jim McGlew, Bice Peruzzi, and Salam Al-Kuntar. I am exceedingly thankful to have worked closely with Kate Gilhuly at Wellesley, who has been an invaluable interlocutor and a dear friend. Of my colleagues at Rutgers, I offer special thanks to Tom Figueira, Azzan Yadin-Israel, and Lowell Edmunds, who read and commented on drafts of the introduction and chapter 1. Last, I have been fortunate to have wonderful graduate students at Rutgers, who taught me much in a seminar on Apuleius, and some of whom read chapters of this monograph at various stages. Special mention goes to Steve Brandwood, Victoria Hodges, and Tobias Philip for help with formatting and clarity of presentation.

Thanks to Rutgers for giving me a pre-tenure leave and to the generosity of the Università di Bologna, which offered me a visiting fellowship in the fall of 2021. I had the wonderful opportunity to present early drafts of chapters 3 and 5 to the FICLIT Department in Bologna, which very kindly hosted me for six weeks in their library. Special thanks to my friends Lucia Pasetti and Francesco Citti for organizing seminars where I could present this material, as well as to Elisa Dal Chiele and Teresa Torcello for discussing Apuleius and translation with me.

Last, it has been a great joy and honor to spend a semester on leave at the Institute for Advanced Study in Princeton (fall 2023)—an utterly unparalleled intellectual experience. I am grateful for the generosity of the Herodotus Fund and the Martin L. and Sarah F. Leibowitz Member Fund, which supported my stay as I finished most of the final revisions of the book in an idyllic *locus amoe-*

nus. I was also very fortunate to spend my time there in conversation with many amazing interlocutors: Felipe Rojas, Linda Gosner, Anastasia Stavroula Valtadorou, Kathryn Morgan, and Matthew Leigh. One can recognize the traces of their influence particularly on the introduction and final chapter.

Many chapters of this monograph have also benefited from the feedback of audiences and readers at many conferences and work-in-progress seminars, from multiple SCS annual meetings to talks at the Universität Heidelberg, Leeds University, Universität Wien, Universität Bonn, Università degli Studi di Milano, Trinity University, Bryn Mawr College, and Columbia University. I know that all these audiences left their marks on the final outcome, and I am grateful for all of the friendships that have grown out of these events. In the rather small community of Apuleius studies, in particular, I am grateful to Evelyn Adkins and Geoffrey Benson, with whom I have had stimulating conversations on the novel and whose recent monographs have influenced my thinking very much. For insight into Apuleius' philosophical work, I am also indebted to Ryan Fowler—who not only introduced me to Latin many years ago, but also generously read and commented on chapters many years later. And I give a whole-hearted thanks to my dear friend Luca Graverini, whose support and conversation over the years has been invaluable. One can discern his influence on many pages of this book.

Beyond the many public lectures, I am also very thankful for the Second Sophistic Colloquium, a yearly work-in-progress seminar that has been vital to my writing of this book. I am grateful to Larry Kim, Kendra Eshleman, Aldo Tagliabue, and Janet Downey for organizing, and special thanks to Kendra and to Emilio Capettini for thoughtful notes on drafts of chapters 1 and 3, respectively, and to all the other members of the group for helpful feedback: Inger Kuin, Jackie Arthur-Montaigne, Scott DiGiulio, Chris Baron, Bryant Kirkland, Brandon Jones, and Rob Cioffi.

Finally, among my many intellectual debts, I am grateful to my editor at the University of Michigan Press, Ellen Bauerle, and to the two anonymous readers. Ellen has shepherded this book through a lengthy process in the reality of the post-COVID world, and the readers (perhaps in rare form these days) engaged with my work at a great level of detail and with deep commitment. Their feedback was invaluable and no doubt, made this a much stronger book than the one I originally sent them. And particular thanks go to Apuleius himself for writing this glorious novel and allowing me to sit on my golden ass for the last ten years thinking about it.

Of course, my debts go far beyond merely the intellectual, and I have received an incredible amount of support from family and friends over the years. Of my friends, special thanks go to Andy and Jessica Zakhari, Kevin Funderburk, Ben Schellack, Ronnie Middlecoop, Aldo Tagliabue, Patrick Glauthier, Ella Haselswerdt, Nick McAvoy, Niti Bagchi, Pete and Sammy Andrews, Tim Bennett, Anthony Sole, Dave Howland and Vicki Banyard, Father J. Brent Bates and the community of Grace Church in Newark, Bice Peruzzi, and Salam Al-Kuntar, all of whom have gone above and beyond throughout this process in giving emotional and intellectual support (and Ben also in supplying high caliber coffee). I am particularly grateful, though, to my family, who has borne with me in my ups and downs through the many years that I have lived with this book in my head. My parents, Kathy and Gary, my brothers, Matt and Dave, and their families, Tanya, Kellyn, Cooper, and Felix, have been a true gift in my life, and I could not have asked for a more loving and supportive family (though I can guarantee they are more surprised than anyone that I have written a book). I am also grateful to my in-laws, Ed and Linda, my sister- and brother-in-law, Liz and Andrew, and my nieces, Vivi and Lucy, for bearing with me on major holidays, as I would wake up early and write (to their bewilderment). But my biggest debt is to my beautiful and incredible wife, Allie, the joy of my life and my best friend in the world, to whom I dedicate this book. We have traveled a long, rocky, and winding road together, and she has been beside me, holding my hand, throughout.

Illustrations

1   Perseus leading Andromeda down from the rock, Pompeian wall-painting from the House of the Dioscuri (first century CE)   156

2   Actaeon being attacked by dogs, marble statue from Lanuvium (second century CE)   161

3   The Punishment of Dirce, statuary group from the Farnese collection (third century CE)   162

4   The Blinding of Polyphemus, statuary group from Tiberius' grotto in Sperlonga (first century CE)   163

5   Hypothetical reconstruction of statues at Sperlonga   164

6   The Striding Diana, marble statue (first-second century CE)   168

7   The Bathing Diana, Roman mosaic found in Syria (third century CE)   169

8   Judgment of Paris with Naked Venus, watercolor reproduction by Wilhelm Zahn of a lost Pompeian wall-painting   182

9   Judgment of Paris with Stripping Venus, Pompeian wall-painting from the House of Jupiter (first century CE)   183

10   The twelve figures from Isis' *anteludia*   262

11   The nine transformations that appear in Plato's The Myth of Er   264

Texts, Translations, and Abbreviations

For the Latin text of Apuleius, I follow the most recent critical editions unless otherwise noted: for the *Met.*, I use Zimmerman 2012; for the philosophical works, Magnaldi 2020; and for the *Apologia* and *Florida*, Jones 2017. All translations are my own unless otherwise stated. Abbreviations for journals come from *L'Année Philologique*. When I abbreviate the names of classical Greek authors, I follow Liddell and Scott's *Greek-English Lexicon* (LSJ). Abbreviations for ancient texts and names of authors follow the conventions of the *Oxford Classical Dictionary*, 3rd edition.

Other abbreviations in this book are as follows:

AAGA 1   B. L. Hijmans and R. Th. van der Paardt, eds. 1978. *Aspects of Apuleius' "Golden Ass."* Vol. 1. Groningen: Bouma.

AAGA 2   M. Zimmerman, V. Hunink, Th. D. McCreight, D. van Mal-Maeder, S. Panayotakis, V. Schmidt, and B. Wesseling, eds. 1998. *Aspects of Apuleius' "Golden Ass."* Vol. 2, *Cupid and Psyche.* Groningen: E. Forsten.

AAGA 3   W. Keulen and U. Egelhaaf-Gaiser, eds. 2012. *Aspects of Apuleius' "Golden Ass."* Vol. 3, *The Isis Book.* Leiden: Brill. https://doi.org/10.1163/9789004224551

DK   H. Diels and W. Kranz, eds. 1952. *Die Fragmente der Vorsokratiker.* 3 vols. 6th ed. Berlin: Weidmann.

OLD   P. W. Glare, ed. 2012. *Oxford Latin Dictionary.* 2nd ed. Oxford.

ThLG   *Thesaurus Linguae Graecae.* University of California, Irvine, 1972–.

ThLL   *Thesaurus Linguae Latinae.* Leipzig, 1900–.

The Groningen commentaries on Apuleius which I cite in this monograph are as follows:

GCA 1985   Hijmans, B. L., R. Th. van der Paardt, V. Schmidt, C. B. J. Settels, B. Wesseling, and R. E. H. Westendorp Boerma. 1985. *Apuleius Madaurensis, "Metamorphoses." Book VIII: Text, Introduction and Commentary.* Groningen Commentaries on Apuleius. Groningen: E. Forsten.

GCA 1995   B. L. Hijmans, R. Th. van der Paardt, V. Schmidt, B. Wesseling, and M. Zimmerman. 1995. *Apuleius Madaurensis, "Metamorphoses." Book IX: Text, Introduction and Commentary.* Groningen Commentaries on Apuleius. Groningen: E. Forsten.

GCA 2000   M. Zimmerman. 2000. *Apuleius Madaurensis, "Metamorphoses." Book X: Text, Introduction and Commentary.* Groningen Commentaries on Apuleius. Groningen: E. Forsten.

GCA 2001   D. van Mal-Maeder. 2001. *Apuleius Madaurensis, "Metamorphoses." Livre II: Texte, Introduction et Commentaire.* Groningen Commentaries on Apuleius. Groningen: E. Forsten.

GCA 2004   M. Zimmerman, S. Panayotakis, V. Hunink, W. H. Keulen, S. J. Harrison, Th. D. McCreight, B. Wesseling, and D. van Mal-Maeder. 2004. *Apuleius Madaurensis, "Metamorphoses." Books IV 28–35, V and VI 1–24. The Tale of Cupid and Psyche: Text, Introduction and Commentary.* Groningen Commentaries on Apuleius. Groningen: E. Forsten.

GCA 2007   W. Keulen. 2007. *Apuleius Madaurensis, "Metamorphoses." Book I: Text, Introduction and Commentary.* Groningen Commentaries on Apuleius. Groningen: E. Forsten.

GCA 2015   W. Keulen and U. Egelhaaf-Gaiser. 2015. *Apuleius Madaurensis, "Metamorphoses." Book XI: The Isis Book: Text, Introduction and Commentary.* Groningen Commentaries on Apuleius. Leiden: Brill.

INTRODUCTION

Encountering the Silenic and Sirenic Socrates

The Aesthetics and Ethics of Reading

Mais par telle légèreté ne convient estimer les œuvres des humains: car vous-même dites que l'habit ne fait point le moine, et tel est vêtu d'habit monacal, qui au dedans n'est rien moins que moine, et tel est vêtu de cape espagnole, qui en son courage nullement affiert à Espagne. C'est pour quoi faut ouvrir le livre et soigneusement peser ce que est y déduit. Lors connaîtrez que la drogue dedans continue est bien d'autre valeur que ne promettait la boîte, c'est-à-dire que les matières ici traitées ne sont tant folâtres comme le titre au-dessus prétendait.

Et, pose le cas qu'au sens littéral vous trouvez matières assez joyeuses et bien correspondantes au nom, toutefois pas demeurer là ne faut, comme au chant de Sirènes, ains à plus haut sens interpreter ce que par aventure cuidiez di ten gaîte de cœur.

It is not proper to estimate so frivolously the works of human beings. For you yourself say that *the habit maketh not the Monk*, that a man may wear a monk-ish habit who is inwardly nothing like a monk, and that another may be clad in a Spanish cape whose courage has nothing which becomes a Spaniard. That is why you must open this book and scrupulously weigh what is treated within. You will then realize that the medicine it contains is of a very different value from that which its box ever promised: in other words, that the topics treated here are not as frivolous as the title above it proclaimed.

And even granted that you do find, in its literal meaning, plenty of merry topics entirely congruous with its name, you must not be stayed there as by the Sirens' song but expound the higher meaning of what you had perhaps believed to have been written out of merriness of mind.[1]

—Rabelais' *Gargantua*

---

1. Translation adapted from M. A. Screech's *Rabelais* (2006).

Rabelais opens his prologue to the *Gargantua* (1534) with this *captatio benevolentiae* to his designated addressee, Erasmus, who had twenty years earlier written the satirical church reform doctrine, *Sileni Alcibiadis* ("the Silenuses of Alcibiades"). After beginning his prologue with a meditation on Alcibiades' enduring image from Plato's *Symposium* of Socrates-as-a-Silenus-statuette,[2] whose outside layer of "onion skin" (*un copeau d' oignon*) and absurd manners hide beneath their surface a "medicine celestial and beyond all price" (*une céleste et impréciable drogue*), Rabelais implicitly appeals to the other image which Alcibiades puts forward at Agathon's banquet, one which emphasizes the philosopher's oral charms: Socrates-as-a-Siren.

With the visual image of the Silenus-statuette, Rabelais suggests that, just as Socrates' grotesque appearance can conceal hidden truth under its risible exterior, books, too, can hide "higher meaning" under frivolous form and thus, may require readers to "open" (*ouvrir*) them like "a box" (*boîte*) and "scrupulously weigh" (*soigneusement peser*) their contents. The issue at hand, however, is not merely the perennial question about the relationship between content and form—about inner and outer, laughably absurd and profoundly serious. It is also about the ethics of reading, about the capacity of and the necessity for the reader to penetrate beneath the surface and be transformed by the encounter.[3] This is where the alternative sensory experience implicit in Alcibiades' second image comes into play: namely, Socrates' oral or verbal charm. Indeed, as Alcibiades continues his mock-encomium in the *Symposium*, he deploys another "image" for Socrates more fitting than the Silenus-statuette, namely, that of Marsyas, the hubristic satyr who had the capacity to enchant his listeners with music (*Symp.* 215c3). This comparison is quickly revealed to be inadequate, however, since Socrates enchants his audience not with an *aulos*, but with "stripped bare speeches" (215c7: ψιλοῖς λόγοις), and in doing so, leaves them utterly "stupefied and possessed" (*Symp.* 215d5–6: ἐκπεπληγμένοι ἐσμὲν καὶ **κατεχόμεθα**). As a consequence of the philosopher's bewitching power, then, Alcibiades claims he must "flee" from Socrates "as if from the Sirens" (*Symp.* 216a6–8: ὥσπερ ἀπὸ τῶν Σειρήνων) for fear of "grow[ing] old beside him" (παρὰ τούτῳ **καταγηράσω**).

---

2.   Hunter 2004, 11–12 and 129–30, notes the long history of this image, pointing both to Erasmus' allegorical (Christianizing) version as well as to the use Rabelais makes of it in order to anticipate his desired reader (11–12).

3.   In this respect, I am influenced by Booth 1988, esp. 483–89, where he, too, uses the metaphors of nourishment (i.e., medicines) and poison.

INTRODUCTION 3

Returning to Rabelais' prologue, we may note that he, too, transitions from likening his novel to a visual mystery, which must be stripped of its deceptive external appearance, to characterizing it as a bewitching song, which ought to be approached with extraordinary caution. Indeed, Rabelais' ideal reader will not "remain" (*demeurer*) stultified beside his book, "as if by the Sirens' song" (*comme au chant de Sirènes*), but will instead take its enchanting spell as an invitation to interpretation "in a higher sense" (*à plus haut sens*). Simply put, the book poses a threat to the reader—the very same threat which the Siren-Socrates posed to Alcibiades—of luring those who encounter it to remain entranced by its charm forever. In this way, readers run the risk of halting their own forward progress or development if they indulge themselves too much in aesthetic pleasure; or in Rabelais' terms, if they get lost in the frivolous merriment of his novel and remain there, mesmerized forever. The reader Rabelais exhorts Erasmus to be, by contrast, is one who engages ethically with this text, or more precisely, one who exercises restraint in his interaction with it and at the same time, utilizes it to achieve some higher state. Take your time and look beneath the pleasurable surface; but do not take so much time that you are bewitched, stultified, and immobilized—so much time that you grow old listening to its charming voice.[4]

I begin this monograph with a meditation on Rabelais' appeal to the "Silenuses of Alcibiades" not only because this episode from Plato's *Symposium* provides an authorizing force for the emergence and evolution of the genre of the novel in antiquity (and indeed, up through the early modern period); but also and relatedly, because it functions as a programmatic image—one to which I shall return time and again in this book—for understanding the deceptive puzzles and Siren-song pleasures which the North African *philosophus Platonicus*, Apuleius of Madaura, invites us to experience through his novel. Indeed, in Apuleius' *Metamorphoses*, we find a very close *comparandum* in antiquity to Rabelais' studied mixture of high and low—a carnivalesque bawdiness which can nonetheless, for the careful and meticulous reader, conceal medicine or secret knowledge beneath its grotesque surface. As I shall argue throughout this monograph, Apuleius appeals to the aesthetic power of the Sirens across his corpus—from popularizing philosophical lectures and epideictic speeches to

---

4. Nor is such an ambivalent reception unique to Rabelais in the early modern period—specifically, concerning the temporalities of reading. For instance, Moore 2020, 43–108, elucidates the widespread love for and anxiety over the Spanish novella *Amadis in Gaule*, demonstrating both its perceived power for the inculcation of virtue among elites as well as its status as a "wanton book."

his burlesque novel about a man turned into an ass, who relishes food, sex, and forbidden knowledge—as a mechanism to invite *lectores* to experience the diverting deceptions of reading but simultaneously, to challenge them to stay focused on higher interpretation; or in other words, to exhort them to remain *scrupulosi* in the face of his literary-rhetorical enticements.

It is worth noting at the outset of this study, then, that the paths which Apuleius criticism has taken—paths especially well-traveled in the forty years since Jack Winkler's seminal study of the novel as an "aporetic" enigma[5]—have often diverged at precisely this fork in the road. Is this journey narrative of an asinine elite, who is transformed and retransformed under the aegis of a foreign goddess, a serious business with a philosophical or religious moral, merely encased in an external form of frivolous merriment?[6] Or alternatively, is it empty diversion and as such, can we simply enjoy the enticements of this seedy tale guilt-free, perhaps even taking added amusement in Apuleius' satire of self-aggrandizing philosophy or religious fervor?[7] In the former camp, we find interpreters attempting to make meaning out of the comic exterior, either by looking at the "seriocomic" or philosophical traditions which Apuleius may be channeling,[8] or relatedly, by finding a "therapeutic" or social-ethical value to the grotesque tale.[9] In the latter, we encounter critics who pick up on literary texture, intertextual cues, performative displays of *paideia*, elements of Milesian ribaldry and comical parody, or even satire of religious authorities as charlatans.[10] What goes overlooked in all of this jockeying between serious and satirical schools of reading, however, is the ethics of aesthetic experience—which are crucial, I would argue, in understanding this

------

5. Winkler 1985. For further discussion of his influence on Apuleius studies, see Ulrich 2020.
6. Most extreme in the camp of religious readers are Reitzenstein 1927; Kerényi 1927; Merkelbach 1962. For Winkler's absurdly tendentious characterization of this approach, see Winkler 1985, 242–47. More nuanced treatments of the religious approach can be found in Graverini 2012b; Tilg 2014a; *GCA* 2015; Benson 2019. It is also salutary to recognize that this is precisely the conundrum found in studies of the early modern novel: see Moore 2020, 309–42; Close 2008.
7. Thus, Perry 1926; Sandy 1972, and many readers after them. See esp. Harrison 2000 and 2013a for the most emphatic statement of the satirical view, on which, more below.
8. On "seriocomedy," see, e.g., Schlam 1992; Graverini 2012a; Hunter 2012, 227–46; Tilg 2014a; and *GCA* 2015. For philosophy in the *Met.*, see DeFilippo 1990; Drews 2012 and 2015; Fletcher 2014, 262–93; Ulrich 2017; and Ulrich 2020.
9. For a therapeutic reading, see Benson 2019. For a social-ethical approach to the therapy, see Adkins 2022.
10. On literary texture, intertextuality, and epideictic display of *paideia*: see Sandy 1997; Harrison 2000 and 2013a. On Milesian ribaldry and comical parody, see Finkelpearl 1998 and 2004; May 2006; Zimmerman 2006; and Kirichenko 2010, 163–99. On satire of religious authority, see, e.g., van Mal-Maeder 1997; Murgatroyd 2004; Libby 2011; Harrison 2013a, 81–94 and 109–22; and MacDougall 2016. For pushback on the satirical thread, which recognizes an interplay between sacred images and religious experience, see Laird 1997 and Elsner 2007, 289–302.

INTRODUCTION   5

text.[11] How much time, if any, should we spend enjoying or dissecting this text? Is there a utility, a social-ethical benefit, or a lesson we are to take away from it? Or should we simply flee, like Alcibiades, afraid of being paralyzed and losing the capacity to move forward?

I would like to begin our journey of retracing Lucius' path in Apuleius' *Metamorphoses* by turning to the novel's (potentially) earliest recorded reception from the *Scriptores Historiae Augustae*[12]—namely, the invective attack the emperor Septimius Severus (allegedly) makes against his political rival Clodius Albinus in the 190s CE,[13] which is persuasive to his audience ostensibly because it presumes a trivializing view of Apuleius' novel. In this derogatory characterization of Apuleius' first readers, I suggest that we discover not merely a disregard for the "serious" elements of the *Metamorphoses* (though Severus, no doubt, intends such a depreciation), but also an underlying suggestion that Apuleius' Milesian tales are, much like Alcibiades' Socrates in the *Symp.*, a Siren-song from which one ought to flee (or so Severus implies). Indeed, in a letter to the senate reproduced in the *Life of Albinus* (*SHA* 12.12), Severus laments that his seemingly learned and politically savvy adversary, in point of fact, spends the better part of his time "growing old" with Apuleius' novel:

> Maior fuit dolor, quod illum pro litterato laudandum plerique duxistis, cum ille neniis quibusdam anilibus **occupatus** inter Milesias Punicas Apulei sui et ludicra litteraria **consenesceret**.

> It was a greater source of pain [to me] that very many of you thought he should be praised as a member of the literati, when, in actuality, he occupied himself with certain old wives' lullabies, growing old amid the Punic Milesian tales of his friend Apuleius and other such literary trifles.

---

11. On which, cf. Grethlein 2021, whose reading usefully elucidates the entanglement of aesthetics with ethics across antiquity.
12. See Gaisser 2008, 20–21, on the early reception of the *Met.*, who cites a (possibly) second-century CE papyrus (PSI 8.919) illustrating *Cupid and Psyche* as the only other early reception of the *Met.* Cf., however, Stramaglia 2010, who argues for a much earlier dating for PSI 8.919 and an earlier iconographic tradition of *C&P*, which Apuleius is incorporating into his myth. See also Grillo 2023, who convincingly proves, in my view, that Tertullian was already reading the *Met.* within a couple of decades of its publication (on which, see the epilogue).
13. While the letter reproduced in the *SHA* is likely fictional, its "dramatic" date, so to speak, is between 194–197 CE—that is, after the death of Pescennius Niger (194 CE) and either before or immediately after the death of Albinus (197). Therefore, the writer of the *SHA* imagines that North Africans are voraciously reading Apuleius by the 190s, esp. since Albinus allegedly attempted to replicate Apuleius with his own Milesian tales (*Alb.* 11.8).

This attestation has long been cited by critics as evidence that Apuleius' ancient readers, save a few injudicious exceptions (e.g., Fulgentius), did not find anything "serious" or substantial to speak of in Lucius' journey narrative, but by and large, disregarded it as *ludicra litteraria*, just as the *Met.*'s Prologue *seems* to suggest.[14] Otherwise—so the argument runs—how could this attack on a political rival have landed with its audience?

Such a straightforward interpretation of this rhetorical diatribe, however, oversimplifies the problem that Apuleius' "old wives' lullabies" (*neniis . . . anilibus*) pose to his readers and thus, obscures the ways in which the *SHA* deliberately situates Apuleius' novel in a more ambivalent register. Needless to say, the implication of Severus' attack is that Clodius Albinus, as a politically involved citizen, ought to be "occupied" (*occupatus*) with important business of state—*negotia*—rather than wasting his time in self-indulgent frivolity. *Occupatus* is a key word in imperial Roman discourse for how one should (or should not) use one's time. For example, in his treatise *On the Brevity of Life*, Seneca laments the *miseri* who keep themselves "occupied" in superficial diversions, such as rhetorical display (*Brev. Vit.* 2.4: *ostentandi ingenii* **occupatio**), external adornment (12.4: *inter pectinem speculumque* **occupatos**), and even antiquarianism (12.1–4); he lambasts even worse offenders who spend their time *occupati* with contaminating enticements like wine and sex (7.1–3) or gladiatorial spectacles (16.3).[15] One ought to direct one's efforts not toward such frivolity, according to Seneca, but rather, toward contemplating one's own mortality and utilizing it to spur on further philosophical meditation and scientific investigation.[16] At the

---

14. On the allusion to the *Metamorphoses* in the *Historia Augusta* as a uniquely disdainful reference which proves the poor reputation of the novel, see, e.g., Gaisser 2008, 41; Carver 2007, 11–12. Recently, however, Graverini 2012a, 96–100, has made the case that Apuleius embeds the discourse of "old-wives' tales" (*aniles fabulae*) into his Prologue in order to anticipate such an ambivalent reception. Cf. also Tilg 2014a, 89. On the Prologue's duplicity in its promise of uncontaminated pleasure, see §§1.4 and 2.4.

15. For discussion of *occupati* as a buzz-word in *Brev. Vit.*, see Leigh 2012. For its imbrication with *curiositas* across the Senecan corpus, cf. Leigh 2013, 153–58. Many thanks to Matthew Leigh for directing my attention to Seneca's usage of this term. As an interesting *comparandum*, we may note that Apuleius' "Socrates" in Aristomenes' opening *fabula* falls in with Meroe precisely because he is initially sidetracked by the "pleasure of a gladiatorial spectacle" (*Met.* 1.7: *voluptatem gladiatorii spectaculi*).

16. Cf., e.g., Sen. *Brev. Vit.* 19.2–3: "Having left the ground, you want to look back toward [scientific wonders] with your mind! Now, while the blood is warm, the vigorous must strive toward higher things . . . no doubt, the condition of all occupied people is wretched, but nevertheless, most wretched is the condition of those who do not even labor in their own occupations, who sleep according to another's sleep and walk by another's gait" (*Vis tu relicto solo mente ad ista respicere! Nunc, dum calet sanguis, vigentibus ad meliora eundum est . . . Omnium quidem* **occupatorum** *condicio misera est, eorum tamen miserrima, qui ne suis quidem laborant* **occupationibus**, *ad*

INTRODUCTION   7

same time, however, Apuleius and his immediate contemporaries use the term in a more overtly utilitarian sense: according to Apuleius' usage in the *Apologia*, for instance, an elite Roman male ought to spend his time "occupied with business" (e.g., *Apol.* 25.3–4: *negotiis occupatum*),[17] or alternatively, "occupied in learning" (*Apol.* 16.11: *discendo occupatus*).

Of course, Severus' attack relies on the notion that Albinus is prodigally wasting his time in the Senecan sense. However, the substance of the trifles with which he "grows old" is likewise ambivalently interpreted in literary-critical and philosophical discourse. As Luca Graverini has demonstrated, "old wives' tales" has a long lineage as a phrase in literary polemics "to identify a lower and contemptible kind of narrative, which has nothing to teach superior minds in search of philosophical truths."[18] Of particular importance for this literary history, according to Graverini, is the closing *mythos* of Plato's *Gorgias*, where Socrates tells a tall tale about the condition of the soul after death—a story which he calls "a very beautiful *logos*" (523a1: μάλα καλοῦ λόγου), but which he fears his interlocutor Callicles will disdain "as if an old wives' tale" (*Gorg.* 527a5–6: μῦθος . . . ὥσπερ γραός). We may add to Graverini's literary history, furthermore, that Socrates has this fear chiefly because of Callicles' brutal attack against philosophy as "nonsense" earlier in the dialogue (*Gorg.* 482–86). Indeed, Socrates' realpolitik interlocutor in the *Gorgias* disparages the whole project of *philosophia* as fitting only for young people insofar as it is beneficial "for the sake of education" (485a5: παιδείας χάριν) and as such, is a perfectly "charming" thing for one to "engage in with moderation during one's youth" (484c6: μετρίως ἄψηται ἐν τῇ ἡλικίᾳ); however, if one "philosophizes beyond one's youth" (484c9: πόρρω τῆς ἡλικίας φιλοσοφῇ)—that is, when one "is already old" (485a6: ἤδη πρεσβύτερος ὤν)—it is "laughable" and it is necessary to call out the "silly talk" (486c7: ληρήματα) and "nonsense" (φλυαρίας) for what it is. Simply put, in a dialogue devoted to discovering the just ends of sophistic rhetoric, the entire activity of *philosophia*, which Seneca was to advocate as the only

---

alienum dormiunt somnum, ad alienum ambulant gradum). This, too, intersects with the discourse of *curiositas* insofar as Seneca uses the term *alienum* (on which, see §§2.1 and 2.3). On Lucius' comic failure to appropriately negotiate between occupation and philosophical self-reflection, see §2.5.

17. We may also compare this usage with the phrasing of Gellius' programmatic statement in the opening of *Noctes Atticae*: the antiquarian excerpts Greek texts, he explains, in order to "free those already occupied in other businesses of life from a deeply shameful and rustic ignorance of matters and words" (*NA praef.* 12: *homines aliis iam vitae negotiis occupatos a turpi certe agrestique rerum atque verborum imperitia vindicarent*).

18. Graverini 2012a, 97.

8 THE SHADOW OF AN ASS

appropriate pursuit with which to "occupy" one's time in the Roman imperial context, is given a strictly demarcated age-restriction by an interlocutor focused on utility, political expediency, and practical outcome. In view of the long history of polemic against *aniles fabulae*, then, Severus' attack on his adversary for being "occupied with old wives' lullabies" suggests that Albinus' behavior is questionable because it is not proper for a Roman elite of a certain age, especially for one who is *meant* to be engaged in politics.

This brings us, finally, to the last significant element of Severus' invective. For he does not complain merely that Albinus *reads* Apuleius, but more specifically, that he "grow[s] old amid [his] Punic Milesian tales" (*inter Milesias Punicas Apulei sui . . . **consenesceret***), where the verb *consenescere* seems also to highlight the inappropriateness of a grown man engaged in such trifles and in fact, activates a parallelism between Apuleius' novel and the ambivalent Siren-Socrates. In support of this latter point, we may note that Alcibiades' flight from Socrates in the *Symposium* is the *locus classicus* in the Greek tradition for an encounter with the Sirens that ends—*not* in death, as in Homer (*Od.* 12.45–46)—but in paralysis;[19] or in other words, only the encounter with the Siren-Socrates leads to aging ceaselessly in the presence of the aesthetic object of speculation. Even more to the point, the precise phrase Alcibiades uses to express his fear of being immobilized next to Socrates—"to grow old beside him" (παρὰ τούτῳ **καταγηράσω**)—is translated in imperial Latin with the very same verb which Severus uses in his invective: *consenescere*. So, in a discourse on learning logic (*NA* 16.8), Aulus Gellius warns that a little knowledge can give birth to a "certain insatiable pleasure of learning" (*NA* 16.8.17: *quaedam discendi voluptas insatiabilis*), which presents to a student the "danger" of "growing old" (***consenescas***) in philosophical twists and windings "as if among the Sirens' rocks" (*tamquam apud Sirenios scopulos*).[20] Even more striking, in fact,

---

19. See, e.g., Hunter 2018, 211: "'Growing old beside Socrates': this is a new vision of the victims of Homer's Sirens—after old age will come wasting and death, unless the gods grant, as some said they did to Tithonus, metamorphosis into a cicada."

20. On *consenescere* as a gloss on (συγ)καταγηρᾶσαι, see *ThLL* 4.0.387.84. On its meaning in the Gellius passage, see *ThLL* 389.24–32, where it is glossed under a specialized usage *de hominibus qui in aliqua re nimis diu commorantur*. See esp. *Inst. Or.* 9.4.112–13, where Quintilian attempts to save "oratory" from "growing old in measuring out feet and counting syllables" (*dimetiendis pedibus ac perpendendis syllabis **consenescat***), since only the "wretched" (*miseri*) are "occupied in the least important things" (*in minimis occupati*) and thus, avoid weighty content. Cf. also *Inst. Or.* 12.11.15–16, where the orator laments that people "spend so much labor in fictional things" (*tantum laboris in rebus falsis consumere*), such as declamation in school, that they fail to move on with their lives: he voices this anxiety, as he explains, "because one should not grow old in one species of practice" (*quia non in una sit [sc. exercitationis] specie **consenescendum***). Both instances

INTRODUCTION 9

is Gellius' discourse at *NA* 10.22, in which he reproduces in Greek the entirety of Callicles' rant against the study of philosophy from the *Gorgias* (discussed above) in order to demonstrate a distinction between "true philosophy," on the one hand, which teaches the "discipline of all virtues" (10.22.24: *virtutum omnium disciplina*), and a "puerile obsession with witty chit-chat" (*puerili meditatione argutiarum*), on the other, with which self-aggrandizing, performative philosophers "grow old in their vain idleness" (**consenescunt** *male feriati*). In other words, Severus couches the encounter with Apuleius' novel in the imperial (and Platonizing) discourse about appropriate and inappropriate responses to aesthetic-philosophical experiences, and in so doing, makes an implicit distinction between legitimate and illegitimate avenues for acquiring knowledge, between seemly and unseemly "occupations." In the end, however, the anxiety over encountering the Sirens is derived from a fear of immobilization—a fear of the loss of one's agency and capacity for choice, and in turn, a halting of forward progress. Fully realizing the metaphorical thrust of Severus' rhetorical diatribe, then, we may say that Albinus made the opposite choice from Alcibiades in deciding to "grow old" beside Apuleius' trifles rather than occupy himself with other activities more "useful" for an elite Roman.

As I suggested above, the paths of Apuleius criticism have diverged precisely at the intersection of Severus' portrait of his rival, in part, because the *Met.*, in its deliberately ambivalent Prologue, appears to demand more from its reader while simultaneously emphasizing its own frivolity.[21] The Prologue speaker famously ends his *captatio benevolentiae*, for instance, with the phrase, "reader, pay attention; you'll be happy you did" (*Met.* 1.1: *lector intende: laetaberis*). And although the "contract" this Prologue negotiates with its reader seems to promote a purely pleasurable or diverting experience,[22] the narrator perpetually lures us into a more active engagement with the text by breaking the fourth wall and explicitly addressing his *lector scrupulosus* (*Met.* 9.30)—by exhorting his reader, just as Rabelais does, to look deep beneath the surface and penetrate the superficiality.[23] Moreover, while my discussion of the "deliberate

---

from Quintilian are thus concerned with appropriate usage or occupation of time and energy in education.

21. For an older, pre-Winklerian recognition of Apuleius' play with the reader, see Kenny 1974; and Svendsen 1978, both of whom I aim to recenter here. For updated discussion, see Kirichenko 2008b.

22. For discussion of the Prologue's "contract," see, e.g., the essays in Kahane and Laird 2001, and esp. Slater 2001 for the language of a "contract." For further discussion of the Prologue, see §§1.4 and 2.4.

23. Cf. Kirichenko 2008b for a useful discussion of the anticipation of the reader in the *Met.*

ambivalence" of Apuleius' novel may appear on its surface similar to Winkler's *aporia*—the "exquisite ambiguity" which refuses to impose a definitive solution on the hermeneutic "games" the *Met.* plays—I would submit that it is, on the contrary, an attempt to recapture an ancient understanding of *aporia*: a Platonic *aporia* meant to engage and challenge its readers through dialectic and thereby, educate them rather than the poststructuralist *aporia* in which theorists of the 1980s reveled.[24]

Indeed, this book is first and foremost about reading, about what a text does to its reader and how it implicates—or we may even say, infects—anyone and everyone who comes into contact with it. The premise of this book is that reading ultimately requires a choice (for which, I leverage the full lexical range of the Latin verb *legere*)[25] and therefore, that engaging with a text invites a particular response or perhaps, a set of responses. For while much excellent work has already been done on the way in which Apuleius interacts with his readers through narrative play, metafiction, and intertextuality, scholars have too often neglected to situate the *Met.* in its own culture(s) of reading and in contemporaneous discourse(s) about philosophical approaches to reading.[26] In this monograph, therefore, I argue that Apuleius, in his studied composition of the *Metamorphoses*, participates in a reader-response movement,[27] which begins with Plato but virtually explodes in the imperial period and Second Sophistic, and which aims to reconceptualize textual engagement itself as a serious enterprise requiring a choice. According to first- and second-century CE articulations of this ancient reader-response theory, reading itself is a crossroads encounter with aesthetic pleasure and one must choose to *make* meaning out of the seductions of a text in order to follow the more correct—or more precisely, heroic—path. Importantly, however, this model of divergent paths also involves an ethics and a temporality. An ethical choice can be a two-roads-diverged,

---

24. For a newfound appreciation for the way in which Plato manipulates his readers in their journey through his educative and dialectical labyrinth, see Collins 2011 and 2015, as well as Cotton 2014. On Apuleius' calculated replication of this procedure in the *Met.*, see Ulrich 2020 and 2022.

25. See OLD, s.v. **lego** 5, 6, 7, and 8.

26. Graverini 2012a offers the most thorough situating to date of the *Met.* in its broader intellectual culture. Cf. also Kirichenko 2010, esp. 87–105, who acknowledges a richer reading culture but ultimately prefers to focus on entertaining elements of mime (e.g., Apuleius as "stand-up comedian"). Tilg's solution of the *Met.* as a "philosophical novel" of the caliber of Voltaire or Murdoch is interesting but anachronistic (Tilg 2014a). On the *Met.*'s relationship to its own world of Middle Platonism, see Moreschini 2015, 59–115; Ulrich 2023.

27. I do mean to invoke as a *comparandum* to ancient reader-response the style of criticism of the same name from the 1970s and 1980s—specifically, the version which grew out of the "School of Constance" (on which, see §0.2 below).

INTRODUCTION 11

momentary and permanent decision—a once-and-for-all choice with simple aspect. However, most ethical choices—and especially, those posed to us in carnivalesque texts such as Rabelais' *Gargantua* or the *Met.*—have progressive-repeated aspect and must therefore be made iteratively. Using the language of the most explicit "conversion" or choice-narrative of antiquity, Augustine's *Confessions*, we can follow the voice telling us to "pick up and read" (*Conf.* 8.12.29: *tolle lege*) and thereby, make that one-time, crossroads decision; but also like Augustine, we may feel the pull of aesthetic (or even erotic) pleasure tugging at our garments, drawing us back to sit beside the text and revel in its more illicit diversions.

I have entitled this monograph *The Shadow of an Ass* after an episode at the close of book 9, which I suggest is representative of the way in which Apuleius inscribes his readers into his novel. At this point in the *Met.*, Lucius-ass is under the care of a lowly gardener who has just had an altercation on the road with a soldier, stolen his sword, and made off to a friend's house to hide. The gardener and his friend tie Lucius-ass up and stash him away in an upper room with a window; and the gardener then hides himself in a "little box" (9.40: *cistulam*). When the soldier arrives with some fellow soldiers to search the house under false pretenses, they find no evidence of the gardener and his ass inside, and a loud quarrel breaks out between the group of soldiers and the gardener's friend. At the sound of this dispute, Lucius' curiosity is piqued and so, he "twists his neck out through a certain small window in his desire to see what the hubbub means" (9.42). By chance, one of the soldiers, "directing his eyes askance at [Lucius'] shadow" (*conlimatis oculis ad umbram meam*), notices it and points it out to his companions. In response, the soldiers reenter the house, at which point, they "look at everything more carefully" (**scrupulosius** *contemplantes singula*), "discover the casket," and haul the gardener off to jail to face the death penalty. Despite the somber end for the gardener, however, the episode concludes with ribald laughter at Lucius' "peeping" (*prospectum*) and with Lucius-auctor explaining to us readers that this incident occasioned the birth of a well-known proverb (*Met.* 9.42):

Unde etiam de prospectu et **umbra asini** natum est frequens proverbium

From here was also born that oft-cited proverb about the peeping of the ass and his shadow.

Commentators have noted that Apuleius cleverly blends two different proverbs here.[28] He likely inherited the first from his Greek model, since a similar incident occurs in the pseudo-Lucianic *Onos* and there, the episode likewise concludes with uncontrollable laughter and with the birth of one of the sayings: "from the peeping of an ass" (*Onos* 45: ἐξ ὄνου παρακύψεως; cf. *de prospectu . . . asini*). The scene in Apuleius differs from the Greek *Onos*, however, in two respects: the soldiers enter the house only once in the pseudo-Lucianic text and only after seeing Loukios (rather than his shadow); and secondly, the proverb— "the shadow of an ass" (*umbra asini*)—seems to be an Apuleian addition and in my interpretation, represents a pointed statement about how one is to encounter this text.[29] In its classical usage, the expression "concerning the shadow of an ass" (περὶ ὄνου σκιᾶς) seems to allude to something that is not worth fighting over. Aside from attestations in Aristophanes' *Wasps* (191) and Plato's *Phaedrus* (260c7), the proverb is connected by a scholiast to an argument made by Demosthenes, in which the orator implies that the substance of an argument is lost when people clash over mere shadows.[30]

Apuleius has done something quite innovative, however, in adding the shadow to this closing episode of book 9, one of the most burlesque books of the whole novel. For the soldiers enter the house and find nothing; then, after one soldier catches sight of a shadow out of the corner of his eye, the whole group of soldiers analyze the inside of the house "more scrupulously" (*scrupulosius*). Only after more careful investigation do they open the "casket" and find what they are looking for. In my view, this seemingly frivolous episode models in miniature the approach to reading that Apuleius provokes from his *lectores scrupulosi*.[31] On the one hand, though Winkler (surprisingly) overlooks the episode, it inscribes into the text his model of "first" and "second" reading, where the soldiers come up empty-handed in the first inspection only to discover what they are looking for after glancing at shadows. In this respect, we will see in §0.3 how the invitation to

---

28. See, e.g., *GCA* 1995, 353–54 *ad loc.* 236, 7–8.

29. Cf. Brancaleone and Stramaglia 2003, 117, who note Apuleius' intervention and creative reworking of a proverb as "un altro 'pastiche,' originale e maliziosamente ironico nella sua allusività," but do not attempt to interpret its significance.

30. According to the *Suda* (O 400), the proverb also occurred in other lost plays, such as Sophocles' *Cedalion* and Aristophanes' *Daedalus*; and Zenobius claimed that it appeared in Menander's *Encheiridion* (*GCA* 1995, 354).

31. So, Hijmans likewise interprets the divergences from the pseudo-Lucianic epitome: "in comparison with the version of the *Onos*, the narrative in the *Met.* invites a more active interpretative engagement from its readers—e.g., the irony is to be discovered. Moreover the ass's stupid mistake is more distressing—and an interpreting reader may well notice that the narrator . . . fails to recognise that stupidity" (*GCA* 1995, 7).

INTRODUCTION   13

retrospective reading—what I call "Palinodic reading"—is, in fact, embedded in the notoriously problematic closing line of the *Metamorphoses*. However, Apuleius has also reinterpreted the "shadow of the ass" proverb—a phrase that originally alludes to something not worth fighting over—so that it refers instead to an incident that appears in philosophical terms much closer to Plato's Allegory of the Cave, where the intellectual path from ignorance to enlightenment is mediated by conjecture based on shadows. After all, shadows and reflections in water (*Rep.* 7.516a6–7: τὰς σκιὰς ... ἐν τοῖς ὕδασι τά ... εἴδωλα) are the first stages of "habituation" in the *Republic*, when the philosopher escapes the cave and attempts to behold the Forms. Similarly, the *Metamorphoses* is filled with shadows and reflections, which, upon scrupulous investigation, are imbued with more significant meaning. As we shall see, the ass-man finds images and reflections in the unlikeliest of places, not only in mirroring pools of water (see *Met.* 1.19 and *Met.* 2.4; on which, see §3.2), but inside rocks, trees, and statues (*Met.* 2.1; on which, see §2.5), and indeed, even in the hair of his lover's head (*Met.* 2.9; on which, see §4.3). The asinine *auctor*'s failed attempts at conjecture—as a fettered prisoner in the cave,[32] so to speak—act as red herrings or false flags, which guide us away from the life-changing experience this text can bring about. This monograph is, in short, an exploration of what it would look like if we were to read Apuleius' burlesque novel within its own reading culture(s)—inherited from Plato but refracted through Second Sophistic and imperial Latin traditions—and thus, were to reenter the text in order to analyze all the nooks and crannies more carefully.

0.1. Reading as a Choice: Heroic Responses to Aesthetic Experience

The critical site of contestation in the *Metamorphoses* has been Lucius' surprise "conversion"[33] and multiple initiations to the goddess Isis (and later, to her con-

---

32. We may note another respect in which this episode with the gardener and the soldier differs from the Lucianic *Onos*—namely, that Lucius' "feet are tied up" (*Met.* 9.40: *complicitis pedibus*) before he is carried up the ladder into the upper room. This episode, furthermore, occurs on the heels of Lucius' experience of being bound up in the mill with his fellow beasts of burden, where he makes conjectures about all the seedy affairs of lovers. The inhabitants of Plato's cave, after all, are "tied up by their feet and fettered at the neck" (*Rep.* 514a5–6: ἐν δεσμοῖς καὶ τὰ σκέλη καὶ τοὺς αὐχένας); but Lucius can move his neck, at least enough to peep out of a window and assess his situation. On the influence of the *Republic*—esp. the Allegory of the Cave—on the *Met.*, see Tarrant 1999, esp. 82–83 on *Met.* 8–10.

33. In the interest of precision, I put Lucius' "conversion" (and not all discussion of conversion) in

14 THE SHADOW OF AN ASS

sort Osiris) after he undergoes anamorphosis into a human. Whereas some readers see real transformation in Lucius' commitment to an ascetic life and his newfound affiliation with a religious community,[34] others read theatrical farce or satire,[35] or even an exposure of the way in which greedy religious officials manipulate willing dupes into paying for charlatan performances of ritual.[36] These issues with Lucius' spiritual transformation are further compounded, as critics have noted, by an apparent narrative problem, namely, that his "conversion" is not anticipated in the prior books of the novel through gradual signs of growth and change or indeed, through any apparent dissatisfaction with the carnal pleasures of the ass, as a proper "novel of development" (*Entwicklungsroman*) ought to point up.[37] The Isis book, meanwhile, is generally regarded as Apuleius' innovation on the Greek "model" (*Vorlage*) he ostensibly translates, Loukios of Patrae's *Metamorphoseis*, and is therefore one of the truly original contributions which the Madauran Platonist makes for the popular subgenre of ass-tales.[38] According to this school of interpretation, though, Isis is merely

---

quotation marks throughout this study because I am attempting here to shift the model we deploy to understand this event, on which, see below.

34. Kerényi 1927 and Merkelbach 1962 represent the most emphatic supporters of the religious interpretation. Tatum 1979, 80–91; and Schlam 1992, 113–22, offer more sensible serious readings and the Groningen commentators on book 11 also skew in the direction of a serious or seriocomic interpretation of the Isis book (*GCA* 2015). Cf. also Graverini 2012b for a study of Isis' *providentia*. Philosophical and seriocomic readings, such as DeFilippo 1990; Drews 2012 and 2015; Graverini 2012a; and Tilg 2014a, bring much weight to bear on the meaning of book 11. Recently, Benson 2019, 134–238, has attempted a more nuanced revival of Merkelbach. Adkins 2022 likewise provides a useful ethical reading of discourse in the novel.

35. Farce is already implicit in Winkler 1985. Slater 1998 and 2003 put even greater emphasis on the cynical reading, and May 2006 connects it specifically to the Roman theater. Cf. also Kirichenko 2007 and 2010. See also Constantini 2018, though he deploys a circular argument in service of the "mere entertainment" approach.

36. See Harrison 2000, 238–52, and 2013a, 81–122. For readings that align with Harrison's general assessment, see van Mal-Maeder 1997; Murgatroyd 2004: Libby 2011: and MacDougall 2016.

37. On the problematic issues surrounding books 7–10 as an *Entwicklungsroman*, see Sandy 1974, 235–36. Cf. Shumate 1996, 43–134, for a more thorough treatment of the slow disintegration of Lucius' world (and world view). For a recent discussion of Lucius' hesitation as a possible sign of "development," see Winkle 2014, 126–29. As the Groningen commentators note (*GCA* 2015, 19–21), moreover, Lucius-ass' appetites do change over the course of the closing books with the result that he seems to slowly become more human.

38. The relationship of Apuleius' ass-tale to the Lucianic *Onos* and its *Vorlage*, Loukios of Patrae's *Metamorphoseis*, is an extremely difficult question and one which I make no pretense to address in this monograph. For general treatments, see Mason 1994 and the recent update of Fletcher 2023. Regarding the Isis book specifically, Walsh 1970, 148, considered it Apuleius' truly original contribution, but recently, Tilg 2014a, 1–18, has made the suggestion that Apuleius inherited the element of conversion from his now-lost *Vorlage* (though I find his arguments conjectural and too reliant on an overly literal reading of Photius). Most convincing to me are proposals that see Apuleius' Latin translation of the Greek ass-tale as a mode of cultural mediation (e.g., Graverini 2002; and Rosati 2003), and my contribution, in

hauled in as a *deus ex machina*, a "ballast" of seriousness for an otherwise frivolous and bawdy text.[39]

This is perhaps the reason why Winkler's "aporetic" solution proved so exciting to a generation of scholars perpetually vacillating between the "time-honored antipodes of Apuleius criticism."[40] For Winkler was the first to propose that we need not solve the problem that the novel seems so deliberately to foreground. If readers want the "conversion" to be real, then it can be for *them*; if readers prefer a skeptical outlook, then the text "authorizes" such an interpretation as well—and to be sure, Winkler, though claiming to disavow any definitive solution, leaned decisively in the direction of skepticism.[41] Insofar as readers' interpretations of Lucius' "conversion" constitute a projection of their desires and commitments onto the text, I am fully aligned with Winkler. For my part, however, I would suggest that the seriousness of this text lies not in its claims about the ass-man—that is, whether *his* transformation is "real" or not—but rather, in its influence on its readers, or more precisely, in the ethical quandaries which it foists readers into as they follow Lucius in his journey,[42] whether as curious voyeurs implicated in his male "gaze"[43] or as participating bystanders whose curiosity is aroused by the pleasure of alien fascination or sadistic delight in senseless violence.[44] In this sense, I am far more interested in the choice(s) the text poses to us—that is, in the profoundly ethical *aporia* (quite distinct from Winkler's deconstructionist *aporia*) that we face at the end of a journey marked by burlesque pleasures and a (possibly fraudulent) "conversion" tacked

---

part, is to suggest it represents specifically a philosophical-cultural mediation (cf. Ulrich 2023).

39. See, e.g., the title of Sandy 1978, which encapsulates the pre-Winklerian discussion of the Isis book: "Book 11: Ballast or Anchor?" Cf. also the now-classic statement of B. E. Perry on Apuleius' motive for writing the Isis book (1926, 244–45): "His main object . . . was to give some kind of ballast to what would otherwise have been regarded as an altogether trivial performance. . . . For the sake of respectability he must bring his story to an edifying conclusion, or give it some serious philosophical tendency, or at least the *appearance* of such, which would serve as a sop to the critics and perhaps to his own conscience" (Perry's emphasis).

40. So Tatum 1979, 103, labeled the problem.

41. So, Winkler's essential summary of the *Met.* as a "philosophical comedy about religious knowledge" (1985, 124).

42. Cf. again Kenny 1974 and Svendsen 1978 for useful antecedents to my reading, and esp. Kenny 1974, 187, who notes of the *Met.*'s playfulness: "The levity is intentionally deceptive, for Apuleius' purpose is at times to deceive the reader in order that he may share in the experience of his hero who so frequently misunderstands the situations in which he finds himself." See also Nì Mheallaigh 2009 on the *Met.* as a *fabula de te*.

43. On which, see Slater 1998 and the insightful intervention of Freudenburg 2007. Cf. also Kirichenko 2008b. For further discussion, see §3.2.

44. On excessive violence in the *Met.* and its visceral representation, see König 2008 and Benson 2019, 149–83. Adkins 2022 also notes the intersections of class, gender, and status in the violence of the *Met.*

on for good measure. Simply put, if we do, in fact, adopt a skeptical outlook and consider Lucius a fraud or a dupe at the end of his journey, is it somehow possible for us to recreate that journey through the intermediary of the text without incurring guilt by implication, without also becoming frauds ourselves? Our criticism of the ass-man should also make us feel uncomfortable about our own wanton participation in his journey.[45]

While I tend to agree, moreover, with Thomas Habinek that conversion as a heuristic category is a red herring for us—or as he phrases, that Apuleius scholars have accepted a particular notion of conversion "under the double impetus of St. Augustine and Arthur Darby Nock"[46]—it is nonetheless worth meditating briefly on the important overlaps between the postclassical, Christianocentric phenomenon of conversion and the model I am proposing of a high-stakes ethical choice. For part of the confusion and critical division over Lucius' "conversion" comes from an oversimplification or misunderstanding of what Molly Murray calls the "paradox" of conversion:

> Conversion can be a deliberate, voluntary action, and the passive receipt of the grace of God. It can be incremental and painfully protracted, and it can be instantaneous and cataclysmic. It can be a matter of refusal and rejection, and a matter of intensifying commitments that already exist.[47]

In other words, conversion has different registers and, much like the episodes of choice we shall encounter in the next chapter, there are multiple temporalities involved in these transformations. Conversion (like choice) can have simple aspect, a once-and-for-all change like Saul on the road to Damascus; or alternatively, it can be a process which happens over time, where one is confronted over and over with the desire to change and simultaneously, with the failure to do so. Hence, it does not make a great deal of sense to complain, as

---

45. In this respect, I am influenced by Freudenburg 2007.
46. Habinek 1990, 49, and see further 50: "Critics privilege a term, conversion, that is for them inherently problematical, then marvel that application of the term to the *Golden Ass* yields a reading of the novel as inherently problematical." Cf. also Bradley 1998 for a compelling rejection of the term "conversion" as well as of the Jamesian model which Shumate 1996 invokes. For a recent survey of the debates and a useful rehashing of the intransigent problems of defining conversion, see Despotis and Löhr 2022. See esp. the contribution Herrero de Jáuregui, who challenges the Christianocentric and evolutionary binary between discursive (i.e., credo-oriented) and experiential approaches to describing conversion and initiation, respectively.
47. Murray 2009, 7. Shumate 1996, 285, offers only brief acknowledgement of this paradox in her book on conversion in the *Met.*

some critics do (cf. n. 37 above), that the ass-man—or more precisely, that Lucius-*auctor* who *represents* the ass-man's experience in his narrative retelling—fails to display signs of regret or repentance before book 11, since the imposition of such restrictive expectations on a narrative representation implicitly assumes only one mode of temporality in conversion, namely, gradual change or development over time.[48]

Furthermore, as Nancy Shumate has argued in her valiant effort to retrofit a modern paradigm of conversion (i.e., of William James) onto an ancient "prototype" (as she labels it), conversion is more accurately viewed as a narrative discourse attempting to represent a subjective experience rather than a mere reflection of a specific psychological process that takes place in a subject.[49] Significantly for Shumate, books 1–10 represent a slow epistemic dissolution of Lucius' world view instead of a gradual moral development of his character. The Isis book, according to her reading, thus constitutes not the fulfillment of a change that has already been in progress—an *Entwicklung* rounded off by a dramatic reorientation in Lucius' course of life—but rather a moment of crisis after too many holes appear in Lucius' world view, and a subsequent paradigm shift, which is compatible with her broader analysis of conversion as a narrative discourse.[50]

However, while I am sympathetic to these prior attempts to make sense of Lucius' dedication to Isis *qua* "conversion"—especially, Richard Fletcher's recent revival of the Nockian notion of a "conversion to philosophy"[51]—I would

---

48. And perhaps more to the point, recent theoretical models for "conversion," especially typological and sociological ones (on which, see Rambo 1993), recognize the paradox as inherent to the narrative form, since the change may be slow and gradual, but the experience of conversion or the recollection of that experience may feel sudden. On this issue, see esp. Brandt's contribution to Despotis and Löhr 2022, which surveys different contemporary models to conversion with a view to their temporalities (Brandt 2022, 17–42).

49. See Shumate 1996, 1–39 and 285–328, and esp. 16, for a representative quotation: "in arguing that the *Metamorphoses* should be reconceptualized as a narrative of conversion, and moreover as a (or even the) prototypical one, I mean that its sophistication as a narrative of subjective experience and its grasp and representation of the complex issues of world building that are often at the center of conversion make it unique in antiquity."

50. On dissolution of world view, see Shumate 1996, 43–134. For Lucius' "conversion" as paradigm shift, see Shumate 1996, 310–28.

51. Nock's oversimplification of Lucius' "conversion" rests chiefly on a comparison with contemporaneous sources which seem to promote a "conversion to philosophy" of the sort which Plato first proposed at *Republic* 7.518c–d (see Nock 1933, 164–86). Shumate 1996, 24, identifies Dio Chrysostom's *Thirteenth Oration* and Lucian's *Nigrinus*—the former sincere, the latter parodic—as two ancient tales of "conversion to philosophy" in Apuleius' milieu. For Fletcher's recent revival of the idea of a "conversion to philosophy" to characterize Apuleius' biography of Plato in *de Platone et eius Dogmate*, see Fletcher 2014, 55–67. Cf. now Despotis 2022 on comparing philosophical and religious conversions (relatively) contemporaneous with Apuleius.

prefer to sidestep potential allegations of using anachronistic *comparanda* (e.g., twentieth-century psychology of religion, or the modern genre of the detective novel),[52] or of resorting to a universal, transcultural discourse of conversion. In fact, to circumvent the innavigable strait of defining conversion—situated as it is between the Scylla of sociological analyses of communal affiliation and the Charybdis of theological or psychological approaches to "repentance"—I appeal instead to a more manifestly ancient paradigm for Lucius' spiritual transformation, namely, that of a high-stakes ethical choice, which has deep roots as a theoretical concept in Homer and Hesiod (cf. §1.1), but which, more importantly for us, undergoes an explosive renaissance in Apuleius' milieu (§1.2).[53] In the final analysis, therefore, I suggest it is more useful to view Lucius' complex and iterative encounters with aesthetic, erotic, and religious pleasure in the *Met.* as a simple choice narrative or even a series of choices posed to Lucius (and by extension, to the reader)—choices inherent in the very act of reading and specifically modeled on heroic archetypes.

For beginning in the imperial period and Second Sophistic (first and second centuries CE) and progressing deep into the fourth (and perhaps even fifth) century, authors, both pagans and Christians in the context of a great amalgamation of philosophical and religious orientations, start to theorize about the influence aesthetic pleasure has on those who encounter it, and moreover, about what constitutes an appropriate or inappropriate response to it. In this burgeoning ancient discourse, authors resort with surprising frequency to one of two heroic archetypes as paradigms for engaging with literature or art: Odysseus in his various temptations (i.e., listening to the Sirens, drinking Circe's magical brew, etc.), on the one hand, and Heracles standing at the crossroads, choosing between virtue and vice, on the other. We encounter these heroic archetypes everywhere in the imperial period, Second Sophistic, and even late antiquity: on the pagan side, in Silius Italicus, Plutarch, Dio Chrysostom, pseudo-Cebes, Lucian, Maximus of Tyre, and Themistius, and among Jewish and Christian authors, in Philo, Justin Martyr, Tatian, Clement of Alexandria, Origen, Basil of Caesarea, and Augustine.[54]

---

52. It is worth noting that, in all the glowing appraisals of Winkler's poststructuralist reading, no one seems bothered in the slightest by the anachronism that bedevils his transformation of the *Met.* into a prototype of the detective novel, a rhetorical maneuver that strikes this reader, at least, as a far more fraught *comparandum* than an autobiographical conversion tale (which can, at the very least, be found in late antiquity).

53. Cf. also Herrero de Jáuregui 2022, 410–12, on the influence of the *homo optans* model on early Christian representations of conversion (e.g., in Clement of Alexandria).

54. On the reception of Heracles in the Second Sophistic (and particularly, in Lucian), see Levine Gera 1995. On Odysseus' *Nachleben*, see Stanford 1963 and the updated assessments of Worman

INTRODUCTION   19

Of course, these heroic archetypes of Odysseus and Heracles can be traced, respectively, back to Homer and Hesiod, and I will demonstrate in §1.1 how the two strands of moralizing criticism in the imperial period evolved from precisely these epic founts. What is unique to the first and second centuries CE, however, is the fact that these two heroes are transformed into philosophical models for how to experience and engage with aesthetic pleasure—from the delight of reading or listening to poetry to the ways in which one ought to look at a painting or watch a theatrical performance.[55] The "text," whether it be a written document, oral performance, or visual display, becomes, in essence, the locus of choice. The recipient of this "text" is encouraged, in turn, to use Odysseus or Heracles as exemplary paradigms for reading, listening, or viewing. The ability to withstand the temptations of aesthetic pleasure—to sail by the Sirens, as it were, or to follow Lady Virtue—is articulated in each case as the mark of a true philosopher, of someone with a "philosophical nature," or similarly, of an ideal reader.

The moralizing and even parodic and ironic criticism from the Second Sophistic, therefore, exhorts readers to make a choice about how to read—to choose to be an "Odysseus" or a "Heracles" in their approach to texts. And Apuleius' *Metamorphoses*, I argue, participates in this strand of criticism, not by explicitly doing the moralizing or even by showing its readers an exemplary "conversion" of this sort, but rather by forcing readers into a bind—into a realization that they have participated in Lucius' voyeurism all along, from his bawdy trysts and bestiality to his violent or scatological outbursts against his various masters. Forced into this bind, readers cannot innocently laugh away Lucius' absurdity at the end of the novel without being implicated themselves in the process. As I will demonstrate in §1.3, Lucius embodies, at different points in his journey, the models of "Odysseus" and "Heracles," and in so doing, recapitulates Socrates' and Odysseus' own journeys in the Platonic corpus (on which, see §5.1). It is not the success or sincerity of this "conversion," however, that invites a mimetic reenactment from readers. On the contrary, in my view, it is precisely the problems of "exquisite ambiguity" in Lucius' life choice—the "gaps" which appear between Lucius' behavior and the heroes he models himself on—and the implication of readers in that ambiguity, in turn, which requires *lectores scrupulosi* to fill in those gaps and

---

1999; Montiglio 2011. On the reception of Heracles, in general, see Galinsky 1972; and the updated assessment in Stafford 2012. For further discussion, see §1.2 with bibliography.

55. Cf. Grethlein 2021, 137–256, who also recognizes a particular entanglement of ethics and aesthetics as an anxiety that resurfaces in the imperial period and Second Sophistic.

make meaning out of "mere" *voluptas*. In this sense, Apuleius invites his reader into an embedded choice about how to respond to this text, about whether s/he wants to derive any benefit (*utilitas*) from this otherwise bawdy and carnivalesque journey narrative.[56]

This engagement of the reader, moreover, is thoroughly Platonic in my reading, insofar as it makes the same demands on the reader which Alcibiades imposes on his auditors in his Silenic and Sirenic images of Socrates at the end of the *Symposium*.[57] We can laugh at the ridiculous satyr whose words are dressed up in an ass-hide—this otherworldly human whom we are tempted to statuize, commercialize, and fetishize by putting him in a museum; or alternatively, we can open him up in order to look more carefully at what is inside—conjecturing from shadows, like the soldiers at the close of *Met.* 9, and appreciating the "statues of gods" hidden beneath the ass-hide.[58] It is significant, in my interpretation of Apuleius' Platonism, that the "Socrates" of Alcibiades' speech in the *Symposium* is transformed into a kind of Odysseus *redivivus*, enduring "labors" (πόνοι) in battle and finally choosing a path of virtue and self-restraint when faced with Alcibiades' erotic seduction.[59] Where the *Metamorphoses* is different, however, is in its method of implicating the reader, that is, by showing us a faux-Odysseus and a mock-Heracles—a failure on all fronts, but one that nonetheless exhorts readers to recognize their own complicity in Lucius' inept striving after transformation. At the heart of my project, then, is a question about how one ought to respond to aesthetic experience. Although Apuleius may appeal to a broad range of audiences—from the elite *litterati*, such as Clodius Albinus, all the way down to Perry's "children and the poor in spirit"—he invites sensitive readers, especially his contemporary ancient readers, to create meaning out of learned, Alexandrian reference, to move beyond the elite appreciation of generic interplay in his otherwise lowbrow experiment in the carnivalesque.[60] The

---

56. Cf. Graverini 2012a, esp. 21–38 and 146–54.

57. Only recently has there been a fuller appreciation in Plato scholarship of the way in which the drama of the dialogues invites certain encoded reactions from readers: see now Collins 2011 and 2015; Cotton 2014; Kaklamanou, Pavlou, and Tsakmakis 2020, esp. Finkelberg's contribution; and Kennedy 2020.

58. See Ulrich 2017 for a fuller discussion of the satyric Socrates in Apuleius' Prologue. See esp. chap. 4 below for how Alcibiades' "statues of gods" becomes a leitmotiv across Apuleius' corpus.

59. On Socrates of the *Symp.* as a latter-day Odysseus, see Hunter 2006, 303–5; Montiglio 2011, 38–65, esp. 52–55. On how this famous scene of restraint gets rearticulated (and parodied) in the Latin novels, see McGlathery 1998; for Petronius' *Satyricon*, Repath 2010; for Apuleius, see Ulrich 2017.

60. See Perry 1967, 5, for the quotation. On elements of play with Alexandrianism in the *Met.*, see Sandy 1997. Cf. also Harrison 2013a, esp. 125–270, on the use of highbrow literature to increase

"conversion to philosophy," which Richard Fletcher proposes as a model for reading Apuleius (n. 51 above), can, therefore, be reframed as a simple philosophical choice narrative (or series of philosophical choices), whereby readers are invited to follow Odysseus or Heracles in their pursuit of knowledge, "scrupulously weighing" the seemingly frivolous narrative.

In the interest of full disclosure, I should note how indebted my approach is to Winkler: it represents a twist, though not an insignificant one, on his do-it-yourself narrative. That is to say, I am perfectly content to regard the *Met.* as a "choose your own adventure" provided that we add this caveat: be very careful what it is you choose. Indeed, warnings to be on guard against the corrupting influence of external forces (witches, sex, goddesses, art, etc.) permeate the *Met.*, and Lucius, out of sheer ignorance or downright stupidity, is repeatedly disregarding those warnings. In a text about reading, seeing, and participating—about the dangers and delights involved in doing so—we should never carelessly wander, like Actaeon in the forest, lest we happen upon something we ought not see. The lesson of the text, simply put, is in how it changes you, the reader, or in what you become when you choose to recapitulate Lucius' journey of voyeurism.

0.2. Methodological Issues

Before rehearsing my introductory case studies of the closing and opening passages of the *Metamorphoses* as exhortations to "active reading," it will be useful to lay bare the methodology of this book, which utilizes reader-response theory (especially, approaches to reader-response emerging out of the "School of Constance")[61] and, to a lesser extent, cognitive narratology,[62] and which com-

---

the stature of the otherwise lowbrow novel. On the *Met.* as an experiment in generic blending, see esp. Finkelpearl 1998.

61. For a history of the Konstanzer Schule, from its origins in the phenomenology of Husserl and the hermeneutics of Gadamer to its evolution in "second-generation" reader-response into a "quasi-pragmatic" approach to reading (Stierle 1975) or a broader "sociology of communication" (Gumbrecht 1975), see Holub 2008. The two primary representatives of the Konstanzer Schule are Hans Robert Jauss (1982a and 1982b), whose focus is directed more to hermeneutics and literary history, and Wolfgang Iser (1974, 1978, 1980, and 1989), who is more interested in the phenomenology of reading. My approach is, in broad terms, aligned more with Jauss, insofar as I aim to situate Apuleius' novel in a literary historical model of reading, but Iser's recourse to "gaps" of indeterminacy will also be a useful paradigm for contextualizing the "deliberate incompleteness" Apuleius creates between Lucius' self-representation and the archetypes on which he models himself (on which, see Winkle 2014, 98, and §2.5).

62. For studies in cognitive narratology, see Jahn 1997; Schneider 2001; Zunshine 2006; for a helpful summary of the theoretical movement of cognitive narratology, see Herman 2013.

bines these theoretical models with more recent work in the field of classics on *ekphrasis* and "mimetic contagion."[63] As I provide a comprehensive scan of the heroic archetypes for aesthetic response in the next chapter (§1.2), it will become clear, I hope, that the philosophical and "active" approach to reading, such as it is articulated in imperial Latin, Second Sophistic, and late antique texts, represents an unmistakable forebear to the intellectualized reader-response movement, which became popular in German literary criticism of the late 1970s and early 1980s.[64] As Hans Robert Jauss points out in his *magnum opus*, the ancient divide between merely searching for "pleasure" (*voluptas*) and pursuing some "utility" (*utilitas*) in the process of reading (a philosophical dispute which Augustine would later come to recategorize in aesthetic terms as a distinction between *voluptas* directed at higher pursuits and mere *curiositas* "to experience the opposite [of that which is beneficial]")[65] is bound up etymologically in the very notion of "enjoyment" (*fructus* or in German, *Genuß*), which connotes both self-indulgent pleasure and productive participation.[66] In the ancient discourse of reader-response, however, the ultimate aim of literary criticism (such as that of Plutarch, Clement of Alexandria, or Basil of Caesarea) is not only to produce capable or "ideal" readers, as in the hermeneutically informed and phenomenological approaches of Jauss and Iser, respectively, but

---

63. For a survey of recent scholarship on *ekphrasis*, see below with n. 75. By "mimetic contagion," I refer specifically to Robert Germany's 2016 elucidation of art's role in manipulating its viewer and the extension of that to literature (on which, see also Whitmarsh 2002 and §3.0).

64. I should note here that I am privileging the theoretical model(s) of the Konstanzer Schule (i.e., Jauss and Iser) over the more anarchic American approaches to reader-response, of which Stanley Fish (1967, 1970, 1972), is the primary representative. In large part, this is because I believe the model of extreme indeterminacy Fish endorses is anachronistic and inappropriate for antiquity (hence, my departure from Winkler), and I would submit that the more culturally embedded approach better approximates how ancient readers imagined the process. For other continental approaches to reader-response, cf. Rifaterre 1966 and Poulet 1972. For a comprehensive treatment of the different models and varieties of reader-response, see the edited volume of Tompkins 1980.

65. See *Conf.* 10.35.55: *his contraria temptandi causa*. For Augustine's fuller discussion, see *Conf.* 10.33–35, and esp. 10.33.49, where he links the threat of aural pleasures (such as the Sirenic Socrates) to their capacity to paralyze a listener: "The pleasures of the ears entangled and bound me more persistently, but you released and freed me. Nowadays, I confess, I take some respite in those sounds which your eloquence brings to life when they are sung with a charming and skillful voice, but not, indeed, to the extent that I am stuck, but such that I get up when I want to" (*voluptates aurium tenacius me implicaverant et subiugaverant, sed resolvisti et liberasti me. nunc in sonis quos animant eloquia tua cum suavi et artificiosa voce cantantur, fateor, aliquantulum adquiesco, non quidem ut **haeream**, sed ut surgam cum volo*).

66. See Jauss 1982a, 22–36 and esp. 22: "Until recently, the enjoyment of art was considered a privilege of the much-maligned *Bildungsbürgertum* and tabooed as such . . . the older, basic meaning of *enjoy*, i.e., 'to have the use or benefit of a thing,' is perceived only in obsolete or technical usage." On the dichotomy between the utilitarian and the pleasurable in ancient assessments of Apuleius, see Macr. *Comm. in Somn. Scip.* 1.2.8 (on which, see §5.3).

more specifically, to develop a notion of reading as a provocation to ethical participation.[67]

In the interest of setting out the theoretical commitments of this book, then, it is worth quickly reviewing Jauss' model, which constitutes, in my view, the most clearly delineated paradigm of reader-response. Coining the phrase "horizon of expectation" (*Erwartungshorizont*), Jauss distinguishes three "horizons" of reading, which one could view simply as relative positions vis-à-vis the text (i.e., immersed vs. distanced; first vs. second reading; etc.) and which are based implicitly on the temporalities of reading.[68] According to Jauss, the first reading, being naïve and linear, is perceptual or "aesthetic" and thus, makes sense of a work as a whole without getting bogged down in troublesome details or lingering questions. This corresponds to the type of absorptive reading phenomenologists and cognitive narratologists analyze (e.g., the "production of presence," which Hans Ulrich Gumbrecht identifies as a counterbalance to hermeneutics).[69] We already saw above, to a certain extent, how the early reception of Apuleius depicts the *Met.*'s readers as absorbed or "occupied" in a useless endeavor. When one attempts a "second reading" according to Jauss' model (*à la* Winkler's "retrospective" approach), however, one's position has changed and therefore, new questions arise relative to the first reading. So also, the "horizon" has changed and for Jauss, the retrospective reading, in setting up a search for new meaning or significance, constitutes a secondary stage of "reflective interpretation" or "perceptual understanding."

In the final analysis of Jauss' framework, furthermore, there is a third reading, which attempts to recuperate the significance a given text had for its first readers, that is, an author's contemporaries who encountered that piece of literature within the intellectual culture for which it was intended:

> An interpretation of a literary text as a response should include two things: its response to expectations of a formal kind, such as the literary tradition prescribed for it before its appearance; and its response to questions of meaning such as they could have posed themselves within the historical life-world of its first readers.[70]

---

67. On the "active reader" in Plutarch and the novels, see Konstan 2004 and 2009, as well as König 2007. For a discussion of the "active reader" in Aulus Gellius, see Howley 2018; DiGiulio 2020.
68. See esp. Jauss 1982a, 10, on the "peculiar" temporality of aesthetic experience. For a useful, brief summary of Jauss' model, see Edmunds 2010, 351–52.
69. See Gumbrecht 2004. For a philosophical exposition of "presence," see also Seel 2005.
70. Jauss 1982a, 146.

On the one hand, as we shall see over the course of this book, Apuleius deliberately entangles his readers with aesthetic pleasure and simultaneously, reveals through Lucius-*actor*'s interactions with religious-erotic art the danger which the act of participating in *mimesis* poses to its viewer (or reader), as the boundaries between art and life are perpetually renegotiated over the course of the novel and in the end, are (arguably) completely dissolved. On the other hand, upon a retrospective reading, which I regard as a "Palinode" in the spirit of Socrates' second speech in Plato's *Phaedrus* (§0.3), the gaps of indeterminacy, which arise from incongruity between Lucius' self-representation and the mythological and philosophical paradigms to which he appeals,[71] function as invitations to readers to take a more distanced stance of "reflective interpretation"—or in other words, to be transformed into *lectores scrupulosi*. So, as we shall see in chapter 1, ancient critics advised readers to take a philosophical approach to texts—even powerfully immersive and potentially contaminating texts—and recommended this approach, moreover, in a manner that anticipates the literary-critical gestures of twentieth-century reader-response. However, whereas the terminologies of Jauss and Iser rely on conceptions of the "informed reader" or the "implied reader," respectively—formulations which attempt to transcend the elusiveness of the "ideal reader," but which amount, in the end, to a valorization of their own superior interpretations—ancient critics, by contrast, discuss at length what it means to be an "active" or "philosophical reader."[72]

Where my theoretical approach fully intersects with Jauss' model (and in turn, diverges from Winkler's) is in my aim to situate the *Metamorphoses* in a literary tradition and more specifically, in a culture of reading recognizable to a second-century CE audience. So, in my conclusion, I suggest that the famous metalepsis near the close of the Isis book, in which Lucius is labeled a "man from Madauros" (11.27: *Madaurensem*), is not simply a "literary seal," or *sphragis*, whereby Apuleius peaks his head out to address his audience, but instead, constitutes an overt incorporation of the local, African reader, likely a member of Apuleius' anticipated readership, into the fictional world of the novel.[73] Apu-

---

71. Such inconcinnity between the lofty ideals of poetry and a character's failed appropriation of them in a prosaic context—what Gian Biagio Conte labels "mytho-mania" (Conte 1996, on which, see also §3.0)—is recognized more generally by Jauss as a "pathology of novel reading" (1982a, 7).

72. For discussions of the "active" reader among Apuleius' contemporaries, see n. 67 above. On the evolution of reading praxis and book culture from the Roman to the Byzantine period, see Cavallo 1999 and 2006. Johnson 2010 is seminal on Roman reading culture in Apuleius' milieu.

73. For a long time, scholars assumed that Apuleius' intended audience was "Romanocentric" (on

INTRODUCTION 25

leius thus not only demands philosophical or "active" reading, but he localizes it to his audience.

While I regard the reader-response theory of the Constance School as the nearest approximation to the discourse of the ancient reading culture I strive to recover, I also utilize other theoretical tools—especially, recent work on *ekphrasis* and "mimetic contagion"—to refine our understanding of the different relative stances a reader can adopt toward a text. Indeed, as I suggested above, I view the first phase of Jauss' readerly engagement as similar to the absorbed type of reading that cognitive narratologists connect with "immersive" texts.[74] One can find the same anxieties we have today about absorption (such as the capacity of virtual reality games to shape the lived reality of their players) in the discussions of imperial, Second Sophistic, and late antique readers, who express palpable concerns over the Sirenic seductions of literature (see above and §1.2[a]). The power that rhetorical "vividness" (*enargeia*) possesses to transport a reader to a scene described in a text—or according to ancient rhetorical theory, to "bring before the eyes the scene on display" (Anon. *Segu.* 96: ὑπ᾽ ὄψιν ἄγων τὸ δηλούμενον) and "transform hearers into viewers" (Nicolaus, *Prog.* 68.12 Felten: θεατὰς τοὺς ἀκούοντας ἐργάζεσθαι)[75]—can corrupt or implicate a reader, and can even enact paralysis or metamorphosis through fascination or

---

which, see, e.g., Harrison 1998a) on the basis of a number of Rome-specific references for readers (e.g., *Met.* 1.24: *forum cuppedinis*). Thus, Dowden 1994 proposes that Apuleius, in fact, writes the novel for Roman readers while living in Rome (in the 150s CE), and Rosati 2003, 278, somewhat more cautiously suggests that the narrating-*ego* is addressing a characterized fictive audience of Roman readers. My approach to reimagining an African readership (on which, see the epilogue with bibliography) takes its starting point from the innovative proposals of Luca Graverini (2002, esp. 66–74, and 2012a, 165–207) as well as from the recent move toward reclaiming Apuleius' African identity (e.g., the edited volume of Lee, Finkelpearl, and Graverini 2014).

74. On "immersion" as a discourse borrowed from virtual reality studies, see Ryan 2001 and 2015. On cognitive narratology, see n. 62 above. See also Ryan 2014. For discussions of so-called "second-wave" cognitive studies and the discourse of enactivism and embodiment, see Kukkonen 2013 and 2014; Kukkonen and Caracciolo 2014. For the usefulness of cognitive narratology for classical texts, see Grethlein 2017; Grethlein and Huitink 2017; Huitink 2019; the edited volume of Grethlein, Huitink, and Tagliabue 2020, esp. the contributions of Allan, Grethlein, de Jonge, and Huitink. On the relationship between "immersion" and *enargeia*, see Allan, de Jong, and de Jonge 2017.

75. On this tradition, see the seminal work of Webb 2009, as well as her application of this rhetorical theory to Second Sophistic texts (e.g., Lucian's *de Domo*) in Webb 2016. On the influence of rhetorical *ekphrasis* on literary models of "mimetic contagion," see Germany 2016. Cf. also Huitink 2019 and 2020; and Allan, de Jong, and de Jonge 2017 on the rhetorical tradition of *enargeia*. I do not take a position here on the "pictorialist" versus "enactivist" accounts of vision, though I am inclined to believe that imaginative experience, such as we find in Lucius-*auctor*'s *ekphrasis* of Byrrhena's atrium (see §3.2), is enhanced through the enactivist model (on which, Huitink 2020 is groundbreaking).

"enchantment."[76] For my purposes, this is particularly important in places where *ekphrasis*, the verbal description of a visual object or spectacle, intersects in ancient aesthetic theory with "mimetic contagion," the anxiety about an artwork "transcending its presumed frame as a mere fiction and propagating itself in the world of the viewer."[77] Thus, in chapter 3, we will consider the ways in which Lucius slowly becomes entangled with what he sees, even to the point of fully replicating the role and position of a mythological figure in a statuary ensemble that he encounters early on in the novel. The fact that he describes his visual experiences in fairly explicit terms—and indeed, at the close of the novel, makes an *ekphrasis* of himself for the reader (who, in turn, inhabits Lucius' earlier role)—renders the reader's willingness to succumb to the seductions of this novel a rather fraught endeavor.

In the final analysis, then, I view the *Metamorphoses* as a text that plays with absorbed and distanced reading. It welcomes, on the one hand, readerly abandon to the pleasures of the text, a "transportation to the fictional world" and a witting overidentification with the asinine *auctor*, Lucius.[78] However, at the same time—or more likely, in a second reading[79]—it invites retrospective reflection on that experience through learned inter- and intratextual reference and indeed, through the "gaps" of indeterminacy which arise between Lucius' quixotic representation of his behavior in heroic garb and the reality laid bare by Apuleius' ultimate exposure of the asinine-*auctor*. By virtue of the narrative "vividness" (*enargeia*) and the pleasure of the *auctor*'s description in the *Met.*, readers are made to sympathize with Lucius in the most literal sense: we look at the world through Lucius' eyes and are thus made to feel desire when he desires, made to feel longing when he drunkenly encounters Photis posing as a *Venus*

---

76. Thus, Ryan 2015, 69, identifies "entrancement" (a close analogue to enchantment) as one of the more intensely immersive states of readers. Alternatively, one may speak of the phenomenon of "presence," which Gumbrecht 2004 relates to the more emotional or phenomenological (rather than hermeneutic) praxis of analyzing texts. On "production of presence" in the *Met.*, see now Benson 2019, 239–59.

77. See Germany 2016 for the theorization of "mimetic contagion" and esp. 18, where he links mimetic contagion to ancient rhetorical discourses on *ekphrasis* (on which, see §3.0).

78. For the role of emotions—of "identification" and "empathy"—see, in particular, Schneider 2001, 613–15.

79. There is an open debate in studies of immersion about whether a passage can be immersive and intertextual *simultaneously* and in that same vein, whether one can be immersed and still recognize allusive play. Grethlein 2017, 20–24, for instance, speaks of immersion as "limited and counterpoised with reflection" (20) and thus, sees one type of aesthetic experience as an oscillation between immersion and reflection. I would argue that the cognitive dissonance one is provoked to feel ought to snap a reader out of a straightforwardly immersed or absorbed reading posture (on which, see below).

Anadyomene in his bedroom, or alternatively, to feel a grotesque and alien fascination with the violent and burlesque world of the Greek countryside. The emotional or affective investment on the part of the reader goes awry, however, when we are led unawares into a bestiality narrative with an aggressively licentious *matrona* only to be dragged back from the abyss of perverted pleasure by a vision of a goddess and the transformation of our previously despicable narrator into a religious ascetic. In short, the unlikely companion to readerly absorption is cognitive dissonance, a discomfort which provokes readers to impose a final meaning on Lucius' journey and by extension, on our own willing participation in it. The reader is forced to oscillate between being absorbed in the narrative and taking a reflective distance from the text.

0.3. Calvus Mimicus: *A Socratic Echo in the* Met.'s *(Anti)-Closure*

I begin my study of the *Met.* with an analysis of the novel's closing line, which has long provided a conundrum to readers,[80] but which, in my view, invites us to reread, reevaluate, and reassess the meaning of the whole text. In this sense, I open with a homage to Winkler's intellectualized approach to retrospective reading, but by contrast to Winkler, I locate the exhortation to reread in the text itself, or more precisely, in its self-conscious allusion to the most famous reassessment in all of antiquity: Socrates' Palinode in Plato's *Phaedrus*. According to this reading, Lucius' narrative representation of his "Romecoming"[81] points the reader to Socrates' own choice to uncover his bald head and redefine the terms of his first speech on erotic love, which had previously been contaminated by Lysias' speech at the outset of the dialogue. The *Metamorphoses* concludes in a notorious anti-closure (*Met.* 11.30):[82]

---

80. For a comprehensive discussion (with bibliography), see Finkelpearl 2004.
81. On Lucius' "Romecoming" as a *nostos* of sorts, see Tilg 2014a, 110–11, and more extensively, Graverini 2012a, 165–207.
82. Many have felt that the *Met.* would have concluded more naturally at 11.25 with Lucius' powerful aretology. For this reason, Finkelpearl 2004 labels 11.26–30 an "epilogue," following Winkler's "epi-epilogue" discussion of Lucius' multiple initiations (1985, 221). Recently, Tilg 2014a, 133–48, has made a case for Apuleius' play with literary closure and anti-closure, though I find the connection he draws between baldness and the "polished" papyrus roll (145–48) unconvincing. I do not entertain here the possibility that the line which constitutes our current ending of the *Met.* in the manuscripts is not the original ending (on which, see van Mal-Maeder 1997, 112–17), but rather, I follow Tilg's recent reinterpretation of the paleographical evidence (2014a, 133–40).

Rursus denique quaqua raso capillo collegii vetustissimi et sub illis Sullae temporibus conditi munia, **non obumbrato vel obtecto calvitio**, sed quoquoversus obvio, gaudens obibam.

Finally, with my head once again shaven completely and **with my baldness neither covered up nor hidden**, but exposed wherever I went, I joyfully carried out the duties of that ancient priesthood, which was established in the time of Sulla.

Most readers who encounter this seemingly incomplete ending have focused on one of two apparent problems: (1) the implications of Lucius' baldness (on which, see nn. 84, 85, and 86 below), and (2) the lack of (or even refusal of) closure with the imperfect verb *obibam*, which (incidentally) can also mean "to die."[83] I will return to the latter issue in the final chapter of this monograph (§5.4). But it is worth analyzing Lucius' baldness at the outset because it is paradigmatic for how Apuleius pulls the wool over our eyes, as it were, and still invites us to try to see through it.

Unsurprisingly, Winkler is the first to analyze Lucius' baldness as a signifier of something more than merely an autobiographical joke about Apuleius' alleged hair obsession, but his interpretation ultimately reduces the interpretive outcomes to a binary choice: Lucius' baldness invites the reader to regard him as either (1) an absurd mime actor (i.e., a *calvus mimicus*), or (2) a sincere initiate of Isis cult.[84] More recent interpretations, such as those of Graverini, Egelhaaf-Gaiser, and O'Brien and James posit a third possibility: Socrates' notorious baldness and its semiotic associations with the philosopher and intellectual in the Antonine period.[85] For Winkler (among others), Lucius'

---

83. On the imperfect tense, see Winkler 1985, 224. Cf., however, Penwill 1990, 24n70, for skepticism about the potential of overstating the importance of the imperfect. On *obire* meaning "to die," see Finkelpearl 2004, 329–30. Tilg 2014a, 141–45, reasserts Penwill's suggestion 1990, 24n70, that *obibam*—"to die"—reverses the closing word of Ovid's *Met.* (15.879): *vivam*.

84. For Winkler (1985, 225–27), there are actually four possible interpretations: (1) Isiac devotees shaved their heads to signify conversion (cf. Juv. *Sat.* 6.533; Plut. *De Is. et Os.* 352C); (2) people who escaped from a shipwreck or slavery thanked a god by deracination (see Lucian *Sal. Post.* 1–2; *Hermotimus* 86); (3) baldness is just plain funny (cf. Eumolpos in Petronius' *Sat.* 109.8–10); and (4) the mime-actor (*calvus mimicus*, μῖμος φαλακρός) shaved his head presumably because of (3) (cf. Lucian *Symp.* 18; Alciphron 3.7). Of course, these are easily reduced to a binary in Winkler's system—"an Isaic priest or a popular buffoon" (226)—which as a strict dichotomy is, as Graverini notes, "somewhat artificial" (2012a, 86).

85. Much of this discussion depends on Zanker 1995, esp. 198–266. On specific connections to Lucius' Socratic baldness, see Graverini 2012a, 82–89; Egelhaaf-Gaiser 2012; O'Brien and James 2006. Cf. also Ulrich 2017.

baldness invites the "open" reading, which, in turn, creates a back door through which more cynical conclusions can creep in. Our asinine narrator has not actually changed or lost his *curiositas*, but merely redirected it from magic, sex, food, etc. to a fetishistic religious devotion.[86]

By contrast to these skeptical readings, I prefer to consider what implications the lack of closure has for the reader. To do so, I take my cue from the third possibility—Socrates[87]—but I push the significance of this anti-closural gesture further by linking it to a particular and especially famous moment in Plato's dramatic depiction of Socrates. For despite the scholarly obsession with Lucius' baldness, readers have not remarked on the strange pleonasm with which Lucius highlights his lack of shame in parading his baldness around: *non obumbrato vel obtecto calvitio*.[88] The mere fact of his baldness is interesting, to be sure; but even more significant for what we take away from this ending is the fact that he parades his baldness around so unabashedly.

I suggest that the key to Lucius' emphasis on the uncovered state of his bald head lies in its self-conscious allusion to the opening of Socrates' Palinode in the *Phaedrus*, where the philosopher apologizes to *Erôs* for a previously corrupted speech, and uncovers his head to deliver a reevaluation (*Phaedr.* 243b4–7):

πρὶν γάρ τι παθεῖν διὰ τὴν τοῦ Ἔρωτος κακηγορίαν πειράσομαι αὐτῷ ἀποδοῦναι τὴν παλινῳδίαν, **γυμνῇ τῇ κεφαλῇ καὶ οὐχ** ὥσπερ τότε ὑπ' αἰσχύνης **ἐγκεκαλυμμένος**.

Before I experience some punishment for slander against Love, I will attempt to atone through a Palinode, with my head uncovered and not concealed, as earlier, out of shame.

---

86. For skeptical readings of Lucius' closing baldness and multiple initiations, see van Mal-Maeder 1997; Murgatroyd 2004; Libby 2011; MacDougall 2016.

87. See esp. Egelhaaf-Gaiser 2012. Cf. also Graverini 2012a, 82–89, for an exemplary treatment of the possible interpretations, esp. 89: "Lucius, a shaven-headed lawyer or rhetorician, is suspended between two hardly compatible worlds: the Forum and the temple. His baldness is, as it was for Socrates, an essential feature of a paradoxical portrait, urging the reader toward both laughter and meditation."

88. This doubling is especially interesting considering that, according to the tradition of rhetorical training, the phenomenon of pleonasm was never a mere happenstance gemination of words. See, e.g., Gellius' discursus on the rhetorical function and significance of pleonasm (*NA* 13.25; on which, see Howley 2018, 54–55).

Socrates, like Lucius, frames his bold act of revealing his head as a way to appease a deity who presides over his speech (and in fact, over the whole text of the *Phaedrus*). More importantly, he also uses pleonasm—a "naked" (γυμνῇ; cf. *non . . . obtecto*) and "unconcealed" (οὐχ . . . ἐγκεκαλυμμένος; cf. *non obumbrato*) head—to explain how his change of attire will transform the content of his speech from debased and sacrilegious to transcendent and true.[89] Given the importance of Socrates' speech in the *Phaedrus* for the shape of the *Metamorphoses* and for Apuleius' broader corpus,[90] and moreover, considering that Lucius' bald pate at the end of book 11 already recalls Socrates,[91] it is not inconceivable to think that the *lector scrupulosus* of the second century would hear Socrates' words echoed in Lucius' closing self-presentation.

Significant for my interpretation of the *Met.*, moreover, Socrates' myth in the *Phaedrus* of the enlightened soul, which is given wings through an erotic encounter, redefines the terms of *erôs* by appealing to an intellective and transcendent effect of desire. His refusal to feel shame at delivering his next speech—uncovering his head, which he earlier concealed (*Phaedr.* 237a4: ἐγκαλυψάμενος) out of a feeling of "shame" (237a5: ὑπ' αἰσχύνης) in a gesture reminiscent of Odysseus covering his head to mask his embarrassment before the Phaeacians (*Od.* 8.83–86)[92]—thus invites his audience (both Phaedrus

---

89. We may note, moreover, that at least one of these phrases—"a naked head" (γυμνή ἡ κεφαλή)—seems to have constituted a *Phaedran* "catchphrase" in the Second Sophistic, as it was frequently alluded to or reworked in second-century CE echoes of Plato. See, e.g., Lucian's *Anacharsis*, where the Scythian interlocutor laments having a "naked head" (*Anach.* 16: γυμνῇ τῇ κεφαλῇ) in an excessively hot *locus amoenus* reminiscent of the *Phaedrus*. See also Clement *Protr.* 7.76.6 and Maximus of Tyre's *Or.* 40.6. Trapp 1990, 147, discusses this as a Second Sophistic "catchphrase," which originated in the *Phaedrus*. The adjective γυμνός, furthermore, may have the secondary meaning of "bald," which is translated in Apuleius by *calvitium*. I am grateful to Andrea Capra for pointing this out to me.

90. It is well established that *Cupid and Psyche* is modeled on the journey of the soul, which constitutes Socrates' second speech (Drake 1968; Kenney 1990a; Kenney 1990b; Panayotakis 2001). Likewise, Apuleius quotes the climax of Socrates' speech in the *Phaedrus* at *Apol.* 64, an otherwise understudied allusion (on which, see §4.1).

91. See Ulrich 2017, 723–30, where I suggest that Lucius' position vis-à-vis Isis (as a *simulacrum deorum*) recollects Alcibiades' image of Socrates as an asinine Silenus with *agalmata theôn* underneath. Cf. also Egelhaaf-Gaiser 2012 and Graverini 2012a, 82–89.

92. Odysseus "draw[s] a great cloak over his head" (8.84–85: μέγα φᾶρος . . . /κὰκ κεφαλῆς εἴρυσσε) in order to "cover over his beautiful face" (κάλυψε . . . καλὰ πρόσωπα) because he feels "shame" (86: αἴδετο) before the Phaeacians. It is also worth noting that this episode of Socrates covering his face out of shame is explicitly alluded to in the work of Apuleius' contemporary, Aulus Gellius. Indeed, when a Roman orator (Antonius Julianus) wants to give an illicit speech in Greek about Venus, he asks permission to "cover his head with his cloak" (*NA* 19.9.9: *operire pallio caput*), just as "they say Socrates did" (*Socraten fecisse aiunt*) when he was making a "somewhat unchaste" (*parum pudica*) speech. Julianus implicitly connects Socrates' head-covering to the Homeric episode, moreover, by accusing the Greeks of "outdoing Alcinous" (19.9.8: *Alcinum vinceretis*) in licentiousness and baseness.

INTRODUCTION   31

internally and the reader outside the text) to see the Palinode as a complete redefinition of *Erôs*. Socrates' Palinode, simply put, redeems the text. Implicit in his two different speeches, after all, is the same dichotomy between two types of Aphrodite/*Erôs* which we find in the *Symposium*—a mechanism which governs not only Pausanias' speech but also Socrates' recollection of Diotima's speech.[93] True philosophical readers or auditors are compelled to feel shame at the first type of *erôs*, the appetitive and animalistic form. However, the delight, pleasure, and wonder brought about by the other type of love, the transcendent kind, is not a source of shame, but of joy.

Of course, it is crucial that Socrates actually delivers a Palinode after this dramatic disrobing, whereas Lucius' phrasing, though a precise translation of Socrates' pleonasm, trails off into oblivion. We could view this cynically with Winkler (et al.) and suggest that there is no Palinode, no redemption for the *Met.* According to this reading, then, Lucius would be more akin to Sosia from Plautus' *Amphitruo*, who claims, in comic burlesque, that he will shave his head and wear the freedman's cap if it turns out he is dead.[94] This is a fine exegesis, to be sure, if we stop after the "first reading," only taking pleasure from the tale and hedonistically moving on to consume the next novel, continuing in our "occupation" with trifles and distractions. In my view, however, this explicit allusion to the most famous refusal to feel shame is, in fact, a provocation to reread the text and in the "retrospective" reading, to reimagine it as a Palinode. Indeed, we may note that, when readers undertake a "Palinodic reading," the first inset narrative they encounter in the opening book is that of a character named "Socrates" "cover[ing] his face which is red from shame" (*Met.* 1.6: *faciem suam . . . punicantem **prae pudore obtexit***) with his cloak and comically "reveal[ing] the rest of his body" (*cetera corporis* ***renudaret***).[95] According to my interpretation, then, the retrospective reading is not merely an opportunity for hermeneutic delight, where a "learned elite" (*pepaideumenos*) can recognize all the embedded clues that point to poststructuralist *aporia*. Rather, it represents a renegotiation of the "contract" formed between *auctor* and *lector* in much the same way that Socrates sets out

93. Apuleius was clearly quite familiar with this dichotomy, moreover, as he cites Pausanias' speech at length in *Apol.* 12 (on which, see Kenney 1990a). See also §4.4.

94. See *Amph.* 461–62: *nisi etiam is quoque me ignorabit: quod ille faxit Iuppiter/ ut ego hodie **raso capite** calvos capiam pilleum*. Plautus' *Amphitruo* figures heavily into Regine May's metatheatrical interpretation of the *Metamorphoses* (May 2006, esp. 216–20 and 314–18). But we ought to note here that, although there is a joke in these lines about Sosia rejoicing in his own non-existence, it is also a profoundly philosophical moment (see, e.g., Caston 2014).

95. Cf. *GCA* 2007, 172 *ad loc.*, who links this gesture at the opening of the *Met.* to Socrates' head-covering in the *Phaedrus*.

to redefine the underlying premises and meanings of the words of his first speech by means of a Palinode to *Erôs*.

One of the episodes where we can see this procedure clearly at work is in Lucius' erotic encounter with his host Milo's slave girl Photis in book 2. For in addition to translating Plato, Lucius' pleonastic phrasing—*non **obumbrato** vel **obtecto** calvitio*—reframes for the *lector scrupulosus* one of the novel's most enticingly erotic encounters. When Lucius sneaks back to his bedroom for an all-night tryst with Photis, which Lucius-*auctor* frames in the language of erotic iconography, the slave girl strips off all of her clothes, and in a gesture reminiscent of the famous *Venus Pudica*, "shadow[s] her shaven privates with her rosy palm out of diligence rather than covering it out of shame" (2.17: *glabellum feminal rosea palmula potius **obumbrans** de industria quam **tegens verecundia***). Simply put, in book 2, there is an attempt to conceal shaven skin, but the illicit object is Photis' depilated privates, which she "shadows over" (*obumbrans*) and "covers" (*tegens*) while deliberately emphasizing in a markedly anti-Platonic gesture that she does so *not* "out of shame" (*de . . . verecundia*).[96] We will return to Lucius' tryst with Photis in §4.3, as it constitutes a calculated reworking of the idealized "lover" and "beloved" tradition from Plato's *Phaedrus*, where the ass-man attempts to replicate Plato's transcendent erotic experience, but parodically fails. For now, however, we may merely note that Lucius' framing of his tryst as a self-aggrandizing *erastês* can be reinterpreted in the "Palinodic reading" as an affair with the *Phaedran* "non-lover."

As I suggested above (§0.1) and will elucidate more fully in chapter 1, there is in the *Zeitgeist* of the second century CE a dichotomy of modes of reading: "active reading" as a philosophical choice versus reading as an act of self-indulgent pleasure. If we understand this bewildering conclusion, though, as an allusion to Socrates' unabashed pate-display in the *Phaedrus*, we can locate the invitation to reread *in the text*. Lucius' *gaudium* at revealing his baldness thus represents a shamelessness on par with Socrates' refusal to be controlled "by shame" (ὑπ' αἰσχύνης) as well as a final reversal of Photis' "shamelessness" in covering over her shaven privates to heighten the *curiositas* and pleasure in her viewer.

---

96. With the phrase *de . . . verecundia*, we may compare Plato's Socrates covering his bald head "out of shame" (ὑπ' αἰσχύνης) and likewise, the Apuleian Socrates attempting to hide his head "from embarrassment" (*prae pudore*).

0.4. *The Prologue's Invitation to the* lector scrupulosus

In light of the realization that the final line of the *Met.* invites readers to engage with the whole novel as a "Palinode," it is now possible to go back to the beginning and reread with fresh eyes, approaching the text with a reoriented evaluation of its religious-erotic implications. To finish off my introductory case studies, therefore, I would like to return to the questions that Rabelais' prologue raised for us at the outset with its appeal to the Silenic and Sirenic Socrates: first, what precisely does it entail to "scrupulously weigh" (*soigneusement peser*) the "serious" content beneath frivolous form? And perhaps more importantly, what kind of attention should we afford to a text which can hold us stultified and entranced by its form "like the Sirens' song" (*comme au chant de Sirènes*), but which may also offer something much different, if a reader adopts a philosophical posture—or in other words, if one takes the time to "interpret it in a higher sense" (*à plus haut sens interpreter*)?

Indeed, if we consider the Prologue from the "Palinodic" perspective, we will see that the marvel this novel offers and the pleasure we are invited to experience does not align so neatly with the *voluptas* a prologist promises in a Roman comedy, as some have contended,[97] or for that matter, with the overtly frivolous and bawdy nature of a Milesian tale, as Septimius Severus characterizes Apuleius' *Punicae Milesiae* in the *SHA*.[98] It is true, to be sure, that the *Metamorphoses* signals its relationship to these playful genres by deploying language vaguely reminiscent of a comic prologue and using generically loaded phrases to gesture overtly to a self-consciously unliterary filiation. In my view, however, Apuleius uses frivolity and merriment to cover over a more serious tale and then provokes his readers nonetheless to assume the posture of *lectores scrupulosi*.

By way of introduction to my high-stakes choice model, I focus on the opening line of the Prologue and analyze how one visual word—*inspicere*—

---

97. On the *Met.*'s Prologue as an invocation of the tradition of the comic prologist in Roman comedy, see Smith 1972; Slater 2001, 213 with n. 2; May 2006, 110–15. Cf. Benson 2019, 251–54 for a useful discussion of the value of *voluptas* in the *Met.* See §2.4 (esp. with n. 88) for further discussion.

98. The phrase *sermo Milesius* (*Met.* 1.1) has inspired too many analyses to list in a footnote. Relihan 1993 remains a useful introduction to Menippean satire, though he excludes Apuleius from his analysis on formal grounds. See also *GCA* 2007, 23–26 and 64–65 *ad loc.* 1,1,1, for a representative treatment. I am particularly partial to Dowden 2006, who excavates a Platonic origin for *sermo Milesius* in the *Symposium*. For a helpful summary of the different takes on the Prologue's generic multiplicity, see now Adkins 2022, 191–99. For fuller analysis with bibliography, see §2.4 (esp. n. 84).

encourages us to take a deeper look into a text that seems otherwise to foreground *divertissement*. The Prologue opens (*Met.* 1.1):

> At ego tibi sermone isto Milesio varias fabulas conseram, auresque tuas benivolas lepido susurro permulceam, modo si papyrum Aegyptiam argutia Nilotici calami inscriptam non spreveris **inspicere**, figuras fortunasque hominum in alias imagines conversas et in se rursum mutuo nexu refectas ut mireris. Exordior. 'Quis ille?'[99]

> But I will weave variegated tales for you in that Milesian style and I will charm your benevolent ears with pleasurable whispering, provided that you do not disdain to look into an Egyptian papyrus inscribed with the cleverness of a Nilotic reed, in order that you may marvel at figures and fortunes of men transformed into other images and turned back into themselves by a mutual knot. I begin my prologue. Who is that?

"Beguilement" (*permulcere*) through "pleasurable whispering" (*lepidus susurrus*); "marvel" (*mirari*) at a "woven together" text (*conserere; exordiri*). The opening line, where the *auctor* bursts into the text *in medias res* with the phrase *at ego tibi*,[100] seems to offer the "first reader" only diversion. Add to this the fact that the Prologue famously concludes with a trivializing break of the fourth wall—"reader, pay attention; you will be delighted" (*lector intende: laetaberis*)[101]—and one can see why critics have almost universally read this as

---

99. I generally follow here the text of Zimmerman 2012, but there is significant debate on how to punctuate this sentence and I retain the manuscript punctuation of *F* (full stop after *mireris*) rather than Helm's change to a comma. Cf. Harrison and Winterbottom 2001, 9, who place a full stop after *inspicere* and take the phrase *figuras fortunasque* as the direct object of *exordior* (meaning, "to weave"). While it may be an elegant critical solution, it also makes the purpose clause adverbial to *exordior* (rather than *inspicere*) and removes the sense of the Prologue as *exordium*. Cf. *GCA* 2007, 53 for discussion.

100. This problematic opening has long been remarked upon. See Leo 1905, 605: "incipit quasi ex medio colloquio"; Helm 1931, vi.; Janson 1964, 114n5; and Scobie 1975, 66. For my own explanation of this issue, see Ulrich 2017, 728–29. See also §2.4 (with n. 87) for fuller treatment.

101. This bold metalepsis has traditionally been read as another trivializing gesture to establish the "contract" of *divertissement* with readers (e.g., Slater 2001), but such an interpretation fundamentally misconstrues the idiom *intendere animum* as a comic gesture akin to the Plautine prologist's metatheatrical call for attention (e.g., *animadvertere*), on which, see May 2006, 111. However, *intendere animum* (to which Apuleius' imperative, *intende*, corresponds) is, in fact, an idiom derived from philosophical discourse (e.g., Cic. *De nat. deorum* 1.52–54; *Hort.* 6.1), and is also used in this way across Apuleius' corpus (e.g., *Plat.* 1.3). Currently, I am working on a short critical note tracing the history of this idiom and the scholarly misrepresentation of it in Apuleius' Prologue.

a generic "contract" between narrator and reader, a binding promise of *merely frivolous* indulgence.[102] As Michael Trapp phrases it:

> Whatever other functions it may perform, the Prologue to Apuleius' *Metamorphoses* strikes a thoroughly hedonistic note, from its fifth word, *Milesio* ("Milesian") to its last, *laetaberis* ("you will revel in this").[103]

Similarly, Luca Graverini connects the "pleasurable whispering" (*lepidus susurrus*) and the "charming of the ears" (*aures permulcere*) to the bucolic *topos* of a *locus amoenus* and the age-old literary-critical debate about the "utility" and "pleasure" associated with literature.[104] Apuleius' Prologue, Graverini explains:

> offers us a "sweet" and *psychagogic* kind of literature, apparently unconcerned with anything *utile*, and able to entice its reader with an almost magical and possibly dangerous power.[105]

In short, Apuleius' narrator appears to promote a decidedly *inutile* kind of poetics; he seems, at least prima facie, to offer only one path to his reader: *voluptas*.

If we look more closely at the usage of *inspicere* here, however, and compare it with its occurrences in Apuleius' broader milieu, this whole assessment of the text begins to unravel much like the variegated threads of these stitched-together *fabulae*, especially for the "Palinodic" reader. I concede, that is, that the initial "horizon of expectation" the Prologue establishes is reading for *divertissement*.[106] But contrary to the erotic and dangerously enchanting visual encounters which we shall see Lucius experiencing throughout the novel—moments when he "gazes upon" (*aspicere*) superficial appearances and takes

---

102. See, e.g., Winkler 1985, 99–122, on the "contract" the Prologue develops with its reader and how it abruptly breaks it with the Isis book. See also Slater 2001, who uses Jauss' terminology of "horizons of reading," but in a somewhat reductive fashion, e.g., to discuss the narrow horizons the auctorial "contract" sets out (213).

103. Trapp 2001, 39. Cf., however, Svendsen 1978, 105, who notes a possible association of *laetor* with "the state of blessedness conferred upon [an] initiate" (on which, see below).

104. In fact, Graverini 2012a, 18–21, connects the *susurrus* of the Prologue specifically to the cicadas' song of *Phaedrus* 258e–259a. Cf. also Hunter 2018, 194–219, on how the distinction between "pleasurable" and "useful" literature is woven into the Sirens episode.

105. Graverini 2012a, 25.

106. See Slater 2001.

delight—the *inspicere*-type of looking represents a philosophical approach to viewing. Thus, Maaike Zimmerman rightly emphasizes how jarring this verb is in the opening line:

> Remarkably, when the reader is asked not to decline to examine this papyrus, the verb *inspicere* is used. . . . In his *Apology* . . . Apuleius uses *inspicere* frequently, always with the connotation of scholarly enquiry, close scrutiny, and philosophical curiosity. . . . As actual readers we too are invited to carry on our careful examination of the text of the *Metamorphoses*, reflecting on what we see reflected there.[107]

As Wytse Keulen points out, furthermore, "*inspicere* [here] may connote carefulness in taking a look at something potentially treacherous."[108] We are confronted, once again, with Rabelais' question: is it medicine or is it poison? To investigate this anxiety, then, it will be useful to scan briefly the usages of this term and a closely related term (*introspicere*) in the works of two authors in Apuleius' broader milieu—Seneca and Aulus Gellius—who together represent the two sides of the "Latin sophist's" polymathic persona: philosophy and rhetoric.

The most famous case in the Senecan corpus is, of course, the textual mirror of *De clementia*, which the philosopher holds out for Nero "to look into" (*De clem.* 1.1: **inspicere**) so that he might "reach the highest of all pleasures" (*perventurum ad voluptatem maximam omnium*).[109] Reading Seneca's treatise, in short, constitutes a means of "looking deep" into one's "conscience" and "dialoguing with oneself" (*loqui secum*).[110] This passage has its own Rabelaisian flavor insofar as *voluptas* constitutes a very strange endpoint for the kind of self-speculation Seneca seems to be advocating,[111] and we will

---

107. Zimmerman 2001, 255.

108. *GCA* 2007, 71 *ad loc*, where he expounds further: "usually *inspicere*, in the sense of taking a look at a written text, is referred to as an indispensable preliminary action in order to gain knowledge of its content, like the action of opening a book." See *ThLL* 7.1.1952.270–53. See also Cavallo 1996, 41, who connects *inspicere* to the *lector scrupulosus*.

109. I have translated *omnium* here as the partitive genitive ("the highest of all pleasures"), but one could also take it as a subjective genitive (i.e., "the highest pleasure of all people"), and I believe that Seneca embeds an intentional ambiguity in this usage. The realization of what *omnium* modifies depends in a sense on what kind of reader Nero is (on which, see Ker 2009).

110. On the dialogic nature of the mirror in general and its extension to the mirror of the text trope, see McCarty 1989, 169. See also Bartsch 2006, 183–88.

111. See Bartsch 2006, 184–85, for an interpretation of the twisted blend of mirror traditions and the underlying sexual implications of this passage, on which, see §2.1 (with quotation).

return to this treatise again in §2.1 when we consider Apuleius' participation in the "mirror of the text" tradition.

Aside from this well-known passage, though, Seneca deploys *inspicere* across his corpus primarily to speak of philosophical (or divinatory)[112] inspection: very often, it concerns general scientific investigation, as in introductory exhortations ("let us investigate")[113] or in directing readers toward the philosophical pursuit of knowledge.[114] Even more relevant for our purposes, however, are moments in his epistolary corpus where Seneca refers to "inspecting" the true character of a person, by which he alludes to penetrating deep beneath the surface-level and superficial ways of evaluating a person. In this vein, Seneca tells his reader in *Ep.* 22 that one has to "look at [people's] true feelings" (22.10: *verum adfectum eorum **inspicias***) in order to know them well. At *Ep.* 115, in turn, he fantasizes about being permitted to "look into the soul of a good man" (115.3: *animum boni viri . . . **inspicere***) and see it shining forth with "justice," "fortitude," "temperance," and "prudence." Perhaps most significant for my argument, though, Seneca explains to his reader at *Ep.* 76 that, if one wishes to know a person's true worth, one must strip away all the adornments and fancy clothes and "look at him naked, to see what sort of a person he is" (76.32: *qualis sit, nudum **inspice***). This notion of "stripping away" external adornments takes its origin from a Platonic philosophical discourse quite familiar to Apuleius,[115] and we shall come back to this leitmotiv at §4.3 when we consider the mock-philosophical fashion in which Lucius strives to "strip away" external features of his beloved to get a look at what is underneath.

Whereas Seneca always uses *inspicere* with a philosophical connotation, it is Apuleius' immediate contemporary, Aulus Gellius, who connects it to "active reading" and who, furthermore, confirms for us that the *inspicere*-type of viewing was taught as regular praxis in second-century CE reading culture.[116] A case-in-point occurs at *Noctes Atticae* 11.13, in which Gellius describes a moment

---

112. The only instance of the latter is *Thyestes* 757.

113. See, e.g., the programmatic opening of *De benefic.* 2.1 (*inspiciamus*); *De benefic.* 5.1; *Ep.* 20.11.

114. A particularly resonant example of this is in *Ep.* 33.5, where Seneca says that one cannot glean wisdom by merely "getting a taste of it" (*degustare*; e.g., by means of epitomes and the like), but rather, the whole of philosophy "must be inspected" (*inspicienda sunt*). This seems an interesting *comparandum* for the character of Lucius who loves to taste things without careful inspection.

115. Cf., e.g., *Alc.* 1 132a5–6, where Socrates claims that, although Erechtheus is "fair-of-face" (εὐπρόσωπος), "it is necessary to see a man stripped" (ἀλλ᾽ **ἀποδύντα** χρὴ αὐτὸν θεάσασθαι) before one can assess his character. This trope also appears in a scene from the opening of the *Charmides*, which Apuleius reworks in *Fl.* 2 (see Harrison 2000, 96 and §4.2).

116. On which, see Johnson 2010; Howley 2018; and Digiulio 2020.

when a teacher of rhetoric, Titus Castricius, admonishes a group of students not to be charmed by a delightful turn of phrase in the speech of a certain Gaius Gracchus. As the young students marvel at the "flow" of the phrase—at how the "rhythm" of the *sententia* "pleases" (11.13.4: *delectabat*) its listeners—Titus Castricius warns them not to let their "ears be charmed by the rhythms . . . and confuse [their] minds with empty pleasure" (11.13.5: *aures . . . modis eblanditae animum . . . voluptate inani perfunderent*). Instead, he urges them to "look deeply into what [the] words mean" (**inspicite . . . penitus,** *quid efficiant verba haec*) and to recognize their lack of substance despite their enchanting form. Castricius exhorts his students, simply put, to take great care with their *aures* and with the influence which "empty pleasure" can have upon their souls.[117]

If *Noctes Atticae* 11.13 reveals to us the performance component of Roman reading culture, even more relevant for our discussion of "active reading" is an essay in book 18 (18.4), in which a public intellectual, Sulpicius Apollonaris, exposes an incompetent *grammaticus* before an audience for claiming to be a "singularly exceptional reader and exegete of Sallust" (18.4.2). While the *grammaticus'* boast is, of course, the object of ridicule,[118] it nonetheless speaks volumes about the second-century CE culture of exegesis and interpretation. Indeed, this braggadocious exegete of Sallust frames his capacity to interpret the historian in medicalized terminology of performing an autopsy on a body: he can "dig down and look deep within not only the first skin and appearance of [Sallust's] thoughts, but even the very blood and innards of [the author's] words" (*NA* 18.4.2: *neque primam tantum cutem ac speciem sententiarum, sed sanguinem quoque ipsum ac medullam verborum eius eruere atque* **introspicere penitus**). Parallel to Castricius' call to "look deeply into" (**inspicite penitus**)[119] a rhetorically charming *sententia* in 11.13, then, the haughty *grammaticus* likewise takes pride in his ability to look beneath appearances and reveal the innards of the text.

We will return to the opening sentence of the Prologue in §2.4 when we consider the text-as-mirror trope in antiquity and the ways in which Apuleius invites us to read his novel through the filters of the *Odyssey*-mirror and the

---

117. Cf. once again Aug. *Conf.* 10.33 (quoted in n. 65 above), which similarly elucidates the dangers of indulging the "pleasures of the ears" (*voluptates aurium*) and their enervating effects.

118. On this passage as a "Socratic exposure" and on Apollonaris as a "Socrates" figure, see Keulen 2009, 71–74; and Howley 2018, 224, respectively.

119. On the level of phrasing, we may also compare Cic. *De orat.* 1.219, where Crassus (allegedly) claims that an orator must "[look] deeply" (**penitus perspexerit**) into the nature of all things in order to influence his audience.

Socratic mirror of self-knowledge. For now, we need only note that Apuleius urges his readers—especially his "Palinodic" readers—to employ a mode of viewing tantamount to the more reflective or distanced approach to reading, which his contemporaries advocate for their respective audiences. Just as Apuleius offers a seductive and sweet rhetoric with which he claims to "charm our benevolent ears," he invites us in the very same breath to look more scrupulously beneath the surface of the seemingly frivolous words.

0.5. The Shape of This Book

To conclude this introduction, I would like to return to the soldiers who see "the shadow of an ass," and decide to reenter the house for a more meticulous investigation. As I suggested at the outset, this episode models a particular approach to a text, which may hide within it precisely what we are looking for, just like the "box" (9.40: *cistulam*) that contains the gardener. In this sense, the soldiers stage a specific paradigm of reader-response—discerning from shadows back to the truth. The rest of this monograph, in turn, will explore the different ways in which Apuleius stages reader-responses for us—various "performances" of meaning within his own contemporary culture—and then, invites us to read "actively," to react philosophically (in many cases, contrary to the response modeled by our asinine *actor* and *auctor*).

Thus, the first part of the book aims to make sense of Apuleius' "performances" of meaning in broader literary-critical traditions. In chapter 1, I situate his staging of reader-responses within (primarily Greek) Second Sophistic and late antique discourse(s) of experiencing aesthetic pleasure. I argue that there is a literary-critical movement in the air, so to speak, which envisions Odysseus and Heracles as model readers and in that sense, as paradigms for resisting or responding to aesthetic experience. In light of this culture of reading, I consider how Lucius' "conversion" can be reframed as a negotiation between these two paradigms of response and more importantly, how Lucius' staged responses ripple out to the reader. In this sense, Lucius retrospectively reframes his transformation as a once-and-for-all, Heraclean type of choice, when, in fact, he has encountered various Sirens, Circes, and Calypsos along the way (and moreover, has implicated us in those encounters).

Then, in chapter 2, I analyze how the allegorical and philosophical approaches to the *Metamorphoses* similarly exist in a tradition of "active reading" and textual engagement. Using the "mirror of the text" as a paradigm, which begins with allegorical readings of the *Odyssey* (e.g., Alcidamas') but continues well into Apuleius' day (and in fact, is utilized by Apuleius himself in *De deo Socratis*), I consider how the opening books of the *Metamorphoses* offer similar invitations to choose to read the allegorical beneath the comic. While Apuleius works within a long tradition of textual engagement as philosophical self-speculation—and especially, responds to his own imperial reading culture, which intensely ramps up the mirroring metaphor for aesthetic engagement—I note that he also anticipates, as it were, the trends of "seriocomic," philosophical speculation which we witness developing later in the early modern novel.

The second part of this monograph turns to the specific choice(s) between absorbed and distanced reading. In particular, I look at the ways in which Lucius overidentifies with his own aesthetic experience—or in other words, how he "mytho-maniacally" imagines himself to be playing the role of the heroes he sees in artistic set-pieces or, in a similar vein, how he refashions his debased and corporeal erotic encounters in the language of idealized Platonic ascent. In this respect, Lucius functions as a model of an immersed but rather incompetent reader, "taking delight" from his aesthetic experiences and reading them, as it were, through the highly filtered lenses of myth and philosophy.[120]

Thus, in chapter 3, I consider Lucius' implication in the Diana-Actaeon statuary ensemble in Byrrhena's atrium (*Met.* 2.4) by analyzing how he uses imaginative experience to transform an innocent statue of the "Striding Diana" into an episode of illicit voyeurism (i.e., a "Bathing Diana"). Moreover, I compare Lucius' role as an external viewer of a statue of Actaeon reflected under Diana's feet with two later recurrences of a spectacle of an eroticized goddess incorporating her viewers: the Judgment of Paris pantomime in book 10, in which a surrogate Venus seductively dances while Lucius-ass looks on from behind the stage curtain; and the spectacle of the initiate Lucius in the final book, standing as a statue on a pedestal and "enjoying" the visual delight of the *simulacrum* of the goddess Isis. These encounters with representations of divinities, each of which constitutes a crossroads choice for Lucius *inside* the text, simultaneously offer an opportunity for readers to assess their own interactions

---

120. Thus, the book-obsessed character of Don Quixote, which Jauss identifies with the "pathology of novel reading" (n. 71 above), has already provided a useful model for understanding the protagonists of the Roman novel: see, e.g., Conte 1996 on Encolpius in Petronius' *Satyricon* and Graverini 2012a on Lucius.

with these religious-erotic encounters from *outside*. Indeed, in each case, Lucius is increasingly incorporated into the representational frame of his visual encounters, from an external human viewer gazing at a statuary ensemble to an asinine viewer looking on as he waits to play a role in the spectacle, and finally, to a statuized human, set up on a pedestal and fully embedded in a statuary ensemble himself. If Lucius' failure to read his visual encounters correctly across the *Met.* leads to his becoming what he sees, then what does reading Lucius' experiences from the (safe?) distance of the text entail for us, his readers?

We turn in chapter 4 to Platonizing transcendent encounters in the *Met.*, which I argue have the power to guide even an absorbed reader to enlightened knowledge. Returning to Lucius' tryst with Photis early on in the novel, I disentangle the way in which the asinine-*auctor* carefully couches his illicit affair in terms of idealized Platonic erotics, but clearly misunderstands or misconstrues the Platonic procedure. This failure of reading, I suggest, ripples out to us as readers, implicating us in Lucius' misinterpretation. In this way, we learn precisely how wrong things can go when one misreads Plato and in a lofty delusion, applies Platonic philosophy to a prosaic, corporeal encounter. Much like the "mytho-maniacal" lens through which Lucius views representations of divinities who role-play episodes from myth, Platonic type-scenes become another locus of choice for Lucius, as he strives to (mis)interpret his quotidian experience in the sublime discourse of Platonic myth. Such misreading presents a mediated crossroads choice, in turn, to the learned reader who recognizes Lucius' failure of interpretation.

Finally, I conclude the book with a new reading of the Isis book as a reworking of Platonic life-choice narratives from the Myth of Er. Indeed, I see Apuleius' incorporation of his *lector* reach a climax in the slippage between author, narrator, and reader in book 11 and therefore, I view the paradigms of life that Lucius-*auctor* stages for us not merely as a comical "symbolic recapitulation" of different characters found inside the novel (*à la* Harrison),[121] but also as an adaptation of Plato's "paradigms of lives" (*paradeigmata biôn*) in end of the *Republic*. The fact that Odysseus reappears at the close of Plato's life-choice narrative in *Republic* 10 and decides to live a life "free of curiosity" is crucial, then, for how we interpret the *Metamorphoses*. Like Plato's Odysseus in the Myth of Er, Lucius in the Isis book gazes upon a curtain call of the different "figures and

---

121. See Harrison 2000, 242–43 and 2012, on which, see further in §5.1.

fortunes transformed into other images," and *allegedly* chooses to abandon his *curiositas* in favor of a more Socratic lifestyle. Lucius also becomes like Socrates insofar as he is stripped of his external, asinine hide and laid bare to reveal (together with Isis) "statues of gods" (*simulacra deorum*). Whether or not we believe Lucius' auctorial representation of his transformation and "conversion," his life choice is put on display for the *lector scrupulosus* who is implicated in reenacting Lucius' choice(s) unless s/he undertakes a different kind of reading, a "Palinodic" reading.

ONE

Setting the Stage for Apuleius

Choice Narratives from Homer to Augustine

Multis et variis exanclatis laboribus magnisque Fortunae tempestatibus et maximis actus procellis, ad portum Quietis et aram Misericordiae tandem, Luci, venisti. Nec tibi natales ac ne dignitas quidem, vel ipsa qua flores usquam doctrina profuit, sed lubrico virentis aetatulae ad serviles delapsus voluptates, curiositatis inprosperae sinistrum praemium reportasti.

After having endured many and various toils, and driven by the great tempests of Fortune and the most powerful winds, Lucius, you have finally come to the harbor of Rest and the altar of Mercy. Neither your lineage nor indeed your dignity, nor even that very learning in which you excel has benefited you at all, but at the precarious point of flourishing youth, you slipped into servile pleasures and carried off the troublesome reward for your unpropitious curiosity.

—Apuleius' *Metamorphoses* 11.15

The fulcrum of any interpretation of Apuleius' *Metamorphoses* seems to hinge on Mithras' moralizing and revisionist rereading of Lucius' transformation in the epigram above.[1] In this notoriously problematic exegesis of books 1–10, Isis' priest declares, on the one hand, that Lucius' asinine misadventures represent the just reward for his unfortunate *curiositas*; on the other hand, he simultaneously implies that Lucius has lost that curiosity through his conversion to Isis. Indeed, Mithras paradoxically pinpoints *curiositas* as both the causal mecha-

---

1. Winkler 1985, 9, notes how Mithras' interpretation "provokes all readers to face the question of meaning."

nism for Lucius' initial suffering at the hands of *Fortuna* and as a tool in Isis' "Economy of Grace" (*Heilsökonomie*), as Christine Harrauer labels it in her unpublished commentary. By doing so, he isolates *curiositas* as the symbol of a larger transformation in Lucius, and readers have long since debated whether or not Lucius, in fact, loses his curiosity at this moment—or in short, whether Lucius has sincerely changed.[2]

It is no coincidence that this is the crucial passage to which Jack Winkler turns at the outset of his study to introduce his deconstructionist model of *aporia*—an approach apropos to the *Zeitgeist* of the late twentieth century, but one anachronistic, to say the least, for understanding Apuleius. The priest's "authorized" interpretation, Winkler suggests, is merely one of many readings, all of which are either "serious" or "satirical," and as interpreters, we choose our mode of reading by a projection of our own desires, prejudices, and inclinations. And while many recent studies of the *Met.* have done much to elucidate the "seriocomic" nature, the emotional power, and the philosophical import of the text as a whole and of book 11, in particular,[3] it is my hope in this chapter to begin to address Winkler's reductive binary for the *Met.* in a different way. Indeed, I aim to resituate Apuleius' narrative about a buffoonish elite, who transforms into an ass and then, retransforms back into a human and converts to the cult of Isis, in its own *Zeitgeist* of imperial and Second Sophistic reading cultures. By doing so, I suggest we can contextualize the "serious" features of the *Met.* within philosophical discussions and literary representations of choice and the role aesthetic experience plays in enacting it.

As I discussed in the introduction, "conversion" as a phenomenon is often framed in the first–fourth centuries CE as a response to text, words, or works of art. Even conversions such as the Pauline "Damascus road" model—a drastic,

---

2. The bibliography on *curiositas* in the *Met.* and meddlesomeness in the novelistic tradition is too vast for a footnote. For the abundant bibliography on *curiositas* in the *Metamorphoses* before Winkler, see Scobie 1975. Schlam 1968, 120–25, also provides a useful discussion. An excellent taxonomy of the different uses of *curiositas, curiosus,* and *curiose* along with a comprehensive summary of scholarship can be found in *GCA* 1995, 362–79. DeFilippo 1990 offers a very compelling reading of *curiositas* in relation to Apuleius' Platonism. Kirichenko 2008b gives a thoughtful analysis of the reader's role in becoming curious; on which, see also Freudenburg 2007. For the most up-to-date treatment (with bibliography), see Leigh 2013, esp. 130–60 for the *Met.*, and Benson 2019, 58–60.

3. A comprehensive list is again beyond the bounds of a footnote. On seriocomedy: see Graverini 2012a; Graverini 2012b; Graverini 2013; Egelhaaf-Gaiser 2012; Tilg 2014a; and the Groningen commentary on the Isis book *GCA* 2015. On emotional power: see now Benson 2019, 239–64. On philosophical import: see DeFilippo 1990; Drews 2012; Drews 2015; Fletcher 2014; Ulrich 2017; and Ulrich 2020.

once-and-for-all sudden alteration of faith, which scholars suggest is largely unattested in classical antiquity[4]—nonetheless feature a voice or text serving as the agent of change. So, Augustine's conversion in book 8 of the *Confessions*, perhaps the most famous literary conversion in antiquity aside from St. Paul's, is likewise enacted by an experience of reading: the numinous voice seems to speak to Augustine, saying, "pick up and read, pick up and read" (*Conf.* 8.12: *tolle **lege**, tolle **lege***). As I suggested in the introduction, a full lexical appreciation of this phrase depends on the inherent connection between reading and choice, since *legere* means both "to read" and "to choose." However, what is interesting about philosophical and religious choice in imperial and Second Sophistic texts, in particular, is the fact that the input-output exchange between reader/auditor/viewer and the textual object is associated, with surprising frequency, with one of two heroic archetypes: Odysseus facing his various temptations (the Sirens, Circe, etc.), or Heracles standing at the crossroads and choosing between Lady Virtue and Lady Vice. These two heroes become philosophical models for how to respond to aesthetic pleasure, from the pleasure involved in reading a written text to the appropriate way to gaze upon a painting. The text, whether verbal or visual, is thus transformed in this sense into the locus of choice, and readers/auditors/viewers are exhorted, according to this model, to follow either Odysseus or Heracles, or in some cases, both. Furthermore, the test of a true philosopher, according to this discourse, is the ability to resist the temptations of aesthetic pleasure and instead, to travel the hard road to virtue—reading "as a philosopher" and gleaning what is "useful" (*utile*/χρήσιμον) from that which is otherwise frivolous or entrapping. In many of these discussions, the text is likened to wine, a sort of intoxicating drink, but the true philosopher waters it down, or uses some kind of *môly* acquired from the hermeneutic tradition to consume the text without transforming into an animal.[5] Thus, "conversion," which has anachronistic associations imported from the Christian tradition and has proven rather difficult to pin down as a concep-

---

4. See esp. Konstan 2010, 168–69 with n. 39: "The idea of a moral transformation in the adult, along the lines of Christian conversion narratives, is foreign to classical biography and to the classical conception of the person in general. Various stories of sudden conversions to philosophy did circulate in antiquity and might even be thought to constitute a motif. But these tales never became the model for a change of character precipitated by remorse over wrongdoing, as happened in nineteenth century and later constructions of forgiveness."

5. On Odysseus' engagement with the Sirens as an exemplary aesthetic experience, see Peponi 2012, 70–94; and Grethlein 2017, 1–17. On the "intoxicated reader" within the *Odyssey* and the way in which the text models paradigms of reading, see Pucci 1987, 201–8. On the reception of the Sirens episode in the later literary-philosophical tradition, see esp. Montiglio 2011, 87–94 and 124–47; and Hunter 2018, 194–219.

tual phenomenon,[6] can be recontextualized for our purposes as a philosophical choice: the text becomes, in short, the locus of choice, a crossroads moment, for the *lector*.

The goal of this chapter, therefore, is simply to reconstruct the reading culture(s)—the *Zeitgeist*, as it were—in which Apuleius is writing his carnivalesque novel. For I believe that he composes his polyglottal and dialectic narrative with a view to the reader-response discourses that are developing in his epoch. And significant for Apuleius, these discourses are steeped in Platonic anxieties about the power of art or literature to contaminate or manipulate anyone who encounters them. Therefore, a majority of my discussion in this chapter may seem somewhat removed from Apuleius, since it is devoted (a) to tracing the origins of Odysseus and Heracles as heroic models of responding to aesthetic pleasure in the archaic and classical periods (§1.1); and (b) to elucidating the appropriation of these heroes specifically as ideal readers in the imperial period, the Second Sophistic, and even in early Christianity (§1.2). While I close this chapter with a reinterpretation of Mithras' crucial intrusion at 11.15 in light of our heroic models (§1.3), I have entitled this "setting the stage" because it will orient my subsequent discussions of Apuleius' approach to allegorizing texts (ch. 2), his leveraging of aesthetic pleasure to implicate his readers in a Platonic fashion (ch. 3), and his invitation to readers to dissociate themselves from Lucius' (mis)readings of sublime encounters with surrogate divinities (ch. 4).

Before we turn to reconstructing the origins of Odysseus and Heracles as archetypal readers, however, it is worth meditating for a moment on a tension inherent in appealing to these two heroes as models, in part because they are so incongruous with one another. Indeed, Odysseus tastes the fruits of every pleasure he is offered but, nonetheless, manages to retain his desire to return home: in this sense, his character trait of being *polytropos* provides an authorization for the pursuit of knowledge[7]—even perhaps illicit knowledge or philosophical

---

6. We may recall how Habinek 1990 laments the inescapability of Nockian and Augustinian versions of "conversion" in studies of Apuleius. On recent attempts to define the concept of "conversion," see Despotis and Löhr 2022. On conversion and categories of religious experience in Apuleius' milieu, see Shumate 1996.

7. On the ambivalence of Odysseus' characteristic *polytropia*, see Stanford 1963, 7, 17, 26–27, and passim. In later interpretation, Odysseus is compared as a *homo duplex* to his heroic opposite, Achilles, the *homo simplex*, on which, see Stanford 1963, 18. On the reception of Odysseus' *polytropia* in Greek rhetoric, esp. in the interactions between Antisthenes and Plato, see Luzzatto 1996. For the ambivalence of *polytropia* in the classical period, see Montiglio 2011, 21–24; for the later Cynic and Stoic interpretations of Odysseus' "versatility" in the Second Sophistic, see 117–19. On *polytropia* in early Christianity, see Glad 1995, 15–52, esp. 19 and 38.

enlightenment achieved through forbidden means; and from the vantage point of his imperial and Second Sophistic reception, Odysseus must face his crossroads continuously, choosing time and again to remain steadfast in the face of aesthetic pleasure. Heracles, by contrast, stands at the crossroads, able to see through the cosmetics and seductive appeal of Lady Vice. He chooses the difficult path of virtue, knowing full well the "labors" (labores/πόνοι) it will entail. In his philosophical decision, therefore, Heracles represents a stark contrast to Odysseus' learning-via-indulgence and the opposite pole of temporality: a once-and-for-all choice, taken at the crossroads of youth.

1.1. The Origins of the Tropes in the Archaic and Classical Periods

I begin my analysis with the two earliest passages that establish the two archetypes, which are found unsurprisingly in the two earliest poets, whose pedagogical value would become a source of anxiety once again in the imperial period and Second Sophistic.[8] Odysseus' encounter with the Sirens (Od. 12.158–200), of course, lies at the forefront of the tradition in the Odyssey; but Prodicus' allegory of Heracles at the crossroads is generally agreed to have been an adaptation of the famous "two roads" passage from Hesiod's Works and Days (286–92).[9] A brief review of the passages from Homer and Hesiod will be useful as we move forward in time to a tradition which adapts them for a Second Sophistic audience and even translates them into Latin.

Odysseus' encounter with the Sirens is already anticipated in the text by Circe's warning at the opening of book 12. Circe foretells of the Sirens, who "charm all men" (12.39–40: πάντας ἀνθρώπους θέλγουσιν) with their "shrill voice," making them forget their wives and children as they "journey home" (12.43: νοστήσαντι). Likewise, it is on Circe's advice that Odysseus "kneads honey-sweet wax" (12.48: κηρὸν δεψήσας μελιηδέα) into the ears of his comrades and has them bind him to the mast in order that he may "delight" (12.52:

---

8. On the second-century CE Certamen between Homer and Hesiod, see Uden 2010. Halliwell 2011, ch. 3, and Rosen 2004 suggest that the Certamen reaches back to an earlier classical tradition, which can be recovered in Aristophanes' Frogs.

9. See Hunter 2014a, 92–100, for the afterlife of Hesiod's "two roads"; Levine Gera 1995 gives a fairly comprehensive treatment of the variations of "Heracles at the Crossroads," esp. in relation to Lucian's Somnium, on which, see below.

τερπόμενος) in the Sirens' voices.[10] When we reach the encounter with the Sirens in the text, we see why Circe advised Odysseus to stop up the ears of his comrades. The Sirens' promise is nothing less than "delight" (12.188: τερψάμενος) together with "greater knowledge" (πλείονα εἰδώς)—indeed, knowledge of "all that has happened on the much-nourishing earth" (12.191: ὅσσα γένηται ἐπὶ χθονὶ πουλυβοτείρῃ). The experience of pleasure accompanied by the acquisition of knowledge constitutes one of the poles of approaches to reading literature in the imperial period and Second Sophistic,[11] and needless to say, will be quite familiar to readers of the *Met.*[12] The anxiety over the power of the Sirens' song—an anxiety which we already saw Plato articulating in the *Symposium*, and which Rabelais was playfully to appropriate two millennia later—resurfaces once again in the first and second centuries CE. Is it possible to feel the intoxicating pleasure of aesthetic beauty and nevertheless, to keep one's mind focused on looking beneath the surface and to leverage that experience into knowledge?[13] It is this scene more than any other in the *Odyssey* that inaugurates the tradition of Odysseus as the *polypragmôn/curiosus* par excellence and thereby, influences his ambivalent reception in later antiquity as an ideal philosopher and simultaneously, a dissolute busybody.[14]

On the opposite pole, both in terms of its approach to virtue and its reception in later antiquity, is Hesiod's "two roads." In an explicitly didactic epic, the narrator of *Works and Days* (hereafter, *W&D*) explains to his brother Perses how and why one ought to pursue justice. The passage of interest to us begins

---

10. Though Peponi 2012, 73–76, notes how cleverly Odysseus communicates Circe's advice about the Sirens to him, i.e., with the "meaningful alteration" (74) that she "commanded" him to listen. See also Peponi 2012, 8, on the semantic overlap between *terpsis* and *hêdonê* (and their cognates) in the archaic and classical periods, respectively: Circe invites Odysseus to experience the right kind of *hêdonê*—i.e., from afar and restrained.

11. On the Sirens as inaugurating a tradition hovering between pleasure and didaxis, see Hunter 2018, 194–231.

12. Graverini 2012a, 150, reads the Apuleian neologism *multiscius*, which appears in the *Met.* only when Lucius explicitly likens himself to Odysseus (9.13), as a Latinized calc on the Sirens' *pleiona eidôs*. Cf. also Kenney 2003. For further discussion (with bibliography), see §1.3 below.

13. On this question, see the discussion of Plato's *Phaedrus* on the Siren-esque cicadas below. See also my discussion of charm and pleasure in Apuleius' Prologue in Ulrich 2017 and §2.5.

14. On Odysseus as a *polypragmôn* in later antiquity, see Leigh 2013, esp. 24–25. Cf. Hunter 2012, 42, speaking of Odysseus in the Myth of Er: "Odysseus' abandonment of the public (and political) life of *philotimia* and *polypragmosynê* is not just a typically Platonic gesture towards the life of the mind, and in particular shows Odysseus choosing the life of a (Platonic) Socrates . . . but may also be understood as a wry comment upon what Odysseus, the archetypal *polypragmôn*, (should have) learned in *Odyssey* 11." See also Ulrich 2020, 688–700, and §5.1. On Odysseus' afterlife as a philosopher, see Montiglio 2011, 66–94 and passim and §2.1. Cf. also Worman 1999 on the reception of Odysseus in tragedy.

at line 286, where the speaker breaks from his recollection of a myth to give advice directly to his addressee (*W&D* 286–92):

σοὶ δ᾽ ἐγὼ ἐσθλὰ νοέων ἐρέω, μέγα νήπιε Πέρση.
τὴν μέν τοι κακότητα καὶ ἰλαδὸν ἔστιν ἑλέσθαι
ῥηιδίως· λείη μὲν ὁδός, μάλα δ᾽ ἐγγύθι ναίει·
τῆς δ᾽ ἀρετῆς ἱδρῶτα θεοὶ προπάροιθεν ἔθηκαν
ἀθάνατοι· μακρὸς δὲ καὶ ὄρθιος οἶμος ἐς αὐτὴν
καὶ τρηχὺς τὸ πρῶτον· ἐπὴν δ᾽ εἰς ἄκρον ἵκηται,
ῥηιδίη δὴ ἔπειτα πέλει, χαλεπή περ ἐοῦσα.

But I will speak to you from my knowledge of what is good, foolish Perses.
To choose wretchedness, and in heaps, is easy:
for the road [to her] is smooth, and she dwells very near.
But the undying gods put sweat in front of virtue:
the path leading to her is long, steep, and harsh, at least, at first.
But once you have arrived on the peak,
then it becomes easy, though it is still difficult.

This first explicit crossroads moment of Western literature, which Koning calls the "Hesiodic passage quoted most often in antiquity,"[15] is generally believed to have been the archetype for Prodicus' allegorization of the moral-ethical choice between virtue and vice.[16] Indeed, as we move forward in the tradition to the imperial and Second Sophistic reception of Heracles, we will see authors treating Hesiod's "two roads" and Prodicus' allegory almost interchangeably, where the heritage of the latter is implicitly assumed to be derived from the former and thus assimilated to it.

In the classical period, these two alternative portraits of heroic virtue are translated in the genre of *Sôkratikoi logoi* into two very different allegories for how one should respond to aesthetic pleasure. In the Platonic corpus, on the one hand, Odysseus' interaction with the Sirens becomes a paradigm for how a true philosopher can avoid being entrapped or stultified when faced with a deceptively pleasurable and charming voice. Important for my argument is the fact that the *Phaedrus* and the *Symposium*, the two most widely read Platonic

---

15. Koning 2010, 144.
16. See Koning 2010, 144–45; and Hunter 2014a, 92–100 and 269–75 on the influence and later reception of Hesiod's "two roads," esp. in the Second Sophistic.

dialogues in the first–second centuries CE,[17] are the texts where Plato most overtly allegorizes the Sirens' song. In the *Phaedrus*, Socrates famously exhorts his young interlocutor to stay wakeful and alert in the pleasurable *locus amoenus*. If the singing cicadas should catch Socrates and Phaedrus "nodding off under their spell" (*Phaedr.* 259a3: νυστάζοντας καὶ κηλουμένους), they will laugh at them, believing that some slaves have "come to a resting-place just like herd animals" (259a5: ἐλθόντα εἰς τὸ καταγώγιον ὥσπερ προβάτια) to take a midday nap. Yet, Socrates explains (259a5–b2):

> ἐὰν δὲ ὁρῶσι διαλεγομένους καὶ παραπλέοντάς σφας ὥσπερ Σειρῆνας ἀκηλήτους, ὃ γέρας παρὰ θεῶν ἔχουσιν ἀνθρώποις διδόναι, τάχ᾿ ἂν δοῖεν ἀγασθέντες.

> if they see [us] dialoguing and sailing by them uncharmed, as if by the Sirens, then perhaps out of admiration they would give [us] the gift which they have received from the gods to give to humans.

There is no wax or physical substance (e.g., *môly*) to counteract or ward off the charm, as in the Homeric version. Rather, Socrates' and Phaedrus' resilience amid the cicadas Siren-song functions as a proof that the auditors are not subject to "laziness of thought" (259a3–4: ἀργίαν τῆς διανοίας),[18] and they are rewarded accordingly. Moreover, the danger the cicada-song poses to its listeners lies precisely in its capacity, as Socrates notes, to transform them into "herd animals." As we turn to Apuleius, we will find a text that not only deploys this Siren-cicada rhetoric to a *psychagôgic* end,[19] but also one that does so, in my view, as a prelude to the ultimate choice it poses to the reader between heroic archetypes and their respective approaches to pleasure.

The cicadas are not, however, the only Sirens in the Platonic corpus whose singing threatens to stultify a listener.[20] As we saw in §0.0, it gets to the very

---

17. See Trapp 1990 on the *Phaedrus*; and Hunter 2012, 155–255, on the *Symposium*. Fletcher 2014, 265, takes it as given how well-known the reception of the *Phaedrus* and the *Symposium* are in the second century CE.

18. Peponi 2012, 70, also notes, interestingly, that the (rare) adjective *akêlêtos*, which Socrates deploys here, only occurs once in the entirety of the Homeric corpus, namely, in the Circe episode.

19. See Graverini 2012a, 12–36, on Apuleius' play with *psychagôgia*.

20. For a full discussion of the reception of the Sirens in Platonic texts, see van Liefferinge 2012. Cf. Hunter 2018, 194–231, and esp. 195, where he notes how the Sirens' promise to Odysseus in the *Odyssey* "inaugurates antiquity's most persistent and influential mode of discussing the nature and effects of literature of all kinds."

heart of Plato's ambivalent relationship to rhetorical and musical pleasure that Alcibiades describes Socrates himself as a seductive Siren, one to be avoided at all costs for fear of remaining entranced beside him forever. So, Alcibiades describes his experience of Socrates to the guests at Agathon's banquet as an encounter with the Sirens and simultaneously, with an Odysseus figure (216a6–8):[21]

βίᾳ οὖν ὥσπερ ἀπὸ τῶν Σειρήνων ἐπισχόμενος τὰ ὦτα οἴχομαι φεύγων, ἵνα μὴ αὐτοῦ καθήμενος παρὰ τούτῳ καταγηράσω.

Thus, stopping up my ears with force, I go away, fleeing [from him] as if from the Sirens, lest I grow old, sitting here beside him.

Socrates' words possess such aesthetic and erotic power that they threaten to bewitch and even stultify his interlocutor; they have the capacity, if not to metamorphose Alcibiades into a quadruped as the cicadas do, nonetheless to immobilize him in such a way that he grows old beside this Silenus statuette. This portrait is, of course, meant to be read with something of a sardonic smirk, as Plato is offering in the *Symposium* yet another apology for his mentor, who is not to blame for Alcibiades' inability to internalize the values Socrates offers.[22] But from this depiction, we see that it is not merely the sweet sounds of the cicadas' chant that possess a Siren-esque quality, to which we must respond like Odysseus; even philosophical rhetoric—and especially Socrates', which is dressed up in the "hide of a wanton satyr" (221e3–4: σατύρου . . . ὑβριστοῦ δοράν)—can beguile its listener. Even Socrates' *logoi*, therefore, must be guarded against with an Odyssean kind of avoidance or responded to with philosophical restraint.

Just as Hesiod exists on the didactic pole opposite to Homer throughout antiquity, so also Xenophon's Socrates represents a vision of the philosopher's project very different from Plato's. So, it is in Xenophon's *Memorabilia* where we find the final mosaic tiles to reconstruct the colorful backdrop against which imperial and Second Sophistic authors develop a reader-response theory.

---

21. On Socrates as an Odysseus *redivivus*, see Hunter 2004, 109–10. See again Peponi 2012 on Platonic texts outlining an appropriate response to *mousikê*.

22. Montiglio 2011, 133–34, interprets Alcibiades' failure to learn as a moment where Plato demonstrates the inappropriate reader-response. See also Hunter 2004, 100–101, on Alcibiades' misunderstanding and Socrates' failure to teach him.

52   THE SHADOW OF AN ASS

Whereas Plato's play with the Sirens demands a philosophical rigor and restraint from those who hear seductive rhetoric, requiring a continuous choice (i.e., with progressive/repeated aspect) to pursue philosophical enlightenment in the midst of aesthetic enchantment, Prodicus' allegory in the *Memorabilia* frames the choice between virtue and vice as a singular, once-and-for-all crossroads moment which the hero faces in his youth. Moreover, while Plato's various Sirens seem to provide a philosophical reworking of the Homeric archetype, the sophist's tale in Xenophon appears to dramatize via allegory Hesiod's advice to Perses. So, Xenophon's narrative begins (Xen. *Mem.* 2.1.21):

φησὶ γὰρ Ἡρακλέα, ἐπεὶ ἐκ παίδων εἰς ἥβην ὡρμᾶτο, ἐν ᾗ οἱ νέοι ἤδη αὐτοκράτορες γιγνόμενοι δηλοῦσιν, εἴτε τὴν δι᾽ ἀρετῆς ὁδὸν τρέψονται ἐπὶ τὸν βίον εἴτε τὴν διὰ κακίας, ἐξελθόντα εἰς ἡσυχίαν καθῆσθαι ἀποροῦντα, ποτέραν τῶν ὁδῶν τράπηται

For [Prodicus] says that Heracles, when he set out from childhood into adolescence—the point in time when young men, just acquiring self-mastery, make it clear whether they will travel in life along the road of virtue or the road of vice—coming out into a quiet place, he sat down, being at a loss as to which of the two roads he should walk.

The "two roads" of Hesiod's *W&D* are transformed into a "life-choice" (*Lebenswechsel*) narrative, wherein a young hero sits at the crossroads "at a loss" (ἀποροῦντα) about which path to take. At this crossroads, which Heracles encounters when he "[comes] out into a quiet place" (much like Socrates and Phaedrus hear the cicadas in a quiet place),[23] personifications of virtue and vice in the form of beautiful women approach the young Heracles. Lady "Vice" (Κακία) is nourished to the point of plump softness, done up with cosmetics, impetuous in her glance, dressed in such a way that her "bloom of youth might shine through" (*Mem.* 2.1.22: ἂν μάλιστα ὥρα διαλάμποι), and "constantly looking at herself" (κατασκοπεῖσθαι ... θαμὰ ἑαυτήν); Lady Virtue, by contrast, is fair to look upon, of liberal appearance, dressed in a white garment, shamefaced, and adorned with *sôphrosynê*.

The former eagerly runs up to Heracles and offers to lead him along "the

---

23. Cf. *Phaedr.* 259a5: ἐλθόντα εἰς τὸ καταγώγιον. For the importance of the solitary place motif and its adaptation in the Latin tradition, see §1.3 below.

SETTING THE STAGE FOR APULEIUS 53

most pleasant and easiest of roads" (2.1.23: τὴν ἡδίστην τε καὶ ῥᾴστην ὁδόν), a path where he will be "inexperienced in griefs" (τῶν δὲ χαλεπῶν ἄπειρος) and will "have a taste of all the delights" (τῶν . . . τερπνῶν οὐδενὸς ἄγευστος) life has to offer: every sort of food and drink, sights and sounds, fancy clothes and smells, soft lovers, and so on. The latter, when she finally catches up to Lady Vice, does not attempt to deceive Heracles "with [any] preludes of pleasure" (2.1.27: προοιμίοις ἡδονῆς) but promises the cold hard facts (2.1.28: μετ᾽ ἀληθείας): the gods have given nothing good or beautiful to humans "without work and diligence" (ἄνευ πόνου καὶ ἐπιμελείας). True to Hesiod's "two roads," Lady Virtue offers only "labors and sweat" (σὺν πόνοις καὶ ἱδρῶτι).[24] In an attempt to dismantle the first speaker's promises, that is, she reveals the true outcome of vice's lifestyle (2.1.30): eating without hunger, drinking without thirst, soft living and coverlets, forcing "erotic pleasure" unnecessarily by "using men as women," and so forth. Heracles' once-and-for-all choice in his youth between these two personified figures thus provides an allegory to explain his later ability to endure so many tasks and especially, the twelve labors for which he is most famous.[25]

As we move forward in the tradition, shifting from classical prose to the literature of the imperial period and Second Sophistic,[26] where these two heroic *topoi* proliferate like dandelion seeds in the soil of the resurging Greek enlightenment, we will see certain facets of the episodes recur time and again, while other elements are creatively elided in new contexts. Odysseus variously becomes an ideal reader/auditor or a dissolute busybody, depending on the author's intention or aim in appropriating the paradigm; and Heracles, in turn, is transformed into a moral exemplar, who heroically resists the temptations of Lady Vice. However, before we turn to adaptations of these heroic paradigms in the first–fourth centuries CE, it is worth noting something that often goes over-

---

24. We may note, in particular, the lexical repetition of "sweat" (cf. W&D 289: ἱδρῶτα) for a description of the path, which Vice later labels a "difficult and long road" (*Mem.* 2.1.29: χαλεπὴν καὶ μακρὰν ὁδόν). See again Koning 2010, 144–45; and Hunter 2014a, 98–99.

25. On which, see Stafford 2012, 23–50 and 104–36. On Apuleius' reception and philosophical intellectualization of Heracles' labors, see *Fl.* 22.3–4 (with Stafford 2012, 126).

26. I do not discuss the reception of Odysseus or Heracles in Greek tragedy because it is not particularly relevant to their reception in Apuleius' milieu and because these topics have been well-treated by Worman 1999; and Lu Hsu 2020, respectively. Similarly, I bypass the reception and representation of Odysseus and Heracles in the Hellenistic period, since a majority of the evidence for the intellectualization of these two heroes in Hellenistic philosophy actually comes from the imperial period (on which, see Montiglio 2011, 66–94 and Stafford 2012, 124–30, respectively); and it is the Platonic and Prodicean allegories of these paradigms, at any rate, that exert the greatest influence on imperial and Second Sophistic approaches to reader-response.

looked here in Xenophon's dramatization of Hesiod's "two roads," namely, that Heracles never actually makes a choice. Indeed, this episode, so often referred to in scholarship as "the choice of Heracles," is, in fact, glossed in Prodicus' allegory as "Heracles' education by Virtue" (2.1.34: τὴν ὑπ᾽ Ἀρετῆς Ἡρακλέους παίδευσιν). The episode concludes, however, in a decidedly open fashion: that Heracles chooses to follow Lady Virtue is only inferred *by the reader*.[27] Moreover, the underlying theme of "Heracles' education" represents at its core the didactic goal of the entire Platonic or Socratic project, indeed, of all *paideia*: namely, to discern what one should call *eudaimonia* and how one ought to go about acquiring it and passing it on to others. It is crucial to keep in mind, then, that Xenophon's failure of closure in "Heracles' education" offers an invitation to the reader to create that closure by making a choice, to impose a final solution on "open" *aporia*. Simply put, at the fount of a tradition that would go on to have a rich afterlife in the imperial period and Second Sophistic, we already see the seeds of reader-response developing.

1.2. The Creation of Heroic Readers in the Imperial Period and Second Sophistic

Given limitations of space, it will not be possible to treat in detail every recurrence of these two heroic paradigms in later antiquity. By my count, "Heracles' education" appears as an exemplary model for imitation at least eighteen times in later antiquity (excluding Apuleius),[28] and Odysseus facing his various temptations is even more prevalent as a philosophical paradigm.[29] What is more ger-

---

27. So, all of the Second Sophistic appropriations of Heracles' "choice" presume. See n. 28 below for a comprehensive list. Lucian's two parodies of the choice, the *Dream* and *Rhetorum praeceptor*, may be highlighting the failure of closure in Xenophon's original, on which, see Levine Gera 1995; and Hunter 2014a, 99–100.

28. Only two of these allusions, moreover, occur in texts which predate the imperial period and Second Sophistic: Cicero's *De off.* 1.117 (on which, see §1.3) and Ovid's *Am.* 3.1. In the first–fourth centuries CE, however, "Heracles' education" is alluded to in the following texts: Persius *Sat.* 5.30–40; Plutarch's *Quomodo quis Sentiat* 77d; Philo *De sacr. ca. et ab.* 20–44; *tabula Cebetis*; Silius Italicus *Pun.* 15.18–128; Dio Chr. 1.66–83; Lucian's *Dream* and *Rhetorum praeceptor*; Maximus *Or.* 14.1; Justin Martyr *Apol.* 2.11; Clement *Paed.* 2.10.110; Philostratus *VA* 6.10; Themistius *Or.* 2.11; Basil *De leg. gr. lib.* 5.55–77, Augustine *Conf.* 8.12. Moreover, the "two roads" motif from Hesiod is adapted as a fable in the anonymous *Life of Aesop* (94). We may also note that Ovid's allusion to the Heraclean choice in *Am.* 3.1—one of only two instances prior to the late first century—constitutes a generic decision for the poetic speaker between Elegy and Tragedy, an antecedent perhaps for Lucian's *Dream*.

29. On which, see Stanford 1963, 118–27; and Montiglio 2011, 87–94 and 124–47. See also §2.1 for further discussion (with bibliography).

mane to my argument is the fact that both models are retooled specifically as an approach to reading and responding to literature and art in Apuleius' milieu. Thus, in the hands of imperial and Second Sophistic authors, aesthetic experience becomes the site of either an Odyssean encounter with the Sirens—dangerous but didactic, if handled correctly—or a Heraclean crossroads choice. Indeed, in the first–fourth centuries CE, these two archetypes are held up as exemplary readers by all sorts of authors, both pagan (e.g., Plutarch, Lucian, Dio Chrysostom, Maximus of Tyre, pseudo-Cebes, Silius Italicus, Philostratus, and Themistius) and Judeo-Christian (e.g., Philo of Alexandria, Justin Martyr, Clement of Alexandria, and Basil of Caesarea). The proliferation of choice-narratives in this period suggests that a discourse about how change, or "conversion," takes place is rapidly evolving in Apuleius' milieu: external stimuli, such as texts or art, have the capacity to seduce or entice a reader, on the one hand, but also the power to bring about a philosophical-religious encounter, on the other.

In the interest of keeping the two tropes separate, I will break from performing my analysis chronologically, preferring instead to treat separately the reception of Odysseus and Heracles as ideal readers. It is worth keeping in mind, however, that in some cases, the boundary between the two heroic paradigms of response becomes porous or blurred, despite the fact that the differences between these mythical figures are so stark. My goal in this section, furthermore, is not to oversimplify by suggesting that all of the texts I treat below—which are composed in very different contexts, genres, and discourse communities—are trying to accomplish the same outcomes or effects through their appropriation of our heroic models. Rather, I aim to sketch the outlines of a specific phenomenon: the appropriation of epic and classical heroes as models of aesthetic response, which was to span four centuries across the whole empire. By doing so, I hope to give a sense of the *Zeitgeist* in which Apuleius is composing his novel.

1.2a. Odyssean Knowledge in the Imperial Period and Second Sophistic

It is not especially unique to the imperial period and Second Sophistic that Odysseus becomes an exemplary model for philosophical inquiry and the acquisition of knowledge. As Silvia Montiglio has shown in her comprehensive study of Odysseus' literary-philosophical afterlife, the metaphorical power of his *nostos* had such purchase as a tale of human experience and exploration that the name of the hero is treated with a certain reverence across antiquity.[30] As we shall explore in more depth in chapter 2, Odysseus is utilized for his allegorical potential as early as Alcidamas (fourth century BCE), possibly even earlier,[31] and the "mirror" of the *Odyssey* becomes a *topos* that takes on a life of its own in the Latin tradition.[32] For instance, a well-known passage of Cicero's *De finibus* presents the Middle Platonist Antiochus of Ascalon's theory of habituation (elucidated by Piso in the dialogue), in which he explains that Odysseus was attracted to the Sirens precisely because of his "desire for learning" (*De fin.* 5.49: *cupiditas discendi*).[33] In later Neoplatonic readings, moreover, Odysseus' journey is even transformed into a spiritual allegory for the *peregrinatio animi*, the fall and redemption the soul undergoes in the process of embodiment and return to the upper realm.[34]

While it is fascinating to gauge the ebb and flow of Odysseus' symbolic status across antiquity (and beyond), what is unique about the first–fourth centuries CE is the fact that Odysseus becomes a model for reading. Paradoxically, he functions as a paragon of virtue precisely in the episodes from the *Odyssey* in which he prefers to indulge himself in pleasure rather than demonstrate any kind of philosophical restraint. It is not the journey in a more general sense that is exemplary as in earlier traditions, where travel is linked to philosophical curiosity and engagement with the world;[35] rather, in the first–fourth centuries, it is precisely *because* Odysseus listens to the Sirens or drinks down Circe's brew, and nonetheless manages to escape, that he becomes a paradigm for how one ought to engage with text or art.[36]

I begin my series of case studies with Lucian's *Nigrinus*, in part because there

---

30. On Odysseus' *Nachleben* across antiquity, see Montiglio 2011. On Odysseus in the Second Sophistic in particular, see Hunter 2018, 92–135.

31. In fact, this method of allegorizing of the *Odyssey* may go back even to the hazy figure of Theagenes of Rhegium, on which, see, e.g., Ford 2002, 68–72; and Domaradzki 2017. See also Buffière 1956, 105, who recognizes Theagenes as "la[ying] the foundations for this allegorical exegesis" (*jetait les bases de cette exégèse allégorique*).

32. See esp. §2.1 and 2.2.

33. Apuleius was clearly aware of this Ciceronian passage, as he alludes to it with the phrase *cupido discendi* in his *laus speculi* in *Apologia* 16, on which, see §2.1 and 2.3.

34. See, e.g., O'Connell 1996, 3–89. See also Ulrich (forthcoming b) on Apuleius' play with "inverted allegory" and his anticipation of this Neoplatonic allegorizing of the soul's journey in *C&P*.

35. Odysseus already possessed a certain philosophical purchase in the late archaic and early classical period for his travels, as Dougherty 2001, 3–13, has well demonstrated. On the connection between wandering and philosophical knowledge, see Montiglio 2005. Cf. again Cic. *De fin.* 5.49–50, where Piso explicitly links Odysseus to wandering philosophers.

36. This is anticipated to a certain extent by Horace's *Epist.* 1.2, which creatively rewrites Odysseus' encounter with aesthetic pleasure (on which, see my discussion in §2.1 with bibliography).

SETTING THE STAGE FOR APULEIUS   57

we see *in nuce* a number of important elements of the Odysseus *topos*. The frame of the dialogue involves a reaction to a speech, which identifies a kind of philosophical madness as the appropriate response to charming discourse. This mania is likened to drunkenness, an overconsumption of undiluted wine. In this instance, philosophical conversion relies precisely on the ability to withstand the temptations of external stimuli. The speaker suggests that an ideal reader ought to be "like Odysseus" in some respects, but rather than using physical restraints to endure temptations, one should rely on a philosophically informed self-control as the proverbial mast to guide one through aesthetic pleasure. Indeed, incorporating Plato's anxieties about the Sirens in the *Phaedrus* and the *Symposium*, certain types of pleasures are to be avoided "like Odysseus," while others are to be indulged, such as listening to the philosopher.

Lucian's Second Sophistic parody on the Academic philosopher Albinus[37] opens with a mock-Platonic recollection of an unnamed speaker's interaction with a famous philosopher named Nigrinus. The speaker, who recounts Nigrinus' encomium of philosophy, describes his experience in terms obviously borrowed from Plato's *Phaedrus*: on hearing the speech, he is "enraptured and drunk with the wine of [Nigrinus'] philosophical discourse" (*Nigrin.* 5: αὐτὸς ἔνθεος καὶ μεθύων ὑπὸ τῶν λόγων περιέρχομαι), just as "Indians are said to experience when first exposed to wine" (οἱ Ἰνδοὶ πρὸς τὸν οἶνον λέγονται παθεῖν). In Nigrinus' response, in turn, we learn that Rome is a school of virtue (*Nigrin.* 19: γυμνάσιον ἀρετῆς) precisely because it is a "test of the soul" (τῆς ψυχῆς δοκιμασίαν): paradoxically, being surrounded by the temptations of so many external stimuli can compel the true philosopher to resist dissolute living.[38] Thus, likening the task of resisting all the sights and sounds of Rome to Odysseus' encounter with the Sirens, Nigrinus explains (*Nigrin.* 19):

> ἀτεχνῶς δεῖ τὸν Ὀδυσσέα μιμησάμενον παραπλεῖν αὐτὰ μὴ δεδεμένον τὼ χεῖρε—δειλὸν γάρ—μηδὲ τὰ ὦτα κηρῷ φραξάμενον, ἀλλ᾽ ἀκούοντα καὶ λελυμένον καὶ ἀληθῶς ὑπερήφανον.

---

37. See Tarrant 1985 on the parody of Albinus in Lucian's dialogue.

38. As with much Lucianic satire, this motif parodies anxieties familiar from Lucian's milieu: for instance, Plutarch's *De curiositate* deals at length with all of the external stimuli (e.g., inscriptions, graffiti, marketplaces, brothels, etc.) which can exercise sway over the *polypragmôn* and even over the wise man who lacks *enkrateia* (see, e.g., *De curios.* 520d); Aulus Gellius seems to extend Plutarch's discussion of external stimuli, moreover, to the value of reading for mastering "enticements," or *inlecebrae* (on which, see Howley 2018, 27–33).

It is necessary simply to imitate Odysseus and sail by them—not bound by your hands (for that is cowardly), nor having guarded the ears with wax, but listening and free and truly contemptuous.

We find out at the end of the dialogue, however, that the ability to listen to and be transformed by an encounter with what is illicit is dependent on a listener's (or reader's) intrinsic nature. As the main speaker concludes the dialogue (*Nigrin*. 37):

οὕτω δὴ καὶ φιλοσόφων ἀκούοντες οὐ πάντες ἔνθεοι καὶ τραυματίαι ἀπίασιν, ἀλλ᾽ οἷς ὑπῆν τι **ἐν τῇ φύσει** φιλοσοφίας συγγενές.

So naturally, not all who listen to philosophers go away enraptured and wounded, but only those who already had something **in their nature**, a kinship with philosophy.

It would seem, therefore, that Lucian's dialogue confirms (if parodically) the sneaking suspicion, which Plato first introduced with Alcibiades in his encomium of Socrates in the *Symposium*,[39] namely, that enlightened inspiration comes only to those who already have philosophical inclinations "in their nature." In order to become a philosophically adept version of Odysseus, we need neither wax nor rope to tie around our hands. Rather, we ought to engage temptations "free" and "truly contemptuous." Only those with inherently philosophical natures, however, will know how to go about achieving this philosophical sublimity.

Next, we turn to Plutarch's *How to Study Poetry*, which similarly presents Odysseus as the paradigmatic reader of seductive verse and thus, constitutes one of the earliest texts to deploy this mode of reader-response.[40] *How to Study*

---

39. On the *Symposium* as Plato's second apology for Socrates, as it exposes Alcibiades' true hybristic nature, see Hunter 2004, esp. 100–101. On Alcibiades' failure to respond appropriately, see Montiglio 2011, 133–34. On Lucian's intertextual engagement with Plato's Sirens generally in the *Nigrinus*, we may also note the reuse of the term *paraplein* at *Nigrin*. 19, which appears in Plato's cicadas episode in the *Phaedrus* (259a7).

40. On Plutarch as the first "modern" reader in this text, see Konstan 2004, though I take some issue with his conflation of "modernity" with deconstructionism. Indeed, Plutarch is "modern" in the sense that he offers a proto-reader-response theory, locating meaning not in the author's intention, but in the reader's response. However, he is by no means a deconstructionist. Rather, he outlines appropriate and inappropriate paradigms of response, thereby suggesting a "correct" approach to the conundrum of meaning-making. Cf. Grethlein 2021, 137–65, for an analysis of Plutarch's ethical approach to aesthetics.

Poetry provides a protreptic guide for educating youths to extract "what is useful" (*Quomodo adul.* 14f: τὸ χρήσιμον) from otherwise pleasurable texts, since young people "need education in their readings even more than in the streets" (15a: ὡς ἐν ταῖς ἀναγνώσεσι μᾶλλον ἢ ταῖς ὁδοῖς παιδαγωγίας δεομένους). In the opening of the dialogue, where the narrator develops a framework for a pedagogy of reading, he alludes explicitly to our Odysseus archetype: he asks his addressee whether one should stop up the ears of the young with wax and have them sail along, avoiding poetry altogether; or alternatively, whether one ought to "direct and guard their judgment by setting them against some correct method of reasoning and binding them to it."[41] Finally, drawing the lesson to its anticipated conclusion, Plutarch explains that young people must use poetry, especially fictional texts, as an exercise in "proto-philosophy" (15f: προφιλοσοφητέον): only by imbibing the pleasure of poetry adulterated by *philosophia* do students become inoculated, "habituating themselves to seek out what is beneficial in their delight" (16a: ἐθιζομένους ἐν τῷ τέρποντι τὸ χρήσιμον ζητεῖν), just as one "mixes wine" (15e: ἡ κρᾶσις τοῦ οἴνου) with water to allow for a tempered pleasure. Once again, we see reading as a dangerous and potentially entrapping activity—one akin to intoxication; and we find Plutarch advocating a specific mode of inculcating virtuous reading habits in young people, exhorting them to be like Odysseus, who could listen to the Sirens only when physically restrained. With this attempt to address Plato's anxieties about poetry,[42] Plutarch suggests (like Rabelais) that literature hides within it a simplified kind of philosophy, and as Hunter notes, seems to advocate for this procedure of "proto-philosophizing" as a means to be "actively engaged in the reading process in a manner which prepares [a young person] for the cut and thrust of philosophical debate."[43] In this case, "some correct method of reasoning" is the mast which holds students fast as they navigate their way through seductive texts.

As we move forward in time, we see Plutarch's advice to young readers retooled for a Christian audience in Basil of Caesarea's *Exhortation to the Young*

---

41. *Quomodo adul.* 15d: ἢ μᾶλλον ὀρθῷ τινι λογισμῷ παριστάντες καὶ καταδέοντες, τὴν κρίσιν . . . ἀπευθύνωμεν καὶ παραφυλάττωμεν.

42. On Plutarch's engagement with Plato in this passage, see Zadorojnyi 2002; and Beneker 2011. Despite a scholarly tradition of viewing Plutarch as a simple-minded moralist in *How to Read Poetry*, Zadorojnyi demonstrates a much more complex pedagogical theory at work. See also Konstan 2004. On the influence of Plato's anxieties over *mimesis* on Second Sophistic discourse, see §3.1.

43. See Hunter 2009a, 172.

60   THE SHADOW OF AN ASS

to Read Pagan Literature, which exhibits the same impulse but puts forward a very different refashioning of the tale.[44] Basil advises his young Christian acolytes that, when poets turn to singing songs about the deeds of evil and dissolute men, "it is necessary to flee the imitation of this by stopping up their ears no less than (they say) Odysseus did when faced with the songs of the Sirens."[45] As Ernest Fortin points out, Basil has offered something of a fictional version of Odysseus, considering that Homer's Odysseus refused to stop up his ears when faced with the Sirens' song, wanting instead to experience the pleasure while avoiding the consequences.[46] *Pace* Fortin, however, we may note that Basil seems here to have been influenced more by the philosophical tradition on the Sirens rather than the original Homeric episode: after all, his description of the appropriate behavior for young readers appears to mirror Alcibiades' reaction to Socrates in the *Symposium*, when he "stops up his ears" (*Symp.* 216a5: ἐπισχόμενος τὰ ὦτα; cf. ἐπιφρασσομένους τὰ ὦτα) and "flees" (φεύγων; cf. φεύγειν) the Siren-song of the philosopher for fear of growing old beside him. Whereas in Lucian and Plutarch, young people must be habituated to experience pleasure in moderation—"free and truly contemptuous," or tied to the mast of reason—in Basil, literature is safe until the point of mimetic contagion: once one begins to replicate the actions of the characters inside the fiction, it is necessary to flee.[47]

We could go on at length about further reworkings of Odysseus as an exemplary reader, from Odysseus the consummate learner and busybody, as in Plutarch's *On Curiosity* (516a–b), to Odysseus as a model for Augustine's *peregrinatio animi* in the *Confessions*.[48] At this point, however, it is necessary only to note that, at the very end of the hermeneutic tradition and in the wake of many imperial, Second Sophistic, and late antique reworkings of Odysseus-the-reader, we find the hero's willingness to indulge himself at every turn applied as

---

44. There has been much discussion on Basil of Caesarea's inheritance of Plutarch's advice in *How to Study Poetry* (see, e.g., Valgiglio 1975; Wilson 1975; and Naldini 1984). Recently, Beneker 2011 has demonstrated that Basil is reading Plato through the lens of Plutarch, much like Apuleius (cf. DeFilippo 1990). On how Basil blends Plutarch's *How to Study Poetry* with his *On Progress in Virtue*—conflating the two heroic archetypes—see below.
45. *De leg. gr. lib.* 4.2: τὴν μίμησιν ταύτην δεῖ φεύγειν, ἐπιφρασσομένους τὰ ὦτα, οὐχ ἧττον ἢ τὸν Ὀδυσσέα φασὶν ἐκεῖνοι τὰ τῶν Σειρήνων μέλη.
46. See Fortin 1981, 190–91 for discussion.
47. On "mimetic contagion" as a phenomenon in antiquity, see Whitmarsh 2002 and Germany 2016, on which, see §3.0. On the reemergence of Platonic anxieties about "mimetic contagion" in the imperial period and Second Sophistic, see §3.1.
48. See again discussion in O'Connell 1994, 174–291. On "Plutarch's patronage of Odysseus," see Montiglio 2011, 128–31.

SETTING THE STAGE FOR APULEIUS   61

an allegory specifically for the reading experience of a Greek novel. Indeed, the late allegorizing interpreter of the *Aethiopica*, "Philip the Philosopher,"[49] reads Heliodorus' late antique rewrite of the *Odyssey* precisely in terms of reader-response:

Ἡ βίβλος αὕτη, ὦ φίλοι, Κιρκαίῳ κυκεῶνι ὠμοίωται, τοὺς μὲν βεβήλως μεταλαμβάνοντας μεταμορφοῦσα εἰς χοίρων ἀσέλγειαν, τοὺς δὲ κατ' Ὀδυσσέα φιλοσοφοῦντας μυσταγωγοῦσα τὰ ὑψηλότερα· παιδαγωγικὴ γὰρ ἡ βίβλος καὶ ἠθικῆς φιλοσοφίας διδάσκαλος, τῷ τῆς ἱστορίας ὕδατι τὸν οἶνον τῆς θεωρίας κεράσασα.[50]

This book, my friends, is very much like Circe's brew: it transforms those who take it in a profane manner into licentious pigs, but those who approach it in a philosophical way, in the manner of Odysseus, are initiated into higher things. The book is educational, teaching ethical philosophy by mixing the wine of contemplation into the water of the tale.

Contemplation (*theôria*) is thus used at the very close of late antiquity to describe how one ought to approach reading an ancient novel.[51] The book is only "pedagogical" (*paidagôgikê*) for the right kind of reader—the one who approaches it *philosophically* "in the manner of Odysseus." Moreover, while the metaphor of intoxication is once again enacted in the context of reading, the wine-consumption can go in two directions: one can be "metamorphosed" into a quadruped (*metamorphousa*), or alternatively, one can be "initiated" into the mysteries (*mustagôgousa*).[52] In fact, we may even note an interesting reversal in "Philip's" language: *theôria* is likened to the intoxicating agent, where transcendent enlightenment becomes the potentially dangerous component, whereas *historia*—the written down version of events—provides the counterbalance. When we return to the *Metamorphoses* (§1.3)—a novel in which the main character attempts to experience magic through a witches' brew but is instead trans-

---

49. For useful discussions of this text, see Lamberton 1986, 148–57; Sandy 2001; and Hunter 2005.
50. The text comes from Hercher 1869, 383, and the translation is adapted from Lamberton 1986, 307.
51. On situating the *Aethiopica* and "Philip the Philosopher's" allegorizing approach in Neoplatonic discourse, see Lamberton 1986, 149–57. On the difficulty of dating the text (the dates of which range from the fifth-twelfth centuries CE), see Sandy 2001, 170–72.
52. Cf. Lamberton 1986, 157: "The *Ethiopica* is, then, a romance that hints a mystical allegory, elevates epic themes, and fills them with a content both adapted to contemporary taste and quite foreign to the works that were the original sources. . . . It is not a systematic allegory, but no doubt it was possible early in its history to read it as one."

formed into a quadruped only to be initiated in the end into a mystery cult—it is no coincidence that the narrator likens his experience explicitly to a quest for Odyssean knowledge.[53] And for our purpose as readers engaging with this book as an intermediary between the grotesque and the sublime, it is significant, in my view, that the asinine *auctor*'s experience is destined to become a *historia* expressed in written form.[54]

1.2b. Heracles at the Crossroads of the Text

Just as Odysseus had a rich afterlife in antiquity for his symbolic potential as a philosophical traveler and model of aesthetic response, so also Heracles was appealed to as a model of choice across antiquity, from being a paradigm of philosophical *enkrateia* to an appropriately stoic figure.[55] Once again, though, I am interested in elucidating here how Heracles is recognized and regarded as an ideal reader in the imperial period and Second Sophistic, since his choice, or "education," at the crossroads represents an approach to pleasure and knowledge strikingly at odds with the Odyssean archetype.

Whereas Plutarch trots out Odysseus as a paragon of virtue in *How to Study Poetry*, he takes a rather different tack in *On Progress in Virtue*. There, he deploys the archaic antecedent to the Heraclean model, Hesiod's "two roads," as a metaphor to describe how one ought to approach pleasurable literature. Opening his text with "Hesiod's very ancient explanation of progress" (*Quomodo quis Sentiat* 77d: τὸ πρεσβύτατον δήλωμα προκοπῆς τοῦ Ἡσιόδου), Plutarch subtly reverses the terms of the Heraclean paradigm. Surprisingly, the path to virtue is "easy, smooth, and accessible" (ῥᾳδίαν καὶ λείαν καὶ δι᾽ εὐπετείας), as long as it has been made smooth "by practice" (τῇ ἀσκήσει). If one has managed to smooth out the path, then "there is a brightness and clarity in philosophizing" (φῶς ἐν τῷ φιλοσοφεῖν καὶ λαμπρότητα), which removes the "confusion and wandering" (ἐξ ἀπορίας καὶ πλάνης) philosophers encoun-

---

53. See *Met.* 9.13 (on which, more below in §1.3). Graverini 2012a, 25, also reads the "sweet poetics" of the *Metamorphoses* in light of this passage from "Philip the Philosopher." See also Hunter 2005, 124; and Ulrich (forthcoming b) on the *Met.*'s merging of "interpretative" and "compositional" allegory.

54. Cf. *Met.* 2.12: *nunc enim gloriam satis floridam, nunc historiam magnam et incredundam fabulam et libros me futurum*, on which, see Adkins 2022, 187–88 (with bibliography).

55. Stafford 2012 is the most up-to-date treatment on Heracles across antiquity. Galinsky 1972 remains very useful.

ter at first.[56] Then, expanding this into a model for reading philosophy, history, and poetry a few sections later, Plutarch explains that one must approach pleasurable texts just as a bee flits from flower to flower looking for honey: while other readers pore over poems "for the sake of pleasure or play" (79c–d: ἡδονῆς ἕνεκα καὶ παιδιᾶς), the one who finds and extracts "something worthy of seriousness" (τι . . . σπουδῆς ἄξιον) makes himself capable of understanding "through habituation and love of the beautiful" (ὑπὸ συνηθείας καὶ φιλίας τοῦ καλοῦ). Here, to be sure, Plutarch weaves very different strands of literary-critical discourse into his archetype of choice. For instance, while the bee already had its own rich literary heritage in antiquity (e.g., in Semonides 7 in Greek lyric, and perhaps even more famously, as a metapoetic device in Vergil's *Georgics* 4 and Horace's *Carmina* 4.2), Plutarch's use of this image to model an approach to reading imbues it with new meaning in the first century CE. Plutarch's bee is not merely an anthologizer in the strict sense of the word, picking out flowers that are particularly pleasurable. Rather, it looks for what is *utile*, what is "worthy of seriousness," amid flowers that most readers experience only as a means to aesthetic pleasure.[57] Finally, after modeling a practice of anthologizing by reviewing himself a number of famous *exempla* who prized the effects of training (e.g., Aeschylus, Diogenes, and Thucydides), Plutarch connects his charming bee analogy back to the *askêsis* involved in making a choice (79f):

οὕτω τὸ **προσέχειν** καὶ τετάσθαι τὴν ἄσκησιν αἰσθητικοὺς καὶ δεκτικοὺς ποιεῖ τῶν πρὸς ἀρετὴν φερόντων ἀπανταχόθεν.

Thus, paying attention and straining in practice makes people perceptive of and receptive to those things which lead to virtue, from whatever source.

In short, the content of literature is unproblematic for Plutarch provided that one "pays attention" in such a way as to leverage the experience toward the acquisition of "virtue."[58] Or in other words, to habituate oneself to the harsh

---

56. We may note the Stoic buzzword of philosophical restraint here in the term *askêsis*: Plutarch's vision entails a certain experience of rejecting pleasure before even arriving at the "two roads."

57. It should not go unnoticed that these are precisely the terms in which the Platonic debate over corrupting rhetoric is articulated in the *Phaedrus* (276d–e): *paidia* vs. *spoudê*. On Apuleius' participation in this debate in the *Met.*, see Graverini 2012a, 36–42, and on aesthetic vs. utilitarian approaches to beauty across Apuleius' corpus, see ch. 4 below.

58. Here, we may recall from §0.4 Apuleius' ambivalent close to his Prologue—*lector intende* ("reader, pay attention") —on which, see fuller discussion in §2.4.

road of virtue (and thereby, make it easy), one must make the necessary philosophical investment.

This model of reading as a Heraclean choice between two paths is refashioned in the following century as an ironic parody of education writ-large in two Lucianic texts: Lucian's pseudobiographical *Somnium*[59] and his "savage . . . invective [against] a counterfeit sophist,"[60] the *Rhetorum praeceptor*. In both texts, there is a choice between two speakers who perform an *agôn* before a young man. The decision is made absurd in each case, however, by presenting no dilemma whatsoever to the ostensible Heracles-figure: for the parallel to Lady Vice in both texts possesses no apparent redeeming qualities. The *Somnium* is a mock-autobiography about a young Lucian's career choice to follow Lady "Education" (Παιδεία) rather than Lady "Sculpture" (Τέχνη), who offers him fame as a craftsman: significantly, Lady *Technê* is ugly, poorly dressed, and covered in dust from sculpting marble, whereas Lady *Paideia* is refined, beautiful, and dressed in fancy clothes. As Deborah Levine Gera has noted, this flies in the face of all other adaptations of Heracles at the crossroads, since the choice is usually between two beautiful women, one of whom has a natural but modest beauty, and the other a seductive, yet artificial attraction.[61] For the reader, however, there is a nagging point at the end of the dialogue, in which Lucian seems to imply that he made the wrong choice by taking the easy road: for on closer inspection, Lady *Technê* possesses the most important qualities of Lady Virtue in all the other Heraclean choice narratives and in fact, appears similar to Socrates or the unshod *Erôs* of Plato's *Symposium*. In short, by assimilating *Paideia* to Lady Vice in "Heracles' education"—whether seriously or in a more parodic spirit—Lucian subtly demonstrates what taking the wrong road might look like.[62]

The *Rhetorum praeceptor* reveals a similarly ironizing approach to the Heraclean archetype by presenting a young man who is embarking on the study of rhetoric with a choice between a long, difficult road (one accompanied by an

---

59. There is some debate about precisely how autobiographical this is: see, e.g., Hall 1981, 16–17; Baldwin 1961, 206; and Jones 1986, 9. Cf. Anderson 1976, 80–81, for skepticism.

60. See Heath 2007, 6, for this assessment.

61. See Levine Gera 1995, 242–43, where she notes at 242: "while a marked contrast between the two women is a standard feature of these tales, it is rare for one of the women to be quite so unattractive as Lucian's *Techne*." Most of the tales "contrast an artless, attractive good woman with an artificial, but alluring, bad one" (243).

62. As Levine Gera 1995, 238, also notes, the fact that Lucian's family trade was masonry links him to "that most famous stonemason of all, Socrates." Lucian's choice thus distances him from a Socratic archetype in his *failure* to pick the right road.

embittered discontent who has already traveled the road to no good outcome) and a short, easy road to sweet success. As Richard Hunter has suggested, this curious diatribe functions, much like the *Somnium*, as "an extensive inversion of Hesiod and of the didactic tradition as a whole . . . a lesson in how to avoid *ponos*":[63] the end goal of the youth's adviser, who mistakenly traveled the hard and difficult road in the footsteps of the likes of Plato and Demosthenes, was ultimately to reach the "highest peak in every vice" (*Rhet. praec.* 25: τὸν ἀκρότατον ἐν πάσῃ κακίᾳ). And yet, although the text is rife with parody and wit in classic Lucianic fashion, it seems at the same time to suggest that the short road to glorious success as a rhetorician has "fruits that are only deceptively sweet."[64] Simply put, in both the *Somnium* and the *Rhetorum praeceptor*, the choice is made to look simple by virtue of the superficially unappealing or ridiculous nature of one of the two options: who on earth would choose to follow the long, hard road, when it seemingly does not lead to where it promises? Much like the bait-and-switch we saw in Apuleius' Prologue, however, the butt of the joke at the end of the text may (surprisingly) be the reader who takes this as mere parody. The choice for the character *inside* the text invites reflection from readers who are *outside* of it on their life choices and in doing so, provokes a protreptic cognitive dissonance.

Just as with the allegorization of Odysseus-as-reader, we could proceed at length with other appropriations of the Heraclean archetype, such as how Dio Chrysostom deploys the "two roads" motif in his first *Oration* on kingship in the late first century CE, or how a half century later, Maximus of Tyre resorts to this trope at the opening of *Oration* 14 to distinguish the flatterer from the friend. Indeed, the *topos* also permeates early Christian discourse within another half century, when Clement of Alexandria, in a tirade against cosmetics and fancy clothing, cites the Ceian Sophist approvingly for "painting [in the allegory of Heracles] images of virtue and vice" (*Paed.* 2.10.110: ἀρετῆς καὶ κακίας εἰκόνας ὑπογράφοντα). Contemporaneously with Clement, Philostratus resorts to "Heracles' education" as a model for choosing different strands of philosophical discourse in the *Vita Apollonii* (6.10.5); and what's more, this passage also attests, as Maaike Zimmerman notes, to the existence of visual

---

63. Hunter 2014a, 98. Cf. also Gibson 2012, who argues that Lucian seems to be mocking a famous pithy saying, or *chreia*, of Isocrates—that "the root of education is bitter, but its fruits are sweet"— which became a popular aphorism on which to elaborate in rhetorical education.

64. Gibson 2012, 92. Cf. also Hunter 2014a, 99, who reads the text as a possible criticism of rhetoric *à la* Plato's *Gorgias* as an unrewarding choice in contrast to the promises of the philosophical life.

66   THE SHADOW OF AN ASS

representations—"picture-books" (ἐν ζωγραφίας λόγοις)—of Prodicus' allegory circulating at this time.[65] Finally, the influence of this tale endures well into fourth-century CE Christian discourse and beyond, as Basil of Caesarea uses Heracles together with Hesiod's "two roads" in his *Exhortation to the Young to Read Pagan Literature*. In a near quotation of Plutarch's *On Progress in Virtue*, Basil explains that, although pagan literature can be dangerous, the young must extract only "as much as is useful" (*De leg. gr. lib.* 4.10: ὅσον χρήσιμον), "just as we keep away from the thorns when plucking flowers from a rose-bed."[66] In Basil's educational treatise, in other words, young readers are fully transformed into Plutarch's flitting bees, becoming anthologists, as it were, of philosophical gems amid otherwise dangerous pleasures. At this point in our story, then, I hope it is clear that "Heracles' education" was tapped for its didactic value as a powerful literary trope time and again in the imperial period and Second Sophistic—most often in the context of reading and education—and so, was in the *Zeitgeist* of the late first–fourth centuries CE.

I would like to conclude my review of the afterlife of the Heraclean model with an analysis of two final passages: the unattributed first-century CE *tabula Cebetis*, and Maximus of Tyre's *Oration* 18. These final two passages are, in a sense, the most important, even though it is speculative to suggest that Apuleius read the former,[67] and the latter only implicitly invokes the moment of choice. Both are representative, however, of the kinds of conversations intellectuals are having about art and text in the resurging Greek enlightenment and in Apuleius' milieu.

The *tabula Cebetis*, an allegorical *ekphrasis* tentatively dated to the first century CE on stylistic grounds,[68] provides an extended meditation on the choice of Heracles, mediated by a "tablet" (*pinax*) discovered by some strangers in a

---

65. Zimmerman 2002, 92–93.
66. *De leg. gr. lib.* 4.8: καθάπερ τῆς ῥοδωνιᾶς τοῦ ἄνθους δρεψάμενοι τὰς ἀκάνθας ἐκκλίνομεν. On Basil's appropriation of Plutarch's *On Progress in Virtue*—specifically, at this moment in Basil's text—see Beneker 2011.
67. We know that the *tabula Cebetis* was widely read in Apuleius' time, as Lucian seems to refer to it twice (*Merc. cond.* 42; *Rhet. praec.* 6) and Tertullian names the author and the work, and even suggests that it had been translated into Latin hexameter verse (*De praescr. haeret.* 39: *Pinacem Cebetis*). On these references, see Nesselrath 2005, 43–45; and Seddon 2005, 177–80. Grethlein and Squire 2014, 287–88, provide helpful discussion of the text's authenticity and influence.
68. Grethlein and Squire 2014, 288n14 with bibliography, for the dating of the text. There seem to be some lexicographical *termini post quem* (Drosihn 1871, 37–39) that make it impossible for the text to be earlier than the first century CE. Others believe that Dio Chrys. 10.30–32 alludes to the text (see Joly 1963, 13–21), which would date it at the very latest to the mid to late first century. Lucian's more obvious references to it make it very plausible that it was vibrant in intellectual discourse by Apuleius' time.

SETTING THE STAGE FOR APULEIUS 67

garden sacred to Kronos. Ekphrastic exegesis of a picture, especially of a sacred object, is another familiar *topos* of Second Sophistic literature, most famously occurring in the opening frame of Longus' *Daphnis and Chloe*.[69] This *pinax* is somewhat different, however, insofar as the *tabula Cebetis* is figured at the outset not only as a sacred offering, but also as an *ainigma*—a riddle to be interpreted, which the exegete compares to the "riddle of the Sphinx" (3.2: Σφιγγὸς αἰνίγματι). Indeed, the old man, who conveniently arrives to provide an extended allegorical explanation of this painted tablet to the strangers, emphasizes that the very act of interpreting this object "furnishes some danger" (3.1: ἐπικίνδυνόν τι ἔχει): for if his auditors "pay attention" (προσέξετε) and "understand" (συνήσετε) his words, they will become "wise and happy" (φρόνιμοι καὶ εὐδαίμονες); but if they do not, they will be doomed to "live in an utterly wretched manner" (κακῶς βιώσεσθε).

Once again, we may recognize at the opening of this text a call to attentive reading. Indeed, just as we saw Plutarch connect the practice of "paying attention" (*Quomodo quis Sentiat* 79f: προσέχειν) to Hesiod's "two roads" by suggesting that readers must develop through *askêsis* a receptivity to that which leads "to virtue" (πρὸς ἀρετὴν), so also, the old exegete demands that his audience "pay attention" (προσέξετε < τὸν νοῦν προσέχειν). Significantly, the exegete suggests, this *pinax* can lead to *eudaimonia*; such an outcome hinges, however, on whether one makes the proper philosophical investment while navigating its enticements. The danger of interpreting this visual object is akin to the danger involved in reading a text: it demands a choice from the interpreter; but it also threatens to stupefy, stultify, and immobilize.[70]

It makes a good deal of sense, therefore, that "Heracles' education" in this first-century CE allegory is reconceived as a choice not between "vice" and "virtue," but ultimately between "deception" (Ἀπάτη) and "true education" (Ἀληθινὴ Παιδεία), the latter of which promises to lead one to the mountain peak of *eudaimonia*. *Apatê* causes all who travel toward her to "drink down her power" (5.2: ποτίζει τὴν ἑαυτῆς δύναμιν), which consists of "wandering and ignorance"

---

69. For a good summary discussion of *ekphrasis* in the novels, see Holzmeister 2014. On the frame of Longus' novel, see Zeitlin 1994 and Ulrich (forthcoming a). The connection to novelistic prologues draws the moralizing-allegorical nature of the *tabula Cebetis* into close contact with the novel (see, e.g., Grethlein and Squire 2014, 291–92; and Haffner 2013, 66). Likewise, there is a similar exegesis of a picture used to open Achilles Tatius' *Leucippe and Clitophon* (on which, see Morales 2004, 36–95). For further discussion of *ekphrasis* and the novel, see §3.1. See also Grethlein 2021, 199–212, on the influence of the *tabula Cebetis* on Lucian and Philostratus.

70. Cf. Haffner 2013, who provides an excellent discussion of the incorporation and immersion of the reader in the *tab. Ceb.* (see esp. 76–81).

(Πλάνος . . . καὶ Ἄγνοια). In the entranceway, over which she stands guard, lie all manner of personified vices (*tab. Ceb.* 6–9): "Opinions" (Δόξαι), "Desires" (Ἐπιθυμίαι), "Pleasures" (Ἡδοναί), "Lack of Self-Control" (Ἀκρασία), "Prodigality" (Ἀσωτία), etc. These vices "leap on" (6: ἀναπηδῶσιν) those who enter, and they "weave themselves" (πλέκονται πρὸς ἕκαστον) around each one with the hope of "lead[ing them] away" (ἀπάγουσι). As a consequence, very few people "travel" (*tab. Ceb.* 15.2: πορεύονται) the road to "true education" because it is "like traveling along some pathless, harsh, and rocky way" (ὥσπερ δι' ἀνοδίας τινὸς καὶ τραχείας καὶ πετρώδους). We may recall at this point the description of the path to virtue in Hesiod's "two roads," which was pervasive in the first–fourth centuries CE: "the path leading to [virtue] is long, steep, and harsh" (*W&D* 290–91: μακρὸς δὲ καὶ ὄρθιος οἶμος ἐς αὐτὴν καὶ τρηχύς).[71]

Aside from the many overlapping associations between the "two roads" and the *tabula Cebetis*, the most crucial element of the *tabula* for my argument is the fact that one can enter through the gate of "deception" and still avoid suffering the ultimate destruction it enacts. Thus, when the strangers ask the old exegete where the vices lead unfortunate souls who become entangled in them, the exegete responds: "some vices lead to salvation; others to destruction on account of their deception" (6.2: αἱ μὲν εἰς τὸ σώζεσθαι . . . αἱ δὲ εἰς τὸ ἀπόλλυσθαι διὰ τὴν ἀπάτην). Simply put, it is possible to return from *Apatê* once one has already walked through her gate. In fact, nearly all of the elements of reader-response, which I traced over the course of this chapter, come into play in this bewildering allegory. The drawing of the *pinax* doubles as a seductive *ainigma* both for the participants *inside* of the text as well as for the reader *outside* of it. There is a danger in the act of exegesis, but for the right kind of listener or reader, drinking down wandering and ignorance can lead paradoxically to "true education" and ultimately to *eudaimonia*. Much as we saw with "Philip the Philosopher's" discussion of drinking down the Circean brew of

---

71. It is tempting also to compare the opening of Plato's *Republic*, which likely plays on this same motif of Hesiod's "two roads": there, Socrates exclaims that he likes dialoguing with old people because they have "traveled" (*Rep.* 328e3–4: πορεύεσθαι; cf. *tab. Ceb.* 15: πορεύονται) a road ahead of us and can therefore tell others whether it is "harsh and difficult, or easy and well-traveled" (τραχεῖα καὶ χαλεπή, ἢ ῥᾳδία καὶ εὔπορος). On the connections between the opening of the *Republic* and Hesiod's "two roads," see Hunter 2014a, 35n86. On the rich pedigree of the allegorical tradition embedded in the *tabula Cebetis* and its connection both to Hesiod's "two roads" and the choice of Heracles, see Fitzgerald and White 1983, 14–15; and Trapp 1997a, 162–63. Grethlein and Squire 2014, 291n33, interestingly suggest that there are also connections between the *tabula Cebetis* and Dio Chrysostom's *Kingship Oration* (*Or.* 1), which likewise deploys the choice of Heracles in a discussion of good rulership. Janzsó 2017 argues that the *tabula Cebetis* may have shared its method of appropriating the Heraclean choice with early Christian texts.

SETTING THE STAGE FOR APULEIUS   69

Heliodorus' novel "like Odysseus," *Apatê* is transformed, in the *tabula*, into an intoxicating drink, which can somehow still provide sublime illumination.

Last, while Heracles is never actually named as the exemplar for making a choice in the *tabula*,[72] the culture hero is nonetheless alluded to through frequent exclamatory invocations. Indeed, the refrain "O Heracles" (ὦ Ἡράκλεις) is repeated multiple times by the strangers (*tab. Ceb.* 4.1; 12.1; 19.1), thereby subtly linking the choice posed by the series of gates to that archetypal decision in the literary tradition, and at the same time, implicating readers in that choice.

Whereas the *tabula Cebetis* presents an overt allegory of choice mediated through a visual and intermedial encounter, our final allusion to a choice between virtue and vice deviates from the Hesiodic/Heraclean paradigm entirely, and instead lays a Platonic veneer over Prodicus' allegory. Indeed, Maximus of Tyre, who is clearly familiar with the Heraclean archetype,[73] opens a series of lectures (*Or.* 18–21) by defending Socrates and his "erotic science" with an analysis of different love relationships gone awry. In doing so, he links the choice between virtue and vice to the well-known "two kinds of Aphrodite" dichotomy from Plato's *Symposium* and moreover, identifies the figure of Socrates as the locus of that choice.[74] At the beginning of *Or.* 18, in particular, after trotting out a number of exemplary lovers, Maximus explains that love is a "two-fold phenomenon" (18.3: πρᾶγμα διττόν): one side is "the provenance of virtue" (τό . . . ἀρετῆς ἐπήβολον) and the other "grows up together with vice" (τό . . . μοχθηρίᾳ συμπεφυκός). Then, attempting to offer an apology of Socrates for the charge of corrupting the youth, Maximus argues that Socrates' "erotic speeches" are similarly ambivalent, insofar as one could interpret them as "ironic" (18.5: εἰρωνεύματα) or "allegorical" (αἰνίγματα).[75] In Maximus' presentation, however, it is up to the reader/listener to decipher the meaning.

---

72. While the *tabula Cebetis* appeals explicitly to the Hesiodic "two roads," that it was associated with Heracles' choice quite early in its reception is clear from Lucian's *Rhet. praec.*, in which the rhetorician-teacher appeals to Cebes as a model for posing a Heraclean choice between two roads to "Lady Rhetoric" (*Rhet. praec.* 6).

73. Cf. *Or.* 14, which I discussed above.

74. For general discussion of *Or.* 18–21, see Trapp 2017, 775–77, and esp. 775, where he notes that Maximus creates "a composite picture" of the erotic Socrates, "put together from Xenophon and Aeschines as well as the Platonic material, and invoking . . . famous moments. . . . [of Socrates'] helplessness in the face of young male beauty." On the structure of *Or.* 18–21, borrowed as it is from the *Phaedrus*, see 777n12.

75. Cf. also *Or.* 3, where Maximus makes another apology for Socrates: he imagines Socrates turning the accusations of corruption and impiety against his Athenian accusers but suggests that the words would have fallen on deaf ears. Trapp 2017, 773 with n. 4 connects this display speech to Lucius' outburst in *Met.* 10.33 about Athenian injustice against Socrates (on which, see §3.3).

70 THE SHADOW OF AN ASS

Finally, Maximus charges Socrates with borrowing Homer's ideas about love but describes Socrates' *erôtikoi logoi* as more "slippery" (18.5: σφαλερούς) and "dangerous" (κινδυνώδεις) than any allegories that Homer produced: Socrates "uses shameful words as allegories for beautiful deeds" (18.5: αἰνίττεται δι' αἰσχρῶν ῥημάτων πράξεις καλάς), "hiding the beautiful with the shameful, and revealing the beneficial through that which is harmful" (τό ... ὑποβαλεῖν αἰσχρῷ καλὸν καὶ τὰ ὠφελοῦντα διὰ τῶν βλαπτόντων ἐπιδείκνυσθαι). Much like the *tabula Cebetis*, text or speech is figured in Maximus' framework as a "riddle" to be solved, but at the same time, that *ainigma* has an ambivalent value for those who listen: it may cause them to "slip" and fall, or alternatively, it may lead to a sublime vision of true beauty. Whereas the *tabula Cebetis* implicitly alludes to the Heraclean archetype, however, by posing a series of life choices between two alternatives and invoking Heracles through playful exclamation, Maximus connects the archetypal choice between virtue and vice to a manifestly Platonic discourse, which influences a great deal of imperial and Second Sophistic thought:[76] the choice between "pandemic" and "heavenly" Aphrodite, a dichotomy to which we shall return at many points over the course of this monograph.

Before we return to our crucial passage from the *Met.*, it is worth reviewing the major through-lines that we have discerned in the respective receptions of Odysseus and Heracles in the first–fourth centuries CE. With the paradigm of Odysseus, we see that aesthetic experience is repeatedly framed as a dangerous and potentially entrapping encounter—one which must be anticipated through philosophical habituation or alternatively, circumnavigated via preventative measures, such as stopping up the ears. At the same time, however, the aesthetic pleasure of literature or art presents an opportunity for "proto-philosophy," an education in heroic resistance that prepares the ideal reader for a lifetime of temptations.[77] Therefore, how one engages with a novel, whether "profanely" or "philosophically" (in "Philip the Philosopher's" phrasing), leads in the final analysis to one of two outcomes: debased transformation into an animal or sublime theorization of the divine.

---

76. Trapp 1997b, 157, notes the "heavy dependence" on the *Symposium* and the *Phaedrus* in all of Maximus' speeches on Socrates' erotic knowledge (*Or.* 18–21).

77. In fact, "Philip the Philosopher's" exegesis of Heliodorus concludes with an exhortation to the reader precisely along these lines: "Let [your] strong will be empowered here! Let it be tested in the furnace of temptations" (387.23–24: ἐνταῦθα τὸ ἀνδρεῖον λῆμα στομούσθω μᾶλλον καὶ τῇ καμίνῳ τῶν πειρασμῶν ἐμβληθήτω). On this passage and its intersection with Platonic views on allegory, see Lamberton 1986, 155.

In contrast to the iterative nature of Odysseus' encounters with pleasure, Heracles' position at the crossroads represents choice as a one-time affair, a decision made at a particular time in one's youth. Nevertheless, our imperial and Second Sophistic appropriations of this famous allegory either reconfigure the choice as a matter of "attention" and habituation through *askêsis*, as in Plutarch; or in more explicitly allegorical treatments, such as the *tabula Cebetis*, textual engagement itself becomes a seductive *ainigma*, a riddle which one must decipher and interpret correctly in order to reach the peak of *eudaimonia*. The path is "slippery" and "dangerous," as we see in Maximus of Tyre's Platonic conflation of "Heracles' education" with the two species of Aphrodite. Nevertheless, seeing through the deceptive guise or standing firm amid enticing temptations presents an opportunity to encounter the divine and reach sublime heights.

As we turn now to Apuleius, we will see many ways in which Apuleius participates in this intellectualized reader-response en vogue in his epoch. The *Met.* not only presents a character who embodies both heroes at different times, and whose "conversion" is framed implicitly in terms of choice; but simultaneously, in my view, that choice ripples out to the reader. In this way, the seductive *ainigma* of Apuleius' burlesque text, which Winkler posited as an aporetic conundrum many years ago, can function alternatively as a crossroads choice—a choice which Lucius-*auctor* claims to make, and which is, by extension, posed to us, whether or not we believe our narrator's claims.

1.3. Odysseus and Heracles at the Crossroads in Cenchreae

It is evident that Apuleius was quite familiar with these reception histories of Odysseus and Heracles. As we shall consider in greater detail in chapter 2, Apuleius appeals explicitly to the allegorizing interpretation of the *Odyssey* as a protreptic mirror for Homer's readers in *De deo Socratis* (hereafter, *Soc.*). Crucially, he closes this treatise on Platonic demonology with a comprehensive review of Odysseus' willing indulgence in dangerous pleasures. In fact, the final sentence of the text (as we have it)[78] homes in specifically on the fact that Odysseus drank the "cup of Circe" (*Soc.* 24.4: *Circae poculum*) without transforming, and "heard the Sirens" (*Sirenas audiit*) without being induced

---

78. The ending of *Soc.* is disputed in the transmission history. See §2.2 with n. 54 for discussion.

to draw near to them. For Apuleius' readers, then, this is presented as a proof that Odysseus cultivated *prudentia* and *sapientia* in equal measure to Socrates, the primary *exemplum* of the whole treatise. So also, Lucius' asinine misadventures in the first ten books of the *Met.* have been recognized as an Odyssean journey of sorts,[79] where Lucius himself is a "failed Odysseus" or an "extremization" of the Homeric wanderer.[80] Indeed, the novel welcomes this kind of comparison already at the outset, when a character named "Socrates" appears but curiously possesses the "wit of Ulysses" (1.12: *Ulixi astu*) and is bewitched by the spell of a "Calypso" figure.[81]

In contrast to his overt appeals to Odysseus as a moral *exemplum* across his corpus, Apuleius nowhere mentions Prodicus' allegory of Heracles in his extant works, although he portrays the hero as an ideal philosopher in both the *Apologia* and the *Florida*.[82] Nevertheless, scholars have increasingly appreciated a subtler engagement with the motif of "Heracles' education" at important interpretive junctures in the novel.[83] In this vein, Maaike Zimmerman has analyzed the various topographies in the *Met.*, noting that Lucius' asinine journey through books 4–9 (with the exception of *C&P*) seems to highlight the harshness of the path he treads.[84] By contrast to the rough roads of the Greek countryside, book 10—where the ass descends into sensual delights and sexual pleasures in Corinth—appears to smooth out the harsh path that Lucius' counterpart walks in the corresponding Greek version, the *Onos*.[85] In his refashioning of the original, therefore, Apuleius may allude to the Heraclean *topos* of Lady Vice

---

79. On the *Met.* as an *Odyssey* of sorts, see Hunter 2006 and Montiglio 2007. See also Graverini 2012a, 141–54.

80. See Graverini 2012a, 133–64, for the characterization of Lucius as an "extremization" of Socrates and Odysseus. Cf. Montiglio 2007, 93, for Lucius as the "opposite of Odysseus, in spite of his own self-presentation."

81. On the many connections between this "Socrates" and the figure of Odysseus, see Hunter 2006, 303–5. Cf. also Münstermann 1995, 8–26; and Smith and Woods 2002. So also, the Chaldean seer in book 2 laments that he endures a "Ulyssean wandering" (2.14: *Ulixeam peregrinationem*), which Krabbe 2003, 474–81, reads as a subtle foreshadowing of Lucius' own Odyssean journey. For further discussion, see §2.5.

82. See *Apol.* 22 and *Fl.* 22, where Apuleius presents Heracles as a proto-Cynic philosopher both in his heroic feats and in his dress. On these passages, see Krabbe 2003, 244–46, where she notes that Apuleius betrays a likely familiarity with the long allegorizing tradition on Heracles.

83. See esp. Zimmerman 2002; and Penwill 2009. See also Krabbe 2003, 217–59, on plays with Lucius as Heracles throughout the novel (on which, more below).

84. See Zimmerman 2002, esp. 86–91, who notes that the Corinthian episode is the only instance in the *Onos* that mentions a difficult road where Apuleius smooths it out (91). See also Schlam 1992, 36–38, who sees travel "on the road" as the organizing motif of *Met.* 8.15–10.31. On the relationship between topography and Lucius' psychology, see De Biasi 2000.

85. Cf. ps.-Luc. *Onos* 49.3.

promising the easier path of pleasure to the hero. Furthermore, the Judgment of Paris—a mythological episode which Second Sophistic authors reconfigured as a Heraclean choice between "pleasure" and "virtue"[86]—occurs in pantomime form at the close of book 10, where Lucius-ass describes a goddess stripping in a lascivious spectacle in front of him. After he is faced with this enticing performance, however, Lucius encounters in quick succession a vision of (a clothed) Isis, who symbolizes a rejection of worldly delights and prompts an unanticipated asceticism in the previously indulgent ass.[87] Thus, J. L. Penwill has argued that the last two books of the *Met.* play with the epic theme of heroic choice: the excessive pleasures of book 10 are set in stark juxtaposition with the restraint, willing self-denial, and fasting (or "religious feasting") of book 11.[88] The harbor of Cencreae, as Penwill notes, stands between a temple dedicated to Aphrodite in Corinth on the one side, and the temples of Asclepius and Isis on the other.[89] In this geographical choice, then, Apuleius reproduces implicitly the crossroads at which Heracles finds himself in Prodicus' allegory.

There is no denying, in other words, that Apuleius self-consciously plays with these two heroic archetypes as models of choice across the novel, and in the chapters that follow, I will explore how these models are manifested in various permutations in Apuleius' oeuvre, from the Odyssean "Socrates" of book 1 (§2.5) to the Heraclean Paris of book 10 (§3.3). However, given the sustained interest in Odysseus and Heracles as paradigms of philosophical choice amid aesthetic experience, as we have seen in our survey of authors in Apuleius' milieu, I would like to return now to the closing books of the *Met.*—and especially, to Mithras' allegorizing reinterpretation of books 1–10—in order to consider how we might assess Lucius' "conversion" not in terms of his internal development or sincerity, but rather, as an oscillation between these two heroic archetypes. For if Lucius represents Odysseus-vis-à-vis-the-Sirens at one time, and Heracles-at-the-crossroads at another—or in other words, if he indulges in aesthetic-erotic pleasure at every turn, but in the end, returns to a crossroads in

---

86. See Athen. *Deipnosoph.* 12.510c, who describes the famous mythological episode as a "judgment of pleasure against virtue" (ἡδονῆς πρὸς ἀρετὴν οὖσαν σύγκρισιν), and explicitly connects it to Prodicus' allegory of Heracles.

87. On the choice between a stripping Venus and a clothed Isis in the transition from book 10 to 11, see further discussion at §§3.3 and 3.4.

88. See Penwill 2009. Cf. also Tilg 2011 on "religious feasting." On the overlaps between the choice and the judgment in antiquity and their reception, see now Davies 2023.

89. So, Pausanias describes the geography (*Periêgêsis* 2.2.3), on which, see Penwill 2009, 94–95 with n. 36. See also Dio Chrys. *Or.* 8.5, who explains that Corinth is "situated as a crossroads of Hellas" (ὥσπερ ἐν τριόδῳ τῆς Ἑλλάδος ἔκειτο).

order to make a one-time decision to travel a different (and arguably, more difficult) path—then what does his final choice entail for the reader, who has also participated in a mediated way in Lucius' aesthetic-erotic delights?

We will first consider how Apuleius blatantly figures Lucius as an Odysseus across the closing books of the *Met.* The most explicit reference, which commentators note is narratively problematic (primarily because Lucius-*auctor*, though an acolyte of Isis at the time of narration, appears nonetheless to revel in his own asinine learning), occurs in book 9, where our narrator makes a one-to-one analogy between his journey and Odysseus' (*Met.* 9.13):[90]

> Nec immerito priscae poeticae divinus auctor apud Graios summae prudentiae virum monstrare cupiens, multarum civitatium obitu et variorum populorum cognitu summas adeptum virtutes cecinit. Nam et ipse gratas gratias asino meo memini, quod me suo celatum tegmine variisque fortunis exercitatum, etsi minus prudentem, multiscium reddidit.

> And it is not without reason that the divine author of ancient poetry among the Greeks, when he desired to represent a man of the greatest prudence, sang of one who acquired the greatest virtues by visiting many cities and coming to know various peoples. For I too remember my time as an ass with thankful gratitude, since covered by its hide and taught by various fortunes, it made me knowledgeable of many things, if not prudent.

Much has been made of the dichotomy here between different categories of knowledge—between *prudentia* and *multiscientia*, true knowledge and mere polymathy[91]—and we will return to this passage again in §2.2, when we reconsider Apuleius' allegorization of Odysseus at the close of *Soc.* What is most

---

90. On the narratological problem of this passage, see Kenney 2003. For a nuanced reassessment, see Lévi 2018.

91. For discussion of Apuleius' neologism, *multiscius*, which occurs only four other times in the Apuleian corpus—of Homer (*Apol.* 31.5), Apollo (*Fl.* 3.9), Hippias (*Fl.* 9.24), and Protagoras (*Fl.* 18.19)—see GCA 1995, 376–79. Kenney 2003 remains an excellent reading of this issue. Lévi 2018 offers the most up-to-date and comprehensive treatment of this Apuleian coinage. Cf. also Graverini 2012a, 141–54; and Ulrich 2020, 700–701, where I discuss how the term *multiscius* translates the opening of the *Odyssey*. Cf. also Ulrich (forthcoming b) on Apuleius' use of Odysseus and "inverted allegory" across the novel. Adkins 2022, 170–73, gives a comprehensive summary of bibliography on this passage and the importance of this term, but departs from the Odyssean reading: following Labhardt 1960, 215, she settles on *multiscius* as a translation for the Greek, *polymathia*, which Plutarch treats in *On Curiosity* (519c) as interchangeable with *polypragmosynê*.

SETTING THE STAGE FOR APULEIUS   75

germane to my argument now, however, is the fact that the Apuleian coinage *multiscius* may, in fact, be a Latin translation of the Sirens' promise to make Odysseus "knowledgeable of more" (*Od.* 12.188: πλείονα εἰδώς).[92] In fact, though it has gone overlooked in discussions of this term, this is precisely how Cicero translates the Sirens' promise in the *Odyssey* in a seminal passage of *De finibus* (5.49), which scholars have otherwise considered significant for Apuleius' broader characterization of Lucius:[93] Cicero's speaker at this point in the dialogue, Piso, appeals to Odysseus as a paradigm for the intrinsic human "desire for learning" (*discendi cupiditas*) and to do so, argues that the Sirens drew people to their rocks not "through the charm of their voices" nor by a "certain novelty and variety of singing," but "because they promised that they knew many things" (*quia **multa** se **scire** profitebantur*).[94] If we take this translational element into consideration, then, not only is Lucius a "failed" or "extremized" Odysseus, but he is, to be more precise, an Odysseus at the very point when he is being seduced by the Sirens' song. Simply put, by suggesting that he has acquired *multiscientia* through his "time as an ass," Lucius-*auctor* reframes his journey in books 1–10 as a Siren-esque encounter with aesthetic pleasure.

Lucius' portrayal of himself as an Odysseus continues through books 10 and 11. As Richard Hunter notes, there is an intertextual connection between the closing line of *Met.* 10, where Lucius is "oppressed by sweet sleep" (10.35: *somnus oppresserat*) at the harbor of Cenchreae, and the opening of *Odyssey* 13, where Odysseus is "conquered by sleep" (*Od.* 13.119: δεδμημένον ὕπνῳ) and abandoned in the harbor of Phorkys.[95] Moreover, as Beate Beer has astutely demonstrated, the sections leading up to our crucial passage in 11.15 further develop the correspondences between Lucius and Odysseus: in fact, from *Met.* 10.35–11.15, Apuleius neatly reproduces the *Odyssey's* plot structure from books 5–8 of (a) sleeping on the beach, (b) bathing in the sea, (c) exposing one's nudity publicly, and (d) listening to one's story retold to an audience.[96]

---

92. Graverini 2012a, 150. Although, elsewhere, I have proposed the opening lines of the *Odyssey*—*pollôn . . . egnô* (1.3)—as a potential target of translation for *multiscius* (see Ulrich 2020, 700–701).

93. See, e.g., Graverini 2012a, 147–49.

94. This translational component may also explain why Apuleius labels Homer *multiscius* at *Apol.* 31.5. I am grateful to one of my anonymous readers for encouraging me to make a clearer articulation of this connection. See §2.1 for further discussion of this passage from Cicero in connection with the allegorizing tradition of the *Odyssey*.

95. See Hunter 2009a, 200.

96. See Beer 2011, 81–86.

So, immediately before Mithras imposes his allegorizing interpretation on books 1–10, Lucius is stripped of his ass-hide and left standing naked before a crowd of people, while attempting to cover himself "with a natural covering" (11.14: *velamento . . . naturali*), much like Odysseus with the olive-branch on the beach in Phaeacia. When we, therefore, reach Mithras' exegesis of the *Met.*, we are prepared through a number of textual cues to witness an Odyssean transformation. And indeed, as I have argued elsewhere, I discern a very specific version of Odysseus in Lucius' problematic loss of *curiositas*: the soul of Odysseus in Plato's Myth of Er, which chooses the "life of an uncurious private individual" (*Rep.* 10.620c6–7: βίον ἀνδρὸς ἰδιώτου ἀπράγμονος) after he ceases from pursuing *philotimia* (as he does in Homer's *Odyssey*).[97] In addition to the Platonic Odysseus expressing his regret over his previous Homeric life, though, I also recognize the heroic archetype of Heracles in the priest's allegorical reinterpretation of Lucius' misadventures. Before we consider the specific nods to "Heracles' education" in our critical passage, however, it will be useful also to review briefly how Apuleius establishes clear correspondences between Lucius and Heracles through overt reference as well as by subtle and suggestive allusion.[98]

Once again, the clearest analogy to Heracles is drawn by Lucius himself at the end of book 2, when he comically likens his slaughter of inflated wineskins to the labor of slaying the three-headed Geryon. After stabbing magically animated wine-bags in a drunken stupor, Lucius immediately "give[s] himself" over to sleep, "which is natural," he claims, "for one worn out from battle with three robbers, just as in the slaughter of Geryon" (2.32: *utpote pugna trium latronum in vicem Geryoneae caedis fatigatum, lecto simul et somno tradidi*). He invokes this paradigm a second time in book 3, expanding it to encompass also Heracles' retrieval of Cerberus. After Photis explains that Lucius in his drunken frenzy became not a murderer, but a "winesack-slayer," our buffoonish mock-hero responds (3.19):

'Ergo igitur iam et ipse possum' inquam 'mihi primam istam virtutis adoriam ad exemplum duodeni laboris **Herculei** numerare, vel trigemino corpori Geryonis vel triplici formae Cerberi totidem peremptos utres coaequando.'

---

97. See Ulrich 2020, 688–701, for my detailed explication, and §§5.1 and 5.2 for further discussion. Cf. also MacDougall 2016, 268–73, who likewise recognizes the Platonic Odysseus' choice in Lucius' loss of *curiositas*. See also Whitmarsh 2011, 186n45; and Hunter 2012, 42, on Odysseus' decision in the Myth of Er.
98. On Heracles as a model for Lucius and Psyche, see Krabbe 2003, 217–59; Harrison 1998b and 2013b.

SETTING THE STAGE FOR APULEIUS   77

"Alright then," I said, "I myself can even count this first distinction of my virtue according to the model of the twelfth labor of Heracles: I equaled the threefold body of Geryon or the triple form of Cerberus with the same number of murdered wine-skins."

What's more, just as Lucius' comic encounter with magically inflated bellies inspires a delusionally heroic and "mytho-maniacal" reframing of his ridiculous behavior,[99] so also, his allegorical counterpart in the central folktale, *C&P*, is characterized as a Heracles in the four impossible tasks, which she humorously fails to accomplish on each occasion: indeed, Psyche's *labores*—especially, her journey to the underworld—have long been recognized as a series of Heraclean feats in miniature.[100]

Aside from these outright allusions to Heracles as a paradigm for our mock-hero in the early books of the *Met.*, Apuleius also prepares his reader for a Lucius-Heracles equivalence by using the same subliminal approach we saw above in the *tabula Cebetis*—namely, through semantic slips in invocations to Hercules (the Latin counterpart to Heracles), such as *mehercule, hercules,* and *hercule.*[101] When Byrrhena's elderly slave recognizes Lucius at the opening of book 2, for example, he exclaims: "By Heracles, it's Lucius" (2.2: *'Est . . . hercules, est Lucius'*). Realizing the full semantic slippage, however, Judith Krabbe points out an alternative possibility: "it's Hercules, it's Lucius."[102] Similarly, at the close of Aristomenes' tale in book 1, Lucius announces his belief in the fabulous tale by swearing an oath to Heracles, which on second glance reinforces the ass-man's implicit equivalence to the culture hero: "For my part, by Hercules, I believe him" (1.20: *ego huic et credo hercules*). Merely capitalize the name, *Hercules*, and it translates: "I also believe him, Hercules that I am."

Most intriguing for the purposes of my argument is the way in which these

---

99. On "mytho-mania" and the Roman novel, see Conte 1996. On Lucius' "mytho-mania" and its significance for our interpretation of the *Met.*, see ch. 3.

100. See, e.g., Harrison 1998b, 61–63, for analysis of the close connections between Psyche's and Heracles' respective labors. See also Harrison 2013b and Krabbe 2003, 225–29.

101. On this tactic in Apuleius, see Krabbe 2003, 219–59, esp. 219 on the invocation "By Hercules" (*mehercule*): "The expression figures in the internal design of the *Metamorphoses* and helps to sustain the allusive relevance of the hero Hercules. By a kind of subversion of its ordinary sense, another sort of metamorphosis, Apuleius also brings into play the 'by Hercules' oath's underlying literal sense." One may note that invocations of Hercules possessed a kind of metatextual significance as early as Plautus' *Amphitruo*, where Hercules is playfully invoked throughout the play, even though the hero is yet to be born until the end of the play: see, e.g., the use of *hercle* at *Amph.* 299, 329, 556, 736, 986.

102. See Krabbe 2003, 219.

formulaic invocations are ramped up in the sections immediately surrounding our central passage. When Lucius first sees Isis' priest, he is holding a crown, which Lucius interprets as a sign of his victory over Fortune (*Met.* 11.12):

> proferens . . . mihi coronam, et **hercules** coronam consequenter, quod tot ac tantis exanclatis laboribus, tot emensis periculis, deae maximae providentia adluctantem mihi saevissime Fortunam superarem.

> He was carrying a crown for me, indeed, fittingly a crown, by Hercules, since by the providence of the greatest goddess, I overcame Fortune, who was striving most savagely against me, after enduring so many and such great labors, and traveling through so many dangers.

Here, not only is the subliminal slippage available to the reader (i.e., "since I, Hercules, overcame"), but it is also connected to a series of labors under the compulsion of a savage goddess, Fortuna, much as Heracles suffered his tasks under the persecution of Hera.[103] Furthermore, after witnessing Lucius' retransformation and hearing Mithras' reinterpretation of books 1–10, the crowd of onlookers interpret the event very differently from the priest: they proclaim Lucius "happy, by Hercules, and thrice-blessed" (11.16: *felix hercules et ter beatus*); or alternatively, Lucius is labeled "a happy and thrice-blessed Hercules." And just in case the reader misses the significance of these invocations to Heracles surrounding 11.15, Lucius names the culture hero one last time in the very sentence before Mithras' crucial exegesis, saying that the priest "addressed [him], by Hercules, with a kind and divine expression" (11.14: *vultu geniali et hercules inhumano . . . sic effatur*).

Through these invocations, in other words, Lucius-*auctor* subliminally represents his actions and his journey as a series of Heraclean *labores*. And Apuleius, in turn, implicitly invites us to travel this path with him—at least, up to a point. When we turn to Mithras' hermeneutic gesture, however, we see that a version of Heracles is, indeed, alluded to, but it is not the Heracles known for his heroic deeds. Rather, in my view, Mithras turns to the Heracles of the philosophical tradition, framing Lucius' journey not as a civilizing feat of Heracles, nor even as an Odyssean encounter with the Sirens, but instead, as a high-stakes choice—one which he made at a particular point in his youth (or perhaps, at a number of

---

103. So, Krabbe 2003, 251 (with notes).

points in his youth) when he took the wrong, anti-Heraclean path. For the sake of convenience, I reprint 11.15 here with my translation:

> Multis et variis exanclatis laboribus magnisque Fortunae tempestatibus et maximis actus procellis, ad portum Quietis et aram Misericordiae tandem, Luci, venisti. Nec tibi natales ac ne dignitas quidem, vel ipsa qua flores usquam doctrina profuit, sed lubrico virentis aetatulae ad serviles delapsus voluptates, curiositatis inprosperae sinistrum praemium reportasti.

> After having endured many and various toils, and driven by the great tempests of Fortune and the most powerful winds, Lucius, you have finally come to the harbor of Rest and the altar of Mercy. Neither your lineage nor indeed your dignity, nor even that very learning in which you excel has benefited you at all, but at the precarious point of flourishing youth, you slipped into servile pleasures and carried off the troublesome reward for your unpropitious curiosity.

In short, Mithras begins his reassessment of Lucius' journey by highlighting the "many and various labors" he had to endure, where *labores* could, of course, refer to Odysseus' sufferings at the hands of various divinities in his *nostos*, but also likely possesses a Heraclean resonance.[104] In particular, if we consider the participle *exanclatis* (in connection with *laboribus*)—an archaizing term that Cicero used earlier in a philosophical context to describe a Heraclean task[105]—we might imagine an ancient reader recognizing an even more palpable echo of the great hero's suffering.

While many commentators have focused on the potential Platonic valences of the phrase *ad serviles delapsus voluptates*,[106] most interesting to me (from the vantage point of Prodicus' allegory) is the clear temporal specification of Lucius' age at the moment of his slip-and-fall: Lucius falls into servile pleasures pre-

---

104. Cf. *Met.* 3.19 (discussed above). Cf. also Krabbe 2003, esp. 229–38; Harrison 1998b, 61–63 and 2013b.

105. See *Acad.* 2.108: *Herculi quendam laborem exanclatum a Carneade* ("a certain labor of Hercules was endured by Carneades"). On the archaizing sound of Apuleius' *exanclo* in *Met.* 1.16, see Finkelpearl 1998, 50.

106. See Graverini 2012a, 115–18 on the Platonic heritage of this phrase. See also *GCA* 2015, 279–80 *ad loc.* 11, 15, 1 (with bibliography). Cf. Fick 1987, 39–40, who links *serviles . . . voluptates* to the Siren-cicada episode from the *Phaedrus*. To these suggestions, we may add that "slipping" on dangerous rhetoric is precisely what the tradition of choice-narratives expresses anxiety over: recall how Maximus of Tyre refers to Socrates' *erôtikoi logoi* as "slippery" (σφαλεροὺς). For further discussion, see §5.1.

cisely "at the precarious point of flourishing youth" (*lubrico virentis aetatulae*). As the Groningen commentators note, *lubricus* is "often used of youth and its passions":[107] they cite as evidence Cicero's famous defense of Caelius, the Roman elite who merely lost himself on the "many slippery paths of youth" (*Pro Cael.* 41: *multas vias adulescentiae lubricas*) in his ill-advised entanglement with Clodia.[108]

We may probe even deeper, however, into this curious little phrase. Indeed, the defining genitive—"of flourishing youth" (*virentis aetatulae*)—specifies a very particular point in one's maturation. Elsewhere in the *Met.*, *aetatula* is used of beloveds, often in a sexual sense: we see Meroe ironically refer to "Socrates," for instance, as a Ganymede who "played with [her] youth for days and nights" (1.12: *diebus ac noctibus inlusit aetatulam meam*). So also, the young boys and girls, who open the spectacle of the Judgment of Paris with a Pyrrhic dance, are said to be "flowering in flourishing youth" (10.29: *virenti florentes aetatula*). In fact, it is even used in the subsequent pantomime as a euphemism for female genitalia: the winds play with Venus' dress in such a way as to reveal the "flower of [her] youth" (10.31: *flos aetatulae*),[109] where Venus' attire explicitly recalls Lady Vice's diaphanous garb in Prodicus' allegory.[110] Simply put, the time specification of Lucius' slip-and-fall is situated by Mithras in the peak of his sexual maturation, when he reaches the point of an ephebe.

With this very specific age in mind, we may recall that "Heracles' education" happens precisely in his transition from boy into ephebe, as Xenophon's text goes out of its way to highlight: "Heracles' education" takes place as he progresses "from boyhood into adolescence" (*Mem.* 2.1.21: ἐκ παίδων εἰς ἥβην).[111] In fact, the *Memorabilia* goes further to specify the exact moment of Heracles' choice by glossing this temporal phrase with an even more precise designation: "the point in time when young men are already acquiring self-mastery" (ἐν ᾗ οἱ νέοι ἤδη αὐτοκράτορες γιγνόμενοι). Lucius, in stark contrast

---

107. *GCA* 2015, 279 *ad loc* 11, 15, 1.
108. See also Zimmerman 2002, 86–89, who observes that soon after Apuleius, the "slippery path" (*lubrica via*) would become a favorite *topos* for the Church Fathers to describe the "road of sin."
109. For a more comprehensive discussion of this phrase across Apuleius, see §3.3 with n. 118.
110. See *GCA* 2000, 376 *ad loc.* 261.24–262.1 and Zimmerman 2002, 86–89. For further discussion of Venus in the Judgment of Paris as a Lady Vice figure, see §3.3.
111. Significantly, the age component is retained in imperial and Second Sophistic receptions of Prodicus' allegory: thus, in Philostratus' allusion to the allegory, Heracles makes the choice "when he is an ephebe" (*VA* 6.10.5: ὡς ἔφηβος ... ὁ Ἡρακλῆς); so also, in Silius Italicus' rewrite of Scipio-at-the-crossroads, the "youth" (*Pun.* 15.18: *iuvenis*) is presented with a choice between *Virtus* and *Voluptas*, as he "sits under a flourishing shadow of laurel" (*lauri residens ... viridante sub umbra*) at a "tender age" (15.17: *rudi ... in aevo*).

SETTING THE STAGE FOR APULEIUS   81

to the heroic paradigm he models himself on, falls into "servile pleasures" (*serviles voluptates*) precisely because he reaches that slippery age of an ephebe and fails to become a "master of himself." As a consequence, he is transformed into a beast of burden, enslaved to the desires and wishes of others.[112]

If we turn to the early reception of the choice of Heracles in Latin literature—in Cicero's *De officiis*, a passage I skipped over in my initial survey—we see that the emphasis on the precise moment of youth for this decision is retained with a similar phrasing. At *De off.* 1.117, Cicero turns to that most difficult decision of life—namely, "who we are, who we want to be, and what kind of life we want [to have]" (*quos nos et quales esse velimus et in quo genere vitae*). Pointing to Heracles, he identifies youth as the most precarious time for this critical choice (*De off.* 1.118):

> Nam quod Herculem Prodicus dicit, ut est apud Xenophontem, cum primum **pubesceret**, quod **tempus** a natura **ad deligendum**, quam quisque viam vivendi sit ingressurus, datum est, **exisse in solitudinem atque ibi sedentem** diu secum multumque dubitasse, cum duas cerneret **vias**, unam Voluptatis, alteram Virtutis, utram ingredi melius esset.

> For this is what Prodicus says of Hercules, as it is in Xenophon—namely, that when [Hercules] was first reaching **the age of puberty**, the **time** which has been given by nature for choosing what path of living each is about to embark on, **he went out into a place of solitude**; and when he saw two roads, one of Pleasure, and another of Virtue, he **sat there for a long time** and debated with himself a great deal as to which of the two would be better to travel.

Beyond the fact that Xenophon's *Kakia* is translated by Cicero as "Pleasure,"[113] with *Voluptas* being both the child of Cupid and Psyche as well as the guiding principle of Lucius' journey, the time of this moment of choice is clearly demarcated: people make choices in the time of flourishing youth, a point in life when it is most hazardous to do so. Thus, Heracles chose between *Virtus* and *Voluptas* when he was first reaching sexual maturation (*cum primum pubesceret*), the "natural" time for making choices. It is further interesting to

---

112. Indeed, the ass is regarded in antiquity as the most servile of animals, on which, see Bradley 2000; Fitzgerald 2000, esp. 94–106; Adkins 2022, 88–117.
113. Cf. *Epist. ad fam.* 5.12.3, where he refers again to Xenophon's *Kakia* as *Voluptas*. Cf. also Sil. Ital. *Pun.* 15.22, where the contest to sway Scipio is between *Virtus* and *Voluptas*.

note that Cicero's version of the Heraclean choice concludes with a discussion of a special class of men, who "adorn themselves with erudition and education, or both" (1.119: *praeclara* **eruditione** *atque* **doctrina** *aut utraque re ornati*) because they carefully choose their life paths in accordance with their "birth" (*quo modo quisque* **natus est**). If we compare this distinction with Mithras' reassessment, it is striking that Isis' priest highlights Lucius' "birth" (*natales*), "station" (*dignitas*), and "education" (*doctrina*), all of which fail to save him from slipping on *voluptates*.[114]

Just as the specific age for Lucius' slip-and-fall matters, so also, the place where he makes his choice is significant. According to Mithras, Lucius "has finally come into the harbor of Quiet" (*ad portum Quietis . . . tandem, Luci, venisti*). We may remember from §1.1 that both Heracles' choice in Prodicus' allegory and Socrates' choice to resist the Siren-cicadas' pleasure in the *Phaedrus* occur when the respective heroes "[come] out into a quiet place" (*Mem.* 2.1.21: ἐξελθόντα εἰς ἡσυχίαν; cf. *Phaedr.* 259a5: ἐλθόντα εἰς τὸ καταγώγιον).[115] Likewise, in Cicero's translation of the Heraclean choice above, the hero has "[gone] out into a place of solitude and sat there for a long time" (*De off.* 1.119: *exisse in* **solitudinem** *atque ibi* **sedentem** *diu*).[116]

As we shall see in the next chapter (§2.5), Lucius begins the novel traveling a "harsh road" (*Met.* 1.2: *iugi . . . aspritudinem*) on horseback and he leaps off the horse because he has been sitting for too long and feels "sedentary fatigue" (*fatigationem* **sedentariam**). We learn later in book 1, moreover, that he is traveling the "pathless wilderness" (1.19: *avias* **solitudines**), when he encounters two interlocutors engaged in an argument and must make a choice between two approaches to fictional accounts. So also, Lucius' second major choice, to which Mithras explicitly refers, takes place when the ass-man sneaks into Pamphile's bedroom to watch her strip and perform magic: as Photis warns him, her mistress only performs magic "hidden away in solitude" (3.20: **solitudinem** *semper abstrusa*); simply put, sitting behind a door "in solitude," Lucius encounters a naked pseudodivinity. So finally, Lucius' "harbor of Quiet" offers yet another

---

114. On the Platonic origins of Mithras' distinction here, see Ulrich 2020, 695. For further discussion, see §§2.4 and 5.0.

115. To my knowledge, only Fick 1987, 38–39, seems to recognize that Mithras' invocation of the "harbor of rest" may to allude to the *katagôgion* of Plato's *Phaedrus* in the Siren-cicada episode.

116. Cf. again Sil. Ital. *Pun.* 15.18, where Scipio is "sitting under a flourishing shadow of a laurel" (*lauri* **residens** *. . . viridante sub umbra*). At the end of this tradition, moreover, when Augustine represents his conversion as a Heraclean choice, he and Alypius "sit as far removed from the house as possible" (*Conf.* 8.8: **sedimus** *quantum potuimus remoti ab aedibus*) and Augustine moves still further to seek out *solitudo* at 8.12.

opportunity for choice, where the metaphorical usage of *portus* signals a different kind of *locus* for philosophical-religious choice.[117] After Lucius makes the wrong aesthetic-erotic choice so many times, pursuing *voluptates* with complete abandon, he is allowed by Isis' divine grace (according to Mithras) to return to a crossroads of solitude and this time, he makes a different choice. While Lucius' decisions in the opening books of the novel lead to corruption and asinine transformation, it may yet be possible, as in the *tabula Cebetis*, to be saved—that is, through a more thoughtful and attentive response to the words of the priest.

But as I suggested in §0.1, I am not particularly interested in relitigating the question of Lucius' "conversion" here. In my view, this final crossroads choice is presented to the reader *outside* of the text as much as to the character *inside* of the text. At the time of narration, the ass-man has already made a number of aesthetic-erotic choices, enchanted as he was by various Sirens and Circes only to be metamorphosed into a herd animal. Whether Lucius is given a second chance is immaterial, I suggest, for a holistic interpretation of the novel. It is the reader, after all, the *lector scrupulosus*, who must "pay attention" (*intende*) and "choose." Every act of reading is a choice, and Apuleius is the master of implicating his reader in that choice. We may even speculate that the choice of Heracles offers the perfect allegory of reading because the hero goes out "into a quiet place" and "sits down at a loss" (*Mem.* 2.1.21: ἐξελθόντα εἰς ἡσυχίαν καθῆσθαι ἀποροῦντα)—the possible location as well as mental and physical posture of a reader.[118] Following "Philip the Philosopher's" allegorizing interpretation of Heliodorus, then, we may prefer to read "philosophically" in order to derive what is *utile* from this otherwise frivolous text. In the final analysis, the *aporia* we experience at its failure of closure becomes a Heraclean or even a Platonic questioning about which path we ought to take in life rather than a deconstructionist confusion that points up an impenetrable uninterpretability. Simply put, the Palinodic reading invites *us as readers* to go into a place of solace, sit down, and be confused about *our* crossroads choice.

---

117. Cf. *ThLL* 10.2.62.84–63.33 for the association of *portus* as a refuge or respite from *negotium* in the philosophical tradition and as a gate of eternal life in early Christian discourse.

118. There is, of course, a rich scholarship on how reading was done in antiquity. See esp. Cavallo 2006, 18, in which he traces the origins of "attentive reading" in solitude. Johnson 2010 offers a comprehensive treatment of reading practice in antiquity. Cf. also Konstan 2004 and Konstan 2009 on Plutarch's "modern" approach to reader-response, and "attentive reading" in the novel. On "active reading" in Aulus Gellius, see Howley 2018; DiGiulio 2020. For further discussion of the posture of the *Met.*'s reader (esp. as we are made *pronus* at certain points in the novel), see §3.2 with n. 95.

TWO

Reading as a Choice in the Apuleian Corpus

The Mirror of the Text and the Demands on the Lector

τὴν Ὀδύσσειαν καλὸν ἀνθρωπίνου βίου κάτοπτρον

The *Odyssey* is a beautiful mirror of human life
—Alcidamas (*apud* Arist. *Rhet.* 3.3.1406b12)

An non apud Homerum, ut <in> quodam ingenti speculo, clarius cernis haec . . . officia

Or do you not discern these duties (of yours) more clearly in Homer, as if in a huge mirror?
—Apuleius *De deo Socratis* 17.3

In the previous chapter, I argued that philosophical and literary critics of the Second Sophistic look to the figures of Odysseus and Heracles as heroic paradigms because of their engagement with and reception of aesthetic pleasure. Both are revered not for their role as culture heroes per se, but rather, for their ability to see and experience visual or aural pleasure (*hêdonê/voluptas*) without being corrupted; and in fact, they even learn from aesthetic pleasure of the sort which would likely lead others astray. I suggested, however, that in the case of Odysseus, in particular, there is an implicit tension in adopting him as a paradigm of experiencing aesthetic pleasure, since he grants readers license to fully enjoy *voluptas*—at least, up to a point. In other words, under the auspices of becoming *prudens/sôphrôn*, Odysseus gives readers an authorization for pursuing illicit or secret knowledge, and even erotic or corrupting pleasure. That is why our imperial and Second Sophistic readers in many cases had to qualify

Odysseus' role as an *exemplum*, from Plutarch's or Lucian's claims that readers ought to "proto-philosophize" or look disdainfully on the pleasure in which Odysseus indulged, to St. Basil's revisionist version of the hero, where he suggests (contrary to Homer) that Odysseus did, in fact, plug up his own ears when he encountered the Sirens' threat.

In this chapter, I home in further on this problem of pursuing virtue amid the aesthetic-erotic pleasures of vice by focusing on two related literary traditions whose proponents likewise grapple with the ambivalent nature of aesthetic experience and also have an unmistakable impact on Apuleius across his oeuvre. First, I consider the tradition of the text-as-mirror and to do so, I turn to an early allegorizing approach to reading the *Odyssey*, which flourishes well into the imperial period and Second Sophistic. Alcidamas' claim (the first epigraph for this chapter) that Homer's epic poem is "a beautiful mirror of human life" is interpretively impenetrable for us modern readers, since this curious bon mot is taken entirely out of context and cited in Aristotle merely as an example of "cold" rhetoric.[1] The allegorizing tradition of Homer's epic took shape, however, on the basis of presumptuous and likely mistaken glosses on puzzling statements such as this, and Apuleius was clearly familiar, if not with Alcidamas' original claim about the *Odyssey* as a mirror for its readers, then certainly with its reception tradition, which was built upon the fourth-century BCE sophist's remark.[2] If the figure of Odysseus can act as a *speculum* for Homer's reader, whether as a philosophical journeyman or alternatively, as a representation of aesthetic-erotic indulgence,[3] then, to be sure, one ought to look upon his character as an *exemplum* of sorts, either as a paradigm for replication or as an opportunity for what Alexei Zadorojnyi labels "ethical therapy by

---

1. See Aristotle *Rhet.* 3.3.1406b12 for the quotation of Alcidamas as an encapsulation of a metaphor that contributes to "cold" (τὸ ψυχρόν) rhetorical style because it is "excessively solemn" and "tragic." Although, even before Alcidamas' meditations on *mimesis* and the mirror of the *Odyssey*, we find Pindar promising the victor in *Nem.* 7.14 that he will provide a "mirror" to reflect his deeds (on which, see Halliwell 2002, 133n4).

2. For Alcidamas' influence on the later poetic reception of the *Odyssey* as a "mirror," see Richardson 1981, 6–9, who further suggests that Plato's antagonism toward the mirror of poetry in *Rep.* 10 may be responding to Alcidamas' original claim. There is great debate, however, on the impact of Alcidamas' "cold" metaphor on ancient literary-theoretical disussions about Homer and the value of poetry: see, e.g., O'Sullivan 1992, 63–66, who, while conceding a broader impact on literary criticism, cautions against Richardson's view of Alcidamas' direct influence on Plato. See also Halliwell 2002, 133n42, who seems more skeptical about the scope of the influence of Alcidamas. On Apuleius' participation in this literary-critical discourse, see Hunter 2014b, 34–35, on which, more below. On Apuleius' general approach to allegorizing Homer, see now Pasetti 2023.

3. For general treatments, see Stanford 1963; Barnouw 2004; and Montiglio 2011. For discussion with more extensive bibliography, see §2.1 below.

deterrence":[4] we should strive either to be *like* Odysseus or to avoid following his erroneous missteps.

The purpose of this chapter, however, is not simply to suggest that Apuleius was familiar with and participated in the long intellectual tradition of allegorizing the *Odyssey*, as such a claim would likely be considered neither terribly innovative nor much disputed in scholarship.[5] Rather, what I am interested in demonstrating here is how Apuleius blends this allegorical tradition with another, especially Roman practice of appealing to the mirror of exemplarity as a prosthetic tool which helps its viewer learn how to "pursue virtue" and "flee vice." As we shall see, quite early in the Roman tradition, authors appeal to biographical depictions for their readers or audience members as a means of regulating and structuring their own lives. In other words, "mirroring," when employed as a "triangulative" instrument,[6] provides an opportunity for ethical self-modeling,[7] and this approach to reflection becomes implicated in the imperial period and Second Sophistic with the practice of reading. Consider, for instance, the famous opening of Seneca's *De clementia*, in which the Stoic philosopher promises "to function as a mirror" (1.1: *speculi vice fungerer*) for Nero through his moral treatise.[8] Somewhat surprisingly, this tradition does not explicitly intersect in Roman literature with the reception of Prodicus' allegory of Heracles' choice between *Virtus* and *Voluptas*. Nevertheless, the thrust of its moral-ethical impulse is aligned quite closely with the educative aim of choice in "Heracles' education": to teach readers the pursuit of virtue and the avoidance of vice.

By no means is Apuleius the first in the Latin tradition to blend the allego-

---

4. Zadorojnyi 2010, 172.

5. On Apuleius' engagement with the *Odyssey*, whether seriously or as parody, see Münstermann 1995, 8–13; Montiglio 2007; Graverini 2012a 141–54; Hunter 2014b. On Apuleius' innovation in the tradition of Homeric *allegorêsis*, see Ulrich (forthcoming b).

6. Cf. Taylor 2008, 20–21, who identifies one function of the mirror of Roman art as "triangulative," "whereby [the subject] might be instructed by the virtues and faults of others, reflected in some metaphorical mirror such as a literary or theatrical account of their deeds." See esp. 19–26 for the "triangulative" mirror in the philosophical tradition.

7. See Bartsch 2006, esp. 23–24. Cf. also McCarty 1989, 169, who points out that the exemplary mirror's function seems to depend on "two properties of the physical device": "its responsiveness, mirroring the observer, change for change, in time; and objectification, capturing his changeable image in space and thus seeming to give it an almost independent being. Creating a personality would, then, be an interactive process: not simply adopting an external image as the self, but discovering the self by correspondence with an external world in which the observer finds himself mirrored. The result is an objectified soul, a personality provoked from without and 'conjured up' from within."

8. On which, see §2.1 below (with bibliography).

rizing approach to Homer with a Roman model of exemplarity. As Richard Hunter has suggested, Apuleius' appeal to the allegorical Odysseus in the closing lines of *Soc.* plays upon a didactic movement enacted in Roman literature at least as early as Horace.[9] Luca Graverini, moreover, has read Lucius' Odyssean heritage in the *Metamorphoses*, which we surveyed in the previous chapter (§1.3), in light of Cicero's exegesis of the Homeric Sirens,[10] and we shall see in §2.3 how Apuleius alludes specifically to Cicero's Sirens in his praise of the ethical value of the mirror in the *Apologia*. What is unique to Apuleius, however, is the fact that he associates this tradition specifically with reading, or more precisely, with a particular type of "active" or "diligent" reading. Indeed, the appropriate response to aesthetic pleasure entails for Apuleius a procedure of stripping away external superficialities and looking deep beneath the surface, much as Alcibiades *claims* to do when faced with the Silenic-Sirenic Socrates in our programmatic passage from the *Symposium*. The exemplary mirror of Roman literature, which is leveraged time and again as a means to teach the pursuit of virtue and the avoidance of vice, is thus fused in the hands of Apuleius with the allegorizing tradition on the *Odyssey* and thereby, transformed into a complex theory of reader-response. Striving after virtue and avoiding vice is nothing less than particularly careful and attentive reading—a practice which we can see Apuleius advocating across his corpus.

In the interest of demonstrating Apuleius' engagement with and appropriation of these two separate traditions, I offer a review of their uniquely Roman strands (§2.1). We will consider, on the one hand, how the exemplary mirror of pursuing virtue and fleeing vice, which evolves into an authorial device employed in self-consciously pedagogical literature of the Augustan and imperial periods (e.g., in satire or biography), traces its origins to Roman comedy of the Republic, a more playful genre which scholars have associated with Apuleius since Macrobius' withering assessment of the *Met.*[11] On the other hand, alongside this "mirror" of Roman comedy, there develops an especially Roman approach to allegorizing the *Odyssey*, which is connected already in Horace's *Epist.* 1.2 to "rereading" in one's leisure time. After surveying the evolution of

---

9. See Hunter 2014b.
10. See Graverini 2012a, 146–49.
11. See *Comm. in Somn. Scip.* 1.2.8, where he (ambiguously) categorizes Petronius and Apuleius under the heading of *comoediae* which only "charm the ears" (*auditum mulcent*), such as the plays of Menander (on which, see §5.3). For the seminal treatment of Roman drama in Apuleius, see May 2006. Cf. also Kirichenko 2010, 11–44, on Apuleius' self-conscious play with theatricality and mime.

these two intellectual currents as a backdrop to Apuleius' theory of reader-response, I will turn to his rhetorical/philosophical texts: the popularizing demonological treatise *Soc.*, and the defense speech he makes when accused of using magic to seduce a widow (the *Apologia*). In the former (§2.2), we will analyze the way in which Apuleius adapts the *Odyssey*-mirror tradition to establish a parallel to Socrates' own cultivation of wisdom through his *daemôn*. There, the approach to acquiring "wisdom" (*sapientia*) and "intelligence" (*prudentia*) involves stripping away external appearances—*aliena* ("external" or "foreign things")—in order to gaze upon an underlying reality beneath. In §2.3, then, we will examine Apuleius' appropriation of the Roman mirror of exemplarity in the *Apologia*'s "eulogy of the mirror" (*laus speculi*), where the *philosophus Platonicus* appeals to none other than Socrates as a paradigm of "ethical therapy by deterrence" (n. 4 above). Aemilianus, Apuleius' accuser, would never have brought a charge against Apuleius, the rhetor suggests, if he had "carefully read" a book and as a consequence, "looked into" a mirror. The relationship between textual engagement and ethical self-modulation thus becomes dependent, in Apuleius' colorful invective, on "diligently reading" Plato.

Finally, having overviewed Apuleius' reception of the Roman allegorical tradition in his rhetorical/philosophical works, I return to the *Met.* to analyze the ways in which our narrator invites *us* to look deeply into this burlesque text. We will look once again at the Prologue in §2.4 and reconsider Apuleius' call to deep reading in light of the novelistic tradition and its perpetual play with hiding weighty content under light and playful form. "To look in" and "marvel" at how "figures" are transformed "into other images" functions, in my interpretation, as yet another programmatic invitation to gaze upon a Socrates-figure—the very sort which Alcibiades eulogizes in the *Symp.* with a deceptive "image" that reveals "statues of gods" when stripped of its external form. After viewing the Prologue as a gesture to the Silenic-Sirenic Socrates, I close out the chapter (§2.5) by analyzing early opportunities for choice in the introductory episodes of *Met.* 1 and 2. Indeed, in the opening episode of the novel, Lucius is faced with a choice about whether he should listen to and enjoy a fictional tale, which can "smooth out the harsh road" he is walking. Having opted to stay on the surface, as it were, and delight in Aristomenes' tale, he wakes up in the town of Hypata at *Met.* 2.1, where, though he recognizes the need for deep reading, he prefers nonetheless to remain on the surface-level and only take in the illusions as they are presented to him.

2.1. The Mirror of the Text Traditions

As I suggested above, the trope of the "mirror of the text" has a long tradition in the ancient world, and much like the figures of Odysseus and Heracles, it proliferates copiously in the imperial period and Second Sophistic.[12] If we can trust the witness of late antique commentators, the first known author of the Roman tradition, Livius Andronicus, allegedly referred to the genre of comedy as a "mirror of everyday life" (Donat. *De com.* 5: *cotidianae vitae **speculum***), since "by reading comedy" (***lectione*** *comoediae*), we "pay attention" (***animadvertimus***) to the imitation of life and habit, just as we gather feint sketches of truth when "intent on the mirror" (***intenti*** *speculo*).[13] So also, Cicero claimed, according to a fragment likewise found in Donatus' fourth-century CE commentary, that "comedy is an imitation of life, a mirror of habit, and an image of truth" (*De com.* 1: *comoediam esse . . . imitationem vitae, **speculum** consuetudinis, imaginem veritatis*). Whereas in the Greek tradition the *Odyssey* is labeled a "beautiful mirror of human life," Roman authors, composing in the wake of Hellenistic ideas about the influence and power of theatrical performance, develop their own inchoate literary tradition by means of an appeal to the moral-ethical reflections of New Comedy.[14]

In fact, writers of Roman comedy, self-consciously aware of the genre's mimetic-ethical function, often deploy mirrors in performances to reflect on theatrical play with identity and exemplarity.[15] The *locus classicus* of such ethical speculation in the Roman comic tradition comes from the *Adelphoe*—from a scene in Terence's masterpiece that would provide the archetype for the "tri-

---

12. Just a few citations will suffice: on the mirror of historiographic biography, see Plut. *Tim.* 1.1; on the mirror of history, see Lucian's *Hist. Conscr.* 51 (with Fox 2001); on the mirror of the dance, see Lucian *De salt.* 72 (with Lada-Richards 2005); on the mirror of philosophical treatises, see Seneca's *De clem. pr.*1 (with Ker 2009 and Braund 2009). See §4.2 for the Second Sophistic reception of the phrase ὥσπερ . . . ἐν κατόπτρῳ (*Phaedr.* 255d5–6), which intersects with this tradition.

13. It is worth noting that Donatus here transforms comedy into a reading experience (*lectio*), and moreover, uses our terminology for careful reading (i.e., *intendere*) interchangeably with the attention demanded by the comic prologist (*animadvertere*). Cf. §0.4 with n. 101.

14. For a useful textbook discussion, see Hunter 1985, 137–51. See, however, Konstan 2018, who interprets the mimetic-speculative image of New Comedy as a larger ideological phenomenon shaping Hellenistic social life.

15. E.g., in Sosia's reference to the philosophical tradition of mirroring when he encounters his doppelganger, Mercury (see *Amph.* 441: *saepe in speculum **inspexi***; on which, see Caston 2014), or in Periphanes' lament in the *Epidicus* that humans do not possess a mirror (*Ep.* 383: *habere speculum*) "to contemplate their life, whenever they looked into it" (386–87: *ubi id **inspexissent**, cogitarent postea/vitam*).

angulative" mirror of exemplarity.[16] Indeed, at *Adelphoe* 414–16, the harsh father-figure, Demea, brags to his slave-cook, Syrus, about how he taught his son, Ctesipho, to regulate his moral-ethical decisions:

denique **inspicere** tamquam **in speculum in vitas omnium**
iubeo atque **ex aliis sumere exemplum** sibi.

Finally, I bid him **to look into the lives of all humans as if into a mirror** and **to take an example** for himself **from others**.

In this second-century BCE drama, we can already note the deployment of our catchword for "active" reading and diligent looking, as we see it later used in Apuleius' milieu: *inspicere*.[17] For a social-cultural system in which one is expected to police one's own behavior by comparison to an external model, it is significant that the "lives" of others are transformed into a *speculum*, by which means viewers can model their behavior. So, Demea boasts to Syrus that he deploys *exempla* as paradigms of pursuit and avoidance: "do this" (417: *hoc facito*); "flee that" (*hoc fugito*); "this is praiseworthy" (418: *hoc laudist*); "that considered vice" (*hoc vitio datur*). Of course, there is an irony in Demea's empty bragging which adds to the comic effect: the stern father congratulates himself on the success of his approach to parenting, even though the audience knows that Aeschinus, the (allegedly) bad son raised under laissez-faire guidance and accused of wantonly stealing a slave girl, took the girl on behalf of his supposedly upstanding brother and Demea's ward, Ctesipho. The humor is amplified, moreover, by Syrus' deflating response, as he immediately laments that "[he] doesn't have the leisure-time **by Hercules** to listen to this" (419: *non **hercle** otiumst nunc mi auscultandi*) and then, proceeds to imitate Demea's high-spun rhetoric when instructing his fellow kitchen slaves. With this subtle appeal to the hero via invocation, it is as if Syrus implies that this grandiose discourse on parenting is not exactly a "choice of Heracles" type of situation.[18]

Nonetheless, this passage from the *Adelphoe* was to be decontextualized

---

16. The first identification of Terence (together with Horace) as fundamental to Roman exemplarity is Kornhardt 1936, 26–34. For fuller discussion, see Mayer 1991, 144–46; Marchetti 2004, 9–17. So also, Chaplin 2000, 11–13, takes Terence (and Horace) as fundamental to the evolution of a culture of exemplarity at Rome.

17. On which, see §0.4 again.

18. Cf. §1.3 (esp. with n. 101), where I suggest that ironic play with the invocation *hercle* has a metatextual significance already in Plautus' usage.

and redeployed as an authorizing model for biographers seeking to legitimize the genre of "lives."[19] "Taking an example" (*sumere exemplum*) establishes the framework, on the one hand, for an emerging culture of exemplarity—a phenomenon which scholars have recognized permeating Roman society in all sorts of ways, from the funerary *imagines* displayed in the atria of elite families to the performance cultures of theater and oratory.[20] Taking one's *exemplum* "from others" (*ex aliis*), on the other hand, simultaneously plays upon a New Comic trope about the "busybody," the *polypragmôn/curiosus* who overeagerly pays attention to *aliena*: "things which pertain to others." Indeed, as Matthew Leigh has shown, Roman Comedy exhibits a keen interest in demarcating the provenance of the busybody, whether we look at the parasite of Plautus' *Stichus*, who "attend[s] with utmost zeal to the affairs of others" (*Stich.* 199: **alienas** res qui curant studio maxumo), or the nosey neighbor of Terence's *Self-Tormentor*, Chremes, who responds to his neighbor's concerns over "caring about others' affairs" (*Heaut. Tim.* 76: **aliena** ut cures) with a line that would ironically be used to encapsulate the humanistic pursuit for ages to come: "I am human: I consider nothing human foreign to me" (77: *homo sum: humani nil a me* **alienum** *puto*).[21]

The blurry line between looking into the lives of others to adopt an exemplary paradigm and overeagerly peering into that which is not one's business is precisely at issue in the variable and shifting meanings of the word *curiosus*, the semantic contours of which range from translating the Greek *polypragmôn* (with all of the attendant negative connotations)[22] to highlighting the scholastic diligence and rigorous care necessary to produce universal history or imperial

---

19. See Mayer 1991; Marchetti 2004, on the influence of Terence's passage on the culture of exemplarity. On biography, see, e.g., Plutarch's proem in the *Timoleon-Aemilius* pair of lives (*Tim.* 1.1): ἐμοὶ τῆς τῶν βίων ἅψασθαι μὲν γραφῆς συνέβη δι' ἑτέρους, ἐπιμένειν δὲ καὶ φιλοχωρεῖν ἤδη καὶ δι' ἐμαυτόν, **ὥσπερ ἐν ἐσόπτρῳ** τῇ ἱστορίᾳ πειρώμενον ἁμῶς γέ πως κοσμεῖν καὶ ἀφομοιοῦν πρὸς τὰς ἐκείνων ἀρετὰς τὸν βίον. On the intentional slippage between text and life here as part of a biographical impulse, see Duff 1999, 32–34.

20. For the seminal work on *imagines* and their relationship with exemplarity, see Flower 1996. See Konstan 2018 on the influence of New Comedy on social life. On exemplarity and its influence on Roman oratory and biography, see Roller 2018; Chaplin 2000 remains an excellent source on exemplarity in historiography.

21. See Leigh 2013, 60–68, for the reception of the *curiosus* in Roman comedy. Cf. also Hunter 1985, 139, who notes that this moralizing one-liner was detached from its context, where it originally mocked "a ploy by a self-important busybody to defend his right to meddle in his neighbor's affairs."

22. For the various Roman attempts to translate the category of *polypragmosynê* into Latin, see Leigh 2013, 54–90. See also Howley 2018, 23–31, for discussion of a meditation in Aulus Gellius (*NA* 11.16) on the difficulties of translating the Greek concept of *polypragmosynê*.

READING AS A CHOICE IN THE APULEIAN CORPUS   93

encyclopedia.[23] As we look to Apuleius' discourse on *curiositas* and "diligent reading," however, we will have to keep in mind a strand of thought distinct from the New Comic associations of the *polypragmôn/curiosus*: that is, a Platonic antagonism toward concerning oneself with "the things of others" (τὰ ἀλλότρια).[24] Indeed, as we shall see in the *Apologia*'s brutal invective against his accuser, Apuleius melds the "triangulative" mirror of exemplarity inaugurated by Terence's *speculum* with Socrates' continued practice across the Platonic corpus of defining justice as the pursuit of self-knowledge: one definition of "justice," Socrates explains in the *Republic*, is "taking care of one's own affairs and not playing the busybody" (*Rep.* 433a8–9: τὸ **τὰ αὐτοῦ** πράττειν καὶ μὴ **πολυπραγμονεῖν**).[25] In short, one can follow Demea's advice and "look into" the lives of others for ethical self-modulation; but from the Platonic perspective, one also runs the risk of overstepping, of becoming a curious voyeur or a nosey busybody.

Before we turn to the reception of the allegorized Odysseus in the Roman tradition, it is worth delving a bit deeper into the afterlife of Terence's mirror of exemplarity, as it connects conceptually with the choice of our other heroic model of aesthetic experience: Heracles. Most famously, in an important programmatic satire, Horace places himself in the genealogy of Ctesipho, the erring child of comedy who was chastised by his stern father: *Sermones* 1.4 tells of how Horace's "best father" regulated his behaviors "by labeling the several vices with examples so that [he] would flee them" (*Serm.* 1.4.106: *ut fugerem exemplis*

---

23. This secondary valence of *curiosus* is derived from its etymological root, *cura* ("care" or "anxiety"). On *curiositas* and Roman imperial knowledge collection, see Leigh 2013, 91–129.

24. See, e.g., *Phaedr.* 229e6 (on which, see more below). See also *Rep.* 443d, where a well-balanced soul is supposed to "not do things belonging to other parts, nor meddle" (*Rep.* 443d1–2: μὴ . . . τἀλλότρια πράττειν ἕκαστον . . . μηδὲ πολυπραγμονεῖν); and *Rep.* 10.606b1–2, where Socrates laments that a good man who is insufficiently educated will indulge in watching tragedy because he "does not think it shameful for him to spectate the sufferings of another" (ἀλλότρια πάθη θεωρῶν καὶ ἑαυτῷ οὐδὲν αἰσχρόν). Cf. also *Charm.* 161b–163c, where Socrates and Critias debate the definition of *sôphrosynê* as "only accomplishing and doing the things belonging to oneself" (162a2–3: τὰ . . . ἑαυτοῦ ἕκαστον ἐργάζεσθαί τε καὶ πράττειν) and "not touching the things of others" (162a1: τῶν . . . ἀλλοτρίων μὴ ἅπτεσθαι). On *allotrion* as a Greek gloss for *alienum*, see *ThLL* 1.1567.21. Leigh 2013, 62, notes the significance of *allotrion* as a translation in the comic discourse of busybodies and its reception (e.g., in Plutarch's *De curios.*), but does not connect it to Socrates-as-busybody (discussed at Leigh 2013, 33–35).

25. One could trace this motif even further back to the Gyges episode in Herodotus. The reason Candaules' servant gives for not wanting to see the king's wife naked is one of the ancient truths that one "must learn from" (Hdt. 1.8.4): "one ought to look [only] at his own things" (σκοπέειν τινὰ τὰ ἑωυτοῦ). On this passage, see Leigh 2013, 96. See DeFilippo 1990 on the influence of Platonic discussion of *polypragmosynê* on the *Met.* For Socrates' own *polypragmosynê* and its influence on Lucius' *curiositas* in the *Met.*, see §5.0.

vitiorum quaeque notando).[26] As Emily Gowers has noted, Horace's satirical realization of exemplary paradigms for "avoidance" (1.4.115: *vitatu*) and "pursuit" (*petitu*) finds its "salient comic antecedent" in the *Adelphoe*'s mirror of others' lives.[27] This appeal to *exempla*, however, is not simply or straightforwardly a "choice of Heracles." For far from highlighting the philosophical benefits of following the path to virtue, it places its emphasis on the practical social harms of failing to avoid vice. So, in an innovative appropriation of the New Comic *polypragmôn/curiosus*, Horace claims that the "opprobrium belonging to others" (1.4.128: *aliena opprobria*) often "frightens young souls away from vices" (*teneros animos . . . /absterrent vitiis*). In short, it is, indeed, appropriate and even vital to look at *aliena*, but the act of looking represents not the nosey peering of a comic busybody nor the Platonic pursuit of justice, but is instead a socially driven and outcome-oriented mode of habituation.

By the Augustan period, therefore, Terence's exemplary mirror had become such a well-recognized *topos* that even historiographers redirect the biographical impulse of Demea's bombast to their own programmatic ends. Thus, Livy's aspiration to provide "specimens of every *exemplum*" (*AUC* 1.*pr*.10: *omnis . . . exempli documenta*) for the reader to "look upon" (*intueri*) in order to take models "for imitation" (*quod imitere*) and "avoidance" (*quod vites*) borrows its conceptual apparatus from Terence.[28] The most noteworthy reception of the "triangulative" mirror, however, occurs nearly a half century later, when Seneca strategically inverts the paradigm in his attempt to educate Nero in the *De clementia*. The opening line of that treatise's prologue retools the ethical mirror of self-modulation into an opportunity for the text's reader/viewer to reach the climax of "pleasure" (*De clem.* 1.1):

> Scribere de clementia, Nero Caesar, institui, ut quodam modo **speculi** vice fungerer et te tibi ostenderem perventurum ad **voluptatem maximam** omnium.

---

26. Text and (adapted) translation of this difficult line come from Gowers 2012, 176 *ad loc.* 106.
27. For the quotation and discussion of the influence of Terence's archetype on Horace, see again Gowers 2012, 176 *ad loc.* 106. In his commentary on Terence's *Adelphoe*, Martin 1976, 168 *ad loc.* 415 takes it as given that Horace was reared on Demea's advice in *Serm.* 1.4. For a more comprehensive discussion, see also Mayer 1991. Cf. also Marchetti 2004, esp. 17–35, who notes the influence, but also elucidates the philosophical (and especially Platonic) backdrop of *Serm.* 1.4.
28. Horace too refers to a negative *exemplum* as a "great specimen" (*Serm.* 1.4.110: *magnum documentum*) for avoidance. So, Mayer 1991, 145, notes that *documentum* is functionally a synonym for *exemplum*. On Livy's engagement with Terence's exemplarity, see Chaplin 2000, 11–13.

I decided to write about clemency, Nero Caesar, in order that I might function in some way like a mirror and reveal you to yourself, destined as you are to come to the greatest pleasure of all.

Immediately following this, however, Seneca paradoxically assimilates the *voluptas* of reading his text-mirror to the acquisition of virtue, suggesting that good action itself is the "true benefit of good deeds" and moreover, that there is "no reward for virtues (*virtutum*) beyond the virtues themselves." Finally, appealing to Terence's exemplary mirror,[29] the philosopher proposes that it will be "pleasing to look into . . . one's good conscience" (*iuvat* **inspicere** . . . *bonam conscientiam*) and thereafter, to "cast one's eyes upon the multitude . . . which exults equally in the destruction of others as well as of itself" (*immittere oculos in hanc . . . multitudinem . . . in perniciem* **alienam** *suamque pariter exultaturam*).

We may recognize here all the specific terminology associated with the Roman comic and satirical discourse on exemplarity—using the external *speculum* for replicating virtuous behavior, "looking into" (*inspicere*) one's own thought processes, and learning from the suffering "which belongs to another" (*aliena*); but interestingly, Seneca has turned the paradigm inside out. Rather than pursuing virtue and fleeing vice *à la* the heroic Heracles, the *praeceptor* has assimilated *voluptas*—an ambivalent "pleasure," which occurs to good outcome nowhere else in tandem with mirror speculation[30]—to the *virtus* of good rulership. In other words, this is not the "triangulative" technique of "ethical therapy by deterrence," but rather, represents a self-satisfied mode of looking, one which requires no ethical transformation from the viewer. So, Shadi Bartsch concludes:

In introducing this terminology . . . Seneca has mingled two mirror traditions: he has introduced the erotic pleasure of the mirror of vanity into the corrective usage of the mirror of self-improvement. And he has done so even though else-

---

29. See Braund 2009, 156 *ad loc.*, who notes a possible echo of Ter. *Ad.* 415 in Seneca's usage of *inspicere*.

30. So, Bartsch 2006, 184, notes: "The terminology of this opening paragraph is deeply problematic. What the mirror of the text promises to show Nero, if he succeeds in ethical rulership, is not self-knowledge . . . or a profitable estrangement from the self, but rather *voluptas*, a term that is distinctly sensual in its connotations." Cf. also Ker 2009, esp. 260–61, on the participation/implication of the reader here and across the Senecan corpus.

96 THE SHADOW OF AN ASS

where he is usually careful to distinguish between *gaudium*, the sober joy born of philosophy, and *voluptas*, whose pleasures are fleeting and of this world.[31]

Indeed, *gaudium*, the philosophical endpoint of Lady Virtue's promise in "Heracles' education," is paradoxically transformed in Seneca's strategic appropriation of Terence's mirror into *voluptas*, virtue's personified antithesis in the Roman reception of Prodicus' allegory.[32]

We shall return to this ethical mirror of exemplarity when we consider Apuleius' *laus speculi* in §2.3, especially since, following Seneca's various appeals to an ethical mirror, the moral-philosophical tradition is linked shortly thereafter to none other than Socrates. However, in the interest of elucidating the other main strand of Apuleius' educative mirror-text—the mirror of Homer—we should briefly review the allegorizing tradition of the *Odyssey* in Latin literature, especially insofar as it intersects with Roman views on exemplarity.

Needless to say, the *Odyssey* is woven into the Roman tradition from its very inception with Livius Andronicus' translation, the *Odusia*, into Saturnian verse. But as with the Greek tradition surveyed in the previous chapter, so also, Odysseus, because of his variable and changeable character in Homeric epic, oscillates between two poles in the Roman philosophical tradition: from the gluttonous parasite, whose delight in hedonic pleasures among the Phaeacians (*Od.* 9.5–10) makes him an ideal Epicurean hero,[33] to the beggar of the latter half of the poem, whose humble rags facilitate his transformation into a philosophical ideal—a proto-Cynic rejecting the comforts of the world[34] or an ideal-

31. Bartsch 2006, 185.
32. Recall from §1.3 (with n. 113) that Xenophon's *Kakia* is translated in Cicero with the Latin *Voluptas*. On Seneca's self-aware inversion of the technical philosophical terminology of *gaudium* and the populist discourse on *voluptas*, see Graver 2016, esp. her discussion of *Ep.* 59.
33. See, e.g., Plautus' *Menaechmi*, where the parasite character is referred to as "my Ulysses" (*Men.* 902: *meus Ulixes*). For the most explicit attack on the Epicurean Odysseus, see Heracl. *Hom. Probl.* 79.2–3, where the allegorist calls Epicurus a "Phaeacian philosopher" (Φαίαξ φιλόσοφος) and lambasts him for stealing "the lies which Odysseus told in playing a role at Alcinous' house" (ἃ γὰρ Ὀδυσσεὺς ὑποκρίσει παρ' Ἀλκίνῳ ... ἐψεύσατο) and making them the "end of life" (τέλη βίου). Cf. also Lucian's *The Parasite* 10–11, in which an Epicurean advocate suggests that Odysseus embraced not the Stoic, but the Epicurean life, so much so that Epicurus "very shamelessly pilfered [from Homer's Odysseus] the goal of the parasite as his endpoint of happiness" (11.1: σφόδρα ἀναισχύντως ὑφελόμενος τὸ τῆς παρασιτικῆς τέλος τῆς καθ' αὑτὸν εὐδαιμονίας τέλος). On the Epicurean reception of Odysseus, see Asmis 1995; Montiglio 2011, 95–100. Cf. also Hunter 2018, 170–80, for a useful discussion of two reworkings—of Horace's *Serm.* 2.5 and Plutarch's *Gryllus*—of Odysseus into a parasite and antihero.
34. On the Cynic reception of Odysseus, see Buffière 1956, 372–74; Montiglio 2011, 66–73. The proto-Cynic, Antisthenes, wrote a work called the *Odysseus* (on which, see Höistad 1948, 94–101) as well as a now lost *On Circe*.

ized Stoic, who endures fate with uncompromising fortitude.[35] For the purposes of assessing Apuleius' reception of the allegorized Odysseus, however, we may begin our scan of the Roman Ulysses with a passage from the late Republic, to which we shall see Apuleius also alluding in the *Apologia*: Cicero's translation of the Sirens episode in *De finibus*.

Indeed, Cicero is one of the first authors we have in the extant Roman tradition to represent Odysseus as an ideal philosophical traveler who offered a paradigm for later thinkers in their intellectual inquiries. In an exploration of the innate "pleasure (*voluptatem*) which [humans] take from learning" (*De fin.* 5.49), Cicero's Piso (the primary speaker, who articulates Antiochus of Ascalon's theory of affection) refers first to the bewitching song of Homer's Sirens as a case in point:

> mihi quidem Homerus huiusmodi quiddam vidisse videtur in iis quae de Sirenum cantibus finxerit. neque enim vocum suavitate videntur aut novitate quadam et varietate cantandi revocare eos solitae qui praetervehebantur, sed quia **multa se scire** profitebantur, ut homines ad earum saxa **discendi cupiditate** adhaerescerent. ita enim invitant Ulixem.

> Homer indeed seems to have recognized [that humans take pleasure from learning] in those tales which he fashioned about the Sirens' songs. For it is not by the charm of their voices, nor by a certain novelty and variety of their singing that they seemed continually to call back those who were passing by; rather, it's because they promised that they knew much, and so men clung to their rocks out of a desire for knowing. Thus, they called to Ulysses.

---

35. See, e.g., Sen. *De const.* 2.1–2: "For our Stoics have pronounced these (i.e., Ulysses and Hercules) wise, since they were unconquered by labors, contemptuous of pleasure, and victorious over all lands" (*hos [sc. Ulixem et Herculem] enim Stoici nostri sapientes pronuntiaverunt, invictos laboribus et contemptores voluptatis et victores omnium terrarum*). On the Stoic reception of Odysseus, see Buffière 1956, 374–77; Stanford 1963, 121–27; Montiglio 2011, 73–83. On Stoic *allēgorēsis* of Homer, see Long 1992; Nussbaum 1993. Cf., however, Seneca *Ep.* 88, where the Stoic mocks the allegorizing traditions that "convince you that Homer was a philosopher" (88.5: *tibi Homerum philosophum fuisse persuadent*), but contradict themselves in suggesting he is "at one time a Stoic, insofar as he approves of virtue alone, flees from pleasures, and does not depart from what is right" (*modo Stoicum illum . . . virtutem solam probantem et voluptates refugientem et ab honesto ne . . . quidem . . . recedentem*), but "at another [time, he is] an Epicurean, who praises the condition of a state which is quiet and spends its life in feasting and song" (*modo Epicureum, laudantem statum quietae civitatis et inter convivia cantusque vitam exigentis*). On this passage and its relationship to Horace *Epist.* 1.2, see Hunter 2014b, 23.

After translating a few lines of *Odyssey* 12 into Latin, Piso then lists exemplary students devoted to study and literature—Pythagoras, Plato, and Democritus—all of whom "traveled to the edges of the world out of a desire for learning" (*De fin.* 5.50: *propter **discendi cupiditatem** . . . ultimas terras esse peragratas*).[36] Finally, linking Odysseus' aesthetic pleasure to philosophical activity, Piso explains that only "curious dilettantes" (*De fin.* 5.49: ***curiosi***) "want to know every sort of thing" (*omnia . . . scire cuiuscumquemodi sint cupere*), whereas the greatest men are led "by the contemplation of greater things toward the desire for knowledge" (*maiorum rerum **contemplatione** ad **cupiditatem** scientiae*).[37]

We already saw the influence of this passage on Apuleius in the previous chapter (§1.3), when we considered how the neologism he coins for Lucius' acquisition of knowledge, *multiscius*, seems to be derived from Cicero's translation of the Sirens episode in *De finibus*: in the *Odyssey*, the Sirens promise their hearer that he will depart "knowledgeable of more" (*Od.* 12.188: πλείονα εἰδώς), but Piso transfers the capacity for comprehensive knowledge to the Sirens themselves, who play upon the innate human "desire for learning" (*discendi cupiditate*) by claiming to "know many things" (***multa se scire***; cf. *multiscius*). Significant for us as we look to Apuleius' *Apologia*, this is the first occasion in the extant Latin corpus where an author speaks of the "desire for learning," a rare phrase associated from Cicero onward almost exclusively with philosophical inquiry.[38] In light of our discussion of *aliena*, we may note that, while Cicero

---

36. With this tradition on the philosophers, we may also compare Democritus' own self-presentation as the intellectual who, "of the men of his time, traveled the greatest amount of earth in search of knowledge" (B 299, 6–8 DK: ἐγὼ δὲ τῶν κατ' ἐμαυτὸν ἀνθρώπων γῆν πλείστην ἐπεπλανησάμην ἱστορέων). Compare also the later reception of Democritus, who "traversed much of the earth" (Ael. *VH* 4.20: πολλὴν ἐπῄει γῆν) in search of wisdom, and indeed, even spent his inheritance to gain wisdom (on which, see Montiglio 2011, 71–72).

37. Graverini 2012a, 147–49, connects this passage from *De fin.* to Lucius' epicizing gesture (*Met.* 9.13), and Hunter 2018, 212–13, follows suit. See also Leigh 2013, 181–83, on the Cicero passage, and 139 (with nn. 61–63) on the connection of this episode to *Met.* 1.2 (on which, see also §2.5).

38. So, Livy speaks of the itinerant philosopher, Pythagoras, who tried to induce followers "to the desire for learning" (*AUC* 1.18.3: *ad cupiditatem discendi*), and Columella advocates in his programmatic preface that people would pursue animal husbandry if they were "more desirous of learning" (*De re rustica* 1.pr.11: *discendi cupidiores*) and did not wish not to seem "imprudent" (*imprudentes*). Closer to Apuleius' milieu, Seneca lays out a program of philosophical study for Lucilius, since he has exhibited a "desire for learning" (*Ep.* 108.2: *cupiditas discendi*). The idiom, which we shall see again in the *Apologia*, is only semantically ambivalent in Gellius: at *NA* 10.12.5, he laments the misdirected interests of philosophers, such as Democritus, who, "rather desirous of learning" (*discendi cupidiora*), pursue the "enticements" (*inlecebra*) of paradoxography; at *NA* 6.17, moreover, Gellius claims to have pursued a pedantic philological discussion—precisely the kind of knowledge associated with *curiosi*—"from a desire for learning" (*discendi . . . cupidine*).

READING AS A CHOICE IN THE APULEIAN CORPUS 99

does not use this specific term from Roman comedy, he nonetheless develops a similar dichotomy between acceptable and illicit forms of knowledge and the pursuit of them. Thus, Piso, responding earlier in book 5 to Cicero's discussion of walking in the footsteps of great historical figures, notes that such "enthusiasms" (*studia*) are "characteristic of superior intellects [only] if they look toward the imitation of the greatest men" (5.6: *si ad **imitandos** summos viros spectant, ingeniosorum sunt*); otherwise, Piso explains, they are merely antiquarian fascinations of the *curiosi*.[39] Here in Cicero's reception of the *Odyssey*, in other words, Piso has reconstructed a thoroughly revised version of the Sirens, where the enchanting creatures sing songs that promise edifying knowledge to the right kind of listener: although he shamelessly indulges in aesthetic pleasure, Odysseus nonetheless becomes, in this strand of the Latin tradition, an *exemplum* of philosophical journeying and thus, a paradigm of the appropriate pursuit of knowledge, which involves the "contemplation of higher things."[40]

The other purple passage to which scholars refer when tracing the Roman afterlife of the allegorized Odysseus is Horace's *Epistles* 1.2,[41] a poem which Richard Hunter has recently argued bears directly upon Apuleius' version of Odysseus in *De deo Socratis*.[42] At the opening of the epistle, Horace spends his free time "**rereading** the author of the Trojan War" (*Epist.* 1.2.1–2: *Troiani belli scriptorem . . . **relegi***), as he tells his addressee Lollius, because Homer "speaks more plainly and uprightly than Chrysippus and Crantor about what is beautiful, what is shameful, what is useful, and what is not" (*Epist.* 1.2.3–4). By naming at the outset of the poem a well-known Stoic and Academic, both of whom had famously transformed the foundational epics into allegorical texts to be mined for lessons,[43] Horace implicitly disregards the philosophical tradition of accommodating Homer to fit into a specific school of thought. This epistle is, as

---

39. With Piso's categories of knowledge pursuit, we may also compare Seneca's *Ep.* 88.7–8, where he laments the kind of Alexandrian scholarly inquisitiveness about Odysseus' "wanderings—e.g., whether or not Penelope was, in fact, chaste—which seems to hinder us from "avoiding continuously wandering" (88.7: *ne nos semper erremus*). Cf. also *Brev. Vit.* 13 for a similar diatribe. For further discussion of Seneca's antagonism toward profitless curiosity, see Leigh 2013, 177.

40. In this respect, Cicero's advocacy of *contemplatio* mirrors "Philip the Philosopher's" philosophical reading of Heliodorus, whose *Aethiopica* "mix[es] the wine of **contemplation** into the water of the tale" (τῷ τῆς ἱστορίας ὕδατι τὸν οἶνον τῆς θεωρίας κεράσασα; text from Hercher 1869, 383). Cf. my discussion in §1.2a.

41. Stanford 1963, 122–23, refers to this poem as "the most famous eulogy" of Homer. For a sampling of treatments of Horace's allegorizing, see also Kaiser 1964; Long 1992; Mayer 1994, 114; Farrell 2004, 269–70; O'Sullivan 2007, 522–23; Montiglio 2011, 137–38; and Hunter 2014b.

42. See Hunter 2014b, 34–35.

43. See, esp., Long 1992, 45–49; Nussbaum 1993 on the Stoic reception of Homer. On Crantor's admiration for Homer, see Diog. Laert. *VP* 4.25–26.

100   THE SHADOW OF AN ASS

Roland Mayer phrases it, "a sort of protreptic, but not towards philosophy."[44] Rather, much like *Sermones* 1.4 with its appeal to Terentian exemplarity, Horace offers practical advice, transforming Odysseus' own anthropological "inspection" into a kind of simplified, "everyday" philosophy.[45] Crucial for the link between Odysseus-as-aesthetic-model and "reading," however, is the fact that Horace flees the enticements of the city to isolate himself at his country estate, where he "rereads" the educational lessons of the Homeric text. So, at *Epist.* 1.2.17–26, Horace adopts Odysseus as a paradigm of *virtus* and *sapientia*:

> Rursus, quid virtus et quid sapientia possit,
> utile proposuit nobis exemplar Ulixen,
> qui domitor Troiae multorum **providus** urbes
> et mores hominum **inspexit**, latumque per aequor,
> dum sibi, dum sociis reditum parat, aspera multa
> pertulit, adversis rerum inmersabilis undis.
> Sirenum voces et Circae pocula nosti;
> quae si cum sociis stultus cupidusque bibisset,
> sub domina meretrice fuisset turpis et excors,
> vixisset canis immundus vel amica luto sus

Again, as to what power virtue and wisdom possess, [Homer] has set before us a useful model in Ulysses, the conqueror of Troy, who looked with prudence upon the cities and customs of many humans, and who endured many difficulties through the broad sea, while he was preparing a return for himself and for his comrades, though he refused to be sunk by the waves which were adverse to his affairs. You know the voices of the Sirens and the cups of Circe. If he had stupidly and eagerly drunk them together with his companions, he would have been shameful and mad under a meretricious mistress, he would have lived like a dirty dog or a sow, friendly to the mud.

In this allegorizing rewrite of the *Odyssey*, we may note, of course, the presence of our significant "reading" term from the Prologue of the *Met.*

---

44. Mayer 1994, 124.
45. Cf., however, Gigante 1984, who uncovers the influence of Philodemus in Horace's exposition of *virtus* and *sapientia*, demonstrating how Horace undercuts his own pragmatic and antiphilosophical allegorizing. See also O'Sullivan 2007, 522–26, who extends this dichotomy of "everyday," philosophical allegorizing to the Roman Odyssey Landscapes.

READING AS A CHOICE IN THE APULEIAN CORPUS   101

(§0.4)—*inspicere*—a term we already saw Terence using in his mirror of lives. As John Moles notes, in contrast with how Horace translates Homer's ἴδεν (*Od.* 1.3: "he saw") in the *Ars Poetica* (142: *vidit*), he uses a "loaded" visual term (*inspexit*) in this allegorizing version of the *Odyssey* in order to enact a procedure we have come to associate with the long tradition of transforming Homer into a proto-philosopher.[46] So also, the adverbial usage of *providus* seems to function as a philosophical gloss on Odysseus' famously ambivalent character trait, *polytropos*.[47]

Importantly for us, Horace's technique of ratcheting up the Homeric phraseology for Odysseus' journey, whether by direct influence or by a shared tradition, is redeployed also in the Greek Second Sophistic reception of the *Odyssey*, as Maximus of Tyre likens the hero's peregrinations to the sprawling journey of the soul. After beginning *Oration* 26 with the opening lines of Homer, Maximus continues to "translate," as it were, the rest of Homer's proem into more philosophically inflected terminology:

αὐτὸς δὲ τῇ ψυχῇ κούφῳ χρήματι καὶ πολυπλανεστέρῳ τῶν σωμάτων, πανταχοῦ περιεφέρετο, πάντα **ἐπεσκόπει**, ὅσα οὐρανοῦ κινήματα, ὅσα γῆς παθήματα, θεῶν βουλάς, ἀνθρώπων φύσεις, ἡλίου φῶς, ἄστρων χορόν

By means of his soul, a light thing that can travel further than bodies, he himself was conveyed everywhere, and **he looked into** all things—all the movements of the heavens, the sufferings of the earth, the counsels of the gods, the natures of men, the light of the sun, and the chorus of the stars.[48]

For Maximus, Odysseus becomes a Platonic metaphysical soul, "carried about everywhere" as if in the circuit of the souls.[49] Strikingly, however, he is said not merely "to see" (ἴδεν), as Homer's Odysseus does, but rather, "to inspect" all things, where *episkopein* represents a more intellectualized procedure of looking than mere visual perception. The ambivalence of this procedure of allegorizing, though, remains perpetually in the background—a feature

---

46. See Moles 1985, 35. Cf., however, Mayer 1994, 155 *ad loc.* 1.2.20, who proposes that *inspexit*, in fact, translates Homer's *egnô*, as "both suggest critical scrutiny, not mere observation."
47. Cf. Hunter 2014b, 34: "*providus* offers a positive and semi-philosophical choice from the many ancient interpretations of Homer's *polytropos*." On the reception of Odysseus' *polytropia*, see §1.0 (with n. 7).
48. Translation adapted from Trapp 1997b, 214–15.
49. See *Phaedr.* 247d. Cf. also *Rep.* 617a.

102   THE SHADOW OF AN ASS

which we can recognize elsewhere in Maximus' corpus, such as when he compares Diogenes the Cynic to the Homeric hero because he "went around **inspecting the things of his neighbors** . . . like Odysseus" (*Or.* 15.9: περιήει **ἐπισκοπῶν τὰ τῶν πλησίον** . . . κατὰ τὸν Ὀδυσσέα). On the one hand, we see the recurrence of overtly philosophizing terminology—*episkopein*—which seems to mirror Horace's usage of *inspicere*; on the other hand, however, gazing upon "the things of neighbors" runs the risk of veering into the wrong kind of activity. From a different vantage point, the founder of Cynicism appears uncomfortably close to the busybody Odysseus, a reincarnation of the comic *polypragmôn/curiosus* whose interest in his neighbors' affairs stands in stark contrast to Plato's approach to justice.

One could go on elucidating the Roman reception of Odysseus by reviewing, for instance, Ovid's adoption of the Homeric hero as a model for the elegiac lover in his elicit pursuit of tawdry affairs,[50] or the "Janus-like" approach to Odysseus in Seneca, who lambasts the hero for cowardice in his dramas, but holds him up in his philosophical works as an ideal Stoic paradigm of responding to aesthetic pleasure.[51] However, since we have covered the elements of the Latin tradition which most inform Apuleius' thought, I would like to close our scan of the Roman Odysseus by returning to Horace's epistle and drawing attention to the way in which the satirist highlights the same kind of ambiguity we saw in the previous chapter between Odysseus-as-ideal-philosopher and Odysseus-as-connoisseur-of-aesthetic-pleasure. For we see also in Horace's revisionist rewrite that Odysseus paradoxically becomes his most philosophical in his encounters with aesthetic pleasure. That is, the satirist establishes an equivalence between the "voices of the Sirens" (1.2.23: *Sirenum voces*) and the

---

50. See, e.g., *Ars amat.* 2.123–24, where the elegist praises Ulysses for "twist[ing] two sea goddesses with love" (2.124: *aequoreas torsit amore deas*). See Stanford 1963, 142–44, on Ovid's identification with Odysseus-as-lover. On the elegists' use of Homer in general, see Michalopoulos 2016.

51. See Stanford 1963, 144–45, who calls Seneca "Mr. Facing-both-ways, a Janus-like figure" in his reception of Odysseus. Cf. also Montiglio 2011, 77–84 and 91–94, for a more thorough, updated treatment. Significantly for us, Seneca speaks approvingly of Odysseus' flight from the Sirens at three points in his *Epistles*. At *Ep.* 56.15, he advocates using the "remedy" (*remedium*) that Ulysses found "against the Sirens" (*adversus Sirenas*) for philosophically enduring aesthetic temptation. In a similar vein, he suggests to Lucilius at *Ep.* 31.2 that he must "close up [his] ears [since] it's not enough [only] to stuff wax in them" (*si cluseris aures, quibus ceram parum est obdere*); rather, he "needs a stronger plug than that which they say Ulysses used for his comrades" (*firmiore spissamento opus est quam in sociis usum Ulixem ferunt*). Last, in *Ep.* 123.12, after ventriloquizing the voice of an Epicurean who advocates living a life of pleasure, Seneca tells his addressee that "these voices must be fled from no differently than those which Ulysses did not want to sail past unless bound" (*hae voces non aliter fugiendae sunt quam illae, quas Ulixes nisi alligatus praetervehi noluit*).

"cups of Circe" (*Circae pocula*), and in so doing, sets up a curious contrafactual: Odysseus *would have* been metamorphosed into an animal *if he had* drunk from Circe's cup. Needless to say, in the Homeric text, he does, in fact, take a drink, but does so without transforming only through the aid of Hermes' *môly*.[52] However, the allegorical rewriting of Odysseus, in which authors creatively elide his overindulgence in pleasure, seems a necessary slippage in the *Odyssey*-mirror tradition. As we turn now to the Apuleian corpus, it is important to keep in mind that this whole system of allegorical modeling—of holding out Odysseus as an *exemplar* of idealized aesthetic response—is intimately connected to the act of reading and *rereading*: Horace can only "look into" (*inspicere*) what Odysseus encountered through his journeys because he spends his *otium* "rereading."

2.2. *The Mirror of the* Odyssey *in* De deo Socratis

Apuleius was clearly familiar with this *Odyssey*-mirror tradition, whether from its source (Alcidamas) or mediated through its later reception, as we see an articulation of the *Odyssey*-mirror on display in the second epigraph for this chapter: "do you not discern things more clearly in Homer as if in some huge mirror?" (*Soc.* 17: *an non apud Homerum, ut <in> quodam ingenti **speculo**, clarius cernis haec*). We can analyze how Apuleius engages with Homeric *allêgorêsis* in the *Soc.* more precisely, though, if we turn to the conclusion of the treatise, where Apuleius composes, as Richard Fletcher phrases it, a "finale of protreptic,"[53] channeling a philosophically inflected version of Odysseus as a paradigm of aesthetic response. Indeed, in the closing passage of *Soc.*, before the manuscript abruptly cuts off,[54] Apuleius concludes his long diatribe on the

---

52. See, e.g., Kaiser 1964, 109–10, who notes Horace's revisionist portrait at *Epist.* 1.2. Cf. Farrell 2004, 269, who describes Horace's reading as "tendentious, but consistent with the interpretive procedures that prevailed in [his] day." The tradition on Hermes' *môly* as philosophical *logos* begins with Xen. *Mem.* 1.3.7, according to which, Odysseus was saved from his fate not only from Hermes' "advice" (ὑποθημοσύνῃ), but also because he had "self-restraint and abstained" (ἐγκρατῆ ὄντα καὶ ἀποσχόμενον). According to the first-century CE grammarian, Apollonius Sophistes, Cleanthes also interpreted this episode "allegorically" (*Lex. Homer.* 114: ἀλληγορικῶς), taking *môly* as equivalent to *logos*, on which, see Montiglio 2011, 79 with n. 38. On *allêgorêsis* in Apuleius' milieu, see Domaradzki 2020, esp. 364–65.

53. Fletcher 2014, 147.

54. There is a possibility that the original conclusion of *Soc.* was lost, as it seems to lack a wrap-up of the whole lecture such as we find in some extracts from the *Florida*. However, as Harrison 2000, 143 notes, though ending somewhat abruptly, there are still closural elements in what currently

mirror of the *Odyssey* and its relationship to Socratic wisdom as follows (*Soc.* 24.3–4):

> Nec aliud te in eodem Ulixe Homerus docet, qui semper ei comitem voluit esse **prudentiam**, quam poetico ritu Minervam nuncupavit. Igitur hac eadem comite omnia horrenda subiit, omnia adversa superavit. Quippe ea adiutrice Cyclopis specus introiit, sed egressus est; Solis boves vidit, sed abstinuit; ad inferos demeavit et ascendit; eadem **sapientia** comite Scyllam praeternavigavit nec ereptus est; Charybdi consaeptus est nec retentus est; Circae poculum bibit nec mutatus est; ad Lotophagos accessit nec remansit; Sirenas audiit nec accessit.

> And Homer teaches you nothing different in this same figure of Ulysses, who always wanted sagacity to be his companion, which [Homer] named Minerva as a poeticism. Therefore, with this same sagacity as his companion, he endured all the most terrifying things and overcame all adversities. Of course, with her as his helper, he entered the cave of the Cyclops, and yet, came out; he saw the cattle of the Sun, and yet abstained; he traveled to the underworld, and came back up; and with this same wisdom as his companion, he sailed by Scylla and was not snatched; he was hedged in by Charybdis, and yet was not caught; he drank the cup of Circe and did not transform; he approached the Lotus-eaters, and did not stick around; he heard the Sirens and did not draw near.

At first glance, we may note that the companionship of *prudentia*, which guides Odysseus on his journey, is also the focal point of Lucius' mock-Odyssean quality in *Met.* 9.13: recall that Lucius explicitly likens himself to Odysseus—"a man of greatest sagacity" (*summae* **prudentiae** *virum*)—but specifies that through his journey, he became "very knowledgeable, if not wise" (*etsi minus* **prudens**, *multiscius*). Furthermore, the only character singled out in the *Met.* for both *prudentia* and *sapientia* is Socrates, the martyr par excellence in the rant of the "philosophizing ass" (*Met.* 10.33). In contrast to *Soc.*, where Odysseus is held up explicitly as a parallel figure for Socrates in respect to his cultivation of wisdom, the *Met.* implicitly calls into question the wisdom of its Odyssean antihero through Lucius' appeal to Socrates at the close of a tirade in response to a pornographic erotic-aesthetic encounter. As we shall see in §3.3,

---

constitutes the end of the lecture (e.g., "an impressively epigrammatic paragraph of balanced sentences on the subject of Ulysses' virtues"). For a full discussion of the textual transmission of (and damage to) *Soc.*, see Harrison 2000, 141–44.

within the structure of the *Met.*, this recourse to Socrates as the paradigm of "providence" and "wisdom" functions to devalue the Homeric Odysseus as a model for Lucius, and in so doing, sets the stage for his life choice in book 11, where he, like Plato's Odysseus in the Myth of Er, prefers a Socratic life free from busybodied wandering.

Returning to the text at hand, however, it is worth recognizing that Apuleius not only participates in but also creatively adapts the long tradition of interpreting the *Odyssey* as a didactic, moralizing text. Much like Horace, for instance, Apuleius adds a philosophical resonance to Odysseus' journey, inasmuch as he translates the quality of *polytropos* with his emphasis on Odysseus' ceaseless cultivation of *prudentia*.[55] Far from simply alluding to Horace, however, he *corrects* the satirist's blinkered retelling, claiming with an emphatic indicative that Odysseus "*did* drink the cup of Circe but did not transform" (**Circae poculum bibit** *nec mutatus est*; cf. 1.2.23–25: **Circae pocula** . . . *quae si* . . . **bibisset** . . . *fuisset turpis et excors*). There is no counterfactual world, in other words, in which Odysseus avoided the *Circae pocula*; rather, in Apuleius' version, he happily and willingly indulged.

What is more, Apuleius' most creative adaptation of this tradition is in his reordering of Odysseus' encounters of books 9–12 to emphasize his idealized response to *voluptas*. That is, he begins with two of the most famous encounters in the *Odyssey*, the Cyclops (book 9) and the Cattle of the Sun (book 12)—episodes which bookend Odysseus' *apologoi* in Homer's epic. As the list continues, however, Apuleius concludes the *Soc.* by highlighting Odysseus' experience of consumptive and aesthetic pleasure: the cup of Circe, the food of the Lotus eaters, and most importantly, the song of the Sirens. For Apuleius, therefore, the moral value of the *Odyssey* lies not in the hero's refusal to indulge himself, but rather, in his ability to habituate himself to pleasure and nevertheless, escape intact. Apuleius' Odysseus, much like Horace's, can indeed teach us about pleasure: but whereas Homer's journey narrative, according to *Epist.* 1.2, teaches readers to "spurn pleasures" (55: *sperne voluptates*), for Apuleius, the epic inculcates readers in experiencing *voluptas* without succumbing to its negative effects.

We have seen, then, how Apuleius inherits, reworks, and develops Alci-

---

55. On the reception of Odysseus' *polytropia* in general, see again §1.0 (with n. 7); on Apuleius' engagement with this tradition, see §2.1 above (with n. 47). In fact, we may note that, in an added nod to Horace's version, Apuleius emphasizes how Ulysses "overcame all adverse things" (**omnia adversa** *superavit*; cf. *Epist.* 1.2.22: **adversis rerum** *inmersabilis undis*).

damas' *Odyssey*-mirror, and moreover, how Odysseus' experience of and simultaneous resistance to aesthetic pleasure constitutes the primary closural device of this popularizing philosophical lecture. And Apuleius, in so tendentiously representing Odysseus' journey, sets the stage for his analysis of the most protreptic paradigm of all: Socrates. Indeed, the logic of Apuleius' argument connects the exemplary figures one finds in Homer's mirror—Nestor, Odysseus, Diomedes, and Calchas—to the Socrates of Plato's *Phaedrus*, who stopped to listen to his divine sign even "when no witnesses were present" (*Soc.* 19.5: *semotis arbitris*).[56] In the final analysis, though, this Socrates contradicts every other *exemplum* cited: he listened not to any random voices in the street, but to "a certain voice" (*Soc.* 20.2), which he perceived "not only with his ears but with his eyes" (20.4: *non modo auribus . . . verum etiam oculis*). Whereas other people "collect their ideas from the voices **of others** and . . . think not with their minds but with their ears" (19.6: *consilia ex **alienis** vocibus colligunt et . . . non animo sed auribus cogitant*), Socrates, by contrast, becomes an *exemplum*—the perfect blend of Nestor's *oratio* and Odysseus' *ratio*,[57] of philosophical awareness and connection to the divine; at the same time, he provides a "reminder" (*Soc.* 21.1: *Socrati exemplo et commemoratione*) to spur us on through zeal for philosophy (*studio philosophiae*) to "desire a likeness to the gods" (*similis numinum [c]aventes*).[58]

This Socratic *exemplum* teaches us, in turn, a procedure of engaging with the world philosophically, of "actively reading" one's surroundings. So, slipping into a digression on "living well" (*Soc.* 22.1: *bene vivere*), Apuleius mounts a tirade against "the rich" for building lavish villas and richly adorning houses, for concealing their empty lives by papering over them with ornate superficialities. They "hunger and thirst" like Tantalus for evasive fruit, Apuleius explains, but do not recognize that they actually desire "true blessedness,

---

56. Cf. Fletcher 2014, 192: "the allegorizing reading of the *Odyssey*, which has been intimated throughout the [*Soc.*], is exploited to signpost the philosophical message of the poem. This message is enacted by the link between Ulysses and Socrates, a link Apuleius makes elsewhere in his corpus."

57. See again Fletcher 2014, esp. 291, for whom the "dressing up of philosophy with *oratio*" is the whole thrust of Apuleius' "aestheticized" version of Platonism.

58. There is a textual problem here, and I follow the text of Magnaldi's 2020 edition. Beaujeu's 1973, 41 *ad loc.* conjecture of *similitudini numinum* for the closing phrase is attractive, however, insofar as it strengthens the connection to the Middle Platonic appropriation of *homoiôsis theôi* ("similarity to the divine"), on which, see Fowler 2016, 224–25 (with footnotes). For Fletcher 2014, 171, this transformation of Socrates from an *exemplum* into a *commemoratio* lies at the heart of the protreptic value of the *Soc.* insofar as "Apuleius turns a speech in praise of Socrates into a discourse on the teaching of the best rhetorical mode of praise."

which is to say, a favorable life and a most fortunate providence" (22.5: *verae beatitudinis, id est secundae vitae et prudentiae fortunatissimae*). The *Soc.* thus instructs its reader that, in order to discover "true blessedness," one must look beneath surface-level appearances and delve into the reality lying underneath the external covering(s). In short, the "rich" must be analyzed, according to Apuleius, "in the very same way that we purchase horses" (22.5: *non . . . aeque . . . ut equos mercamur*): we do not "consider [a horse's] trappings" (23.1: *phaleras* **consideramus**), "inspect the brightness of its girdle" (*baltei polimina* **inspicimus**), and "contemplate the wealth adorning its neck" (*ornatissimae cervicis divitias* **contemplamur**); rather, after "removing all of those ornaments" (*Soc.* 23.2: *istis omnibus exuviis amolitis*), we "contemplate the horse itself naked" (*equum ipsum nudum . . .* **contemplamur**). So also, "when considering people" (23.4: *in hominibus* **contemplandis**), the philosopher explains, we ought to "consider the very person deep within" (*ipsum hominem* **penitus considera**), looking not at his "external features" (***aliena***)—his parentage, fortune, nobility, lineage, birth, and wealth (23.5)—but rather, at his education, erudition, and ultimately, wisdom. We must "observe him as a pauper" (23.4: *ipsum . . . pauperem specta*), that is, "much as [we do with] master Socrates" (*ut meum Socratem*).

Throughout this unanticipated digression, we may note that Apuleius uses the terminology for inspecting people which we have come to associate in this study with meticulous reading and deep philosophical engagement: *contemplari, inspicere, considerare*, and so on. What's more, in this lengthy and meandering diatribe, situated between his "mirror of Homer" and his closing *exemplum* of Odysseus, Apuleius deploys the ambivalent discourse of *aliena*, which, as we saw above, has associations with both the New Comic busybody who eagerly spies on his neighbors and the Platonic articulation of justice as not looking into "things belonging to others." Apuleius' creative adaptation of this discourse, far from focusing on the Platonic pursuit of self-knowledge or ethical self-modulation, advocates instead looking carefully into other people's business, but it does so by stripping away externalities and superficialities in a complex fusion of Terence's model of exemplarity with later philosophical articulations of the "reflexive" mirror.[59]

---

59. On the "reflexive" function of the mirror (in contrast to its "triangulative" usage), where "the subject would see himself, along with . . . his faults and virtues, and adjust his life accordingly," see Taylor 2008, 20. Cf. also McCarty 1989, 168–69 and 171–73, on the complex tradition of exemplary mirroring.

As we look forward to the *Met.* and apply Apuleius' reception and manipulation of the two strands of the text-as-mirror from the *Soc.*, it is worth recalling that Lucius has long been recognized as an "anti-Socrates" and simultaneously, as an "extremization" of Odysseus.[60] Indeed, Lucius could easily be said to "collect his ideas from the voices of others" (*consilia ex alienis vocibus colligunt*), much like the fools of *Soc.* Thus, as we shall see in §2.5, his refusal to engage in myth-rationalization in the opening narrative passage of the novel (1.3–1.4), rather than functioning as an emulation of the Platonic Socrates who avoids inspecting *allotria*, amounts instead to what we might call a theory of voyeuristic listening—a novelistic realization of the New Comic *curiosus* retrospectively reframing his pursuit of knowledge in pseudo-philosophical terms.[61]

We may also recall that Lucius in the *Met.* is well-endowed in terms of status, education, and appearance—at least as much as any of the wealthy audience members whom Apuleius addresses in the *Soc.* In the Prologue, the narrator brags about his elite lineage (1.1: *vetus prosapia*)—derived from Athens, Corinth, and Sparta;[62] and at the opening of the first narrative passage, Lucius-*auctor* boasts of his noble parentage, which connects him intellectually to famous Middle Platonic philosophers of the first century CE, Plutarch of Boeotia and Sextus of Chaeronea (*Met.* 1.2). The skeptical interlocutor of book 1 notices Lucius' fancy dress (*Met.* 1.20) and infers from those *aliena* that Lucius would not be bamboozled by Aristomenes' tale.[63] Thus, it is significant that at the close of the novel (as we saw in §1.3), Isis' priest emphasizes in his reinterpretation of books 1–10 that Lucius did not benefit from his "birth" (*natales*), "station" (*dignitas*), or "education" (*doctrina*), but instead, was dogged by *Fortuna* throughout his journey.[64]

All of this is to say that Lucius is a character who, according to the frame-

---

60. On Lucius as an "anti-Socrates," see O'Brien 2002, 40–44; on Lucius as an "extremization" of Socrates, see Graverini 2012a, 118–31. See also Smith and Woods 2002; Keulen 2003 on Lucius' "Socratic-Cynic" pedigree, esp. in relation to Apuleius' "Socrates." On Lucius as a mock-Odysseus, see n. 5 above.

61. On which, see Ulrich 2020, 680–88. Cf. Winkle 2014, 100–107, on Lucius' "Typhonic choice." On learning through the ears as a faux-historiographic motif in the *Met.*, see Graverini 2012a, 141–46.

62. On the issue of who narrates the Prologue—whether it is Lucius, Apuleius, or some hybrid of the two—see §2.4 below (with bibliography).

63. Cf. also *Met.* 2.2, where Lucius' aunt Byrrhena recognizes his beauty, which aligns, as Keulen 2006 has demonstrated, with the idealized external traits discussed in physiognomic treatises of the second century CE.

64. This reading of Lucius' conversion through the lens of the *Soc.* is anticipated, to a certain extent, by Tatum 1979, 119–22.

work of *Soc.*, appears on the surface to be successful—clearly, a member of the class of the "rich"—but is actually a fool when stripped of his *aliena*. The ass into which he transforms reveals his actual character[65] and thus, exposes his failure of interpretation and his misapplication of Platonic ideals.[66] Part of the pleasure of the *Met.*, therefore, consists in watching a buffoon retrospectively misconstrue his absurd behavior in terms of sublime myth and Platonic enlightenment.[67] Considering Apuleius' awareness and creative adaptation of allegorizing interpretations of Homer, however, I suggest that his bait-and-switch invitation in the Prologue and Lucius' refusal to myth-rationalize in the opening passages of book 1 (on which, see §2.4 and §2.5 below) pose a choice to the reader about how to engage with this novel. If the exemplary nature of the *Odyssey* and the figure of Socrates ultimately teach us to look beneath surface-level appearances—to inspect the essence of something after "removing all of the ornaments"—then the *Met.*'s opening request "to look in" (*inspicere*), in my view, demands a similarly active procedure of textual engagement.[68] The fact that we read in the *Met.* about a character who represents, at different points in time, extremizations or failed versions of Odysseus and Socrates should give us pause about our own involvement in this narrative—or more precisely, about how our image, too, appears in the frame of this strange Odyssean tale.

2.3. The "Triangulative" Mirror of Socrates and Deep Reading in the Apologia

Before returning to the opening of the *Met.*, it will be worthwhile to take one final detour—this time, into the *Apologia*—where Apuleius' *laus speculi* develops a similar analogy between mirror-gazing and diligent reading. Indeed, if Apuleius resorts in *Soc.* to the allegorizing tradition of the *Odyssey*-mirror to implicate his audience in a didactic program of deep reading, he turns in the

---

65. Cf. Lytle 2003 for a particularly useful treatment of Lucius' ordinary ass-like nature, and the disjunct between his narrative presentation and actual behavior.
66. See Ulrich 2020. See also ch. 4 for a paradigmatic example of Lucius' studied misinterpretation of Plato.
67. See esp. §4.3 for further discussion. Lucius' Platonizing gestures are akin to Encolpius' epicizing and philosophizing gestures in the *Satyricon*; in this sense, my reading aligns with Conte's interpretation of Encolpius (1996, 2), "the *scholasticus*, victim of his own literary experiences, who naively exalts himself by identifying with heroic roles among the great mythical and literary characters of the past."
68. So, Svendsen 1978 suggests in broad-brush strokes.

Apologia to the exemplary, "triangulative" mirror to counter the accusation that he regularly adorned himself before a *speculum*. Thus, in an impressive display of oratorical virtuosity, Apuleius concludes the *Apologia* by reviewing each subsidiary charge with a laconic, two-word summary (*Apol.* 103.2–3): "shiny teeth" (*dentes splendidas*), "look[ing] into mirrors" (*specula **inspicis***), "mak[ing] verses" (*versus facis*), "inspect[ing] fish" (*pisces exploras*), "consecrat[ing] wood" (*lignum consecras*), and "tak[ing] a wife" (*uxorem ducis*);[69] he answers each charge, in turn, with a two-word rebuttal, and responds to the particular charge of "looking into mirrors" with the dubious and otherwise unsupported claim—"a philosopher ought to" (*debet philosophus*). In short, although the specific accusation of "looking into mirrors" hinges on the *speculum*'s association with effeminate behavior in men and is intended to portray the accused as a magic-obsessed fop,[70] Apuleius rhetorically manipulates the situation by explaining that mirror speculation constitutes a sine qua non of philosophical activity, one authorized by earlier *exempla*.

Indeed, Apuleius defends his own mirror usage in his *laus speculi* by pointing to Socrates as its first paradigmatic user, who deployed it, in the spirit of the Terentian *speculum*, with a view toward "ethical therapy by deterrence" (*Apol.* 15.4–7; see again n. 4 above for quotation):

> An turpe arbitraris formam suam spectaculo assiduo explorare? An non Socrates philosophus ultro etiam suasisse **fertur** discipulis suis, crebro ut semet in speculo **contemplarentur**, ut qui eorum foret pulchritudine sibi complacitus, impendio **procuraret** ne dignitatem corporis malis moribus dedecoraret, qui vero minus se commendabilem forma putaret, **sedulo operam daret** ut virtutis laude turpitudinem tegeret? Adeo vir omnium sapientissimus speculo etiam ad disciplinam morum utebatur.

> Do you judge that it is shameful to explore one's own form in a continual spectacle? Isn't Socrates the philosopher said to have actually exhorted his students to contemplate themselves frequently in the mirror in order that one who

---

69. On the powerful rhetorical display of this two-word summarization of and response to the charges, see Hunink 1997, 248 *ad loc.* 103.2.

70. See the discussion that opens *Apologia* 13–16 in Hunink 1997, 58: "Apart from magic and luxury, there is also a strong link with erotic purposes: mirrors were a common attribute of Venus and their use was conventionally restricted to women for erotic or related purposes. . . . Use by men was often condemned, since it implied effeminacy." See also McCarty 1989, 179–84; Taylor 2008, 7, on the connection between the mirror, magic, and erotics.

READING AS A CHOICE IN THE APULEIAN CORPUS   111

pleased himself with his beauty might take great care not to disfigure the dignity of his body with evil character, and one who considered himself less commendable in form might assiduously labor to hide his ugliness with the praise of virtue? In this way, the wisest man of all used a mirror even for the discipline of character.

We can recognize here another familiar tradition on the mirror to which I alluded above, namely, the "reflexive" mirror of ethical modulation. Seneca obliquely refers to this apocryphal anecdote in his excursus on Hostius Quadra in book 1 of *Natural Questions*, when he claims that "mirrors were invented so that a person might "know himself" (1.17.4: *se nosset*): a beautiful man, so that he may flee infamy (*ut **vitaret** infamiam*); and an ugly man, so that he might recognize that, whatever is lacking regarding his form, has to be compensated for by virtues" (*redimendum esse **virtutibus***). Seneca appeals, on the one hand, to the Socratic ideal of the mirror of self-knowledge, a prosthetic tool of the Delphic maxim (*se nosse*), as an ironic set-up for this episode in which a mirror-gazer's twisted delusion heightens his *voluptas*. Simultaneously, however, this advice, which is attributed to the figure of Socrates shortly after Seneca's invocation of this ethical *speculum*, seems to constitute a paradoxical reworking of Terence's mirror of "pursuit" and "avoidance," one which is entirely dependent on the viewer: in both cases, the mirror aids the pursuit of virtue; for the "beautiful" man, however, that pursuit is paradoxically an avoidance of the social consequences of ill-repute *à la* Horace's *Sermones* 1.4, whereas the ugly man is invited by the *speculum* to make recompense for his grotesque external appearance by supplementing it with virtues.

It makes a good deal of sense, then, that Socrates, the notoriously ugly and satyr-like philosopher, becomes the figurehead of this tradition in Plutarch and afterward.[71] In *Advice to the Bride and Groom*, Plutarch explains that "Socrates" bid "mirror-gazing youths" (141d1: τῶν ἐσοπτριζομένων νεανίσκων) who were ugly to "correct their form with virtue" (141d1–2: ἐπανορθοῦσθαι τῇ **ἀρετῇ** . . . τὸ εἶδος) and in turn, exhorted the beautiful among them "not to dishonor their form with vice" (μὴ καταισχύνειν τῇ **κακίᾳ** τὸ εἶδος). Plutarch's "Socratic" mirror, modeled also on Terence's *speculum*, poses a Heraclean choice to its viewer, in other words—a choice between virtue (*aretê*; cf. *virtutis laude* in Apuleius' version) and vice (*kakia*; cf. *malis moribus*). But much as with Sene-

---

71. On this tradition, see again McCarty 1989, 171–73; Bartsch 2006, 18–28.

ca's articulation of this tradition, the "correct" choice regardless of external appearance is "virtue."[72]

In his citation of Socrates as the figurehead of mirror-speculation, therefore, Apuleius makes it clear with an "Alexandrian footnote" (i.e., *fertur*)[73] that he is participating in this imperial and Second Sophistic tradition of tracing the "reflexive" ethical mirror back to the philosopher who most eagerly championed the pursuit of the Delphic maxim. Apuleius' departures from this tradition, however, are more interesting than his mere reception of the anecdote. It is significant, for instance, that he phrases Socrates' advice in the discourse of *curiositas*, but relates it specifically to the meticulous kind of *cura*. Socrates thus advises his disciples to engage in "contemplation" (**contemplari**) in the mirror; the ugly, in particular, are exhorted "assiduously" (*sedulo*) to put their efforts toward covering their grotesque appearance.[74] The beautiful, by contrast, are told to "take great care" (*impendio* **procuraret**) not to destroy their *dignitas* with evil habits—and here, Apuleius is perhaps weaving into Socrates' ethical advice the New Comic strand on *curiosi*, who attend with utmost zeal to "the affairs of others" (*Stich.* 199: **alienas** *res*), but have "nothing of their own to take great care over" (200: *nulla est res quam* **procurent** *sua*). Apuleius' Socrates, in short, advocates that those of his disciples who possess *dignitas* (one of the external *aliena* noted in the *Soc.*) should carefully ensure that their internal *mores* match their outer appearance.

It is crucial, therefore, that at the close of *Apol.* 16, as Apuleius wraps up his rebuttal to the charge of owning a mirror, he turns to his primary accuser, Aemilianus, and implies that his misunderstanding of Apuleius' mirror-usage stems ultimately from a failure of reading. A final exemplary mirror-user is conjured up, Archimedes of Syracuse, who wrote a "huge volume" on mirrors— the now-lost *Katoptrika*[75]—and who is especially memorable "because he had looked often and diligently into a mirror" (16.6: *quod* **inspexerat** *speculum saepe ac diligenter*). Apuleius goes on (*Apol.* 16.7):

---

72. Cf. also *De ira* 2.36.2, where Seneca claims it is beneficial (*profuit*) for men "to look at a mirror" (*aspexisse speculum*) because the recognition of their disfiguration will bring them back to themselves.

73. On the "Alexandrian footnote," see Hinds 1998, 1–5, who defines the phenomenon as "the signaling of specific allusion by a poet through seemingly general appeals to tradition and report" (1–2).

74. Here, *sedulo* represents one of the key adverbs (together with *scrupulose*) that Apuleius deploys across the *Met.* to characterize Lucius' *curiositas* (on which, see Leigh 2013, 142 with n. 78).

75. See Hunink 1997, 65 *ad loc.* 16.6, for the identification of the text.

Quem tu librum, Aemiliane, si nosses ac non modo campo et glebis, verum etiam abaco et pulvisculo te dedisses, mihi istud crede, quamquam teterrimum os tuum minimum a Thyesta tragico demutet, tamen profecto **discendi cupidine speculum inviseres** et aliquando relicto aratro **mirarere** tot in facie tua sulcos rugarum.

If you had come to know this book [i.e., Archimedes' *Katoptrika*], Aemilianus, and if you had given yourself over not only to the field and clods, but also to the abacus and chalk, believe me about this, even though your utterly grotesque face differs minimally from the tragic Thyestes, you would nonetheless **be looking into a mirror out of a desire for learning** and at some point, after leaving the plow aside, **you would be marveling** at the very many furrows of wrinkles on your face.

Embedded in this brutal invective is a robust theory of the purpose and effect of reading, and relatedly, of the role that aesthetic pleasure plays in learning. Aemilianus' failure consists primarily in his refusal to engage with a particular book, one which would have imparted to him a "desire for learning" (*discendi cupido*). We may recall here our purple passage from Cicero on the Sirens (§2.1), which, beyond inaugurating the Roman reception of Odysseus-as-philosopher, constitutes the first instance in the Latin tradition of the rare idiom *discendi cupiditas* (see n. 38 above). In fact, I would posit that Apuleius, in his attack on Aemilianus' lack of intellectual curiosity, alludes quite explicitly to this *locus classicus* on the Sirens as a Homeric authorization for philosophical journeying. For in the chapter of *De finibus* immediately following his discussion of the Sirens, Cicero's Piso tells an anecdote about the very same Archimedes, who once became so engrossed in his learning, "so intently" (*De fin.* 5.50: *attentius*) drawing geometrical figures in the dust, that he did not notice when his homeland was captured. The attentive pursuit of knowledge, which Apuleius represents in his defense speech with such adverbs as *attente* (*Apol.* 13.3; cf. 65.4), *sedulo* (3.8; 15.6; 36.8; 48.5; etc.), *diligenter* (13.4; 16.7; 61.5; 64.5), and *curiose* (39.2), becomes thoroughly intermingled across the *Apologia* with the act of reading, and so much so that, when Apuleius concludes his treatment of the subsidiary charges with a direct quotation of Plato, he claims Maximus will easily recognize it since "he has diligently read [about the upper realm] in the *Phaedrus*" (64.5: *legit in Phaedro **diligenter***).[76]

---

76. For a fuller treatment of this passage in the context of Apuleius' well-developed reader-response

Returning to Apuleius' invective, then, it is noteworthy that Aemilianus' engagement with a book in the counterfactual scenario would inspire not only a "desire for learning" (*discendi cupido*), but simultaneously, would somehow function as the catalyst for an encounter with a mirror: if Aemilianus had read Archimedes' *Katoptrika*, Apuleius suggests, he would have "looked into a mirror" (*speculum inviseres*) and would have "marveled" (*mirarere*) at his own appearance. Here, it is striking that Apuleius conjures a grotesque mythical character from the Roman stage: Aemilianus would have recognized his physical likeness to the "tragic Thyestes"—or more specifically, to the "utterly grotesque" theatrical mask representing him[77]—and would have, in turn, attempted to cover over his deformity, as the quintessential philosopher once advised his ugly disciples, with "the praise of virtue." For Aemilianus, in short, such a text-mirror encounter *could* have been the beginning of a philosophical journey.

Finally, in his closing treatment of the charge of mirror-ownership, Apuleius reveals what it is he offers to Aemilianus (and by extension, to Maximus and his audience): a choice between types of lives, between the philosophical life and the obscure rustic life.[78] Crucially, this choice represents an ironic twist on the Platonic Socrates' engagement with the Delphic maxim in Plato's *Phaedrus*. For at the end of chapter 16, Apuleius compares his own ethical-intellectual behavior, as he is "occupied with learning" (16.11: *discendo occupatus*), with Aemilianus' nosey investigations into the deeds of others:

> et tibi umbra ignobilitatis a probatore obstitit, et ego numquam studui male facta cuiusquam cognoscere, sed semper potius duxi mea peccata tegere quam **aliena indagare**.

> while the shadow of obscurity has shielded your character from scrutiny, I have never been zealous to learn about the misdeeds of anyone else, but instead, I have always worked to conceal my own faults rather than track down those of others.

---

theory, see §4.1. On Apuleius' incorporation of his judge throughout his speech, see the astute assessment of Harrison 2000, 46. See also Riess 2008a, 52, for Apuleius' strategic affiliation with the image of Socrates to appeal to Maximus.

77. Cf. May 2006, 85, who reads this in light of comic invective, suggesting that Aemilianus, with his real face, possesses the dramatic accoutrement that Apuleius disavows using at *Apol.* 13.

78. Fletcher 2014, 199, again comes close, but does not fully articulate the issue: "Apuleius mobilises the 'philosophical situation' of the trial to offer an idealized portrait of the author as Platonic philosopher and also to once again dramatize the two strands of Platonic philosophy in the form of the learned judge and the rustic Aemilianus."

This "concealment of faults" appeals one final time to the "Socratic" specular encounter, insofar as the ugly, according to Apuleius' reception of this tradition, ought to "cover over" (*Apol.* 15: **tegeret**; cf. *mea peccata* **tegere**) their grotesque appearance with the praise of virtue. In a subtle twist, however, the marked phrase **aliena** *indagare* is implicated simultaneously in the wider discourse of *curiositas*, conjuring up again two distinct and conflicting traditions on how to interact with *allotria/aliena*. If Aemilianus is figured in Apuleius' invective as the New Comic busybody, sticking his nose where it does not belong and as a consequence, overlooking his own faults, the *philosophus Platonicus* has taken a different tack toward *aliena*, indeed, channeling one of the most famous Socratic choices—Socrates' decision in the *Phaedrus* to pursue the Delphic maxim rather than to rationalize away an unbelievable myth (*Phaedr.* 229e5–230a1):

> οὐ δύναμαί πω κατὰ τὸ Δελφικὸν γράμμα γνῶναι ἐμαυτόν· γελοῖον δή μοι φαίνεται τοῦτο ἔτι ἀγνοοῦντα **τὰ ἀλλότρια σκοπεῖν**.

> I am not yet able to know myself in accordance with the Delphic maxim; and indeed, it seems laughable **to inspect the matters of others** while I am still ignorant of this fact.

"Inspecting the matters of others" (τὰ ἀλλότρια σκοπεῖν), when one is still ignorant of one's own unbridled and monstrous nature,[79] is the primary issue in the original Platonic context, and Apuleius, adapting this crucial passage on Platonic self-knowledge to a new occasion, gives a precise translation into Latin: *aliena indagare*. To phrase it differently, borrowing from a scene in the *Phaedrus* well-known to readers in the second century CE[80]—one where Socrates reveals his own engagement with the literature and myth of the past as

---

79. So, Socrates expands the investigation to "whether [he] happen[s] to be some beast more complicated . . . than Typhon" (*Phaedr.* 230a3–4: εἴτε τι θηρίον ὂν τυγχάνω Τυφῶνος πολυπλοκώτερον), on which, see §2.5.

80. It is generally accepted that the "Typhonic choice" had a powerful impact on later antiquity. See Trapp 1990 on the importance of the *Phaedrus* in the first–second centuries CE. See also Hunter 2012, passim and esp. 4, where he notes: "the opening of the *Phaedrus* has become a 'classic,' the object of discussion, imaginative recreation, imitation, and indeed drama; it is a text which has gathered around itself a body of metatextual commentary and interpretation, which has almost coalesced with the Platonic text itself." For more discussion and bibliography, see §2.5 and §4.1 with n. 1.

116 THE SHADOW OF AN ASS

a philosophical choice about how to fulfill the Delphic maxim—Apuleius simultaneously poses a choice to his accuser, to his audience members, and most importantly, to his learned judge, Maximus. Will we choose to be like Socrates, Archimedes, or indeed, Maximus, in our decision to "diligently look," "diligently listen," or "diligently read"? Or will we lazily content ourselves with the unsavory and inappropriate interest, or even overeager voyeurism, of a busybody like Aemilianus?[81]

Apuleius' revisionist reframing of the value of mirror-speculation and its relationship to literary engagement is, of course, embedded in an invective speech, and we must always be cautious in attending to the constraints of genre when assessing the sincerity or value of such philosophical allusions. In my view, however, the philosophical concerns undergirding the *Apologia* cannot be so easily dismissed as mere self-fashioning and display.[82] On the contrary, I would suggest that Apuleius uses allusion and intertext—in both public discourse and philosophical treatises addressed to individual readers, across genres and in different modes of discourse—to teach his readers and listeners to engage actively with his texts. That is why looking into a mirror or playfully indulging in writing erotic epigram can be considered consistent with the philosophical life, a part of the same endeavor as "inspecting fish" or performing careful exegesis of the Greek in Pudentilla's letter.

2.4. *The Prologue as Embedded Choice:* inspicere . . . ut mireris *(Met. 1.1, again)*

Now that we have surveyed the discourse of mirror-speculation and the connection Apuleius draws in his philosophical-rhetorical works between the act of reading, the pursuit of self-knowledge, and the process of stripping away superficialities (*aliena*), it is time to turn back to the *Met.* and consider the ways

---

81. Cf. Fletcher 2014, 217, where he connects Platonic quotation with being a "careful reader": "Apuleius focalises Maximus at a moment of Platonic quotation, yet rather than the usual play on Platonic *anamnesis* we have Apuleius imagine him as a 'careful reader' of Plato."

82. On which, see, e.g., Harrison 2008, 3, for a characteristic assessment of the *Apologia*: "In this work we find the sophist in court ranging in learned play through the whole field of literature, stressing both his own versatile authorship and his wide reading of Latin and Greek authors, wittily demonstrating his cultural capital, both as a key tool in his self-defense and as an advertisement for his intellectual prestige and sophistic standing to the type of Roman North African audience before whom he was to make his subsequent career." Cf. Helm 1955, 86, who famously referred to the *Apologia* as "Ein Meisterwerk der zweiten Sophistik."

READING AS A CHOICE IN THE APULEIAN CORPUS   117

in which this seriocomic novel—modeled simultaneously on the *Odyssey* and Menippean satire, on Platonic dialogue and Roman comedy—positions itself in this distinguished tradition of the text-*speculum*. On the one hand, I propose, it creates an amalgam of the New Comic, "triangulative" mirror of exemplarity and the Socratic, "reflexive" mirror of self-knowledge. In short, we are shown a mock-(auto)biographical life: when we initially encounter it, we are invited to "look into" (*inspicere*) the book (as Apuleius suggested Aemilianus *should* have done), and "marvel" (*mireris*) at shifts in "figures and fortunes." As the "Palinodic" reader would undoubtedly recognize (§0.3), moreover, these transformations are explicitly associated with a mock-Socrates and an "extremized" Odysseus. The educative value of this novel, however, lies not simply in its display of ethical paradigms for replication or avoidance *à la* Terence's *speculum*, but rather in its exposure of the asinine character of the *actor* (and *auctor*) and thereby, its implication of us, Apuleius' readers, in Lucius' buffoonery. We return in this section, therefore, to the Prologue in order to reassess its invitation to a more introspective mode of looking, before moving on to two early crossroads moments for Lucius in books 1 and 2. As we shall see, in light of the Prologue's self-conscious call to a more careful inspection of the identity of its speaker, Lucius' choice to willfully delude himself and lend credence to Aristomenes' *fabula*, and to take delight, in turn, in the surface-level deceptions manifest in the city of Hypata reveals a potential difference between Lucius-*auctor* and his reader.

As we saw in §0.4, the opening line of the *Met.* appears—at least, prima facie—to foreground the novel's promise of mere *divertissement*, striking, as Michael Trapp points out, "a thoroughly hedonistic note":[83]

> At ego tibi sermone isto Milesio varias fabulas conseram, auresque tuas benivolas lepido susurro permulceam, modo si papyrum Aegyptiam argutia Nilotici calami inscriptam non spreveris inspicere, figuras fortunasque hominum in alias imagines conversas et in se rursum mutuo nexu refectas ut mireris. Exordior. Quis ille? Paucis accipe.

> But I will weave variegated tales for you in that Milesian style and I will charm your benevolent ears with pleasurable whispering, provided that you do not refuse to look into an Egyptian papyrus inscribed with the cleverness of a

---

83. Trapp 2001, 39. On my punctuation of the text here, see §0.4 with n. 99.

Nilotic reed, in order that you may marvel at figures and fortunes of humans transformed into other images and turned back into themselves by a mutual knot. I begin my prologue. Who is that? Listen in a few words.

The first sentence gestures, as scholars have long recognized, to a variety of genres, incorporating programmatic terminology to highlight the *Met.*'s literary filiation to Menippean satire (i.e., *Milesius*) or even more traditional Roman satire (i.e., *sermo*),[84] but simultaneously blending it with generic markers of Roman comedy and *Sôkratikoi logoi*.[85] Thus, on the one hand, as Wytse Keulen describes the Prologue's poetics:

> [It] is concerned with education, both the education that shaped its speaker and the education that its audience brings to their reading of the text . . . it presents us with a choice of "genre" (*sermone isto Milesio*), alluding to Aristides' *Milesiaka* and the Latin translation of this work by Sisenna.[86]

As intimated above, however, this "choice" of genre is a bait-and-switch. For beyond conjuring the burlesque satire of Aristides of Miletus and its overtly moralizing counterpart (i.e., Horatian *sermo*), the Prologue seems to highlight, on the other hand, its likeness to a Roman comic *exordium* and simultaneously, to emphasize its pedigree of Platonic dialogue. Indeed, the illusion of a spoken dialogue is accomplished through the manufactured pretense of the reader's entering a conversation midway (*at ego tibi*);[87] that exchange is immediately interrupted, however, by a second and even more jarring contrivance: the question (*quis ille?*), which has usually been interpreted as a metaliterary appeal akin to a New Comic prologue, where an actor breaks the

---

84. On the nature of "Milesian tales," see Relihan 1993, though he excludes Apuleius from his study on formal grounds. On their influence on the genre of the ancient novel, see Bowie 2013. For discussion of the *Met.*'s filiation to *Milesiaka*, see Harrison 1998b; Graverini, Keulen, and Barchiesi 2006, 47–50; *GCA* 2007, 64–65 *ad loc.* 1,1,1; Kirichenko 2010, 178–84; Tilg 2013; Graverini and Nicolini 2019, 141 *ad loc.* 1.1. On the Prologue's and Apuleius' more general interaction with Roman *sermo*, see Gowers 2001 and Zimmerman 2006.

85. On interactions with New Comedy, see n. 88 below. On mock-dialogic associations, see Scobie 1975, 66; Morgan 2001; De Jong 2001; Trapp 2001; Ulrich 2017, 728–30, on which, more below.

86. *GCA* 2007, 8.

87. So, Leo 1905, 605, notes: "incipit quasi ex medio colloquio." Cf. also Helm 1955, vi.; Janson 1964, 114n5; Scobie 1975, 66. Morgan 2001, 161, phrases the issue in a lucid fashion: "In the very first sentence, the emphatic position of *At ego tibi* . . . implies a previous storytelling *tu mihi* ('you to me . . .') . . . we are plunged into the position of overhearing part of a larger narrative exchange already in progress." See also Gowers 2001, 85–86, for useful reflections.

READING AS A CHOICE IN THE APULEIAN CORPUS 119

theater's fourth wall to name and identify the major players and plot-points of the upcoming drama.[88]

Whereas *quis ille?* seems to possess the generic flavor of a Plautine prologist entreating his audience for a favorable reception, the introductory phrase *at ego tibi*, which opens the novel *in medias res* with the adversative conjunction *at*,[89] has been interpreted instead as a nod to symposiastic literature affiliated with Socrates:[90] Xenophon's *Symposium* famously opens with the phrase, "but it seems to me" (*Symp.* 1: ἀλλ᾽ ἐμοὶ δοκεῖ), a signal phrase used to highlight the dialogue's "feigned orality";[91] so also, Plato's *Symposium* registers significant transitions in speakers at Agathon's banquet with versions of this formula.[92] Recall, for instance, Alcibiades' ingratiating introduction to his speech, where he presents an image for Socrates which I have adopted as programmatic for Apuleius' novel: "**but I** will attempt to praise Socrates, my friends, through images" (*Symp.* 215a4–5: Σωκράτη **δ**᾽ **ἐγὼ** ἐπαινεῖν, ὦ ἄνδρες . . . ἐπιχειρήσω, δι᾽

---

88. On the intrusion as a gesture to a Roman comic prologue—a popular solution to the problem— see Smith 1972; Harrison 1990, 509; May 2006, 110–15; Kirichenko 2010, 163. The suggestion is already implicit in Winkler 1985, 195n25, who, however, puts greater emphasis on the intentionally puzzling nature of the speaker's identity as "a nexus of connected identities, an enigma that offers itself to be resolved, humorously over-coded as a challenge for every kind of reader from the naïve to the sophisticated" (1985, 203). On identity in the Prologue, see also Too 2001. For resistance to the Prologue's parallelism with a New Comic *exordium*, see Slater 2001, esp. 218. The identity of the Prologue speaker and the answer to *quis ille?* have been something of an obsession of Apuleius scholarship, especially of the twentieth–twenty-first centuries: see, e.g., the essays in Kahane and Laird 2001 for a survey of approaches, most of which land on Apuleius, Lucius, or some combination of the two as the Prologue speaker (though not without significant complications). For updated discussions, see Adkins 2022, 195–97; Graverini and Nicolini 2019, 138–40 (with bibliography). For a generic solution, see Graverini 2012a, 1–50. For the speaker's identity as a matter of rhetoric and performance, see *GCA* 2007, 11–14. Drews 2006 has proposed there is a change in speaker in the middle of the Prologue. Relatedly, Tilg 2014a, 21–24, combines aspects of all the solutions—Lucius, Apuleius, and the speaking book—to suggest that the speaker's identity flags a literary filiation to Loukios of Patrae's *Metamorphoseis*. On the speaker as a *daemonic* voice, see Benson 2019, 29–49. For the speaker's identity as a Platonizing gesture—a solution I favor—see Trapp 2001; Kirichenko 2008a; Fletcher 2014, 266–67; Ulrich 2017.
89. The introduction of a poetry book within a larger collection with *at* is exceedingly rare, and indeed, *at* is unparalleled in Latin as the opening word for an entire work of literature. See Scobie 1975, 66, for discussion of the enigmatic *at*, which earlier scholars attempted to emend away. For recent treatments of the mock-dialogic *at*, see Graverini 2012a, 2–10, who reads it as a metaliterary claim, and Tilg 2014a, 25–32, who sees it as a programmatic stylistic gesture.
90. Xenophon's *Symposium* is already suggested as a model by Scobie 1975, 66, a suggestion on which Tilg 2014a, 29, expands by noting the stylistic influence of the "inceptive ἀλλά" on Second Sophistic authors. De Jong 2001 extends this notion of a one-sided dialogue which starts *in medias res* to the Platonic corpus, and I have argued elsewhere that this is particularly evocative of exchanges between speakers in a symposium such as Agathon's (see Ulrich 2017, 728–30).
91. On the colloquial flavor of the opening ἀλλά, see Deniston 1954, 20–21. On its reception as "*fingierte Mündlichkeit*" in the Prologue of the *Met.*, see Fowler 2001.
92. See Ulrich 2017, 728–30, for my fuller discussion of Apuleius' engagement with this Platonic model in the Prologue.

εἰκόνων). Crucial for my reading, this dialogic situation in the *Symposium*, where a primary speaker addresses an audience about an idiosyncratic individual—and what's more, one who is transformed by means of that speech-act from one medium of representation (215a5: εἰκόνες) into an entirely different figural form (215b3: ἀγάλματα ... θεῶν)—is reproduced in a strikingly parallel manner with the Prologue's initial promise: "in order that *you* may marvel at *figurae* transformed into other *imagines* and then back again." It is especially worth keeping in mind, then, the parallel of Alcibiades bursting into Agathon's banquet to give a parodic rewrite of Socrates' eulogy of *Erôs*: for as we shall see in §2.5, the interruption of a two-way conversation with the addition of a third (unanticipated) interlocutor is replicated very quickly in Lucius' first crossroads choice.

Recognizing these transitional, dialogic signals in the opening words of the *Met.*, therefore, I am inclined to follow Richard Fletcher's suggestion that the question—*quis ille?*—is better translated as "who speaks?" By rendering it in this way, Fletcher reframes the mystery of the Prologue's narrator as a "rephrasing of basic issues of impersonation at the heart of philosophical writing and identity."[93] The "choice" of genre, which Keulen identified with the Prologue's overt terminological cues, thus hinges on implicit generic markers, which point to the unknown identity of the narrator and to the character of this strange, new literary form. How we read *quis ille?*, simply put, determines whether this is a comedy or a Socratic dialogue, both of which are genres with noteworthy histories as "mirrors" for their readers.

In fact, while it has generally gone overlooked in scholarship,[94] the closing passage of Plato's *Phaedrus*—a text which some interpreters have discerned lurking behind the *Met.*'s Prologue (with its reference to Egyptian papyrus and its manifest obsession with writing)[95]—also homes in on the identity of the speaker of any *logos* as a locus of anxiety for certain types of readers/listeners. So, after delighting Phaedrus with charming "Egyptian *logoi*" (*Phaedr.* 275b3–4), Socrates concludes this extraordinary meditation on the relationship between *Erôs* and self-knowledge with an explicit rebuke of the sophistic lines of inquiry which his young interlocutor earlier espoused: "it was sufficient for the priests in the shrine of Zeus at Dodona," Socrates claims, "to listen to an oak

---

93. Fletcher 2014, 266–67.
94. See, however, Ulrich 2023 for the influence of this episode of the *Phaedrus* across Apuleius' corpus, and esp. 98–99 for its influence on the Prologue.
95. See Trapp 2001; Kirichenko 2008a; Ulrich 2017.

READING AS A CHOICE IN THE APULEIAN CORPUS   121

or a stone out of their simplicity, so long as it spoke the truth" (275b5–c1);[96] "but to you" (σοὶ δ'; cf. *at ego tibi*), Socrates complains to Phaedrus, "it matters who the speaker is and where he comes from" (διαφέρει τίς ὁ λέγων καὶ ποδαπός). As we have already seen, the question of "who speaks" the Prologue is a difficult conundrum for readers of this text. Needless to say, the issue of "where he comes from" (cf. ποδαπός) presents another bewildering problem to Apuleius' readers, particularly since the Prologue initially traces "[Lucius'] ancient lineage" (1.1: *mea vetus prosapia*) to Athens, Corinth, and Sparta,[97] and the *auctor* links his mother's line to Plutarch of Boeotia and Sextus of Chaeronea (*Met.* 1.2), but at the end of book 11, the narrating *ego* is repatriated to North Africa, transformed in an unanticipated shift in identity into a "poor man from Madauros" (11.27: *Madaurensem sed admodum* **pauperem**).[98]

We will return to the *Madaurensem*-problem in the epilogue to this monograph, where I reconceptualize the identity-shift as an appeal to Apuleius' African reader and by doing so, bring to fruition the reader-response approach I have been tracing out for the whole novel.[99] For now, however, it is necessary only to emphasize that the interpretive conundrums the Prologue poses to its readers—issues of identity which direct our attention specifically to Lucius' *aliena*—are entirely stripped away from the ass-man in the end. Therefore, not only is Lucius paradoxically transformed over the course of the novel from an elite Greek of the most venerable origins into an undistinguished provincial from a backwoods town in North Africa, but he is also completely dispossessed at the novel's close, stripped of his "ass hide" (*corium*) and displayed "naked" (*nudus*) in front of a crowd of observers (11.14). In fact, even after his conversion and successful incorporation into Isis-cult (which, of course, involves being further deprived of his hair), he arrives at the house of Asinius Marcellus, the priest who officiates his second initiation, where he is received as a Madauran and a "poor one at that": no one has, to my knowledge, sufficiently explained

---

96. Cf. Ulrich 2023, 89–91, where I argue that Apuleius alludes explicitly to this line of the *Phaedrus* in the opening of *Soc.*

97. Cf., however, Graverini and Nicolini 2019, 138, who note of this remarkable citation of these important cities in Greece: "questi dettagli sembrano infatti indicare più una generica ascendenza culturale greca attribuita al romanzo che non il luogo d'origine del suo protagonista."

98. The unanticipated shift in ethnic identity of the narrator in book 11 is, much like the identity of the Prologue speaker, an issue of great debate in Apuleius scholarship. See Harrison 2000, 228–35; and *GCA* 2015, 465–67, for thorough discussion of and extensive bibliography on the many different approaches to this apparent authorial intrusion. See the now-classic van der Paardt 1999; Smith 2012; Graverini 2012a, 186–88; Tilg 2014a, 107–31 for recent treatments of the problem. For further discussion, see the epilogue with bibliography.

99. For which, I am influenced by Luca Graverini 2012a, 188 and *per sermones*.

why Lucius is labeled a *pauper*, when we have already been told in no uncertain terms that he comes from an elite (and likely wealthy) background[100] and easily goes on to a lucrative career declaiming in the Roman forum.[101]

If, instead, we take into consideration the mode of viewing, which the Prologue requests from us and which Apuleius elsewhere suggests one should deploy when "discerning in the mirror of Homer," we realize that "active" or diligent reading demands removing the *aliena* and looking at the very person— that is, "naked" (*Soc.* 23.2: *nudum*), as one would inspect a horse. So, we may recall, Apuleius' "finale of protreptic" in *Soc.* suggests that, in order to ascertain a person's character (especially, when confronted with someone "rich"), one must not "esteem *aliena*" (23.4: *aliena aestimare*), but rather, ought to "consider the very person deeply and look at him as a *pauper*, like master Socrates" (*sed ipsum hominem penitus considera, ipsum ut meum Socratem **pauperem** specta*). In other words, although the Prologue highlights the mutable identity of a wealthy, distinguished, and educated elite whose native origins connect him to all the cultural power centers of the Mediterranean world, we can nevertheless reread the Prologue in our "Palinodic" reading with the knowledge that, at the end of the novel, Lucius-ass is to be dispossessed of these markers of identity and put on display, like a "poor Socrates," for an audience in Cenchreae as well as for us readers to gawk at.

Thus, if we update Winkler's "retrospective" model in light of the call to "Palinodic" reading in the closing line of the *Met.* (cf. §0.3), we may imagine that the *lector scrupulosus*, after watching Lucius parade his bald head around Rome in book 11, is invited to roll this "Egyptian papyrus" back to the beginning. There, encountering the Prologue again, one discovers—not merely an "open," aporetic call to interrogate the identity of the Prologue speaker, to disentangle "the nexus of connected identities" or decipher an unsolvable "enigma" (n. 88 above)—but rather, specific literary paradigms, which the novel parades before us in adulterated forms. As I have argued elsewhere, the Prologue presents us with an "embedded choice between Homeric and Platonic modes of

---

100. So, Rhode 1885, 78–79, first noted this textual inconsistency.

101. Van Mal-Maeder 1997, 103, cites Lucius' poverty as proof that he is an investment to be capitalized on by manipulative priests, but the reasoning is tendentious. While the Groningen commentators assume that *sed admodum pauperem* must refer to Lucius' pennilessness in Rome, arguing that the text never explicitly acknowledges Lucius' wealth (*GCA* 2015, 467–68 *ad loc.* 11,27,9), it is pretty clear that (1) though he presents himself as penniless, Lucius is not a *pauper* for very long at all, given his ability to pay for costly initiations within a short period of time; and (2) Lucius has elite connections (e.g., a letter of introduction from a Corinthian noble) which would be available only to a rich person.

viewing, listening, and reading."[102] Keeping in mind Apuleius' deep engagement with the mirror of Homer, therefore, and the interchangeable *exempla* of Odysseus and Socrates, we can reconsider the opening sentence, which promises its "scrupulous reader" an experience of "marvel at figures and fortunes of humans transformed into other images and then turned back again" (1.1: *figuras fortunasque hominum in alias imagines conversas et in se rursum . . . refectas ut mireris*). In my view, a truly retrospective interpretation of the *Met.* asks readers to look behind its initial promise of marvel, where they can recognize the guise of a very particular Socrates—Alcibiades' Socrates in Plato's *Symposium*, where a parodic encomium refashions him as a latter-day Odysseus.[103]

Returning to our programmatic Platonic passage, we may recall that Alcibiades' objectification of Socrates at the end of the *Symposium* sets the philosopher up as a visual-aural spectacle meant to inspire didactic and philosophical wonder in those who encounter him. At first, Alcibiades promises to praise Socrates through "images" (*Symp.* 215a5: εἰκόνες), and his opening "image" immediately deploys an alternative representational metaphor: Socrates is akin to one of those Silenus statues, which one must "open up" (215b2: διοιχθέντες) in order to find "statues of gods" (215b3: ἀγάλματα θεῶν) buried within. This *eikôn* is insufficient, though, because it is purely visual, and Socrates' marvelous qualities derive more from his oral charms: his "speeches are most similar to the Silenuses which one can open up" (221d8: οἱ λόγοι . . . ὁμοιότατοί εἰσι τοῖς σιληνοῖς τοῖς διοιγομένοις) because they are covered in the "hide of a hubristic satyr" (221a1: σατύρου δή τινα ὑβριστοῦ **δοράν**); when one strips away all the talk, however, of "donkeys" (ὄνους) and "pack-asses" (κανθηλίους), one discovers "statues of virtue" (222a4: ἀγάλματ' ἀρετῆς) underneath.

While this metaphor of unveiling, revealing, or exposing something divinely beautiful under an absurd exterior is characteristic of novels both ancient and modern (§0.0), we may note in the specific case of Apuleius an even closer engagement with the *Sileni Alcibiadis*. For much like Alcibiades' Socrates, Lucius is also slowly transformed into a series of spectacular representations over the course of book 11: most surprisingly, at the close of the novel, he stands "as a statue" in front of a statue of Isis (*Met.* 11.24: *me . . . in vicem **simulacri** constituto*); and if we consider that he is dressed as a Helios or even Osiris

---

102. Ulrich 2017, 708.
103. See Hunter 2004, 109–10, on Alcibiades' Socrates as a reincarnated Odysseus. Cf. Ulrich 2017, 720–30, for fuller discussion.

figure,[104] he seems together with Isis to constitute an ensemble of *simulacra deorum* (cf. ἀγάλματα θεῶν). What is more, this transformation takes place only after he has been stripped of his "ass-hide," the *corium* (=δορά)[105] of a beast which is "hateful to [Isis]" (11.6: *mihi . . . detestabilis . . . beluae . . . corio*). For the retrospective reader, in other words, the promise of an opportunity to "marvel" (*mirari*) at *figurae*, which are "transformed" (*conversas*) before our eyes "into other images" (*in alias imagines*), activates a figural metamorphosis of our asinine "anti-Socrates" in much the same way as Alcibiades publicly lays bare the Platonic Socrates in the *Symposium*.[106]

Whereas Socrates is transformed from *eikones* into *agalmata theôn* through a process of "stripping away" his ugly external features, Lucius, in a stunning parodic reversal, must be stripped of his *aliena*—his lineage, parentage, fortune, learning, good looks, and high birth—transformed, in turn, into *imagines*, and finally, exposed to reveal the *simulacra deorum* underneath. In fact, even Socrates' "ass-talk," which reveals "statues of virtue" when "opened," seems to be replicated in Lucius' self-description as a *rudis locutor* in the Prologue: "crude" (*rudis*) speaking is etymologically linked, as Winkler himself recognized long ago,[107] to the verb *rudere*, the "braying" of an ass. Not only must this ass-man be stripped of his external *corium* to reveal the "statues of gods" underneath, but as with Alcibiades' Socrates, the words of the Prologue—the braying buffoonery with which Lucius-*auctor* dresses up his *vita*—must also be exposed if one hopes to find the "statues of virtue" hidden below its surface.

We will return to this image again in the following chapters, as this procedure of stripping Lucius to his bare figural form must guide our interpretation not only of his role as a *simulacrum* increasingly incorporated into Isis' statuary ensemble (§3.4), but also of our own fraught interaction with the representational form(s) put on display in this text (§4.5). As we close our discussion of the Prologue, however, it is necessary for the moment to meditate on the "marvel" we are offered if *we* "look into" this text. This, too, is an experience which hovers between philosophical investigation and aesthetic delight, inasmuch as

---

104. See *GCA* 2015, 404–6.

105. Cf. *ThLL* 4.0.951.79 for the Greek gloss of δορά for the Latin *corium*.

106. On Lucius as an "anti-Socrates," see again O'Brien 2002, 40–44. Once again, Fletcher 2014, 171n111, seems to hint at Apuleius' appreciation of the way in which Alcibiades commodifies Socrates at this moment in the Platonic corpus, but only loosely connects it to the exemplary (*sc.* objectified) Socrates of the *Soc.*

107. See Winkler 1985, 196; Gowers 2001, 80–81, who notes that "there is just the shadow of a braying ass in *rudis locutor* to hint that he has an asinine past too, that this philosophy teacher is a former donkey."

READING AS A CHOICE IN THE APULEIAN CORPUS 125

its educative value depends on the object of one's marvel. So, Plato and Aristotle regularly speak of "wonder" (θαυμάζειν) as the beginning of philosophy;[108] and Longus, sprinkling this pedagogical flavoring into his more sensuous novel, opens *Daphnis and Chloe* with the unnamed narrator "looking" (ἰδόντα) and "marveling" (θαυμάσαντα) at a painting—an aesthetic encounter which inspires him, in turn, to write his novel as an "offering to love." In fact, we know from Photius' summary of the lost work most scholars consider the very first novel—Antonius Diogenes' *Incredible Wonders beyond Thule*[109]—that the main narrative seems to have been motivated by an encounter with an inscription on a coffin: "stranger, whoever you are, open (me), in order that you may learn marvelous things" (Phot. *Bibl.* 116: Ὦ ξένε, ὅστις εἶ, ἄνοιξον, ἵνα **μάθῃς** ἃ **θαυμάζεις**). Indeed, this novelistic episode of opening a box and looking inside is similar to the reader's encounter with beauty in the *Met.*: as we shall see in §4.4, Psyche cannot stop herself from indulging her curiosity to "open" and "look into" Proserpina's *pyxis* of true beauty, which leaves her immobilized by infernal sleep.

We have seen, however, that marvel and specifically marveling at the mirror of the text, can also be educative in Apuleius' corpus, as our "Latin sophist" adapts (perhaps parodically) Plato's and Aristotle's claims about wonder as the catalyst for the pursuit of philosophy. Recall again Apuleius' suggestion in the *Apologia* that Aemilianus would have "looked into" (*Apol.* 16.7: *inviseres*) a mirror, if he had read Archimedes, and as a result, could have "marveled" (*mirere*) at his aspect. Careful reading leads to mirror-speculation, which, in turn, produces "marvel" by triangulating one's appearance through dramatic *exempla* and simultaneously furnishing self-knowledge. Using this idea of marvel as a spur to philosophy, Apuleius concludes his brutal invective by pointing up his own peculiar reception of Socrates' choice to fulfill the Delphic maxim: Apuleius prefers to "conceal [his] own faults rather than track down those of others" (16.11: *mea peccata tegere quam **aliena indagare***). So also, as we readers of the

---

108. Socrates in the *Theaetetus*, for instance, famously remarks that "wonder is precisely the experience of the philosopher" (*Theaet.* 155d2–3: μάλα γὰρ φιλοσόφου τοῦτο τὸ πάθος, τὸ **θαυμάζειν**) and that "there is no other beginning to philosophy than that" (οὐ γὰρ ἄλλη ἀρχὴ φιλοσοφίας ἢ αὕτη). Cf. also *Alc. 1* 103a1. For further references on the importance of philosophical "wonder" in the dialogues, see Denyer 2001, 83 *ad loc. Alc. 1* 103a1; Nightingale 2004, 253–68. Similarly, at *Metaphysics* 982b12–13, Aristotle claims that "it is on account of wondering that humans, both now and at first, began to philosophize" (διὰ γὰρ τὸ **θαυμάζειν** οἱ ἄνθρωποι καὶ νῦν καὶ τὸ πρῶτον ἤρξαντο φιλοσοφεῖν).

109. Although this text is undatable (see Morgan 2007), we may note that Photius believed it predated all the other novels.

Met. vicariously "look into" the *aliena* of the ass-man, we may likewise marvel; and yet, we are invited to respond differently from Aemilianus.

2.5. Lucius, "Socrates," and Surface-Level Looking

I suggested above that part of the pleasure of reading the *Met.* lies in the way in which it parades around a buffoonish character, one who constantly misconstrues his own behavior in terms of mythological and philosophical models, but fails to make good on those comparisons in his everyday life.[110] Insofar as this involves Apuleius' complex method of allusion, I concur with Harrison's notion that Apuleius playfully incorporates his elite readers with learned winks to the highbrow literature of the past.[111] I diverge from Harrison, however, in believing that readers are meant to stop there. Rather, across his corpus Apuleius is deeply invested in a program of "active reading"—that is, in forcing his readers to look beneath the surface of things and "discern in the mirror of Homer," so to speak, appropriate and inappropriate paradigms for the philosophical life. To conclude this chapter, I turn to two key moments of resolutely *inactive* viewing in the early books of the *Met.*: the first narrative passage of book 1 (1.2–1.4), and Lucius' first morning in Hypata (2.1). In both cases, Lucius is presented with spectacles that are not quite what they seem to be; and on both occasions, he stubbornly refuses to look below the surface level. In fact, he cannot bring himself to do anything but delight in the pleasure of a story or a spectacle.

The opening episode of the *Met.* (directly following the Prologue) poses to Lucius the first of many consequential choices. As our narrator travels the "harsh" and "slippery" road to Thessaly, he leaps from his horse's back to "shake off the wearied fatigue from sitting" (1.2: *fatigationem sedentariam*) and encounters two interlocutors engaged in conversation. As I have argued at length elsewhere, the context and terrain of this journey is already implicated

---

110. On which, see chs. 3 and 4 below. This aspect of my reading aligns with Gian Biagio Conte's seminal interpretation of Petronius' *Satyricon*, insofar as he elucidates a pointed disjunction between Encolpius the actor, Enclopius the narrator, and Petronius the author. See, e.g., Conte 1996, 23–24: "So Encolpius, scholastic addict of myth, the naïve character obsessed with models of great literature that he uses as parameters of interpretation for the events of daily life, also wants to be a sincere and trustworthy narrator; but he is certainly a 'mythomaniac narrator' . . . even if he does not consciously intend to falsify the narrative, he lacks the ability to keep separate in his account the level of mythical fantasy, inspired by literature, and the level of events around him."

111. See Harrison 2000, 210–59; 2013a.

READING AS A CHOICE IN THE APULEIAN CORPUS   127

in the discourse of choice by comparison to another famous literary-philosophical type-scene: Socrates' refusal to rationalize myths in the opening of the *Phaedrus*.[112] In that *locus classicus* of bucolicism, Socrates and Phaedrus undertake their walk outside the walls of Athens as a solution to the weariness from "sitting for too long" (*Phaedr.* 227a4: συχνὸν . . . χρόνον καθήμενος), since walks along the roads are "better for removing weariness" (ἀκοπωτέρους) than following public walkways in the city.[113] However, in stark contrast to Lucius, who seeks a diverting conversation to alleviate the discomforts of traveling "on business" (1.2: *ex negotio*), Socrates emphasizes repeatedly in his opening exchange with Phaedrus the need for "leisure-time" (σχολή) in the pursuit of self-knowledge. Indeed, he even quotes Pindar that it is "a matter more important than business" (*Phaedr.* 227b9: ἀσχολίας ὑπέρτερον πρᾶγμα) to listen to and analyze Lysias' and Phaedrus' prior exchange. In short, the motivation and topography of Lucius' first crossroads-choice already exhibits a complex engagement with its ostensible Platonic antecedent: Lucius portrays his Thessalian travel as an opportunity to replicate Socrates' pursuit of self-knowledge in his own dialogic exchange; but, far from taking an extramural leisure-walk to engage in philosophical inquiry, Lucius traverses a "rough" landscape with no intention to abandon his business interests, but merely in search of some distraction.[114]

It is in the context of this anti-Platonic landscape that Lucius "make[s] himself a third to two companions" (1.2: *duobus comitum . . . tertium me facio*) in conversation and overhears one of the travelers, in turn, blurt out with biting laughter: "stop telling such absurd and monstrous lies." Lucius demonstrates with his response both a failure to fulfill the Delphic maxim with which Socrates concerned himself and a countertheory of the value of *fabulae* (*Met.* 1.2):

> Isto accepto, sititor alioquin novitatis, "Immo vero" inquam "impertite sermones non quidem curiosum, sed qui velim scire vel cuncta vel certe plurima. Simul iugi quod insurgimus aspritudinem fabularum lepida iucunditas levigabit."

---

112. See Ulrich 2020, 680–81. See also Winkle 2014; Graverini 2012a, 137–40.

113. Graverini 2012a, 137, labels the walk-from-fatigue "a detail that in passing might seem trivial [but] confirms the intertextual relationship between the beginning of the *Metamorphoses* and the beginning of the *Phaedrus*." Cf. also O'Brien 2011, 127, on the shared motif.

114. Lucius walks in precisely the opposite landscape from that of the *Phaedrus* (*Met.* 1.2): *Postquam ardua montium et lubrica vallium et roscida caespitum et glebosa camporum <emensus> emersi.* On the deliberate superimposition of a Platonic motif onto the wrong landscape, see Ulrich 2020, 681.

When I heard that outburst, being thirsty for novelty in general, I said, "Please share your conversation with me! Not that I am curious per se, but I'm the sort who wants to know all things, or at the very least most things. At the same time, the charming pleasure of stories will smooth out the harshness of the ridge we are climbing."

As Matthew Leigh points out, Lucius here makes a distinction "of dubious validity" between *curiositas* and knowledge of all things,[115] and we should recall that Cicero's Piso in his discussion of the Sirens claims it is only the *curiosi* who "want to know all things of any sort whatsoever" (*De fin.* 5.49: *omnia . . . scire cuiuscumquemodi sint cupere*).[116] In Cicero's version, this dilettantish curiosity is juxtaposed with the contemplation of higher things—the *scientiae cupiditas* that enchanted "so great a hero" (5.49) as Odysseus and kept so great an intellect as Archimedes "deeply attentive" (5.50: *attentius*); or as Apuleius phrases it in his *Apologia*, the *discendi cupido* that Aemilianus *should have* had.[117]

Lucius, by contrast, lacks that innate human impulse toward philosophical inquiry. Rather, the reason Lucius values tales is revealed in his very next statement: the "charming pleasure" of *fabulae* will "smooth out the harshness of the ridge," where the rare term *aspritudo* (used of topography only by Apuleius)[118] mirrors the discourse about the "harsh road" which we saw deployed in the Heraclean choice narratives and their reception (§1.2).[119] Needless to say, our curious narrator is not invested in self-knowledge; quite

---

115. Leigh 2013, 139. See also Winkler 1985, 28.

116. Compare this to a fragment of Menander found in one of Cicero's letters to Atticus, which claims that "nothing is sweeter than to know everything" (Men. *Epit.* fr. 2a Arnott: οὐδέν ἐστι γὰρ/ γλυκύτερον ἢ πάντ᾽ εἰδέναι); and Cicero connects this sentiment to his own insatiable curiosity (Cic. *Att.* 4.11.2: *ut homini curioso*). See the discussion of Leigh 2013, 61, with n. 38, for the original citation. Cf., however, DeFilippo 1990, 478.

117. With Lucius' dilettantish desire for *fabulae*, we may compare a scholastic rant from Aulus Gellius on a particular episode from Pliny's *Natural Histories* in which the latter misattributes a series of *fabulae* to the great philosopher Democritus. There, Gellius laments the "fallacious enticement of such marvels" (*NA* 10.12.4: *de istiusmodi admirationum fallaci inlecebra*) and complains that certain *ingenia*—"especially those more desirous of learning" (*ea . . . potissimum, quae* **discendi cupidiora** *sunt*)—will be captivated by such marvels and as a consequence, will slip and "fall" (**elabuntur**). Both Lucius and Psyche succumb to their temptations after listening to *fabulae*, and both moments of youthful weakness are described as "falls" (cf. 5.24: *delabitur*; 11.15: *delapsus*). On Psyche's fall, see §4.4 (esp. with n. 86). On the scene from *NA* and its import for second-century CE reading culture, see Howley 2018, 29–30 and 135–40.

118. *ThLL* 2.0.846.73–74. In most uses, *aspritudo* is a medical term used of a particular eye disease. Cf., however, the usage of the etymologically related *asperitas*, which is regularly used of difficult roads or paths (e.g., Cic. *Phil.* 9.2), on which, see *ThLL* 2.0.821.48–73.

119. See Zimmerman 2002, 89–91, on "harsh" roads in the *Met.* See esp. *Met.* 9.10 on the *iter arduum* (on which, see also Ulrich *forthcoming* b).

the contrary, Lucius longs only for a kind of escapism, a diversion from the long hard journey.

In fact, as Jeffrey Winkle has demonstrated, Lucius' subsequent reaction to the skeptic exposes a gaping chasm between the ass-man and his Platonic ancestor.[120] For in the *Phaedrus*, after Socrates and his young companion walk a distance outside the walls of Athens, they discover the spot where Boreas (allegedly) snatched Oreithyia, and Phaedrus asks Socrates if he "believes the tale" (229c4: μυθολόγημα) to be true. In response, Socrates dismisses the entire project of myth-rationalization as laughable sophistry since he has not yet fulfilled the Delphic maxim (see quote in §2.3 above). But more precisely, as Socrates explains, he prefers to disregard questions about the truth-value of myths and instead, to use them to "investigate . . . [himself]" (*Phaedr.* 230a2: σκοπῶ . . . ἐμαυτόν) in order to discover "whether [he] happen[s] to be some beast more complicated and furious than Typhon, or a gentler and simpler animal" (*Phaedr.* 230a3–4). Readers of Plato have long recognized that this framing question about Socrates' composite nature—what Winkle calls a "Typhonic choice" in the *Met.*—is programmatic for the rest of the dialogue, from its foreshadowing of the image Socrates later uses for the soul of a human-animal hybrid (a charioteer and winged-horse pair) to its lingering presence in the Siren-cicada episode:[121] after all, the reason Socrates advocates that he and Phaedrus should sail by the cicadas uncharmed is so that they can prove they are not quadrupeds (see §1.1).

Whereas Socrates uses the category of myth as an exhortation to self-examination and more specifically, as an opportunity to reflect on the complicated nature of his own soul, Lucius, by contrast, advocates unquestioning belief in the fabulous, since the payout in his view—escape from the discomforts of the body—outweighs the intellectual risks. So, after hearing the skeptical interlocutor's complaints about the absurd tales of Meroe's magic, Lucius affirms Aristomenes' *fabula* (before hearing it!) and in turn, berates the skeptical interlocutor for his disbelief (*Met.* 1.3):

> Minus hercule calles pravissimis opinionibus ea putari mendacia quae vel auditu noua vel visu **rudia** vel certe supra captum cogitationis **ardua** videantur; quae si paulo **accuratius exploraris**, non modo compertu evidentia, verum etiam factu **facilia** senties.

---

120. See Winkle 2014.

121. For a sampling of discussions, see, e.g., Ferrari 1987, 9–12; Nicholson 1999, 14–34; and Morgan 2012. See also Hunter 1997 on the influence of this same question on Longus' *D&C*.

130   THE SHADOW OF AN ASS

You do not understand, by Hercules, that it is because of people's distorted notions that those stories which seem new to the ear or unfamiliar to the eye or even difficult beyond the mind's grasp are thought to be lies. If you look into these things with a little more care, you will feel that they are not only clear to ascertain, but also easy to do.

This crossroads of interpretive choice, much like Mithras' reinterpretation of books 1–10, opens with an invocation to Heracles, which playfully hints at that inaugural crossroads moment (cf. §1.3). Thus, in walking a harsh road and attempting to "smooth [it] out," Lucius evidently prefers the promise of Lady Vice in Prodicus' allegory, who offers an "easy and short road to happiness" (Xen. *Mem.* 2.1.29: ῥᾳδίαν καὶ βραχεῖαν ὁδὸν ἐπὶ τὴν εὐδαιμονίαν) instead of Lady Virtue's "difficult and long road" (χαλεπὴν καὶ μακρὰν ὁδόν). What is more, when he rebuts the skeptic, Lucius deploys topographical terminology for the thorny problems of intellectual inquiry—things which seem "unfamiliar" (*rudia*) or "difficult" (*ardua*)[122]—but simultaneously, he suggests that such issues are made to "[feel] easy" (*facilia senties*) as long as one uses the tools of philosophical investigation: *explorare* is another verb for intense intellectual scrutiny, such as with Apuleius' claim in the *Apologia* to "inspect fish" (*Apol.* 103: *pisces* **exploras**) on Aristotle's authority,[123] while *accuratius* has its origins in the discourse of "active" reading.[124] In short, Lucius depicts his credulous approach to *fabulae* as a similarly "Typhonic choice," where he is to decide whether and how to perform intellectual inquiry; paradoxically, though, such meticulous scrutiny leads neither to rationalizing the tales away (as the skeptical interlocutor would prefer) nor to striving doggedly after self-knowledge (as his philosophical model would advocate), but rather, to a kind of lazy acceptance of entertaining pleasure.

It is striking, therefore, that Lucius, after actually hearing Aristomenes'

---

122. Needless to say, the primary meaning of *arduus* is topographical, relating to rough and mountainous terrain (see *ThLL* 2.0.492.54–59) and only by extension, to the "harsh road to virtues" (e.g., Sen. *De ira* 2.13.1). On *rudis*, see OLD, s.v. 1c for the primary semantic contour connected with land "not yet cultivated, virgin."

123. Recall that Apuleius' two-word rebuttal to the charge of "inspecting fish" is that "Aristotle teaches [it]" (*Apol.* 103.2: *Aristoteles docet*). For further discussion, see §4.3 (with n. 73).

124. It shares the etymological root of "care," we may note, with *curiose*: see *ThLL* 1.0.343.31, where the adverb is glossed as *diligenter*, and 1.0.343.40–78 on its use *cum verbis discendi, scribendi, sim.* Cf. *Met.* 1.26, where Milo, in an episode of failed hospitality (cf. *GCA* 2007, 36–37), interrogates Lucius "rather carefully" (*accuratius*) and "explores" his background "most scrupulously" (*scrupulosissime explorans*).

absurd tale about an anti-Platonic "Socrates,"[125] delights in the pseudo-philosopher's tragedy (like a *curiosus/ polypragmōn*),[126] and thanks his interlocutor with another invocation to Heracles (*Met.* 1.20):

> Sed ego huic et credo hercules et gratas gratias memini, quod lepidae fabulae festivitate nos avocavit, asperam denique ac prolixam viam sine labore ac taedio evasi.

> But I, by Hercules, believe him and I remember him with grateful thanks, because he distracted us with the merriment of his charming tale. Thus, I ascended a harsh and long road without toil or tedium.

By bookending Lucius' reactions to "unbelievable tales," in short, with metaliterary appeals to Heracles that are accompanied by implicit allusions to the hero's own choice between a sweat-filled path and an easy shortcut, Apuleius lays bare Lucius' underlying asinine character.[127] Although Lucius fashions himself an advocate of diligent looking, it becomes abundantly clear by the end of this "Typhonic choice" that he has no intention to look beneath the surface. It is no surprise, then, that—just like the curious gossips of *Soc.*, who creep through the streets "think[ing] not with their mind but with their **ears**" (*Soc.* 19.6: *non animo sed **auribus** cogitant*) and furthermore, in contrast with Socrates of that same treatise, who sought to receive the voice of his *daemôn* "not only with his **ears** but also with his eyes" (20.4: *non modo **auribus** eum verum etiam oculis*)—Lucius rejoices that, in sating his curiosity with Aristomenes' charming tale, he was carried "not on the back [of his horse], but by [his] **ears**" (*Met.* 1.20: *non dorso illius sed meis **auribus***).

By the same token, we can analyze how Lucius' failure to read scrupulously has serious consequences for his own life. For instance, the proof he cites for his theory of *fabulae* is eerily replicated inside Aristomenes' tale.[128] So, after Lucius tells his interlocutors how he almost died from eating too much cheesy polenta,

---

125. See n. 60 again.
126. See, e.g., *GCA* 2007, 367 *ad loc.* 1.20.5: "Lucius' taking pleasure in this account of misfortunes . . . characterizes him as a *polypragmōn*."
127. This is further accomplished through the verb *evadere*, which can be equivalent to *in altitudinem ascendere* (*ThLL* 5.2.989.31–61). In other words, Apuleius self-consciously activates a term embedded in the discourse of ascent. On Apuleius' awareness of and playful appropriation of (Platonic) topological language, see Ulrich *forthcoming* b.
128. See Ulrich 2022 on the "ontological metalepsis" between Lucius' rationalization and the inset tales he hears.

but on the very next day, marveled at the performance of a sword-swallower whom he "saw with his own eyes" (1.4: *isto gemino obtutu . . . **aspexi***), it is striking that *within* the subsequent inset tale, Aristomenes' "Socrates" is stabbed in the throat, but magically wakes up the next day and walks to a *locus amoenus*, where he chokes on a hefty bite of cheesy bread and dies. This early instance in the novel of a seepage between frame and inset tale introduces for *lectores scrupulosi* the crux of Plato's anxieties over *mimesis* (see §3.1): it should give us pause, in other words, that the boundaries between a reader, listener, or viewer and the content they consume (whether narrative, theatrical, or artistic) are disconcertingly porous. For now, however, we need only note that Lucius' preference, when faced with a "Typhonic choice," is not to "look beneath" the surface of the trick, but rather, to employ superficial looking: *adspicere* rather than *inspicere*. In so doing, Lucius chooses to enjoy aesthetic pleasures as mere diversions. Thus, whereas Plato's Socrates refuses to waste his *scholê* on dissecting *mythoi*, preferring instead to use *logos* to pursue the truth about himself, Lucius is uninterested in self-knowledge and "giv[ing] *logos* the meaning of *fabula*,"[129] hopes only to pass his time in distractions while "on business."

The deliberate "gaps" Apuleius creates between Lucius and the Platonic Socrates, however, do not merely offer an invitation to triangulate Lucius' character with the moral-ethical *exemplum* of Socrates and point out the particular ways in which he falls short of his philosophical model.[130] Beyond prompting the procedure of "looking into" Lucius' *vita* and using it as a tool for enacting "ethical therapy by deterrence," we may also consider Apuleius' use of the *Phaedrus* from a different vantage point, inasmuch as the dialogue, at its fundamental level, poses a series of life choices to its readers: a choice between "inspecting the matters of others" and striving after self-knowledge, a choice between Socrates' first and second speeches on the nature of *Erōs*, and finally, a choice over how to respond to the aesthetic pleasure of the Siren-esque cicadas. It is thus vital for any interpretation of the *Met.* to recognize that Lucius himself, when faced with this parodic *Phaedran* crossroads in the opening of the

---

129. See Graverini 2012a, 138, for quotation and discussion.

130. Others have recognized the way in which Apuleius highlights deliberate gaps between Lucius' experience and his model(s): so, Hunter 2012, 232, notes that "the difference between the Apuleian text and its [Platonic] model" should influence our interpretation, and Benson 2019, 99 and passim, extends this also to the gaps between the *Met.* and Apuleius' philosophical works. Winkle 2014, 98, notes a "deliberate incompleteness" in Apuleius' references to Plato. Relihan 1993, 29, suggests that such philosophical parody might have been endemic to Menippean satire.

READING AS A CHOICE IN THE APULEIAN CORPUS   133

novel, decides, in a comical exposure of his antiheroic character,[131] to take the easy road of aesthetic indulgence.

Furthermore, on the heels of Aristomenes' *fabula* about a mock-Socrates, stripped of his Platonic heritage and dressed up in Odyssean garb,[132] Lucius arrives at his host Milo's house, where he participates in a farcical episode of "perverted hospitality"[133] and ends up going to bed on an empty stomach, "having feasted on tales alone" (*Met.* 1.26: *cenatus solis fabulis*). When he awakes the following morning in Hypata, the central city in the land of magic, Thessaly, we see a similar exposure of our asinine *auctor* for his failure to read scrupulously (*Met.* 2.1):

> Ut primum nocte discussa sol novus diem fecit, et somno simul emersus et lectulo, anxius alioquin et **nimis cupidus cognoscendi** quae rara miraque sunt, reputansque me media Thessaliae loca tenere, quo artis magicae nativa cantamina totius orbis consono ore celebrentur, fabulamque illam optimi comitis Aristomenis de situ civitatis huius exortam, suspensus alioquin et voto simul et studio, **curiose singula considerabam**. Nec fuit in illa civitate quod **aspiciens** id esse crederem quod esset, sed omnia prorsus ferali murmure in aliam effigiem translata, ut et lapides quos offenderem de homine duratos, et aves quas audirem indidem plumatas, et arbores quae pomerium ambirent similiter foliatas, et fontanos latices de corporibus humanis fluxos crederem; iam statuas et imagines incessuras, parietes locuturos, boves et id genus pecua dicturas praesagium, de ipso vero caelo et iubaris orbe subito venturum oraculum.

> When first the night was shaken off and the new sun brought about the day, I arose both from sleep and from my bed, generally uneasy and excessively desiring to become acquainted with things which were rare and marvelous; and I was thinking that I was in the very middle of Thessaly, where the native incantations of the magical art are celebrated with the harmonizing mouth of the whole world, and indeed, that that tale of my best comrade, Aristomenes, arose from the place of this city. On tenterhooks in general from both my expectation and my excitement, I diligently inspected everything. There was nothing in that city

---

131. So, Keulen 2003.
132. On which, see Münstermann 1995, 8–13, who speaks of the transformation of Socrates into Odysseus as one of the fundamental "literarische Metamorphosen." For further connections, see Hunter 2006, 303–5. See also Ulrich 2020, 696–700 and §5.1, for my own discussions of Apuleius' use of the Socrates/Odysseus models in the Isis book.
133. On "perverted hospitality and debased literary paradigms," see *GCA* 2007, 36–42.

which, I would believe, upon gazing at it, was what it was, but all things had been transformed absolutely into another appearance, as if by a deadly murmuring: I thought the stones which I encountered had been hardened out of man, and the birds which I heard had grown their plumage from the same place, and the trees which surrounded the city walls had gotten their leaves in a similar way, and even the liquid fountains had flowed from human bodies; [I believed] that the statues and images were already about to walk, the walls about to speak, and the cattle and chattel of this sort would begin to presage, indeed, that an oracle would come suddenly from the very sky itself and from the disk of the sun.[134]

After opening this second book with a Homeric tag-line,[135] Lucius tries once again to spin his aesthetic response and cloak it in the discourse of careful philosophical reading: he claims to follow the method of inquiry we saw Apuleius advocating in the *Apologia*—namely, using his external surroundings (e.g., books, Sirens, mirrors, etc.) to conceive of a "desire for learning." However, just as with his "Typhonic choice" in book 1 and the subtle incongruity between his own analytical procedure and the paradigms on which he models himself, Lucius-*auctor* deploys a slight but significant shift in idiom in his depiction of this encounter with novelties—one which exposes a chasm between his illicit curiosity and the acceptable forms of knowledge pursuit.

Indeed, whereas Cicero's Odysseus and Archimedes were driven by an innate human "desire for learning" (*discendi cupiditas*), Lucius is "excessively desirous of becoming acquainted" (*nimis cupidus cognoscendi*) with "rare marvels," things which would most certainly fall under Apuleius' category of *aliena* in *Soc.*[136] What's more, although Cicero uses the idiom *cognoscendi cupiditas* (*Tusc. Disp.* 1.44) once to describe "desire to see the truth" about the heavens which "is naturally in our minds," by Apuleius' time, this phrase had semanti-

---

134. I borrow "on tenterhooks" as a translation of *suspensus* from Slater 1998, 25, who further notes: "Lucius is eager, indeed too eager to find magic and metamorphosis in, as well as under, every rock. He sees the present as an unstable moment between past and future transformations—transformations he hopes to witness and (as we know on second reading of the novel) gain power over."

135. See *GCA* 2001, 53 *ad loc.* 2,24,17–24, which compares Verg. *Aen.* 12, 669 (*ut primum discussae umbrae et lux reddita menti*) with our passage (*ut primum . . . fecit*).

136. So, Graverini and Nicolini 2019, lxvii: "Lucio dichiara di essere *nimis cupidus cognoscendi*, ma questo non lo qualifica certo come filosofo, né lo avvicina a quei Plutarco e Sesto da cui si vantava di discendere a 1, 2, 1. La sua non è l'insaziabile *cupiditas cognoscendi* esaltata da Cicerone in *Tusc.* 1, 44, diretta alle cose celesti e alla verità: lui stesso ci informa che il suo desiderio di conoscere è diretto verso *quae rara miraque sunt*."

cally deviated from describing the legitimate pursuit of knowledge, and had instead become thoroughly associated with popular diversions of spectacle, such as distracting novelties and deceptions. So, Seneca the Elder, in the preface to book 4 of the *Controversiae*, compares himself to "gladiator-producers" (*Contr.* 4.pr.1: *munerarii*) who strive "to intensify an audience's suspense" (*ad expectationem populi detinendam*): the rhetor attempts to sprinkle "novelty" (*novitas*) into his *libellus* because the "desire for becoming acquainted with unknown things" (*cupiditas ignota cognoscendi*) is more intense than when an orator merely repeats familiar *topoi*. Likewise, the Younger Seneca in his treatise *On Anger* speaks of deploying "either pleasing or novel conversation" (*De ira* 3.39.4: *sermones . . . vel gratos vel novos*) to subdue a patient and thereby, "call [him] away with the desire of becoming acquainted with it" (*cupiditate cognoscendi avocabit*). Lucius' "desire to become acquainted" with paradoxographical novelties in Hypata, far from constituting a philosophical inclination to "[strip] off the surface reality of things in order to see beneath,"[137] seems instead aligned with Lucius' theory of *fabulae* which are about "distraction" (*avocare*) rather than education: Lucius revels in the marvels themselves instead of penetrating them.

It is thus a perfect encapsulation of Lucius' self-representation as a philosophically inclined viewer—what I label his "philosophico-mania" (see chap. 4)—that he parrots the discourse of "active" reading with the claim that he "diligently inspected everything" (*curiose singula considerabam*), but immediately undercuts his careful viewing by exposing his unwillingness to look beneath. Once again, he "sees" (*adspicere*) things which are not what they seem to be on the surface, but chooses not to "look into" (*inspicere*) them; he recognizes that everything has been made into "another appearance" (*omnia . . . in aliam effigiem translata*), just as the Prologue promised it would be (cf. *figuras fortunasque hominum in alias imagines conversas*), but rather than learning from the marvel he experiences, he delights in the excitement and the promise of metamorphosis. Indeed, Lucius has precisely the wrong reaction to marvel, the Alcibiadean kind which strips the external appearance only for a consumptive pleasure, like a visitor to a museum of curiosities.

Shortly after this episode, Lucius encounters a statuary scene, the close inspection of which charges him with erotic excitement and renders him unable to control his desires—a scene to which we shall return in the next chapter (§3.2).

---

137. Slater 1998, 24.

To close, however, I would like only to suggest that Lucius' failure to read "actively" and inspect his surroundings "diligently" works in tandem with the gaps Apuleius exposes between Lucius and his models. Thus, Graverini rightly connects Lucius' asinine gullibility in avidly consuming stories to "novelistic heroes such as Don Quixote or Lewis Carroll's Alice."[138] Simply put, the ass-man embodies precisely what Socrates had hoped to avoid when he encountered the cicadas. In the next chapter, we turn to developing a clearer theorization of the effects of Lucius' misreading on us by analyzing how this "mytho-mania" intersects with anxieties about the contagious nature of *mimesis*.

---

138. See Graverini 2012a, 140.

THREE

Entranced by the Mirror of Myth

Mimetic Contagion, Mytho-Mania, and Readerly Choice

> Fulvia's bedroom was a deeply carpeted octagon, lined, walls and ceiling, with rose-tinted mirrors that multiplied every gesture like a kaleidoscope. A bevy of Fulvias stepped, naked as Botticelli's Venus, from the white foam of their discarded dresses and converged upon him with a hundred outstretched arms. A whole football team of Morris Zapps stripped to their undershorts with clumsy haste and clamped hairy paws on ranks of peach-shaped buttocks receding into infinity.
>
> —David Lodge, *Small World*

In David Lodge's justly famous satire of the itinerant academic life, *Small World*, there is a scene that encapsulates the ambivalence of erotic aestheticism and the looming ethical danger of trying to visualize the divine represented on earth. Morris Zapp, a bloviating literary critic, finds himself to his own surprise in the bedroom of a beautiful, younger Italian scholar, Fulvia Morgana. Fulvia's bedroom is "lined, walls and ceiling, with rose-tinted mirrors that [multiply] every gesture like a kaleidoscope." As Lodge describes the affair with the epigram above, "a bevy of Fulvias stepped, naked as Botticelli's Venus, from the white foam of their discarded dresses and converged upon [Morris] with a hundred outstretched arms." The episode in *Small World* ends, to be sure, in calamitous humor, as Fulvia's husband returns home unexpectedly and Morris Zapp comes to realize that the whole affair was planned as a set-up for ménage à trois. The titillating and immersive power of description in this episode, however, combined with a vision of the (surrogate) goddess illuminates *in nuce* what we turn to in this chapter: the potentially contaminating influence of aesthetic experience and the danger of interacting with (representations of) the divine in the *ekphrases* of the *Metamorphoses*. Whereas we considered in the previous chapter a didactic-ethical tradition of mirror-gazing and its relevance for the kind of looking Apuleius invites from us as we read the *Met.*, this chapter will explore how Lucius' interactions with different representations of divinities have the potential to expand beyond the boundaries of their physical media and shape Lucius' (and perhaps, even our) life in a very real way.

On the one hand, this episode from *Small World*, where the narrator appeals to "Botticelli's Venus," replicates an auctorial gesture quite familiar to a reader of the Roman novel. This narratorial voice is similar, after all, to the "mythomaniacal" *auctor* that Gian Biagio Conte recognized in Petronius' Encolpius—a character who perpetually colors his quotidian erotic and consumptive encounters in the grandiose shades of the lofty myths of the past.[1] Others, such as Luca Graverini, have likewise recognized this same mytho-mania in the asinine narrator of Apuleius' *Metamorphoses*, who also appeals to figures of the mythical past—Heracles and Odysseus (cf. §1.3)—to make sense of his own transformation into an ass and his subsequent misadventures.[2] We may think, by comparison, of the book-obsessed Don Quixote, who models for his early modern readers precisely the debased approach to fiction that the experience of Cervantes' novel may strive to teach us to eschew.[3]

This episode from *Small World* is representative, though, of another, related phenomenon in ancient art-critical discourse, an anxiety widespread across antiquity from Plato onward: namely, the capacity of art to break out of its own representational limits and reproduce itself in the lives of those who interact with it. This is a phenomenon Robert Germany recently theorized as "mimetic contagion," which is not merely "the conceit that life may be drawn into imitation of art,"[4] in which the one-way direction of influence is surprisingly revealed to be a two-way street, but more precisely, that an artwork, through the mechanism of mimetic desire, can "[transcend] its presumed frame as a mere fiction and propagat[e] itself in the world of the viewer."[5] With this theoretical frame-

---

1. See Conte 1996, passim and esp. 27–28. We may recall that Jauss 1982a, 7, labeled this the "pathology of novel reading."
2. For an application of Conte's theoretical framework to Lucius-*auctor*, see Graverini 2012a, 140.
3. See Close 2008. Cf. Moore 2020, 109–76, on the reception of Cervantes in English liteature. See also Graverini 2012a, 140, on Lucius as a predecessor of the great novelistic heroes of the early modern novel (quoted in §2.5).
4. See Germany 2016 (6 for quotation). For a related discussion of "ontological metalepsis" in Apuleius, where inset tales seep into frame narratives in uncanny ways, see Ulrich 2022.
5. See Germany 2016, 18, where he links mimetic contagion to the ancient rhetorical *Progymnas-*

ENTRANCED BY THE MIRROR OF MYTH   139

work in mind, another way to view Morris Zapp's erotic encounter with Fulvia Morgana as a surrogate for "Botticelli's Venus" is in light of the ancient discourse on the dangerous and contaminating way in which aesthetic pleasure can affect (or we may even say, infect) those who experience it. It can arouse desire in a viewer to make that which is represented into a reality in his or her own life. A reader can be carried off by immersion or identification to the point of delusion or self-deception; and this anxiety over art's capacity to manipulate us through its seductive naturalism can be traced all the way back to Plato's famous critique of *mimesis* in book 10 of the *Republic*.[6]

While mimetic contagion will concern us more generally in this chapter, as our comprehension of Lucius' encounters with representations of divinities—his crossroads choices—depends, to a certain extent, on a shared appreciation of iconographies, which are culturally diffuse and widely appreciated, we will also be interested in a more specialized subspecies of this phenomenon—what Tim Whitmarsh has labeled "*ekphrastic* contagion": "the power of the visual icon to infect its surrounding discourse with ontological and perceptual uncertainty."[7] Indeed, *ekphrasis*—the ancient rhetorical-poetic practice of describing anything from a work of art to a hippopotamus[8]—"seep[s]" beyond its borders, as Whitmarsh phrases it, and this is in large part because of the well-recognized relationship in antiquity between *enargeia/evidentia* (usually translated "vividness") and *phantasia/visio*, the "mental image" which, according to materialist optical theories, would make a physical impression on the mind like a signet-ring in wax.[9] Descriptions are powerful over their hearers or

---

mata, which describe *ekphrasis* as a "descriptive speech that vividly (*enargeia*) brings the subject on display under the eyes (*hyp' opsin*)." On this discourse, see also Webb 2009 and §0.2 with n. 75.

6. On the relationship between "immersion" and deception, see Grethlein 2021, and esp. 75–106, on the influence of Plato's ideas about *mimesis* on the development of an ancient aesthetics of deception. On Plato's rejection of *mimesis*, see the masterful discussion of Halliwell 2002, 37–148, and esp. 118–48. Cf. also Germany 2016, 72–94.

7. See Whitmarsh 2002, 111.

8. On which, see Webb 2009, whose fundamental insight is that ancient authors understood the subjects of *ekphrasis* to reach far beyond merely *objets d'art*. The function and affective influence of *ekphrasis* writ large has been of increasing concern to scholars in the last thirty-five years, and the bibliography, both modern and ancient, is too abundant to treat within the bounds of a footnote. Noteworthy contributions are as follows. Modern studies of *ekphrasis*: Mitchell 1986; Krieger 1992; Heffernan 1993; Mitchell 1994; Wagner 1996. For ancient studies: Fowler 1990; Putnam 1998; Webb 1999; Elsner 2002; Bartsch and Elsner 2007; Webb 2009; Squire 2009; Squire 2014; Dufallo 2013.

9. On Aristotelian memory theory, see Sorabji 1972, esp. 11–17. On the influence of Aristotelian theory on Roman discourses of mnemotechnics, see Penny Small 1997, 72–121. On *phantasia* across antiquity, see Watson 1988. On the influence of philosophical and rhetorical discussions of *phantasia* on the Roman novels, see Slater 1997.

140 THE SHADOW OF AN ASS

readers—indeed, even possessing the capacity to "enslave" (*De sublim.* 15.9: δουλοῦται) or "totally dominate" (*Inst. orat.* 8.3.62: *plene dominatur*) them, according to 'Longinus' and Quintilian (respectively)—primarily because they rely on a storehouse of memories, a "picture gallery" in the mind, upon which a rhetor could draw in his *ekphrasis*.[10] Over the course of this chapter, we shall see how Apuleius quite literally plays with iconographic set pieces, borrowing from a cultural "picture gallery" to create new and even more powerful illusions, or *phantasiae*. But also for the purposes of this chapter, we will need to employ our own "horse-jumping knowledge" (1.1: *desultoria scientia*)—the very skill which the *Met.*'s narrator claims to deploy at the opening of the novel—by leaping back and forth between mimetic and *ekphrastic* contagion: for inside the narrative world of the *Met.*, on the one hand, Lucius-*actor* encounters representations of divinities which threaten to overstep their representational frames and transform Lucius into a (witting) participant; outside the narrative world, however, sits the reader, the recipient of the rich rhetorical *ekphrases* provided by Lucius-*auctor*. We as readers are invited to "[succumb] to the seductions of visualization," as Whitmarsh phrases it, and with that invitation come all the anxieties about what it means to read this text with self-control and whether it is possible to do so.[11]

To elucidate mimetic contagion more clearly by way of a particularly striking instance of it in the genre of the novel, it is worth meditating briefly on the complicated conception of Charicleia in Heliodorus' *Aethiopica*, an example which forms the basis of Whitmarsh's analysis and on which Germany's reading of erotic art also relies.[12] I am referring, of course, to the explanation provided in book 4 of the *Aethiopica* for the white pigmentation of Charicleia, the daughter of two dark-skinned, Ethiopian parents. As the Egyptian priest Calisiris translates a letter written in Ethiopic script from Charicleia's mother, Persinna happens to gaze upon a painting of the naked, white Andromeda at the moment of Charicleia's conception (*Aeth.* 4.8):

---

10. See esp. Webb 2009, 107–30, on the role of *phantasia* in *ekphrasis*. Once again, I do not intervene in debates here on "pictorialist" versus "enactivist" accounts of perception here (see §0.2 with n. 75), but regard both as valuable contributions to our understanding of *enargeia*. For my own "enactivist" reading of Encolpius in the picture gallery of Petronius' *Sat.*, see Ulrich *forthcoming* c.

11. See Whitmarsh 2002, 122, for quotation and discussion of reading with self-control (*sôphrosynê*).

12. See Whitmarsh 2002, 115–19; Germany 2016, 66–67 for discussion.

ἐπειδὴ δέ σε λευκὴν ἀπέτεκον, ἀπρόσφυλον Αἰθιόπων χροιὰν ἀπαυγάζουσαν, ἐγὼ μὲν τὴν αἰτίαν ἐγνώριζον ὅτι μοι παρὰ τὴν **ὁμιλίαν** τὴν **πρὸς** τὸν ἄνδρα **προσβλέψαι** τὴν Ἀνδρομέδαν ἡ **γραφὴ παρασχοῦσα** καὶ πανταχόθεν ἐπιδείξασα γυμνὴν (ἄρτι γὰρ αὐτὴν ἀπὸ τῶν πετρῶν ὁ Περσεὺς κατῆγεν), ὁμοιοειδὲς ἐκείνῃ τὸ σπαρὲν οὐκ εὐτυχῶς **ἐμόρφωσεν.**

When I gave birth to you, white as you are and revealing a skin color foreign to the Ethiopians, I realized the cause: a painting furnished Andromeda for me to look upon, at the moment when I was mingling with my husband, and exhibited her naked from every angle (as she was when Perseus was just leading her down from the rocks); and unfortunately, [the painting] transformed your skin so as to make it similar in form to her.

In Persinna's retelling of the tale, this *graphê*, "furnishing" the naked body of the mythical heroine for Persinna "to look upon" (προσβλέψαι), imprints the form of Andromeda on the fetus through its own agency, thereby replicating itself inside her body. According to Whitmarsh, "Charicleia can almost be said to be a walking *ekphrasis*" or an "illusionistic artwork"; "her white skin . . . the canvas upon which a wholly misleading cultural portrait is sciagraphed."[13] Significant for our discussion of mimetic contagion, however, is an astute point raised by Sarah Olsen about the active role this painting plays in the sexual intercourse between Hydaspes and Persinna. The painting as the focus of Persinna's gaze during intercourse participates, on the one hand, in something akin to a ménage à trois with the queen and her husband; on the other hand, the encounter is at once both procreative and contaminating, managing not only to accomplish what Hydaspes and Persinna could not over the course of ten years of normal intercourse—namely, pregnancy—but also uncannily adulterating that offspring with the interference of a third element.[14] Simply put, the painting has agency over its viewer, and far from Persinna having control over her own gaze, the dynamics of visuality, whereby a seemingly one-way street is suddenly transformed into a two-way interaction, can subtly shift at any moment and enact a transformation in the viewer.[15] This anxiety is brought to the fore

---

13. Whitmarsh 2002, 111.
14. See Olsen 2012, 310–13.
15. Cf. Olsen 2012, 312: "On some level, Andromeda plays a highly active role in the conception of Charicleia, imprinting the fetus with her own image. In a sense, she impregnates Persinna. As the

142   THE SHADOW OF AN ASS

again, moreover, in the recognition scene at the end of the novel, as the Ethiopians turn to the painting—that is, the *mimesis*—in order to authenticate, so to speak, the legitimacy of Charicleia's Ethiopian identity.

To set the stage for our consideration of mimetic contagion and divine intermediaries in the *Met.*, it will be necessary first to do a deep dive into Apuleius' own theory of *mimesis* in the *Apologia* and explicate its Platonic origins (§3.1). As we saw in this monograph's introduction, the danger of aesthetic pleasure lies in its threat of stultification and an end to forward movement or progress. In a reworking of Plato's anxieties over the pleasure(s) of imitation and its capacity to impede one's progress, then, Apuleius' opening praise of the mirror at *Apologia* 14 exposes his fears about *being* represented in a fixed, static medium—about having his representational afterlife established and legislated as unalterable.[16] For Plato, as we shall see, *mimesis* poses the risk not only of deception or misinterpretation, but also of contaminating one's progeny or afterlife, and Apuleius extends this concern in the *Apologia* to the reception of his own representational afterlife. If an encounter with aesthetic pleasure and *mimesis* is a fundamentally erotic experience in Plato's view—one which has the potential to contaminate one's spiritual offspring (according to the various metaphors of spiritual pregnancy and birth across Plato's corpus)[17]—Apuleius seems, at least prima facie, to endorse an illegitimate means of representation: Apuleius utilizes the "mirror" (*speculum*), which has the "fidelity" of a courtesan according to *Apol.* 14, to avoid the stultification or representational failures inherent in other mimetic media (e.g., statuary or painting).

After elucidating Apuleius' indebtedness to Platonic ideas and their reception in the *Apologia*'s discussion of mirrors and *mimesis*, we will turn to the *Metamorphoses* and analyze Lucius' programmatic encounters with three different *mimeses* of divinities: the Diana-Actaeon sculptural group in book 2, which Lucius imaginatively brings to life in an eroticizing *ekphrasis* (§3.2); a pantomime of the Judgment of Paris in book 10, in which the asinine *actor* sensuously describes the pornographic dance of a surrogate Venus in a mythi-

---

object of impregnation, fertilized physically by Hydaspes and visually by Andromeda, Persinna is rendered twice-passive." On the importance of children appearing similar to their parents, see, e.g., Hes. *W&D* 235: τίκτουσιν . . . γυναῖκες ἐοικότα τέκνα γονεῦσιν.

16. See *Fl.* 16 on Apuleius' own anxieties about the Carthaginians' dedication of a statue. Cf. also *Fl.* 7 on Alexander the Great's attempt to control any artistic rendering of his *imagines*. On the relationship between these epideictic speeches and Apuleius' theory of *mimesis* in the *Apologia*, see Too 1996, who also explores Apuleius' anxieties over the fixity of representation ("*rigor mortis*"). Cf. also Slater 1998 for a similar approach.

17. On Plato's reworking of the "pregnant male" tradition, see Leitao 2012, 182–226.

ENTRANCED BY THE MIRROR OF MYTH   143

cal farce (§3.3); and finally, another sculptural group of a goddess and a voyeur—
this time, of Isis standing on a pedestal and beside her, Lucius playing the role
of "statue" (*simulacrum*) integrated into the artistic ensemble (§3.4). What we
shall find in these three significant, interpretative episodes is not only a corresponding relationship between the divinities who direct Lucius' journey,[18] nor
for that matter a straightforward "evolution" (*Entwicklung*) in Lucius' relationship to sensuous versus spiritual delights;[19] but even more so, we shall discover
that Lucius is increasingly incorporated into the representational frame of the
mimesis. Indeed, because of the power *mimesis* possesses to break out of its
container, transgress the boundaries separating art and life, and thereby, propa-
gate itself in the life of its viewers, Lucius goes from being an outside (human)
observer of a fixed representation to becoming himself a (quadrupedal) participant in a spectacle, and finally, to being transformed into a figural representation in the sculptural group of a goddess.

Thus, as we shall see in §3.2, in the Diana-Actaeon statuary ensemble,
Lucius encounters himself by chance in the "reflection" (*Met.* 2.4: *simulacrum*)
of the mirroring water through which he views a "statue" (*simulacrum*) of
Actaeon. In so doing, he could (and should) recognize the implications of this
artistic representation for his life, namely, that he is a witting voyeur who is
about to be transformed into a quadruped and destined to suffer the threat of
being "ripped apart" (*sparagmos*).[20] Fast-forward to book 10, and Lucius once
again plays the role of voyeur providing an *ekphrasis* of what he sees—except,
in this case, he is *already* a quadruped and is slated to perform the final act in
the spectacle: a mimic reproduction of Pasiphaë, which would inevitably end
with beasts ripping him to shreds in an actual *sparagmos*.[21] By a narrow escape,

---

18. That the surrogate goddesses, or representations of goddesses, mirror or foreshadow Isis has long
    been recognized: see, e.g., Tatum 1969, 492; Gwyn Griffiths 1975, 29; Singleton 1977; Schlam 1992,
    118; *GCA* 2001, 409–11; Krabbe 2003, 580–87; Libby 2011, 302–5.

19. Whether or not the *Met.* is an *Entwicklungsroman*, or "novel of development," was one of the
    central concerns in assessing Lucius' "conversion" for Apuleius scholars before Winkler: see, e.g.,
    Nethercut 1968; Tatum 1969; Sandy 1974; Sandy 1978. Cf. also Finkelpearl 1991, who connects
    Lucius' failure of growth to his aesthetic experience and response to the erotic pantomime of
    Venus.

20. On the representation of Actaeon as a foreboding omen of Lucius' transformation and the per-
    petual threat of *sparagmos* in the subsequent books, see Heath 1992, 102–21. Others have noted,
    of course, the significance of the Diana-Actaeon atrium as a proleptic device: see, e.g., *GCA* 2001,
    115–16 *ad loc.* 2.4, who refers to this episode as a *"mise en abyme proleptique"* (91). Cf. also Shu-
    mate 1996, 67–71; Slater 1998; Freudenburg 2007.

21. On Lucius-ass' public copulation with a criminal as a potential Pasiphaë mime, see Zimmerman-
    de Graaf 1993; May 2008, 351 with n. 39. Cf. also *GCA* 2000, 26, on the relationship between the
    Diana-Actaeon *ekphrasis* and the pantomime of Venus (on which, see §3.3 below).

Lucius manages to avoid his own public humiliation and immolation. Fleeing to a nearby beach at Cenchreae and falling asleep, he wakes up in the middle of the night and gazes once again into mirroring water, where he encounters the *simulacrum* ("reflection" or "appearance") of a goddess. Then, after a series of initiations into Isis' cult, Lucius proudly stands on a pedestal in a sculptural group of his own—as a *simulacrum* ("statue") contemplating the *simulacrum* of a goddess with "delight" (*voluptas*); the internal audience for this spectacle, in turn, wanders around him to gaze upon the ensemble, as Lucius-*auctor* offers his readers an *ekphrasis* of himself. At the very end of the novel, in short, Lucius is stultified, transformed into an immobilized statue sitting beside a statue of the goddess and delighting in her erotic-religious aspect forever.

That Lucius is represented as a motionless statue after his human anamorphosis actualizes, on the one hand, Apuleius' anxieties from the *Apologia* about the capacity of *mimesis* to bring an end to temporality and impede forward progress. The thoroughly asinine Lucius may very well experience the *rigor mortis* of becoming a representational intermediary, especially if we consider that Diophanes' prophecy about Lucius "becom[ing] books" (*Met.* 2.12: *libros me futurum*) comes true in the end through the finalization of the textual medium by which our asinine *actor*'s tale is relayed to us. However, what I am more interested in analyzing in this chapter is the way in which Apuleius-as-author, through these episodes strategically placed in the architecture of his novel, reveals the risks that *mimesis* poses to those who interact with it and moreover, how he threatens to implicate *us* by our absorption in Lucius' narrative. Indeed, by revealing Lucius' increasing incorporation into the scenes with which he interacts, Apuleius invites us, I argue, to question our own attachments to this book, to interrogate our encounters with aesthetic pleasure, and to rethink our approach to viewing the divine in art.

3.1. Specular Fidelity: Mirror(ing) Magic in the Apologia and the Limits of Representation

In chapter 2, we looked at one of Apuleius' rebuttals to the charge of owning a mirror, which his accusers leveled at him as evidence of engaging in magic. In his *tour de force* summation and response to the subsidiary charges in the *Apologia*, Apuleius laconically addresses the accusation of "look[ing] into mirrors" (*Apol.* 103: *specula inspicis*) by portraying catoptric speculation as an

ENTRANCED BY THE MIRROR OF MYTH   145

inherently philosophical activity: "a philosopher must" (*debet philosophus*). While the previous chapter focused on situating Apuleius' *laus speculi* in a shared cultural and ethical-philosophical tradition of mirror-gazing, this section turns to the opening of the *Apologia*'s encomium of the mirror, where Apuleius eulogizes the *speculum* as a mimetic tool over against other forms of artistic representation, such as painting and sculpture. Indeed, beyond possessing all of the individual qualities that other artforms lack, Apuleius argues, the mirror can register motion or change over time in its subject. Other art forms, by contrast, fix or even stultify the object of depiction in a static and immobilized state, thereby literalizing the anxieties we surveyed in the introduction about the temporalities of aesthetic experience (e.g., Alcibiades' fear of permanent immobilization beside the Sirenic Socrates). This capacity to accommodate diachrony in representation thus transforms reflection into the ideal metaphor for metamorphosis.[22]

Although this stance on *mimesis* may seem at first glance anti-Platonic[23]—merely deployed as a rhetorical sleight-of-hand which Apuleius uses to defend himself against a legitimate charge of magical practice[24]—I suggest, on the contrary, that all of the Platonic anxieties about *mimesis*, which are later dramatized in the novels and novelistic texts,[25] collide in this clever treatment of the different registers of representation. As we shall see shortly, one of the primary metaphors Plato uses across his corpus to express concerns over *mimesis'* influence on its viewer comes from the realm of erotic love and from his anxieties over the "offspring" that issues thereof (i.e., whether it is legitimate or adulterated). As Diotima phrases it in her speech from the *Symposium*, to give birth to legitimate and lasting offspring constitutes the goal of all erotic and poetic experience, since "all men are pregnant in body and soul" (*Symp.* 206c1-3:

---

22. In this way, the *speculum* (according to Apuleius' analysis) overcomes the problems of "representing metamorphosis" in literature and art (on which, see Sharrock 1996) because it can simultaneously register synchronicity (i.e., a complete picture) and diachronicity (i.e., reading over time). Cf. also Paschalis 2002, 137–38, on the capacity of the mirror (esp. Apuleius' *speculum*) to exist in between the plastic and the poetic arts.

23. While Too 1996, 135, suggests that Apuleius "firmly reiterates the Platonic line on the inferiority of imitation," we may recall, in fact, that Plato's critique of *mimesis* in *Rep.* 10 works, first and foremost, by analogy to the empty and unreal images produced by a mirror, on which, cf. Libby 2011, 309–10.

24. On the legitimacy of the accusers' link between mirrors and magic, see Hunink 1997, 57–58. On the use of mirrors in magic more generally, see McCarty 1989.

25. The topics of *mimesis* and representation in the novels are well covered in the scholarship. For a representative sampling: see Whitmarsh 2002; Hermann 2007; Kahane 2007; Kirichenko 2013; Whitmarsh 2013; Dufallo 2013, 178–205; Bierl 2018; Grethlein 2021, 232–56.

κυοῦσιν . . . πάντες ἄνθρωποι καὶ κατὰ τὸ σῶμα καὶ τὴν ψυχήν) and all types of copulation—whether men "associate" (209c2: ὁμιλῶν) with women and it leads to human offspring or alternatively, with the Form of beauty itself and it leads to poetic output or "true virtue"—represent attempts to produce "offspring" (209d2: ἔκγονα) and thereby attain immortality. Simply put, through *homilein* ("associating"), humans attempt to overcome the diachronic experience of perpetual metamorphosis to which we are all subject in our mortal bodies. Temporality, transformation, and choice all cease to exist, according to Diotima, when one sits in the presence of divine beauty. As Stephen Halliwell has aptly noted, however, a fundamental problem of *mimesis*, which Plato raises in his censorious attack in *Republic* 10, is its likeness to "a courtesan engaging in a liaison which produces defective offspring."[26]

Significant for our purposes, Apuleius similarly presents his preference for the *speculum* over other forms of *mimesis* in the language of erotics, both in its connection to legitimate offspring and in its power to produce an adulterated representational afterlife. Much like Plato, the underlying anxieties at play for Apuleius are diachrony and metamorphosis. Let us first consider how Apuleius phrases this preference for the *speculum* in chapter 14, where we shall see him engaging more deeply with the Platonic position than scholars have previously recognized (*Apol.* 14):[27]

Cedo nunc, si et inspexisse me fateor, quod tandem crimen est **imaginem suam nosse** eamque non uno loco conditam, sed quoquo velis parvo speculo promptam gestare? An tu ignoras nihil esse aspectabilius homini nato quam formam suam? Equidem scio et **filiorum cariores esse qui similes videntur** et publicitus **simulacrum suum** cuique, quod videat, pro meritis praemio tribui. Aut quid sibi statuae et imagines variis artibus effigiatae volunt? Nisi forte quod artificio elaboratum laudabile habetur, hoc natura oblatum culpabile iudicandum est, cum sit in ea vel magis miranda et facilitas et similitudo. Quippe in omnibus manu faciundis imaginibus opera diutina sumitur, neque tamen si-

---

26. See Halliwell 1988, 135 *ad loc.* 603b1. See also 156 *ad loc.* 607e4: "Poetry is implicitly the kind of seductive *hetaira*, courtesan . . . with whom young men may fall disastrously in love, but from whom older and mature men, despite some lingering affection, will keep their distance." Cf. also Grethlein 2021, 75–106.

27. Too 1996, 135, who offers the most comprehensive reading of this passage, initially suggests that Apuleius "goes further than Plato in his critique of conventional modes of representation." In the end, however, and in a nod to Winkler, she makes it a matter of identity and self-fashioning. Cf. Slater 1998; Lateiner 2001 for similar readings of the *Apol.* onto the *Met.*

militudo aeque ut in speculis comparet; deest enim et luto vigor et saxo color et picturae rigor et **motus omnibus, qui praecipua fide similitudinem repraesentat**, cum in eo visitur imago mire relata, **ut similis, ita mobilis et ad omnem nutum hominis sui morigera**. Eadem semper contemplantibus aequaeva est **ab ineunte pueritia ad obeuntem senectam**, tot aetatis vices induit, tam varias habitudines corporis participat, tot vultus eiusdem laetantis vel dolentis imitatur. Enimuero quod luto fictum vel aere infusum vel lapide incusum vel cera inustum vel pigmento illitum vel alio quopiam humano artificio adsimulatum est, **non multa intercapedine temporis dissimile redditur et ritu cadaveris unum vultum et immobilem possidet**, tantum praestat imaginis artibus ad similitudinem referundam levitas illa speculi fabra et splendor opifex.

Look now, even if I confess that I looked into [a mirror], tell me, what accusation is there in knowing one's own image and in carrying it around wherever you want—not hidden in one place, but available in a small mirror? Or don't you know that nothing is more worthy for a mortal human to look at than his own appearance? Indeed, I know that children who appear similar [to their parents] are more beloved and likewise, that each person who deserves rewards is granted his own statue in public in order that he may see it. Or what else do statues and images fashioned through various arts signify? Unless perhaps that which is fashioned through artifice (i.e., sculpture) is considered praiseworthy, but this one offered by nature (i.e., a reflection in a mirror) is to be judged blameworthy, even though in it the facility and similarity of representation are perhaps more marvelous. Clearly, in the crafting of all images by hand, long labor is spent, and still, they never attain to a similarity that compares with that which is found in mirrors. For clay is lacking in vigor, rock in color, and painting in firmness, and all of them are lacking in motion, which conveys similarity with noteworthy fidelity. Since in [a mirror], an image is seen, marvelously rendered, both similar and mobile, and subservient to every nod of its man. For those who are looking into it, it always remains at their same age from the entrance of boyhood to dying old age. It adopts so many changes of age, participates in so many varying appearances of the body, and imitates so many expressions of the same man, when he takes pleasure as well as when he endures pain. For anything molded from clay or cast in bronze or carved in stone or imprinted in wax or spread with color or imitated by any other human skill is rendered dissimilar in no great space of time; in the manner of a corpse, it possesses one motionless face. So

148   THE SHADOW OF AN ASS

much does that skillful smoothness and artistic shine of a mirror surpass the representational arts in terms of returning similarity.

At the outset of this passage, Apuleius explicitly situates his eulogy of the mirror in the Platonic self-knowledge tradition discussed in §2.3. We may recall, for instance, that Seneca, in his own appropriation of this tradition, claims that mirrors were invented "so that man himself might know himself" (*Quaest. nat.* 1.17.4: *ut homo ipse se **nosset***; cf. *imaginem suam **nosse***).[28] Unlike Seneca, however, Apuleius quickly directs his argument to the mimetic value of offspring in particular. Children who "appear similar" to their parents (i.e., legitimate)[29] are "more beloved" and their likeness is implicitly compared to statues—*simulacra* or physical representational media, which publicly declare an individual's deserts. In a striking reversal of Diotima's discourse about the desire for immortality attained through offspring, then, Apuleius renders the production of progeny merely another mode of imitative representation, one appreciated for its mimetic verisimilitude and thus, akin to other forms of "plastic" arts.

In the next section of chapter 14, Apuleius attacks other forms of *mimesis* in an attempt to recuperate his self-image from the control that society might leverage over it—or, in Yun Lee Too's reading, to avoid a kind of representational death.[30] What has similarly gone overlooked in this paradoxical privileging of specular *mimesis*, however, is the direct line Apuleius draws between erotics and motion. The *speculum* possesses its "noteworthy fidelity" (*praecipua fides*) because it registers "motion" (*motus*) over time, and this representational metaphor implicitly borrows from the discourse of marital—or more precisely, sexual—faithfulness.[31] By contrast, the problem Apuleius identifies with other

---

28. We may further link this play with the Socratic *gnôthi seauton* tradition to Narcissus, about whom Tiresias delivers the inverted prophecy—"provided he does not know himself" (*Met.* 3.348: *si se non **noverit***). On this as Ovid's intentional play with Socrates' dictum from the *Phaedrus*, see Bartsch 2006, 84–85. See also Taylor 2008, 19–26, who reads the passage from Seneca as an allusion to the self-knowledge tradition from *Alc. 1*.

29. For the *locus classicus* on similarity in childbirth, see Hes. *W&D* 235 (n. 15 above). See also Cat. 61.215–24 and Mart. *Ep.* 6.27. In Apuleius' milieu, see Charit. *Callirh.* 2.11.2. On the importance in Greek culture of similarity of appearance for claims of legitimacy, see Whitmarsh 2002, 115, who cites Gow 1952, 2.334 with references.

30. See Too 1996, 135: "The author suggests . . . that art is a device for murdering people, as it induces into its subjects, not the *rigor* of the three-dimensional object which a painting is said to lack, but *rigor mortis*. Art annihilates the vitality of its subjects and transforms them into corpses." Cf. also Lateiner 2001 on immobilization.

31. The *locus classicus* for representational fidelity in Latin literature is Horace's *Ars poet.* 133–34: *nec verbo verbum curabis **reddere** fidus / interpres, nec desilies imitator in artum* (on which, see Cope-

modes of representation, both two-dimensional painting and three-dimensional sculpture, is the fact that they do not change with the subject and thus, quite literally objectify him or her in a static state. For this reason, Apuleius complains of the "corpse-like manner" (*ritu cadaveris*) in which other mimetic media cast a subject in a fixed and unchanging image, one which is "rendered dissimilar in no great space of time" (*non multa intercapedine temporis dissimile redditur*). Alternatively, the *speculum* registers change over time, mirroring its subject "from the entrance of boyhood to dying old age" (*ab ineunte pueritia ad obeuntem senectam*).

It is crucial to note here that Apuleius eulogizes the mirror not only in the discourse of mimetic "fidelity" (*fides*), but subliminally links it to the ambivalent association with a courtesan. His highest praise for the *speculum*'s verisimilitude, after all, is the fact that it is "both similar and mobile and subservient to every nod of its man" (*ut similis, ita mobilis et ad omnem nutum hominis sui* **morigera**), where *morigerus* is a term associated with prostitutes and courtesans as early as Roman comedy.[32] It is evident that Apuleius was well aware of the erotic undertones of *morigerus*, since he employs it elsewhere to describe, for instance, the men whom Pamphile transforms into "cattle or any other creature she wants" (2.5: *in pecua et quodvis animal*) in a mere "moment of time" (*puncto*) because they are "less submissive" (2.5: *minus* **morigeros**) to her.[33] Indeed, the danger of interacting with Pamphile—"all-love," by name, and another Circe or Siren figure in the *Met.*[34]—is identical to the seductive power of the encounter with aesthetic pleasure, which we surveyed in chapter 1. One risks metamorphosis into a "herd animal," the temporality of the transformation is immediate, and perhaps most importantly, even when one thinks s/he has control over the interaction, one quickly becomes "subservient," losing

---

land 1991, 28–30). The notion of mimetic "return" (*reddere*) is precisely what is at issue in the Apuleius passage (cf. *redditur*). On the more regular function of *fides* in erotic contexts, see *ThLL* 6.1.679.71–680.12. The term usually relates to betrayed fidelity (esp., in elegiac contexts) as in Horace C. 1.5.5–6, where the narrator "lament[s] the changed faithfulness and divinities [of his beloved]" (**fidem**/*mutatosque deos flebit*). See also C. 1.33.1–4.

32. See *ThLL* 8.0.1491.4–8, where the usage is delimited *speciatim in re veneria*. See also Adams 1982, 164, for the development of the idiom *morem gero* and its later associations with passive sexual behavior.

33. With this passage, cf. *Met.* 2.16, where Lucius begs Photis to let her hair down "in order to be more submissive to [him]" (*ut mihi* **morem** *plenius* **gesseris**). See also *Apol.* 74.7, where Apuleius lambasts Aemilianus for debased behavior (as a receiving partner) in his youth: "once, in his boyhood, before he was deformed by that baldness, [Aemilianus] was submissive to his pederasts in all manner of unspeakable behaviors" (*olim in pueritia, priusquam isto calvitio deformaretur, emasculatoribus suis ad omnia infanda* **morigerus**).

34. See, e.g., Schlam 1992, 68–69.

mobility or temporality and instead, being fixed in a perpetual state of inanimation.

Before we turn to the *ekphrasis* of Byrrhena's atrium (§3.2), where we shall see Apuleius narrativize these anxieties about illegitimate erotics, stupefaction, and metamorphosis in Lucius' encounter with a Diana-Actaeon statuary ensemble, it will be useful to review more comprehensively the Platonic origins of Apuleius' (seemingly) oxymoronic position on the *speculum* and to consider the influence that such philosophical discourses had for understanding mimetic contagion in the novels writ large. After all, the *katoptron*—specifically, a handheld mirror, which one can point at different objects, like Apuleius' *speculum* in the *Apologia*—constitutes the first analogy to which Socrates appeals in order to critique the metaphysical deception of *mimesis*. At 10.596e1–3, Socrates suggests that his interlocutor could create the entire universe—the sun, the heavenly bodies, the earth, himself, animals, and so forth—if only he "took up a mirror and carried it around with him everywhere" (596d9–e1: λαβὼν κάτοπτρον περιφέρειν πανταχῇ; cf. *Apol.* 14: *quoquo uelis paruo speculo promptam gestare*).

Of course, scholars have long debated this analogy of Plato's, which, in the words of Ernst Gombrich, "haunted the philosophy of art ever since."[35] Yet, in doing so, they have focused primarily on issues of dimensionality and deception—for example, on Socrates' problematic lack of an account of statuary (three-dimensional *mimesis*) in his treatment of imitation[36] or alternatively, his famous dictum that *mimesis* is some "third-level removed from reality" (10.599a1: τριττὰ ἀπέχοντα τοῦ ὄντος).[37] Although we shall see these elements of the critique ironically reconfigured in Byrrhena's statuary ensemble and in the pantomime of Venus, an oft-overlooked feature of Plato's censorious position is the fact that it is phrased metaphorically in terms of an unhealthy erotic attachment. Socrates' banishment of Homer and the poets from his ideal society in *Rep.* 10 is based not on the aesthetic or ethical qualities of the poetry per se (as in *Republic* 2 and 3),[38] but rather on the potential

---

35. Gombrich 1977, 79. For a recent treatment of this issue, see Grethlein 2021, 75–106 with bibliography.

36. See, e.g., Murray 1996, 200 *ad loc.* 598b6–8: "The generalization from painting to mimetic art as a whole . . . is slipped in unobtrusively; but the argument just used in relation to painting cannot be straightforwardly applied to a three-dimensional medium like sculpture, let alone poetry."

37. Cf., however, Halliwell 1988, 116 *ad loc.* 597e3, who connects this "metaphor of 'two removes'" to "the language of family inheritance, royal succession, etc."—situations, that is, where anxiety about the legitimacy of offspring is palpable.

38. On the traditional disjunction scholars have drawn between the discussion of *mimesis* in books

ENTRANCED BY THE MIRROR OF MYTH 151

for inferior issue or even bastard offspring, which results from engaging with representation and falling in love with it.[39] Thus, at *Rep.* 10.603a7–b2, Socrates likens painting to a courtesan, with whom one can associate to the detriment of one's "pure" bloodline:

τοῦτο τοίνυν διομολογήσασθαι βουλόμενος ἔλεγον ὅτι ἡ γραφικὴ καὶ ὅλως ἡ μιμητικὴ πόρρω μὲν τῆς ἀληθείας ὂν **τὸ αὑτῆς ἔργον** ἀπεργάζεται, πόρρω δ᾽ αὖ φρονήσεως ὄντι τῷ ἐν ἡμῖν **προσομιλεῖ** τε καὶ **ἑταίρα** καὶ φίλη ἐστὶν ἐπ᾽ οὐδενὶ ὑγιεῖ οὐδ᾽ ἀληθεῖ.

It was with the aim of getting agreement on just this point that I said that painting, and the mimetic art as a whole, produces work which is far from the truth; and far from wisdom too is the element within us with which it consorts like a courtesan and beloved, for no sound or true purpose.

The anxiety expressed here concerns the "outcome" *mimesis* accomplishes in its viewer, and the progeny that issues forth from such an erotic entanglement is, as Socrates suggests, potentially inferior or even illegitimate (10.603b4):

φαύλη ἄρα φαύλῳ συγγιγνομένη φαῦλα γεννᾷ ἡ μιμητική.

And so, the mimetic art—an inferior artform copulating with an inferior counterpart—begets inferior offspring.

It is thus because of its capacity to engender unhealthy erotic attachment and the undesirable issue that results from such copulation with *mimesis* that Socrates excludes Homer and the poets from his state, "just like those who have fallen in love with someone, but nevertheless restrain themselves even by force, if they believe the love to be unbeneficial" (*Rep.* 10.607e4–5: ὥσπερ οἱ ποτέ του ἐρασθέντες, ἐὰν ἡγήσωνται μὴ ὠφέλιμον εἶναι τὸν ἔρωτα, βίᾳ μέν, ὅμως δὲ ἀπέχονται).[40]

2–3 and that of *Rep.* 10, see Murray 1996, 3–6. For further discussion and one possible solution, see Germany 2016, 78–85. See also Halliwell 2002, 48–61, on the contours of the earlier and latter discussions of *mimesis*.

39. See esp. Grethlein 2021, 77–91, on "immersion" in Plato's aesthetic theory.

40. On which, see Halliwell 2002, 55: "it is revealing that the *Republic*'s second treatment of mimesis, in book 10, is framed by quasi-confessional expressions of Socrates' (and, at some level, Plato's) closeness to the poetry he criticizes . . . at the end of the section . . . he goes on to speak in the

The same anxiety recurs in the *Phaedrus*—a dialogue devoted, in general, to exploring healthy and distorting forms of *erôs*. There, Socrates tells a *mythos* about the invention of writing in Egypt and concludes with a famous analogy between speeches and painting (*Phaedr.* 275d4–e5):

δεινὸν γάρ που, ὦ Φαῖδρε, τοῦτ᾽ ἔχει γραφή, καὶ ὡς ἀληθῶς ὅμοιον ζωγραφίᾳ. καὶ γὰρ τὰ ἐκείνης **ἔκγονα** ἕστηκε μὲν ὡς ζῶντα, ἐὰν δ᾽ ἀνέρῃ τι, σεμνῶς πάνυ σιγᾷ. ταὐτὸν δὲ καὶ οἱ λόγοι· δόξαις μὲν ἂν ὥς τι φρονοῦντας αὐτοὺς λέγειν, ἐὰν δέ τι ἔρῃ τῶν λεγομένων βουλόμενος μαθεῖν, **ἕν τι σημαίνει μόνον ταὐτὸν ἀεί**. ὅταν δὲ ἅπαξ γραφῇ, κυλινδεῖται μὲν πανταχοῦ πᾶς λόγος ὁμοίως παρὰ τοῖς ἐπαΐουσιν, ὡς δ᾽ αὕτως παρ᾽ οἷς οὐδὲν προσήκει, καὶ οὐκ ἐπίσταται λέγειν οἷς δεῖ γε καὶ μή. πλημμελούμενος δὲ καὶ οὐκ ἐν δίκῃ λοιδορηθεὶς τοῦ πατρὸς ἀεὶ δεῖται βοηθοῦ· αὐτὸς γὰρ οὔτ᾽ ἀμύνασθαι οὔτε βοηθῆσαι δυνατὸς αὑτῷ.

For writing has this strange sort of quality, Phaedrus, and is, in reality, similar to painting. On the one hand, its offspring stand as if living, but if you ask them something, they remain very solemnly silent. Speeches also have this same quality: you would think that they speak as if they have some thought, but if you ask them about any of the words spoken because you want to learn, they indicate only one and the same thing always. Once it has been written, however, every speech is tossed about from mouth to mouth everywhere similarly among those who know, just as much as it is bandied about among people for whom it is not at all fitting, and it does not know to whom it ought to speak and to whom it shouldn't. And when [a speech] is wronged or abused unjustly, it always needs its father as a helper: for on its own, it is able neither to defend nor help itself.

While Socrates here avoids the more explicit language of bastardy, the same problem with *mimesis* persists—namely, the inferiority or failure of representation's "offspring" (ἔκγονα). Socrates together with Phaedrus thus seeks to find the "legitimate brother" (276a1–2: ἀδελφὸν γνήσιον) of a written *logos*, which is "born better and stronger than it."[41] We may note, furthermore, that the illegitimacy of mimetic offspring, in the case both of painting and written speech, comes from its inability to register change over time in the viewer/listener.

language of a regretful, nostalgic lover, withdrawing from a *grande passion* yet only able to relinquish it with immense psychological effort."

41. For the classic discussion of the role of paternity and legitimacy in the written-ness of the *logos*, see Derrida 1972, 271–83.

There is a slippage, however, in Apuleius' reorientation of the Platonic anxiety: whereas the fear of adulterated offspring in the Platonic criticism of written speech relates to a failure of education and the complications of interpretation that arise from the static nature of the object represented, Apuleius prefers the "courtesan" fidelity of the mirror precisely because it transforms in relation to its subject. In that sense, the viewer or listener maintains control over the "off-spring" *mimesis* produces rather than "possess[ing] one motionless face in the manner of a corpse."

If the *Republic* and the *Phaedrus* exhibit anxieties about the power of representation to infect its viewer/hearer with illegitimate ideas and to produce bastard offspring, Diotima's speech in the *Symposium* extends the reproduction metaphor to all aesthetic experience and in so doing, makes a distinction between categories of viewers, or in the case of erotic-aesthetic experience, between types of lovers (i.e., physical and spiritual).[42] As we saw above, Diotima argues in her discourse on *Erôs* that "all men are pregnant" but later differentiates between those who are "teeming in body" (208e1–2: οἱ μὲν . . . ἐγκύμονες . . . κατὰ σώματα) and those "teeming in soul" (208e5–209a1: οἱ δὲ κατὰ τὴν ψυχήν). The former category of men "turn their attentions toward women and are erotic in this way" (208e2–3), and so, believe that they produce "immortality," "memory," and "happiness" through their human offspring. The latter category of men, on the other hand, produce "thought" and "virtue," which we see most evidently from the "offspring" (209d2: ἔκγονα) of Homer, Hesiod, and the other poets. Through "grasping beauty and associating with it" (209c2–3: ἁπτόμενος . . . τοῦ καλοῦ καὶ **ὁμιλῶν** αὐτῷ; note the verb *homilein*), therefore, this kind of pregnant soul "gives birth and produces those things with which it was long teeming" (ἃ πάλαι ἐκύει τίκτει καὶ γεννᾷ). Diotima concludes, then, that a soul in this category, which is further "educated in erotic matters" (210e2–3: πρὸς τὰ ἐρωτικὰ παιδαγωγηθῇ) "gives birth not to images of virtue, since it has not grasped an image, but rather to true virtue, since it has grasped the truth" (212a3–5: τίκτειν οὐκ **εἴδωλα ἀρετῆς**, ἅτε οὐκ εἰδώλου ἐφαπτομένῳ, ἀλλὰ ἀληθῆ, ἅτε τοῦ ἀληθοῦς ἐφαπτομένῳ).[43] Once again, this concerns the

---

42. For the most thorough discussion of the categorical distinctions between different kinds of pregnancies in the *Symposium*, see Sheffield 2001, who distinguishes throughout between the "lover of the lower mysteries" (LLM) and the "lover of the higher mysteries" (LHM). Cf. also Ferrari 1992, esp. 253–62, on the connection between those pregnant in soul and the birth of discourse.

43. There is an irony in the phrase *eidôla aretês*, as Alcibiades' goal in stripping Socrates and his *logoi* of their external satyr hide deploys a near (but importantly, distinct) repetition: if one opens up Socrates' laughable *logoi*, according to Alcibiades, s/he will see *agalmat' aretês* (222a4)—similarly

paradox and danger of education, which we already saw thematized in §0.0 and which Apuleius ironically reproduces with his praise of the courtesan-like "fidelity" of the *speculum*: if you "sit beside" the object of aesthetic pleasure, you may just stay there for the rest of your life; and this aesthetic experience could be transcendent or toxic depending on the nature of the object (i.e., medicine or poison) and whether it will give birth to legitimate or adulterated children inside of you.

Therefore, while we can trace the roots of Apuleius' mimetic doctrine on the *speculum* in the *Republic* and *Phaedrus*—as they are concerned, respectively, with producing "legitimate" offspring and preserving representational fidelity—we learn from the *Symposium* that there is something akin to our ancient reader-response theory associated with erotic-aesthetic experience. The kind of "offspring" that issues forth from an encounter with beauty is dependent, after all, on the character of the viewer—or in my framework, on the seriousness of the *lector*. We can see that the anxieties about contaminated reproduction which are associated with *mimesis*, moreover, permeate the ancient novels in all sorts of ways, from Achilles Tatius' *Leucippe and Clitophon*, which opens with an *ekphrasis* of the rape of Europa,[44] to Longus, whose "Dionysiac paintings" adorning the walls of a temple at the opening of *D&C* 4 threaten retrospectively to reshape the inner world of the characters through mimetic contagion.[45] In fact, Robert Germany's chapter on cultic and erotic art concludes with an analysis of the Babylonian canopy of the tryst between Ares and Aphrodite which hangs over the bed of the idealized couple at the opening of Xenophon of Ephesus' *Ephesiaca*.[46] There, the "inserted image," or *Bildeinsatz*,[47] functions not only to model divine paradigms for our hero and

---

a representational device, but a divine intermediary rather than an illusory reflection. As I have argued elsewhere (Ulrich 2017) and as we shall see further in §4.1, Apuleius is well aware of the representational play in Alcibiades' speech in the *Symposium*: he redeploys the phrase *simulacra deorum* across his corpus to invoke this precise distinction between "reflections" and "statues" of gods/virtue.

44. On the role of *L&C*'s opening *ekphrasis* in staging episodes of *mis*reading, see Morales 2004, 37–48, and esp. 48: "The painting of Europa/Selene is programmatic in its foregrounding of visual appearance as a site of error. . . . Reading is thus staged as erring, or, more specifically, monoscopic reading is staged as erring, as misreading." On the ways in which the painting of Europa infiltrates not only the main narrative, but also the mini-inset narratives of *L&C*, see Reeves 2007.

45. See Zeitlin 1994, 157–65, on the significance of Dionysophanes' garden park in book 4 for the whole novel. Cf. also Ulrich forthcoming a for an updated interpretation of the "Dionysiac paintings."

46. See Germany 2016, 65–71.

47. On *Bildeinsätze* and their significance more generally in the ancient novels, see Steiner 1969. On the significance of such encounters with art in the Greek novels and Petronius, see, e.g., Dufallo 2013, 191–96.

ENTRANCED BY THE MIRROR OF MYTH   155

heroine, but also, through the physical transfer of vision and the psychological impact of art, enacts a transformation in the heroine from a chaste and pure Artemis to a seductive and sexually voracious Aphrodite.

If we return, however, to our *locus classicus* of mimetic contagion discussed above—Charicleia's contaminated birth due to Persinna's ménage à trois with her husband and a painting of the naked Andromeda—we may now view this motivating episode for Heliodorus' entire novel as an overly literal narrativization of Plato's ontological and perceptual anxieties about *mimesis*. In the midst of a "legitimate" experience of intimacy between husband and wife, where Heliodorus points up the ambivalence of this encounter by using Plato's word for "consorting" with a *hetaira* (*proshomilein*) as well as the term for more "legitimate" copulation (*homilia*) to describe Persinna's and Hydaspes' afternoon delight (*Aeth.* 4.8.4),[48] an artistic rendering, which displays a tantalizing erotic nude, foists itself upon Persinna at a moment of sexual (and perceptual) vulnerability. In doing so, it transforms acceptable erotic love between married partners into ménage à trois and ultimately, influences the procreative outcome of the sexual encounter.

This episode, moreover, dramatizes Platonic anxieties about dimensionality and perspective in *Rep.* 10, which I hinted at above and to which we shall see Apuleius also allude in the next section. For as Olsen notes, the two-dimensional painting in the bedchamber seems to become three-dimensional in Persinna's erotic encounter with it, since she sees the naked body of Andromeda "from all sides" (πανταχόθεν);[49] the painting comes to life, in a sense, stepping out of its frame for a full-frontal visual experience. Some have even conjectured, in fact, that Heliodorus engages with a real iconographic tradition from Roman wall-painting, as some frescoes (e.g., fig. 1) seem to represent Perseus' darker hand supporting Andromeda's white arm as he "lead[s] her down from the rocks" (ἀπὸ τῶν πετρῶν . . . κατῆγεν).[50] As readers familiar with the novel will recall, the only remnant of Charicleia's Ethiopian identity is a ring of dark skin around

---

48. In fact, it is tempting to suggest that Heliodorus deliberately inverts the terms of legitimate and illegitimate encounters. We may recall that, in Plato's critique of *mimesis* in the *Republic*, Socrates speaks of our souls "consorting with" (10.603b1: προσομιλεῖ) *mimesis* as with a *hetaira*; but in the *Symposium*, Diotima describes souls "associating with" (209c2: ὁμιλῶν) beauty. In Heliodorus, Persinna first describes her "legitimate" encounter with her husband in terms of "consorting"— "your father was consorting with me" (4.8.4: μοι **προσωμίλει** τότε ὁ πατὴρ ὁ σός)—but only later uses the language of "associating" (*homilia*) after the painting furnishes a naked Andromeda.

49. See Olsen 2012, 311 with n. 1.

50. On these frescoes, see esp. Phillips 1968. Most renditions of Andromeda's rescue represent the chains on the wrist, not the upper arm; but there is also an eighth-century illuminated manuscript drawing, which may have had an earlier archetype and which has dark chains or rings on the upper arms (on which, see Phillips 1968, 18 with plate 16).

Fig. 1. Perseus leading Andromeda down from the rock. Pompeian wall-painting from the House of the Dioscuri (VI.9.6), first century CE
(Courtesy of the Ministry of Culture, National Archaeological Museum of Naples.)

her white arm. Though admittedly speculative, the ring of dark skin around Charicleia's arm in that case would not merely be a vestigial marker of Hydaspes' paternity, the last remnant of the identity of her "legitimate" father, but could also very possibly represent a full realization of Plato's fears about *mimesis*. A specific iconographic type of Andromeda, a portrait of her naked but with Perseus' darker hand surrounding one of her snow-white arms, has inter-

ENTRANCED BY THE MIRROR OF MYTH   157

fered in the intercourse and adulterated the conception of the heroine, leaving a ring as a remnant of the contagion.[51]

In the next section, we shall see how Apuleius engages in precisely the same kind of play with aesthetic allusion and mimetic contagion in Byrrhena's atrium. The sculptural ensemble of Diana-Actaeon functions, on the one hand, like the *Bildeinsatz* ("image insert") in Xenophon of Ephesus' *Ephesiaca* inasmuch as it models a potential paradigm for Lucius' interactions with the divine and furthermore, enacts a transformation in him through his visual encounter with art. The *Met.* is unlike the Greek novels, however, since its *telos* is not the reunification of the idealized, elite couple followed by marriage and the production of "legitimate" offspring. What we shall see Lucius give birth to—or more precisely, what his interactions with artistic representations will give birth to *in him*—is of a rather different kind, and this is why it has been useful to review Apuleius' theory of *mimesis* and its Platonic filiation. Lucius, first through seeing himself reflected in a mirror embedded within the statuary ensemble, is inspired to reenact the representation in his own life, and this sets the tone for his aesthetic encounters throughout the rest of the novel. However, if specular fidelity is that of a courtesan (as it is in the *Apologia*), then we may be invited to question Lucius' own incorporation and later statuization in a series of further representational ensembles, which play with statues, motion, and reflections.

3.2. Simulacrum Actaeon, *Mimetic Contagion, and the Viewer in Byrrhena's Atrium (Met. 2.4)*

Now that we have seen both the Platonic origins of Apuleius' treatment of *mimesis* in the *Apologia* and the discernible influence of Plato's reception on the ancient novelistic tradition, it is fitting to turn to our scene in the *Metamorphoses*, where Lucius-*actor* lights upon a grand-scale statuary ensemble in his aunt Byrrhena's atrium, and so moved by the naturalistic verisimilitude of the artistry, he sets out to describe it in the mode of a poeticizing *ekphrasis*. How this *ekphrasis* functions within the novel—whether it is a plot device, a didactic or prophetic warning, or merely an impressive display piece—has long been a

---

51. This reading is subliminally suggested in Olsen 2012, 315, but I am indebted for this interpretation primarily to Emilio Capettini, who generously read and commented on an earlier draft of this chapter.

source of debate in Apuleius criticism.[52] What has largely escaped the notice of scholars, however, is the way in which this atrium scene propagates itself rather disconcertingly in Lucius' life at the end of the *Metamorphoses* and threatens, furthermore, to ripple out even into the real life of readers, if they do not "actively" read.[53]

For as we shall see, the statuary ensemble puts on display a *simulacrum* of a voyeur already (partially) transformed into a quadruped for his voyeurism and gazing upon a goddess mediated through a mirror. As I suggested in the introduction to this chapter, Lucius-*actor* ultimately replicates what he sees in this atrium in his own life in two different encounters with goddesses: first, as an asinine voyeur himself describing the striptease of a goddess; and then, as a *simulacrum* of an already transformed voyeur standing next to the *simulacrum* of a goddess and mirroring her. Simply put, as a result of mimetic contagion, Lucius becomes not only a version of Actaeon from myth, nor merely the wittingly voyeuristic instantiation of "Actaeon" represented in Byrrhena's atrium. Rather, through his illicit fascination with a representation—and in particular, through the mechanism of the "courtesan" *mimesis* of the *speculum*—he is transformed into a *simulacrum* of a person who has undergone metamorphosis for seeing illicit sights and is thereafter fixed in a goddess' statuary ensemble. Or to phrase it in Platonic terms, Lucius "consorts with" different *mimeses* of erotic love and magic, and as a consequence, those imitative arts reproduce or give birth to something in him: an illegitimate desire to experience and participate in that which is represented.

It is necessary to note that cynical readers of the *Metamorphoses* have already recognized Lucius' stultification and statuization under the "gaze" of the goddess. For Niall Slater, for instance, Lucius' loss of control over his own gaze is paralleled by his own transformation "into a virtually inanimate thing":[54]

> Although not actually turned to stone in the process, Lucius has become part of a reconstituted sculpture group, under the gaze of Isis.[55]

---

52. For copious discussion and bibliography on this passage, see *GCA* 2001, 91–113. For particularly useful and compelling readings, see Heath 1992, esp. 121–28; Shumate 1996, 67–71; Slater 1998; Paschalis 2002; Freudenburg 2007.
53. On Apuleius' use of this kind of "ontological metalepsis," see Ulrich 2022. Grethlein 2021, 206, recognizes a similar collapsing of inner and outer receptions, and an analogous pedagogical impulse in a near predecessor to Apuleius, the *tabula Cebetis*.
54. Slater 1998, 40.
55. Slater 1998, 39. Cf., however, the discussion of the Groningen commentators (*GCA* 2015, 415–16), who see a different iconographic transformation of Lucius here—that is, into a representation of Apollo or Helios.

ENTRANCED BY THE MIRROR OF MYTH   159

Once again, though, my interest here is not in assessing Lucius' "conversion" in the Isis book, but rather in analyzing the way in which Apuleius assimilates us, his readers, to the internal audience. In book 11, as we shall see, sensitive readers are placed in the very same position Lucius inhabits in Byrrhena's atrium: they become spectators of a statuary ensemble that may implicate them without their conscious awareness. In that sense, *lectores scrupulosi* are confronted with the desires this text reproduces in them through their encounter with it. Indeed, Apuleius makes it clear through his use of the internal audience that we cannot read this text without being contaminated like Lucius by a kind of Actaeonic voyeurism.[56]

Let us turn now to the text itself, where we will see a statuary ensemble transformed into a motive, erotic narrative via the mirroring water into which the narrator invites us to look (*Met.* 2.4):

> Ecce lapis Parius in Dianam factus tenet libratam totius loci medietatem, signum perfecte luculentum, veste reflatum, procursu vegetum, introeuntibus obvium et maiestate numinis venerabile. Canes utrimquesecus deae latera muniunt, qui canes et ipsi lapis erant. His oculi minantur, aures rigent, nares hiant, ora saeviunt, et, sicunde de proximo latratus ingruerit, eum putabis de faucibus lapidis exire; et—in quo summum specimen operae fabrilis egregius ille signifex prodidit—sublatis canibus in pectus arduis pedes imi resistunt, currunt priores.
>
> Pone tergum deae saxum insurgit in speluncae modum muscis et herbis et foliis et virgulis et sicubi pampinis et arbusculis alibi de lapide florentibus. Splendet intus umbra signi de nitore lapidis. Sub extrema saxi margine poma et uvae faberrime politae dependent, quas ars aemula naturae veritati similes explicuit. Putes ad cibum inde quaedam, cum mustulentus autumnus maturum colorem adflaverit, posse decerpi, et si fontem, qui deae vestigio discurrens in lenem vibratur undam, pronus aspexeris, credes illos ut rure pendentes racemos inter cetera veritatis nec agitationis officio carere. Inter medias frondes lapidis Actaeon simulacrum, curioso optutu in deam <deor>sum proiectus, iam in cervum ferinus et in saxo simul et in fonte loturam Dianam opperiens visitur.

And behold, Parian marble fashioned into the effigy of Diana occupied the middle of the whole area in balance, a very brilliant statue, with its garment

---

56. In this sense, my reading of Byrrhena's atrium expands on the work of Heath 1992, 121–28; Freudenburg 2007; and Kirichenko 2008b, the last of whom views the implication of the reader as a fundamental function of the novel.

blowing in the wind, vividly running forward, coming to meet those who enter, and venerable with the majesty of a divinity. Dogs guarded the flanks of the goddess on either side, and the dogs themselves were also made of marble. Their eyes were threatening, their ears stiff, their nostrils flared, and their mouths were raging, and if any barking burst in from nearby, you would think that it came from the marble's jaws—and the aspect in which that excellent sculptor exhibited the greatest proof of his craftsmanship—with the dogs lifted high so as to show their chest, their hind feet stood firm but their front feet seemed to run.

Behind the back of the goddess, the rock rose in the manner of a cave, with moss, grass, leafage, bushes, here vines, there little trees all blossoming out of the marble. Inside, the statue's shadow glistened from the sheen of the marble. Under the furthest edge of the rock, apples and skillfully polished grapes hung down, which art vying with nature displayed to resemble reality. You would think that certain things from there could be plucked for food, when the wine-bringing autumn breathed in the ripening color, and if you bent down and looked into the fountain that runs along by the goddess' feet shimmering in a gentle wave, you would believe that those clusters, hanging there as if in the country, did not lack the quality of motion among other aspects of reality. In the middle of the marble's foliage, a statue of Actaeon was seen, both in the rock and in the fountain's reflection, leaning over with a curious stare downward toward the goddess, already wild and turning into a stag and awaiting Diana about to bathe.

Considering Plato's anxieties about the capacity of *mimesis* to delude its viewer and produce illegitimate offspring, it is striking that Apuleius, a self-proclaimed *philosophus Platonicus*, has mediated a three-dimensional sculptural group through the two-dimensional medium of mirroring water. Indeed, it is worth pointing out, in light of Apuleius' own theory of *mimesis*, that there remains no corresponding Diana-Actaeon statuary ensemble of this size or detail in the extant material record.[57] The closest analogue we have in the material remains is the famous Lanuvium Actaeon (fig. 2 [also this book's jacket]), which displays a life-sized statue of an untransformed Actaeon, holding a deerskin and being attacked by dogs: that is, "representing" metamorphosis "by

---

57. See Schlam 1984; Slater 1998.

Fig. 2. Actaeon being attacked by dogs. Marble statue from Lanuvium, second century CE (Courtesy of the © Trustees of the British Museum.)

implication."[58] We know of other statuary scenes of a nearly comparable scale and level of detail, however, such as the Punishment of Dirce from the Baths of Caracalla (fig. 3) or the Polyphemus group from Tiberius' grotto at Sperlonga (fig. 4). In the former, a viewer can perceive minute detail, such as foliage growing out of the marble, whereas in the case of the latter, we know that the sculptural group was displayed over mirroring water (fig. 5) to enact precisely the kind of illusory optical effects that Lucius-*auctor* recounts in his *ekphrasis*.

Yet, while no three-dimensional Diana-Actaeon sculptural group corre-

---

58. See Sharrock 1996, 107–16, for a discussion of "representing" metamorphosis.

Fig. 3. The Punishment of Dirce. Statuary group from the Farnese collection, third century CE
(Photograph by Marie-Lan Nguyen. Courtesy of the Ministry of Culture, National Archaeological Museum of Naples.)

Fig. 4. The Blinding of Polyphemus. Statuary group from Tiberius' grotto in Sperlonga, first century CE
(Photograph by Carole Raddato. Courtesy of the Ministry of Culture, Sperlonga Archaeological Museum.)

sponds to Apuleius' expansive verbal representation, this scene weaves together a pastiche of motifs and iconographic conventions from Roman wall-painting and smaller, individual statuary representations.[59] Taking this into consideration, we may propose that Apuleius creates through *ekphrasis* a grand-scale statuary scene of an episode that likely never appeared in the sculptural repertoire—or in other words, that he "sculpturalizes" a motif borrowed from Roman wall-painting[60]—but expands the boundaries of imaginative potential and by doing so, twists the plausible.[61] Much as Heliodorus' wall-painting comes to life

---

59. See, e.g., Slater 1998, 27: "While no set of surviving artifacts precisely represents this sculptural group, a number of pieces of Roman art can help us see what might have been in the author's mind." Cf. Schlam 1992, 71, who calls Byrrhena's atrium "a composite of famed Hellenistic images."
60. I am grateful to Ann Kuttner, who discussed this particular feature with me at length. Cf. also Dufallo 2013, 246, who speaks of this "imaginary sculpture in a parodic, make-believe Greek world served up for the viewer's titillation and delight."
61. So, Andrew Laird (1993, 18–19) speaks of a distinction between description of an actual picture or object, and "imaginary *ekphrasis*," in which the picture is "utterly dependent on . . . words for its existence."

Fig. 5. Hypothetical reconstruction of statues at Sperlonga
(Reproduced with permission of Michael Squire, from Spivey and Squire, *Panorama of the Classical World* [London, 2004], fig. 230, and modified after a diagram by G. Lattanzi, in B. Conticello and B. Andreae, *Die Skulpturen von Sperlonga* [Berlin, 1974] (AntP 14), fig. 11.)

in three dimensions and displays the naked body of Andromeda "from all sides," so also, Apuleius transforms a motif from two-dimensional wall-painting into a three-dimensional sculptural group, and then mediates it visually *back* through the two-dimensional mirror. In this way, Apuleius literalizes Plato's anxieties about *mimesis* being some "third remove from reality" (*Rep.* 10.599a1).

Turning to the text itself, the first half of the *ekphrasis* describes a scene of particularly impressive artistic realism in the expected mode of a rhetorical or poetic *ekphrasis*. It opens with a traditional technique of focalization to direct the reader's attention: *ecce*, similar to the Philostratean "look!" (ἰδού) which Norman Bryson has identified.[62] Moreover, the narrator incorporates the reader into the description with a series of second-person singular verbs: if any barking comes forth, "you will think" (*putabis*) that it is coming from the mar-

---

62. See Bryson 1994, 266.

ENTRANCED BY THE MIRROR OF MYTH 165

ble.[63] Even this play with sound and motion—the illusion of barking, the apparent movement of the statue with its refluent robe[64]—highlights the problems of intermediality: the narrator reminds us time and again that we are looking at "marble" (*lapis*) even as he describes how it seems to step out of its still life.[65] Diana is not the goddess herself but is emphatically representational and material: "marble fashioned into Diana" (*lapis . . . in Dianam factus*).[66] The dogs as well as their imaginary barking are likewise sculpted from *lapis*. In a reversal of Ovid's Actaeon, however, the *auctor* is also sure to remind us that this is "art emulating nature" (*ars aemula naturae*), that art "arranged" the natural setting so as to seem "similar to the truth" (*veritati similes*). In Ovid's version of the Actaeon story, after all, the young hunter unsuspectingly enters into a grove so beautiful that it seemed as if "nature had imitated art with her genius" (*Met.* 3.158–59: *simulaverat **artem** ingenio **natura** suo*).[67] Apuleius, by contrast, highlighting the constructed-ness or materiality of Byrrhena's ensemble, reconstitutes the appropriately subordinated relationship of art to nature—***ars** aemula **naturae***—at least, until we are invited to look into the mirroring water.

However, as the focalization changes, as the speaker's narrative-camera zooms in closer on the figure of Diana and then refocuses the reader's attention on the mirroring water beneath her feet, the whole *ekphrasis* is transformed from the "Striding Diana" into a different scene from iconography: namely, the "Bathing Diana."[68] This is accomplished strikingly through the statuary ensemble seeming to step out of its fixed boundaries (*à la* Andromache in Heliodorus) and to move via the imaginative potential of the mirror. The narrator says in an emphatic future-more-vivid:[69] "if you look down (*pronus aspexeris*) into the fountain, you will believe" (*credes*) that the scene "does not lack the quality of motion" (*agitationis officio*). *Officium*, we should note, is an erotically and magically charged term, synonymous with *morigerus* elsewhere in the

---

63. On the proliferation of second-person verbs in *ekphrasis*, see Bartsch 2007, 83. A practitioner of rhetorical *ekphrasis* could employ a number of methods to incorporate a reader into the act of "viewing" the imagined scene. Importantly for us, phrases like "one would have said" or "you would think" are "a standard ekphrastic marker, hypothesising a viewer taken in by the illusion" (Whitmarsh 2002, 114).

64. Cf. Laird 1993 on "disobedient *ekphrasis*."

65. So, Shumate 1996, 70, speaks of "the almost badgering recurrence of *lapis*."

66. We may contrast this, e.g., with the opening of Callistratus' Narcissus-*ekphrasis*, which highlights how the mythical person is "made from rock" (*Descr.* 5.1: Νάρκισσος ἐκ λίθου πεποιημένος).

67. On which, see van der Paardt 2004, 29. Cf. also Krabbe 1989, 54–55.

68. On the iconographic play, see Schlam 1984.

69. O'Sullivan 2016, 201, notes that Lucius "switches to the future-more-vivid, as if he knows for sure that if we just bend over we will see it."

Metamorphoses.[70] Rephrased according to Apuleius' mimetic theory from the *Apologia*, the mirroring water provides the "fidelity" of a courtesan maintaining the simulation of motion for a viewer even as it reflects a static statuary ensemble. And so, we may ask: to which kind of offspring will this "officious" mirror give birth? Indeed, as Lucius-*actor* walks closer to the statue and "bends over" (*pronus*) the water, the reader's focus is shifted from the whole statuary ensemble, where a clothed Diana stands amid her dogs, to reflections in water, which somehow seem to represent her "about to bathe" (*loturam*).

It is worth taking a moment, in fact, to analyze carefully the final sentence of this *ekphrasis* in order to dissect the way in which Apuleius provides a paradoxical aesthetic encounter and thereby, invites readers to make a choice over how to experience this complex representation. For the sake of convenience, I reprint the Latin:

> Inter medias frondes lapidis Actaeon simulacrum, curioso optutu in deam <deor>sum proiectus, iam in cervum ferinus et in saxo simul et in fonte loturam Dianam opperiens visitur.

Here, we encounter Actaeon "in the middle" but his status as the Actaeon familiar from a mythical tradition is immediately qualified by the term *simulacrum*[71]—a word which emphasizes not only that this is a *version* of Actaeon (i.e., a fixed representation), but simultaneously plays upon the dual medium through which Actaeon is seen. *Simulacrum* is, of course, a term for both a statue and a reflected image in a mirror.[72] Lucretius seems to derive its etymol-

---

70. On erotic (or pseudoerotic) uses of *officium* in the *Met.*, see 4.31, 5.28, 5.25, and 10.3. On magical-religious uses, see 2.30 and 11.9. On the erotic undertones of *officium*, which seems to have developed into a double entendre for the passive partner in a homoerotic encounter (cf. Adams 1982, 163), see OLD, s.v. **officium** 1c.

71. Wowerius 1606 deleted this word as an unnecessary gloss (on which, see Zimmerman 2012, 25 *app. crit. ad loc.* 15).

72. Apuleius uses *simulacrum* almost uniformly to mean "statue," though the term refers primarily to specular reflection in other texts (e.g., in Lucretius), as it is a translation of the Greek *eidôlon*. See Bailey 1947, 1183 *ad. loc.* 30, for Lucretius' use of mirroring terms; cf. also Hardie 1988 for a discussion of the significance of this Lucretian word in Ovid's Narcissus episode. *Simulacrum* appears 26 times in the Apuleian corpus, 22 of which refer to a physical statue or stand-in for a divinity. Twice the word alludes to a ghostly vision (*Met.* 1.6; 8.12). *Met.* 2.4 is one of only three places where Apuleius plays with the dichotomy between statues and mirrors; another ambiguous case occurs at *Apol.* 42.21, where *simulacrum* describes a vision of Mercury in water (i.e., a mirroring medium). In this instance, however, the *simulacrum* is clearly not a reflection but an epiphany of a god, much like the dream-like *simulacrum* of Isis in *Met.* 11.3, where it is also dually reflected in the water of the sea (on which, see §3.4 below).

ENTRANCED BY THE MIRROR OF MYTH   167

ogy from the phrase *simul ac*: "as soon as" you place an object in front of the reflective surface, it creates an image.[73] Actaeon's status as representation is further underscored, in Lucius-*auctor's ekphrasis*, by the phrase *et in saxo simul et in fonte*: Actaeon is seen in two places at once—both . . . and (*et . . . et*)—but the lexical element *simul*, beyond playfully appropriating Lucretius' etymology for the *simulacrum* (i.e., with *simul et*),[74] also invites the reader to strive to do the impossible.[75] Simply put, if *lectores* were to follow Lucius-*auctor's* suggestion and "lean over" (*pronus*) the pool, it would be impossible for them to look at the statue *and* its reflection *at the same time*.

Furthermore, Actaeon is already getting punished for a crime that he has not yet committed. In short, with the phrase *iam in cervum ferinus*, Apuleius "represents metamorphosis" in a diachronic process.[76] By contrast to Ovid's version, Apuleius' Actaeon has not yet seen the naked goddess. Indeed, if we triangulate this scene through Ovid's Actaeon, where the narrator famously intrudes with an apology that there was no fault on Actaeon's part, but only "wandering" (*Met.* 3.142: *error*), we can see that Apuleius is again playing with the Latin poetic tradition by eliding the role of *error*.[77] While Ovid's Actaeon is also seen by internal viewers (i.e., Diana's nymphs)—expressed with a related vision verb (see 3.178-79: *nudae **viso** sua pectora nymphae / percussere **viro***)—Apuleius' Actaeon in his act of incidental viewing "is seen" (*visitur*) as a witting voyeur, lying in wait (*opperiens*) to catch a glimpse of the goddess, who is "about to bathe" (*loturam*).[78]

---

73. See *DRN* 4.211 for the implicit etymologizing (on which, see Hardie 1988, 73n3).
74. Given Apuleius' high level of "controlled gamesmanship" (as Winkler 1985, 170, phrases it), it is tempting to suggest that Apuleius plays even further in an etymological sense with the phrase *simul et*. That is, if you read the sentence in order (i.e., before you reach the main verb *visitur*), *simul-et* could function as the potential subjunctive of *simulare* (the other etymology Lucretius provides for *simulacrum*; cf. Hardie 1988, 72–73). Thus, we could translate at the subliminal level: "the *simulacrum* of Actaeon would even pretend that Diana is about to bathe in the fountain."
75. I am grateful to Emilio Capettini for this suggestion.
76. Cf., e.g., Slater 1998, 29: "the parts of this imagined sculptural group are curiously scattered along the axis of time: Actaeon is already undergoing the punishment for his curiosity by being metamorphosed into a stag, but the naked object of that curiosity is not present before his eyes." In my view, Paschalis 2002, 136–37, puts excessive emphasis on the completed aspect of the metamorphosis of Actaeon, when he says: "*Iam in cervum ferinus* means that Actaeon 'has already taken the shape of a beast.' In other words, *iam* here marks not a beginning but a completed action." *Pace* Paschalis, there are no extant visual representations from antiquity which represent Actaeon *fully* transformed because, as Sharrock 1996 notes, such a representation would fail to signify the myth without some suggestion of diachronicity. See also *GCA* 2001, 112–13 *ad. loc.*; and Dufallo 2013, 246, on the phrase.
77. On which, see Krabbe 1989, 55; and Krabbe 2003, 581.
78. On this transformation of Actaeon into an intentional voyeur, see Heath 1992, 104. There also seems to be a pointed pun on *in fonte loturam*, as Schlam 1984, 105 notes: the goddess is "about to bathe in the fountain." Cf. also Krabbe 2003, 581.

Fig. 6. The Striding Diana. Marble statue of Diana, first-second century CE, now in the Louvre
(© Musée du Louvre, Dist. RMN-Grand Palais / Thierry Ollivier / Art Resource, NY)

Whereas Actaeon's status is complicated "along the axis of time" (n. 76 above), Diana is transformed in her iconographic type by the agency of the mirror. Indeed, as Carl Schlam demonstrated, Apuleius blends two very different iconographic traditions—the "Striding Diana" (fig. 6) and "Bathing Diana" (fig. 7)[79]—which Lucius-*auctor* conflates in his *ekphrasis*.

We will return to this *ekphrastic* confusion of undressing goddesses in the next chapter, where we shall see Lucius-*auctor* retrospectively portraying his seedy tryst with Photis in the highbrow discourse of Platonic enlightenment, in

---

79. Figures 6 and 7 are not unique but rather exemplary of two different iconographic traditions widespread across geography and time in the imperial period, on which, see Schlam 1984, 87–106, and esp. 106.

Fig. 7. The Bathing Diana. Roman mosaic found in Syria, third century CE
(Mosaic in the As Suwayda National Museum, image courtesy dbtravel / Alamy Stock Photo.)

part, by enacting a transformation of iconographic types in his description. More important for our present discussion, however, is the fact that the mirroring water acts as the agent of the iconographic transformation of Diana.

I have delineated these striking features of the *ekphrasis* of Byrrhena's atrium here—the illusory play with dimensionality, the transformation of mythical and iconographic traditions, and most importantly, the emphasis on the complex temporality of viewing the *simulacrum* in the mirror—not merely to highlight Apuleius' echoing of Platonic anxieties in his descriptive technique, but also to demonstrate that the aesthetic danger of the statuary ensemble lies in the vacillation between mimetic contagion and the mytho-maniac's approach to art. Lucius-*actor* believes, on the one hand, that he can participate in this spectacle, that he can project himself onto the scene, without suffering any of the consequences Actaeon endured in the mythical tale. Like the mythomaniacal Encolpius, that is, he imagines that he can play the role of Actaeon *up to a point* and still avoid replicating the rest of the tale. Thus, we may wonder whether the imaginary *simulacrum* of Actaeon in the statuary ensemble would have, in point of fact, possessed a "curious gaze," as Lucius claims, or whether the *curiosus optutus* represents a mytho-maniacal assimilation of the object of *mimesis* to the character of the spectator.[80] The mirror is superior to other mimetic forms, after all, because it is "similar and mobile, and subservient to every nod of its man" (*ut similis, ita mobilis et ad omnem nutum hominis sui* **morigera**).

On the other hand, we are invited to recognize a striking analogy between Actaeon and Lucius[81]—and in turn, between Lucius and ourselves—through the *simulacrum* which he (and we) encounter(s). Indeed, as Winkler shrewdly notes, in order for Lucius to see the *simulacrum* of the voyeur "in the fountain" (*in fonte*), he would likely need to be leaning far enough over the water to encounter a *simulacrum* of himself at the same time—except that it is not Lucius who "leans over" the pool.[82] Instead, if we follow the exhortation of our mytho-maniacal narrator, it is we who are bent over the fountain to gaze upon the water: he says, "if *you* look down" (*pronus aspexeris*). Indeed, in a brilliant demonstration of the power of mimetic contagion, the rippling pool of water conflates the object of representation in the mirror, and as a consequence, the subject of *visitur* (not to mention, the agent) is left deliberately ambiguous: Is it a version of the mythical Actaeon? A "statue" (*simulacrum*) of Actaeon? A "mirror-image" (*simulacrum*) of a "statue" (*simulacrum*) of Actaeon? Or is the "reflection" (*simulacrum*) actually Lucius bent over the water, looking at himself *as if* he is Actaeon? Might the reader, in fact, be reflected in the frame, as s/he gazes "downward" (*pronus*) at the book and through the words, at the mirroring pool? We cannot see all of these different representations *at the same time*, but the narrator nonetheless invites us to choose a representational point of reference.

This is where it is necessary, then, to perform our "horse-jumping" maneuver between mimetic and *ekphrastic* contagion. For while the term *pronus* gestures forebodingly for Lucius toward his bent over posture as an ass (i.e., mimetic contagion), it also simultaneously reflects back *on us*, as we sit bent over our books and are invited to visualize (i.e., *aspexeris*) the scene through Lucius' description. In fact, if we look closer at this term *pronus*, we may note that there

---

80. Cf., e.g., Paschalis 2002, 137.
81. See, e.g., Riefstahl 1938, who was the first to note the one-to-one correspondence between Actaeon and Lucius.
82. Cf. Winkler 1985, 170: "Since my estimate of Apuleius's controlled gamesmanship is high and since I believe him to be maneuvering the reader into a dilemma to choose among interpretations, I think that *pronus aspexeris* should be fully visualized. If you *did* lean forward to look into the water you would see not only a second Actaeon but yourself" (original emphasis).

ENTRANCED BY THE MIRROR OF MYTH   171

is a philosophical tradition reaching back to Plato and Xenophon[83]—a tradition with which Apuleius was clearly familiar[84]—which posits that the main distinction between animals and humans is a difference in posture: between "terrestrial" and "celestial" posture, between looking down at the earth and looking up at the stars. "Terrestrial" posture is symbolic of excessive desire for food and sex.[85] Thus, according to some Platonic treatments of metempsychosis, quadrupeds were originally humans whose lack of interest in "looking up" and contemplating the heavens enacted their metamorphosis into herd animals.[86]

The threat that aesthetic pleasure poses of transforming those who experience it into herd animals is already familiar to us—for example, from the Sirenesque cicadas in the *Phaedrus*, which would laugh at Socrates and his interlocutor if, charmed by the cicadas' song, they should fall asleep "like sheep" (259a5: ὥσπερ προβάτια; cf. §1.1). On a very physical level, then, Lucius-*auctor* invites us to replicate this transformation *outside of the text* through *ekphrastic* contagion, and this is brought to the fore even for the first-time reader by the very close intratext of another famous figure, hunched over and gazing into mirroring water. Indeed, a mere twelve sections earlier in the *Met.*, readers will have just encountered a fan-fiction "Socrates," who escaped punishment in Athens and fled to Thessaly in order to live as an "Odysseus" entrapped by a "Circe" or "Calypso."[87] This "Socrates," we may recall, is immediately corrupted by spectacle, drunkenness, and sexual desire in another extraordinary literalization of Platonic anxieties (*Met.* 1.6–1.9). But the scene directly parallel to our implica-

---

83. See O'Sullivan 2016. Cf. also Fitzgerald 2000, 102–3.

84. See, e.g., *Apol.* 7, where Apuleius describes the placement of the mouth of a quadruped, which is "humble and turned downward toward the feet, nearest to track and pasturage" (*humile est et deorsum ad pedes deiectum, uestigio et pabulo proximum*). Cf. also *De mund.* 17, where Apuleius categorizes the different types of *animalia* as "creeping on their belly" (*in alvum **prona***) and "flying" (*proiecta*).

85. See O'Sullivan 2016, 203–5. This semantic coloring for *pronus* is everywhere in the *Met.*: we first encounter the term at *Met.* 1.2, where Lucius' horse "leans over with his face twisted to the side" (*ore in latus detorto **pronus***) in order to "consume an ambulatory breakfast" (*ientaculum ambulatorium... **adfectat***). Then, shortly after encountering Byrrhena's atrium, Lucius "leans over [Photis]" (2.10: ***pronus** in eam*) in order to snatch some open-mouthed kisses; and Photis responds, in turn, in "leaning desire" (2.10: ***prona** cupidine*). Psyche replicates Lucius' posture in a gesture of *agalmatophilia* (cf. §4.3 and 4.4), when she finally sees Cupid's beautiful body, by "lean[ing] over him" (5.23: ***prona** in eum*).

86. See, e.g., *Phaed.* 81e and *Rep.* 9.586a–b.

87. As O'Brien 2002, 37–40 notes, Socrates' friends advise him in the *Crito* to escape to Thessaly (*Crit.* 53b–e). Moreover, Hunter 2006, 303–5, points out that, when in Thessaly, this Socrates becomes eerily similar to Homer's Odysseus. So, Meroe even explicitly refers to herself as a Calypso deserted by "the wit of Ulysses" (1.12: *Ulixi astu*), on which, see below. On the significance of the transformation of Socrates to Odysseus (and vice versa in the Isis book), see Ulrich 2020, 699, and further discussion in §5.1.

tion as readers in Byrrhena's atrium is the death of "Socrates" after he enters a *locus amoenus* marked as a precise duplicate of the place where Socrates warns Phaedrus about the dangers of aesthetic pleasure. Indeed, after being pierced in the throat by Meroe's sword but plugged up with a sponge to survive the puncture wound (*Met.* 1.13), "Socrates" and Aristomenes meander to a bank along a river—one noted for its Phaedran "plane tree" (1.18: *platanum*).[88] Rather than resisting pleasure and engaging in philosophical discourse like his Platonic counterpart, however, Apuleius' dissolute reincarnation of the famous philosopher incidentally consumes too much cheesy bread, and so, desperately reaches for water to wash it down. As Aristomenes narrates the affair, this Socrates-*redivivus* "folds himself to his knees and leans over [the water], greedily attempting to take a drink" (1.19: *complicitus in genua adpronat se avidus adfectans poculum*), at which point, the wound in his throat opens back up, the sponge falls out, and he keels over and dies.

At first glance, this "Socrates" seems a comic parody of the Platonic archetype: scholars have recognized in this figure an inversion or "extremization" of the Platonic Socrates,[89] a symbolic gesture toward "comic ambiguity" in the novel,[90] or even an example of Apuleius' "comic deflation" of philosophical ideas by placing famous philosophers in inappropriate situations and settings.[91] If, however, Apuleius was familiar with and playing upon the philosophical tradition of posture as a means of distinguishing humans from animals, then it is more than mere comic appropriation that Socrates—the figure in antiquity most associated with the Delphic oracle and the *gnôthi seauton* tradition[92]— enters into the very same grove where he advocated in the *Phaedrus* for the pursuit of self-knowledge, but far from striving to achieve self-knowledge, "leans" (*pronus*) over a glassy, reflective surface and dies.

Keeping this Narcissus-like "Socrates" in mind, then, we may look back at

---

88. The "plane tree" here is generally agreed to be a complex allusion to the *Phaedrus*, on which, see Drake 1968, 108n29; van der Paardt 1978, 83; Münstermann 1995, 12; Sandy 1997, 253; O'Brien 2002, 77–78; Smith and Woods 2002, 191; *GCA* 2007, 338–39 *ad loc.*; Graverini 2012a, 18 and 135; Winkle 2014, 98–100; and Ulrich 2022, 264–65. For a comprehensive discussion of the reception of Plato's *locus amoenus* in the Second Sophistic, see Trapp 1990, 141–48 and 171 for an appendix. Cf. also Hunter 2012, 4, for the importance of the opening of the *Phaedrus*: "[it is] . . . a 'classic,' the object of discussion, imaginative recreation, imitation, and indeed drama."
89. See, e.g., Smith and Woods 2002; Graverini 2012a, 133–64.
90. See Keulen 2003, esp. 110–13.
91. See Kirichenko 2008a, 93–96, who refers to philosophical figures and scenes placed in "deflating context[s]." Cf. Finkelpearl 1991 for a similar interpretation of Lucius' tirade after the pantomime of Venus (on which, see §3.3 below).
92. Cf. *Apol.* 15 for Apuleius' interpretation of this (on which, see §2.3). See also *Met.* 10.33, where Apuleius refers to Socrates but elides his name (on which, see §3.3).

ENTRANCED BY THE MIRROR OF MYTH   173

the *ekphrasis* of Byrrhena's atrium, which uniquely invites readers to direct *their* gaze at a *simulacrum* while "bent over" mirroring water. While we have seen how Lucius projects his own desires onto the statuary ensemble—how he makes it come to life, as it were, and act out an illicit scene of a stripping goddess—first-time readers are given no other option *but* to participate in Lucius' viewing. We are compelled, in short, to lean over the pool ourselves, much as we are bent (*proni/ae*) over our books, and to indulge in the fantasy which Lucius urges us to visualize. It is significant, in this respect, that the earliest instance of solitary reading in antiquity comes from the first book of Achilles Tatius' *L&C*—a text with which Apuleius was very possibly familiar.[93] There, the narrator Clitophon, in an effort to peep at his beloved Leucippe without being caught, "lays hold of a book" (*L&C* 1.6.6: βιβλίον . . . κρατῶν) and "bends over it and pretends to read" (ἐγκεκυφὼς ἀνεγίνωσκον).[94] Although it is speculative in the world of scholarship on the sociology of reading in antiquity,[95] it is nonetheless suggestive that the posture Clitophon adopts—that is, bent over a book and feigning interest in one text (most likely, a novel)[96] in order to feast his eyes on the spectacle of another (i.e., the female body)—seems to mirror the posture that Lucius-*auctor* invites us to assume in the atrium. As we move from the threat mimetic contagion poses to Lucius to that which *ekphrastic* contagion presents to us, we are left wondering whether we can, indeed, read this book with self-control or *prudentia*, or whether like Apuleius' metempsychosis

---

93. On the possibility that Apuleius was familiar with *L&C*, see Freudenburg 2007, 239. For a recent article on *L&C* as a major site of intertextuality in the second–third centuries CE, see D'Alconzo 2021. I am in the process of finishing an article on the kitchen-seduction scene of the *Met.* and its intertextual engagement with *L&C* and the pseudo-Lucianic *Amores*.

94. It is significant, in my view, that Achilles Tatius uses the same verbal root for reading a book (ἐγκύπτω) which Plato employs in the *Republic* to describe herd animals, who are "always looking down and bent to the earth in the manner of cattle" (9.586a7–8: βοσκημάτων δίκην κάτω ἀεὶ βλέποντες καὶ **κεκυφότες** εἰς γῆν).

95. On the sociology of reading (about which I make no claims here), see Cavallo 1996; Johnson 2010 (with bibliography). That this is the physical posture of reading is further suggested by a near-contemporaneous *comparandum* in Sextus Empiricus, who speaks of "bending over a book" (*Pyrrh.* 1.45: ἐγκύψαντες βιβλίῳ) after gazing upon the sun and seeing optical illusions in the letters. Although I could find no attestation in Latin where *pronus* refers to the physical posture of leaning over a book, it is perhaps implied in usages which connect *pronus* to the mental/intellectual posture of being receptive to *fabulae*, gossip, or poetry. Hence, Statius, after listing the feats of Vettius Bolanus to his son, tells Crispinus to "drink down such lore with prone ears" (*Silv.* 5.2.58–59: *bibe talia **pronis**/auribus*); and Tacitus claims that "malicious disparagement is received with prone ears" (*Hist.* 1.1: *obtrectatio et livor **pronis** auribus accipiuntur*). So also, Suetonius claims that Nero is "prone to poetry" (*Nero* 52: *ad poeticam **pronus***) and [Quintilian]'s major declamations discuss an old man who is "prone to fables and vulgar chit-chat" (*Decl. Maiores* 18.2.2: *ad fabulas vulgaresque sermones **pronus***).

96. Thus, Bowie 2006, 61, notes that Clitophon's reading is likely a metaliterary gesture to the novel itself or the wider genre. So also, Goldhill 1995, 70–71 and Morales 2004, 78–79. Whitmarsh 2020, 146 *ad loc.* 1.6.6, speaks of "an obviously self-referential dimension" to this scene.

of an asinine "Socrates," we, too, will suffer some unfortunate fate from leering at the text's seedy delights.

The *ekphrasis* of Byrrhena's atrium concludes, as is traditional in novelistic descriptions of artworks, with the entrance of an exegete to offer an interpretation for the internal viewer.[97] As Lucius becomes immersed in his own imaginative world, Byrrhena snaps him out of it with a seemingly hospitable gesture that, in retrospect, doubles as foreboding warning (*Met.* 2.5):[98]

> Dum haec identidem **rimabundus** exinde **delector**, "Tua sunt" ait Byrrhena "cuncta quae vides."

> While I stood there, inspecting the scene closely and taking great pleasure from it, Byrrhena said, "it's yours, everything you see."

Lucius reveals, on the one hand, exactly what kind of reader he strives to be: Apuleius' coinage *rimabundus* is derived from the root-noun *rimae*,[99] the "cracks" or "chinks" in a door through which one voyeuristically looks at those sights which are illicit.[100] Rather than striving to be a *lector scrupulosus*, however, by applying this statuary scene to his life in a self-reflective way, Lucius prefers to "take pleasure" in the spectacle. Here, we may note that the verb form *delector* subliminally incorporates the reader into the nexus of self-indulgent

---

97. On the exegete as a figure traditionally associated with *ekphrasis*, see Bartsch 1989. We may note the arrival of an exegete in Petronius' *Satyricon* (83–89; on which, see Ulrich *forthcoming* c), in the prologue of Longus' *Daphnis and Chloe*, and most allegorically, in the *tabula Cebetis* (on which, see Grethlein and Squire 2014). On Byrrhena as the traditional *exêgêtês* of an *ekphrasis* in the scene, see Paschalis 2002, 139.

98. See Winkler 1985, 168, who calls this line, "a lovely ambiguity, read as hospitable by the first-reader, as ominous by the second-reader." Cf. also James 1987, 128.

99. See OLD, s.v. **rimabundus**, where the word is defined as "examining closely (with the eyes or mind)." The only other extant instance comes from the *Soc.*, where it is used of "carefully contemplating the gods with our intellect" (on which, see below). On *rimabundus*, see also Freudenburg 2007, 243: "The word is likely to be Apuleius' own invention, built on analogy with adjectives of the *mirabundus* type. . . . In fact I think what Apuleius has done here is simply switch the *r* and *m* from the familiar *mirabundus* to invent *rimabundus* so that you still hear one word inside the other enhancing its meaning."

100. See, e.g., *Met.* 3.21, where Lucius watches Pamphile's transformation into an owl "through a certain chink in the doors" (*per . . . **rimam** ostiorum quampiam*). Cf. also Petron. *Sat.* 26, where Quartilla "appl[ies] her curious eye to the chink [in the door] which she had wantonly split" (*per **rimam** improbe diductam applicuerat oculum curiosum*). A particularly intriguing usage, for our purposes, occurs in Horace's *C.* 3.14, where the speaker claims that "whitening hair" alleviates "spirits desirous of a shameless crack" (3.14.26: *rixae cupidos protervae*); and in his *scholion* to this line, Porphyry glosses *cupidos*: "old age mitigates the spirits of youths which are haughty and *leaning over* a crack" (*In Carm.* 3.14.26: *superbos iuvenum vel rixae **pronos** animos [senectus] mitigat*).

ENTRANCED BY THE MIRROR OF MYTH   175

desires, which Lucius has confounded in his *ekphrasis*.[101] Thus, although this statuary ensemble could function as a transcendent encounter with a daemonic intermediary and we readers could take this opportunity, as Apuleius advocates in *Soc.*, to "contemplate [the gods] through careful investigation with our intellect" (*Soc.* 2: *intellectu eos* **rimabundi** *<contemplamur>*), Lucius nonetheless entraps us in a kind of voyeuristic and autoerotic desire.

Whereas Lucius-*auctor* implicates us with mytho-maniacal (mis)interpretation, Byrrhena's response to Lucius' creepy ogling, in which she performs the traditional role of exegete, may also invite us to escape from Lucius' entrapment, especially in the "Palinodic reading." The phrase "it's yours, everything you see" (**tua** *sunt . . . cuncta quae vides*), which reoccurs after the *ekphrasis* of Cupid's palace (5.2: *tua sunt haec omnia*), is ironic, since Lucius is soon to undergo his own metamorphosis only to be perpetually threatened by a *sparagmos* akin to Actaeon's punishment.[102] But the feature most interesting to me, and one which has not been fully explored in relation to Byrrhena's words,[103] is the fact that at the end of the novel, Lucius encounters two more representations of divinities in rapid succession—encounters which establish a contest, as it were, between *Venus vulgaris* in the pantomime of book 10 and the "true" revelation of Isis in book 11. He ultimately rejects the former only to be fully incorporated into a representational ensemble of the latter. As we turn our attention now to Lucius' anxiety over being incorporated into a public spectacle at the close of book 10, we must keep Byrrhena's *tua* at the forefront of our minds, as it may reach beyond Lucius' life, threatening to seep through the boundaries of the text and implicate "you" inside the *ekphrasis* (cf. *aspexeris*).

3.3. *The Seductions of Venus, the Primitive Choice, and the "Philosophizing Ass" (Met. 10.29–35)*

Between Lucius' imaginative play in Byrrhena's atrium and the sensuous *spectaculum* in which he is slated to participate eight books later, the ass-man narrates many encounters with surrogate divinities, from Photis' and Pamphile's illicit stripteases (see §4.3) to the *simulacrum* of Epona and the veneration of

---

101. On *delector* as a playful incorporation of the *lector*, see Freudenburg 2007, 245 and 247.

102. See *GCA* 2001, 115–16 *ad loc.*, who also refers to this episode as a "*mise en abyme proleptique*" (91). For Actaeonic threats to Lucius, see Heath 1992, 102–21.

103. Heath 1992 and Slater 1998 come closest to recognizing the striking parallelism, but both miss the intermediary step of Venus' pantomime.

Psyche, who is explicitly labeled "another Venus" (4.28: *Venerem aliam*; on which, see §4.4). The reason for us to fast-forward at this point to the pantomime of Venus, however, is because there are structural and thematic connections between the Diana-Actaeon statuary ensemble and its spectacle counterpart in book 10—most significantly, in their shared status as elaborate *ekphrases* of *representations* of stripping goddesses.[104] The connection between these two episodes is made clear in the very opening line, as Lucius strategically positions himself to gaze on the spectacle before the curtain lifts (10.29):

> ac dum ludicris scaenicorum choreis primitiae spectaculi dedicantur, tantisper ante portam constitutus pabulum laetissimi graminis, quod in ipso germinabat aditu, **libens adfectabam**, subinde **curiosos oculos** patente porta spectaculi prospectu gratissimo reficiens.

And while the opening acts of the spectacle were dedicated to playful choruses of mime-actors, I was situated in front of the gate, happily pursuing the nourishment of the lushest grass springing up in the very entrance, while frequently refreshing my curious eyes with the most pleasing sight of the spectacle through the open gate.

In the frame of the *ekphrasis*, Lucius-*actor* represents himself *pronus*, and mimicking the ambulatory breakfast his horse takes at the very beginning of the novel (cf. *Met.* 1.2: *ientaculum ambulatorium . . . pronus adfectat*)—a scene already echoed, we may recall, by the breakfast (1.18: *ientaculum*) which kills the reincarnated "Socrates" as he likewise "leans over" (1.19: *adpronat*) and "greedily pursues the cup" (*avidus adfectans poculum*). At the same time, however, Lucius gazes at the theatrical *mimesis* from behind an open doorway (*patente porta*), replicating his position as voyeur peeping through the chink of the door (cf. 3.21: *rimam ostiorum*), as he feasts his "curious eyes" (*curiosos oculos*) on the spectacle. The set-up thus reproduces, in many respects, the scenario of the *simulacrum Actaeon* in the atrium of Byrrhena. There, the statue, while representing Actaeon-as-voyeur with a "curious gaze" (2.4: *curioso optutu*), is paradoxically "already wild and turning into a stag" (*iam in cervum ferinus*; cf. n. 76

---

104. Cf., e.g., *GCA* 2000, 26, on the structural connection between the Diana-Actaeon *ekphrasis* and the Paris pantomime. See also Singleton 1977, 44 and 47–49. For the most substantial treatments of this episode to date, see Fick 1990; Finkelpearl 1991; Zimmerman-de Graaf 1993; Kahane 2007; May 2008; Kirichenko 2008a.

above)—or in other words, is already changing into a *pronus* quadruped under threat of being ripped apart by animals. So also, although Lucius seems to leisurely enjoy this spectacle as a parallel activity to his consumption of grass (and surprisingly, as a disinterested observer),[105] it should not escape our notice that Lucius-*actor* is, one could say, a man "already wild and turned into an ass" (i.e., *iam in asinum ferinus*) and furthermore, is poised to suffer a very real *sparagmos*. Thus, when Lucius finally returns to his senses after getting immersed in the spectacle, he remembers that he is "utterly tortured by the fear of death" (10.34: *metu etiam mortis maxime cruciabar*) because he is slated to *become* the show: after he is set on stage to perform a bestial sex-act with a criminal woman, beasts are to be sent in to "tear to shreds the woman attached to [his] side," and he fears that they will not "spare [him] as if . . . innocent." In quite a literal sense, then, Lucius has suffered from mimetic contagion. In book 2, he delights and luxuriates in the atrium scene of Diana-Actaeon which, though unbeknownst to him at the time, is to become a reality in his life. Then later, in book 10, he gazes once again upon a surrogate goddess in a representational frame with the slight (but substantial) difference that this time, he has a designated role to play in the display. As he waits for *this* goddess to strip, he simultaneously anticipates his own (rather than the mythical Actaeon's) *sparagmos*.

The parallelism between Byrrhena's atrium and the Venus pantomime is further heightened for readers in the opening description of the setting for the theatrical spectacle, which plays with different levels of representation much like the *simulacrum Actaeon* (10.30):

> Erat mons ligneus ad instar incliti montis illius quem vates Homerus Idaeum cecinit, sublimi instructus fabrica, consitus virectis et vivis arboribus, summo cacumine de manibus fabri fonte manante fluviales aquas eliquans. Capellae pauculae tondebant herbulas, et in modum Paridis, Phrygii pastoris, barbaricis amiculis umeris defluentibus pulchre indusiatus adulescens, aurea tiara contecto capite, pecuarium simulabat magisterium.

> There was a wooden mountain, built with lofty craftsmanship like that famous Mount Ida, which the bard Homer sang of; it was planted with sod and living

---

105. May 2008, 352–58, emphasizes how far Lucius-*auctor* is from being immersed in the spectacle, inasmuch as he perpetually highlights its artifice and acts as if he is not about to participate. It may be Lucius-*actor*, however, who is describing the scene (on which, see Zimmerman-de Graaf 1993, 155; and n. 119 below)—hence, my use of that designation here.

178 THE SHADOW OF AN ASS

trees, and at its highest peak, poured out river waters from a fountain flowing down from the hands of the craftsman. A few little goats munched on herbs, and a youth—beautifully clothed in foreign cloaks flowing down from his shoulders in the manner of the Phrygian herdsman, Paris, and with his head covered by a golden tiara—was feigning mastery of the herds.

Much as we saw above with the sculptural group, this display twists the relationship between the illusionary and the real—in this case, through extraordinary stage pyrotechnics. As Ahuvia Kahane has demonstrated, Apuleius' play with levels of representation even in the first noun-adjective phrase constitutes an elaborate reworking of Plato's anxieties about imitation: *mons ligneus* can stand for (1) the "wooden mountain" constructed on stage, (2) the actual mount Ida in the Troad (punning on "Ida," which is Doric for "timber"), (3) the poetic construct sung by Homer in his epic poems, or (4) the mythical setting for the Judgment of Paris.[106] Moreover, inasmuch as the "Judgment of Paris" pantomime is doubly enacted—on the primary level, performed on stage for an internal audience, but mediated on a secondary level through a vivid *ekphrasis* for us readers—this episode could be described "in Platonic terms as twice removed from 'reality.'"[107]

We may also note, however, that this *ekphrasis* not only mirrors the atrium of Byrrhena in its naturalism, but even amplifies the illusion of mimetic verisimilitude.[108] If Byrrhena's atrium was, in pointed reversal of Ovid, "art emulating nature" (2.4), the pantomime spectacle has, in turn, co-opted actual elements of nature into its representation. Thus, whereas the atrium *represents* foliage in sophisticated detail—there are, after all, six different types of vegetation which seem to "flower from the marble" (2.4: *de lapide florentibus*)—this theatrical *spectaculum* has "living trees and foliage" (*virectis et vivis arboribus*) planted into its backdrop. And while both displays have running water—"a fountain ... running along by the goddess' feet" (2.4: **fontem**, *qui deae vestigio discurrens*) compared with "a flowing fountain" (10.30: **fonte** *manante*)—the "lofty craftsman" even adds some live "goats" (*capellae*) grazing on the actual foliage for good measure.

When Lucius, therefore, comes to describe the central figure of the spectacle, a surrogate Venus dancing seductively in a diaphanous garb, the danger of enchantment and entrapment of the viewer is even more palpable (10.31):

---

106. See Kahane 2007, 253.
107. Kahane 2007, 252.
108. So, May 2008, 357–58 labels it "meta-pantomime."

ENTRANCED BY THE MIRROR OF MYTH   179

Super has introcessit alia, visendo decore praepollens, gratia coloris ambrosei designans Venerem, qualis fuit Venus cum fuit virgo, nudo et intecto corpore perfectam formonsitatem professa, nisi quod **tenui pallio bombycino inumbrabat spectabilem pubem**. Quam quidem laciniam curiosulus ventus satis amanter nunc lasciviens reflabat, ut dimota **pateret flos aetatulae**, nunc luxurians aspirabat, ut adhaerens pressule membrorum voluptatem **graphice deliniaret**.

After these [i.e., Juno and Minerva], another entered, exceedingly surpassing in beauty to look upon, representing Venus with the grace of her ambrosial color, just as Venus was when she was a virgin, making a display of her perfect beauty with her naked and uncovered body, except for the fact that she was shadowing over her spectacular privates with a thin, silken covering. Indeed, a curious little wind was quite lovingly blowing this little garment back and forth—now in a lascivious mood in order to lay bare the flower of her youth with the covering removed, and now breathing luxuriantly in order to graphically accentuate the pleasure of her limbs, pressing it closely [against her body].

There are, of course, many overlaps between this description and the erotic gesticulations of Photis in book 2, from the replication of iconographic Venus types (see 2.17: *in speciem Veneris quae . . .* ; cf. 10:31 *qualis fuit Venus cum . . . virgo*)[109] to the playful and seductive covering of the private parts (see 2.17: *obumbrans*; cf. 10.31: *inumbrabat*).[110] We will return to this vision of a surrogate goddess in the next chapter, when we consider Lucius' delusional representation of his tryst with Photis.

For now, what I am interested in is: (1) the way in which nature colludes with the mimeticism of the *actor*'s *ekphrasis* in order to paint the scene with *enargeia* (i.e., *ekphrastic* contagion); and (2) how the description of the goddess and Lucius' subsequent response to her performance construe this pantomime as a crossroads choice for Lucius. To the first point, it is striking not only that the "curious little wind" (*curiosulus ventus*) creates actual motion for the viewer (rather than the illusion of motion), but also that the narrator describes the performance precisely in the language of naturalistic painting and *ekphrasis*.

---

109. See, e.g., Zimmerman-de Graaf 1993, 152, who underlines all of the verbal parallelisms between Photis in the kitchen-seduction scene (2.7) and Venus on stage. See also *GCA* 2000, 375–76 *ad loc.* 261.24–262.1.

110. See Singleton 1977, 49.

The phrase *graphice deliniaret*, in particular, borrows rare art-critical terminology from the discourse of painting, which we find in Pliny the Elder, Aulus Gellius, and elsewhere in the Apuleian corpus, to transform this mobile spectacle of dance into a static, eroticized portrait. *Deliniare*, for instance, appears in Apuleius' set-piece display speech on Alexander's attempt to legislate the production of his portraits (*Fl.* 7):[111] anxious about devaluing his representational afterlife with *imagines* fashioned by inferior artists, Alexander put out an edict that "only Polycletus could represent [his image] in bronze, only Apelles could paint it with colors, and only Pyrgoteles could forge it in relief" (*Fl.* 7.6: *solus eam Policletus aere duceret, solus Apelles coloribus deliniaret, solus Pyrgoteles caelamine excuderet*). Likewise, the adverb *graphice* constitutes a rare transliteration of Greek from art-critical discussions of *ekphrasis*.[112] Thus, in a famous explication of Simonides' bon mot about "painting as silent poetry," Plutarch quotes a battle description from Demosthenes and claims that it encapsulates "pictorial vividness" (*de glor. Athen.* 347c1: γραφικῆς ἐναργείας). So also, in Gellius' *Noctes Atticae*, the adverb is used to emphasize the *enargeia* of Chrysippus' verbal description of personified Justice. The titular line for essay 14.4 reads: "that Chrysippus appropriately and pictorially painted an image of Justice with rhythms and colors of words" (*quod apte Chrysippus et graphice imaginem Iustitiae modulis coloribusque verborum depinxit*). In short, words have the power both through cadence and rhetorical devices to paint a portrait. In Lucius-*actor*'s description of the pantomime, however, the "pleasure of Venus' limbs," which are *actually* moving in a dance, are vividly put on display for external viewers via *ekphrastic* contagion: wind colludes with our narrator, becoming a scene-painter and transforming a mobile spectacle into a fixed portrait in words.[113]

It is significant for our interpretation of this pantomime, therefore, that a favorite iconographic motif of Roman wall-painting is that of Venus in a flitting, diaphanous garb in the Judgment of Paris. A painting from the House of Melea-

---

111. Cf. Too 1996 on this episode and its exposure of Apuleius' own anxieties about being represented.

112. So, the *ThLL* 6.2.2197.4–5 glosses *graphice* as: *fere 'quasi in pictura.'* Cf. also *GCA* 1985, 236 *ad loc.* 198.11–16.

113. So, Paschalis 2002, 139–41, notes that the structure of the pantomime resembles "a series of tableaux." Cf. Fick 1990, 225, who speaks of an "Ästhetik der Bewegung" in this passage characteristic of the Second Sophistic.

ENTRANCED BY THE MIRROR OF MYTH   181

ger (fig. 8), for instance, shows a representation of Venus in thin gossamer (cf. Apuleius' *pallium bombycinum*), whereas one from the House of Jupiter (fig. 9) seems to evoke the wind lifting Venus' garment to expose her privates.[114]

If the atrium of Byrrhena fuses and "sculpturalizes" different iconographic repertoires of Diana-Actaeon, the pantomime of Venus, by contrast, describes an *actual* three-dimensional mime—one likely very familiar to Apuleius' readership[115]—in the language of two-dimensional wall-painting, the iconography of which was culturally diffuse.[116]

Moreover, while the pantomime episode mirrors and amplifies the sculptural group of Byrrhena, relying upon the "picture gallery" inside a reader's mind, the most striking way in which the *spectaculum* duplicates the atrium of book 2 is in its function as another crossroads choice. Sixty years ago, T. C. W. Stinton suggested an ancient link between the allegorical strand of the Judgment of Paris and Prodicus' version of Heracles at the crossroads: Aphrodite and Pallas function, Stinton explains, as stand-ins for "pleasure" (*hêdonê*) and "wisdom" (*phronêsis*) in the later reception of the tale, near parallels, that is, to personified *kakia* and *aretê* in Prodicus' allegory.[117] But, looking beyond structural correspondences between the judgment and the choice, and analyzing more closely Lucius-*actor's ekphrasis*, the explicit description of the goddess as she first appears—"shadow[ing] over her spectacular privates with a silken covering" (*tenui pallio bombycino inumbrabat spectabilem pubem*)—manifestly echoes the depiction of Lady Vice in Prodicus' "Education of Heracles." We may recall from §1.1 that, when she first appears in Xenophon's text, *Kakia* is wearing a "cloak through which her privates, in particular, would appear" (*Mem.* 2.1.22:

---

114. Figure 9 is only preserved in a water-color reproduction from 1825 by Wilhelm Zahn (housed in the Antikensammlung, Staatliche Museen zu Berlin), but claims to represent an original from the House of Meleager. For this theme across Roman art, see Clairmont 1951, 108–10. In particular, Aphrodite's nudity and her "garment fluttering" (*flatternde Gewandstück*) in the wind is a Roman innovation. See 82–86 for a comprehensive list of instances.

115. On the regularity of the Judgment of Paris as a theme for theatrical mimes in the Roman period, see, e.g., Singleton 1977, 47–48, who cites, among other things, Lucian's reference to the "Judgment of Paris" pantomime (*de Salt.* 45: ἡ ἐπὶ τῷ μήλῳ κρίσις). See also Finkelpearl 1991, 229; Robert 2012, 102–3.

116. In this respect, we find a striking *comparandum* in the opening passage of Achilles Tatius' *L&C*, where the narrator produces a sensuous *ekphrasis* of an eroticized painting of Europa: her "body appear[s] through her garment" (*L&C* 1.1.11: τὸ . . . σῶμα διὰ τῆς ἐσθῆτος ὑπεφαίνετο), and the heroine's cloak clings so tightly to her limbs that it "become[s] a mirror of her body" (ἐγίνετο τοῦ σώματος κάτοπτρον).

117. See Stinton 1965, 1–12. Cf. now Davies 2023, esp. 101–4.

Fig. 8. Judgment of Paris with Naked Venus. Wilhelm Zahn's watercolor reproduction of a lost Pompeian wall-painting originally from the House of Meleager (VI.9.2), first century CE
(Courtesy of Staatliche Museen zu Berlin, Antikensammlung/Johannes Laurentius CC BY-SA 4.0, Archiv Antikensammlung SMB-PK, Rep. 4 Graphothek, W. Zahn Nr. 65.)

Fig. 9. Judgment of Paris with Stripping Venus. Pompeian wall-painting from the House of Jupiter (V.2.16), first century CE
(Reproduced with the permission of the Ministry of Culture, National Archaeological Museum of Naples. Photograph credit: Mondadori Portfolio / Hulton Fine Art Collection, courtesy of Getty Images.)

ἐσθῆτα δὲ ἐξ ἧς ἂν μάλιστα ὥρα διαλάμποι) and so, I would venture to suggest that Venus' *flos aetatulae* in Lucius' *ekphrasis* could function as a gloss on Lady Vice's *hôra*.[118]

It is crucial for our interpretation of this episode, then, that Lucius-*auctor* links the pantomime explicitly to choice in his famous tirade—and here, I follow Maaike Zimmerman's suggestion that the sensuous *ekphrasis* of the *spectaculum* is offered by Lucius-*actor* (i.e., expressing his sentiments at the time), whereas the subsequent rant of the "philosophizing ass" (10.33: *philosophantem asinum*) is delivered retrospectively by the Isiac acolyte, Lucius-*auctor*.[119] At 10.33, Lucius breaks the fourth wall, and in the most extreme apostrophe of the *Met.*, addresses his readers directly:

> Quid ergo miramini, vilissima capita, immo forensia pecora, immo vero togati vulturii, si toti nunc iudices sententias suas pretio nundinantur, cum rerum exordio inter deos et homines agitatum iudicium corruperit gratia, et originalem sententiam magni Iovis consiliis electus iudex rusticanus et opilio lucro libidinis vendiderit, cum totius etiam suae stirpis exitio? Sic hercules et aliud sequens iudicium inter inclitos Achivorum duces celebratum, vel cum falsis insimulationibus eruditione doctrinaque praepollens Palamedes proditionis damnatur, virtute Martia praepotenti praefertur Ulixes modicus Aiaci maximo. Quale autem et illud iudicium apud legiferos Athenienses catos illos et omnis scientiae magistros? Nonne divinae prudentiae senex, quem sapientia praetulit cunctis mortalibus deus Delphicus, fraude et invidia nequissimae factionis circumventus velut corruptor adulescentiae, quam frenis coercebat, herbae pestilentis succo noxio peremptus est, relinquens civibus ignominiae perpetuae maculam, cum nunc etiam egregii philosophi sectam eius sanctissimam praeoptent et summo beatitudinis studio iurent in ipsius nomen?

---

118. See *GCA* 2000, 376 *ad loc.* 261.24–262.1. Although the *ThLL* treats the extended usage of *flos* in a rather Victorian sense as "nearly the same as beauty" (6.1.935.49–74), it is clear that, in Apuleius' usage here as well as elsewhere in his corpus and milieu, the term can be a euphemism for "privates." So, at *Apol.* 76.4, Apuleius chastises Rufinus' daughter for her "despoiled chastity and withered flower" (*pudore dispoliato, **flore** exsoleto*). More scandalously, Suetonius uses *flos aetatis* to describe Caesar's prostituted youth according to rumors that floated around: "the flower of his youth, sprung from Venus, was contaminated in Bithynia" (*Vit. Iul.* 49.3: ***florem** . . . aetatis a Venere orti in Bithynia contaminatum*).

119. See Zimmerman-de Graaf 1993, 155, who argues that the change in tense from the imperfect (i.e., the description of the experiential "I") to the present (i.e., alluding to the time of narration) signals this transition in narratorial voice. In his characteristic preference for the cynical interpretation of the *Met.*, Winkler 1985, 242n66, reads the "philosophizing ass" as "the master signifier for the rest of the text," but this is largely because he obscures this likely change in speaker.

Why, then, do you marvel, you cheapest lives, nay, you forensic herds—or better yet, you vultures in togas—if all judges these days trade their opinions for a price, when at the very beginning of time, beauty corrupted a judgment which was negotiated between gods and humans, and a rustic, shepherd judge, chosen by the plans of great Jupiter, sold his primitive opinion for the price of lust, even at the destruction of his entire stock? So also, by Hercules, another later judgment is celebrated among the famous leaders of the Argives, such as when Palamedes, excellent in erudition and doctrine was convicted of treachery on trumped-up charges, or when mediocre Odysseus was preferred to the greatest Ajax, extraordinary in martial virtue. What sort of judgment, moreover, was that one among the law-giving Athenians, those sagacious teachers of all wisdom? Surely you remember the old man of divine prudence, whom the Delphic god preferred to all mortals for his wisdom? After being attacked by the fraud and envy of the worst faction as if he was a corruptor of the youth (which he, in fact, checked with reins), wasn't he killed by the harmful juice of a poisonous herb, thus leaving a stain of perpetual disgrace on the citizens, since even now the most noteworthy philosophers prefer his holiest sect and in the highest pursuit of happiness, swear by his name?

If Byrrhena played the role of *exêgêtês* for Lucius, telling him in a foreboding harbinger, "it's yours, everything you see," Lucius-*auctor* here assumes her mantle, fulfilling the requisite function of *ekphrastic* exegete for his reader in this reconfiguration of the earlier episode. Yet, while he physically embodies the position and posture of Byrrhena's *simulacrum Actaeon* within the representational frame in a realization of mimetic contagion—i.e., as a *pronus* quadruped gazing upon a stripping goddess with "curious eyes"—he simultaneously accosts *us* as if he were an enlightened interpreter of the spectacle. Lucius-*auctor* chastises his readers—*quid ergo miramini* ("Why do you marvel . . . ?")—in the discourse of art criticism and immersion: "marvel," of course, is one of the experiential phenomena which characterizes *ekplêxis*, or "stupefaction," at beauty, naturalistic verisimilitude, or even erotic seduction.[120] When he addresses us in the vocative, moreover, he calls us "herds of the forum" (*forensia pecora*), thus actualizing the threat which aesthetic experience, especially the

---

120. On which, see 4.2 (with n. 26). *Mirari* is the goal of the Prologue's variegated display (1.1: *ut mireris*), which is in line with other novelistic prologues, such as Longus' *D&C* and the fragment of the *Incredible Wonders beyond Thule* we considered earlier (see §2.4). On the philosophical origins of the *topos* of "marvel" in Apuleius, see Graverini 2010; Ulrich 2017, 722–23.

186   THE SHADOW OF AN ASS

pleasure of verbal charm, poses to its audience: it can transform those who experience it into beasts of burden.[121]

For many scholars—and particularly, for the cynical school of criticism—this rant has provided an alternative "master signifier" (n. 119 above) to counterbalance Mithras' moralizing recasting of books 1–10 at *Met.* 11.15 (see §1.0). Of course, Lucius' world-weariness and staunch rejection of *Venus vulgaris* in the pantomime represented for an earlier generation of criticism a sign of "evolution" (*Entwicklung*), whether we read the tirade as "the voice of human consciousness within the animal" or as a symbol of "the inadequacy of human understanding of Venus and her charms."[122] In post-Winklerian criticism, however, and especially in light of Winkler's (mis)identification of the Isiacpriest-Lucius as the speaker of the *ekphrasis*,[123] the consensus has largely settled (with a few noteworthy exceptions)[124] on emphasizing the comic incongruity of Lucius—a debased and horny ass, who sensuously describes his Pasiphaëan affair with a Roman *matrona* a mere twelve sections earlier (10.22)[125]—suddenly recoiling in disgust at the victory of *Venus vulgaris* and lecturing his readers about not giving themselves over to aesthetic-erotic pleasure.[126]

What scholars have significantly overlooked about this tirade on the corruption of justice, however, is how Lucius reframes the Judgment of Paris as a "primeval" choice narrative (cf. *originalem sententiam*) and links it, moreover,

---

121. Cf. *Phaedr.* 259a and my discussion of it in §1.1. So also, Apuleius' discussion in the *Apologia* of Plato's *Venus vulgaris* alludes to its power over "herd animals and beasts" (12.2: *pecuinis et ferinis*). Cf. Zimmerman-de Graaf 1993, 157.

122. See Schlam 1978, 103, and Tatum 1979, 79–80, respectively, for quotations. The debate over Lucius' progress or moral development still raged among readers of this earlier generation. Cf., e.g., Sandy 1978, 123, who recognizes the rant as a gesture of "sign-posting comic incongruity."

123. Winkler 1985, 146.

124. See Fick 1990 and Zimmerman-de Graaf 1993. Cf. now Adkins 2022, 199–204.

125. That Lucius is about to replicate his mytho-maniacal affair with the *matrona* in a Pasiphaë mime is suggested by Schlam 1992, 55. To link this episode to choice further, we may note that Lucius alludes subliminally to the "Education of Heracles" through an exclamation "by Hercules" (*Hercules*) at the climax of his tryst with the Roman *matrona*: "pressing my spine in a tighter embrace, she clung [to me] such that I, by Hercules, believed that I was even lacking something for fulfilling her lust" (10.22: *spinam prehendens meam adpliciore nexu inhaerebat, ut **hercules** etiam deesse mihi aliquid ad supplendam eius libidinem crederem*). On the significance of these playful invocations of Hercules, cf. §1.3.

126. The starkest statement of Lucius' failure to change can be found (pre-Winkler) in Wlosok 1969, 69: "Auch zeigt er keine Spur eines inneren Reifwerdens oder gar einer Läuterung, die ihn der Erwählung zum Isisdienst entgegenführt. Er bleibt töricht, geil, gefräßig, neugierig und lernt im Grunde nichts dazu." For cynical views of the rant, see Finkelpearl 1991; and Kirichenko 2008a, 91–93. Cf., however, Kirichenko 2010, 115–21, who presents a more nuanced view of Lucius' outburst. Moreover, Finkelpearl, in my opinion, threads the needle nicely (esp. 234–36) by reading the tirade as an episode shot through with references to moralizing literature which Lucius himself misunderstands and misconstrues.

ENTRANCED BY THE MIRROR OF MYTH   187

to our preferred paradigms of choice in Second Sophistic reader-response. For after lamenting the corruption of this trial "at the beginning of time" (*rerum exordio*), Lucius invokes Hercules (*sic hercules*), and in so doing, subliminally connects Paris' choice between goddesses to Prodicus' allegory, a phenomenon familiar from our discussion in §1.3 and one which Lucius replicates in his affair with the *matrona*.[127] More explicitly, though, the other *exempla* Lucius cites— the betrayal of Palamedes, the judgment of arms between Odysseus and Ajax, and the trial of Socrates at Athens—initiate the process of devaluing Odysseus as a heroic paradigm and of privileging Plato's Socrates, in turn, as the ideal model of a life-choice. We may recall from §1.3 that Lucius likens himself specifically to Odysseus at 9.13 for his *multiscientia*. However, as Apuleius transitions here from the degraded world of books 1–10 to the transcendent realm of the Isis book, he foreshadows a paradigm shift, according to which Lucius (allegedly) loses his *curiositas* and thereby, replicates Odysseus' choice in *Plato's Myth of Er* to adopt the life of an "unmeddlesome private citizen" (*Rep.* 10.620c6–7: ἰδιώτου ἀπράγμονος).[128]

When we look closely at these corrupted mythical judgments, then, it is significant that in each case, Lucius alludes not to the allegorized version of Odysseus as exemplary reader and model of self-restraint (as we surveyed in §2.1), but rather to the treacherous trickster and devious schemer, whose machinations in the *Iliad* led to the downfalls of heroes.[129] So, in referring to the "trumped-up charges" (*falsis insimulationibus*) of Palamedes, Lucius cites the well-known story of the hero's demise at the hands of Odysseus, who allegedly planted evidence of betrayal in Palamedes' tent and exposed him to his fellow Greeks.[130] Similarly, Lucius' next *exemplum* of corrupted *iudicium* turns to the famous tale of the judgment of arms between Odysseus and Ajax—this time, devaluing Odysseus as a paradigm by labeling him with an adjective that encapsulates Greek self-restraint and simultaneously, heroic failure: "mediocre" (*modicus*).[131] Uncoincidentally, these first two exempla mirror Plato's debased version of Odysseus in his *Apology*: indeed, at one point in *his* defense speech, Socrates imagines commiserating in

---

127. See n. 125 above. Cf. Krabbe 2003, 217–59.
128. On which, see §5.1. See also Ulrich 2020, 688–700.
129. On Odysseus' diminished reputation in tragedy, see Stanford 1963, 102–17 and Worman 1999. On his variable reception in fourth-century BCE philosophy, see Montiglio 2011, 38–65.
130. This story was likely in Euripides' now-lost *Philoctetes* (on which, see Dio Chrys. *Or.* 59.8). Cf. also Lucian's *Calumniae*, where the narrator laments that betrayal by Odysseus.
131. On the primary, earlier sense of *modicus* (derived from Greek *metrios*), see *ThLL* 8.0.1228.42 and 8.0.1228.59. See *ThLL* 8.0.1231.39–51 for the evolution of the adjective's more pejorative association.

188   THE SHADOW OF AN ASS

Hades with Odysseus' victims—Palamedes and Ajax[132]—and expresses a desire, in turn, to "track down and question" (*Apol.* 41b5–6: ἐξετάζοντα καὶ ἐρευνῶντα) supposedly great Homeric heroes about their wisdom, first and foremost, the treacherous Odysseus. In short, Apuleius reproduces Plato's own questioning of paradigms of wisdom, transforming the *auctor*'s response to the pantomime of Venus and the venal judgment of Paris into an opportunity to expose Lucius' doubly mytho-maniacal reflection.

It is fitting, therefore, that Lucius-*auctor* concludes his list of miscarriages of justice with the greatest failed *sententia* of all, the historical Socrates, an "old man of divine prudence, whom the Delphic god preferred to all mortals" (10.33: *divinae prudentiae senex, quem . . . praetulit cunctis mortalibus deus Delphicus*). As Luca Graverini has shown, this is only one of two instances in the *Met.* where Apuleius singles out "shining paradigms of *prudentia*":[133] the former is Odysseus at 9.13; the latter this historical Socrates, set in stark contrast to the Homeric hero. Or to phrase it differently, at the end of book 10, after Lucius endures a mock-*Odyssey* which culminates in a myth about an originary choice in an *agôn*, Lucius-*auctor* appeals to the figure of the historical Socrates as the model of choice, not only for the Delphic god who "prefers" him to all mortals, but also for "noteworthy philosophers" (*egregii philosophi*) throughout time. Indeed, famous thinkers "choose" (*praeoptent*) Socrates over others as a model for life, swearing by his name in their "highest zeal for happiness" (*summo **beatitudinis** studio*). Through the reference to this famous philosopher, Lucius connects his reaction to Venus' pantomime to philosophical "blessedness" (*beatitudo*), the Latin translation for Greek *Eudaimonia*, which, we may recall, is precisely what Lady Vice's friends call her in Prodicus' allegory (cf. Xen. *Mem.* 2.1.26: οἱ μὲν ἐμοὶ φίλοι . . . καλοῦσί με **Εὐδαιμονίαν**). Simply put, this citation of Socrates as a paradigm of life brings us full circle, back to the central question of this chapter, and indeed, of this monograph: namely, what influence does (or should) aesthetic experience have on us? Will we suffer mimetic (or *ekphrastic*) contagion if we indulge ourselves and take pleasure in its seedy delights? Or will we be like Alcibiades, fleeing Socrates "as if he is a corruptor of [our] youth" (*velut corruptor adulescentiae*), when he speaks to us in *logoi* hidden beneath the "hide of a hybristic satyr" (*Symp.* 221e2–3: σατύρου . . . ὑβριστοῦ δοράν)?

---

132. Cf. Adkins 2022, 203n61, who notes *Apol.* 41b as the "philosophical source for this diatribe."
133. See Graverini 2012b, 92–93.

ENTRANCED BY THE MIRROR OF MYTH 189

Lucius famously concludes his tirade with a comical metalepsis by imagining a "characterized fictive reader" impatiently interrupting him:[134] "look now, will we suffer an ass philosophizing to us?" (10.33: *Ecce nunc patiemur philosophantem nobis asinum*). As noted above, this "philosophizing ass" becomes the "master signifier" for cynical readers, even though it may activate Lucius' associations with the asinine Socrates of the *Symposium*, the *rudis locutor* par excellence who hides "statues of virtue" (222a4: ἀγάλματ᾽ ἀρετῆς) in his *logoi* about "donkeys and pack-asses" (221e4: ὄνους . . . κανθηλίους).[135] The Judgment of Paris concludes, in turn, with a final feat of pyrotechnics, where the earth opens up and swallows the stage, while a pipe from the ceiling rains down saffron-infused wine and "dyes" (10.34: *maculatae*) the sheep yellow. But Lucius, recognizing that his keepers are dumbstruck at "the sensuous spectacle" (10.35: *voluptario spectaculo*), and fearing to suffer not only a "contamination" (10.34: *contagium*) but also a *sparagmos*, flees to a beach at Cenchreae. There, he falls asleep in an explicit replication of Odysseus' long-awaited slumber on the sands of Phaeacia/Phorkys,[136] and this anticipates Lucius' transition from a debased Odysseus to an incurious Socrates.[137] As we turn now to book 11, we will consider how the juxtaposition of Isis with the spectacle of Venus sets the stage for Lucius' final incorporation into the cortege of the Egyptian goddess.

3.4. Simulacrum Lucius, *Ekphrastic Contagion, and the Actaeonic* Lector *(Met. 11.24–25)*

If Venus through her seduction in the pantomime makes an offer akin to that of Lady Vice from Prodicus' allegory, it points up Lucius' crossroads choice that he is immediately faced with the *simulacrum* of another goddess when he comes to at the opening of book 11. Indeed, at 11.1, Lucius wakes up in a state of terror, purifies himself in the sea, and says a prayer to a numinous presence still unknown to him. Immediately, he narrates his vision of a goddess (11.3)—"look, a divine face in the middle of the sea" (*ecce pelago medio . . . divina facies*)—and

---

134. See Zimmerman-de Graaf 1993 for the "characterized fictive reader," which Adkins 2022, 187–218, deploys for her excellent discursive approach to the novel.
135. Cf. Adkins 2022, 204, on the resonance with the *Symp.* here.
136. On the closure of book 10 as a marked, epic book-ending, see Harrison 2013a, 192. On this moment as an allusion to Odysseus on the beach of Phaeacia or Phorkys, see Beer 2011, 79–86; and Hunter 2009a, 200, respectively.
137. See Ulrich 2020, 696–700; and see further §5.1.

190 THE SHADOW OF AN ASS

when the deity raises her face above the waves, a "very clear simulacrum" (*perlucidum simulacrum*) seems to stand before him. Here, once again, Lucius is *pronus* (i.e., still asinine), as he gazes upon the *simulacrum* of a goddess via mirroring water. This time, however, the goddess is clothed in stark contrast to *Venus vulgaris*: she replicates, in short, Lady Virtue in the "Education of Heracles"[138] and simultaneously, reverses Lucius' thought experiment in book 2 of "stripping" Venus of her elaborate clothes (see 2.8; on which, see §4.3).

Although this striking choice between goddesses is related to the central question of Apuleius criticism in the last century, we remain focused in this chapter on how Lucius engages with *representations* of goddesses and moreover, how he becomes increasingly incorporated into their figural displays. To that end, we consider in the closing section of this chapter the way in which Lucius becomes not the mythical Actaeon, who is merely put on display as a representation in Byrrhena's atrium, but rather and more peculiarly, becomes Actaeon as an *object* of representation in the statuary ensemble of a goddess. Simply put, he becomes a *simulacrum* of a person *in a state of transformation*, who is featured in a sculptural group as he gazes upon a (clothed) goddess and describes *himself* to *us* via *ekphrasis*. Whether or not such stultification as a statue is a desirable outcome for a curious buffoon, who (until meeting Isis) enjoys casting his gaze every which way, remains an open and unanswerable question. Indeed, readers can interpret the *simulacrum Lucius* together with his textualization at 2.12 as yet another act of fixing the object of representation *ritu cadaveris*—"in the manner of a corpse" (cf. *Apol.* 14.7).[139] However, an ancient aporetic reading—which is to say, one that embraces a dialectical *aporia*, which requires readerly participation (rather than a poststructuralist one)—would ask not whether Lucius' transformation is "real," but rather what Lucius' transformation means *for us*, his interlocutors; or more precisely, what demands this text places on *us*.[140] In that respect, I would submit that at the close of the Isis book, we as readers are disconcertingly thrust (via *ekphrastic* contagion) into Lucius' earlier position vis-à-vis Byrrhena's atrium, assimilated to external viewers who may be "drawn into imitation" of the scene.[141]

---

138. Cf. Xen. *Mem.* 2.1.22 for a description of *Aretê*: εὐπρεπῆ τε ἰδεῖν καὶ ἐλευθέριον φύσει, κεκοσμημένην τὸ μὲν σῶμα καθαρότητι, τὰ δὲ ὄμματα αἰδοῖ, τὸ δὲ σχῆμα σωφροσύνῃ, ἐσθῆτι δὲ λευκῇ.

139. Again, Too 1996 reads immobility as sinister. Similarly, in a nod to Winkler, Lateiner 2001, 239–40, sees continuity rather than difference in Lucius' *agalmatophilia* (on which, see ch. 4).

140. For a fitting lament about the effect of Winkler's "aporetic" approach on Apuleius criticism, see Dowden 1998. On the *Met.*'s demands on its readers, see again Kenny 1974; and Svendsen 1978.

141. Cf. Germany's definition of mimetic contagion (n. 4 above). On the reader's implication in Apuleius' text, see Kirichenko 2008b. See also Nì Mheallaigh 2009.

ENTRANCED BY THE MIRROR OF MYTH 191

Let us turn, therefore, to Lucius' self-description during his initiation, where we learn that the anamorphosed ass-man is put on public display in an elaborate outfit decorated with representations of hybrid animals. At 11.24, Lucius delivers a brief *ekphrasis* of *himself* with vivid *enargeia* (once again incorporating his reader with a second-person singular subjunctive):[142]

> Namque in ipso aedis sacrae meditullio ante deae **simulacrum** constitutum tribunal **ligneum** iussus superstiti, byssina quidem, sed floride depicta veste conspicuus ... Quaqua tamen **viseres**, colore vario circumnotatis insignibar animalibus; hinc **dracones Indici**, inde **grypes Hyperborei**, quos in speciem pinnatae alitis **generat** mundus alter.

> For in the very middle of a sacred temple, I stood (as I was ordered) on a wooden dais situated in front of the *simulacrum* of the goddess: indeed, I was distinguished in a silken garment, one painted with flowers. ... Wherever you looked, I was notably marked with animals of variegated color embroidered all over; on this side, Indian dragons; on another, Hyperborean griffins, to which another world gave birth in the guise of a winged bird.

Niall Slater rightly notes that Lucius *becomes* the spectacle—no longer in control of the "gaze," but subject to it—and thus, finds his apparent loss of identity and subordination to the goddess "less appealing than appalling."[143] Without recognizing how Lucius reproduces *both* Byrrhena's atrium *and* Venus' pantomime in different ways, however, Slater has, I fear, missed the point: Apuleius-the-author invites *us* to enjoy this spectacle, to "[succumb] to the seductions of visualization" (n. 11), while at the same time exposing the danger of doing so. For, on the one hand, Lucius is situated not in a domestic atrium for happenstance viewers, but in a thoroughly public context: "in the very middle" (*meditullio*) of a temple like both the *signum* of Diana *and* the dancing Venus,[144] but displayed on a "wooden" (*ligneum*) stage (akin to the *mons **ligneus*** in the Judgment of Paris).

---

142. See *GCA* 2015, 412, on *quaqua tamen viseres*: "by the use of the second person, the narrator tries to involve the readers in the description, who become, in a way, part of the audience admiring Lucius' outfit."

143. Slater 1998, 40. Cf. also Slater 2003, 100, where he links the transformation from spectator to spectacle to the *Risus* festival.

144. Cf. 2.4, where the representation of Diana holds the "balanced middle" (*libratam ... **medietatem***). Venus, too, takes "center stage" (10.32: *in ipso **meditullio***) just prior to her dance. On these "middling" representations as potential intermediaries in Apuleius' demonological framework, see Ulrich 2023, 95–97, and further discussion in §5.4.

This *ekphrasis* does not, however, highlight the artistry and naturalistic verisimilitude of the scene, or for that matter, its elaborate pyrotechnics; there is no illusion of motion via mirroring water nor any sensuous play from the wind. Rather, Lucius points up his otherworldly quality, insofar as he is decorated with hybrid creatures, Indian dragons and Hyperborean griffins—both of which as winged quadrupeds mirror the very form which Lucius-ass had longed to assume throughout the novel.[145] These are creatures, in other words, to which "another world gave birth" (**generat** *mundus alter*)—and here, the connection between *mimesis* and (contaminated?) offspring is brought full circle. Lucius, therefore, remains tethered to his composite nature as a "half-transformed" man in this spectacle, much as the *simulacrum Actaeon* in Byrrhena's atrium represents a mythical personage "already wild and turning into a stag" (*iam in cervum ferinus*). But whereas the object (and agent) of the gaze were obscured in Byrrhena's atrium, as the passive *visitur* of 2.4 had a complex representational medium as its subject, the very *same* verb is used in a pointedly personal manner for this *ekphrasis*—*viseres* ("*you* would see!"). Or in other words, the familiar *ekphrastic* device of the second-person singular verb (see n. 63), when triangulated through the earlier encounter with the ambiguously focalized *simulacrum Actaeon*, pointedly casts the reader in the role Lucius plays in book 2.

Dressed in such a multivalent costume, then, Lucius is situated as a *simulacrum* on a *tribunal* beside Isis' *simulacrum* for public exhibition (11.24):

Sic adinstar Solis **exornato me** et in vicem **simulacri** constituto, repente **velis reductis** in **aspectum** populus **errabat**.

Adorned like Sol in this way and set up in the manner of a *simulacrum*, with the curtains suddenly drawn, the people wandered about me looking for a glance.

Moreover, while Lucius-*actor* eventually moves from this position (and indeed, even travels to Rome), his closing word of the novel—his *final* verbal utterance—is a prayer, in which he promises to "mirror" the goddess secretly in his heart for eternity (11.25):

---

145. See *Met.* 6.30 and 8.16 (on which, see Winkle 2014, 120–22). On Lucius' comical obsession with becoming a winged quadruped (like Pegasus), see Ulrich 2020, 687–88. In this respect, Lucius realizes Socrates' (Delphic) question at the opening of the *Phaedrus* about whether he is a composite creature or a simpler being (on which, see Morgan 2012).

ENTRANCED BY THE MIRROR OF MYTH   193

Divinos tuos vultus numenque sanctissimum intra pectoris mei secreta conditum perpetuo custodiens **imaginabor**.

I will **image** your divine face and most holy deity, guarding it hidden in the secret places of my heart forever.

On the one hand, in the first passage, *simulacrum Lucius* is situated on a dais behind curtains much like the *spectaculum* of book 10. Indeed, just as the wooden stage for Venus' pantomime was revealed after the "canopy was lifted and the scene curtains rolled up" (10.29: *aulaeo **subducto** et complicitis sipariis*), so also, the representational display of Lucius invites spectation after the "curtains are drawn" (*velis **reductis***). Thus adorned with composite hybrids on his cloak, he stands on the *tribunal*—this time, as a *simulacrum* of one "already wild and turned into an ass" (*iam in asinum ferinus*). Furthermore, as a central figure in this sculptural ensemble, he spends his time gazing upon the *simulacrum* of a goddess. But even after he moves from the *tribunal,* on the other hand, he promises in our second passage to function *for eternity* (*perpetuo*) as a specular *imago* of the goddess. Simply put, he offers to keep a representational facsimile of the goddess "in the secret places" of his heart and in fact, transformed into a book, he continues to perform this function today. It is, of course, disturbing to our modern notions of subjectivity and self-actualization that Lucius' final word of the novel is *imaginabor*: he seems to lose himself in his reflection of the goddess and to become a representational device, which exists merely to register (a *representation* of) the goddess.

At the same time, though, our interpretation of Lucius' final position vis-à-vis the goddess is somewhat more complicated. For while Lucius is still on display as a *simulacrum* in the ensemble of Isis, he claims to feast for three days, "enjoy[ing] the ineffable pleasure of the goddess' statue" (11.24: *inexplicabili **voluptate** simulacri divini **perfruebar***). Indeed, stripped of his ass-hide and attired in clothes which symbolize his composite (and possibly divine)[146] nature, he banquets among the gods, thus unveiling for us *simulacra deorum* (i.e., Plato's "statues of gods").[147] It is in this exposure of Lucius' inner (divine) representation, then, that we return to the connection between mimetic contagion and progeny/offspring. For Lucius narrates how he "enjoy[s] the ineffable

---

146. See, e.g., *GCA* 2015, 415 *ad loc.* 11.24.4, and 404–6. For the notion that the spectacle of Lucius standing next to Isis could foreshadow the advent of Osiris, I am indebted to Luca Graverini (*per sermones*).

147. Cf. Ulrich 2017, 723–28, on this intertext and see further §5.5. On stripping Socrates, see §4.3.

pleasure" of Isis' statue, and in so doing, describes his religious experience in the language of an erotic entanglement: throughout the *Met.*, *voluptas* refers almost exclusively to a debased form of pleasure—one experienced in illicit sexual liaisons which produce contaminated offspring.[148] Likewise, the verbal component of his *voluptas*—*perfruor* ("to enjoy")—has erotic connotations akin to the "delight" that Lucius-*auctor* takes in the statue of Diana he imaginatively undresses.[149] Is Lucius' stultification as a statue and absorption before Isis' *simulacrum*, therefore, a new, religious-philosophical form of *voluptas*—a "pleasure" somehow redeemed under Isis' "economy of grace"? Or is it merely a redirection of his debased *voluptas*, a fetishization of the goddess' statue in yet another autoerotic, imaginative exercise? This remains, of course, the irreconcilable question about the *Met.*, and we shall return to it again in the next chapter when we consider Lucius' attempts to experience *agalmatophilia* in his religious-erotic encounters with surrogate goddesses.

But more interesting to me is to consider the influence that this encounter with the *simulacrum* Lucius (via *ekphrastic* contagion) is meant to have on us, the readers *outside* of the text. In this respect, it is worth noting that the people of Cenchreae who witness Lucius on the dais are said to "wande[r] about [the *simulacrum*] for a glance" (11.24: *in aspectum populus* **errabat**). Simply put, *error*—the most significant element from Ovid's Actaeon, which Apuleius deliberately elides in Lucius' *ekphrasis* of Byrrhena's sculptural group (see §3.2 with nn. 77 and 78)—enters the novel at the very end in the form of the internal audience's reaction to this new statuary ensemble. Whereas the Actaeon of *Met.* 2.4 was no victim of innocent "wandering," but rather a witting voyeur lying in wait for a clothed goddess to undress, we readers at the close of the Isis book are assimilated to the viewers *inside* of the text, the *populus* which "wanders," perhaps unwittingly, into a spectacle of metamorphosis mediated through a figural

---

148. See Bartsch 2006, 184–85, on *voluptas* as "a term that is distinctly sensual in its connotations." Of the 30 times that *voluptas* is used in the *Met.*: 13 allude explicitly to erotic pleasure (1.8, 2.10 [twice], 2.17, 2.18, 4.27, 5.31, 7.21, 10.4, 10.20, 10.23, 10.31, and 10.32), 5 to the pleasure of indulging in illicit spectacle (1.7, 4.13, 4.14, 5.26, and 10.17), and 6 loosely to consumption or generally to illicit behavior (7.11, 8.12, 9.19, 11.15, 11.23, and 11.28). The two ambiguous cases are in *C&P*, when Psyche "gives birth" (6.24: *nascitur*) to a daughter named "Pleasure" (personified!), and here at 11.24.

149. On the erotic valence of *fruor*, see *TLL* 6.1.1424.22–51 (*de amore, libidine*) and Adams 1982, 198. Cf. also *GCA* 2001, 161 *ad. loc.*, who notes: "Dans les *Met.*, *perfrui* est le plus souvent employé avec nuance érotique." See also Adams 1982, 197–98, who treats *delecto* in the same section as *fruor.* Cf., however, Apuleius' *Plat.* 2.22, where *frui* is used of the "wise man's" (*sapiens*) perpetual "delight" in happiness and security.

representation and reflected, in turn, in the mirror of Lucius' heart. Ovid's narrator famously asked of his Actaeon's incidental sacrilege—"what crime [is] there in wandering?" (*Met.* 3.142: *quod . . . scelus **error** habebat*). Nevertheless, we may feel some discomfort as solitary readers of a bawdy and carnivalesque novel, "bent over" (*proni/ae*) our texts and gazing upon a *simulacrum*. In this closing spectacle of the novel, then, we are reminded of our earlier posture and "consumptive gaze" in the visual spectacle of Byrrhena's atrium. Simultaneously, though, we are invited to feel a productive cognitive dissonance, to attempt to distinguish our experience here from Lucius-*auctor*'s delusional fantasy of a "Striding Diana" transforming into a "Bathing Diana" before his eyes. For us, at the very least, there is the possibility that we have merely "wandered" into this text, and perhaps it is also still possible for us to escape it unscathed.

FOUR

Visualizing the Goddess

*Religious-Erotic Choice in Mock-Platonic
Encounters with the Divine*

In the wake of Lucius' encounter with Byrrhena's statuary ensemble, in which he uses the power of aesthetic imagination to transform a "Striding Diana" into a "Bathing Diana," he returns home to his host Milo's house. Aroused from the magic of artistic verisimilitude, he determines to seduce Milo's slave girl, Photis. In the tryst that follows, we shall see on full display what I refer to in this chapter as Lucius' "philosophico-mania": parallel to his delusions of grandeur in seeing himself playing the role(s) of mythical heroes, that is, he similarly attempts to rationalize his own overly corporeal and debased erotic experiences in terms of famous transcendent moments from Platonic dialogues. The immersive pleasure of reading Lucius' tawdry description of his affair is complicated for the *lector scrupulosus*, however, by the recognition of how highbrow, Platonic reference is contaminated with alternative models of erotics— for example, with Roman models from erotic poetry and art, and even with the literary reception of Platonic ideals in the Second Sophistic.

As we shall see, the idealized model(s) of Platonic erotics, which we find comprehensively explicated in the two dialogues most important for imperial and Second Sophistic education—the *Phaedrus* and the *Symposium*[1]—entails at

---

1. On the role of the *Phaedrus* in Second Sophistic education, see Trapp 1990. On the reception of Plato (both *Phaedr.* and *Symp.*), see Hunter 2012. On the *Phaedr.* in Apuleius' contemporaries— Achilles Tatius, Petronius, and Longus—see respectively Nì Mheallaigh 2007; Repath 2010; Hunter 1997. Recently, cf. Fletcher 2014, 265–76, on the origins of "Platonic fiction" in these two dialogues in particular.

its outset a choice over how to respond to beauty: that is, whether to appreciate it aesthetically or whether to leverage it to some other, more transcendent end and "climb the ladder," so to speak, to the Forms. As Radcliffe Edmonds has recently demonstrated, this Platonic choice is made especially clear through the way in which Plato uses the image of a divine statue.[2] One can attempt, on the one hand, to mount the beloved "in the manner of a quadruped" (*Phaedr.* 250e4: τετράποδος νόμον) or sexually assault a statue of a divinity, like the black horse of Socrates' Palinode in the *Phaedrus* or the lover in the cautionary tale of *agalmatophilia* in the pseudo-Lucianic *Amores*. However, there is also a "correct" way, according to Platonic erotics, to use an image or to respond to the encounter with beauty: to "track" (*ichneuô*) the sign or follow the "trace" (*ichnos*) in a mnemonic chain to recollect the Form of beauty which the soul encountered in its precorporeal state.[3]

This Platonic distinction is, of course, what is at stake in our programmatic encounter with aesthetic-erotic experience from the *Symposium*: Alcibiades flees the Sirenic Socrates precisely because he can only see the aesthetic (and *not* the utilitarian) value in sitting next to the marvelous philosopher; he does not know how to "scrupulously weigh" what is underneath the surface (*à la* Rabelais' Prologue). That Apuleius was well aware of this Platonic distinction between aesthetic and utilitarian modes of viewing is evident from, among other things, his treatment of statuary in the *Apologia* and the *Florida*.[4] Indeed, we shall see in the next section (§4.1) that Apuleius leverages the choice over how to view statuary to powerful rhetorical effect in the *Apologia* by linking the sight of his little statuette of Mercury—the etiolated *sigillum* which the prosecution attempts to interpret as another sign of Apuleius' involvement in

---

2. See Edmonds 2017. On statuary in Greek religion in general, see Steiner 2001, esp. 198–204 on Plato; Kindt 2012, esp. 155–89 on *agalmatophilia* in the Second Sophistic; Platt 2011.
3. See, e.g., *Phaedr.* 252e7–253a5: ἰχνεύοντες δὲ παρ᾽ ἑαυτῶν ἀνευρίσκειν τὴν τοῦ σφετέρου θεοῦ φύσιν εὐποροῦσι διὰ τὸ συντόνως ἠναγκάσθαι πρὸς τὸν θεὸν βλέπειν, καὶ ἐφαπτόμενοι αὐτοῦ τῇ μνήμῃ ἐνθουσιῶντες ἐξ ἐκείνου λαμβάνουσι τὰ ἔθη καὶ τὰ ἐπιτηδεύματα, καθ᾽ ὅσον δυνατὸν θεοῦ ἀνθρώπῳ μετασχεῖν. Moreover, in Socrates' final words in the *Phaedo*, he exhorts his followers to "live (by following) in the tracks of the things discussed now and earlier" (*Phaed.* 115b9–10: ὥσπερ κατ᾽ ἴχνη κατὰ τὰ νῦν τε εἰρημένα καὶ τὰ ἐν τῷ ἔμπροσθεν χρόνῳ ζῆν). Importantly, Plato connects this process of "following the tracks" to the seriocomic act of writing at the end of the *Phaedr.* (see 276d1–5): ἀλλὰ τοὺς μὲν ἐν γράμμασι κήπους, ὡς ἔοικε, παιδιᾶς χάριν σπερεῖ τε καὶ γράψει, ὅταν [δὲ] γράφῃ, ἑαυτῷ τε ὑπομνήματα θησαυριζόμενος, εἰς τὸ λήθης γήρας ἐὰν ἵκηται, καὶ παντὶ τῷ ταὐτὸν ἴχνος μετιόντι, ἡσθήσεταί τε αὐτοὺς θεωρῶν φυομένους ἁπαλούς. On following the "tracks" of the divine through images in Plato, see Edmonds 2017.
4. See esp. *Apol.* 63–64 (on which, see below) and *Fl.* 15. On *mimesis* and statuary in the *Apol.*, *Fl.*, and *Met.*, see Too 1996; Slater 1998. Lateiner 2001 deals with the role of statuary and immobility in the Risus festival.

magic—to the upper-realm from Socrates' Palinode in the *Phaedrus*, about which his learned judge, Maximus, has "diligently read" (*Apol.* 64.5: *legit . . . diligenter*).[5] His accusers, Apuleius implies in his rebuttal, merely misunderstand how to deploy the utilitarian mode of appreciating statues and thus, misinterpret his ownership of a statuette as magical praxis, when, in point of fact, it is a philosophical and in particular, Platonic pursuit of *anamnêsis*—one rooted in a procedure of following "tracks" or "traces" (*vestigia*; cf. *ichnê*) of beauty on earth to the divine. In fact, it is clear from the opening of the *Soc.* that Apuleius translated Plato's concept of "tracking" (*ichneuô*) the Forms across his corpus with the verb *vestigare*: according to Apuleius' demonology, "we track down some [gods] only by intellection" (*Soc.* 1.2: *alios intellectu* **vestigamus**).

After elucidating how Apuleius frames his statue-appreciation in Platonic terms in the *Apologia* (§4.1), I aim in this chapter to situate the religious-erotic encounters that Lucius has with surrogate goddesses (e.g., Photis, Venus) as well as his epiphany (real or imagined) of Isis in a Second Sophistic, Platonizing discourse of erotic and religious modes of viewing (§4.2). For as Jas Elsner has demonstrated in his penetrating epilogue to *Roman Eyes*, Apuleius seems to have chosen ancient erotic and religious art—the "Striding Diana" pose and the Cnidian Aphrodite—as "the key image[s] . . . around which mimetic and religious gazes collide" in the *Metamorphoses*.[6] Indeed, the two modes of viewing that Elsner elucidates throughout *Roman Eyes*—"horizontal viewing," which plays upon desire invested in "social and personal relationships with others (as evoked through images),"[7] and "vertical viewing," which attempts to commune with the divine via artistic representation—"turn out to flip as two sides of a coin about a single image."[8] The religious and erotic types on which readers focus, moreover, are "not legislated by any means other than the viewer's choice."[9] As one might expect, I concur with Elsner's innovative suggestion that the *Met.* requires from its readers a choice in the mode of viewing they deploy,

---

5. On this instance of self-fashioning as the "ultimate directing of Platonism into a protreptic for philosophy," see Fletcher 2014, 216–18, 218 for quotation.

6. Elsner 2007, 301.

7. Elsner 2007, 289.

8. Elsner 2007, 302. Cf. also Kindt 2012, 166, who similarly takes religious and erotic gazing to be a difference in intention: "The religious and the erotic both relied on the visual as the primary medium of interaction. Both dimensions of human life together informed the way in which the statue was approached. Religious gazing can be oriented along the ritualistic functions of religious objects. But . . . it also encompasses another way of looking on as fundamentally a mental (cognitive) activity. . . . Erotic gazing, in contrast, is driven by the desire to touch and to possess (in sexual union), to traverse and penetrate."

9. Elsner 2007, 301.

and moreover, that this choice is potentially fraught with danger. I will push this further, however, by linking the viewer's choice to readerly choice.

Furthermore, a place where I break significant new ground in this chapter is in my interpretation of the erotic tension in the buildup to and consummation of Lucius' tryst with Photis (§4.3), bookended as it is with artistic representations of goddesses. For beyond alluding to well-known iconographic types in Lucius' epiphanic encounters with surrogate goddesses in the early books of the *Met.*—for example, the "Striding Diana" transformed into a "Bathing Diana,"[10] or Photis metamorphosed into the Cnidian Aphrodite[11]—Apuleius represents Lucius, his philosophico-maniacal narrator, retrospectively reframing his tryst with a slave girl in highbrow, idealized Platonic discourse. It is, of course, playful on the iconographic level, given that the model for the *Venus Pudica* type presented a notorious art-critical problem even in antiquity: according to Athenaeus, Praxiteles allegedly based his Aphrodite on a courtesan named Phryne, who was long associated with both Praxiteles and Apelles.[12] In light of this arthistorical discourse, then, it is interesting that Lucius goes home after ogling a marvelous statue of a goddess, and attempts to statuize a low-class slave girl *as if* she were Venus, replicating in reverse the procedure that Praxiteles (supposedly) performed. However, while the art-critically aware reader will look at these different representations of goddesses in various states of undress and see how Apuleius invites an encounter which potentially verges on sacrilege,[13] the *lector scrupulosus*—one who has "diligently read" the *Phaedrus* like Apuleius' judge in the *Apol.*—will recognize how Lucius rationalizes his own *agalmatophilia* ("statue-loving") through his (mis)appropriation of the procedure outlined in the *Phaedrus* (and elsewhere).

As we shall see, at the *ekphrastic* climax of his foreplay with Photis, Lucius gazes upon the back of Photis' head and quotes a most famous and sublime moment from the *Phaedrus*, when the beloved looks into the lover's eyes and sees himself, "as if in a mirror" (*Phaedr.* 255d5–6: ὥσπερ . . . ἐν κατόπτρῳ). This phrase—"as if in a mirror"—had its own afterlife in Second Sophistic, Platonic erotics, appearing in texts which explicitly foreground their *Phaedran* ancestor,

---

10. On the history of these two archetypes and Apuleius' fusion of them, see Schlam 1984. See also my fuller discussion in §3.2.
11. See, e.g., Slater 1998, 20–24.
12. For the tale, see Athen. *Deipnosoph.* 13.590f–91b. On the biographizing tendency of authors in the Second Sophistic to link Phryne to Praxiteles, see Havelock 1995, 42–49. See also Squire 2011, 100–101.
13. On potential transgressions of religious-erotic epiphanic viewing, see Platt 2011; Kindt 2012.

such as Plutarch's *Amatorius*,[14] as well as those which model a novelistic poetics on this transcendent moment of the erotic self-knowledge tradition, such as Achilles Tatius' *Leucippe and Clitophon*.[15] Apuleius, however, in a style of Platonic parody well-known to readers of the *Met.*, represents Lucius eulogizing Photis' *hair* for its "likeness to a mirror" (*Met.* 2.9: *ad instar speculi*), thereby turning the beloved around and transforming this transcendent encounter into an episode of fetishized fantasy. This Platonic archetype, which provided the basis for a range of discussions on the intersubjective nature of *erôs* and its power to grant self-knowledge to lovers, is thus transformed into a subject-object interaction susceptible to narcissism; and Lucius' feigned "erotic reciprocity," the mutual desire which subordinated beloveds are said in the *Phaedrus* to experience,[16] is revealed instead to be *agalmatophilia*, a rather strange obsession of the Second Sophistic.[17]

In fact, it is part of the brilliant parody that Lucius reverses the direction of Platonic enlightenment. Whereas in Plato, the lover sees beauty, attempts to sacrifice to the beloved "like a statue or a god" (251a6: ὡς ἀγάλματι καὶ θεῷ), and eventually follows the "trace" of beauty back to its source, Lucius sees a statuary ensemble of a fully dressed goddess and imagines her naked. Then, so aroused by Diana's mimetic verisimilitude that he imaginatively undresses the goddess with his "curious gaze" (2.4: *curioso optutu*), Lucius returns home to transform a human into another iconographic type—in this case, the *Venus Pudica*. That is to say, while sexual arousal functions in Plato as a vehicle to encounter the divine, in Lucius' philosophico-mania, the divine offers merely another opportunity for sexual arousal, both with the *simulacrum* of Diana and with his statuized Photis. After elucidating the Platonic patina Lucius layers over his tryst (§4.3), we will consider how this approach to viewing the divine ripples through the rest of the novel, influencing Psyche's religious-erotic

---

14. See Plut. *Amat.* 765f6–7 for the phrase in context (on which, see §4.2). On the influence of the *Phaedrus* on the *Amat.*, see Trapp 1990, 157–61; Hunter 2012, 185–222. On the influence of the *Amat.* on the idealizing Greek romances, see Goldhill 1995, 144–61.

15. See *L&C* 1.9.4–5. It is generally agreed that there are significant echoes of the *Phaedrus* in Achilles Tatius (Marincic 2007; Nì Mheallaigh 2007). Morales 2004, 130–35, deciphers a great deal of the *Phaedrus* in this specific passage. Cf. also Goldhill 1995, 66–102.

16. On Plato's revolutionary development of "erotic reciprocity," see Halperin 1986, though I do not fully subscribe to his idealizing reading. On Platonic "specular reciprocity," see Pellizer 1987; on its influence on later versions of the Narcissus myth (or vice versa), see Egan 2004.

17. On which, see Steiner 2001, 185–250; Platt 2001, 186–88, 199–201; Kindt 2012, 155–89. Lateiner 2001, 239–40, also connects Lucius' behavior to *agalmatophilia*, though he (mis)reads such "statue-loving" into the Isis book when, in fact, Lucius breaks with procedure (on which, see §4.5 below).

encounter in *C&P* (§4.4) as well as Lucius' concluding choice of Isis at the opening of book 11 (§4.5). However, whereas other readers might take these episodes strictly as parody—satire-for-the-sake-of-satire—I read the philosophico-mania of our asinine *auctor* as a comment on how not to read Plato and moreover, as a choice posed to the *lector scrupulosus* over whether to continue following the incompetent *auctor* down the primrose path, so to speak.[18] As we shall see, careful, "active" reading of the *Met.*—much like "diligent reading" of the *Phaedrus*—can lead to the appropriate epiphanic experience: following the trace of the divine back to its source rather than replicating the *agalmatophile*'s pleasure. At issue here once again is aesthetic versus utilitarian modes of viewing, and once more, the choice is up to the reader. Let us turn now to Apuleius' concluding rebuttal of the subsidiary charges in the *Apol.*, where we can derive Apuleius' terms for this approach to statuary in the rhetor's clear juxtaposition of his own and his accusers' modes of viewing.

4.1. *Aesthetic and Utilitarian Viewing in the* Apologia

We may recall again Apuleius' whirlwind conclusion to the *Apologia*, in which he summarizes each of the charges with two words and responds, in turn, with a two-word rebuttal. In §2.3, we saw Apuleius answering the charge of "looking into a mirror" (*Apol.* 103.2: *specula inspicis*) with the response: "a philosopher must" (*debet philosophus*). Likewise, he summarizes the last of the subsidiary charges and rebuts it in two words: "'You worship wood': Plato advises it" (103.3: '*lignum consecras*': *Plato suadet*). It is, to be sure, an extraordinarily creative form of self-fashioning to claim that Plato would endorse Apuleius' specific practice of carrying around a little wooden statuette of Mercury, which he refers to as his "king" (*Apol.* 64.8: *Basileus*). If we look back at the conclusion of the subsidiary charges, however, we see a distinctly Platonic approach to leveraging beauty—and especially, the beauty of statues—to recollect the divine by following "traces" back to the Forms.

At *Apol.* 63, Apuleius turns to the "third lie" of the prosecution, namely, that he had a habit of "carrying around wherever [he] went a *simulacrum* of a certain god hidden within his books" (63.3: *quoquo eam, simulacrum alicuius dei inter libellos conditum gestare*) and moreover, that he "prayed to it on festal days

---

18. In this respect, my reading builds on Heath 1992, 121–28; Penwill 1990.

with incense, wine, and sometimes even with a sacrificial victim." Apuleius does not dispute this accusation. Instead, he suggests that the prosecution has merely misinterpreted—or we may say, misread—Apuleius' mode of engaging with his *simulacrum*. They failed not only to appreciate the aesthetic beauty of his little *sigillum* (62.2), which they suggested was "grotesque," "etiolated," and even "cadaverous," but also to understand the utilitarian value of statue-worship and in particular, the way in which statues function as intermediaries between humans and the divine. Indeed, renewing the charge of atheism that Apuleius had put forward earlier in his speech,[19] he claims that Aemilianus never looks at "statues of gods" (*Apol.* 63.9: ***simulacra deorum***) and as a consequence, "neglects them all" (*omnia neglegit*).

Simulacra deorum, as I have suggested in this book and elsewhere,[20] is an important tag-line across the Apuleian corpus, alluding as it does to our programmatic passage from Plato's *Symp.*: there, Alcibiades eulogizes Socrates as a metamorphic spectacle whose external hide conceals *agalmata theôn* underneath.[21] Here in his own *Apologia*, therefore, Apuleius deploys a brilliant rhetorical maneuver, transforming Aemilianus into an Alcibiades-figure, but one who has failed even to recognize the "statues of gods" (*simulacra deorum*) Apuleius possesses "hidden within" (*conditum*). In fact, this rebuttal to the charge of Apuleius' fraught ownership of a statue is mirrored in a ring-composition with the first of the subsidiary charges—the charge that Apuleius is "beautiful"—to which he responds with an invective against his own disgusting hair. Indeed, at *Apol.* 4, Apuleius complains that far from remaining beautiful, his "perpetual literary labor" has ruined his youthful glow, sucking dry "his sheen" and removing his "color" and "vigor." Then, he points to his hair as the prime example (4.11–13):

> vides quam sit amoenus ac delicatus horrore implexus atque impeditus, stuppeo tomento adsimilis et inaequaliter hirtus et globosus et congestus, prorsum inenodabilis diutina incuria non modo comendi, sed saltem expediendi et discriminandi.

> You see yourself how "charming" and "delicate" it is: it's horribly tangled, knotted and unkempt like flaxen cushion-stuffing, shaggy and unequal in length, so

---

19. See Hunink 1997, 168 *ad loc.* 63 for discussion.
20. Ulrich 2017. See also my introduction for its programmatic nature.
21. Cf. also O'Brien 2002; Graverini 2012a, 118–31; Egelhaaf-Gaiser 2012.

204   THE SHADOW OF AN ASS

bunched up, coiled, and mangled by my prolonged carelessness not only of arranging [it], but even of untangling and combing [it].

This grotesque hair represents, on the one hand, Apuleius' external appearance *pars pro toto*. At the close of the subsidiary charges, however, our brilliant rhetor reveals his "*simulacrum* of a certain god," which he carries "hidden within books" (*inter libellos conditum*)—a *simulacrum* which discloses Apuleius' true character. Deploying not only a shared vocabulary of beauty, linked through obscure lexical terms such as *sucus*,[22] but even the same construction for epideictic display (i.e., *vides quam . . . sit*), Apuleius unveils his little statuette for the court (*Apol.* 63.7–8):

> Em vide, quam facies eius decora et suci palaestrici plena sit, quam hilaris dei vultus, ut decenter utrimque lanugo malis deserpat, ut in capite crispatus capillus sub imo pillei umbraculo appareat, quam lepide super tempora pares pinnulae emineant, quam autem festive circa humeros vestis substricta sit.

> Behold! Look at how beautiful its appearance is, how full of wrestling sheen, how charming the face of the god is, how pleasantly the youthful wool creeps down on both cheeks, how the hair on his head appears to curl under the edge of the shadow of his cap, how charmingly his perfect little wings stick out from his temples, how handsomely his cloak is draped about his shoulders.

The small effigy thus becomes a fitting representation of Apuleius' own *simulacra deorum*: the rhetor strips himself, so to speak, of his external appearance and reveals his true Socratic or Satyric character—a maneuver which Yun Lee Too has recognized in the ring-composition between *Apol.* 4 and 64, and which others have seen at work elsewhere in Apuleius' corpus.[23]

What is significant for my interpretation, however, is not the "methodologi-

---

22. *Sucus* is rarely used to describe the appearance of humans in Apuleius: apart from these two passages, this usage only occurs in an *ekphrasis* of the statue of Bathyllus at *Fl.* 15. That *ekphrasis* likewise begins with a description of hair and then moves down to the neck (*cervix*), which is *suci plena* (15.7). Elsewhere, *sucus* is used to refer to poison or the juice of plants, such as in Lucius' tirade on the death of Socrates at *Met.* 10.33.

23. See Too (1996, 148), who interestingly adds that the Silenus-statuttes in Plato's *Symposium* are found in "Hermes factories" (215b1: *hermoglypheiois*), which may explain "why Apuleius' effigy is a Mercuriolum." On Apuleius' treatment of Marsyas in *Fl.* 3 as part of his self-fashioning, see, e.g., Finkelpearl 2009; Fletcher 2014, 228–34.

cal impersonation" of Plato in Apuleius' self-fashioning,[24] but rather the fact that he connects the "correct" mode of viewing this divine statue explicitly to the practice of "diligently reading" Plato's *Phaedrus*. After displaying the beautiful statuette and attacking Aemilianus for his sacrilege, Apuleius explains why Maximus (his judge), by contrast, will recognize the utilitarian value of religious statuary (*Apol.* 64.3–5):

> Ceterum Platonica familia nihil novimus nisi festum et laetum et sollemne et superum et caeleste. Quin altitudinis studio secta ista etiam caelo ipso sublimiora quaepiam **vestigavit** et in extimo mundi tergo stetit. Scit me vera dicere Maximus, qui τὸν ὑπερουράνιον τόπον et οὐρανοῦ νῶτον legit in Phaedro diligenter.

> But we in the Platonic family are aware of nothing but what is joyous and happy and solemn, what is of the upper realm and heavenly. Indeed, that sect, out of its zeal for the sublime, has even followed the tracks of certain matters higher than the very sky and has stood on the outermost ridge of the cosmos. Maximus knows that I speak the truth, since he has diligently read in the *Phaedrus* about the "place beyond the heavens" and the "ridge of heaven."

The appropriate reaction to a statue of a god or goddess, in other words, is to recognize the "traces" of the divine, the "loftier matters" (*sublimiora*) the soul once "followed the tracks of" (*vestigavit*) when it stood on the ridge of the cosmos. This "correct" mode of viewing, however, is available only to a "diligent reader" of the *Phaedrus*. What's more, the *lector scrupulosus* of the *Apologia* will recall that it is the duty of philosophers to "track down and inquire into all things" (cf. *Apol.* 16.1: *videntur . . . debere philosophi haec omnia* **vestigare** *et inquirere*).[25] Thus, just as Plato outlines "correct" and "incorrect" modes of viewing beauty, where the "correct" approach involves "following in the tracks" (*ichneuô*) of the "traces" (*ichnê*) left behind on earth and using them in a mnemonic chain to recollect the original experience of the Form, so also, Apuleius suggests that the charge laid against him of owning a statuette hinges on how

---

24. The concept of methodological impersonation is developed in Fletcher 2014. On Apuleian allusion and self-fashioning in the *Apol.* in general, see Harrison 2008, esp. 12–14 on Platonic allusion.

25. Fletcher 2014, 125–30, extends this phenomenon also to the "catascopic flight" of personified Philosophy in *De mundo*.

one "reads" it. One could, like the uneducated Aemilianus, choose to appreciate it solely in aesthetic terms by viewing it "horizontally" for its implications in the social panopticon (*à la* Elsner). The "correct" reading, however—the one endorsed by the "Platonic family" and practiced by Apuleius and Maximus—is to utilize the statue to achieve a higher end, to recollect the "place beyond the heavens" (*hyperouranion topon*).

Before we turn to the *Metamorphoses* to look at Lucius' philosophico-maniacal privileging of aesthetic over utilitarian modes of viewing, it will be useful to consider briefly the Platonic backdrop and its afterlife in Apuleius' milieu (§4.2). For we shall find in Plato the terms of the discourse that Lucius deploys, especially in describing the arousal he feels building up to his tryst with Photis. Moreover, the afterlife of this Platonic discourse in Second Sophistic literature represents how badly the transcendent pleasure of visualizing beauty can turn out for the wrong kind of viewer/reader. Indeed, a hyperphysical and overly sexualized response to divine beauty can lead to a distorted form of *agalmatophilia* rather than a Platonic *anamnêsis* of one's previous experience as a disembodied soul. This aesthetic versus utilitarian mode of viewing divinity, beyond constituting the philosophical backdrop for Lucius' fetishized tryst with Photis, will also provide the foundation for my interpretations of two thematic and structural parallels in the *Met.*—namely, "Soul's" epiphany of *Amor* in *C&P* as well as Lucius' final epiphany of Isis at the opening of book 11. In both cases, the divinity's hair represents the physical feature which enacts the erotic-religious epiphany. However, whereas Psyche follows in Lucius' footsteps by pursuing an overly sexualized touch of the god—even to the point of wounding the god, like the *agalmatophile* in the pseudo-Lucianic *Amores*—the asinine Lucius of book 11 along with his fellow worshippers of Isis deploy the appropriate procedures of handling, viewing, and utilizing the statue of the goddess to a divine, epiphanic end.

4.2. Platonic Transcendence and Its Afterlife in Roman Literary and Second Sophistic Epiphany

The initial phenomenological experience of gazing upon beauty, according to a number of Platonic dialogues, is *ekplêxis*: a mixture of stupefaction and amazement, simultaneously paralyzing as well as transcendent.[26] In particularly

---

26. See, e.g., *Symp.* 192b7, 211d5, and 216d3; *Phaedr.* 250a6 and 255b4. On the origins of *ekplêxis* and its reception in Plato (and Aristotle), see Belfiore 1992, 218–22. See also Nightingale 2004, 157–68, esp. 158–59 for discussion of theorizing the beloved in the *Phaedrus*. *Ekplêxis* is labeled the natu-

heightened visions of beauty on earth, *ekplêxis* leads to an out-of-body experience and the viewer describes the feeling as being wholly "outside of oneself." Thus, at the opening of Plato's *Charmides*, all the bystanders who witness the entrance of the beautiful young *erômenos* are "dumbstruck and entirely bewildered" (*Charm.* 154c4: ἐκπεπληγμένοι τε καὶ τεθορυβημένοι ἦσαν) at the spectacle. Similarly, the *erastês* in the *Phaedrus* experiences his religious-erotic encounter not only in terms of *ekplêxis*, but also as an escape from corporeality: "whenever [souls] see some likeness to the things in the other world, they are dumbstruck and are no longer in themselves" (*Phaedr.* 250a6–7: ὅταν τι τῶν ἐκεῖ ὁμοίωμα ἴδωσιν, ἐκπλήττονται καὶ οὐκέτ' <ἐν> αὐτῶν γίγνονται).[27] It is unsurprising that this form of stupefied amazement ripples out in the Hellenistic period into the discourse of ancient art-criticism, as the appropriate viewer reaction to beautiful art—and especially, to heightened naturalism or mimetic verisimilitude—is expressed in these terms.[28] Moreover, Luca Graverini has already recognized this Platonic religious-erotic motif at work in Psyche's vision of Cupid in *C&P*, where "Soul," gazing at her beloved for the first time, is said to be "terrified at so beautiful a sight and not in control of her mind" (*Met.* 5.22: *tanto aspectu deterrita et impos animi*).[29]

Significantly, this initial experience of visualizing beauty is universal, but the "correct" and "incorrect" responses are clearly delineated in the Platonic procedure. After undergoing *ekplêxis* at beauty, the onlookers in the *Charmides* gaze at the beautiful youth "as if upon a statue" (*Charm.* 154c9: ὥσπερ ἄγαλμα). Likewise, the initial reaction of the lover in the *Phaedrus* is to "feel religious awe, as if looking upon a god" (*Phaedr.* 251a5: προσορῶν ὡς θεὸν σέβεται); and given the opportunity, he would "make a sacrifice to his darlings as if to a statue

---

ral response to beautiful poetry and rhetoric as early as Gorgias (DK B11) and Aristophanes (*Fr.* 961–62), and certainly flows into Platonic discourse through these rivulets (see *Symp.* 198b5 and 215d5–6; *Phaedr.* 234d1 and 259b8).

27. In the reception of this *topos* in imperial rhetorical theory (e.g., in 'Longinus'), *ekplêxis* leads to *ekstasis* (i.e., "standing outside of oneself"), on which, see de Jonge 2020.

28. See, e.g., Hardie 2002, 185, on Aeneas' reaction to himself in Dido's temple (on *stupor*, the Latin equivalent to *ekplêxis*): "The line between the two kinds of amazement, at a work of art and at a supremely beautiful human being, is one that is difficult to draw within the reactions of both Aeneas and Perseus to the objects that hold their gaze. But the attempt to discriminate is misguided, given the routine interference in ancient writing on art between aesthetic and erotic responses." *Ekplêxis* likewise becomes a critical term in rhetorical treatises and scholia for discussing the effects of powerful poetry on the reader, on which, see Hillgruber 1994, 94–95 on Ps.-Plut. *Hom.* 6; Nünlist 2009, 144–45.

29. With this Latin phraseology, cf. τεθορυβημένοι ἦσαν; οὐκέτ' ἐν αὐτῶν γίγνονται, on which, see Graverini 2010. Cf. also Lateiner 2001, 227–32, though he does not recognize the Platonic heritage of this trope. See also Popescu 2014, 39–41, who detects a similar play with *ekplêxis* as a philosophical/reader-response oriented phenomenon in Lucian's *VH*.

or a god" (251a6: θύοι ἂν ὡς ἀγάλματι καὶ θεῷ τοῖς παιδικοῖς). And once again, of course, Alcibiades satirically worships Socrates in the *Symp.* by stripping his grotesque, external hide to see the *agalmata theôn* hiding beneath (*Symp.* 215b3) and the "statues of virtue" (222a4: ἀγάλματ᾽ ἀρετῆς) concealed in his words. Although Alcibiades feels the universal initial reaction to Socrates' marvelous beauty, being himself "dumbstruck and spellbound" (*Symp.* 215d5–6: **ἐκπεπληγμένοι** ἐσμὲν καὶ **κατεχόμεθα**), he notoriously refuses to be educated appropriately and ultimately, is revealed to have failed to respond philosophically.[30]

In fact, there is a lovely irony woven into the intertextual play between the *Charmides*, the *Alcibiades 1*, and the *Symposium*. At the opening of the *Charmides*, as the bystanders marvel at the eponymous *erômenos*, one of Socrates' companions, Chaerephon, approaches the philosopher and inquires after what he thinks of the young beauty. Attempting to emphasize the unparalleled nature of Charmides' external appearance, Chaerephon suggests: "If [Charmides] were willing to strip, he would seem faceless; so utterly beautiful is his form" (*Charm.* 154d3–4: οὗτος μέντοι, ἔφη, εἰ ἐθέλοι **ἀποδῦναι**, δόξει σοι ἀπρόσωπος εἶναι· οὕτως τὸ εἶδος πάγκαλός ἐστιν). To this rather odd fetishism, Socrates responds with a similarly discomfiting suggestion—one which would become a leitmotiv of Platonic philosophical procedure. Only one thing will reveal Charmides to be an unrivaled beauty: if his internal form, his soul, matches his external beauty. To investigate this, Socrates asks (*Charm.* 154e4–6):

> τί οὖν . . . οὐκ **ἀπεδύσαμεν** αὐτοῦ αὐτὸ τοῦτο καὶ ἐθεασάμεθα πρότερον τοῦ εἴδους; πάντως γάρ που τηλικοῦτος ὢν ἤδη ἐθέλει διαλέγεσθαι.

> Why, then, don't we strip that very part of him and behold it before [we look at] his form? For being of a ripe age already, I'm sure he'll be willing to dialogue.

This play with internal and external beauty is part of the tradition we saw Apuleius tapping into above with his "*simulacrum* of a certain god" in the *Apologia*. As we saw in §0.4, this notion of stripping the beloved was widespread in

---

30. Cf., e.g., Montiglio 2011, 133–34, who interprets this scene in the *Symp.* as a moment when Plato demonstrates the inappropriate reader-response: "Alcibiades' deafness characterizes him as one of Odysseus' companions, whereas, had he been a model disciple of Socrates, he would have absorbed more of his teacher's charm than Odysseus did of the Sirens'. For the correct attitude vis-à-vis Socrates the Siren is not even that of Odysseus, who chose to listen to the song and yet to protect himself from it, but total and permanent abandonment."

Apuleius' milieu, connected both to "active" reading and philosophical looking. In this vein, we may recall how Seneca advises his reader in *Ep.* 76: to know a person's true worth, one must remove all external circumstances and even "take off the body itself" (76.32: *corpus ipsum exuat*)—indeed, "look at him naked" (*nudum inspice*) and "contemplate his soul" (*animum intuere*). We may further note that this passage from the *Charmides* was well-known to Apuleius, since he alludes to it at the opening of *Florida* 2.[31] This idea of "stripping" the beloved, however, arises in another Platonic dialogue important for imperial education: *Alcibiades 1*.[32] There, Socrates suggests to his putative *erômenos* that, in order to see what external "beauty" (*Alc. 1* 132a5–6: εὐπρόσωπος) really is, "it is necessary to behold [people] stripped naked" (ἀλλ᾽ **ἀποδύντα** χρὴ αὐτὸν θεάσασθαι).

It speaks to Plato's rich (and generally, underappreciated) humor that this is precisely what Alcibiades attempts to do to Socrates: to strip him and his words of their external "hide" (221e3–4: δοράν) in order to behold what is underneath. But Alcibiades' aesthetic appreciation of the *agalmata theôn* under Socrates' skin models the "incorrect" reaction to beauty, insofar as the *erômenos* attempts to leverage his epiphany into erotic pleasure and in particular, into an overly corporeal and hypersexualized encounter with Socrates.[33] Rather than using the *ekplêxis* induced by Socrates as a tool in the mnemonic chain to recollect the original source of beauty, Alcibiades transforms the philosopher into a kind of curiosity in a museum, and even attempts to sexually violate this statue of the divine.[34]

---

31. So, *Fl.* 2 opens with Socrates encountering a "beautiful youth" (2.1: *decorum adulescentem*), and upon inspecting him, he exclaims: "In order that I may see you, say something too" (2.2: *ut te uideam . . . aliquid et loquere*). On this opening as an allusion to the *Charmides*, see Harrison 2000, 96. Cf. also Lee 2005, 67 *ad loc.*; Fletcher 2014, 232.

32. On the *Alc. 1* in antiquity, see Denyer 2001, 14; Pradeau 1999; and the introduction to Segonds' text of Proclus' commentary on the *Alc. 1* (Segonds 1985). For more references, see Bartsch 2006, 41. We know that Apuleius read the *Alc. 1* and considered it authentic, since he quotes it directly at *Apol.* 25.11.

33. Alcibiades acknowledges his role reversal in the coded *erastês-erômenos* sexual dynamics (217b4–5: ἅπερ ἂν ἐραστὴς παιδικοῖς ἐν ἐρημίᾳ διαλεχθείη; 217c7–8: ὥσπερ ἐραστὴς παιδικοῖς ἐπιβουλεύων). On this inversion of the Athenian norm, see Usher 2002, 214. That this is how this episode is received in the Latin tradition is evidenced by the Croton episode in Pet. *Sat.*, where Encolpius suffers from impotence and Giton laments his "Socratic faithfulness" (*Sat.* 128.7: *Socratica fide*), claiming that "Alcibiades never laid so untouched in his master's bed" (*non tam intactus Alcibiades in praeceptoris sui lecto iacuit*).

34. The term that Alcibiades deploys in his complaint over how Socrates treats his youth is *hybrizein* ("to assault"), though the young *erômenos* is the one who breaks procedure by adopting the role of pursuer and striving after sheer bodily pleasure. See *Symp.* 219c5 and 222a8. Cf. Hunter 2004, 99: "Alcibiades . . . turns the sober world of Agathon's symposium upside down: now it is *erômenoi*, not their lovers, who get insanely jealous . . . it is they who are enslaved to their teachers . . . and it is sexual abstinence which is characterized as outrage (*hybris*, 219c5)."

When we turn to the kitchen-seduction scene in Apuleius, we shall see Lucius-*auctor*, in addition to adopting the philosophical discourse of *ekplêxis* to cloak his erotic encounter with Photis in Platonic garb, also attempt to "strip" (*despoliare*) his beloved—*not* of her external appearance in order to see her soul, but rather of her *hair* in order to imaginatively heighten his fetishistic pleasure. Most important for Apuleius' method of framing Lucius' erotic entanglement in the discourse of idealized Platonic encounters, though, is the transcendent power that *hîmeros* is said to have at the narrative denouement of Socrates' Palinode. For when Socrates' myth reaches its climax, the philosopher elucidates the effects of desire not only on the *erastês*, but also on the *erômenos* (*Phaedr.* 255c1–e1):

ἡ τοῦ ῥεύματος ἐκείνου πηγή, ὃν ἵμερον Ζεὺς Γανυμήδους ἐρῶν ὠνόμασε, πολλὴ φερομένη πρὸς τὸν ἐραστήν, ἡ μὲν εἰς αὐτὸν ἔδυ, ἡ δ' ἀπομεστουμένου ἔξω ἀπορρεῖ· καὶ οἷον πνεῦμα ἤ τις ἠχὼ ἀπὸ λείων τε καὶ στερεῶν ἁλλομένη πάλιν ὅθεν ὡρμήθη φέρεται, οὕτω τὸ τοῦ κάλλους ῥεῦμα πάλιν εἰς τὸν καλὸν **διὰ τῶν ὀμμάτων** ἰόν, ᾗ πέφυκεν ἐπὶ τὴν ψυχὴν ἰέναι ἀφικόμενον καὶ ἀναπτερῶσαν, τὰς διόδους τῶν πτερῶν ἄρδει τε καὶ ὥρμησε πτεροφυεῖν τε καὶ τὴν τοῦ ἐρωμένου αὖ ψυχὴν ἔρωτος ἐνέπλησεν. ἐρᾷ μὲν οὖν, ὅτου δὲ ἀπορεῖ· καὶ οὔθ' ὅτι πέπονθεν οἶδεν οὐδ' ἔχει φράσαι . . . **ὥσπερ δὲ ἐν κατόπτρῳ ἐν τῷ ἐρῶντι ἑαυτὸν ὁρῶν** λέληθεν. καὶ ὅταν μὲν ἐκεῖνος παρῇ, λήγει κατὰ ταὐτὰ ἐκείνῳ τῆς ὀδύνης, ὅταν δὲ ἀπῇ, κατὰ ταὐτὰ αὖ ποθεῖ καὶ ποθεῖται, **εἴδωλον ἔρωτος ἀντέρωτα ἔχων·**

The fountain of that stream, which Zeus named "desire" when he was in love with Ganymede, flows in abundance; it is carried into the lover, sinking into him, and when he is filled, it overflows outside; and just as the wind or some echo bounces back from smooth, hard surfaces and is carried back from whence it originated, so the stream of beauty travels back into the beautiful one through the eyes, the [path] through which it naturally enters into to the soul. It stirs the soul up and waters the passages of the feathers and inspires it to grow wings, filling the soul of the beloved with love. Thus, he is in love, but he is confused about the object of his love; he neither knows what he is experiencing nor can he explain it . . . he does not realize that he is seeing himself in his lover as if in a mirror. And whenever the lover is with him, he is free from his pain as is his lover; but whenever the lover is absent, he feels the same desire his lover feels for him, possessing love's image, reciprocal love.

The "flow of desire" is imagined to be a physical substance which travels back and forth between lover and beloved "through the eyes" (διὰ τῶν ὀμμάτων), functioning as a kind of nutritive liquid, which waters the pathways of the feathers and makes the soul "grow wings." In fact, even before this narrative climax, Socrates describes the "transformation" (*Phaedr.* 251a7: μεταβολή) the *erastês* undergoes from "receiving the flow of beauty through his eyes" (251b1–2: τοῦ κάλλους τὴν ἀπορροὴν διὰ τῶν ὀμμάτων): deploying a thinly veiled euphemism, Socrates claims that the "flow" nourishes the roots of the feather and the "shaft of the feather" (251b6: ὁ τοῦ πτεροῦ **καυλός**) grows swollen or erect.[35] The incorporeal soul, to put it bluntly, gets an erection.

In the buildup to Lucius' entanglement with Photis, we will find all of these elements from the Platonic archetype deployed in a manner so parodic that it exposes the extent to which Lucius-*auctor* embodies an incompetent exegete of Plato. Lucius-*actor* also grows an erection (albeit a very corporeal one) from gazing upon Photis from behind, while she makes a nutritive liquid, a sausage soup, into which Lucius longs to "dip his finger." In that mock-Platonic exchange between *erastês* and *erômenê*, however, Lucius displaces the locus of the "flow" from the eyes, the Platonic "windows to the soul," to Photis' hair, thereby transforming an intersubjective, transcendent encounter into an episode of fetishistic fantasy.

Before turning to the tryst proper, however, we should also note that Plato's idealized encounter has an afterlife of its own in imperial and Second Sophistic literature, as this fount of desire feeds into many subsequent rivers, becoming a source for imitation across antiquity. Shadi Bartsch has recognized a twisted distortion of this "erotic reciprocity" in Narcissus' and Hostius Quadra's encounters with the mirror in Ovid and Seneca, respectively.[36] For instance, Tiresias' foreboding promise—"provided he does not know himself" (*Met.* 3.348: *si se non noverit*)—seems to represent an inversion of the famous Delphic dictum (*gnôthi seauton*) with which the *Phaedrus* passage is also conceptually engaged.[37] Moreover, Rory Egan has convincingly argued that the mutuality of

---

35. *Kaulos* is used in the Hippocratic corpus to refer to the phallus (see, e.g., *Int.* 14). Hence, Frontisi-Decroux 1996, 95, speculates that the swelling psyche looking upon the beautiful boy in this passage is, in fact, the phallus. On botanical-phallic metaphors and the reception of the *kaulos* in Latin, see Adams 1982, 26–27.
36. See Bartsch 2006, 84–114. Toohey 2004, 271–76, likewise connects Hostius Quadra and Narcissus as models of failed (Platonic) self-knowledge.
37. On self-knowledge as a unifying theme of the *Phaedrus*, see Griswold 1986, 2–9 and passim. On its reception in this Ovidian reworking, see Bartsch 2006, 85. Cf. also Taylor 2008, 59.

212 THE SHADOW OF AN ASS

desire—that is, the feeling of relief when the lover is present, and the experience of reciprocal desire when the lover is away (cf. κατὰ ταὐτὰ αὖ ποθεῖ καὶ ποθεῖται)—is dramatized in Ovid's archetype of self-love: "while he seeks, he is sought; and he equally kindles and is kindled" (*Met.* 3.426: *dumque petit, petitur, pariterque accendit et ardet*).[38]

Aside from parodic or distorted appropriations of Plato's ideal in the Latin literary tradition, there is also a clear link between this Platonic archetype of erotic reciprocity and Second Sophistic Greek discourses on love.[39] This link is most clearly evidenced, in my view, in the afterlife of a particular phrase from the *Phaedrus* passage above—"as if in a mirror" (ὥσπερ . . . ἐν κατόπτρῳ)[40]—a concept which proliferates in the Second Sophistic, and which Apuleius also translates into Latin in Lucius' religious-erotic epiphanies. The power of specular reflections to offer simultaneously transcendent epiphany as well as access to self-knowledge becomes a *topos* of the Second Sophistic; and a simple *ThLG* search reflects the resurgence of this phrase, which curiously leaps from the fourth-century BCE world of Platonic dialogue directly into the texts of authors such as Plutarch, Lucian, Achilles Tatius, Aelius Aristides, and even into early Christian texts (e.g., pseudo-Clement and Gregory of Nyssa).[41] In the interest of space, I will explicate only two examples, which not only signal their imitation of the *Phaedrus* manifestly, but also bear clear relevance to my discussion of Apuleius' reception of Plato's aesthetic-versus-utilitarian approaches to desire. It is worth noting, however, that, beyond the many attestations of versions of this Platonizing phrase in the Second Sophistic, the erotic discourse of Plato and the "flow of desire" is similarly palpable everywhere in Apuleius' milieu.[42]

---

38. See Egan 2004, 149–50: "The Ovidian collocation of self-knowledge, self-love, repudiation of the love of others, auditory or echoic reciprocity, and specular reciprocity matches a constellation in the *Phaedrus*."

39. On which, see Goldhill 1995, 46–111.

40. This phrase also appears in the *Alcibiades 1* (133a1), another dialogue centered on the *gnôthi seauton* tradition.

41. To offer a list of examples of variations of this Platonic catchphrase: Pl. *Phaedr.* 255d4, *Alc. 1* 133a1, and *Leg.* 905b4; pseudo-Arist. *Problem.* 915b29 and *De mund.* 395a33; Plut. *Quaest. Plat.* 1002a8 and *Amat.* 765f6; Philo *De somn.* 2.206.3 and *De op. mund.* 76.3; Luc. *De salt.* 81.8; Ael. Arist. *Pan.* 196.10; Achill. Tat. *L&C* 1.9.4 and 6.6.1; Diog. Laert. *VP* 7.152.9; pseudo-Galen *Ad Gaur. Quomod. Anim. Fetus* 6.1.6; Philostr. *VA* 2.30.30 and 8.7.399; pseudo-Clement *Hom.* 5.26.1; Greg. Nys. *Epist.* 19.3, *Orat. viii de Beat.* 44.1105.33, and 44.1272.21. Aside from early Christian texts, this list includes examples only up to the time of Apuleius. Note that the phrase largely falls out of usage between Plato and the Second Sophistic, and then curiously reenters philosophical (erotic) discourse.

42. See Bartsch 2006, 57–114; Goldhill 1995, 46–111 and 2001 on the influence of atomist optics (particularly from the *Phaedrus*) on Latin and Second Sophistic theories of eroticizing vision, respectively. See also Morales 2004 on Platonizing optical theory in Achilles Tatius.

VISUALIZING THE GODDESS   213

The first case of this phrase in the Second Sophistic appears in a work of Lucius' "ancestor," Plutarch (cf. *Met.* 1.2):[43] the *Amatorius*. Beyond replicating a discourse about love in a Platonizing style, this dialogue explicitly marks its filiation to the *Phaedrus* in the opening lines, when the primary interlocutor, Flavian, demands that the young Autobulus (Plutarch's son) dispense with all the trappings of the *Phaedran* generic landscape, such as "Plato's Ilissus, his famous chaste tree and the gentle grass-grown slope."[44] At 765b–f, then, Plutarch (the character in the dialogue) begins a discourse on Pausanias' famous two kinds of love from the *Symposium*: "Heavenly Love" (*ouranios Erôs*) and the love of "the many" (*hoi polloi*). "Heavenly Love," he claims, puts beautiful bodies before the eyes of lovers and in so doing, fashions "beautiful mirrors of the Beautiful" (*Amat.* 765b1–2: ἔσοπτρα καλῶν καλά). According to Plutarch's exegesis, then, the "true lover," upon reaching the heavenly realm and "consorting with true beauty" (766b6–7: τοῖς καλοῖς **ὁμιλήσας**; cf. §3.1 for discussion of *homilein*):

> ἐπτέρωται καὶ κατωργίασται καὶ διατελεῖ περὶ τὸν αὐτοῦ θεὸν ἄνω χορεύων καὶ συμπεριπολῶν, ἄχρι οὗ πάλιν εἰς τοὺς Σελήνης καὶ Ἀφροδίτης λειμῶνας ἐλθὼν

> becomes winged, is initiated into the mysteries, and continues to dance and accompany his god up above until the point when he comes back into the meadows of Selene and Aphrodite.

To be sure, this imagery of winged-ness, inflamed desire, and orgiastic dancing in the upper realm takes its impulse from the *Phaedrus*. Paradoxically, however, a version of our Platonic catchphrase—ὥσπερ . . . ἐν κατόπτρῳ— appears in Plutarch's description of the behavior of "the many," where he draws up a negative paradigm by which to distinguish the "incorrect" approach to beauty (*Amat.* 765f9–766a1):

> ἀλλ᾽ οἱ πολλοὶ μὲν ἐν παισὶ καὶ γυναιξὶν **ὥσπερ ἐν κατόπτροις εἴδωλον** αὐτοῦ φανταζόμενον διώκοντες καὶ ψηλαφῶντες οὐδὲν ἡδονῆς μεμιγμένης λύπῃ δύνανται λαβεῖν βεβαιότερον.

---

43. On Lucius' genealogical connection to Plutarch as a form of "kinship diplomacy" and the scholarly issues associated with it, see *GCA* 2007, 94 *ad loc*. On the reception of Plutarch in the *Met.*, see Walsh 1981; DeFilippo 1990; Keulen 2004; Hunink 2004; Kirichenko 2010, 91; Van der Stockt 2012.

44. *Amat.* 749a3–4: τὸν Πλάτωνος Ἰλισσὸν καὶ τὸν ἄγνον ἐκεῖνον καὶ τὴν ἠρέμα προσάντη πόαν πεφυκυῖαν.

But the many, pursuing and groping after the image of [Love] which appears in boys and women **as if in mirrors**, are able to take away nothing more stable than pleasure mixed with pain.

There are, in fact, two types of "mirrors": the "beautiful mirrors of the Beautiful," for which Plutarch uses the term *esoptra*; and alternatively, the "as-if" mirror—the *katoptra*—which *hoi polloi* exploit for mere pleasure. The former method of viewing constitutes the utilitarian approach to leveraging beauty in order to undergo a transcendent ascent and acquire self-knowledge; the latter, by contrast, deploys the aestheticizing approach merely to enjoying the incidental pleasures of beauty. It is not without significance, then, that the ideal lover is likened to the bee-readers that we encountered in §1.2(b): just as bees "leave behind many green flowers, if they do not possess honey" (765d2–3), Plutarch claims, so also, lovers ought to read the bodies of beloveds, searching for "some trace of the divine" (ἴχνος τι τοῦ θείου). Once again, the aesthetic-erotic experience is reduced to reading bodies: external vs. internal, form vs. content, and superficial vs. depth. The beautiful body of a beloved becomes another text, so to speak, to be mined for useful content and leveraged accordingly.

Aside from Plutarch's Platonizing gestures in the *Amatorius*, our Platonic catchphrase recurs in another important passage from Apuleius' milieu: the opening book of *Leucippe and Clitophon*. In this second-century CE Greek romance, Achilles Tatius represents his ideal hero, Clitophon, receiving consolation for his amorous situation from his cousin Clinias, who advises him in markedly Platonizing discourse. Unlike in Plutarch, however, this gesture of filiation to the *Phaedrus* playfully appropriates the Platonic ideal, insofar as Clinias makes a paradoxical distinction between sight and touch: seeing is "more pleasurable" than the act of consummation. Elucidating the physics of desire in terms reminiscent of Zeus' "fount" of *hîmeros*, Clinias explains (*L&C* 1.9.4–5):

Οὐκ οἶδας οἷόν ἐστιν ἐρωμένη βλεπομένη· μείζονα τῶν ἔργων ἔχει τὴν ἡδονήν. Ὀφθαλμοὶ γὰρ ἀλλήλοις ἀντανακλώμενοι ἀπομάττουσιν **ὡς ἐν κατόπτρῳ τῶν σωμάτων τὰ εἴδωλα**· ἡ δὲ τοῦ κάλλους ἀπορροή, δι᾽ αὐτῶν εἰς τὴν ψυχὴν καταρρέουσα, ἔχει τινὰ μίξιν ἐν ἀποστάσει· καὶ ὀλίγον ἐστὶ τῆς τῶν σωμάτων μίξεως· καινὴ γάρ ἐστι σωμάτων συμπλοκή.

You don't know how great the sight of the beloved is: [seeing] holds greater pleasure than doing it. For the eyes, reflecting one another, make imagistic

VISUALIZING THE GODDESS   215

impressions of each other's bodies, **as in a mirror**. And the flow of beauty, flooding through them (i.e., the eyes) and into the soul, proffers some mingling in its emanation. And it is a small taste of the mingling of bodies: for it is a novel kind of embrace of bodies.

Again, we have the clear trappings here of a *Phaedran* allusion: the "flow" of beauty going "through the eyes" and "into the soul."[45] To add to these topological similarities, we may note that Clinias later on in this passage advises Clitophon on how to "give birth to reciprocal love" (1.9.6: τίκτει . . . ἀντέρωτα) in Leucippe—only the second occurrence of the word *anterôs* in extant Greek literature after Plato.[46] Clinias' greatest consolation to Clitophon, however, is that he gets to remain perpetually present with his beloved, since he lives next door to Leucippe and so, is never compelled to suffer the pain of being apart, such as we saw described in our *Phaedrus* passage and dramatized in Ovid's Narcissus. In fact, in a hilariously mock-Platonic gesture, Clinias explains that the *hêdonê* derived from looking is even "greater than the act," thereby transforming the philosophical ideal of leveraging beauty to track the divine into a parody of Plato's look-but-don't-touch, incorporeal approach to erotics. The aesthetic pleasure of presence is the only end, and gazing into the mirror of the beloved's eyes is somehow better than the consummation of desire which ensues.

It is clear from my exposition, then, that not only the *Phaedrus* as a whole, but this scene, in particular, was foundational for philosophical erotics and indeed, underwent a peculiar renaissance in Apuleius' milieu.[47] When we turn to the *Met.* in the next section, we will see a similar kind of parodic appropriation of this Platonic ideal: rather than witnessing a transcendent erotic encounter, we are invited as readers to look on as a character reminiscent of Plutarch's

---

45. Morales 2004, 130–35, questions whether the *Phaedrus* is the primary allusion here and Goldhill 2001, 178–79, seems to split the difference between Platonizing and Stoicizing models of optics. However, Bartsch 2006, 68–69 and 79, argues for a syncretism of Platonic and atomist theories of optics in *L&C* and a *Phaedran* filiation, in particular, for the phrase *hê . . . tou kallous aporroê*. Moreover, our catchphrase—*hôs en katoptrôi*—is distinctly Platonic, as Whitmarsh 2020, 157–58 *ad loc.* 1.9.4, notes in passing.

46. There is evidence that Epicrates of Ambracia wrote a comedy entitled *Anterôs*. Aside from that, however, the only other extant usage of the term *anterôs* prior to Achilles Tatius occurs in the *Life of Alcibiades* (4.4.7), where Plutarch is, in fact, *quoting* Plato's *Phaedrus*. That Achilles Tatius is "borrow[ing]" from Plato here is noted by Whitmarsh 2020, 158 *ad loc.* 1.9.6, though he does not comment further on the rarity or significance of this term.

47. On the *Phaedrus* in the Second Sophistic in general, see Trapp 1990; Hunter 2012. Given space, we could also consider Lucian's *De salt.* (81), which likewise deploys our Platonic catchphrase in a gesture of filiation to the *Phaedran* mechanics of desire.

hoi polloi pursues an "image of love" in the "mirror" of the female body. Before turning to Lucius' liaison, however, it will be useful to explicate briefly one final element that fills out the Platonic backdrop to Lucius' religious-erotic epiphanies: the "incorrect" approach to beauty, which Plato outlines in the *Phaedrus* and which is reconfigured as *agalmatophilia* in its Second Sophistic reception. For, as we shall see, Lucius-*actor*'s behavior in his encounter with Photis undercuts Lucius-*auctor*'s philosophico-maniacal attempt to reframe the tryst retrospectively. Simply put, while Lucius-*auctor* deploys all of the elements of the *Phaedran* archetype we have elucidated—a (meta)physical erection, stripping the beloved, reflection in the "mirror" of the beloved, and "erotic reciprocity"— Lucius-*actor* reveals his ultimate affiliation with the *Phaedran* black horse in his uncontrolled leap onto the beloved.[48]

Thus far, we have considered how recognizing, appreciating, and even worshipping the beloved as a "statue" (*agalma*) represents the "correct" reaction in Platonic erotics to the out-of-body experience of *ekplêxis*. The alternative response, however, is of one who has not been "recently initiated" into love or has even been "corrupted" (*Phaedr.* 250e1–251a1):

> ὁ μὲν οὖν μὴ νεοτελὴς ἢ διεφθαρμένος οὐκ ὀξέως ἐνθένδε ἐκεῖσε φέρεται πρὸς αὐτὸ τὸ κάλλος, θεώμενος αὐτοῦ τὴν τῇδε ἐπωνυμίαν, ὥστ᾽ οὐ σέβεται προσορῶν, ἀλλ᾽ ἡδονῇ παραδοὺς τετράποδος νόμον βαίνειν ἐπιχειρεῖ καὶ παιδοσπορεῖν, καὶ **ὕβρει προσομιλῶν** οὐ δέδοικεν οὐδ᾽ αἰσχύνεται παρὰ φύσιν ἡδονὴν διώκων.

> Thus, the one who is not newly initiated or is even corrupted is not carried swiftly from here to there (i.e., to Beauty itself), when he beholds its namesake here; thus, he does not worship it when he looks upon it; instead, giving himself over to pleasure, he attempts to mount [the beloved] in the manner of a quadruped and to beget children; having intercourse with it through sexual violence, he feels neither fear nor shame at pursuing pleasure contrary to nature.

This cautionary paradigm for how not to appreciate beauty seems prima facie to describe the asinine-Lucius of books 1–10, who is, to be sure, still "uninitiated" and perpetually gives himself over to pleasure, even to the point

---

48. Cf. Winkle 2014, 107–25, who, expanding on Drake 1968, reads Lucius as the *Phaedran* black horse, esp. as he is reunited with *Candidus*.

of attempting to "mount" various beloveds "in the manner of a quadruped."[49] In this respect, we may recall how Platonic anxieties about "consorting" (*proshomilein*) with mimetic pleasure are articulated in terms of adulterated offspring and inferior issue.[50] The specter of Plato in the *Met.* becomes even more apparent, though, when we consider how the "incorrect" approach is similarly appropriated in a text very likely in Apuleius' milieu (one perhaps even familiar to him): pseudo-Lucian's *Amores*, variously dated from the second to the fourth centuries CE.[51] For there, we find the Lucianic narrator dramatizing Plato's anxieties about the aestheticizing response to beauty in a mock-dialogic debate, which takes place around Praxiteles' famous statue of Aphrodite in Cnidos.[52]

The Cnidian Aphrodite, as we already noted, is one of "the key images . . . around which mimetic and religious gazes collide" in the *Met.* (see n. 6 above). In the *Amores*, therefore, it is significant that pseudo-Lucian reproduces (in Platonizing fashion) a heated debate between two overly sexualized characters—a boy-crazy Athenian, Callicratidas, and a girl-obsessed Corinthian, Charicles—as they walk around the statue of the goddess in her temple and anatomize her particular body parts. For our purposes, it is important to note that both characters have an excessively corporeal response to the statue: the hetero-oriented Charicles "stretche[s] his neck out as far as possible to kiss [the statue]" (*Am.* 13: ἐφ᾽ ὅσον ἦν δυνατὸν ἐκτείνων τὸν αὐχένα κατεφίλει); and while the homoerotic Callicratidas "closely observes the boyish parts of the goddess" (*Am.* 14.1: **τὰ παιδικὰ μέρη** τῆς θεοῦ κατώπτευσεν) and shouts out exuberantly, Charicles stands silently "dumbstruck" (ἐπεπήγει)—save for a certain "flowing sensation in his eyes" (**ῥέον** ἐν τοῖς ὄμμασι πάθος). The other details of this episode are not necessary for us to review, except to point out the dialogue's obvious indebtedness to the *Phaedrus* and its parodic participation in Second Sophistic Platonic erotics.

---

49. On Lucius' asinine posture as a meaningful interpretative element, see O'Sullivan 2016 and §3.2. On his attempts to "mount" various beloveds, see §4.3 below.

50. Recall the distinction we perceived in §3.1 (esp. n. 48) between legitimate "associating" (*homilein*) with beauty (or a spouse) and illegitimate "consorting" (*proshomilein*).

51. Personally, I believe this playful little dialogue to be authentically Lucian, since Apuleius seems to allude to Plato *through* it in the kitchen-seduction episode. I will continue to refer to it as pseudo-Lucian, however, since this is not the appropriate venue to take a stance on its authenticity. On its dating and authenticity, see Bloch 2019 (originally published in 1907), whose pronouncements on the text went largely unchallenged (see Helm 1927; Macleod 1967; Jones 1984) until very recently (see, e.g., Jope 2011) and even then, usually in footnotes (see, e.g., Dowden 2006, 46n11; Elsner 2007, 119n26).

52. For the most extensive analysis of the erotic debate in the *Amores*, see Haynes 2013. For its interaction with Second Sophistic romance, see Goldhill 1995, 102–11; D'Alconzo 2021.

What is paramount for us, however, as we look forward to Lucius' interactions with Photis-Venus-Isis in the following sections is (1) the description of the statue's posture, which curiously mirrors Photis' transformation at the opening of her tryst with Lucius; and (2) the cautionary tale the temple keeper tells of a young *agalmatophile*, who became so obsessed with the masterpiece that he spent the night with the statue. As to the former feature, the brief *ekphrasis* the narrator, Lycinus, offers of the Cnidian Aphrodite's form is, importantly, the "first extant reference to the specific gesture of Aphrodite's right hand."[53] Thus, Lycinus begins his description (*Am.* 13):

πᾶν... τὸ κάλλος αὐτῆς ἀκάλυπτον οὐδεμιᾶς ἐσθῆτος ἀμπεχούσης γεγύμνωται, πλὴν ὅσα τῇ ἑτέρᾳ χειρὶ τὴν αἰδῶ **λεληθότως** ἐπικρύπτειν.

Her entire beauty was revealed, uncovered with no garment surrounding her— except to the extent that she hid her privates imperceptibly with one hand.

Here, we may think again of the evocative dress of Lady Vice in Prodicus' allegory: while clothed in a garment (unlike the Cnidian), she nonetheless chooses a thin gossamer intended to reveal her "youth" (*Mem.* 2.1.22: ὥρα)— and *hôra* can be a euphemism for "privates" (see §3.3 with n. 118). I also suggested in the previous chapter that the pantomime of Venus in *Met.* 10 alludes to that archetype of female seduction, since the surrogate Venus, like Lady Vice, "shadow[s] over her spectacular privates" (10.31: *inumbrabat spectabilem pubem*) with a silken chiffon in order to "lay bare the flower of her youth" (*pateret flos aetatulae*). Whereas Lady Vice and her counterpart Venus in the *Met.* strive to titillate via deliberately revealing clothing, however, the Cnidian Aphrodite plays coy with her outright nudity by covering her privates "imperceptibly"—and here, *lelêthotôs* (a rare adverb derived from the verb *lanthanô*) is connected already in the first century CE to *curiositas* and its power "imperceptibly" to suggest the illicit to the mind of a viewer.[54] It is no coincidence then, in my view, that Photis, when she aims to entice Lucius into a sex-

---

53. So Havelock 1995, 28, argues.
54. Cf., e.g., Plutarch's *De curiositate* 520e4–5, where he explains the harm of *reading* graffiti, which appears at first glance to be harmless: "things which seem *not* to harm just by being read, nonetheless do harm imperceptibly by creating a desire for seeking out that which is illicit" (ἃ δοκεῖ μὲν οὐ βλάπτειν ἀναγιγνωσκόμενα, βλάπτει δὲ **λεληθότως** τῷ μελέτην παρεμποιεῖν τοῦ ζητεῖν τὰ μὴ προσήκοντα).

ual liaison, mimics the pose of the Cnidian Aphrodite: after stripping off all her clothes and letting her hair down, she "shadow[s] her shaven privates with her rosy palm out of diligence rather than covering it out of shame" (2.17: *paulisper etiam glabellum feminal rosea palmula potius obumbrans **de industria** quam tegens verecundia*).[55] And while the statue of Venus seems to signal with its coquettish hand-gesture a conscious "awareness of being seen,"[56] the posture of Photis—at least, according to Lucius' (admittedly skewed) interpretation of it— appears quite intentionally to draw attention to the "shaven privates": *industria* here, as the *ThLL* notes, seems to communicate a purposeful intention, a design to heighten the intoxicating pleasure.[57]

However, if Charicles' and Callicratidas' erotic reactions to the *agalma* begin to verge on sacrilege, replicating as they do the "incorrect," overly corporeal approach to beauty, they are stopped in their tracks, so to speak, when they notice a "stain" (*Am.* 15: σπίλον) on the goddess' thigh. At that point, they are regaled with a "strange story of an incredible fable" (*Am.* 15: ἀπίστου λόγου καινὴν . . . ἱστορίαν) by the temple keeper. According to her account, the stain came from a young man who, in Pygmalion-esque fashion,[58] spent the night with the statue and marred it from his lovemaking (*Am.* 16):

> πέρας αἱ σφοδραὶ τῶν ἐν αὐτῷ πόθων ἐπιτάσεις ἀπενοήθησαν, εὑρέθη δὲ τόλμα τῆς ἐπιθυμίας μαστροπός· ἤδη γὰρ ἐπὶ δύσιν ἡλίου κλίνοντος ἠρέμα λαθὼν τοὺς παρόντας ὄπισθε τῆς θύρας παρεισερρύη καὶ στὰς ἀφανὴς ἐνδοτάτω σχεδὸν οὐδ' ἀναπνέων ἠτρέμει, συνήθως δὲ τῶν ζακόρων ἔξωθεν τὴν θύραν ἐφελκυσαμένων ἔνδον ὁ καινὸς Ἀγχίσης καθεῖρκτο. καὶ τί γὰρ ἀρρήτου νυκτὸς ἐγὼ τόλμαν ἢ λάλος ἐπ' ἀκριβὲς ὑμῖν διηγοῦμαι; τῶν ἐρωτικῶν περιπλοκῶν **ἴχνη** ταῦτα μεθ' ἡμέραν ὤφθη καὶ τὸν **σπίλον** εἶχεν ἡ θεὸς ὧν ἔπαθεν ἔλεγχον.

---

55. So, if we take Lucius' description of Photis in 2.17 to be alluding to the Praxitelean masterpiece, then either the *Amores* is authentically Lucian (and thus, has priority), or Apuleius' description is, in fact, the "first extant" literary reference to this gesture. I am currently in the process of publishing an article which aims to situate the *Amores* between Achilles Tatius and Apuleius via intertextual reference, thus supporting Havelock's claim (1995, 28).

56. For an excellent discussion of this posture and its interpretation across antiquity (and into modernity), see Squire 2011, 69–114, and 75 for quotation.

57. See *ThLL* 7.1.1276.31–41, where it is listed as *adverbialiter, i.q. consilio, consulto, ratione, dedita opera.* Cf. OLD, s.v. **2**.

58. For this tale as a Pygmalion-type of story, see Elsner 2007, 118–20. On the youth's suicide as possessing an "Actaeon-esque flavor of divine punishment," see Platt 2011, 186–87. Cf. also Squire 2011, 104–6, who suggests that the Actaeon archetype must always have been associated with the transgressive and fatal potential of Praxiteles' masterpiece.

220 THE SHADOW OF AN ASS

At last, the excessive intensity of the desires inside him made him lose all sense and audacity was discovered as a pimp for his desire. For already when the sun was leaning toward its setting, quietly escaping the notice of those present, he slid behind the door, and standing unseen in the innermost shrine, he trembled almost not even taking a breath; and when the temple attendants dragged the gate to a close from the outside as per usual, the new Anchises was shut inside. And why would I be so chatty as to narrate to you precisely the audacity of that unspeakable night? At daybreak, these traces of the erotic embraces were seen, and the goddess had a stain as proof of the things she suffered.

This cautionary tale clearly had significant purchase in the imperial period and Second Sophistic, as Pliny the Elder and Clement of Alexandria also allude to it, and Lucian narrates another version of it in his *Imagines*.[59] Most important for my purposes, though, is the fact that this episode dramatizes, in a sense, the behavior of the "uninitiated" or "corrupted" lover of the *Phaedrus*.

Upon hearing this story, the boy-loving Callicratidas concludes that, from the location of the "stain" on the goddess' thigh, it is clear that the boy tried "to have intercourse with the stone like a boy" (*Am.* 17: παιδικῶς τῷ λίθῳ προσωμίλησεν)—or in Platonic terms, to "[have] intercourse through sexual violence" (*Phaedr.* 250e5: ὕβρει προσομιλῶν), "mounting" the beloved "in the manner of a quadruped." So also, we may note that Lucius, in his extended tryst with Photis, attempts to use her "like a boy," when she offers him the "boyish bonus" (*Met.* 3.20: *puerile . . . corollarium*) out of her generosity. The unnamed noble of the *Amores*, however, commits such an "audacity" that it would be an act of excessive chattiness to narrate it. Instead, the whole episode is glossed over merely with a vague reference to the "traces" (*ichnê*) of erotic embraces, the "stain" on the goddess' leg. The *ichnê* which remain, however, are not the Platonic traces which lead to *anamnêsis*—the "tracks" one follows in a mnemonic chain back to the Form of beauty. Rather, these traces only provide an admonition against the *agalmatophile*'s approach to erotics, illuminating what happens to people who eroticize statues of goddesses to purely aesthetic ends and fail, in turn, to leverage them into a sublime encounter. As we turn now to

---

59. Pliny is the only other source to refer to the "stain" which the *agalmatophile* leaves on the statue as a "sign of desire" (*NH* 36.21–22: *ferunt amore captum quendam, cum delituisset noctu, simulacro cohaesisse, **eiusque cupiditatis esse indicem maculam**). For other versions of the cautionary tale, cf. Clement's *Protr.* 4.51: Ἀφροδίτη δὲ ἄλλη ἐν Κνίδῳ λίθος ἦν καὶ καλὴ ἦν, ἕτερος ἠράσθη ταύτης καὶ μίγνυται τῇ λίθῳ; and Lucian's *Imag.* 4: ἐρασθείη τις τοῦ ἀγάλματος καὶ λαθὼν ὑπολειφθεὶς ἐν ἱερῷ συγγένοιτο, ὡς δυνατὸν ἀγάλματι.

the *Met.* in section 4.3, we will likewise see a cautionary tale of a character who becomes "a great story and an incredible tale" (2.12: *historiam magnam et incredundam fabulam*; cf. *Am.* 15: ἀπίστου λόγου καινὴν . . . ἱστορίαν); and so also, we will encounter a similarly maniacal approach to theorizing the goddess.

4.3. Mock-Platonic Erotics in Hypata: Epiphany and (Meta)Physics in Lucius' Affair with Photis

As I suggested in the beginning of this chapter, Lucius embarks upon his liaison with Milo's slave girl, Photis, as a direct response to his sexual arousal at the sight of Byrrhena's *atrium* ensemble; and moreover, in order that Photis might play the role of intermediary between himself and Milo's wife, Pamphile, a magical sorceress about whose power Byrrhena cautions Lucius (*Met.* 2.5). We may remember from §3.2 that Lucius initially looks at the sculptural group in Byrrhena's *atrium* by examining it with a careful, "voyeuristic" gaze (*Met.* 2.5: *rimabundus*) and taking "excessive delight" (*eximie delector*) in the display: *delector*, I suggested, constitutes one approach to reading[60]—one which, we can now say, represents the aesthetic rather than utilitarian mode of appreciating beauty. It is thus quite poignant that, when Lucius hastens "his footstep" (*Met.* 2.6: **vestigium**) back to Milo's house after hearing "the much-desired name of magic," he does so "out of his mind" (*vecors animi*) and "similar to a madman" (*amenti similis*); he must caution himself to "stay wakeful and remain within himself" ("*age*," *inquam* "*o Luci, evigila et* **tecum esto**"). Lucius phrases his erotic excitement, therefore, in Platonic terms: following the "trace" (*vestigium*) back to the source and undergoing a kind of out-of-body *ekplêxis*.[61]

Lucius' initial response, however, reverses the Platonic procedure, inasmuch as he looks at a statuary ensemble of mimetic verisimilitude and heightened eroticism, and then follows *his own* "footstep" (instead of the "trace") back to his host's house in order to entangle himself in a bawdy liaison. To phrase it differently, Luicius chooses a human (almost at random)[62] to statuize instead of

---

60. Cf. Freudenburg 2007, 245, who gestures at the relationship between the *lector* and *delector*.
61. With the Latin phrase—*tecum esto*—cf. *Phaedr.* 250a7: οὐκέτ' <ἐν> αὐτῶν γίγνονται. Thus, Graverini 2010, esp. 75–82, suggests that the allusions to being "outside of oneself" in the novels have a Platonic (and particularly, *Phaedran*) resonance.
62. Photis' sex-appeal (*Met.* 2.6: *forma scitula*) and (alleged) attraction to Lucius are mentioned for the first time here, after Lucius has grown aroused from looking at Diana and from hearing about magic. This is a classic problem of the *Met.*'s unity, which *GCA* 2001, 240 *ad loc.*, explains on the

being philosophically dumbstruck at the sight of beauty on earth and as a consequence, treating his beloved *like* a divine *agalma* (as in the Platonic approach to utilizing arousal as a vehicle for sublime experience). Upon finding Photis at home cooking a sausage stew, Lucius describes her sensuous swaying and vibrations in highly eroticized terminology. She is dressed in the garb of a Roman courtesan with a "shiny red band girding up her very breasts" (2.7: *russea fasceola praenitente altiuscule sub ipsas papillas succinctula*).[63] As she "rotates the stew-pot in a circle with her flowery hands" (*cibarium vasculum floridis palmulis rotabat in circulum*),[64] she "frequently shakes and softly slides her limbs in circling bends" (*in orbis flexibus crebra succutiens et simul membra sua **leniter** inlubricans*), while her "hips supply wiggle" (*lumbis sensim vibrantibus*) and she "ripples her moving spine in a gently sexy shake" (***spinam mobilem** quatiens **placide** decenter **undabat***). As is well-recognized, this erotic movement clearly foreshadows the pantomime dance of *Venus vulgaris* in book 10, where the surrogate Venus "moves herself gently" (10.32: ***placide** commoveri*), and seems to promise, "by means of her slowly hesitating footstep" (*cunctanti . . . lente vestigio*) and "gently fluctuating spine" (***leniter fluctuante spinula***), to give Paris a wife "similar in form to herself" (*forma . . . sui . . . consimilem*).[65] The "Palinodic" reader can easily read Venus' performance, moreover, back into Photis' eroticized cooking dance and thus, recognize the kitchen-seduction scene (together with Byrrhena's warning) as an early crossroads choice for Lucius.

However, in light of our exegesis of Platonic paradigms of aesthetic-versus-utilitarian modes of response, it is crucial that Lucius describes his immediate reaction to the seductive movements of *this* surrogate Venus in mock-Platonic terms (*Met.* 2.7):

---

    principle of "narrative economy" (on which theory, see also van Mal-Maeder 1995, 105–8; Graverini 2001, 431). I would prefer to explain it in terms of characterization, whereby the *agalmatophile* Lucius retrospectively rewrites the past.

63. On Apuleius' play here with the iconography of Roman prostitutes, esp. from Roman wall-painting, see *GCA* 2001, 413–15; Hodges forthcoming. Adkins 2022, 134, notes that Photis adopts the *Venus pendula* sexual position which we encounter in the low-class art of Roman brothels. In the wake of our discussion of erotic iconography in ch. 3, we may note the fusion of high and low art, as the Diana-Actaeon statuary ensemble is here refracted through the iconographic signifiers of a Roman brothel. Cf. also Graverini 2001 for this scene as blending high epic (esp. Vergilian allusion) with burlesque.

64. On the *vasculum* as a euphemism for vagina, see Schmeling and Montiglio 2006, 32–33.

65. On the clear philological connection between these two scenes (esp. with the metaphor of waves), see Zimmerman-de Graaf 1993, 151; *GCA* 2000, 389–90 *ad loc.* 263.13–19; *GCA* 2001, 148; Schmeling and Montiglio 2006. Cf. Harrison 2013a, 215–28, who discusses "waves" as a general epic metaphor for the emotions in the *Met.*

Isto aspectu defixus obstupui et mirabundus steti; steterunt et membra quae iacebant ante.

Fixed at that sight, I was dumbstruck and I stood, marveling; parts of me which were lying limp before also stood erect.

The language of *ekplêxis* (of stultification, marvel, and paralysis) is all too familiar from the critical tradition of art appreciation and *ekphrasis*. This phraseology recalls, for instance, Aeneas' reaction to the paintings of the Trojan war on the walls of Dido's temple, where he is similarly "fixed in one gaze" (*Aen.* 1.495: *obtutu . . . defixus in uno*) and dumbstruck (*stupet*) at the marvels appearing before him.[66] Ovid likewise borrows from this Vergilian archetype to depict Narcissus' reaction to the mirror of his beloved.[67] When Narcissus sees himself (*Met.* 3.418–19):

adstupet ipse sibi vultuque immotus eodem
haeret, ut e Pario formatum marmore signum.

He is dumbstruck at himself, and clings, unmoving in one and the same face, just like a statue formed from Parian marble.

Whereas Aeneas reacts in the aesthetically appropriate (if self-deluded)[68] way and Narcissus is deceived even to the point of worshipping his beloved as a divine statue—a *signum* whose "hair" he likens to Bacchus' or Apollo's (*Met.* 3.421)—Lucius responds to the erotic seductions of a slave girl only after he is aroused from looking at a statue of a divinity and playing out an erotic story in his mind.[69] Lucius' erotic excitement, in other words, leads to a reaction akin to

---

66. Finkelpearl 1998, 46–47, discusses this under "comically incongruous allusion to Vergil." Westerbrink 1978, 65, cited in Finkelpearl, suggests that *Aen.* 2.774 (*obstipui, steteruntque comae*) is the primary referent, though, as I will argue, Apuleius is most likely alluding to Plato's *Phaedrus* through Vergil. Cf. also Graverini 2001, 437, on this phrasing as "un vero e proprio *pastiche virgiliano*."

67. See Hardie 2002, 146: "Narcissus' astonishment at what he sees (418 *adstupet*) is the typical reaction of the beholder of a masterpiece of illusionist art, like Aeneas looking at the reliefs in the temple of Juno at Carthage." See also Lateiner 2001, 227–32, on *stupor* in the *Met.* On engagement with Ovidian erotics in this scene, see Graverini 2001, 439–41.

68. Most critics recognize that Aeneas has an uncritical response to the artistic representations in Juno's temple, since they celebrate the destruction of the Trojan people. See, e.g., Farrell 2012, 298–304.

69. The parallelism between Lucius' eroticization of Diana's statue and of Photis' undulation is fur-

224   THE SHADOW OF AN ASS

agalmatophilia rather than the measured, religious-erotic worship of the Forms. His peculiar language of *ekplêxis* thus literalizes his Platonic archetype.

Indeed, we may recall that the *erastês*, as a consequence of receiving the "flow" of beauty "through his eyes," is nourished in his soul to such a point that the "shaft of the [soul's] feather" (*Phaedr.* 251b6: ὁ τοῦ πτεροῦ **καυλός**) grows erect: *kaulos*, as noted above, represents an obviously phallic euphemism. According to the Platonic model, therefore, beauty causes a kind of metaphysical erection, and this transfer of desire provides the catalyst for the soul to "grow wings" (*Phaedr.* 255d2: πτεροφυεῖν).[70] By contrast, our philosophico-maniacal narrator, though obsessed with gaining wings and taking flight,[71] nonetheless mistakes the transcendent experience of beauty, which is described *metaphorically* in corporeal terms by Plato, for a very physical and bodily interaction. Rather than acquiring a metaphysical erection and becoming winged, Lucius' "parts" (*membra*) stand straight up, and he remains physically erect (albeit *pronus*) for much of the rest of the novel—a feature of his asinine metamorphosis he perpetually spotlights.[72]

This misconstrual of the Platonic approach to erotics becomes more explicit, as the narrative moves from embodied *ekplêxis* to *ekphrastic* fantasy. After exchanging some erotic banter with Photis, Lucius "explores [her body] diligently" (2.8: *diligenter . . . explorassem*), where *explorare* is a term used more regularly of reading texts and engaging in philosophical speculation;[73] he

---

ther emphasized by the near-identical, phonetic relationship between *rimabundus* and *mirabundus* (on which, see Freudenburg 2007, 243).

70. Cf. also *Phaedr.* 249c (πτεροῦται), a metaphor which is imitated frequently in the Second Sophistic (e.g., in Plut. *Amat.* 766b7: ἐπτέρωται).

71. At *Met.* 3.22, Lucius begs Photis to make him a winged Cupid: *ac iam perfice ut meae Veneri* **Cupido pinnatus** *assistam tibi.* Then, the image of becoming a winged Pegasus occurs at 6.30, 8.16, and 11.8 (on which, see §2.5 and §5.1). On the fascination with "Icarianism" in *C&P*, see James 1998. On wings and winged-ness in the *Met.* as an allusion to the *Phaedrus*, see Winkle 2014, 118–25. Cf. also Ulrich 2020, 687–88, on how Lucius comically misapplies this image to his body.

72. After transforming into an ass, Lucius takes solace in the growth of his *natura* at 3.24; then, when threatened with castration in book 7, he laments the possible loss of his "most recent acquisition" (7.24: *in novissima parte*). Moreover, the *matrona* in book 10 adores Lucius primarily for his huge member (10.22: *tam vastum genitale*). We may compare the close of the pseudo-Lucianic *Onos* (56), where the corresponding matron character rejects the retransformed Loukios because of his shrunken genitals. Some have even read Lucius' loss of tail (*cauda*) at 11.13 as a form of castration (see, e.g., Winkle 2014, 124–25). On the priapic associations of the ass (with reference to Lucius' metaphorical castration), see van Mal-Maeder 1997, 108–9. Cf. also Graverini 2001, 437–38, who reads *membra* as a novelistic deflation of the *Aeneid*, where the hero's "hair" (*comae*) stands on end.

73. As noted in §2.3, *explorare* is used throughout the *Apologia* almost exclusively of philosophical activity, and often, of reading specifically: at *Apol.* 15.4, of introspective mirror-gazing (*assiduo*

then offers an encomium of her hair, which he begins with a very strange thought experiment (*Met.* 2.8):

> denique pleraeque indolem gratiamque suam probaturae lacinias omnes exuunt, amicula dimovent, nudam pulchritudinem suam praebere se gestiunt, magis de cutis roseo rubore quam de vestis aureo colore placiturae. At vero—quod nefas dicere, nec quod sit ullum huius rei tam dirum exemplum!—si cuiuslibet eximiae pulcherrimaeque feminae caput capillo **spoliaveris** et faciem nativa specie **nudaveris**, licet illa caelo deiecta, mari edita, fluctibus educata, licet inquam Venus ipsa fuerit, licet omni Gratiarum choro stipata et toto Cupidinum populo comitata et balteo suo cincta, cinnama fragrans et balsama rorans, calva processerit, placere non poterit nec Vulcano suo.

> Very many women take off all their clothes in order to prove their own nature and gracefulness. They remove their outer garments and they desire to show their naked beauty, hoping to be more pleasing from the rosy blush of their skin than from the golden color of their clothing. But truly—and this is criminal to say, and may there be no such wretched example of this!—if you strip the head of any exceptional woman—indeed, even the most beautiful woman—of its hair, and if you expose her appearance in its native guise, even if she's descended from heaven, begotten in the sea, and reared in the waves—indeed, even if she's Venus herself, attended by a whole chorus of Graces and accompanied by a whole population of Cupids, girded with her belt, breathing cinnamon and sprinkling fragrant balsam around—if she goes out bald, she will not be able to please, not even her husband Vulcan.

In this rhetorically rich hypothetical, Lucius retrospectively reframes his behavior as if it were modeled on the philosophical ideal, likening his beloved to a goddess, much as the dumbstruck *erastês* does in the *Phaedrus* (cf. 251a6). Moreover, just as we saw Socrates advocating in the *Charmides* and *Alcibiades 1*, Lucius-*auctor* attempts to "strip" the beloved to see what is underneath. Indeed, we may recall that Chaerephon in the *Charmides* suggests viewers

---

explorare); at 36.8, of continual reading (*sedulo explorare*); at 40.6, of reading Aristotle's books (*explorare studio*); at 103.2, of studying fish on the advice of Aristotle (*pisces exploras*); and most importantly, at 73.7 where Apuleius speaks himself of "testing the qualities of [Pudentilla's] virtues" (*virtutium eius dotes explorassem*). Cf. also *Apol.* 85.3, where Apuleius laments that Pudens reads his mother's feelings in her letters in an illicit or voyeuristic way (*adfectiones exploras*). This is retooled in a comical, philosophico-maniacal way in the *Met.* (e.g., in 1.3 and 1.26).

ought to "strip" (*Charm.* 154d4: ἀποδῦναι) the beautiful *erômenos* to look at him "faceless"; and to this proposal, Socrates responds that viewers ought rather to "strip" (*Charm.* 154e4–5: ἀπεδύσαμεν) Charmides' external appearance to "behold" his soul. Apuleius, quite familiar with this Platonic leitmotiv (see n. 31 above), represents Lucius likewise "stripping" (*spoliaveris*) his beloved in order to "lay bare" (*nudaveris*) her appearance. Our asinine narrator is not interested, however, in illuminating her true character—in uncovering what Socrates hopes to reveal in the *Charmides*. Instead, Lucius' goal in "stripping" his beloved is to heighten the pleasure of fetishism: whereas Chaerephon proposes that Charmides' body is so beautiful that, if he were to "strip," he would seem "faceless," Lucius imagines Venus herself stripped not only of her clothes, but even of her *hair*; and he muses over her inability to "delight" (*placiturae . . . placere*) her lover under those strange contrary-to-fact conditions.

This bewildering thought-experiment leads, in turn, to Lucius' encomium of hair, which engages explicitly with the central Platonic passage discussed in §4.2. Turning to Photis' hair, Lucius elaborates (2.9):

> Quid cum capillis color gratus et nitor splendidus inlucet, et contra solis aciem vegetus fulgurat vel placidus renitet, aut in contrariam gratiam variat aspectum et nunc aurum coruscans in lenem mellis deprimitur umbram, nunc corvina nigredine caerulus columbarum colli flosculos aemulatur, vel cum guttis Arabicis obunctus et pectinis arguti dente tenui discriminatus et pone versum coactus **amatoris oculis occurrens ad instar speculi reddit imaginem gratiorem**?

> What is it like when hair has a pleasing color and its brilliant luster shines and it flashes lively against the rays of sun, or softly reflects or changes its appearance for an opposite charm; now gleaming gold, it is compressed into the smooth shadow of honey; now dark blue with raven-black, it imitates the little flowers on pigeons' necks; or when it is anointed with Arabian myrrh and parted with a sharp comb's fine tooth and gathered at the back, it **comes to meet the lover's eyes and just like a mirror, returns a more pleasing image**?

This is an intertextually rich passage with models ranging from elegy and epic to more playful references.[74] According to Suetonius, for instance, Domi-

---

74. For the most comprehensive reading of this passage, see Finkelpearl 1998, 62–67, who sees a fusion of the Vergilian Circe with the elegiac beloved of Propertius and Ovid. See also Graverini 2001, who expands on Finkelpearl's epic intertexts. Cf. Schmeling and Montiglio 2006 on the play

tian allegedly wrote a treatise on haircare (*Dom.* 18.2: *De cura capillorum*); and in Petronius' *Satyricon*, Encolpius delivers an "elegy of hair" (*Sat.* 109.8: *capillorum elegidarion*). In fact, a late antique bishop, Synesius of Cyrene, wrote an *Encomium of Baldness* supposedly in response to a now-lost *Encomium of Hair* written by Dio Chrysostom a generation before Apuleius. What I am interested in here, however, is the way in which Apuleius blends these more lowbrow texts with highbrow reference to the transcendent experience of "erotic reciprocity." For this is not merely a playful encomium of hair in the Second Sophistic tradition of flashy rhetoric on nugatory themes.[75] Nor is it simply portraying Lucius' encounter as a Circean distraction or a tryst with an unfaithful, elegiac beloved (although it accomplishes that as well).[76] Rather, if we look more closely at the last line of this encomium, we not only see our Platonic catchphrase—where *ad instar speculi* provides a Latin translation of ὥσπερ . . . ἐν κατόπτρῳ—but we also encounter a complex and studied engagement with the entire Platonic tradition of the flow of desire. A glance at the following table reveals how carefully Apuleius has reworked his archetype:

διὰ τῶν ὀμμάτων *ἰόν*	**oculis** <u>*occurrens*</u>
ἐν τῷ <u>*ἐρῶντι*</u>	*amatoris*
ὥσπερ δὲ ἐν κατόπτρῳ	*ad instar speculi*
<u>**εἴδωλον**</u> ἔρωτος <u>ἀντέρωτα</u>	**imaginem** gratiorem

This erotic interaction does occur "through the eyes," but it is only the eyes of the lover (and not those of the beloved) which participate; and they interact *not* through the "flow" of desire, where an intersubjective encounter between self and other makes the feathers of the soul to grow, but instead, they delight in the color and sheen of hair in fetishistic delusion. In other words, the specular reflection remains—there is still an *imago/eidôlon*—but rather than an eye-to-eye intersubjective encounter of reciprocal desire, this is an eye-to-hair

---

with "waves" in the seduction scene writ large. See also Montiglio 2005, 58–61, who reads Lucius' description of Photis' hair as an expansion on the Homeric epithet *kalliplokamos* applied to Circe.

75. *Pace* Sandy 1994, 1568–69, who remarks on fatuousness of this ebullient *ekphrasis*. On Apuleius' nugatory obsession with hair, see Englert and Long 1973.

76. On the Ovidian heritage of this encomium, see *GCA* 2001, 171 *ad loc.* See also Finkelpearl 1998. On elegiac *topoi* in books 1–3 in general, see Mathis 2008; Hindermann 2010. Cf. also Adkins 2022, 127–28. I am not particularly convinced by Harrison's suggestion 2013a, 130–32 (expanded on by Graverini 2001, 441–43), that this episode portrays Photis as a Nausicaa figure, since the parallels seem relatively weak compared to Vergilian, Ovidian, and Platonic intertexts.

objectification of the beloved.[77] Indeed, Photis becomes her hair, the body part a *pars pro toto* substitution. Even Venus herself would not be Venus without her hair! The *imago* is not praised, in turn, for its mimetic verisimilitude, but on the contrary, is said to be *gratior*. One might ask: "more pleasing" than what? A more pleasing reflection of Lucius, the agent of desire? It may be worth recalling at this point Achilles Tatius' parodic reception of Plato's specular archetype, in which Clinias describes seeing as offering "a greater pleasure" (cf. again *L&C* 1.9.4: μείζονα . . . τὴν ἡδονήν) than the act. Much as in Achilles Tatius or even in the Hostius Quadra episode from Seneca's *Natural Questions*, self-knowledge and the technologies deployed to acquire it are transformed into opportunities and tools for self-deception, for taking excessive pleasure in false appearances.[78]

As the foreplay continues and Lucius-*auctor* leaves off his encomium, Lucius-*actor* enters the scene to consummate his pleasure and there, we find a perfect Apuleian coinage to translate the Platonic neologism *anterôs*—the "erotic reciprocity" with which Plato endows the beloved in a culturally revolutionary act.[79] For when Lucius-*actor* leaps as an *agalmatophile* onto his fetishized beloved, he "leans over top of her" (*Met.* 2.10: **pronus in eam**) in order to "place a kiss" (*savium impressi*) on the peak of her head, much as Charicles in pseudo-Lucian's *Amores* "stretches his neck out to kiss" the statue of the goddess (*Am.* 13). Photis responds, in turn, with an intense reciprocity of desire like the *erômenos* of the *Phaedrus*—or so, Lucius suggests in his revisionist reconstruction (*Met.* 2.10):

> Iamque **aemula libidine in amoris parilitatem** congermanescenti mecum, iam patentis oris inhalatu cinnameo et occursantis linguae inlisu nectareo **prona cupidine** adlibescenti, "Pereo,' inquam 'immo iam dudum perii, nisi tu propitiaris."

> Now, her rivaling desire blossoms together with mine to an equal point of love, with the cinnamony breath of her now open mouth and the nectar-sweet strikes of her attacking tongue; and as she grew aroused with inclined desire, I said, "I'm dying; no actually, I'm already long gone, unless you appease me."

---

77. Alternatively, we could speak of Apuleius contaminating an idealized Platonic model with Roman paradigms of sexual subjectivity, such as the penetrator/penetrated model, or the more recently discussed agency-oriented model (see, e.g., Kamen and Levin-Richardson 2015).

78. See Bartsch 2006, 103–14; Toohey 2004, 261–82. Cf. my discussion of *voluptas* in §3.4.

79. See again Halperin 1986.

In characteristically decadent Apuleian prose, Lucius depicts Photis' mirroring desire growing "to an equal point of love" (*in amoris parilitatem*), deploying (like Plato with *anterôs*) a term for erotics that appears nowhere in extant Latin before this bawdy episode. We already saw in the previous section how rarely *anterôs* is used in antiquity, reoccurring only for the second time in a Platonizing scene from Apuleius' near contemporary, Achilles Tatius. Moreover, a careful analysis of the prosody of the Apuleian line reveals Photis' mirroring desire on the level of metrics and phonetics: Photis' *aemula libidine* is transformed through open-mouthed kisses and an exchange of scents and tastes into *prona cupidine*, an erotic responsion to Lucius' posture. Simply put, Photis' "desire" (*cupido*) adopts Lucius' *pronus* posture in the exchange of erotic pleasure. This brilliant narrative reconstruction is undercut, however, by the overtly physical nature of the exchange. What in Plato is merely a metaphor for heightened erotic desire, where *hîmeros* is imagined to be a physical substance flowing between subjects like a liquid or stream, becomes in Lucius' narrative imagination an actual transfer of desire through breath and physical exchange of fluids—through nectar and cinnamony kisses.

Just as Lucius' vision of the statuary ensemble in Byrrhena's atrium establishes a model for interpreting his subsequent encounters with (representations of) divinities throughout the *Met.* (§3.2), so also, Lucius' encounter with Photis in book 2 sets the tone for his successive religious-erotic epiphanies in the *Met.*—scenes which we can now read in light of the philosophico-maniacal tendencies of our asinine narrator. Indeed, at a number of points in the novel Lucius attempts to "mount beloveds" in unnatural ways: in book 7, Lucius' sadistic driver labels the ass an *amator* and grumbles that he pursues "unheard of lusts" (*Met.* 7.21: *incognitas . . . libidines*) with any "girl or soft boy" that passes by, attempting even to "mount a woman" (*mulierem . . . **inscendere***) when "Venus is opposed" (*aversa . . . Venere*);[80] and in the bestiality scene in book 10, Lucius wonders how he will "mount the delicate matron" (10.22: *delicatam matronam **inscendere***) with so many legs and such an oafish body. Yet, despite Lucius' manifest impulse toward *agalmatophilia*, the *auctor* perpetually reframes his excessively corporeal encounters in the highbrow terms of Platonic enlightenment, even to the point of "raising his face to Jove" (*dentes ad*

---

80. The fact that book 7 contains another "charioteer" moment strengthens Drake's theory 1968, 106–9, since Lucius-ass lunges like the black horse at a series of beloveds before he himself gets mounted and brought under control/harmony in 7.24. See also Winkle 2014, 110–17, on the various "charioteers" that guide Lucius as a black horse.

Iovem elevans)[81] in the *spurcum additamentum* when the *matrona* massages his groin in book 10—a gesture of sublime enlightenment physically impossible for a quadruped.[82] In the space that remains, however, it will be useful to analyze two structural and thematic counterparts to Lucius' philosophico-mania in the kitchen-seduction episode not only to assess Apuleius' clear refashioning of Platonic archetypes in the novelistic landscape, but also to understand how this method of appropriation acts as an invitation to the reader to choose his or her own path. It is to the first of those that I now turn.

4.4. The Soul Encounters the Divine: Platonic Epiphany in C&P

Ever since antiquity, the central and longest inset tale in the *Metamorphoses*, *Cupid and Psyche* (hereafter, *C&P*), has been recognized for its Platonic and allegorizing elements.[83] To begin with, the *fabula* seems to be modeled on the Platonic dichotomy in the *Symposium* between "Heavenly Aphrodite" (*Venus caelestis*) and "Pandemic Aphrodite" (*Venus vulgaris*).[84] Furthermore, the most obvious Platonic allusion in the entirety of the *Met.*—save perhaps the "plane tree" in book 1[85]—occurs at the end of Psyche's epiphany of Cupid: she attempts to grab his leg when he flies off in anger, thereby trying to become winged; and she holds on in his flight until she "finally grows weary" (*Met.* 5.24: *tandem fessa*), like the journeying soul from the *Phaedrus* (248c7–8: βαρυνθεῖσα), and

---

81. This potentially spurious passage is found in the bestiality episode with the *matrona* (*Met.* 10.20–22) and the fuller context reads as follows: "and when the beautiful woman moved from my balls to the head of my penis rapidly, whinnying and raising my teeth to Jove, by Priapus, I began to grow intensely erect because of the frequent rubbing" (*et cum ad inguinis cephalum formosa mulier concitim veniebat ab orcibus, ganniens ego et dentes ad Iovem elevans Priapo<n> frequenti frictura porrixabam*). See Zimmerman 2012, xxiii–xxv for text and discussion. The *spurcum* is found in the marginalia notes in manuscript φ in the Laurentian library, and its authenticity has since been a source of great debate. On its authenticity and function as a representation of Lucius' tendency to refashion his animal behaviors in rational terms, see Lytle 2003, esp. 356–64. Winkler 1985, 192–93, speaks of critics "castrat[ing] the text at its most graphic moment." For a skeptical (if uncompelling) response to Lytle, however, see Hunink 2006. See also Carver 2007, 68–71, for a thorough history of the debate and some cautious solutions to the problem.

82. Cf. §3.2. On asinine posture, see again O'Sullivan 2016; Fitzgerald 2000, 102–3.

83. See esp. Carver's discussion of Tertullian, Martianus Capella, and Fulgentius on the philosophical import of *C&P* in late antiquity and the Middle Ages (Carver 2007, 36–47). See also Graverini 2012a, 110–13, on *C&P*'s relationship to other *aniles fabulae* that straddle the line between pleasurable satire and philosophically useful texts. On the shared Gnostic and Middle Platonic elements in *C&P*, see Moreschini 1978, 1–42; Dowden 1982.

84. Apuleius was clearly familiar with the dichotomy, as he paraphrases it in detail at *Apol.* 12. See Kenney 1990a, 19–20, on Apuleius' innovation in deploying this dichotomy in *C&P*.

85. On which, see §3.2 with n. 88.

VISUALIZING THE GODDESS   231

"falls down to the earth" (*delabitur solo*; cf. ἐπὶ τὴν γῆν πέσῃ). In this way, Psyche mirrors the soul's process of embodiment in accordance with the dynamics of Platonic metempsychosis in the central myth of the *Phaedrus*.[86]

There is no disputing that Platonic allegory and that the *Phaedrus*, in particular, are woven into the narrative fabric of *C&P*. The scholarly debate hinges rather on the significance of that Platonic allegorical reference, whether it is a mere sprinkling of learned flavoring—one spice among many others, such as epic or satire[87]—or whether it is more fundamental and symbolic.[88] Moreover, although Ben Edwin Perry famously labeled the Isis book a "ballast" to give weight to Apuleius' otherwise frivolous text in his 1967 Sather Lectures (see §0.1 with n. 39), one might offer the counterpoint that *C&P*—at least in its reception history, often detached as it is from the frame of the novel in which it is situated and published separately as a lofty folktale[89]—functions as the Platonic anchor for this carnivalesque text.

As my "scrupulous reader" will surely have noticed, I have mainly avoided basing my Platonic reading of the *Met.* on the central *anilis fabula* because, of all the central interpretive moments in the novel, it has received the most commentary on its Platonic heritage.[90] A thread running through *C&P* which has regrettably been overlooked in scholarship, however, is its relationship to the Lucius-Photis tryst, especially when we consider how Psyche replicates Lucius' mock-*Phaedran agalmatophilia* and his fetishistic approach to religious-erotic experience in book 2.

In the character of Psyche ("Soul"), we trace Lucius' erotic journey in reverse. She begins her life "as a wondrously crafted statue" (4.32: *ut **simulacrum** fabre politum*), which visitors come from far and wide to behold and "marvel at" (*mirantur omnes*), much like the Cnidian Aphrodite. In those who

---

86. See Walsh 1970, 206–7; Schlam 1970, 485; Kenney 1990b, 184–85. Cf. Graverini 2012a, 112, who claims that a reader familiar with the *Phaedrus* "cannot avoid a sense of *déjà vu*" when they encounter this scene. See also *GCA* 2004, 294–97, for a summary of scholarship on the allusion. On Platonic metempsychosis as a more significant factor in the Isis book, see §5.1.

87. See, e.g., Harrison 2013a, esp. 125–78, 197–213, and 243–55 on "literary topography" in *C&P* (and the *Met.* more broadly).

88. Tilg 2014a, 57–83, for instance, makes *C&P* central to his analysis of "Platonic fiction." See Kenney 1990a, 12–28 and esp. 27, for discussion of historical approaches. For my own reading of *C&P* as an "inverted allegory" which causes readerly bewilderment, see Ulrich forthcoming b.

89. Graverini 2012a, 95, notes how stand-alone editions of *C&P* have shaped its reception history. On the reception of *C&P*, see Moreschini 1994, 5–96.

90. On Platonism in *C&P*, see Kenney 1990a; Kenney 1990b; James 1998; Dowden 1982; Dowden 1998; Dowden 2006; Panayotakis 2001; Tilg 2014a. On Platonic elements as generic interplay and enrichment of literary identity, see Graverini 2012a; Hunter 2006; Hunter 2009b; Hunter 2012.

behold this *simulacrum*, moreover, she causes "dumbstruck wonder" (4.28: *admiratione stupidi*) and speechless awe at "her inaccessible beauty"; and viewers are even led to "worship her in religious adoration as if she were truly Venus herself" (4.28: *ut ipsam prorsus deam Venerem <venerabantur> religiosis adorationibus*). As the drunken old narrator tells us, all of Venus' temples and cult sites are abandoned and grow marred through disuse (4.29), and Venus herself laments that her name suffers the "uncertainty of substitutionary worship" (4.30: *vicariae venerationis incertum*). Simply put, in this erotic matrix, Psyche constitutes not only an *erômenê* whose beauty inspires the anticipated Platonic reaction from viewers (i.e., *ekplêxis*, marvel, stultification, etc.), but she is also worshipped as an *agalma*, a stand-in for the divine.

We may recall here that the ideal lover is supposed to respond to beauty by "worshipping" his beloved "as a god" (*Phaedr.* 251a5: ὡς θεὸν σέβεται) and by "making sacrifices to his darlings as if to a statue or a god" (251a6: θύοι ἂν ὡς ἀγάλματι καὶ θεῷ τοῖς παιδικοῖς). As we saw in the previous section, Lucius, our philosophico-maniacal narrator, attempts retrospectively to reframe his actions toward Photis in terms of the ideal Platonic lover: he statuizes her, treats her as a surrogate Venus, and strips her of her outer appearance in order to facilitate a "true" encounter with the divine.

Psyche, however, after an extended period of objectification under the masculine "gaze,"[91] strives to take an active role in her religious-erotic epiphany of Cupid in one of the most sublime scenes in all of Latin literature.[92] Though Psyche is not explicitly labeled an *erastês/amator*, the drunken *anus* nonetheless marks her attempt to transform into one when she explains how Psyche enters the bedroom where her unseen husband lies (*Met.* 5.22):

Tunc Psyche, et corporis et animi alioquin infirma . . . et prolata lucerna et adrepta novacula sexum audacia mutavit.

Then Psyche, generally feeble in both body and mind . . . dragging in a lamp and seizing a razor, changed her sex through her hubris.

---

91. Though he does not specifically treat *C&P*, Slater 1998 remains the best treatment of the "gaze" in the *Met.* On the visual dynamics of *C&P*, which play with who gets to see and what remains invisible, see Benson 2019, 98–148.

92. On the transcendent description, see Braund 1999.

VISUALIZING THE GODDESS   233

Here, I would submit that Psyche attempts, much like Alcibiades in Plato's *Symposium*, to reverse roles with her *erastês*.[93] Up to this point in the *fabula*, that is, she plays the role of the beloved whom others statuize and marvel at— the one who is subordinated to the god. Through her *audacia*, however, she aims to redefine her sexual role in her relationship with Cupid. Attempting to penetrate him with her eyes (via the *lucerna*), and then with a "small razor" (*novacula*)—almost certainly a phallic gesture—"Soul" strives to "see" the divine.

Before moving to the *ekphrasis* of Cupid, where Psyche's fetishism of the god's hair recalls Lucius' earlier philosophico-mania, it is worth highlighting how Psyche's *audacia* mirrors Alcibiades' *hybris* in the *Symp.*, to which the young *erômenos* playfully alludes in his closing speech. Alcibiades is, of course, the hubristic player in his interactions with Socrates, insofar as he acts as hunter, pursuer, and *erastês*, although it is socially inappropriate for him to do so. It is worth reiterating, for instance, that Alcibiades, in the consummate (mis)interpretation of Socrates' advice to "strip" his beloved, aims to remove the philosopher's satyric hide as a parodic attempt to encounter the divine. Bearing this in mind, it is suggestive, in my view, that the tool Psyche brings with her to accomplish her erotic role-reversal is *not* a *gladius*, like the dagger which Meroe brings with her to pierce Socrates' throat in book 1,[94] but rather a *novacula*—a razor for sheering the head of its hair.[95] Psyche enters the bedroom of her beloved, in other words, intending *not* to "strip" him in order to look beneath the surface level and gaze upon his "soul" underneath, but instead, to shave his head, just as Lucius-*auctor* strives to do with his Photis-as-hairless-Venus experiment in book 2.

Replicating Lucius' failure, however, to utilize erotic epiphany to follow beauty's "trace" back to its Form, Psyche revels in the aesthetic and hyperphysical pleasure of her beloved. With her first glance at Cupid's beauty, Psyche undergoes the expected Platonic experience of *ekplêxis*: she is "terrified at so great a sight" (*Met.* 5.22: *tanto aspectu deterrita*), "out of control of her spirit"

---

93. See n. 33 above on this role-reversal. On the influence of this speech on Apuleius, see Egelhaff-Gaisser 2012; Ulrich 2017; Ulrich 2022; Adkins 2022, 204.

94. Cf. *Met.* 1.13: *et capite Socratis in alterum dimoto latus per iugulum sinistrum capulo tenus **gladium totum** ei demergit.*

95. See OLD, s.v. 1 *novacula.* Cf. esp. Martial *Ep.* 2.66.7, who proposes that Lalage "denude" (*nudet*) her head of its hair with a *novacula.* See also Cels. *De med.* 6.4.3, who suggests "shaving daily with a *novacula*" as the best solution for bald spots.

234   THE SHADOW OF AN ASS

(*impos animi*), and "trembling" (*tremens*).[96] Even her *novacula*, the instrument by which she strives to "change her sex," grows wings: out of fear, the *anus* explains, the razor "slips out of [Psyche's] insolent hands and flies off" (5.22: *manibus temerariis delapsum evolasset*).[97] Much as Lucius misconstrues the Platonic metaphysical erection of the soul's "feather" (*kaulos*), Psyche literalizes her erotic flight, imagining that her phallic instrument "grows wings." Her epiphanic delight reaches its climax, then, when she sees Cupid's hair, which is described via *ekphrasis* at *Met.* 5.22:[98]

> Videt capitis aurei genialem caesariem ambrosia temulentam, cervices lacteas genasque purpureas pererrantes crinium globos decoriter impeditos, alios antependulos, alios retropendulos, quorum splendore nimio fulgurante iam et ipsum lumen lucernae uacillabat. Per umeros volatilis dei pinnae roscidae micanti flore candicant et quamvis alis quiescentibus extimae plumulae tenellae ac delicatae tremule resultantes inquieta lasciviunt. Ceterum corpus glabellum atque luculentum et quale peperisse Venerem non paeniteret.

> She sees the pleasant hair of his golden head drenched in ambrosia; (she sees) curls of hair wandering over his milky neck and purple cheeks, beautifully arranged, some hanging in front, some behind, and at the glow of their excessive brightness, the lamplight itself wavered. Along the shoulders of the flying god, dewy wings gleam in the manner of a glistening flower, and even with the wings at rest, the tips of the soft and delicate little down-feathers ripple tremulously and restlessly play. The rest of the god's body is smooth and splendid— just the sort that Venus would not be ashamed to have given birth to.

Apuleius marks the relationship between this religious-erotic epiphany and the Lucius-Photis tryst through a number of verbal and thematic correspon-

---

96. Cf. *Phaedrus* 251a2–7 for the description of the *erastês* looking upon true beauty: ὅταν θεοειδὲς πρόσωπον ἴδῃ κάλλος εὖ μεμιμημένον ἤ τινα σώματος ἰδέαν, πρῶτον μὲν ἔφριξε καί τι τῶν τότε ὑπῆλθεν αὐτὸν δειμάτων, εἶτα προσορῶν ὡς θεὸν σέβεται, καὶ εἰ μὴ ἐδεδίει τὴν τῆς σφόδρα μανίας δόξαν, θύοι ἂν ὡς ἀγάλματι καὶ θεῷ τοῖς παιδικοῖς. Note the confluence of fear, shuddering, and worship. Cf. Graverini 2010 on the *Phaedran* interplay here in *C&P*.

97. The razor's "flight" (*evolare*) is thus parallel to Pamphile's flight when she transforms herself into an owl (3.21): *mox in altum sublimata forinsecus totis alis evolat*. That Apuleius uses the same verb for the Icarian flight of an owl and for a razor suggests that this represents Psyche's attempt to grow wings.

98. See esp. Braund 1999 on the sensuous delight of the rhetorical description here.

VISUALIZING THE GODDESS   235

dences. The focalization begins with the "hair of the golden head" (*capitis aurei . . . caesariem*), which reproduces the encomium of hair in 2.9 in its kaleidoscopic color display and its bright sheen.[99] Moreover, the arrangement of Photis' hair, as it "hang[s] down over the nape and is dispersed across the neck . . . heaped together in a glob at the top" (*Met.* 2.9: **cervice dependulos** *ac dein per colla dispositos . . . paulisper ad finem* **conglobatos**), mirrors Cupid's hairdo, which "wander[s] over his milky neck and purple cheeks, beautifully arranged, some hanging in front, some behind" (*cervices lacteas genasque purpureas pererrantes* **crinium globos** *decoriter impeditos, alios* **antependulos**, *alios* **retropendulos**). The clearest sign that we are expected to read this passage in tandem with the Lucius-Photis tryst, however, is the depiction of Cupid's body, as the narrator's focalization moves downward. As Psyche directs her gaze at Cupid's lower parts, Apuleius redeploys a special coinage—*glabellus* ("hairless")—which he first used at the close of Lucius' liaison: Photis, when she lasciviously strikes the pose of the Cnidian Aphrodite, covers "her hairless privates" (2.17: **glabellum** *feminal*) with her hand.[100]

It is quite clear, then, that the *lector scrupulosus* is meant to read Psyche's epiphany in light of Lucius' philosophico-maniacal and revisionist retelling of his liaison in book 2.[101] So, it is unsurprising that, when we arrive at the heightened climax of transcendent experience, we see another reworking of the mirroring, "erotic reciprocity" motif and another appropriation of our paradigmatic Platonic passage. Psyche, after directing her gaze from her beloved's hair down to his body, recognizes his "weapons" (5.22: *tela*) at his feet; out of "excessive curiosity" (*Met.* 5.23: *satis et curiosa*), she fetishizes them, "examining her husband's arms, feeling them up and marveling at them" (**rimatur** *atque pertrectat et mariti sui miratur* **arma**; where *arma* represents another obvious phallic reference).[102] Taking an overly tactile approach to erotics, much like

---

99. With the variegated color description of Cupid's hair, cf. 2.9, where Photis' hair "varies its appearance" (*variat aspectum*), at one time dark golden, at another bluish-black. Furthermore, just as Cupid's hair causes the lamplight to waver "at the glow of its excessive brightness" (**splend**ore *nimio* **fulgura**nte), so also, Photis' hair has a "shiny brightness" (2.9: *nitor* **splend**idus) that "shimmers" (**fulgurat**).

100. This Apuleian neologism, outside of its usage here and at 2.17, appears only in the *Florida* to describe Apollo's "hairless" body (*Fl.* 3.9).

101. In view of my analysis above, I naturally disagree with Kenney 1990b, 183, when he claims: "the spirit of the description is closer to that of Isis in her great epiphany . . . than to the raptures of Lucius over the charms of Photis."

102. See OLD *s. v.* **10a** *arma*. Cf., e.g., Mart. *Ep.* 6.73.6 and *Carm. Priap.* 31.3.

Lucius' voyeuristic "inspection" (2.5: *rimabundus*) of Diana in Byrrhena's atrium, Psyche does not realize, in turn, that she is transformed through erotic reciprocity (5.23):

> Sic ignara Psyche sponte in Amoris incidit amorem. Tunc magis magisque cupidine fraglans Cupidinis, prona in eum efflictim inhians patulis ac petulantibus saviis festinanter ingestis, de somni mensura metuebat.

> In this way, Psyche willingly (if unwittingly) fell in love with Love. Then, more and more on fire with desire for Desire, she leaned over him gazing passionately and though eagerly heaping upon him wanton open-mouthed kisses, she was afraid that he might wake up.[103]

The marked wordplay (*in Amoris . . . amorem . . . cupidine . . . Cupidinis*) has long been recognized as more than mere rhetorical luxuriance.[104] This moment of epiphany has been seen by some as a transformation of Psyche's affections from "pleasure" to "love,"[105] or at the very least, as a play on the "two kinds of love" dichotomy which functions as the organizing principle for *C&P*.[106] Rereading this scene in light of Apuleius' deeper engagement with the *Phaedrus*, however, we may note that the careful prosody of the line represents something akin to Photis' *amoris parilitas*—that is, the Platonic *anterôs* which Photis achieves through the transformation of her *aemula libido* into *prona cupido*. Psyche's affections similarly take on the character of her beloved, even to the point of mirroring his various names through a striking polyptoton. "Erotic reciprocity," in other words, reaches such a climax that "Soul" manifests in an embodied sense the different appellations of the god.

Despite her epiphany of *Amor* and her "erotic reciprocity," however, Psyche responds to Cupid's beauty with the "incorrect" Platonic approach: "leaning over him" (***prona in eum***) in a replication of Lucius' own *agalmatophilia* toward

---

103. Here, I have retained some of the word play from the translation in Kenney 1990a, 77.

104. See Kenney 1990b, 184: "unless Apuleius is merely reveling in verbal exuberance for its own sake (something he does, I believe, less often than some critics make out), the point would appear to be that Psyche, still unaware (*ignara*) of her husband's true identity, is still worshipping him under his false or factitious one."

105. See, e.g., Hooker 1955, 38.

106. See *GCA* 2004, 286–87 *ad loc.* 121, 6–8, who sees this "double word-play" as "point[ing] to the two aspects of love."

Photis (2.10: **pronus** *in eam*), she "eagerly heap[s] wanton open-mouthed kisses" (*patulis ac petulantibus saviis festinanter ingestis*) upon her beloved, just as Lucius plants a kiss on Photis' forehead. It is no surprise, then, that the lamp Psyche brings with her cannot contain its excitement at the sight of the god, but in an "audacious" (*audax*) gesture of erotic climax, "spews forth a drop of hot oil" (5.23: *evomuit . . . stillam ferventis olei*). In so doing, she burns the god (*sic inustus*), leaving him stained with a wound—a sign of his suffering (see *Met.* 6.11: **vulnus**; *Met.* 6.21: **cicatrice**)—much like the cautionary tale of the young noble in the *Amores*. Psyche's excessively desirous lunge at Cupid, simply put, reproduces the wrong way to respond to erotic epiphany, insofar as she sneaks into the room of the god at night, sees what she ought not, and consummates her desire by marking the god with a remnant sign of her sexual violence.

The second half of *C&P* famously morphs from a Platonic journey of the soul into an epic journey narrative—one which is modeled on Odysseus' and Heracles' *labores*, and which culminates in Psyche's underworld *katabasis*.[107] And yet, our Platonic discourse of following "traces" (*ichnê/vestigia*) back to the divine and striving to gaze upon true beauty continues: at the opening of book 6, Psyche is "intent on the traces of her husband" (*Met.* 6.1: *mariti* **vestigationibus intenta**);[108] and after enduring her underworld journey, Psyche must "retrac[e] her earlier steps back to that chorus of heavenly stars" (6.19: *recalcans priora* **vestigia** *ad istum caelestium siderum redies chorum*).[109] Psyche fails, of course, to accomplish that return on her own, as she cannot restrain herself from "look[ing] into" (6.19: **inspicere** *illam . . . pyxidem*) the box of beauty Proserpina gives her, but instead, strives once again to see the Forms without first undergoing the appropriate steps of initiation.[110] Nevertheless, Psyche is apotheosized at the end of her tale by the sheer grace of a divinity. Moreover, although Psyche botches the procedure of "attentively reading" Cupid's body, she nonetheless experiences the *voluptas* our narrator promises *us*, even to the point of giving birth to a child by that name—a clearly ambivalent close to the

---

107. Psyche's labors have been linked to Aeneas, Heracles, Jason, and Odysseus (on which, see, e.g., Harrison 2013a, 167–73; Harrison 2013b; Finkelpearl 1998). On the theme of *katabasis* in *C&P* and its link to Platonism, see Panayotakis 2016; Ulrich forthcoming b.

108. I follow here the text of Kenney 1990a, 88, which preserves van der Vliet's conjecture (*intenta*).

109. On this line as an allusion to the circuit of the souls in Plato's *Phaedrus* refracted through *Aen.* 6, see Ulrich forthcoming b.

110. For our purposes, it is worth noting that Apuleius' drunken *narratrix* implicates the reader by deploying the precise terminology of the Prologue's exhortation to the reader: "look into" (*inspicere*) my text; "pay attention" (*intende*; cf. *intenta*).

charming tale, which foreshadows Lucius' own undeserved anamorphosis and his "inexplicable pleasure" in the presence of Isis.[111]

As we move to our final religious-erotic epiphany—that of Isis, whom we saw in §3.4 subtly figured as Lady Virtue in a crossroads choice between goddesses—we return not only to the question of Lucius' philosophico-mania in his representation of this encounter with the goddess, but also to the demands which this text places on the *lector scrupulosus*. For we will see in Lucius' epiphany of Isis, on the one hand, similarities to and continuities with his erotic encounter with Photis and in turn, with Psyche's religious-erotic epiphany of Cupid: a shared fetishization of hair, a Platonic *ekplêxis* at a kaleidoscopic color display, and an apparent reframing of the scene as a kind of *Phaedran* encounter—especially, given an alternative translation of our Platonic catchphrase. We will also find, however, some stark differences between the human-Lucius' response to Photis—or for that matter, Psyche's overly tactile pursuit of a bodily encounter with Cupid—and the more hesitant, measured, and contemplative reaction of the converted ass-man of book 11. Most strikingly, he does not try to strip the goddess and imagine her naked in his religious-erotic encounter. While the text may not come down on one side or the other about Lucius' final transformation—whether it is a satire of religious cult, a mocking poke at our asinine protagonist, or a sincere representation of religious conversion—it nevertheless implicates its reader in its *aporia* and thus, requires a choice from us between Elsner's "horizontal" and "vertical" viewing of the divine. Indeed, the *lector scrupulosus*, who has "diligently read" (*Apol.* 64.5: *legit . . . diligenter*) the *Phaedrus* like Apuleius' judge Maximus, cannot help but think of the Platonic invitation to contemplate the divine after watching an asinine buffoon so thoroughly misconstrue his tawdry affairs as sublime moments of enlightenment.

4.5. Lucius' Philosophico-Mania for Isis: Platonic Epiphany in the Isis Book

Lucius' epiphany of Isis in book 11 lays bare, in many ways, the Platonic clues we have considered throughout this chapter. As we saw in §3.4, the Isis book opens with our narrator still in asinine form (and therefore, still *pronus*) waking up on

---

111. On the ambiguity of *voluptas* (esp. in the Isis book), see §3.4.

VISUALIZING THE GODDESS   239

a beach in Cenchreae and experiencing a vision of the goddess by looking down at reflections of the moon on the seascape.[112] Immediately, he decides to wash himself in the sea, in a philosophico-maniacal gesture of ritual "purification" (*Met.* 11.1: *purificandi studio*).[113] Then, he addresses by a number of different names the goddess whose providential presence he senses: Ceres, Venus, Diana, and Proserpina. These names not only "symbolically recapitulate" the earlier episodes, where goddesses appear in the novel in surrogate forms (in, e.g., Byrrhena's atrium, *C&P*, or the Judgment of Paris),[114] but they are also redefined, as it were, in entirely new terms. Most strikingly, Lucius designates Isis as "heavenly Venus" (11.2: *caelestis Venus*), thus implying retrospectively that the species of Venus who presides over books 1–10 is "pandemic" (*vulgaris*).[115] Isis, in turn, subsuming all the named divinities under her godhead in an act of religious syncretism, curiously labels herself "Paphean Venus" (11.5: *Paphiam Venerem*)—that is, the more ancient and religious version of Venus, who is associated with the "Ouranian" Aphrodite of Plato's *Symposium*, and whose cult *simulacrum* is, according to Tacitus, "of inhuman likeness" (*Hist.* 2.3: *non effigie humana*).[116] In short, Lucius turns to a new Venus for his salvation—not a stripping goddess whose aesthetic-erotic pleasure can titillate with visual delights, but a clothed, almost inhuman form, whose otherworldly aspect invites transcendent speculation. Once again, therefore, the debate over book 11—over whether Isis represents continuity with or opposition to Lucius' previous aesthetic-erotic experience in books 1–10—is, at the fundamental

---

112. I know of no one who has noted that Lucius-*actor* at the opening of book 11 must still be *pronus*, and thus, can only see the moon through reflections in the water (i.e., can only look downward). This is signified perhaps by the phrase *marinis emergentem fluctibus* (11.1), which, as the Groningen commentators note, plays on the "apparent image of the moon which almost 'comes out' of the waves" (*GCA* 2015, 89 *ad loc.*). It is tempting to compare this to the philosopher who has just escaped the cave in Plato's *Republic* and can only see things via "reflections in water" (516a7: ἐν τοῖς ὕδασι τά . . . εἴδωλα), looking first at the "light of the moon and the stars" (516a9–b1: τὸ τῶν ἄστρων τε καὶ σελήνης φῶς). Cf. Libby 2011, 309–10.

113. See Kelting 2021 on the philosophical heritage of Lucius' Pythagorean purification.

114. See Harrison 2000, 242–43, on "symbolic recapitulation," expanded in Harrison 2012. See also §5.1 for fuller discussion of this phenomenon.

115. See again n. 84 above.

116. *GCA* 2015, 159 *ad loc.* 11.5.2, notes the ancient associations in the second–first centuries BCE, particularly in Asiatic Greece, between Isis and Aphrodite. On the many parallels in the *Met.* between Isis and Venus, see Tilg 2012, 148–49. To my knowledge, it has gone overlooked in scholarship that Paphean Venus of Cyprus is the very one whom Pausanias refers to as *Ouranian*: "the older [Aphrodite], who's motherless and the daughter of Ouranos" (*Symp.* 180d6–7: ἡ . . . που πρεσβυτέρα καὶ ἀμήτωρ Οὐρανοῦ θυγάτηρ) is the one labeled "Cyprus-born" in Hesiod's *Theogony* (199: Κυπρογενέα). Hence, Isis deploys the unique epithet *fluctuantes* (on which, see again *GCA* 159 *ad loc.* 11.5.2) to translate, in my view, the Hesiodic epithet πολύκλυστος (*Theog.* 199: "beaten with many-a-wave").

level, a question of whether or not key thematic terms (e.g., *voluptas* or *perfrui*; cf. §3.3) change their meaning under Isis' "economy of grace."

After Lucius experiences this epiphany of the goddess and addresses her by various names, he gazes upon her *simulacrum* (here, "dream-vision") in a manner that rehearses his earlier erotic epiphany of Photis as well as Psyche's religious-erotic epiphany of Cupid. At the same time, however, the context differentiates this new experience from the others in crucial ways. On the one hand, he initially focuses on Isis' hair, which, in accordance with iconographic depictions of the goddess,[117] is crowned with a mirror-like disk. This encomium of hair, as has long been recognized, alludes intratextually to Lucius' encounter with Photis.[118] I print below Lucius' two *ekphrases* of hair (*Met.* 2.9 and 11.3, respectively):[119]

Sed in mea Photide non operosus sed inordinatus ornatus addebat gratiam. **Uberes enim crines** leniter remissos et cervice dependulos ac *dein per colla dispositos* <u>sensimque</u> sinuato patagio residentes paulisper ad finem conglobatos in summum **verticem** nodus **adstrinxerat**.

But in the case of my Photis, the unelaborately worked up, but unarranged adornment added pleasure. For her abundant hair—gently let down and hanging over her neck, and then dispersed across the neck, until resting on a softly fluctuating border, and gathered together in a glob at the end—had been bound together in a knot at the top of her head.

Iam primum crines uberrimi prolixique et <u>sensim</u> intorti *per divina colla passive dispersi* molliter defluebant. Corona multiformis variis floribus sublimem **<u>destrinxerat verticem</u>**, cuius media quidem super frontem plana rotunditas in modum speculi, vel immo argumentum lunae, candidum lumen emicabat, dex-

---

117. See Gwyn Griffiths 1975, 124–25 *ad loc.*, on the *Realien* of Lucius' *ekphrasis* in Isis-cult iconography.
118. See, e.g., *GCA* 2001, 22: "Il est généralement admis que les similitudes entre ces deux passages servent à mettre en évidence l'opposition entre Isis et Photis, c'est-à-dire, une fois encore, entre le livre 11 et les dix premiers livres. Selon cette interprétation, Photis serait l'image négative d'Isis et la description de sa chevelure serait à lire en contraste avec celle de la chevelure de la déesse." Cf. also Alpers 1980, 201–2. Schmeling and Montiglio 2006, 37–38, make a compelling argument for the significance of the echo, but read into it "elements of eroticism" and thus, "continuity" rather than "opposition." On the interrelation of religious and erotic gazing, see again Kindt's quotation (n. 8 above).
119. For the sake of comparison, I have marked in bold, underline, and italics all of the verbal and conceptual parallels.

tra laevaque sulcis insurgentium viperarum cohibita, spicis etiam Cerialibus desuper porrectis <ornata. Vestis> multicolor, bysso tenui pertexta, nunc albo candore lucida, nunc croceo flore lutea, nunc roseo rubore flammida; et quae longe longeque etiam meum confutabat optutum palla nigerrima splendescens atro nitore.

First of all, her hair, extremely full, long, and gently curled, flowed down softly, freely strewn over her divine neck. A manifold crown, (woven) with variegated flowers, lightly rested on the top of her lofty head. At its midpoint, above her forehead, a flat circular disc like a mirror—or rather, a representation of the moon—was conspicuous with a white light. The disc was embraced on the left and right by coils of snakes rising up and adorned with ears of wheat spreading out on top. Her cloak, woven of thin flax linen, was multicolored, now brilliant with white brightness, at another time yellow with golden flower, and now fiery with rosy redness; and the thing which far and away confounded my sight was a deep black cloak gleaming with dark brightness.

Even a cursory glance at the noteworthy parallels reveals that we are invited to read these two elaborate descriptions side-by-side. We may note, for example, that Isis' aspect, much like Photis' (and Cupid's), displays a kaleidoscopic color palette which changes over time.[120]

The question remains, however, as to whether this reveals a unity or disjunction between books 1–10 and 11. For the satirical reader, Isis' *crines uberrimi* functions as an amplification of Lucius' delusion: Lucius-*auctor*, still taking excessive pleasure in his peculiar fetishes, encounters in Isis' locks a superlative and thus, even more pleasurable manifestation of Photis' *uberes crines*.[121] This interpretation is rendered problematic, however, not only by the way in which words seem to take on new meanings under Isis (cf. §3.4), but also by the fact that Lucius' focus and reaction are strikingly different. First of all, he looks into the hair-mirror of Isis' head, where *in modum speculi* replicates (in differenti-

---

120. In particular, Lucius' description of Isis' multicolor cloak, which changes colors "at one time . . . and then another . . . and then another" (**nunc** *albo candore lucida,* **nunc** *croceo flore lutea,* **nunc** *roseo rubore flammida*), mirrors the *nunc . . . nunc . . . vel cum* of Photis' hair-mirror (see §4.3 above). On the "color palette" of Apuleius throughout the *Met.*, see Krabbe 2003, 521–66.

121. See, e.g., Libby 2011, 302–5, who places herself firmly in the Harrison-school of cynical readers. Cf. also GCA 2001, 180–82 *ad loc.* 32,22–33,2 and 409–11; Schmeling and Montiglio 2006, 37–38. The Groningen commentators on the Isis book seem to suggest that this repetition could be explained merely by Apuleius' "lexical preferences" (GCA 2015, 130 *ad loc.* 11.3), but I personally find this proposal uncompelling for an author so adept at linguistic manipulation.

ated Latin terms) our Platonic catchphrase, "as if in a mirror" (ὥσπερ . . . ἐν κατόπτρῳ). And there, he sees *not* a pleasurable, delusory vision of an objectified beloved, but the "bright light" (*candidum lumen*) of the moon.[122] Although it is not an eye-to-eye, intersubjective encounter which leads to self-knowledge, it is also not an eye-to-hair fetishization of a beloved. By contrast to his earlier instrumentalizing gaze, Lucius looks into an actual mirror-like device and leverages it to a more sublime, religious reflection on the cosmos.[123]

More importantly, although Lucius stands at the beginning of book 11 in the same position which he inhabited vis-à-vis Diana in Byrrhena's atrium—namely, looking "downward" (*pronus*) at a *simulacrum* reflected in water[124]—he does *not* attempt to undress the goddess in his imagination. Instead, he appreciates her clothed aspect for its invitation to wonder. In fact, given Apuleius' appropriation in the Photis episode of the art-critical tradition on the Cnidian Aphrodite,[125] it is suggestive that, according to Pliny the Elder, Praxiteles actually made two Venuses: one "clothed" (*NH* 36.20: *velata specie*) and a second nude version, which "many sailed to Cnidos to see" (*quam ut viderent, multi navigaverunt Cnidum*). According to that tale, moreover, the people of Cos, who were given the choice by Praxiteles between the two Venuses, initially chose the clothed one on the grounds that "it was the dignified and chaste thing [to do]" (*severum id ac pudicum*). Lucius' encounter with the *Venus caelestis* of book 11, in other words, Platonizes a well-known art-critical episode from the imperial era by representing a second version of the goddess—one who possesses an aspect which recollects even at the verbal level the earlier surrogate of Venus from book 2. But, whereas the first Venus figure "stripped her clothes off and let her hair down" (2.17: *laciniis cunctis suis renudata crinibusque dissolutis*) in order to "transform charmingly into the guise of Venus rising up from the waves" (*in speciem Veneris quae marinos fluctus subit pulchre reformata*), this *Venus caelestis* remains clothed, much like the second Praxitelean original or even the *simulacrum* of "Paphian Venus," which is "of inhuman likeness" (cf. Tac. *Hist.* 2.3: *non effigie humana*). Simply put, with the epiphany of Isis, we are

---

122. Libby 2011 makes, in my view, a very tendentious argument about the *lumen* of the moon being "borrowed" and therefore, artificial. On the contrary, in light of the Platonic tradition of looking into "as-if" mirrors to acquire self-knowledge, Isis' hair-mirror seems far less cynical or satirical. On the "mirroring" of mirrors in books 2 and 11, see Krabbe 2003, 580–87.

123. Cf. Krabbe 2003, 581–83, who links the *speculum* of Isis to the *specula candelabri* from which Pamphile prophesies the future at *Met.* 2.11.

124. Lucius refers to Isis as a "radiant image" (11.3: *perlucidum simulacrum*), which, as Heath 1992, 106, points out, "directly recalls his description of the statue of Diana": *signum perfecte luculentum* (2.4). See again §3.2 for further discussion of this episode.

125. See Slater 1998, and cf. §4.0 above.

faced once more with a choice between goddesses—as in the "Education of Heracles" or the Judgment of Paris. This time, however, our asinine narrator attempts neither to strip *this* Venus in his imagination nor even to shear her of her hair; instead, he delights in her "marvelous appearance," clothed as it is.

The other feature that "serious" readers of the Isis book might point to is the fact that, although Lucius undergoes the same Platonic religious-erotic experience—namely, *ekplêxis*, marvel, and looking into the "mirror" of the beloved—he does not lunge at the goddess in an attempt at *agalmatophilia*, but in contrast to his earlier behavior, shows restraint, hesitantly approaching her with wonder.[126] Indeed, after he awakens from his epiphanic dream of the goddess, Lucius "marvels at the clear presence of the . . . goddess" (11.7: *miratus deae . . . tam claram praesentiam*), but remains "intent on her great commands" (*magnis . . . imperiis eius **intentus***). He is physically immobilized, in turn, at the sight of the goddess, unable to "move further than a nail's breadth" (11.17: ***ungue latius** indidem **digredi***) from her, as he "focuse[s] on the manifestation of the goddess" (***intentus** <in> deae specimen*).

Of course, as we saw in §3.1, stultification and the loss of mobility is precisely what causes Apuleius anxiety in his discussion of *mimesis* in the *Apologia*. In that respect, we may note that Photis, too, is "unwilling for [Lucius] to move further than a nail's breadth from her" (2.18: *invita quod a se **ungue latius digrederer***).[127] Once more, however, the nature of the immobilizing object and the posture of the viewer toward that aesthetic object are fundamental. By contrast to the earlier scene, Lucius cannot move in the Isis book because of intense focus, where *intentus* reproduces the readerly call to *intendere*.

Indeed, it is paramount for us that, when Lucius finally undergoes his anamorphosis, he depicts his response in terms reminiscent of his philosophicomania toward Photis, but with a drastically different bodily response (11.14):

> At ego stupore nimio defixus tacitus haerebam, animo meo tam repentinum tamque magnum non capiente gaudium, quid potissimum **praefarer** primarium, unde **novae vocis** exordium caperem, quo **sermone** nunc renatam **linguam felicius** auspicarer, quibus quantisque verbis tantae deae gratias agerem.

---

126. Thus, Winkle 2014, 110–17, reads Lucius being "tamed" by various charioteers as the possible "development" (*Entwicklung*) in the asinine books.

127. Heath 1992, 121–28, points up the repetition of this phrase in the Photis-Isis episodes. Moreover, the criminal woman with whom Lucius-ass is slated to copulate publicly in book 10 is condemned, in part, because she poisons a doctor and then refuses to allow him "to depart further than a nail's breadth from her" (10.26: ***ungue latius** a se discedere*).

244   THE SHADOW OF AN ASS

But I, dumbstruck with excessive stupefaction, was silently fixed, as my spirit could not comprehend so sudden and such great joy. [I was at a loss] as to what principal prefatory statement I should make first, or from where I should take up the *exordium* of my new voice, with what speech I should auspiciously inaugurate my now-renewed tongue, or with what such powerful words I should give thanks to so great a goddess.

Luca Graverini has ingeniously demonstrated how this sentence functions as "a sort of new prologue, the starting point of a new narrative segment": it opens with the cryptic *at ego* of the first line of 1.1 and incorporates the terminology of an *exordium*.[128] For Graverini, then, this represents a final transformation of our narrator from the previously asinine teller of tales to a newly converted initiate.

This is not *merely* an invitation, however, to envision a new narrative segment, in which we see the Prologue appropriated to new ends. Taking our Platonic aesthetic-erotic experience into account, we may also point out that Lucius adapts again the discourse of *ekplêxis* he used in his earlier encounter with Photis, where he was likewise "fixed in one aspect" (2.7: *isto aspectu* **defixus**; cf. **defixus**) and "dumbstruck with wonder" (*obstupui* et **mirabundus**; cf. **stupore** nimio and **miratus**). There is one exception to this repetition, however: in this case, Lucius' "spirit" (*animus*) and not his "member" (*membra*) takes its pleasure from the marvelous wonder. He is, to be sure, subservient to the goddess, as the satirical school of readers would hasten to point out;[129] and in fact, Lucius' posture after he is stripped of his ass-hide replicates Photis' *Venus Pudica* gesture in 2.17. That is, he (and *not* his beloved) is "stripped" of his external appearance (11.14: *nefasto tegmine* **despoliaverat** *asinus*), where the term *despoliare* is recycled from book 2 (cf. 2.8: *caput capillo* **spoliaveris**); and in a comic repetition of Photis' posture, the anamorphosed ass-man stands naked before an audience, "closing his legs tightly and drawing his hands carefully over top" (*compressis in artum feminibus et superstrictis accurate manibus*). Needless to say, this is another mock-Platonic moment recalling Alcibiades' hubristic stripping of Socrates, as Lucius, too, is stripped of his ass-hide (*corium*)

---

128. With the bold words above, compare the terms from *Met.* 1.1: *praefamur*; *vocis immutatio*; *sermone . . . Milesio*; *linguam Atthidem*; *glebae felices*. See Graverini 2012a, 52, for the quotation and a careful analysis of the parallels.

129. See, e.g., Slater 1998; Harrison 2013a; Murgatroyd 2004; Libby 2011; MacDougall 2016.

VISUALIZING THE GODDESS   245

to reveal the inner man.[130] By contrast with our programmatic passage, however, Lucius does not interact with the goddess in an overly bodily or corporeal fashion: indeed, when the *asinus* "strips" Lucius to reveal his inner character, it is possible that it even takes with it the phallic device with which the *agalmatophile* does sexual violence to the goddess (if, indeed, Lucius' loss of the *cauda* represents a kind of castration).[131]

Lucius concludes the novel in a series of increasingly introspective and symbolic encounters with the goddess.[132] As we saw in §3.4, he describes how he spends the days after his initiation "enjoying the inexplicable pleasure of her divine statue" (11.24: *inexplicabili* **voluptate** *simulacri divini* **perfruebar**). And at 11.25, he luxuriates in his knowledge of the goddess, "reflect[ing] and perpetually guarding her holiest divinity hidden within the secret places of his heart" (*numen . . . sanctissimum intra pectoris mei secreta* **conditum** *perpetuo custodiens imaginabor*). I suggested in §3.4, furthermore, that, although he deploys the same terminology for his earlier debased erotic experience, it is quite possible to read this *voluptas* instead as a "pleasure" associated with feasting among the gods. However, while I remain agnostic about Lucius' "conversion" (though I tend toward sincerity), Lucius' final posture vis-à-vis Isis—that is, guarding a representation of her divinity "hidden" (**conditum**) within his heart—brings us back to where we began this chapter: namely, to Elsner's distinction between "vertical" and "horizontal" viewing, and to Apuleius' own relationship to divine statuary in the *Apologia*. Indeed, reading across his corpus, we may recall that Apuleius, rather than deny the accusation in the *Apologia* that he carries "the *simulacrum* of a certain god hidden within his books" (*Apol.* 63: *simulacrum alicuius dei inter libellos* **conditum**), boldly acknowledges his utilitarian approach to contemplating the divine. Apuleius uses the opportunity presented by the trial to strip himself of his external appearance by linking this little statuette to the *simulacra deorum* of Platonic philosophy, and more specifically, to the act of reading the *Phaedrus*. Whether or not we trust Lucius-*auctor's* representation of his "conversion," we are nonetheless shown a portrait of another

---

130. See Ulrich 2017. Cf. also Egelhaaf-Gaiser 2012; O'Brien 2002.

131. See Winkle 2014, 125, where he suggests that Apuleius' reference to the tail reproduces a phallic pun from the *Phaedrus*, in which the black horse "stretches out its tail" (*Phaedr.* 254d6–7: ἐκτείνας τὴν κέρκον). Although taking *cauda* as a phallic euphemism is problematic, I am convinced by Winkle's reasoning (125n85), where he shows how it parallels Lucius' *natura* elsewhere in the novel and particularly, in his initial transformation at 3.24. Cf., however, van Mal-Maeder 1997, 108–9.

132. See Benson 2019, 184–238, on "narratological invisibility" and Adkins 2022, 177–85, on Lucius' ritual/symbolic silence.

character who conveys an "image" (*imaginabor*) of the divine "hidden deep within" (*intra . . . conditum*). It is quite possible, of course, to read Lucius' "conversion" horizontally within the social panopticon of viewing: for instance, many scholars find Lucius' attempts to achieve a certain social status within a small religious community through performative devotion to be disingenuous or even downright foolish. Even if this is the case, however, sensitive readers have likewise been implicated, provoked or even compelled to recognize a sort of buffoonish misconstrual of Plato. As *lectores scrupulosi*, therefore, we are invited to follow Apuleius' lead and leverage this opportunity to pursue the appropriate, "vertical" encounter with the divine. We must avoid at all costs neglecting the *simulacra deorum* as Aemilianus does and instead, must approach our aesthetic-erotic encounters like Maximus, Apuleius' judge. In short, we must "diligently read" the *Phaedrus* (*and* the *Metamorphoses*); if we do, we cannot help but be transformed.

FIVE

Paradigms of Life

Platonic Choice and Reader-Response in the Isis Book

καὶ τελευταίῳ ἐπιόντι, ξὺν νῷ ἑλομένῳ, συντόνως ζῶντι κεῖται βίος ἀγαπητός, οὐ κακός. μήτε ὁ ἄρχων αἱρέσεως ἀμελείτω μήτε ὁ τελευτῶν ἀθυμείτω.

Even for the one who goes last, if he makes his choice intelligently and lives intently, there is still available for him a life of contentment, and not a bad one. Let the one who begins [choosing] not be careless about its choice, and let the one who concludes not be despondent.

—*Republic* 10.619b3–6

So, the "prophet of Lachesis" announces the eschatological choice of lives episode in the Myth of Er, one of the most bewildering and controversial scenes in the whole of the Platonic corpus.[1] In this surprise conclusion to a dialogue devoted to investigating the pursuit of justice for its own sake, Socrates' mouthpiece—Er the Pamphylian, who temporarily died and experienced firsthand an afterlife encounter of the judgment of souls—closes his *mythos* with a haunting spectacle of choice, in which disembodied *psychai* arrive in an intermediary place between the upper and lower worlds, and are asked to "choose" (αἱρεῖν) their next life in accordance with a complex system of lots. While the episode highlights the arbitrariness of fortune and chance in how one's life turns out, it simultaneously emphasizes that a "life of contentment" (βίος ἀγαπητός) con-

---

1. See Annas 1981, 344–54, for a classic study of the problems of the Myth of Er. For the most substantive treatments of the Myth of Er's complex interpretive issues, see Segal 1978; Halliwell 1988, 17–23 and 2007; O'Connor 2007; and Barney 2010.

247

248 THE SHADOW OF AN ASS

tinues to be available for the person who "chooses intelligently" (ξὺν νῷ ἑλομένῳ) and "lives intently" (συντόνως ζῶντι). As the episode unfolds, readers are given an illuminating window into the process of metempsychosis as well as an encore of characters, the most famous names from the Greek epic cycle, deciding to live very different lives from their prior incarnations in the texts of Homer.[2] The moral lesson of the initial life-choice (Rep. 10.619b7–c8)— the soul which obtained the first lot, but disregarded the prophet's warning, made its *hairesis* haphazardly, and picked the life of a tyrant—is glaringly clear: it is necessary to "inspect [one's choice] at leisure" (10.619c2: κατὰ σχολὴν σκέψασθαι), and one who makes the wrong decision can only "blame [one]self" (10.619c4–5: ἑαυτὸν αἰτιᾶσθαι), not "fortune, *daemones*, and everything else" (τύχην . . . καὶ δαίμονας καὶ πάντα). So, after nine books of meticulously trying to develop a philosophical rationale for pursuing justice for its own sake, Plato's Socrates resorts to this jarring afterlife story as a closure to his philosophical masterpiece—a *mythos* which seems to contradict all prior attempts in the dialogue to advocate for the self-fulfilling benefits of pursuing justice,[3] but which, at the same time, aims to promote "choosing a moderate life" (10.619a5–6: τὸν μέσον . . . βίον αἱρεῖσθαι) and "fleeing excess" (φεύγειν τὰ ὑπερβάλλοντα).

I begin the final chapter of this monograph with a meditation on this strange scene from the *Republic* not simply because the *hairesis* episode overlaps conceptually with the emphasis I have placed throughout this book on philosophical choice as a lens through which to analyze encounters with aesthetic pleasure in Apuleius, but more precisely, because, with the Platonic life-choice paradigm in view, we return to the interpretative crux with which I opened the first chapter of this book (§1.0): Mithras' reevaluation of books 1–10 of the *Met.* according to an Isiac framework. Turning back to the Isis book, I argue that Apuleius' jarring closure for his carnivalesque novel is modeled in significant ways on Plato's Myth of Er (especially, on the concluding episode of *hairesis*). In particular, I suggest that Lucius' religious "conversion"—his anamorphosis and subsequent initiations to the cults of

---

2. See Segal 1978, esp. 329–33 on Plato's general indebtedness to Homer in the Myth of Er. Cf. Halliwell 1988, 189 *ad loc.* 619e6; and Montiglio 2011, 49–51 on Plato invoking the Homeric parade of souls from the *Odyssey*.
3. See, e.g., Annas 1981, 349, for a characteristic assessment: "The Myth of Er is a painful shock; its vulgarity seems to pull us right down to the level of Cephalus, where you take justice seriously when you start thinking about hell-fire . . . if we take it seriously, it seems to offer us an entirely consequentialist reason for being just, thus undermining Plato's sustained effort to show that justice is worth having for the agent in a non-consequentialist way."

Isis and Osiris—acquires a new symbolic value when we recognize that his choice is patterned not merely on an allegorizing paradigm of the Homeric Odysseus, but in point of fact, on a specific, revisionist portrait of Odysseus: namely, Plato's Odysseus at the end of the *Republic*, who chooses, by contrast to the other characters in the parade of heroes, to become human and indeed, to be reincarnated in the "life of an unmeddlesome private individual" (620c6–7).[4] In this final meditation on book 11, therefore, we return not merely to the tired question about the nature of Lucius' "conversion"— whether he is a gullible dupe of greedy priests,[5] or the genuine specimen of a transformed acolyte[6]—but rather, to the *aporia* inherent in our choice to participate in this journey of a debased Odysseus and to the related question of how *we* might be expected to respond to his transformation.[7]

This Platonic episode of life-choice provides a fitting closure to this monograph, since in demonstrating Apuleius' deliberate engagement with Plato's *mythos* in the Isis book, we revisit a number of questions underlying this study. Throughout this monograph, I have argued that the *Met.* offers a meditation on how one should engage with aesthetic pleasure—that is, on what the Prologue's request to "pay attention" (1.1: *lector, intende*) entails, and how one should go about being a *lector scrupulosus*. As we have seen in the preceding pages, no figure from mythology is more implicated in the positive and negative associations of "meddlesomeness" than Odysseus, and Lucius appeals to this Homeric hero, both explicitly and implicitly,[8] as an authorizing model for his own misdirected *curiositas*. However, Odysseus' overeager interest in scrutinizing his

---

4. So, Segal 1978, 333, notes that Odysseus is the "only [Homeric figure] who chooses a human form of his own sex, undeceived by externals," and expounds that "this passage is a summation, in mythic terms, of the struggle throughout the *Republic* between 'human' and 'savage,' civilized and bestial." For earlier treatments of the significance of this Platonic Odysseus for Lucius' loss of *curiositas*, see MacDougall 2016, 268–73; Ulrich 2020, 688–700.

5. On Lucius as a gullible dupe of rapacious religious authorities, see Winkler 1985, 212; van Mal-Maeder 1997, 102–5; Harrison 2000, 244–45. On the "unambiguously corrupt" priests of the Syrian goddess as a "narrative precursor" to the cult of Isis, see Harrison 2000, 248–49. Cf. also Murgatroyd 2004; Libby 2011; MacDougall 2016. For a useful corrective, see Graverini 2012a, 69–75.

6. Most "serious" readings of Lucius' "conversion" take on an allegorical flair: thus, Reitzenstein 1927; Kerényi 1927; and Merkelbach 1962 provided the most famous (and notoriously problematic) allegorical reading. For Lucius' "conversion" as a spiritual rise from debased magic to philosophical and religious "conversion," see Harrauer 1973; Münstermann 1995. On the philosophical significance of Lucius' "conversion," see DeFilippo 1990; Dowden 1998; Drews 2012 and 2015. For "seriocomic" approaches, which grant a certain genuine sincerity to Lucius' "conversion," see Graverini 2012a; Tilg 2014a.

7. Cf. Drews 2015, 528, for a similar proposal in light of philosophical themes.

8. See again *Met.* 9.13 (on which, see §1.3 with discussion and bibliography).

250   THE SHADOW OF AN ASS

surroundings, and even his debased participation in aesthetic-erotic pleasure, are set at odds in the literary tradition (especially, in the Platonic corpus) with the philosophical busybody par excellence, Socrates, who was put to death for a meddlesomeness verging on sacrilege,[9] but was resuscitated, in Plato's various apologies across the dialogues, as a philosopher merely striving to fulfil the Delphic maxim—one who directed his intellectual pursuits exclusively toward self-knowledge.

So, while the philosopher was deemed by some in antiquity the quintessential *polypragmôn* because of his natural curiosity toward the outside world,[10] Plato aims nonetheless to redefine the parameters of Socrates' *polypragmosynê*, to give a rebuttal to the (quite legitimate) charge that his teacher was excessively interested in the affairs of others.[11] In light of this, Odysseus' choice in *Rep.* 10 is nothing less than an attempt to redirect the epic hero's curiosity in his Homeric life to a kind of philosophical (and "Socratic") *apragmosynê* in his Platonic metempsychosis.[12] And Lucius' analogous reorientation of *his curiositas* from the darker side of magic to the saving light of Isis, when viewed through the lens of Apuleius' engagement with the Myth of Er, seems to reincarnate in a novelistic landscape this metamorphosis of the Homeric Odysseus in the *Republic*.

While the life-choice episode in Er's fabulous tale offers us a chance to

---

9. So, at least one of the accusations against Socrates seems to have been that he "went around giving counsel and playing the busybody" (*Apol.* 31c5: συμβουλεύω περιιὼν καὶ **πολυπραγμονῶ**). Moreover, in the official language of the accusation, this meddlesomeness verged on sacrilege, insofar as he was "seeking the things under the earth and in the heavens" (19b5: ζητῶν τά τε ὑπὸ γῆς καὶ οὐράνια).

10. See Hunter 2009b, 52.

11. See Plato's *Apol.* 19b4, where Socrates addresses the charge of "doing wrong and being meddlesome" (ἀδικεῖ καὶ **περιεργάζεται**) in his philosophical searches (on which, see Leigh 2013, 33–35). Perhaps more important for my study, Socrates is regarded in his Second Sophistic reception as an *apragmôn*, whose interests are redirected toward self-analysis. See, e.g., Plut. *De curios.* 516c, where Socrates' *periergia* is directed toward the correct objects of investigation and its *telos* is "to recognize one's own vices and to be rid of them" (516c7: ἐπιγνῶναι τὰ ἑαυτοῦ κακὰ καὶ ἀπαλλαγῆναι). Cf. Kirichenko 2010, 87–89, on how Socrates' turn to *apragmosynê* became a paradigm for the "conversion to philosophy," esp. in the Second Sophistic.

12. So, Montiglio 2011, 49–51, notes that Plato "invents" this "quiet Odysseus" as a fantasy, in which Odysseus' soul dispenses with the *philotimia* characteristic of political involvement and instead, "reincarnates in a philosopher." Cf. also Hunter 2012, 42: "Odysseus' abandonment of the public (and political) life of φιλοτιμία and πολυπραγμοσύνη is not just a typically Platonic gesture towards the life of the mind, and in particular shows Odysseus choosing the life of a (Platonic) Socrates . . . but may also be understood as a wry comment upon what Odysseus, the archetypal πολυπράγμων, (should have) learned in Odyssey 11." Cf. also Tilg 2014a, 73–78, who reads Lucius' loss of *curiositas* as an allusion to Plato's *Gorg.* (523a–527e), where a philosopher is one "who . . . does not play the busybody" (526c4: φιλοσόφου . . . οὐ πολυπραγμονήσαντος).

PARADIGMS OF LIFE   251

revisit, on the one hand, the question of "attentive" reading and its imbrication with misdirected *curiositas*, it also allows us, on the other hand, to view Lucius' initial metamorphosis, along with his subsequent "conversion" and initiations, as participating in a broader Platonic discourse about metempsychosis—that is, about the continuity of identity across bodily transformations. Of course, an earlier generation of scholarship on the *Met.* deciphered a Platonic resonance in Lucius' asinine transformation.[13] In the *Phaedo*, for instance, Socrates famously claims that souls in between bodily incarnations are likely to "be attached to the sorts of characters" (*Phaed.* 81e2: ἐνδοῦνται . . . εἰς τοιαῦτα ἤθη) they happened to cultivate in their previous life; and according to Socrates' classification of metempsychoses, those souls which pursued "gluttony, wantonness, and drunkenness" in a former incarnation are wont to "sink into the species of asses and other such beasts" (81e6–82a1: εἰς τὰ τῶν ὄνων γένη καὶ τῶν τοιούτων θηρίων . . . ἐνδύεσθαι). In this sense, Lucius' "[slip] into servile pleasures" (11.15: *ad serviles **delapsus** voluptates*) at the crossroads of youth seems to reenact the "sinking" of a soul into embodiment in the *Phaedo*,[14] especially when we consider the associations of the adjective *serviles* with the donkey.[15]

However, while I believe that the *Phaedo*'s categorization of soul-types is, of course, relevant for Lucius' asinine transformation, we turn in this chapter to the parade of heroes reincarnated in the Myth of Er because this second eschatological tale can be used to explain Lucius' anamorphosis and "conversion"—and indeed, it gets to the very heart of the question about continuity and change which has haunted scholarship on Lucius' "conversion" and initiation(s), espe-

---

13. See, e.g., Schlam 1970, 480. For recent revivals of this proposal, see Winkle 2014, 97–98; Tilg 2014a, 70. Cf. also Smith 2023, 3–4, who notes a loose connection between the Platonic line on asinine metempsychosis and the demonization of the ass in fable.

14. Important for recognizing Apuleius' use of the phraseology of metempsychosis here is the fact that Psyche, when she attempts a *Phaedran* winged flight but "grows weary and falls to the earth" (5.24: *tandem fessa **delabitur** solo*; cf. §4.4 with n. 86), reproduces the embodiment of souls in the *Phaedrus* in precisely the same terminology: *delabor*. On the Platonic origins of the phrase *serviles . . . voluptates*, see Graverini 2012a, 114–18, who, however, follows a different text for 5.24 and therefore, denies that Lucius' *delapsus* echoes Psyche's *dilabitur* (115). Here, I follow Zimmerman 2012, 115, who prints *delabitur*.

15. On the donkey and its natural submission to *servitium*, see Col. *De re rust.* 6.37.4. On the asinine associations of *serviles*, see Fitzgerald 2000, 103–5. Cf. also Bradley 2000, 124–25, who argues (*contra* Sandy 1974 and Penwill 1975) that *serviles voluptates* cannot refer to servitude or enslavement to pleasure, but rather, must associate Lucius with a slave in the *types* of pleasures he enjoys. Interestingly, Fick 1987, 39–40 links *serviles . . . voluptates* to the Siren-cicadas' enslavement of auditors through rhetoric in the *Phaedrus* (on which, see §1.1).

cially since Winkler.[16] Simply put, Isis' *anteludia* exhibits reincarnations of previous characters from the burlesque books of the novel and in so doing, functions as a (parodic) reproduction of Er's epic heroes rejecting their Homeric lives. In light of this detailed reproduction of life-choice from the Myth of Er, then, Lucius' loss of *curiositas* invites us to speculate not simply about the sincerity of his "conversion" or the continuity of his character in his Isiac incarnation, but also about the deadly seriousness of his choice, framed as an epilogue of sorts to a hair-raising eschatological tale. Is it possible that his success or failure in choosing carefully could somehow rebound upon us readers?

I open this chapter (§5.1), therefore, by demonstrating the way in which Apuleius fashions the most enigmatic elements of the Isis book not only on a generalized model of Platonic metempsychosis, but in very specific ways, on the bewildering *hairesis* episode from the Myth of Er. Indeed, Lucius' decision to enter the "voluntary servitude" (11.15: *iugum . . . voluntarium*) of Isis can be contextualized as the culmination of her *anteludia*, a procession of characters who publicly enact "symbolic recapitulations" of earlier episodes from the novel.[17] Thus, when a priestly representative of a goddess stands up after this staging of reincarnated characters and declares Lucius saved from *curiositas* (=*polypragmosynê*),[18] it is difficult not to think of the Myth of Er and its closing *exemplum* for the parade of Homeric heroes choosing new lives under the aegis of a *prophêtês*.

After showing that Isis' *anteludia* parallels, in many respects, the parade of Homeric heroes in the Myth of Er, I turn in §5.2 to Lucius' initiation into the cult of Osiris, which I regard as the final element in Apuleius' reproduction of Plato's *mythos*—namely, the allocation of an "intermediary divinity." Indeed, in the Platonic model, each soul, after making its choice, approaches Lachesis, from whom it obtains a *daemôn* to guide it through its next life. This process is

---

16. On which, see my discussion in §0.1 (with bibliography). For a representative recent discussion of "continuity" and "ambivalence" in the Isis book, see, e.g., Keulen 2015. For the most ardent supporter of a marked antithesis between books 1–10 and the Isis book, see Frangoulidis 2008, 175–203.

17. On "symbolic recapitulation," see Harrison 2000, 242–43 and 2008. See also Fick-Michel 1991, 420–23. On the *Ploiaphesia* as a recapitulation of the *Risus* festival, see Frangoulidis 2008, 179–90; and MacDougall 2016, though they arrive at opposite conclusions.

18. Indeed, recent scholarship has reached a consensus that *curiositas* appears to be a Latin gloss for two related Greek concepts, *polypragmosynê* and *periergia* (see, e.g., DeFilippo 1990, 479; Hunter 2009b; and Leigh 2013). On the broader relationship between *polypragmosynê* and *curiositas* in Middle Platonism, see DeFilippo 1990. On Lucius' *curiositas* as a realization of Plutarch's discussion in *On curiosity* (*Peri polypragmosynê*), see Kenney 2003, 163–67; Van der Stockt 2012.

not simply a designation by lot, but involves an active choice made by a soul in the intermediate position between lives. As the *prophêtês* of Lachesis cryptically claims: "the responsibility lies with the chooser; the god is blameless" (617e4–5: αἰτία ἑλομένου· θεὸς ἀναίτιος).[19] So also, in the Isis book, while the responsibility for Lucius' asinine metamorphosis is complicated by competing interpretations offered by Mithras and the crowd of onlookers,[20] the priest of Isis nonetheless assigns Lucius a *numen*—a term used interchangeably with *daemôn* for Socrates' guardian divinity in the *Soc.*[21]—which is to guide the remainder of his life. And Lucius reaffirms this choice of an "intermediary," in turn, by enduring yet another initiation—this time, into the cult of Osiris, one of the few *daemones* explicitly named in *Soc.* (15.10). In other words, read in light of Er's life-choice episode, Lucius' final initiation becomes not simply additional evidence to confirm his exploitation at the hands of greedy priests (n. 5 above), but instead, is portrayed as a specific choice of an "intermediary divinity" to take charge of his post-asinine life.

In §5.3, I depart from my comparative analysis in order to turn my attention to the seemingly shared receptions of these two *fabulae* in the analytical framework of an ancient witness: Macrobius. Indeed, just as I began this monograph with Septimius Severus' brutal reception of Apuleius' novel as "old wives' lullabies," I return in this final chapter to the late antique reception of the *Met.*, arguing that ancient readers took great pains to distinguish Plato's cryptic closure for the *Republic* from the "merely pleasurable" subgenre of fiction, with which Apuleius "sometimes played." Given more space to elaborate, one could demonstrate clear thematic and conceptual links between the (primarily North African) Latin reception of the Myth of Er and Apuleius' representation of Lucius' *katabasis* in his initiation to Isis (and in fact, as a prelude to future work on Apuleius' situating of the Isis book in this tradition, I have drawn a diagram in the **appendix** tracing out the nine overlapping categories these two *fabulae* share). For the purposes of this chapter, however, we need only focus on Mac-

---

19. Tatum 1979, 38, implicitly suggests this Platonic moral underlies Lucius' earlier encounters with the fantastic.

20. Indeed, one of the famously problematic issues with Mithras' exegesis is the fact that it is immediately undercut by the crowd of onlookers, who interpret Lucius' "retransformation" (11.16: *reformavit*) as a sign of his "innocence" and "fidelity" in the eyes of a divinity (on which, see Ulrich 2020, 690–91). Cf. also Fletcher 2023, 99–109, who questions the mutual exclusivity of the different audience reactions.

21. See, e.g., *Soc.* 14.7, 15.6, 15.9, 20.6, and 21.1.

robius' distinction between *fabulae* which merely "charm the ears" and tales which are more didactic or philosophically oriented—in large part, because it brings us back to the underlying question of this monograph: the ethics of fiction. So, while modern critics of the *Met.* routinely invoke the antiquarian's strict dichotomy as evidence for a disdain in antiquity for Apuleius' trifles, they never, in fact, situate this dichotomy in its original context—namely, as a late antique attempt to make an apologia for Plato's Myth of Er, which was derisively mocked from the Hellenistic period onward. In light of this, I suggest that Apuleius does not merely allude to the Myth of Er as a loose model for Lucius' "conversion," but seems, in fact, to welcome a comparison also at the conceptual and lexical levels between Plato's controversial conclusion to the *Republic* and his own "ballast" to his burlesque tale of pleasure and pursuit of illicit knowledge. In other words, if the Myth of Er rewrites *Odyssey* 11 with the Pamphylian's claim to narrate "no tall tale to Alcinous" (*Rep.* 10.614b2: Ἀλκίνου γε ἀπόλογον), Apuleius affirmatively recreates Plato's most controversial *mythos* with his own *katabasis* tale and thereby, functions as an *interpres* of Platonic philosophy for his African readers.[22]

Finally, to conclude (§5.4), I return in my own ring-compositional gesture to the final line of the *Metamorphoses* with which I began this book in order to show how the closing depiction of Lucius, "joyfully carrying out the duties" (*munia . . . gaudens* **obibam**) of Osiris' priesthood, invites comparison not to a buffoon repeating his initiations *ad infinitum* nor to someone undergoing a metaphorical death, but rather to the *daemones* of Apuleius' *Soc.*, which "carry out duties between men and gods" (*Soc.* 7.3: *inter homines ac deos* **obeunt**). If Lucius' "Romecoming" is thus a gesture of mediation—not only a cultural negotiation of translating a Greek original for a Romano-Carthaginian audience,[23] but also a philosophical mediation where the ass-man functions as *daemôn* for his readers—then the sincerity of his conversion is not the only factor that bears upon the "seriousness" of the text. Rather, alert readers are forced to decide how to cultivate this *daemôn*—how to *make* an educational encounter through "actively" reading the *Met.*'s asinine and frivolous form.

---

22. On Plato's myth as a rewrite of Homer's underworld, see O'Connor 2007; Halliwell 2007. On Apuleius as an *interpres* for Plato, see Fletcher 2014, 145–72; Ulrich 2023. Cf. also the epilogue to this book on his role as *interpres* for an African audience.

23. On which, see Graverini 2012a, 179–97; and Tilg 2014a, 110–11.

5.1. "Paradigms of Lives" (παραδείγματα βίων) in the Isis book

At many points in this monograph, I have ruminated on the figures of Odysseus and Socrates, analyzing the way in which these two heroic characters, as forefathers of the genre of the novel,[24] function as paradigms on which Lucius models himself across the *Met.* To phrase it more precisely, I have aimed to demonstrate that, throughout Apuleius' corpus—and especially, in the closing books of the *Met.*—there is a negotiation between the figures of Odysseus and Socrates, where the Homeric hero is sometimes set against the Athenian philosopher as a competing *exemplum*, but at other times, the two paradigms are confused or intermixed. So, as we saw in his response to an eroticized pantomime of Venus (§3.3), Lucius appeals to Socrates as the highest *exemplum* of *prudentia* and *sapientia* and in fact, pointedly alludes to the philosopher's own desire in Plato's *Apology* to investigate whether Odysseus was truly wise or disastrously treacherous (*Apol.* 41b). Moreover, as I noted in §1.3, the analogies Lucius-*auctor* draws between himself and Odysseus extend even further than the explicit comparison he makes in *Met.* 9.13, from the closing sentence of book 10 where Lucius is "oppressed by sweet sleep" (*Met.* 10.35: *dulcis somnus oppresserat*) on the "sands" of Cenchreae, to his exposure naked before a crowd of onlookers after he is stripped of his ass-hide (*Met.* 11.14). The former scene, of course, recalls Odysseus being "overpowered by sleep on the sand" (*Od.* 13.119: ἐπὶ ψαμάθῳ . . . δεδμημένον ὕπνῳ) as he is abandoned by the Phaeacians in the harbor of Phorkys,[25] whereas the latter replicates the Homeric hero's nudity before Nausicaa and her companions on the shores of Scheria—except for the fact that Lucius has to cover his privates "with the natural covering" (11.14: **velamento** . . . *naturali*) of his hands rather than with an "olive-branch" (*Od.* 6.128: πτόρθον).[26]

---

24. The role of Socrates as an archetypal figure for the genre of fiction was recognized as early as Nietzsche in *The Birth of Tragedy* (see chap. 14). So also, Bakhtin 1981 located the origins of the novel's multivocality in Platonic dialogue. For discussion of Socrates *and* Odysseus as novelistic forefathers, see Hunter 2012, 224–26.

25. On which, see Hunter 2009a, 200. Cf. also Harrison 2013a, 191–93, on the epic signals in the book ending and beginning of 10 and 11, respectively.

26. *Pace* Keulen 2015, 32–35, who usefully notes that Loukios does not attempt to cover himself in the *Onos* (54), but prefers to read Lucius' bashfulness as a Roman imposition of the value of *pudor* on the scene (rather than an Odyssean echo). Vander Poppen 2008, 171, notes in passing the resonance with the *Odyssey*. For fuller discussion of the linkages between Lucius and Odysseus in the early chapters of the Isis book, see Beer 2011. In fact, I would go further to suggest that Apuleius deliberately uses the word *velamentum* here, as it refers in its extended meaning to an "olive branch wrapped in wool" (OLD, s.v. **velamentum** 2b) which a suppliant would carry and therefore, translates, so to speak, the "olive branch" (πτόρθον) Odysseus grabs in *Od.* 6.

In fact, it speaks to Apuleius' manifold play with these two paradigms of aesthetic-erotic response that a character named "Socrates" appears in the first inset tale of the *Met.*—indeed, in a literary context which evokes the *locus amoenus* of the *Phaedrus* (§2.5)—but is conjured up as a parodic reincarnation in Odyssean garb. Thus, Apuleius' "Socrates" is disguised as a beggar, who covers his face in comic imitation of Odysseus' shame before the Phaeacians (*Od.* 8.83–86), and is overtly figured by the witch Meroe as a "Ganymede who played with [her] youth" (*Met.* 1.12: *Catamitus qui . . . illusit aetatulam meam*), while she, in turn, was "abandoned like Calypso by the wit of Ulysses" (*Ulixi astu deserta vice Calypsonis*).[27] These are, to be sure, "literary metamorphoses" (*literarische Metamorphosen*),[28] but they are much more than mere literary play, especially for the "Palinodic" reader. That is, in light of Lucius' pointed allusion to Socrates' Palinode in the *Phaedrus* at the close of the Isis book (§0.3), the fact that this debased metempsychosis of "Socrates" is characterized as an Odysseus, who betrays his lover-goddess, and at the same time, as a Ganymede, who refuses to fulfil his role as a submissive *erômenos*, acquires a new symbolic meaning for the retrospective reader. Zeus' cup-bearer, we may recall, is the primary mythological paradigm of the "beloved" to which Socrates alludes at the climax of his Palinode in the *Phaedrus*;[29] and as we saw in §4.3, Lucius deliberately echoes the transcendent "fountain of desire" image from that dialogue in his attempt to reframe his bawdy tryst with Photis in idealized Platonic terms. In short, what seems at first glance to be mere literary or intertextual play—the sprinkling of various spices from different genres, or an agonistic game of bringing the highbrow texts of Homer and Plato down to the seedy underworld of the novel—constitutes, upon closer inspection, a more complicated maneuvering between these models of aesthetic response.

It is with this "horse-jumping" (*Met.* 1.1) vacillation between Homeric and Platonic paradigms in mind, then, that we return to the Isis book to dissect the ways in which Apuleius portrays Lucius' encounter with Isis' devotees and his "conversion" to her cult similarly as a series of mock-reincarnations. To do so, we turn to the Myth of Er—a *mythos* which has recently been recognized as a potential model for the Isis book,[30] and which frames the conclu-

---

27. For these connections between the Apuleian "Socrates" and the Homeric Odysseus, see Hunter 2006, 303–5 and Ulrich 2020, 696–700.
28. See Münstermann 1995, 8–13 for this phrase.
29. See *Phaedr.* 255c1–e1, on which, see §4.2.
30. Already before Winkler, Tatum 1979, 91, suggested a loose comparison, but without providing detailed exegesis. For a more thorough analysis, see Ulrich 2020, 688–700, which I expand on here. Cf. also MacDougall 2016, though he arrives at very different conclusions from me.

sion of the whole *Republic* as a tale of philosophical choice. While I believe that there are, in fact, many detailed overlaps between Lucius' *katabatic* vision of the *navigium Isidis* ("the ship-festival of Isis," or *Ploiaphesia*) and Er's after-life encounter with a judgment day spectacle,[31] I focus here on the parade of epic heroes in the *Republic* who choose their next incarnation from an assemblage of *paradeigmata biôn* because, by recognizing this episode as the target of allusion for the *anteludia*, we can link Lucius' "conversion" more overtly to the ancient discourse of choice.

Before turning to the *anteludia* proper, however, it is worth noting at the outset of my analysis that Isis' train is put on display before Lucius' eyes only after he experiences an epiphany of a universal goddess—one who labels herself a "singular deity" (*Met.* 11.5: *numen unicum*),[32] and whose "star-spangled" (11.4: *stellae dispersae*) cloak conceals seven robes adorned with detailed cosmological symbols.[33] Significantly, as Byron MacDougall has argued, the kaleidoscopic vision of the goddess elegantly reproduces the "Spindle of Necessity" in the Myth of Er, inasmuch as Plato's complex machine (the instrument of reincarnation) constitutes a *mimesis* of the cosmos with eight nested "whorls" representing the planets and exhibiting a dizzying array of multicolored lights.[34] If Mac-Dougall is correct that Isis' "star-spangled" cloak is reminiscent of the "dappled" (616e9: ποικίλον) outermost whorl and moreover, that the variegated cosmos is evoked by her seven-layered dress,[35] then it is certainly no coincidence that Lucius awakes from his epiphanic dream, sprinkles himself with sea-spray in anticipation of a new beginning,[36] and immediately encounters a parade of characters performing an encore of earlier episodes from the novel given new meaning under Isis' "economy of grace."

In addition to the cosmological, color parallels between Lucius' epiphany of the goddess and Er's description of the "Spindle," Isis' *anteludia* is attended,

---

31. E.g., Lucius' reunion with his *familiares* at Isis' *Ploiaphesia* (*Met.* 11.18), which replicates Er's description of souls encountering their "family members" (*Rep.* 10.614e3–4: γνώριμαι) when they take their rest "at a festival" (ἐν πανηγύρει). For further discussion of points of contact, see Ulrich 2020, 691–700.

32. Cf. Drews 2015 on Isis as an "inclusive goddess," who incorporates all other divinities into herself and thereby, functions as a Platonic demiurge or *nous*. So also, Fick 1987, 34–35, notes the Platonic and Middle Platonic associations of this phrase (*numen unicum*).

33. On the *Realien* of Isis being "seven-robed" and its cosmological implications, see Marcovich 1986.

34. See MacDougall 2016, 256–59. Cf. also Martijn 2022.

35. See esp. Martijn 2022, 160, who frames the color-scheme in terms of Platonic metaphysics: "the colors of her robe may tell us that Isis represents, not just the moon as the partner of the sun, but a whole cosmos."

36. So, GCA 2015, 193 *ad loc.* 11,7,1 note the poetic association of *marino rore* with a new day or beginning.

258   THE SHADOW OF AN ASS

much like Er's parade of souls, by the joyful harmonizing of nature in its aural response. Thus, at 11.7, the "golden sun" (*sol . . . aureus*) rises suddenly, bringing about a peaceful day:

> ut **canorae** etiam **aviculae** prolectatae verno vapore concentus suaves adsonarent, matrem siderum, parentem temporum orbisque totius dominam blando **mulcentes** adfamine

> so that even melodious birds, enticed by spring's warmth, resounded in pleasing strands, charming the mother of the stars, the parent of times, and the mistress of the whole earth with their seductive address.[37]

At the same time, flowering trees, stirred up by the "southerly winds" (11.7: *austrinis . . . flatibus*), come to life and express their joy at the presence of the goddess by "whisper[ing] sweet sounds with the gentle motion of their arms" (*clementi motu bracchiorum dulces strepitus* **obsibilabant**). In fact, as nature approaches a climax of cosmic tranquility, Lucius claims that the entire "heavens . . . glow with the naked and clear brilliance of its own light" (*caelum . . .* **nudo sudoque luminis** *proprii* **splendore** *candebat*)—a phrasing nearly identical to the "light . . . which is like a rainbow, but brighter and clearer" (10.616b5–6: φῶς . . . τῇ ἴριδι προσφερές, **λαμπρότερον** δὲ καὶ **καθαρώτερον**), and shines forth at the "Spindle's" cosmic pole "through the whole heaven" (10.6164: διὰ παντὸς τοῦ **οὐρανοῦ**). That is to say, the fact that Apuleius represents Sirenesque birds singing in "pleasing strands," while personified trees whisper a sweet melody in reply, establishes a clear point of comparison to the synaesthetic experience of the *hairesis* scene. So, we may recall that in the Myth of Er, the Sirens, the most dangerously enchanting singers from Homer, are inexplicably reincarnated in the architecture of the "Spindle," sitting atop each whorl and "inton[ing] one harmony together" (10.617b7: μίαν ἁρμονίαν **συμφωνεῖν**),[38]

---

37. On the Platonic associations of the "mother of the stars" and the "parent of times" as a demiurgic principle, see Drews 2015, 523–24.

38. On the Sirens' role in the Myth of Er, cf. Halliwell 2007, 447: "the integration of (eight) Sirens into a model of cosmic harmony . . . rewrites their status as (two) seductive but destructive demons in *Odyssey* 12." It is worth further noting that the parallelism of the two processions is emphasized once again with the musical performance of Isis' *peculiaris pompa* after the *anteludia* (at 11.9). That is, Isis' procession includes "charming symphonies" (**symphoniae** . . . *suaves*) performed on pipes and flutes, to which a "chorus shining in their snow-white best" (*veste nivea et cataclista praenitens . . . chorus*) sings, while "rehearsing a charming song which the poet gifted with the favor of the Muses sang out" (*carmen venustum iterantes, quod Camenarum favore sollers poeta modulatus*). In this mirroring of nature in the festival celebration, there are verbal (e.g., *symphonia*) as well as visual parallels with the Myth of Er (e.g., the Fates in the *Republic* are garlanded and dressed in white).

while the Fates "hymn in answer to the harmony of the Sirens" (10.617c3–4: ὑμνεῖν πρὸς τὴν τῶν Σειρήνων ἁρμονίαν). In light of this parallelism, we may note that Apuleius utilizes the very terms that characterize the Sirens in Latin to describe the "melodious" (*canorus*) tune the *aviculae* sing to "charm" (*mulcere*) the highest divinity.[39] All of this is to say, in the location where Isis' procession is set to take place, a multicolor visual spectacle is followed by an aesthetically enticing verbal response, which creates the backdrop for a spectacle of choice.

Thus, as nature and the cosmos align under Isis' divinity, Lucius-*auctor* turns his attention to the *anteludia* of Isis in what Stephen Harrison has labeled an "analeptic *ekphrasis*,"[40] a "symbolic recapitulation" where earlier figures from the novel reappear in a kind of narrative "curtain-call"[41] (11.8):

> Ecce pompae magnae paulatim praecedunt anteludia votivis cuiusque studiis exornata pulcherrime. Hic incinctus balteo militem gerebat, illum succinctum chlamide crepides et venabula venatorem fecerant, alius soccis obauratis inductus serica veste mundoque pretioso et adtextis capiti crinibus incessu perfluo feminam mentiebatur. Porro alium ocreis, scuto, galea ferroque insignem e ludo putares gladiatorio procedere. Nec ille deerat qui magistratum fascibus purpuraque luderet, nec qui pallio baculoque et baxeis et hircino barbitio philosophum fingeret, nec qui diversis harundinibus alter aucupem cum visco, alter piscatorem cum hamis induceret. Vidi et **ursam** mansuem, cultu matronali, quae sella vehebatur, et **simiam** pilleo textili crocotisque Phrygiis Catamiti pastoris specie aureum gestantem poculum, et **asinum** pinnis adglutinatis adambulantem cuidam seni debili, ut illum quidem Bellerophontem, hunc autem diceres Pegasum, tamen rideres utrumque.

---

39. So, Ovid's Sirens are transformed into "birds" (*Met.* 5.553: *pluma pedesque **avium***) with human faces in order that their *canor* ("melody") might be fit "for charming the ears" (*Met.* 5.561: ***mulcendas . . . ad aures***), and it is likely that Apuleius made these cosmic singers *aviculae* in a nod to the Ovidian tradition on the Sirens. Cf. also the mock-Circe in Petronius' *Satyricon*, whose "sweet sound . . . charms" (*Sat.* 127.5: *dulcis sonus . . . **mulcebat***) the air such that "you'd believe the harmony of the Sirens was singing" (*putares . . . **canere** Sirenum concordiam*). Interestingly, Apuleius applies this Siren terminology to his philosophical master in his biography of Plato, who becomes a "swan" in a dream of Socrates and takes flight from the altar of Cupid, "charming the ears of gods and men with his musical melody" (*Plat.* 1.1: ***canore** musico auditus hominum deorumque **mulcentem***), on which, see Ulrich 2017, 731–34 and more below. On *mulcere* and its link to the Sirens' *thelgein*, see Graverini 2012a, 31–36.
40. See Harrison 2012, which expands on Harrison 2000, 242–43.
41. So, MacDougall 2016, 254–56, labels the *anteludia*, as he notes its significance in comparison to the Myth of Er.

And lo! The preludes to [Isis'] great procession advanced slowly, very beautifully adorned in the desired garb of each's choice. Here, one man, girding himself with a belt, was playing the soldier, and another girded with a Greek cloak
was represented as a hunter by his high-boots and spears; another, putting on
gilded socks, silken clothing, and dressed in pricey ornamentation with his hair
woven on his head, pretended he was a woman with his fluid gait. Further
along, another, noteworthy for his greaves, shield, helmet, and sword, you'd
think was coming from a gladiatorial game. Nor was there lacking one who
role-played a magistrate with his fasces and purple, or one who feigned the
philosopher with his mantle, staff, sandals, and goatish beard. There was one
who represented a fowler through his different sticks with birdlime, and
another, a fisherman with his fishhooks. I even saw a tame bear in the dress of
a Roman matron, who was being conveyed on a sedan, and an ape in a stitched
cap and Phrygian saffron dress, mimicking the guise of the shepherd Ganymede carrying a golden cup. Lastly, [I saw] an ass with wings glued on its back,
walking beside some debilitated old man, such that you would think the latter
was Bellerophon, and the former Pegasus, and you would laugh at both.

This seemingly absurd spectacle—observed from Lucius-*actor*'s vantage
point, but relayed to the reader from the auctorial perspective—has inspired
many different interpretations. Some have wanted to take a historical approach,
connecting this procession to other carnivalesque *ludi* which preceded major
rituals and spectacles, such as those we know of from the imperial *pompa Cir-
censis*.[42] Others, however, have taken literary or metaliterary approaches, pointing to the ways in which these characters replay in miniature different episodes
from the novel.[43]

The domesticated *matrona*-bear, for instance, seems to combine the Trojan
bear episode of book 4 (*Met.* 4.13–21) together with the licentious matron of
book 10 (10.19–22) into a hybrid creature—one which renegotiates the blurred
boundaries separating human and animal in the novel and simultaneously,

---

42. For a useful discussion of approaches to the *anteludia*, see Gianotti 1986, 78–95. See also the summary of various approaches in *GCA* 2015, 205–6. For historical *comparanda* (e.g., of Cybele cult
and Emperor Cult), see Gianotti 1986, 84; and Fredouille 1975, respectively. Cf., however, Fick
1987, 35–36, who points out that there is no extant evidence of a pre-*ludi* to the *navigium Isidis*.

43. See, e.g., Harrauer 1973; and Fick-Michel 1991, 420–23, the latter of whom anticipates, to a certain
extent, the reflections in Harrison 2000, 242–43 and 2012. Cf. also Fick 1987, 36–37, who suggests
that the purpose of the *anteludia* lies in its stark contrast with the *peculiaris pompa*—or in other
words, in the juxtaposition between the parodic-burlesque and the sublime-serious.

PARADIGMS OF LIFE   261

highlights the threat involved in becoming a beloved of the gods. Indeed, Gwyn
Griffiths even discerned in the matron-bear a likely gesture to the figure of Callisto, who, in Ovid's version of the tale, suffered punishment at the hands of
Juno for her erotic entanglement with Jupiter.[44] According to Stephen Harrison's model of "analeptic *ekphrasis*," an "alert reader" can look upon these recycled figures from the previous books and take pleasure in what Lucius cannot
see—namely, his own unanticipated implication in the spectacle.[45] This interpretation has a certain purchase, to be sure, since Lucius' futile attempt to
become winged in his asinine metamorphosis calls up the hybrid image of
Pegasus to which he continually returns—and importantly, this image is derived
from Socrates' refusal to rationalize myths in the *Phaedrus*.[46] On two previous
occasions in the novel, that is, Lucius likens himself to this mythical creature.[47]
So, the fact that he sees a comic embodiment of his own failure to become
winged—or more precisely, that he sees a literalization of a Platonic image for
the soul, which he had foolishly applied to his very physical body[48]—is, no
doubt, an invitation to ribald laughter.

In my view, however, this "symbolic recapitulation" may also urge the *lector
scrupulosus* to step outside the text and meditate on life-choice narratives more
broadly, and especially, on Er's parade of souls, since many of Plato's eschatological myths engage in playful speculations on the manifold outcomes of reincarnation. To see how Apuleius incorporates Platonic metempsychosis, then,
let us take a closer look at the specific characters on exhibition in Isis' *anteludia*,
and for the sake of simplifying the argument, I merely enumerate here the different roles devotees play in the goddess' train (fig. 10).

I need not exhaustively rehash an argument I have made elsewhere that the
specific number of participants in the *anteludia* (twelve), taken together with
the particular breakdown of human-animal metempsychosis (i.e., nine human
and three animal performers), evinces a general connection to Platonic metem-

---

44. See Ovid *Fast.* 2.177–86. On the tamed *matrona*-bear as a Callisto figure, see Gwyn Griffiths 1975,
     179.

45. So, Harrison 2000, 242–43 concludes: "The effect of this symbolic recapitulation of various
     themes from the novel, unrecognized as usual by the thoughtless Lucius, who here as in the obvi-
     ously cautionary inserted tales fails to see what is plainly relevant to himself, is entertaining and
     witty. The stress for the alert reader is plainly on comic effect and the anticipation of the work's
     coming closure." On the danger(s) of getting implicated in a spectacle, however, see ch. 3 above.

46. Cf. §2.5. On Lucius' "Typhonic choice," see Winkle 2014, 100–107. On the seriocomic effect of
     Lucius' channeling Socrates here, see Ulrich 2020, 680–88.

47. See *Met.* 6.30 and 8.16. Cf. Winkle 2014, 121–23 for discussion.

48. Cf. Ulrich 2020, 687–88 for further analysis.

> 1. a soldier
>
> 2. a hunter
>
> 3. a cross-dressing man
>
> 4. a gladiator
>
> 5. a magistrate
>
> 6. a philosopher
>
> 7. a bird-catcher
>
> 8. a fisherman
>
> 9. a tame she-bear dressed as a *matrona*
>
> 10. a monkey dressed as Ganymede
>
> 11. an ass with wings labeled Pegasus
>
> 12. an old, debilitated Bellerophon accompanying the winged-ass

Fig. 10. The twelve figures from Isis' *anteludia*

psychosis narratives. Indeed, there are three animal species in the *Phaedo* to which soul-types can be "bound,"[49] whereas in the *Phaedrus*, Socrates enumerates nine human categories into which different souls can be reincarnated.[50] Nor is it necessary to thoroughly review Harrison's treatment of the previous figures to which these twelve performers correspond in the novel, though it is perhaps worth bearing in mind his interesting proposal that the Ganymede-monkey (*samia*) constitutes a reincarnated "Socrates" (who is referred to as a *Catamitus* in book 1), but is simultaneously reminiscent of the Judgment of

---

49. See *Phaed.* 81e5–82b9 for the three animal types, which fall roughly into quadrupeds (asses), predatory animals (wolves, hawks, and kites), and nobler hive-creatures (bees, wasps, and ants). The first animal-type is clearly meaningful for Lucius' asinine conversion (on which, see above with n. 13).

50. See *Phaedr.* 248c5–e3 for the human types. Cf. Ulrich 2020, 698–99 for fuller discussion. While the parallelism is not perfect—as Socrates lists the types, in order, as a philosopher, a king/governor, a commercial trader, a physical trainer or doctor, a mystical seer, a mimetic poet, a farmer, a sophist, and finally, a tyrant, whereas Isis' *anteludia* only contains a few clear analogues (e.g., soldier, magistrate, gladiator, etc.)—it speaks to Apuleius' general method of blending different Platonic type-scenes into his narrative (on which, see Ulrich 2023).

PARADIGMS OF LIFE 263

Paris episode at the close of book 10 (i.e., with the mention of the monkey dressed as a Phrygian *pastor*).[51] Whereas Harrison suggests that such recapitulations ought to remind Lucius-*actor* of earlier warnings he should have heeded about the danger of magic (and so, in his view, they signal to the "alert reader" a continuity between Lucius' asinine transformation and his "conversion"), I would argue, on the contrary, that the dual symbolism of the Ganymede-monkey, in point of fact, recalls two significant crossroads moments for Lucius, the first of which misled him into magic, while the second offered him his first "free choice" in the novel.[52]

However, while we could go character-by-character, attempting to decipher the interpretive significance of each, I am more interested in taking a macro-level view and analyzing the way in which the *anteludia*, via this mechanism of "symbolic recapitulation," does not simply evoke the encore of heroes in the Myth of Er, but in fact, fully realizes its conclusion. So first, we may consider *which* mythological characters appear in Er's dramatization of choice, and furthermore, *what sort* of *paradeigma biou* each of them chooses. Indeed, after the first soul fails to devote the requisite *scholê* to its choice, Er describes how figures from myth step forward in this judgment day spectacle—heroes reminiscent of the cast of characters who appear before Odysseus in the Homeric *nekyia*[53]—and after contemplating their previous (Homeric) lives, choose a new one. Thus, Orpheus, nursing his hatred for women because of his *sparagmos* at their hands, chooses to become a swan, whereas Ajax and Agamemnon decide to be reincarnated as predatory animals—a lion and an eagle, respectively—since they "remembered" the suffering they endured in their Homeric existence. By and large, the major mythical characters prefer to become animals in their next life as a consequence of recollecting their previous one and harboring resentment over it. Only three, however, decide to remain human, and only one chooses the same gender: Atalanta becomes a male athlete, Epeius (the creator of the Trojan horse) a "female craftsman," and Odysseus an "unmeddlesome private individual." In the interest of comparing

---

51. For the specific comic evocations of earlier episodes in the novel, see Harrison 2012, 379–85. On this dual echo, see also Fick-Michel 1991, 423.

52. Cf. Drews 2015, 525–26, who notes that the first instance in the novel when Lucius is granted "free choice" (10.35: *liberum . . . arbitrium*) is at the close of the Judgment of Paris (on which, see §3.3).

53. As Segal 1978, 323, points out, Er's parade of heroes at the close of the *Republic* rewrites Homer's own display of heroic characters in Odysseus' journey to the underworld. Cf. also Halliwell 2007. On the presence of Ajax and Agamemnon, and the curious absence of Achilles, see Montiglio 2011, 48–49.

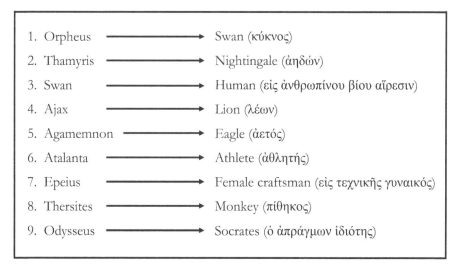

Fig. 11. The nine transformations that appear in Plato's The Myth of Er

these transmigrations with the parade of Isis' devotees in figure 10, I have mapped out the nine metempsychoses Er enumerates in figure 11 (*Rep.* 10.620a–d), and it is worth emphasizing here that these reincarnations are described in the language of metamorphosis (μεταβάλλειν).

In narrating the "metamorphoses" of famous heroes, then, Er explains that each makes his choice "in accordance with the character of [its] previous life" (620a2: κατὰ συνήθειαν ... τοῦ προτέρου βίου), which implies not only a "continuity of memory" between the present life and its next iteration, but also a theory of shared identity between souls before and after metempsychosis.[54] This is, uncoincidentally, how performers in the *anteludia* are "adorned" (*exornata*) in their new life under Isis, with "each" dressed "in the desired garb of choice" (11.8: *votivis cuiusque* **studiis**).[55] But once again, though it is a fascinating exercise to compare the transformations in the *Republic*'s encore with

---

54. On the paradox involved in the "continuity of memory," see Halliwell 1988, 21–23 and 189 *ad loc.* 620a.
55. While the Groningen commentators correctly note that there is a stronger religious meaning for *votivus* than "choice" (*GCA* 2015, 207 *ad loc.* 11,8,1), I would submit that there is also a translational component in this description of the characters in the *anteludia*: *studium* (OLD, s.v. **1b**) glosses the Greek term for inclination/habituation (συνήθεια), while *votivus* suggests that this new affiliation depends on the desires of "an earlier life."

Lucius' "analeptic *ekphrasis*,"[56] it is more useful, to my mind, to recognize that these human-animal transmigrations of figures from myth are remarkable emblems of a larger spectacle, where fortune and free will are mutually implicated in the process of life-choice, and the only control an individual can exert over future outcomes is through the act of "recollecting" one's previous life and choosing wisely in light of it.

So now, we come to the final choice in the Myth of Er, which, I suggest, establishes the paradigm for Lucius' "conversion." Once all of the other mythical figures choose new *paradeigmata*, the soul of Odysseus steps forward to make *its* choice (*Rep.* 10.620c3–d2):

κατὰ τύχην δὲ τὴν Ὀδυσσέως λαχοῦσαν πασῶν ὑστάτην αἱρησομένην ἱέναι, **μνήμη δὲ τῶν προτέρων πόνων φιλοτιμίας** λελωφηκυῖαν ζητεῖν περιιοῦσαν χρόνον πολὺν **βίον ἀνδρὸς ἰδιώτου ἀπράγμονος**, καὶ μόγις εὑρεῖν κείμενόν που καὶ παρημελημένον ὑπὸ τῶν ἄλλων, καὶ εἰπεῖν ἰδοῦσαν ὅτι τὰ αὐτὰ ἂν ἔπραξεν καὶ πρώτη λαχοῦσα, καὶ **ἀσμένην** ἑλέσθαι.

And by chance, the soul of Odysseus drew its lot last of all and came forward to make its choice; mindful of its previous toils and ceasing from ambition, it went around for a long time looking for the life of an unmeddlesome private individual. It barely found one lying around and neglected by others, and upon seeing it, [the soul] claimed that it would have done the same thing even if it had obtained the first lot, and it happily chose it.

As the concluding *hairesis* of the whole episode, the soul of Odysseus provides a fitting juxtaposition with the first choice—that of the soul which failed to "inspect [its choice] at leisure" (10.619c2: κατὰ σχολὴν σκέψασθαι) but nonetheless refused to "blame itself" (10.619c4: ἑαυτὸν αἰτιᾶσθαι) for its misery in

---

56. We may note, for instance, that the three animals in Isis' train reappear specifically as mythological characters and thus, playfully invert the transformations of Er's tale. Epeius' transformation in the Myth of Er is especially interesting as a *comparandum*, since he is known in the *Odyssey* as the creator of the Trojan horse (*Od.* 8.493), and the "tamed *matrona*-bear" (*ursam mansuem*) of Isis' *anteludia* recapitulates the "Trojan bear" episode from book 4 (Harrison 2012, 384); there, the robber Thrasyleon parodically dresses in a bear-costume to besiege a city, but fails to live up to his Odyssean predecessor. Simply put, the novel's earlier bear, which mimicked the Trojan horse, is reincarnated as a domesticated woman like Er's Epeius. On the Thrasyleon episode as an "inverted fall of Troy," see Frangoulidis 1991. As far as I can tell, Slater 2003, 95, is the first to label this the "Trojan bear" episode, although its associations with the Vergilian *Iliupersis* were recognized much earlier (La Penna 1985; Frangoulidis 1991; Finkelpearl 1998, 92–96).

266   THE SHADOW OF AN ASS

the next life.[57] The Homeric journeyman, by contrast, takes a meticulous look at his options, "going around for a long time to seek after" (ζητεῖν περιιοῦσαν χρόνον πολὺν) the "life of an unmeddlesome (ἀπράγμονος) individual" in much the same way that Socrates "goes around seek[ing] after" (*Apol.* 23b5: περιιὼν ζητῶ) a paragon of wisdom in the *Apology*.[58] Whereas the other Homeric heroes in this encore make grudging choices after "recollecting" their previous suffering, Odysseus leverages the "memory of his previous toils" (μνήμη . . . τῶν προτέρων πόνων) to a positive outcome—namely, to the abandonment of *philotimia*, where "honor-loving" is a pejorative term related to the *allotria/aliena* esteemed by the many.[59]

In this respect, it is also worth comparing this "curtain call" in the Myth of Er with Socrates' "Typhonic choice" in the *Phaedrus*. For we may recall that there, the philosopher is similarly faced with a parade of characters from myth—Centaurs, Chimaeras, Gorgons, and Pegases—but decides, in contrast to the first soul in the *hairesis* episode, that it would require "a great deal of leisure-time" (*Phaedr.* 229e3: πολλῆς . . . σχολῆς) to "investigate the matters of others" (230a1: τὰ ἀλλότρια σκοπεῖν), and prefers instead to pursue the Delphic maxim in seeking after the life of a "gentler and simpler animal" (230a4: ἡμερώτερόν τε καὶ ἁπλούστερον ζῷον).[60] If Lucius parodically alludes to the "Typhonic choice" in his first crossroads encounter but comically fails to recognize its significance,[61] then it is a powerful ring-composition, to be sure, that

---

57. So, Montiglio 2011, 51, notes the importance of this juxtaposition, comparing it with the metempsychosis episode of the *Phaedrus*, where "the two souls occupy again diametrically opposite positions, with the tyrant's as the last to be mentioned, while the philosopher's is the first."
58. The parallelism is further accentuated by a later passage in the *Apology*, where Socrates attempts to refute the charge of "going around and playing the busybody" (31c3: περιιὼν καὶ πολυπραγμονῶ).
59. On which, see §2.3. On the *philotimos* as an explicit contrast with the *philosophos*, see, e.g., *Phaed.* 68c and 82c, where the "honor-lover" is guided by "the fear of dishonor and disrepute" (82c7). Cf. also *Rep.* 581a–b, in which *philotimia* is associated with the "spirited" part of the soul in contrast to the philosophical part. As Montiglio 2011, 49–50, points out, *philotimia* is juxtaposed explicitly with *apragmosynê* in Euripides' (now-lost) *Philoctetes*, and Dio Chrysostom's précis of this text (*Or.* 59) brings this conversation into Apuleius' milieu.
60. The intertextual connection between Socrates' refusal to myth-rationalize in the *Phaedrus* and Er's description of the *hairesis* is further strengthened by the closing line of the Myth of Er's choice, in which many human-to-animal transmigrations occur (and vice versa): "the unjust transform into wild creatures, whereas the just transform into gentle species" (10.620d4–5: τὰ μὲν ἄδικα εἰς τὰ ἄγρια, τὰ δὲ δίκαια εἰς τὰ ἥμερα μεταβάλλοντα). The choice is ultimately between a "wild/uncivilized" (ἄγρια; cf. *Phaedr.* 229e3: ἀγροίκῳ τινὶ σοφίᾳ) creature and a "gentle" species (ἥμερα; cf. *Phaedr.* 230a5: ἡμερώτερον).
61. On Lucius' "Typhonic choice," see n. 46 above. Cf. §2.5 for fuller discussion. Lucius' response to Aristomenes' tale, in particular, acquires a new symbolic value for the "Palinodic" reader: "I judge nothing impossible, but however the fates decree it, so all things happen to mortals" (*Met.* 1.20: *nihil impossibile arbitror, sed utcumque **fata** decreverint, ita cuncta mortalibus provenire*). Read

Apuleius brings us back to that opening choice by conjuring up a parade of animal-human transmigrations in the *anteludia*, which once again raise the specter of Socrates' question about hybrid identity.

Setting aside Plato's literary-philosophical goal in representing Odysseus' reincarnation as a Socrates, though, it is more significant for my purposes that Isis' train of reincarnated figures concludes with precisely the same spectacle—that is, with a priestly authority standing in front of a stripped-bare Odysseus-figure and announcing his new *Fortuna* in the wake of his previous toils (11.15):

> Multis et variis exanclatis laboribus magnisque Fortunae tempestatibus et maximis actus procellis ad portum Quietis et aram Misericordiae tandem, Luci, venisti. Nec tibi natales ac ne dignitas quidem, vel ipsa qua flores usquam doctrina profuit, sed lubrico virentis aetatulae ad serviles delapsus voluptates, curiositatis improsperae sinistrum praemium reportasti.

> After having endured many and various toils, and driven by the great tempests of Fortune and the most powerful winds, Lucius, you have finally come to the harbor of Rest and the altar of Mercy. Neither your lineage nor indeed your dignity, nor even that very learning in which you excel has benefited you at all, but at the precarious point of flourishing youth, you slipped into servile pleasures and carried off the troublesome reward for your unpropitious curiosity.

Turning back to Mithras' surprise exegesis, in other words, we can read Lucius' anamorphosis and "conversion" as an overt nod to Plato's Odysseus in the Myth of Er and at the same time, as a reversal of the opening transformation in book 1 of a debased "Socrates," who abandoned his wife and entangled himself in an affair with a "Calypso." Thus, the priest opens his exegesis with a reference to the "many and various toils" Lucius suffered, explicitly linking his *labores*, in turn, to an Odyssean kind of wandering ("driven by the great tempests of Fortune").[62] What is more, Mithras points directly to the impotence of *aliena* to save Lucius from slipping into asininity, where "high-birth" (*natales*), "station" (*dignitas*), and "education" (*doctrina*) correspond neatly with the ele-

---

through the Isis book's play with Plato's most haunting myth on the indeterminate relationship between fate and free will (on which, see esp. Halliwell 2007), Lucius' concession to *fata* here implicates him as a character that fails to take the requisite *scholê*, much like the first soul in the *hairesis* episode.

62. As Hunter 2009a, 200, suggests, Mithras, in fact, echoes here Lucius' earlier prayer to "let [his] labors be enough" (11.2: *sit satis laborum*), which strengthens the Odyssean resonance.

ments of a *paradeigma* which complicate one's choice (according to Socrates' aside).[63] In fact, diminishing the extraordinary role that "chance" (*tychê/fortuna*) plays in his asinine life, Mithras suggests that Lucius' quadrupedal *katabasis* was, in the most basic terms, a "troublesome reward for unpropitious curiosity." Simply put, Mithras (like the *prophêtês* of Lachesis) rewrites books 1–10 as a cautionary tale of personal responsibility: "the responsibility lies with the chooser; god is blameless" (617e4–5).

So, when Mithras concludes his interpretation by pointing to Lucius as a paradigm for learning from one's mistakes in a previous life, we can see that he, more or less, translates the closing phrasing of Odysseus' choice in the *Republic* (11.15):

> en ecce **pristinis aerumnis** absolutus Isidis magnae providentia **gaudens** Lucius de sua Fortuna triumphat.

> Look, freed from earlier toils by the providence of great Isis, Lucius gladly triumphs over his *Fortuna*.

Just as Odysseus "ceases from ambition" (φιλοτιμίας λελωφηκυῖαν) because he remembers his "earlier toils" (τῶν προτέρων πόνων), the omnipotent *providentia* of Isis ensures that Lucius is immediately "freed from his earlier toils," where *pristinis aerumnis* nicely parallels Odysseus' recollection. "Remember[ing]" (11.6: *memineris*), after all, is the sole demand Isis makes of Lucius, when she appears to him and promises to enact a "sudden transformation of [his] figure" (*figuram tuam repente mutatam*). What is more, Mithras suggests here that Lucius triumphs over *Fortuna* "happily" (*gaudens*), much as Odysseus makes his choice (cf. **ἀσμένην** ἑλέσθαι) in accordance with *tychê*— and here, the (adverbial) participle anticipates Lucius' self-presentation in the final line of the novel: at 11.30, Lucius uncovers his bald head in Socratic fashion, and "[goes] around happily fulfilling his duties" (*munia . . . **gaudens** obibam*) as an incurious *pastophorus*.

The parallels between the Myth of Er and the Isis book are, indeed, striking when we set the structure of Apuleius' surprise "ballast" for his novel side-by-side with Plato's chilling eschatological tale. In fact, as we shall see in the next

---

63. So, in *Rep.* 10.618b–619b, Socrates refers to "nobility of birth" (εὐγενεία; cf. *natales*), "office" or "station" (ἀρχή; cf. *dignitas*), and "teachability" (εὐμάθεια; cf. *doctrina*) as the complicating factors involved in making a life choice (on which, see Ulrich 2020, 695).

section, to complete the analogy with Plato's *mythos*, Lucius is allocated a *daemôn* to guide the rest of his life, and undergoes, in turn, an Er-like *katabasis* in his initiation ritual after his "conversion." For the moment, however, I would like to revisit the question of continuity of identity across metamorphosis and in doing so, to return to the controversial question about Lucius' "development" (*Entwicklung*) in the closing books of the novel. For one of the perennial problems with approaching the *Metamorphoses* as an *Entwicklungsroman* is the *auctor*'s recurring request to be "return[ed] to his former self." At 10.29, he longs for "roses which could return [him] to [his] earlier Lucius" (*rosae, quae me **priori** meo Lucio **redderent***), whereas in his prayer addressed to the universal goddess at the opening of book 11, he simply requests a "return to [his] Lucius" (11.2: **redde** *me meo Lucio*):[64] the former is depicted as a Homeric Odyssean desire for a return to a former self or life (i.e., a return to the *same*), whereas the latter, with the removal of the key adjective *prior*,[65] might suggest a more extreme kind of Platonic transformation into something different. So also, in Platonic metempsychosis tales, there is an ambiguity about the nature of psychic-somatic transmigration. For instance, Socrates claims in the *Phaedrus* that, after ten thousand years of metempsychosis, "each soul [comes back] to the same place from where it came" (248e5–6: εἰς . . . τὸ αὐτὸ ὅθεν ἥκει ἡ ψυχὴ ἑκάστη); and likewise, in the *Phaedo*, there are some souls—particularly, those of a "gentle species" (82b6: ἥμερον γένος)—which "[go] back into the same human species" (82b7: εἰς ταὐτόν γε πάλιν τὸ ἀνθρώπινον γένος) for their next lives. This is, of course, the question raised by the opening line of the *Met.'s* Prologue, which promises that readers will be amazed not only by "the transformation of figures and fortunes of humans into other images" (1.1: *figuras fortunasque hominum in alias imagines conversas*), but also (and paradoxically), by "their restoration back into themselves" (*in se rursum . . . refectas*). While Plato, in his theory of psychic transmigration, certainly allows for the restoration of a soul into the same type of body—and indeed, even suggests that such a simple return is a reward for cultivating the "gentle" nature Socrates himself hoped to find in his own soul in the *Phaedrus*—it is crucial for any interpretation of the *Met.* that the final "transformation of a figure" (11.6: *figuram . . . mutatam*) Isis enacts in book 11 is to strip Lucius of his Odyssean ass-hide and thereby, reveal a Socrates underneath.

---

64. See *GCA* 2000, 357 *ad loc.* 10.29; and *GCA* 2015, 120–21 *ad loc.* 11.2, for discussion of these two important "returns."

65. See Gianotti 1986, 43 w. n. 29: "l'assenza di *priori* sembra anticipare la nascita di un Lucio nuovo."

5.2. Lucius' Allocation of a Daemôn and Er-Like Katabasis to the Divine

While I am clearly sympathetic to a more "serious" reading of the Isis book, these questions about Lucius' final life-choice(s)—about whether they exhibit sameness or difference, continuity or change—remain, in my view, intractable from the vantage point of any criticism which would seek to make definitive claims about Lucius' psychological state.[66] Once again, however, I am less interested in arguing that Lucius' loss of *curiositas* is "real," or for that matter, that it represents a religious redemption of our previously asinine *actor*. Instead, as I noted in §0.1, I am more invested in elucidating the choices the Isis book poses to *lectores scrupulosi* who become entangled in Lucius' journey. And in light of the Isis book's sustained pattern of allusion to the Myth of Er, I would argue that Apuleius scholars have too haphazardly neglected the way in which the closing chapters of the novel, where Lucius undergoes multiple and increasingly more expensive initiations into Isis and Osiris cult, can be read as part of Apuleius' broader reception of Platonic demonology—and especially, the demonology of the *Republic*.[67] We may note, for instance, that Lucius' final initiation is not into the cult of Isis' usual consort Serapis (as one might expect),[68] but into that of Osiris. Significantly, according to Apuleius' demonology in the *Soc.*, Osiris was merely human at one time, but was later granted ceremonial rites because he "charted the **course of his life** justly and prudently" (*Soc.* 15.9: *iuste ac prudenter curriculo vitae gubernato*), and as a consequence, was revered as a *daemôn* in Egypt (15.10: *in Aegypto Osiris*).[69] This corresponds, in broad-brush strokes, to a handbook kind of Middle Platonic demonology, as Plutarch classifies both Isis and Osiris originally as "intermediaries" (δαίμονες) who, in fact, "trans-

---

66. *Pace*, e.g., Harrison 2000, 248–49, and 2013a, 117, who confidently divines that Lucius' dream-visions are "self-generated," but willfully overlooks the fact that other characters in the Isis book (e.g., Asinius Marcellus) have parallel dreams (on which, see Vannini 2018, 239). For the history of this debate in Apuleius scholarship, see again §0.1 (with bibliography).

67. The most thorough treatment to date of Platonic demonology and its influence is Timotin 2012 (see esp. 259–86 on Apuleius' demonology). For treatments comparing Apuleius' demonology with his contemporaries, see Moreschini 1989; Trapp 2007; Benson 2016. For a basic review of Apuleius' demonology, see Constantini 2021. On Apuleius as a translator of Platonic demonology, see Ulrich 2023.

68. So the preponderance of documentary evidence and our knowledge of Isis cult would suggest. See *GCA* 2015, 450–51 for a discussion of Isis' traditional consort Serapis, and the literary-historical reasons for why Apuleius may have resorted to Osiris instead.

69. Cf. van Mal-Maeder 1997, 95, who notes that Osiris appears in *Soc.*, but claims (with little support) that this Osiris "has little in common with the one of the *Metamorphoses*."

formed" (*De Is. et Os.* 361e2: μεταβαλόντες) into divinities "on account of their virtue" (δι᾽ ἀρετήν).[70]

Given Osiris' status as a *daemôn* because he virtuously managed his *curriculum vitae*, it is no coincidence that our asinine hero, though he longs in his heedless youth to "dive headlong into the very abyss" of illicit magic (*Met.* 2.6), is nonetheless reclaimed by a universal goddess who utilizes this same "track of life" metaphor. When Isis appears to Lucius in an epiphany at the opening of book 11, she exhorts him to "clearly remember, and always keep hidden deep within [his] heart, the fact that the remaining track of [his] life is devoted [to her]" (11.6: *plane memineris et penita mente **conditum** semper tenebis mihi reliqua **vitae tuae curricula***). In short, Isis patterns Lucius' post-asinine life on the paradigm of Osiris from the *Soc.* What is more, Apuleius borrows this "track of life" metaphor from the preliminary discussion of the Myth of Er, where the "unjust," even if they manage to "escape people's notice when they're young" (10. 613d6–7: νέοι ὄντες λάθωσιν) like Gyges with his ring, eventually get caught "at the end of the track" (ἐπὶ τέλους τοῦ **δρόμου**), and become "laughable" (καταγέλαστοι) to spectators.[71] Lucius, too, made his first crossroads choice "at the precarious point of flourishing youth (11.15: *lubrico virentis aetatulae*)," and spent the burlesque books of the novel "covered by [an ass's] hide" (9.13: *celatum tegmine*) and escaping the notice of onlookers through a Gyges-like invisibility.[72] And yet, at this critical juncture in his life, Isis reorients Lucius' *curriculum vitae* so as to regulate it like Osiris' in *Soc.*

We may further point out that Lucius' description of his relationship to Isis in the closing chapters of book 11 closely mirrors the way in which Apuleius himself frames his own practice in the *Apologia* of carrying around a *simulacrum* of Mercury, the "intermediary between those above and those below" (*Apol.* 64.1: *superum et inferum **commeator***), "hidden within his books" (63.3: ***inter** libellos **conditum***). I suggested in §4.1 that Apuleius uses this little statuette of Mercury to represent his internal character to his judge, Maximus, and

---

70. Cf. also *De Is. et Os.* 362e4: "so, Osiris and Isis altered from good *daemones* into divinities" (ὁ μὲν γὰρ Ὄσιρις καὶ ἡ Ἶσις ἐκ δαιμόνων ἀγαθῶν εἰς θεοὺς μετήλλαξαν). On the significance of Plutarch's mediation of Platonic demonology for Apuleius, see DeFilippo 1990, 483–89.

71. Although the "track of life" metaphor can be found in Latin before Apuleius (e.g., in Cicero), it only refers to the temporal span of one's life and is not yet transformed into an assessment of virtuous living until Apuleius (*ThLL* 4.0.1506.73–1507.2). Apuleius' usage, however, marks a clear evolution in the metaphor's semantic capacity, as it acquires a (Platonic) moral resonance (on which, cf. also *Apol.* 96.7). See also Ulrich 2020, 693–94.

72. On Lucius' invisibility as a nod to the *Republic*'s ring of Gyges thought-experiment, see Benson 2019, 62–97.

that he strips himself, as it were, of his external appearance to reveal *simulacra deorum* underneath. But now, with Apuleius' reception of Platonic demonology in mind, we may also consider, by comparison, how Lucius addresses Isis in his final spoken words of the novel (11.25):

> divinos tuos vultus **numen**que sanctissimum intra pectoris mei secreta **conditum** perpetuo **custodiens** imaginabor.

> Perpetually guarding your divine face and your holiest divinity hidden within the secret places of my heart, I will reflect them.

Therefore, just as Apuleius carries around a physical representation of his tutelary *daemôn* "hidden" (*conditum*) on his person—a statuette his accusers mistakenly call a *daemonium* (*Apol.* 63.6), but which he reinterprets for his judge through the lens of Platonic demonology[73]—so also, Lucius "guards" his own intermediary goddess (*numen*) as a symbolic representation "hidden (*conditum*) within the secret places of his heart."

Returning to the Myth of Er as an archetype for book 11, then, it is interesting to recall that the encore of *hairesis*, in which Homeric characters come forward to choose new lives, concludes with each soul being assigned a new *daemôn*—one which corresponds to their new "paradigm of life," and which will guide them in their next life (10.620d6–e1):

> ἐπειδὴ δ᾽ οὖν πάσας τὰς ψυχὰς τοὺς βίους ᾑρῆσθαι, ὥσπερ ἔλαχον ἐν τάξει προσιέναι πρὸς τὴν Λάχεσιν· ἐκείνην δ᾽ ἑκάστῳ ὃν εἵλετο **δαίμονα**, τοῦτον φύλακα συμπέμπειν τοῦ βίου καὶ ἀποπληρωτὴν τῶν αἱρεθέντων.

> Therefore, when all the souls had chosen their lives, they went off to Lachesis in the order in which they were assigned. And she sent with each the demon which it had chosen as a guardian of its life and a fulfiller of its choices.

We know that Apuleius was quite familiar with this passage, since he creatively translates it in his own demonological treatise.[74] At *Soc.* 16, Apuleius

---

73. See again *Apol.* 64, on which, see §4.1 and §5.4. Cf. Hunink 1997, 162–63 and 170–73 on Apuleius' marvelous rhetorical reversal in this maneuver.

74. On Apuleius' method of translating demonology, see now Ulrich 2023. Cf. also Hijmans 1987; and Hoenig 2018a, on Apuleius' techniques of translation in his philosophical texts.

PARADIGMS OF LIFE   273

names famous *daemones* universally regarded throughout the world (e.g., Osiris), and then explicates the roles they play in Platonic eschatology as "witnesses and guardians" (16.3–4: *testes et custodes*) for people as they go through life: "though visible to no one, they are always present as judges of all actions and thoughts" (*nemini conspicui semper adsint, arbitri omnium non modo actorum verum etiam cogitatorum*).[75] More interesting than Apuleius' reworking of this passage in the *Soc.*, however, is the fact that the choice of *daemôn* features as one of the only elements that appears in a second-century CE Middle Platonic, Latin précis of the Myth of Er, the *Compendiosa Expositio*, which Justin Stover has recently postulated is the "lost third book" of Apuleius' *De Platone*.[76] So, after a brief remark on the judgment of souls "from the underworld" (*Exp.* 8: *de inferis*), the author (likely Apuleius)[77] summarizes Plato's *mythos* primarily as a spectacle of choice:

> Ceterum defunctorum animas interdum transire in mutorum animalium corpora et in vicem horum in hominum transfigurari, ita tamen ut quamdiu non transierint **prioris vitae meminerint**. nam et uniuscuiusque hominis proprium δαίμονα, quem nos genium appellamus.[78]

> [Plato says] that the souls of the dead meanwhile cross into the bodies of mute animals, and the souls of these (i.e., animals), in turn, are transfigured into the bodies of humans, but in such a way that, as long as they have not crossed, they recall their earlier life. For each human has its own *daemôn*, which we call a *genius*.

This oversimplified summation of human-animal "transfiguration" (*transfigurari*) seems to fit nicely with the pattern of the *Met.* discussed above, as the novel dramatizes Lucius' "cross-over" into the body of a "mute animal." It is also

---

75. Whereas Apuleius relies primarily on the *Symposium*'s demonology earlier in the *Soc.* (on which, see Timotin 2012, 116; and Dillon 2004), this summary of the *daemones*' involvement in human justice clearly channels the language of the *Republic*, since their role as "witnesses and guardians" (*testes et custodes*) renders into Roman juridical terms the *daemôn*'s function in Er's myth as the "guardian . . . of life and fulfiller of life-choices" (φύλακα . . . τοῦ βίου καὶ ἀποπληρωτὴν τῶν αἱρεθέντων).

76. Stover 2016.

77. On Apuleian authorship of the *Expositio*, I concur with Hoenig 2018b that Stover successfully demonstrates it is very likely a second-century CE North African text and possibly even authentically Apuleius, but I am not fully convinced that it constitutes the "lost third book" of the *De Platone*.

78. Text comes from Stover 2016, 104–6.

striking, furthermore, that the interest in recollection *across* metempsychosis remains intact in this Middle Platonic treatment: "they recall their prior life," much as Lucius longs to go back to a *prior* version of himself. But most significant is the fact that the allocation of a *daemôn* takes pride of place in this précis, so much so that the Greek is retained and then glossed in terms of a specifically Roman demonology.

Therefore, considering that Apuleius knew this conclusion to the Myth of Er well, it is problematic, to say the least, to disregard the fact that Lucius, after replicating the Platonic Odysseus' transformation into an unmeddlesome Socrates, similarly undertakes a *katabasis* to the underworld and afterward, is allocated a new tutelary *daemôn* to guide him through his next life.[79] As he describes the details of his initiation to Isis at 11.23, Lucius-*auctor* breaks the fourth wall one final time, demanding unquestioning belief in his Er-like *katabasis*:

> Quaeras forsitan satis anxie, studiose lector, quid deinde dictum, quid factum. Dicerem si dicere liceret, cognosceres si liceret audire. Sed parem noxam contraherent et aures et lingua[e], <illicitae intemperantiae ista>, illae temerariae curiositatis. Nec te tamen desiderio forsitan religioso suspensum angore diutino cruciabo. Igitur audi, sed crede, quae vera sunt. Accessi confinium mortis et, calcato Proserpinae limine, per omnia vectus elementa remeavi; nocte media vidi solem candido coruscantem lumine; deos inferos et deos superos accessi coram et adoravi de proxumo. Ecce tibi rettuli quae, quamvis audita, ignores tamen necesse est. Ergo quod solum potest sine piaculo ad profanorum intellegentias enuntiari, referam.[80]

> Perhaps you seek anxiously enough, my eager reader, what was said at that time and what happened: I would say, if I were permitted to say, and you would learn if it were permitted (for you) to hear. But your ears and my tongue would bring about equal injury—my tongue for its illicit chattiness, and your ears for their rash curiosity. Yet, since you are perhaps on tenterhooks with religious longing, I will not torture you with prolonged anguish. Therefore, listen and believe

---

79. On the *Met.* as a *katabasis* akin to the *Republic*, see Tarrant 1999. See also Sabnis 2013; and Panayotakis 2016. On the *katabasis* theme in the *Met.* as an "inverted allegory," cf. Ulrich forthcoming b.

80. I follow the conjecture of Nicolini 2010 here, which she suggests may solve the problem of Lucius' continued *curiositas* (on which, more below).

things which are true. I approached the boundary of death and, after traipsing upon the threshold of Proserpina and being conveyed through all of the elements, I returned; in the middle of the night, I saw the sun flashing with a bright light; I approached the gods below and the gods above face to face and I revered them from very nearby. Lo! I've reported things to you which, even though you've heard them, nonetheless you must remain ignorant of them. Therefore, I will report only that which can be divulged to the understanding of the profane without the need for expiation.

This passage has long been a site of critical contestation for scholars, as the apostrophe to the reader is left ambiguous as to whether it confirms or contradicts Mithras' assessment in 11.15.[81] For some readers, Lucius' disclosure about his *katabatic* journey appears to exhibit precisely the kind of *temeraria curiositas* our *auctor* claims to eschew, and the ass-man simply cannot restrain himself from the act of narration.[82] Others, however, decipher a certain restraint here, as Lucius claims to "report only that which can be divulged . . . without the need for expiation" and in fact, seems not to "divulge[e] any real secrets here."[83]

More significant than the question of whether or not Lucius exhibits sacrilegious *curiositas*, however, is the fact that readers are fully incorporated through this rhetorical metalepsis, as they undergo a transformation from *scrupulosi* to *studiosi* in a surprise role-reversal with the narrator. As the Groningen commentators astutely point out, while Lucius-*auctor* in book 9 presumes his "scrupulous" readers are "inquisitive and challenging"—or more precisely, that they doubt his knowledge and skeptically question his access to information— the "eager" readers of the Isis book are themselves rendered *curiosi*, infected with the (appropriate?) "religious desire" born out of "anxiety" and "suspense."[84]

---

81. See esp. *GCA* 2015, 383–85 (with bibliography) on this passage as a "crucial interpretive problem" (384), particularly in how it collapses the distinction between Lucius and the reader. See also Kirichenko 2008b, 360–67, who argues that Apuleius implicates his "characterized fictive reader" through this apostrophe. Cf. also *GCA* 2000, 21, for discussion of how the text makes us readers guilty of *curiositas* in book 10, and then pulls the rug out from under us in 11.23.

82. So, e.g., Harrison 2013a, 118–20 suggests, though he neglects the potential restraint Lucius seems to display (e.g., in narrating only details well-known to the uninitiated).

83. See *GCA* 2015, 384, who suggest that most of the details of Lucius' description were publicly known. See also Kirichenko 2008b, 366. Cf. Benson 2019, 184–238 (and esp. 211–16), who recognizes an increasing "narratological invisibility" in Lucius' focalization of his experience. Adkins 2022, 180–85 concurs that Lucius' discourse becomes vaguer and indeed, "highly symbolic" (183) in the close of the Isis book.

84. See *GCA* 2015, 393–94 *ad loc.* 11,23,5–6 for the distinction between *scrupulosus* and *studiosus*. On Lucius' willingness to divulge secrets as a form of initiating the reader, "an appetizer . . . intended to tantalize his audience's curiosity, but not to satisfy it completely," see *GCA* 2015, 385.

Simply put, all of a sudden and without warning, our reading experience is transformed from an intellectual engagement, where we participate in the act of narrating, to an emotional investment, and nowhere is our role as witting voyeurs more evident than here.

It is crucial, then, that Lucius frames his initiation in the discourse of *katabasis*, translating, in a sense, the afterlife narrative of Er. So, Lucius "journeys" (*remeavi*; cf. *Rep.* 10.614b8: πορεύεσθαι) to the "boundary of death" (*confinium mortis*; cf. 10.614b4: τελευτήσας), "conveyed through all the elements" (*per omnia vectus elementa*) like the Pamphylian narrator in his afterlife encounter (cf. *Rep.* 10.614b6: κομισθείς). Moreover, after reaching Persephone's threshold, he approaches an intermediary, dislocated place—akin to the cryptic "divine realm" (10.614c1: τόπον τινὰ δαιμόνιον) to which Er travels—and there, he simultaneously "approach[es] the gods below and those above" (*deos inferos et deos superos accessi*). And just as Er sits in a place "in between" (*Rep.* 10.614c4: μεταξύ) the upper and lower realms, tasked with functioning as "a messenger to humans" (10.614d2–3: ἄγγελον ἀνθρώποις) and thence, relaying "everything he hears and beholds" (ἀκούειν τε καὶ θεᾶσθαι πάντα), so also, Lucius returns from his *katabasis* in order to reprise this role, "announcing" (*enuntiari*) to the uninitiated "what was said and what happened" (*quid... dictum, quid factum*). That is to say, Lucius—after witnessing a parade of souls transformed under Isis and then, himself enduring a metempsychosis from an Odysseus to a Socrates—brings his transformation to completion by fully inhabiting the role of Er himself and channeling a *katabatic* vision of a haunting eschatology (much as Socrates ventriloquizes the Pamphylian). With Lucius' transmigration into a Socratic narrator of an afterlife tale, we return to the question of the ethical value of the *Met.* and the underlying purpose of fiction.

For the Myth of Er—and indeed, the entire *Republic*—concludes with Socrates' cryptic claim that "myth was saved" (10.621b8–c1: μῦθος ἐσώθη) by Er's narration and moreover, that "it would save us too, if we believed it" (καὶ ἡμᾶς ἂν σώσειεν, ἂν **πειθώμεθα** αὐτῷ). And perhaps this claim about the redemptive power of *mythos* makes a certain amount of sense in the context of a dialogue devoted to justice and the importance of pursuing it for its own sake—though many commentators have found Socrates' appeal to a nightmarish judgment day quite jarring.[85] However, in a novel that foregrounds its status as a "lie" (*Met.* 1.3: *mendacium*) with the intrusion of a skeptic in the very begin-

---

85. See again Julia Annas' assessment (n. 3 above).

ning and what is more, calls into question all of the narrators of inset tales who insist on the truth-value of their obviously fantastic claims (cf., e.g., 1.5: *vera comperta*),[86] the cognitive dissonance of Lucius' request that we "listen and believe in things which are true" (11.23: *audi, sed crede, quae vera sunt*) is all the more striking.[87] Implicit in Lucius' final demand for our credulity is the claim that this tale "would save us too, if we believed it," and just as in the case of the Myth of Er, we, too, are left wondering how a *fabula* could save its reader.

5.3. The Purpose(s) of Fiction: The Shared Receptions of the Myth of Er and the Isis Book

As I suggested in the introduction to this monograph, novelistic texts from Plato to Rabelais delight in straddling the line between danger and didaxis, poison and medicine, the frivolous and the sublime. The seriocomic image of the Silenic-Sirenic Socrates, which I have argued is programmatic for Apuleius' entire corpus, spotlights the ambivalence of the genre of fiction from its very inception. The fact that Plato's philosophical masterpiece, in which he dramatizes the power of dialectical method over the course of nine books, astonishingly concludes with such a (potentially) trivializing "old wives' tale" was not lost on ancient commentators and in fact, was to become a source for biting criticism by later philosophical schools.[88] Now that we have analyzed the elaborate correspondences between the Isis book and the Myth of Er, it is possible to take a step back from the text and consider the reasons why Apuleius, a self-proclaimed *philosophus Platonicus* who regularly performed his allegiance to

---

86. On the deliberate inconsistencies in Aristomenes' claim to recount "true events experienced firsthand," see GCA 2007, 145 *ad loc.* 1,5,1. On this play with the truth-value of representation as a Platonic narrative strategy, see Ulrich 2022, 257–58 (with n. 49 on *comperta*).

87. Cf., however, GCA 2015, 396 *ad loc.* 11,23,5–6, who recognize in the formulation—*audi, sed crede*—a disjunction with earlier tales: "it describes a new mode of reception the audience needs to adopt here, which is absolutely different from other modes of reception previously encouraged in the novel." So, Gwyn Griffiths 1975, 294 *ad loc.*, likens the appeal to true testimony to similar claims in the New Testament.

88. For instance, we know of the brutal critique of a certain Epicurean named Colotes, who is the target of a polemical treatise by Plutarch, and is specifically quoted in Macrobius (on which, see below). There were other readers, of course, who also took Plato's mysticism with a certain levity: cf., e.g., the assessment of the fragmentary Greek historian of India, Megasthenes (c. 300 BCE), who explains, according to Strabo's summary, how the Brahmans "also weave together tales, just like Plato, about the immortality of the soul and the choices in Hades and other such nonsense" (Strabo 15.1.59: παραπλέκουσι δὲ καὶ μύθους, ὥσπερ καὶ Πλάτων περί τε ἀφθαρσίας ψυχῆς καὶ τῶν καθ᾽ ᾅδου κρίσεων καὶ ἄλλα τοιαῦτα).

278   THE SHADOW OF AN ASS

Plato in North Africa,[89] might have chosen to model his surprise transition to seriousness in book 11 on Plato's own self-consciously fictional tale.

While no answer to this speculative historical question can be wholly satisfactory, I suggest that Apuleius, by self-consciously inviting a comparison between the "ballast" for his burlesque novel and the *Republic*'s jarring eschatology, channels once again the role he plays in the *Soc.* of "interpreter of Plato's divine sentiment" (*Soc.* 16.5: *Platonis divinam sententiam me **interprete***).[90] In particular, I posit for the sake of argument (though, it is admittedly conjectural) that Apuleius works within a Latin reception tradition—a critical discourse on the Myth of Er, which can be traced (in all likelihood) back to Cicero, and which was shaped, in turn, by Cicero's decision, out of fear of the snide ridicule of Epicurean readers, to close his Latin translation of the *Republic* with a dream narrative (instead of a reincarnation tale).[91] While I will only sketch here the lines of this tradition of translating and reinterpreting Plato's myth in broadbrush strokes,[92] I appeal to it nonetheless because it allows us, ultimately, to revisit our underlying question of the ethics of fiction—that is, whether the value of *fabulae* lies (as our asinine *auctor* claims in book 1) in their capacity to "distract [us]" (1.20: *avocavit*)[93] and help us "escape the long and harsh road" (*asperam . . . ac prolixam viam . . . evadi*) of life, or whether they can, alterna-

---

89. We know from an extant epigraph originally attached to a statue of Apuleius that he was clearly regarded as a Platonic philosopher in Carthage (on which, see Too 1996; and Gaisser 2014, 55). On Apuleius' performance of philosophy before large audiences in North Africa, see esp. *Fl.* 18.1–2: *Tanta multitudo ad audiendum conuenistis, ut potius gratulari Carthagini debeam, quod tam multos eruditionis amicos habet, quam excusare, quod philosophus non recusaverim dissertare. nam et pro amplitudine civitatis frequentia collecta et pro magnitudine frequentiae locus delectus est.* On this passage as evidence that Apuleius addressed audiences of different levels of literacy and education in Carthage, see La Rocca 2005, 263–65. Cf. also Bradley 2005, 19–21.
90. On Apuleius as translator of Plato, cf. Fletcher 2014, 145–72 (and esp. 172): "*De deo Socratis* is the most radical expression of his self-fashioning because Apuleius not only speaks for Plato's *sententia*, but also adopts the Platonic dramaturgic role of portraying the *persona* of Socrates the *sapiens* before his audience as the perfect *exemplum* of philosophy as a way of life." In my view, Apuleius functions as a translator of Platonism for a North African audience across his corpus (on which, see also Ulrich 2023).
91. See esp. the explanation offered by Macrobius: "although Cicero lamented that this *fabula* (i.e., Plato's) was derided by the uneducated—as if himself aware of the truth—he nevertheless shunned the paradigm of crude censure and preferred, instead, to have his narrator wake up rather than come back to life" (*Comm. in Somn. Scip.* 1.1.9: *hanc fabulam Cicero licet ab indoctis quasi ipse veri conscius doleat irrisam, exemplum tamen stolidae reprehensionis vitans excitari narraturum quam reviviscere maluit*). We know for certain that Colotes' criticism of Plato was alive and circulating in Apuleius' milieu, as Plutarch wrote a treatise *Against Colotes* in defense of Plato's mythologizing tendencies. On Colotes' view as found in Proclus, see Halliwell 2007, 460.
92. Cf. the **appendix** for a more detailed analysis.
93. This theory of fiction is repeated, we may recall, by the drunken old *narratrix* of *C&P*: she opens the tale with the promise to "distract [Charite] with charming fictions and old wives' tales" (*Met.* 4.27: *Sed ego te narrationibus lepidis anilibusque fabulis protinus **avocabo***), where once again the idiom of *aniles fabulae* is deployed in a deliberately self-deprecatory gesture.

tively, function as an exhortation to virtue. In reproducing Plato's most controversial *mythos* in a novelistic landscape, then, Apuleius simultaneously develops an apology for and an *agôn* with Plato, recreating Plato's own homage to and competitive emulation of Homer in his vision of the underworld.

To come back to this question, therefore, let us turn our attention first to a passage well-known to Apuleius scholars, where the late antique commentator Macrobius makes a distinction between the two kinds of fiction and their respective ends (*Comm. in Somn. Scip.* 1.2.7–8):

> Fabulae, quarum nomen indicat falsi professionem, aut tantum conciliandae auribus voluptatis aut adhortationis quoque in bonam frugem gratia repertae sunt. **auditum mulcent** vel comoediae, quales Menander eiusve imitatores agendas dederunt, vel argumenta fictis casibus amatorum referta, quibus vel multum se Arbiter exercuit vel **Apuleium non numquam lusisse miramur**.

> Fables, whose name already implies an admission of falsehood, were discovered for two reasons: either to provide mere pleasure to the ears, or also to exhort [the listener] to good fruit. So, comedies charm the ears, such as those Menander and his imitators wrote for production, as do plots stuffed full of the fictionalized downfalls of lovers: Petronius Arbiter occupied himself with those all the time, and to our surprise, Apuleius even sometimes played with them.

So, it would seem that *fabulae* were categorized in late antiquity along the very lines we have been interrogating throughout this study. If we apply the antiquarian's dichotomy to the *Met.*, Lucius' approach to utilizing *fabulae* for *divertissement* (*tantum . . . voluptatis*) is juxtaposed with Mithras' protreptic reframing of books 1–10 as a means to "exhort" a reader "to good fruit" (*in bonam frugem*)—and here, we may note that Macrobius' use of the agricultural metaphor (*frux*) seems to come not from Plato's protreptics "to virtue," but rather, from Mithras' reframing of the ass-man's journey and its "fruitful benefit" (*fructus*).[94]

On a superficial analysis of this passage, Macrobius seems closely aligned,

---

94. So, at *Met.* 11.15, Mithras rewrites Lucius' journey as a tale that encapsulates the "fruit of [his] freedom" (*fructum tuae libertatis*). Cf. also *Comm. in Somn. Scip.* 1.1.5, in which Macrobius notes that Plato resorted to an afterlife *fabula* because he knew that nothing would serve to "implant affection for justice in [people's] hearts" (*ad hunc . . . iustitiae affectum pectoribus inoculandum*) except for the knowledge that "its fruitful benefit" (*fructus eius*) would not pass away at the end of life. On Macrobius' use of terminology from the *Met.* to offer a critical assessment of it, see below (with n. 98).

280   THE SHADOW OF AN ASS

to be sure, with modern critics of the *Met.* who tend to group Apuleius with the likes of Menander and Petronius in his goal *merely* to "charm the ears" (*auditum mulcere*).[95] Taking this ancient criticism prima facie, however, overlooks a number of its subtler features. Some critics, for instance, have interpreted Macrobius' "marvel" (*miramur*) at Apuleius' participation in this subgenre of *fabulae* as evidence that ancient readers expected something rather different from a legitimate Platonist.[96] Similarly complicating for those wanting to read Macrobius' claim straightforwardly is his qualification that Apuleius "sometimes" (*non numquam*) indulged in such trivialities.[97] That is, if Apuleius, the master of "controlled gamesmanship," is merely another incarnation of Petronius (as some modern critics would have it), then why does he only "sometimes" play with *comoediae* (in contrast to the *arbiter elegantiae*, who indulges "a lot")? In fact, as Luca Graverini has astutely noted, Macrobius seems even to resort to terminology borrowed from the *Metamorphoses* itself—or more precisely, from its Prologue (1.1: *aures . . . permulceam*)[98]—to develop his sweeping characterization of a subgenre which strives only to "charm ears," though this analysis, too, is complicated by the fact that Macrobius' specific phrase (*auditum mulcere*) is pilfered directly from the opening of Apuleius' *Plat.*, where he represents Plato "charming the ears (*auditus . . . mulcentem*) of people and gods with his musical chant."[99]

---

95. Many commentators juxtapose Macrobius' "satirical" or trivializing interpretation of the *Met.* with the alternative, excessively allegorizing tradition in antiquity, such as we find in Fulgentius' *Mythologiae*. See, e.g., the passing references in Sandy 1978, 125 (with n. 18); van Mal-Maeder 1997, 92 (with n. 18); Harrison 2013a, 13–16.

96. See, e.g., Regali 1983, 220 *ad loc.*, who sees *miramur* as a positive assessment of Apuleius' generic variety; Stahl 1952, 84n5, by contrast, takes the marvel here as a kind of disgust or disappointment in a fellow Platonist for dabbling in such trivialities. See also Keulen 2007, 115n25; Graverini 2012a, 97n134.

97. See, e.g., Keulen 2007, 115 (with n. 25), who takes it as a statement of generic diversity: "*non numquam* also indicates Macrobius' awareness that Apuleius was more prominent in other genres, as opposed to Petronius, who engaged in such exercises considerably (*multum*)." It is not immediately clear (to me, at least) that *non numquam* applies to the entirety of the *Met.* (in contrast to his *philosophica*) rather than to certain books of the *Met.*, such as book 9—a book which is, indeed, "stuffed full of the fictionalized downfalls of lovers" (*fictis casibus amatorum referta*). However, no one, to my knowledge, has suggested this possibility.

98. See Graverini 2012a, 23–24, where he points out that both Macrobius and the *SHA* frame their criticisms in words borrowed from the *Met.* See also Keulen 2007, 114.

99. This scene opens the biography of Plato, where the talented youth appeared to Socrates as a cygnet in a dream and after sitting in his lap, "sought the sky, charming the ears of people and gods with his musical chant" (*Plat.* 1.1.5: *caelum petisse canore musico **auditus** hominum deorumque **mulcentem***). It speaks to the ambivalence of Plato's own flirtations with novelistic narrative that Macrobius resorts to Apuleius' characterization of Plato in his attempt to create a strict dichotomy between categories of *fabulae*. On this opening of *Plat.* as a translation of the close of Agathon's speech in the *Symp.*, where *Erôs* is said to "chant a song, charming the thought of men and gods" (*Symp.* 197e5: ᾄδει θέλγων πάντων θεῶν τε καὶ ἀνθρώπων νόημα), see Ulrich 2017, 731–34.

While I have suggested, then, that Macrobius' assessment of the *Met.* is more ambivalent even on its face than scholars have appreciated, I would, in fact, go one step further, arguing that the most complicated feature of this dichotomy—one which is universally overlooked—is the fact that Macrobius develops it as a deliberate attempt to provide an apologia for Plato's Myth of Er; and to do so, furthermore, he utilizes Plato's own censorious "treatise of wisdom" (*Comm. in Somn. Scip.* 1.2.8: *sapientiae tractatus*; i.e., books 2–3 of the *Republic*) as a means of removing the trivializing *fabulae* "from Plato's sanctuary" (*e sacrario suo*) and banishing them, in turn, "to nurses' cradles" (*in nutricum cunas*). The reason this added contextualization makes our reading of Macrobius so precarious, in other words, is because it reveals that many ancient readers—indeed, critics from the Hellenistic period on—put Plato's Myth of Er in the same general category as the trivializing *argumenta* of Menander, Petronius, and Apuleius. The great deal of effort our antiquarian commentator expends, therefore, in trying to disentangle Plato from these merely pleasurable *comoediae*, constitutes a form of special pleading.

The most notorious critics of the Myth of Er, as Macrobius explains in his preliminary discussion of Cicero's *Somn.*, were the Epicureans—and here, Macrobius names a particular student of Epicurus, a certain Colotes, who pilloried Plato for "pollut[ing] the very door for seeking truth with a lie" (*Comm. in Somn. Scip.* 1.2.4–5: *ipsam quaerendi veri ianuam mendacio polluerunt*). Interestingly, the substance of Colotes' criticism (i.e., that Plato resorted to a resurrection myth) is couched in the discourse of theater: Plato composed "a scene of fiction" (*scaena figmenti*), Colotes claimed, and to this end, sought out a *persona* and "a novel form of death" (*casus . . . novitas*). According to this cynical assessment, Plato is transformed not merely into a jarringly inconsistent philosopher, but in fact, into a New Comic playwright. The Myth of Er, in turn, is not merely deceptive, but is "polluting," contaminating the pursuit of truth with a *mendacium*.

As noted above, this criticism was widespread across antiquity—so much so that Cicero sought to avoid replicating Plato's flirtations with eschatological fiction in his *Somn.*, and Plutarch felt compelled to defend his philosophical master from the influential Epicurean attack.[100] Significantly for us, though,

---

100. See n. 91 above for Cicero's anxious assessment. See also Plutarch's *Against Colotes* for a general defense of Plato against the Epicurean. Cf. also *Quaest. conv.* 740b–c, where a character (Lamprias) responds to an attack on the absurdity of the Myth of Er by suggesting that Plato "uses the intellect most when he mixes some myth with a *logos* about the soul" (740b5–6: ὅπου δὲ μῦθόν τινα τῷ περὶ ψυχῆς λόγῳ μίγνυσι, χρῆσθαι μάλιστα τῷ νῷ), and then cites an "allegorical" (740b8: αἰνιττόμενον) reading of the end of the *Republic*.

this critical posture also reshaped discourse on the intersection of magic and philosophy in Macrobius' milieu—a fact which suggests that at some earlier point in time, North African Latin criticism, in all likelihood, became a locus for debate about Plato's playful speculations on the afterlife. So, in his brief nod to the Myth of Er, Augustine hand-waves away Plato's implausible closure, claiming that Cicero's treatment of the philosopher's "resurrection" story in his "books on the *Republic*" confirms "that [Plato] was merely playing around" (*De civ. D.* 22.28: *lusisse*) instead of "intend[ing] to say something true" (*uerum esse . . . dicere uoluisse*). Similarly (but with a more hostile tone), the fourth-century CE Carthaginian rhetor and pupil of Augustine, Favonius Eulogius, opens his *Disputatio* on the *Somn.* by praising Cicero for refusing to resort to the "lies of dreaming philosophers" (*Disp.* 1: *somniantium philosophorum . . . commenta*) or "unbelievable tales" (*fabulas incredibiles*) akin to those derided by the Epicureans. Rather, the rhetor appreciatively notes, Cicero appealed more plausibly to a dream, which Eulogius labels the "conjectures of the prudent" (*prudentium coniecturas*).

Augustine's dismissal, on the one hand, utilizes the same phrasing we saw Macrobius employing to describe Apuleius' composition of *fabulae* which "charm the ears"—namely, that he sometimes "played" (*lusisse*) with this subgenre—whereas Eulogius appears, in fact, to channel Lucius' description of his own transformation into "books." With the rhetor's derision of Plato's *fabulae incredibiles* in mind, we may recall what the Chaldean seer Diophanes prophesies about Lucius' life in book 2 of the *Met.*—namely, that he will become "a great history and an unbelievable *fabula*" (2.12: *historiam magnam et incredundam fabulam*). Of course, these lexical similarities could merely be coincidental usages of commonplace phrases borrowed from traditional rhetorical discourse[101]—except for the fact that they occur in the specific context of a late antique North African criticism of Plato's *mythos* and moreover, that they intersect curiously with Macrobius' assessment of Plato's *mythos*, where the antiquarian treats the "noble lie" in tandem with Apuleius' burlesque play.

Turning back to Macrobius, then, we may note that he strives to defend Plato from the onslaught of criticism and simultaneously, to set the stage for

---

101. For instance, *ludere*, as Keulen 2007, 114–15 notes, can be placed within the discourse "of rhetorical exercise and literary entertainment." *Incredibilis fabula*, by contrast, is a surprisingly rare collocation in extant Latin, occurring only in Cicero's *Part. or.* (40), where it alludes to moving listeners emotionally through rhetorical manipulation. In the *Quaest. Nat.*, moreover, Seneca gives a retort to people who exclaim *fabulae* when they hear "something incredible" (3.17: *res incredibilis*). Thus, it is possible that the idiom was more common and we merely lack attestations of it.

Cicero's understandable retreat from potential critics. To do so, he offers a basic outline of the Myth of Er at the opening of his commentary (1.1.9):

> sed ille Platonicus **secretorum relator** Er quidam nomine fuit, natione Pamphylus, miles officio, qui cum vulneribus in proelio acceptis vitam effudisse visus, duodecimo demum die inter ceteros una peremptos ultimo esset honorandus igne, **subito seu recepta anima seu retenta**, quicquid **emensis inter utramque vitam diebus** egerat videratve, tamquam publicum professus indicium **humano generi enuntiavit**.

> But that Platonic **reporter of mysteries** was a certain man named Er—Pamphylian by race, and a soldier in his duty. After he seemed to die from wounds received in battle, and was finally to be honored on the twelfth day with the last fire among the others who had died, suddenly, whether **regaining his soul or retaining it**, he **announced to the human race**, as if making a public proclamation, whatever he had done and seen **in the days he spent between his two lives**.

Setting our analysis of Lucius' *katabasis* from §5.2 against this Latin summary of Plato's tale, we can note a number of striking lexical and thematic overlaps. First of all, Er is labeled by Macrobius a "reporter of mysteries," where the Pamphylian's afterlife encounter constitutes a revelation of *secreta* (or *arcana*); or in other words, Er's eschatological tale functions as a sacred discourse one must carefully guard from the view of the "profane."[102] What is more, Er's vision is likened to a human-animal transmigration, whereby the antiquarian elides the difference between Er's afterlife experience and that of the souls in the Homeric encore. In this vein, Macrobius suggests, it is unclear whether Er "retains" or "recovers" his *anima* in the intermediary space "between his two lives." Simply put, he frames Er's journey in terms reminiscent of metempsychosis in the *Met.*, such as in the parodic episode of the "Trojan bear" in book 4. There, Thrasyleon does not "forget his prior virtue" (4.20: *pristinae virtutis*

---

102. In fact, it is worth noting that Macrobius creates the distinction between *fabulae* precisely because he wants to clarify what tales "[philosophy] excludes as if profane from the very entranceway of sacred discourse" (1.2.6: *velut **profana** ab ipso vestibulo sacrae disputationis excludat*). Furthermore, he later claims that Plato resorted to the "fabulous" precisely because that is how nature intended it: she hid herself "from the vulgar senses of humans" (1.2.17: *vulgaribus hominum sensibus*) because she "wanted her secrets to be handled through fables [only] by the prudent" (1.2.17: *a prudentibus **arcana sua** voluit per fabulosa tractari*).

oblitus) when he reaches the "end of his life," but instead, maintains the theatrical "scene" (*scaena*) for as long as he "retains his mind" (*anima **retinens***). So also, immediately after his asinine metamorphosis, Lucius makes a show of his *ingenium* to his reader to help us discern "whether [he] became an ass in both mind and sense" (4.6: *an mente etiam sensuque fuerim*).

In fact, in the late antique reception of the *Met.*, this continuity of the *mens/anima* across transmigration is precisely what is at issue. Thus, Augustine explains the fabulous tales of metamorphosis, which are regularly recited in the Italian countryside, and which he takes Apuleius' "fiction" to be representative of, by appealing to this question of psychic continuity. According to his famous confusion of Lucius-*auctor* with Apuleius-the-author,[103] those who are transformed into beasts of burden do not, as a consequence, acquire "the mind of an animal" (*De civ. D.* 18.18: *mentem . . . bestialem*), but rather, "preserve a rational human [mind]" (*rationalem humanamque seruari*). So Apuleius "indicated" (*indicauit*), Augustine continues, under the circumstances when "he became an ass with his mind retained" (***animo permanente** asinus fieret*). In short, the conceptual underpinnings of metempsychosis in Plato's Myth of Er, on the one hand, and metamorphosis in Apuleius' *Met.*, on the other, converge at the question of continued psychic identity across bodies,[104] and this is reflected, I argue, in their eerily similar (Latin) receptions in late antiquity.

Most important for our comparison of Lucius and the Pamphylian journeyman, however, is the fact that Er is resurrected, according to Macrobius, as an eschatological spectacle and put on display, in turn, to "mak[e] a public proclamation" and "announce to the human race" what he had done and seen. So also, in Lucius' *katabasis* to the "threshold of Proserpina," he coyly "report[s]" (11.23: *referam*) to us "what was said and what happened" in the intermediary space where he encountered "the gods below and those above." Moreover, he offers as the pretext for preserving the "secret" rites (*secreta/arcana*) that he has "reported" in his narration only what can be "announced" (*enuntiari*) to the "the understanding of the profane" (*ad profanorum intellegentias*) without sacrilege. Although he sees the gods "face-to-face" (*coram*)—and indeed, even

---

103. See Whitmarsh 2013, 64–67, on Augustine's narratological confusion. Cf. also Gaisser 2008, 33–34 on the influence of Augustine's conflation of author and narrator on the Medieval and Renaissance reception of the *Met.* as an autobiography. I do not address here the alternative name of the *Met.*, which we learn about from Augustine's assessment: *The Golden Ass* (*Asinus Aureus*), on which, see Winkler 1985, 292–321; Bitel 2000; most recently, Roskam 2014.

104. On the different ass novels and their complex questioning of identities across bodies, see Whitmarsh 2013, 75–85.

closes the novel with an unmediated vision of Osiris, "the loftiest and mightiest of the gods," who visits him *in propria persona*—he nonetheless remains "devot[ed] to [his] sacred rites" (11.30: *sacris suis . . . deservirem*) as a formal representative of the divine, putting his bald pate on display for us as a public proclamation of his "intermediary" status.

We will turn in the final section to this concluding chapter of the *Met.* in order to see how it fashions Lucius as a *daemôn* for us readers, as he fulfils his duties as a *pastophorus* in the cult of Osiris. I hope here, however, to have provided one possible proposal to the mystery of why Apuleius concludes his Latin translation of the original Greek ass-tale with the Isis book.[105] Indeed, far from simply tacking on a "ballast" as a pretext for writing such frivolity in books 1–10—or for that matter, using the closing book of the *Met.* as an opportunity to satirize religious authorities and those duped by their performative manipulations—Apuleius models a tale ripe for speculations about reincarnation on Plato's own incursions into the mythical realm. In short, by translating Er's *katabatic* encounter into an initiatory context, and by doing so in the precise terms in which Plato's ancient critics disparaged him,[106] I suggest that he offers both a homage to his philosophical master and simultaneously, a pointed response to his detractors.

5.4. Quaedam divinae mediae potestates: *Lucius as a* daemôn *for the Reader*

In this closing chapter, I set out to address the *Met.*'s theory of fiction by demonstrating how Apuleius reenacts a Platonic procedure—and indeed, reverses Cicero's precedent of avoiding Plato's resurrection narrative in *Rep.* 10—when he concludes his burlesque novel with a reworking of Plato's eschatological *mythos* in the *Republic*. Apuleius finishes off his novel, in short, with a narrative structure closely modeled on the Myth of Er: an epiphany, a spectacle of

---

105. We may recall that the *Onos* does not end with a religious transformation. Therefore, either Apuleius inherited it from the lost Loukios of Patrae's *Metamorphoseis* or he created it *ex nihilo*. See Tilg 2014a, 1–18, on Apuleius' inheritance of the religious ending from Loukios of Patrae. Cf. also Fletcher 2023, 171–79, who offers a subtler claim for Apuleius' dependency, namely that the *Metamorphoseis* may have included some role played by a divinity in its concluding book. However, both Tilg and Fletcher, in my view, rely too heavily on Photius' claim that Loukios wrote his novel "in earnest" (*Bibl.* 129: σπουδαίων) to fashion a tale about Apuleius-as-translator.

106. Cf. again **appendix** for a fuller comparison of the terminological overlaps.

human-animal *paradeigmata biôn*, the transformation of an "Odysseus" into a "Socrates," an allocation of a *daemôn*, and finally, an underworld *katabasis* of the (anti)hero. What is more, he constructs this Platonic narrative architecture by utilizing much of the terminology we later find associated with the Myth of Er in the late antique Latin critical tradition (but which may have been already circulating in Apuleius' time). Either these features of the Isis book represent an extraordinary coincidence, or Apuleius deliberately modeled the Isis book on the Myth of Er as an anchor (and emphatically not a ballast)[107] for a "Greek-ish tale" already ripe for Platonic eschatological manipulation.

To conclude this chapter, then, I would like to return to my reader-response approach and propose a demonological reading of the *Met.* To do so, we come back again to the interpretively vexed final line of the novel, which I analyzed in §0.3 as a "Palinode," but which I propose also figures Lucius as a *daemôn* for us readers.[108] Before we turn to *Met.* 11.30, however, it is worth meditating briefly on how we can recast Lucius' aesthetic-erotic experiences across the novel, in light of Apuleius' homage to Plato, as potential religious encounters with the divine. For when interrogating Apuleius' Platonism and the philosophical-heuristic value of this burlesque text, one of the questions we are immediately confronted with is what Plato himself accomplished by creating via mimetic representation the character of Socrates in his corpus of dia-logues.[109] Nowhere is this question more significant for our interpretation of Plato than in our programmatic passage from the *Symposium*, where Socrates functions as a material representation of the divine—"statues of gods" (*Symp.* 215b3: ἀγάλματα . . . θεῶν)—and at the same time, as a *daemôn* himself. He is transformed in Alcibiades' closing speech, after all, into an embodiment of *Erôs*, and through this metamorphosis, becomes an instantiation of the inter-mediary Diotima describes.[110] Or phrased in terms of philosophical choice, readers of the *Symposium* face a decision at the end of the dialogue over how they intend to engage with the *agalmata theôn* Socrates manifests and indeed,

---

107. *Contra*, e.g., Perry 1967, 244–45 (quoted in §0.1 n. 39). Cf. also Sandy 1978.

108. This builds on Geoffrey Benson's recent suggestion (2019, 28–61) that the Prologue's voice is that of a *daemôn* addressing the reader. So also, in my view, Lucius becomes that *daemôn* in his adap-tation of the "Palinode" in 11.30.

109. Cf. Fletcher 2014, 291, who takes this same question as the guiding principle of his full-corpus study: "all philosophy must come to terms with Plato's 'creation' of Socrates in the act of writing, his dressing up of philosophy with *oratio*." See also Laird 2003 for an important demonstration of how an author in Apuleius' milieu (i.e., Lucian) dealt with this question. Cf. also Kahane 2007.

110. See Sheffield 2006, 187–88, on the striking correspondences between the *daemonic Erôs* and Alcibiades' depiction of Socrates. Cf. also Hunter 2004; Usher 2002.

over what kind of reading experience they hope to have: do they simply want to enjoy a comedy (with Aristophanes) or are they willing to plumb the depths in a confrontation with tragedy (with Agathon)? For Socrates—the nagging busybody who famously compels Aristophanes and Agathon to acknowledge that the same person could write comedy and tragedy (*Symp.* 223b–d)—sits on the couch between these two playwrights and plays the role of intermediary, straddling the two genres and thereby, creating a seriocomic encounter with the sublime.[111]

We may recall from chapter 4 that Lucius, too, encounters many representations of divinities over the course of his journey, but in most cases—far from utilizing the visions of *simulacra deorum* to come into contact with the divine—he leverages them to heighten his aesthetic-erotic pleasure. In view of Apuleius' reception of the *daemonic* Socrates from the Platonic corpus, however, we may look back at Lucius' encounters with "statues of gods" and consider how they simultaneously offer Lucius-ass an opportunity to cultivate *daemones*. For the primary Middle Platonic thread, which runs through the whole of Apuleius' *On the God of Socrates*, is the notion that "there are certain divine powers *in the middle*" (*Soc.* 6.2: *quaedam divinae mediae potestates*).[112] Significantly, these intermediaries have a specific location and function in the cosmos, possessing a "middling nature in accordance with the middle-ness of their place" (*Soc.* 9.2: *pro loci medietate media natura*)—and Apuleius uses the rare marked term *medietas* to delineate the region of *daemones*.[113] Thus, in his attempt to offer clarification, he gives an analogy to explicate in common parlance the cosmology of *daemones* in "the balanced middle space" (*Soc.* 10.1: *huius libratae medietatis*): just as clouds inhabit an intermediary place in the air, moving up or down based on the amount of moisture they contain, so also, *daemones* traverse the "middling" realm between heaven and earth, albeit invisible to the human eye.

For my purposes, then, it is noteworthy that all of the mimetic representations of divinities across the *Met.* are likewise said to inhabit a middle space,

---

111. On Socrates' position between Agathon and Aristophanes as a marker of the *Symposium* as tragicomedy, see Clay 1975. For up-to-date treatments, see Hunter 2004; and Sheffield 2006.

112. On this Middle Platonic demonology, see esp. Habermehl 1996; and Ulrich 2023.

113. This rare neologism was apparently coined by Cicero to translate the term μεσότητες from Plato's *Timaeus* (36a) in his own *Timaeus* (23): "For I scarcely dare to speak of *medietates*, which the Greeks call μεσότητες; but let it be imagined that I said such a thing, for that will be clearer" (*vix enim audeo dicere medietates, quas Graeci μεσότητας appellant; sed quasi ita dixerim, intellegatur; erit enim planius*).

whether in the middle of an atrium, a shrine, or a stage. So, when Lucius-*actor* encounters the very first divine *simulacrum* of his journey (Byrrhena's statuary ensemble), the *auctor* of the *ekphrasis* describes how the marble representation of Diana "holds the balanced middle of the whole place" (2.4: *tenet **libratam** totius loci **medietatem***)—and here, we may note that Apuleius deploys the precise coinage from *Soc.* to emphasize the marble statue's *daemonic* position in Lucius' field of vision (cf. *Soc.* 10.1: ***libratae medietatis***). So also, shortly after his transformation, Lucius-ass comes across a small shrine to the goddess Epona in the stable to which he has been relegated, and according to his (retrospective) description, "a *simulacrum* of the goddess was situated in nearly the very middle of the small temple" (3.27: ***in ipso fere meditullio** . . . deae simulacrum residens aediculae*).[114]

Furthermore, embedded in the central inset tale of the *Met.*, we encounter Psyche, an avatar for Lucius who wakes up in the divine palace of Cupid, which the drunken *narratrix* claims is situated "in the middle-most middle of a grove" (5.1: ***medio luci meditullio***). Thus, it was "built," she explains, "by divine arts" (*aedificata . . . divinis artibus*) and "fashioned for gods' conversing with humans" (*ad conversationem humanam . . . fabricatum*).[115] It is paramount, then, that immediately before his encounter with Isis, Lucius witnesses an eroticized mime performance of the Judgment of Paris, in which the most seductive figure—an almost nude Venus and a representational embodiment of Lady Vice in Lucius' crossroads choice—takes her place "in the very middle of the stage" (10.32: ***in ipso meditullio** scaenae*), where she dances alluringly for Paris and wins the prize for beauty.

In short, by the time we reach book 11, Lucius has encountered a number of divine representations—either in statuary, theater, or fable—all of which function (in the discourse of Middle Platonism)[116] as potential intermediaries for coming into contact with the divine. Indeed, as we may recall from §3.4, it is significant that, promptly following this spectacle of a surrogate Venus, Lucius experiences an epiphanic vision of Isis' "divine face" (11.3: *divina facies*), which rises from "the middle of the ocean" (*ecce pelago **medio***)—activating once again

---

114. Note the similarly unique and related coinage, *meditullium*, likewise attested before Apuleius only once in Cicero (*Top.* 37). On the significance of this statue of Epona as a foreshadowing of Isis, see Winkle 2015.

115. Benson 2019, 98–148, hints at a *daemonic* reading of *C&P*, but does not pick up on the recurrence of "middling" divinities in Lucius' encounters.

116. On which, see Ulrich 2023.

the "middling" component of Lucius' representational encounters.[117] From the perspective of demonology and its implications for the *lectores scrupulosi*, however, we may recognize one final spectacle of a *simulacrum* "in the middle": indeed, in the statuary ensemble of Isis and Lucius—in which the ass-man stands as a *simulacrum* on a pedestal with the goddess and we readers, in turn, wander about him in search of a glance—the sculptural group is placed, yet again, "in the very middle of the sacred temple" (11.24: **in ipso** *aedis sacrae* **meditullio**). Simply put, the fact that Lucius missed many opportunities to cultivate a *daemôn* is emphasized by the "middling" nature of the representations of gods he encounters; at the end of the novel, however, whatever the reality of Lucius' "conversion," we are confronted with our own vision of "statues of gods," set up, once again, "in the middle," and we are offered a choice, in turn, as to how we will engage with this new aesthetic object.

Considering, therefore, this possibility of reinterpreting Lucius' aesthetic experiences over the course of the novel as encounters with *daemones*, we may turn now to the last word of the *Met.*—*obibam*—which, in my view, brings about one final metamorphosis in Lucius, transforming him this time from a buffoonish mime into a *daemonic* intermediary for his readers. For just as Lucius' baldness has caused ambivalent consternation among critics but alludes, in point of fact, to a specific portrait of Socrates (§0.3), so also, the final word of the novel, while leaving critics in *aporia* over how skeptically one should read the anti-closure,[118] can similarly be reframed in light of Apuleius' demonology. Let us recall how the *Met.* ends (11.30):

> Rursus denique quaqua raso capillo collegii uetustissimi et sub illis Sullae temporibus conditi munia, non obumbrato uel obtecto caluitio, sed quoquouersus obuio, gaudens **obibam**.

---

117. On the strong verbal connections between Photis and Isis (esp. in Lucius' descriptions of their hair), see Krabbe 2003, 580–87. Isis' echoes of Photis and Diana have long been recognized: see, e.g., Tatum 1969, 492; Gwyn Griffiths 1975, 29; Schlam 1992, 118; *GCA* 2001, 409–11; Libby 2011, 302–5. See §4.5 for a fuller comparison of Photis' and Isis' hair.

118. Whitmarsh and Bartsch explain well the "disorienting wedge" of the Isis book, which *obibam* intensifies (Whitmarsh and Bartsch 2008, 252): "[Lucius'] readers are left in some confusion, for here the story abruptly stops with the verb 'I was going' (*obibam*). There is no link back to the beginning, to our charming whisper, to the pre-transformed narrator, or to the production of the narrative we are reading. And while we hear twice that Lucius will be the subject for a book ... we never hear that he will *write* this book himself, nor that he will do so as a priest of Isis and Osiris" (their italics). On the problem of anti-closure, see Finkelpearl 2004. For bibliography and further discussion, see §0.3 with n. 82 and 83.

Finally, with my head once again shaven completely and with my baldness neither covered up nor hidden, but exposed wherever I went, I joyfully carried out the duties of that ancient priesthood, which was established in the time of Sulla.

Aside from the other problems with this line (cf. §0.3), scholars have been particularly bothered by its final word. On the one hand, the imperfect tense—*obibam*—seems to imply an incompleteness of the tale[119] or to suggest, in more general terms, that Lucius' transformation is still in progress, that his pricey initiations into cult religion will continue *ad infinitum*.[120] Some critics add to this complication, moreover, the wrinkle that the verb *obire*, which seems here to mean to "conduct" or "carry out," can also carry a more sinister connotation: "to die."[121] According to this reading, "conversion"—at best, an incomplete process, which greedy priests can use to manipulate gullible fools into paying ever higher fees for initiation—can also constitute a kind of personal death, an end to subjectivity and to one's pleasurable desires.[122] Indeed, the fear of an end to temporality—the threat of the loss of subjectivity and of all the ambitions one might have in life—is precisely why Alcibiades flees from the Sirenic Socrates at the close of the *Symposium*.

However, readers who color *obire* with this secondary semantic meaning are (begrudgingly) forced to acknowledge that such a connotation can, at best, be subliminal in this context:[123] for when *obire* means "to die," it is intransitive (orig-

---

119. Winkler 1985, 224, citing Callebat 1968, 500, on "*le sourire complice du narrateur*," sees the imperfect as a knowing "taunt" to the reader about the distance that separates the narratorial voice and recently converted actor. Cf. Penwill 1990, 24n70, for skepticism about the limits of Winkler's narratological approach in this reading.

120. See esp. van Mal-Maeder 1997; Harrison 2000, 238–52; Murgatroyd 2004; Libby 2011; MacDougall 2016. All of these emphasize that Lucius appears in the closing chapters of book 11 to be a dupe suffering at the hands of manipulative religious authorities.

121. OLD, s.v. 7 and 8. Cf. Laird 2001, 275, who notes this potential (though he adopts an epitaphic rather than cynical interpretation). See also Finkelpearl 2004, 329–30, for helpful discussion. Even recently, Tilg 2014a, 141–45, has reasserted this interpretation as a reversal of Ovid's closing *vivam*, which revives the suggestion of Penwill 1990, 24n70.

122. See, e.g., Too 1996 on the phrase *ritu cadaveris* (*Apol.* 14) for the potential of static *mimesis* to fix an object of depiction in a kind of death of self. Cf. also Slater's assessment (1998, 46–47): "My own experience of reading and re-reading Apuleius, however, has not left me balanced between two interpretations of the novel (either as an entertaining adventure with no deeper meaning or as a narrative of progress toward salvation) but more and more convinced of the irony of the ending and its final objectification of Lucius under the gaze of Isis. If we as readers wish to avoid her petrifying gaze, we would do well to observe the dynamics of that gaze as reflected in the viewpoint in the water."

123. See *GCA* 2015, 516 *ad loc* 11.30, for the admission that one cannot read *obire* with the primary semantic valence of "death" here.

inally from *mortem obire*—"to go to meet one's death");[124] but in the passage in question, *obire* has *munia* as its direct object ("I was carrying out the duties"). The verb appears a few chapters earlier in this same construction, when Lucius is patiently awaiting his first initiation into Isis cult and claims that "for so many days, [he] was carrying out the office of honoring the sacred rites" (11.22: *quot dies* **obibam** *culturae sacrorum ministerium*). Shortly thereafter, Lucius is placed on his *tribunal* as a *simulacrum* together with Isis "in the very middle of the sacred temple" (11.24: *in ipso aedis sacrae* **meditullio**). Or if we phrase it in terms of the demonology of the *Soc.*, Lucius becomes one of the "certain intermediary divine powers" (*Soc.* 6.2: *quaedam divinae mediae potestates*) which exist on earth to facilitate interactions between humans and the gods.

The key to recognizing Lucius as an intermediary for his readers, moreover, lies in how we interpret this closing word of the novel. For the verb *obire* is also used in *Soc.* to describe the movement of intermediary *daemones*, as they travel between the heavens and earth, "fulfilling their duties." In particular, at *Soc.* 7, Apuleius explicates how *daemones* are tasked with various "duties, works, and cares" (7.1: *munus atque opera atque cura*)[125] in order to carry out the will of "heavenly divinities." After delineating the different "provinces" (6.4: *provinciae*) of demons—that is, whether they are tasked with sending dreams, or manipulating entrails or bird omens—Apuleius explains (*Soc.* 7.3):

Quae omnia, ut dixi, mediae quaepiam potestates inter homines ac deos **obeunt**.

All of these are duties which, as I have said, certain intermediary powers between humans and gods **fulfill**.

The primary antecedent of *quae* here is the phrase *munus atque opera atque cura* and thus, the direct object of *obire* here constitutes a fitting parallel to the idiom Lucius-*auctor* deploys in the closing line of the novel (cf. *munia . . . obibam*). If Lucius has, indeed, traveled to the underworld and "approached the gods below and the gods above face to face" (11.23: *deos inferos et deos superos accessi coram*), it is telling that Lucius afterward reprises the role of the *Soc.*'s

---

124. The idiom is derived from the phrase *mortem obire* (on which, see *ThLL* 9.2.46.16–48) and develops an intransitive usage in later Latin (*ThLL* 9.2.48.45–50), but neither makes sense in our context here.

125. Here, I follow the text of Jones 2017 (rather than Magnaldi's deletion of *atque opera*).

"certain intermediary powers" (*mediae quaepiam potestates*), as he tells us how he joyously "fulfills his duties" in Rome. Indeed, just as "Socrates" of the *Soc.* becomes a *daemôn* through cultivation of his *daemonion* and in so doing, is transformed (like *Erôs* or Osiris) into a semidivinized human,[126] so also, Lucius (at least, in his self-representation) worships Isis and Osiris until he reaches such a stage of initiation that he can function daemonically.

Once again, we need not believe Lucius-*auctor* or endorse his own assessment of his "conversion," even if he demands (like Socrates in the Myth of Er) that we "listen and believe." As we have explored throughout this book, every time Lucius is faced with an aesthetic encounter, he seems to miss its transformative potential, whether because he overidentifies with the mythical Actaeon without following the tale to its well-known conclusion (§3.2), or because he misconstrues his debased (animalistic) responses to aesthetic pleasure by adding a patina of philosophical coloring to his narrative reproduction (§4.3). However, if we as readers choose only to take *divertissement* from Lucius' failures of interpretation, how do we avoid replicating them in a nearly identical fashion, when we, too, are put in the position of Lucius—that is, when we, too, approach a spectacle of *simulacra deorum*, which mediates "between gods and humans" for readers and viewers alike (precisely as *daemones* do)?

We may recall from §4.1 that Apuleius' most trenchant attack against Aemilianus in the *Apologia* is over his failure to cultivate a religious *daemôn* and hence, his inability to recognize the Platonic *Basileus* in the glorious wooden *sigullum* of Mercury that Apuleius carries with him. Indeed, at the climax of the subsidiary charges, he suggests that, if Aemilianus misinterprets the significance of his (Apuleius') figural *daemôn*, then "he has either never even seen any statues of gods or he neglects them all" (*Apol.* 63.9: *profecto ille simulacra deorum nulla videt aut omnia neglegit*). To conclude his invective, then, he calls down all manner of curses upon his accuser, praying that "that intermediary god between the upper and lower gods" (64: *deus iste superum et inferum commeator*) will return just deserts to Aemilianus in recompense for his lies about *daemones*. Apuleius' judge Maximus, by contrast, does recognize the *daemonic* significance of Apuleius' cult practice (according to Apuleius' stroking of his ego) because he has "diligently read about the 'place beyond the heavens' and

---

126. See, e.g., *Soc.* 17, on Socrates as a *vir apprime perfectus* who cultivated his *daemôn* as a *Lar contubernio familiaris.*

the 'ridge of heaven' in the *Phaedrus*" (*Apol.* 64: τὸν ὑπερουράνιον τόπον *et* οὐρανοῦ νῶτον ***legit*** *in Phaedro* ***diligenter***). Simply put, reading—and more specifically, reading Plato—becomes the locus of choice and the means of undergoing a transcendent experience. Aemilianus could have seen *simulacra deorum*, had he only taken the time to read his Plato.

So also, at the close of the *Met.*, I have argued that we encounter *simulacra deorum*—a seriocomic spectacle of a man transformed from human to ass to *daemôn*, mirroring the transformation that Socrates himself undergoes in Alcibiades' speech. When we begin our "Palinodic" reading, therefore, we encounter for a second time the false flag or red herring that has beguiled so many critics (1.1): *lector intende: laetaberis*. We could (much like Lucius) take the *laetitia* this Prologue promises as an invitation to indulge in superficial reading.[127] That is to say, we could decide merely to "take delight" (*delector*) from this tale, deluding ourselves that we can watch the spectacle of an ass-man and nonetheless, remain free from its contamination. If we do so, however, without becoming *lectores scrupulosi*—without exercising the necessary discernment and leveraging the tale to see the traces of the divine imprinted on it (or us?)—then will we not also be transformed into asses?

This is precisely, then, where choice reenters the discussion. For some readers may prefer to be asses—some may find it more interesting or more pleasurable to travel the world "hidden under the cover of an ass-hide" (cf. 9.13: *celatum tegmine*), playing the voyeur undetected, and spying on neighbors from the mediated distance of the text. And to be sure, this carnivalesque novel offers us that opportunity, should we choose merely to enjoy its seedy delights. As we saw in chapter 3, however, we cannot safely look on without being implicated in the pleasures of the text, without being incorporated into the spectacle ourselves. And so, we sit, as I have suggested throughout, in the hearing of the Sirens, in the presence of Lady Vice, or in the overgrown palace of Circe, ready to take pleasure in the sounds or greedily drink down the contaminating brew. This is the power aesthetic experience can have on its viewer or listener (or reader). But Apuleius' *lector scrupulosus*—the one who simultaneously "reads" and "chooses" (*legere*)—follows the advice of the late antique commentator on Heliodorus (§1.2a): though the text is "like Circe's brew," possessing the capacity

---

127. See Adkins 2022, 199, who notes the ambiguity of the verb *laetor*, which can denote either earthly or spiritual pleasure, as was regularly acknowledged in scholarship before Winkler (cf., e.g., Svendsen 1978, 105).

to transform its readers into pigs, it also has the power to "initiate" (μυσταγωγοῦσα) us into "sublime things" (τὰ ὑψηλότερα)—that is, as long as we read it "philosophically." It is fitting for Apuleius, the "playboy" and the "showman," to revel in the burlesque pleasures of the novel.[128] But perhaps it is even more appropriate for the Carthaginian *philosophus Platonicus*, translating Platonic mysteries into Latin for a new set of readers, to demand a life choice from his *lectores studiosi*.

---

128. So, the tongue-in-cheek assessment of Swain 2001, 269.

Epilogue

Asinine Priest, "Madauran" Reader

We have explored throughout this monograph instances in the *Metamorphoses* where Lucius-*actor* (and by extension, the reader) is situated at a crossroads and compelled to decide about a future path. In Lucius' case, I have argued, he tends to make the wrong decision, to travel down the indulgent path of aesthetic pleasure rather than the enlightened path of restraint. I have suggested all along, though, that these moments simultaneously demand a choice from us about how to read—about precisely what it means to "pay attention" (1.1: *lector intende*), or how one can become a *lector scrupulosus* (9.30). On the one hand, we are encouraged to follow heroic paradigms of aesthetic response (ch. 1) and indeed, to look meticulously beneath surface-level appearances, stripping away deceptive outer layers like an "onion skin" (ch. 2). At the same time, however, the novel self-consciously highlights the dangers of rashly participating in its *serviles voluptates*. It showcases its capacity to contaminate its readers who "take delight" (2.5: *delector*) in the spectacles on display (ch. 3); but simultaneously, it exposes its frivolous narrator as a philosophico-maniacal buffoon, as he reframes his debased erotic encounters in the discourse of idealized Platonic response (ch. 4). The Isis book, of course, drastically changes the stakes, as frivolous indulgence in aesthetic pleasure unexpectedly becomes deadly serious with the introduction of a hair-raising eschatological tale of philosophical choice. The question readers are thus left with at the end of the Isis book is, at its root, a Platonic one: namely, "whether [they] happen to be some beast more complicated and furious than Typhon, or a gentler and simpler animal" (*Phaedr.* 230a3–4).

We have thus oscillated in our discussion between the first two modes of reader-response, which Hans Robert Jauss identified in his literary-historical approach to stages of aesthetic experience: the naïve and linear (or "aesthetic") stage of reading, on the one hand, and the secondary level of "reflective interpretation," on the other. In this brief epilogue, I want to turn back to Jauss' theory of reader-response, and analyze the third stage of aesthetic experience—namely, "questions of meaning such as they could have posed themselves within the historical life-world of [a text's] first readers."[1] To address this vexed historical question about Apuleius' novel (for which any answer is inevitably conjectural), we come back to the famous *Madaurensem* problem at *Met.* 11.27—an issue I already touched upon in §2.4, but which I return to here as a pendant to my reader-response approach. In this epilogue, I suggest that, with the astonishing entrance of a "man from Madauros" into the novel, Apuleius not only pierces the illusion of an impermeable boundary between fiction and reality, but also subtly implicates his North African readers, assimilating them to Lucius-*actor* as he approaches a priest named "ass-man" in order that he may encounter the divine. Here, yet again, the *Met.* constitutes a generic experiment in translating Platonism for a Carthaginian audience, as Apuleius plays the role simultaneously of cultural intermediary and philosophical *interpres*.[2] Before we return to this troublesome narratological problem, however, it is necessary first to address the intractable question of *who* Apuleius' intended audience was, and *what* his aims might have been in appealing to them. A few preliminary words on the transmission and reception of the *Met.* are, therefore, necessary.

The readership of the ancient novels has, of course, long been a source of great speculation, with scholars conjecturing about whether these texts were meant for the consumption of a middle class, bourgeois audience in search of lowbrow literary experience, or alternatively, whether their authors hoped to reach educated readers (i.e., *pepaideumenoi*) in concentrated centers of culture and power.[3] While the last few decades of research on the genre have convinc-

---

1. Jauss 1982a, 146.
2. For further discussion of Apuleius' role as translator of Platonic demonology, see Ulrich 2023. For general treatments of Apuleius' demonology, cf. §5.2 n. 67.
3. On the out-of-date view of a middle-class readership, see Perry 1930, esp. 97–98; Schmeling 1974. Hägg 1983, 90–101, offers a more sympathetic, if still patronizing, view of the readership (e.g., 90: "rootless, at a loss, restlessly searching"). This modern fantasy was called into question in the 1980s–1990s, and scholars have since recognized the novels' appeal to a more educated readership through a variety of pieces of evidence: e.g., literacy rates and papyrus production (Stephens 1994), sophistication (Wesseling 1988; Bowie 1994), allusion to classical texts (Bowie 1996), etc. For a useful overview and discussion, see Hunter 2008. An interesting *comparandum* for what I will argue here is the fact that some have discerned a geographical limitation in the "intended" audience of the earliest Greek romances, namely, Asia Minor (Hägg 1994, 70n32) and perhaps

ingly put to rest any elitist notions that the novels were composed for "children and the poor in spirit,"[4] it has generally been assumed in Apuleius scholarship (at least, until recently) that the *Met.* was intended for Roman readers—and perhaps, that Apuleius even wrote the novel while living in Rome.[5] With the publication of Julia Haig Gaisser's comprehensive study of the transmission and reception of the *Met.*, however, there has been an increasing awareness of the "African connection" and the role it played in Apuleius' survival.[6] In short, the majority of extant sources which preserve the earliest memories of Apuleius— whether through statuary commemorating his popularity as a "Platonic philosopher,"[7] or literary references to his reputation as a magician[8]—have come down to us almost exclusively through African writers and readers.[9] As Gaisser notes, however, while the chain of transmission exhibits a clear link to Africa, there is nonetheless a period of approximately 150 years where our *philosophus Platonicus* seems to have been erased from the literary record.[10] We may recall from this book's introduction, for instance, that in the 190s CE, the

---

even more specifically, Aphrodisias (Bowie 1996, 90–91), whence Antonius Diogenes (possibly the first novelist) likely hailed (Bowersock 1994, 38–41).

4. See Perry 1967, 5.

5. So, Grimal 1985, presumes that certain details point to a Roman provenance (e.g., the size of the spectacle in the Judgment of Paris episode, which seems more fitting for the Colosseum than a provincial amphitheater), though such speculations have been called into question (Graverini 2012a, 180–82). Dowden 1994 is the most forceful proponent of a "Roman market" and indeed, attempts to redate Apuleius' composition of the *Met.* to his Roman period in the 150s CE (424–28). See also Hunink 2002, who supports Dowden's assumption. Cf. Coarelli 1989 for a (conjectural) hypothesis that Apuleius lived in a specific house in the suburbs in his Roman period (the so-called Casa di Apuleio in Ostia), and wrote the *Met.* in honor of his patron, Q. Asinius Marcellus. On this theory, see also Beck 2000; Vannini 2018 (on which, more below).

6. Gaisser 2008. See also Gaisser 2014 and more generally, the essays in Lee, Finkelpearl, and Graverini 2014.

7. The earliest attestation to Apuleius is an inscription dedicated by the Madaurans to "[their] Platonic philosopher," which adorned a statue erected in honor of Apuleius either in his lifetime or shortly thereafter. On the dedication of this inscription, see Tatum 1979, 105–8; Winkler 1985, 277. On its relationship to Apuleius' anxieties over *mimesis*, see Too 1996. On its usefulness as evidence for the "African connection," see Gaisser 2014, 55.

8. On Apuleius' early reputation as a magician beginning in the early fourth century CE (again in North Africa), see Gaisser 2008, 21–29; Carver 2007, 11–25.

9. This curious fact of transmission is perhaps best encapsulated by Augustine's claim in an epistle to his friend Marcellinus that Apuleius would come more readily to his mind than to that of his Iberian correspondent because "as an African . . . he is better known to us Africans" (*Ep.* 138.19: *Apuleius . . . qui nobis Afris Afer est notior*).

10. So, the first time Apuleius' name occurs in the literary record is in the *Divine Institutes* (written between 305 and 313 CE) of a fellow North African, Lactantius. Though many have speculated that Apuleius and Tertullian very likely crossed paths—"that the two might have met" (Smith 2023, 85n2) or at the very least, that "Tertullian cannot have remained unaware either of Apuleius' activities as a sophist . . . or of his writings" (Barnes 1971, 257)—no one found a convincing link until Luca Grillo (2023), on which, see below. On Apuleius' likely intersection with North African Christianity, see Smith 2023, 75–87.

emperor Severus (allegedly) accused his fellow North African, Clodius Albinus, of overindulging in Apuleius' *Punicae Milesiae*. But of course, such a rhetorical diatribe could just as well be a dramatic fiction of the *Historia Augusta* (c. fourth century CE?) rather than an accurate representation of any *Realien* of North African literary culture in the late second century CE.

If transmission is one approach scholars have taken to hypothesize the possibility of an African readership, others have considered the provincial spin Apuleius puts on quintessentially Roman intertexts as proof of the *Met.*'s self-conscious engagement in a cultural negotiation.[11] In this vein, Luca Graverini has suggested that Apuleius' Africa-oriented adaptation of important episodes and themes from Vergil's *Aeneid*, the unrivaled nationalist Roman epic, bespeak a more direct encounter with an African (and particularly, Carthaginian) audience.[12] Indeed, the very fact that Lucius' journey ends in Corinth—a once-great cultural center razed to the ground by the Romans in the second century BCE and transformed into provincial outpost for the metropolis of Rome (much like Carthage)—functions, in Graverini's view, as a form of Romanization for an African audience. Simply put, Corinth constitutes a site of a cultural negotiation for a provincial client state of Rome seeking to achieve its own literary-intellectual prestige.[13]

While the "African connection" has survived largely through incidental, late antique polemics or scholarly conjectures about the provincial patina which Apuleius layers onto his allusions, the evidence is mounting, I believe, for a sweeping reevaluation of Apuleius' readership—one which begins with a recent article by Luca Grillo, where he uncovers compelling proof that North Africans were likely reading the *Met.* as early as the beginning of the third century. Indeed, in "The Early Reception of Apuleius," Grillo claims to have found in Tertullian's *Adversus Valentinianos* an allusion—in my view, an irrefutable

---

11. See Finkelpearl 1998, 134–48 for an early articulation of this approach.

12. For example, Apuleius' decision to rewrite Aeneas' slighted African queen Dido with his more positive presentation of the heroine Charite offers a "correction" to Vergil's antagonism to Africa (on which, see Finkelpearl 1998, 143; Graverini 2012a, 201), whereas Juno's unwavering love for Venus in *C&P* constitutes a provocative "literary amnesia," since the *Aeneid* famously opens with Jupiter's consort seething with eternal rage and plotting to use Carthage as a tool to enact her vengeance (Graverini 2012a, 204). That Apuleius appealed to an African audience in the *Florida* and the *Apologia* is generally acknowledged. For instance, on Apuleius' performance of philosophy in Carthage—indeed, even to very large audiences—see *Fl.* 18 (esp. 14–16), on which, see Graverini 2012a, 200–201. Cf. also Bradley 2005 on the diversity of Apuleius' Carthaginian audience. On his advocacy for the importance of Africa and a pan-Mediterranean literary culture, see *Fl.* 20 (with Adkins 2022, 222).

13. See Graverini 2002, which is reworked in 2012a, 165–75.

EPILOGUE   299

one—to a troubling scene from book 8 of the *Met.* The argument is dense and detailed, but it is worth briefly reviewing its primary claims, since its implications are, indeed, far-reaching.

The target of Tertullian's allusion comes from the low-point of Lucius' time under the care of the debased priests of the Syrian goddess. After witnessing a number of charlatan religious performances aimed at pilfering money from unsuspecting audiences, Lucius is confronted with the most "extraordinary crime" (8.29: *tale facinus*), when the priests of the goddess brutally rape an unwitting youth whom they had invited to dinner. Unable to stand idly by as he witnesses such a horror, Lucius attempts to intervene (8.29):

> '**Porro Quirites**' proclamare gestivi, sed viduatum ceteris syllabis ac litteris processit 'O' tantum, sane clarum ac validum et asino proprium, sed inopportuno plane tempore.

> "Give way, citizens," I wanted to shout, but only a bare "O" came forth, stripped of other syllables and letters; and though it was clear and strong and indeed, appropriate for an ass, it obviously [came] at an inopportune time.

This is one of many occasions where Lucius-ass attempts to speak, but is comically frustrated by his inability to produce anything but a sound "appropriate for an ass" (*asino proprium*). Significant for reassessing Apuleius' readership, however, is the fact that Tertullian seems clearly to echo this passage in his *Adv. Valent.*, a polemic which depends, to a certain extent, on a Greek apologetic archetype (Irenaeus' *Adversus haereses*), but which adorns the Latin translation with localizing references that could appeal to a Carthaginian audience (*à la* Apuleius). In the specific passage of *Adv. Valent.* which alludes to Apuleius, Tertullian is attacking the Valentinians' theory of Aeons (intermediary demigods), whose power Christ's intervention has diminished. Among this group of Aeons, however, there is a certain Horos who continues to exert a destructive influence on the life of a daughter of Christ, Enthymesis or "Inclination," and Tertullian describes his continued power over her at *Adv. Valent.* 14.3–4:

> tamen temptavit et fortasse adprehendisset, si non idem Horos . . . nunc tam importune filiae occurrisset, ut etiam inclamauerit in eam 'Iaô!', quasi '**porro Quirites!**' aut 'fidem Caesaris!' inde inuenitur Iao in scripturis.

300   THE SHADOW OF AN ASS

[Enthymesis] tried and would perhaps have taken hold of [Christ's light], had not the same Horos . . . just then stood in the daughter's way so rudely that he even shouted against her "Iaô," as if to say, "give way, citizens!" or "by the good faith of Caesar," and from there, the name Iao is found in the scriptures.

Grillo notes a number of overlaps between these two passages—from the comic (almost Apuleian) procedure of likening the religious cry Iaô to the braying "O" of an ass, to the desire to "shout" (*inclamauerit*; *proclamare*) an authoritative invocation at an "inopportune time" (*tam importune*; *inopportuno plane*). The decisive link, however—one which confirms the *Met.* as the indisputable target of the allusion—is the unique exclamatory phrase Tertullian deploys: "give way, Roman citizens" (*Adv. Valent.* 14.3–4: *porro Quirites!*). For aside from Lucius' usage in *Met.* 8, this exclamation only occurs one other time in extant Latin—in a mime of Liberius found in Macrobius' *Saturnalia* (*Sat.* 2.7: *porro Quirites! Libertatem perdimus*), an unlikely source of imitation, to be sure, for the North African apologist.[14]

Thus, while scholars have long envisaged some convergence between Apuleius and Tertullian[15]—whether through a passing acquaintance, or in a more sustained interaction—I believe that Grillo has decisively shown a clear connection in the densely allusive pattern of Tertullian's appeal to the ass-man's exclamation. For my purposes, moreover, the downstream implications of the Christian apologist's adaptation of the *Met.* are far more significant. For if, indeed, the intertextual relationship is sound, it suggests not only that Tertullian was reading Apuleius' novel within thirty to forty years of its publication,[16]

---

14. What is more, I would add something that goes unrecognized in Grillo's analysis, namely, that the second exclamatory phrase in Tertullian's polemic—"by the good faith of Caesar" (*fidem Caesaris*)—also has an Apuleian flair. Indeed, the first time in the Latin language that Caesar's *fides* is called upon *as* an authoritative invocation occurs in the "shadow of an ass" episode in *Met.* 9.42, where the soldiers "implore by the good faith of Caesar" (*fidem . . . Caesaris . . . implorantium*) that they have received trustworthy information as to the whereabouts of the gardener and his ass, while the gardener's friend "appeals to a divine intermediary" (*deum numen obtestantis*).

15. See n. 10 for scholars' speculative musings. Moreschini 1968 claimed to have discovered an allusion to Apuleius' *Soc.* in Tertullian's *De anim.*, but this has been refuted by Barnes 1971, 256–58. So also, Fredouille 1981, 117, has noted a number of lexical oddities and semantic deviations which the two authors share, but this can only point to and cannot confirm engagement or influence. I currently have a PhD student, Tobias Philip, working on the influence of Apuleius' Judgment of Paris on Tertullian's *De spect.*, and he has likewise discovered a more detailed intertextual engagement.

16. Assuming the traditional publication date for the *Met.* in the 170s (cf. Harrison 2000, 10) and the more precise dating for Tertullian's treatise (between 207 and 210 CE). Of course, dating the publication of the *Met.* is notoriously difficult, and some have proposed a much earlier period of composition: e.g., Coarelli 1989 suggests the 140s, and Dowden 1994 the 150s. However, the *argu-*

EPILOGUE 301

but also that he expected his African audience (or at the very least, some of them) to be able to appreciate the humor of invoking the ass-man's bray in his polemical refutation of the Valentinians. Simply put, the widely held view that Apuleius published the *Met.* for Roman readers—a premise assumed a priori merely because Apuleius would otherwise be unique in Latin literature in appealing to a provincial audience[17]—is invalidated by the likelihood of an ancient reading population already enjoying his novel within a generation of its publication.

And if Apuleius intended his novel for an African audience (as with the *Florida*), then the metalepsis at the end of his novel takes on a much different meaning from how scholars have hitherto interpreted it. So, let us now turn to this final intervention of the *auctor* on the narrative, where the designation *Madaurensem* constitutes another jarring intrusion of reality on the fictional world. The passage occurs at *Met.* 11.27, where Lucius-*actor*, having undergone all the rigors of initiation into Isis' cult, surmises he should embark on one final initiation into Osiris' sect, and his suspicions are quickly confirmed when he encounters an initiate of the Egyptian god in a dream. The next day, we learn, Lucius meets this initiate *in propria persona*, who turns out to be a *pastophorus* ("priest") of Osiris, and who, ironically, goes by the name Asinius Marcellus. After recounting his own dream to this priest, Lucius discovers that the *pastophorus* likewise had a dream on the very same night, in which the god Osiris spoke directly to him about his impending encounter with Lucius (11.27):

> nam sibi visus est quiete proxima, dum magno deo coronas exaptat [et], de eius ore, quo singulorum fata dictat, audisse mitti sibi Madaurensem sed admodum pauperem, cui statim sua sacra deberet ministrare; nam et illi studiorum gloriam et ipsi grande compendium sua comparari providentia.

> For he dreamt on the previous night, while he was fitting out crowns for the great god, that he heard from the god's very mouth, by which he prophesies the

---

mentum ex silentio for its publication after the *Apologia* (158/59 CE) remains insurmountable, in my view, since the prosecution would almost certainly have produced the novel as evidence of Apuleius' flirtation with magic, just as they utilized his other literary output against him (cf. *Apol.* 9). Hunink's suggestion (2002, 227) that Apuleius' accusers may not have understood the *Met.* and that Apuleius, in turn, would want to avoid a nuanced interpretive debate with unintelligent people seems rather weak to me, since the context would have required a response to a formal charge had they brought one.

17. So, Dowden 1994, 422: "if he had been primarily addressing provincial audiences in his published works, he would be practically unique." See Graverini 2012a, 183–85 for a nuancing of this stance.

302   THE SHADOW OF AN ASS

fates of each person, that a man from Madauros was being sent to him, one who was very poor, to whom he (Asinius) was immediately to administer his (Osiris') sacred rites; indeed, he dreamt that the god's providence ordained fame for that one (i.e., the Madauran) from his intellectual pursuits and a good amount of money for him (i.e., Asinius).

As I noted in §2.4, this dream is problematic from a narrative perspective, since Lucius-*actor*—who initially traces his "ancient lineage" (1.1: *vetus prosapia*) to Corinth, Athens, and Sparta, and is descended from Plutarch of Boeotia and Sextus of Chaeronea (1.2)—is somehow repatriated as "Madauran" by a divine voice at the end of his story. An older generation of criticism took this as a paradigmatic example of Apuleius' careless and haphazard composition.[18] So, Oudendorp claimed that "Apuleius shamefully forgot himself here" (*Turpiter vero hic sui oblitus est Appulejus*),[19] whereas others, passing the inconsistency off onto the manuscript tradition, sought to emend the problem via conjecture.[20]

However, in the wake of Winkler's postmodernist approach to Apuleius, in which inconsistencies merely function as "puzzles of authority,"[21] scholars have adopted a more nuanced attitude toward this intrusion of the authorial voice. Some have suggested a metaliterary or comic-sophistic approach, where the *pastophorus* seemingly misunderstands the signifier *Madaurensem* (which, in actuality, points to Apuleius outside of the text),[22] whereas others have read the intrusion as a *sphragis* ("a literary seal")[23] or even a cultural mediator between

---

18. See Helm's subsection *de rebus neglegenter compositis* (Helm 1910, xv–xvii.) in his *praefatio*, although Helm applies the judgment to the whole of book 11 (among other things) rather than the specific issue of the *Madaurensem* problem. Cf. also Perry 1967, 236–84, for a fuller assessment of Apuleian inconsistencies.

19. Oudendorp 1776 *ad loc*. For the only modern commentator who endorses the "error" theory, see Scobie 1969, 81.

20. Goldbacher 1872, 410, was the first to suggest a conjecture (*mane Doriensem*); Robertson 1910 *ad loc*. gives a thorough discussion of the issue, suggesting *mandare se <religiosum>*. See van der Paardt 1999 on the history of the problem and *GCA* 2015, 465 *ad loc*. 11,27,9 and in general, 464–67 for a more up-to-date treatment of interpretations and solutions to the inconsistency.

21. See Winkler 1985, 218–19. Even before Winkler, van der Paardt 1999 (originally published in 1981) suggested that this inconsistency represents a kind of metalepsis, a temporary collapse between the intradiegetic fictional world of the narrator and that of the extradiegetic author. On the history of appreciating Apuleius as a literary artist capable of more nuanced and self-conscious inconsistency, see Harrison 2013a, 13–37.

22. On this episode as metafiction, see Penwill 1990, 13–16. Harrison 2000, 228–31, expands on Penwill's argument to endorse a "comic-sophistic" approach. For a similar effect, in which Apuleius plays with his reader's expectations, see Graverini 2012a, 186–87.

23. On *sphragis*, see Tilg 2014a, 125–31, who revives this notion from an earlier generation of critics

EPILOGUE 303

Apuleius' fringe North African identity, on the one hand, and the overpowering gravitational force of Rome, on the other.[24] Within the discourse of the Second Sophistic, after all, the *sphragis* as a tool for negotiating between a normative, imperial discourse and a parasitic, novelistic reworking of that discourse from the periphery seems especially apropos for a Latin translation of a Greek popularizing text written by a North African.[25] That is to say, to scholars writing in a time of hybridized identity and complicated negotiations between urban and provincial, approaching the *Madaurensem* problem as a cultural negotiation seems an attractive solution.[26]

However, with the scales now tipping in favor of an African readership, and furthermore, in the spirit of recuperating the *Met.*'s original "questions of meaning" for Apuleius' first readers, I suggest that the designation—"a man from Madauros"—could also incorporate what we might call a "contemporary reader" of the *Metamorphoses* by elegantly mapping the reader's situation onto the Lucius-Asinius dream scenario.[27] For out of nowhere and unawares, a Madauran approaches a *pastophorus* who happens to be named "ass-man" in order to be "administered into the initiatory rites" of the cult of a divinity. In fact, Lucius goes out of his way to emphasize the irony of the priest's name and its significance for the central transformation(s) of the *Met.* (11.27):

quem Asinium Marcellum vocitari cognovi postea, reformationis meae <minime> **alienum** nomen.[28]

Afterward, I learned that he was called Asinius Marcellus, a name not at all foreign to my transformation.

(e.g., Lesky 1941, 44; Paratore 1942, 65; Walsh 1970, 184n4). See also Smith 2023, 157–71, who links it to authorial metalepses in the New Testament and Early Christian texts.

24. On cultural negotiation, see Finkelpearl 1998, 215–16 and 2007, 273; Graverini 2012a, 187–88.

25. Cf., e.g., Whitmarsh 1998, 96–99, who endorses precisely this kind of interpretation of the named author at the end of Heliodorus' *Aethiopica*.

26. For a particularly useful discussion of the *Madaurensem* problem and its narratological implications within the Isis book, see Whitmarsh and Bartsch 2008, 251–55.

27. This reception-oriented approach to the *Madaurensem* problem was initially inspired by a discussion I had with Luca Graverini (*per sermones*). See also Graverini 2012a, 188, where he entertains the "possibility that [*Madaurensem*] is a subtle nod to an African audience, who have thereby been invited to sympathize with a protagonist/author who comes from their own province."

28. Here, I follow the conjecture of Robertson 1946, 165 *ad loc.*, though I do not specifically endorse any definitive textual solution (on which, more below).

The pronounced act of naming Osiris' priest, which uniquely (in the novel) includes both a *nomen* and *cognomen*, has caused a great deal of speculation among scholars. Some have attempted to identify a historical figure from the Asinius Marcellus family (well-known from the late first century CE)[29] and in so doing, to offer more definitive answers to biographical questions about Apuleius' life (e.g., where he lived outside of Rome, or whether Asinius Marcellus was possibly a patron for his literary output?);[30] others, in turn, have (more plausibly) recognized the name as an elaborate kind of wordplay, a characteristically Apuleian pun to complement the jarring bait-and-switch with identity in Lucius' sudden shift in nationality.[31]

However, considering the way in which the Isis book, at many points, assimilates the reader to the internal audience for Lucius' exposure as a spectacle of transformation,[32] it is possible to view the sudden intrusion of a Madauran character—indeed, one who enters the novel at the precise moment when s/he encounters an intermediary *pastophorus* named "ass-man"—not simply as the authorial *persona* peeking out of the text to wink at the reader in a "rhetorical metalepsis," but also as the reader him- or herself unwittingly (and perhaps unwillingly) transcribed onto the text.[33] Significantly for us, this metaleptic inconsistency compels every reader—even the most immersed reader,

---

29. So, Vannini 2018, 240, notes that "il nome Asinio Marcello era caratteristico di una delle famiglie consolari più in vista dell'età imperiale." He cites an Asinius Marcellus who lived under Nero (according to Tacitus' *Ann.* 14.40), and a Q. Asinius Marcellus who served as consul in 97 (or 99) CE and who himself had a son (a consul under Hadrian?) of the same name (according to the speculation of Coarelli 1989, 34–35). Vannini, therefore, attempts to revive Coarelli's (1989) thesis that Apuleius had a house in Ostia, which had an inscription in the base with the name Q. Asinius Marcellus.

30. Adkins 2022, 219–25, follows Vannini's (2018) proposal that the name Asinius Marcellus may have been a family name associated with Apuleius' patron and thus, that the authorial intrusion represents not only a literary *sphragis*, but also a homage to Apuleius' anticipated "real" reader. However, this is where I find Vannini's (2018, 239–48) speculative conjecture of a patron who funded the publication of the *Met.* in Rome rather far-fetched. This patronage relationship would require that Apuleius wrote the *Met.* in the late 140s–early 150s (on which, see n. 16), and the creation of a "real," historical patron (Q. Asinius Marcellus) ignores the compelling evidence for an African (instead of a Roman) readership, as it depends exclusively on the "Roman market" theory (on which, see n. 5 above).

31. See, e.g., van der Paardt 1999, 244, who notes that Asinius' "name underlines [his] fictionality." Cf. esp. Nicolini 2012 for discussion of the pun (with bibliography).

32. See again my discussion in §3.4.

33. For a discussion of metalepsis in *Met.* 11.27, see Whitmarsh 2013, 71-72. On "rhetorical" and "ontological metalepsis" in Apuleius generally, see Ulrich 2022, where the former represents a temporary breach in the fictional illusion (e.g., an Aristophanic *parabasis*), while the latter constitutes a complete renegotiation of the boundaries between diegetic levels. I would thus interpret *Madaurensem* as an "ontological metalepsis," insofar as it changes the substance of the tale in a jarring breach of narrative levels by merging the reader with Lucius in a collision of worlds.

who is utterly entranced by the Siren-song jingle of Apuleius' playful rhetoric—to take a step of distance away from the textual encounter, to puzzle in reflection over the surprise shift in characters' identities. One cannot simply be "lost in a book," to borrow a metaphor from immersion theory, when such apparent contradictions pile up so incongruously. So, just as the *Madaurensem* rouses the North African reader to identify with the narrator, so also, the fact that "ass-man" Asinius is not foreign to Lucius' *reformatio* suggests that he is not foreign to the reader's transformation either—and here, two pertinent questions arise, one textual and one interpretive.

For, on the one hand, most scholars agree that something seems to be missing from the text in the closing phrase of Lucius' punning play, which reads in manuscript *F reformationis meae alienum nomen*. It seems to require, in short, a qualifying adverb to clarify its meaning: for instance, *non* or *minime* (i.e., "a name not at all foreign to my transformation"),[34] or perhaps the adverb *iam* to emphasize the disjunct between Asinius' name and Lucius' newly recovered form (i.e., "a name at that time foreign to my retro-transformation").[35] Just as the textual puzzle seems to leave us poised to give way to poststructuralist *aporia*, so also, there is an ambiguity in the meaning of *reformatio*, as the term is used to describe Lucius' initial asinine metamorphosis (3.24) as well as his later anamorphosis into a human (11.13).

While I have followed Robertson's conjecture in printing <*minime*>, I do not mean to take a definitive stance on either puzzle and in fact, I concur with Winkler that the *Met.* seems to challenge its readers even in its enigmas of textual transmission.[36] Rather than solving the problem, then, I have elaborated on the issues involved in this pronounced act of naming because, parallel to the disorienting insertion of a "man from Madauros," it confronts North African readers once again with the question of identity—with anxieties over how "foreign" they, in fact, are to the ass-man, and whether the voyeuristic pleasure they have taken in his *reformatio* may somehow involve them as well. To phrase it

---

34. See *GCA* 2015, 462–63 *ad loc.* 11,27,7 for discussion. The Groningen commentators, however, follow Zimmerman 2012, 280 *ad loc.* in leaving out any adverb. Robertson 1946, 165 *ad loc.* (whose text I print) conjectures <*minime*>, since it is often abbreviated in manuscripts as *me* (with a dash) and thus, could easily have fallen out after *meae.*

35. See Nicolini 2012, 29–30, for this clever conjecture and for discussion of the ambiguity of *reformatio.*

36. Cf. Winkler 1985, 170n67 (referring to a textual error in *Met.* 2.4): "The *AA* seems to be the kind of composition in which even mistakes make sense; for the problematic equation of Actaeon with Lucius with Apuleius makes the echo *-sum proiectus* (which would mean 'I was projected') an intriguing, even teasing, riddle for the second-reader."

differently, Lucius jokingly points out that Asinius' name is, in some sense, *alienum* to his metamorphosis (or anamorphosis?). On a deeper level, however, with the implication of "a man from Madauros" in mind, the question can, alternatively, be directed outward to the reader. How "foreign" is this asinine priest from *my* transformation? Is this *reformatio* a simple *fabula* of human-animal transmigration—one which I can enjoy from afar? Or is this unexpected restoration of a wandering ass to a mystical priesthood, on the contrary, a *fabula de me*?[37] After getting lost in this carnivalesque tale of magic, sex, and pleasure, is it possible to recognize any distance at all (<*minime*>) between myself and Lucius?

Returning to the *Madaurensem* problem, therefore, we may note a heightened ambiguity of reference in Asinius Marcellus' recollection of his dream. As Stephen Harrison has pointed out, in this bewildering vision of the god (which is further distanced via indirect statement), there are reflexive pronouns and possessive adjectives (*sibi . . . sua . . . sua*), which subtly shift referents over the course of the sentence (i.e., from Asinius to Osiris); likewise, there is a studied ambiguity in the weak demonstrative (*eius*) and the intensifier (*ipsi*).[38] Although one can, to be sure, step back from being immersed in the narrative and create a diagram of who's-who in this prophetic vision,[39] the swirl of identities confounds the "active reader" precisely at a moment of intense reflection. Thus, it is most significant, in my view, that the dream concludes with "fame for **that one** from his literary pursuits" (***illi** studiorum gloriam*), where *studia* can refer both to literary composition and readerly reception,[40] and the strong demonstrative (*ille*) seems contextually to point to the "Madauran." In short, it is no coincidence that "Palinodic" readers, after encountering this *ille* renowned for "literary pursuits," can turn the papyrus roll back to the opening of the novel, where they will find another demonstrative—the other famous enigma of the Prologue's *quis ille?*—pointing at an unknown person in disconcerting ambiguity. Is it Lucius, Apuleius, or the reader? The difference between *actor*, *auctor*, and *lector* is, in retrospect, elided.

Indeed, I suggested in §2.4 that the break of the fourth wall with the open-

---

37. See Nì Mheallaigh 2009 on the *Met.* from the reader's perspective as a *fabula de se.*
38. Harrison 2000, 231.
39. As, e.g., Vannini 2018, 236–37, does in an overcorrection of Harrison's point about the deliberate confusion of the reader.
40. See OLD, s.v. **studium** 7. See, e.g., Cic. *Pro Arch.* 4.4 "on the liberal arts" (*de studiis humanitatis*). Cf. the closing of Stat. *Theb.* (12.815), which is most explicitly about reading. See also Pliny *Ep.* 3.1.9 on *studia* as sympotic literary reception.

ing *quis ille?* can be contextualized as a philosophical question akin to that of Socrates at the close of Plato's *Phaedrus* (275b5–c1): thus, Socrates explains to Phaedrus that *allotria/aliena*, such as "who is speaking?" (275c1: τίς ὁ λέγων), matter perhaps to "wise" people, but the priests of Dodona listened to a rock or an oak "provided it spoke the truth." So also, at the close of the *Met.*, we encounter an intermediary priest who claims to speak the truth (cf. 11.23: *sed crede, quae vera sunt*), even though his words are transmitted through an ass's bray. When we approach the "Palinode," however, as Apuleius' first readers might have—that is, as "foreigner(s) to these studies" (1.1: *advena* **studiorum**)—the indeterminate question of identity (*quis ille?*) can take on a whole new meaning. Indeed, far from a mere generic game akin to a Plautine prologist's stage-setting, or even a Platonic nod to the problems inherent to dialogue (i.e., "who is speaking?"), this *ille* might, in fact, point unnervingly out to the Madauran reader, who approaches an asinine *pastophorus* in search of the divine. As it gestures to someone outside of the text, breaking all the boundaries separating fiction from reality, it asks: "who is reading?" That is, after a nightmarish journey through a quadruped's *katabasis* followed by an eschatological vision of judgment day, I would submit that, when this asinine *pastophorus* points at us and says—"reader, pay attention; you will be happy"—we would do well to "listen and believe."

Appendix

This appendix compares the Latin commentary tradition on the Myth of Er (*left-hand column*) to the lexical choices Apuleius makes across the *Met.*, and especially in the Isis book (*right-hand column*) along nine shared thematic axes. The commentary tradition on the Myth of Er spans from Valerius Maximus' first-century CE collection of sayings to Apuleius' own demonology (e.g., *De deo Socratis*) and the (likely Apuleian) second-century CE Middle Platonic summary of dialogues (*Expositio*) and finally, to the myth's late antique reception (i.e., Macrobius' *Comm. In Somn. Scip.*, Augustine's *De civitate Dei*, and Favonius Eulogius' *De Somn. Scip.*).

Myth of Er, Commentary Tradition	Apuleius, *Metamorphoses*
1. *Retaining the Mind:*	
Macr. *In Somn. Scip.* 1.1.9: *seu* **recepta anima** *seu* **retenta**	4.20 [of Thrasyleon]: **anima retinens**
	4.6: *an* **mente** *etiam* **sensu**que *fuerim asinus*
Aug. *De civ. D.* 18.18: *humano* **animo permanente**	
2. *Journey to the Underworld:*	
Eul. *De Somn. Scip.* 1: *multa . . .* **de inferis** *secreta*	11.6: **ad inferos** *demearis*
	11.18: *reducem . . .* **ab inferis**
Expositio 8: **de inferis**	cf. 11.23: **deos inferos** *et deos superos accessi . . . calcato* **Proserpinae limine** *. . . remeavi*
3. *Reportage of Secrets:*	
Macr. *In Somn. Scip.* 1.1.9: **secretorum relator**	11.1: *opacae noctis silentiosa* **secreta**
Eul. *De Somn. Scip.* 1: **multa** *. . . de inferis* *secreta*	11.21: *ad* **arcana** *purissimae religionis* **secreta**
	11.23: **rettuli** *. . .* **referam**

4. Enunciation of Rites to the Uninitiated:

Macr. *In Somn. Scip.* 1.2.12: *rerum* **sacrarum
enuntiatio**
Macr. *In Somn. Scip.* 1.1.9: **enuntiavit**

11.22: *piissimis* **sacrorum** *arcanis*
11.23: *ad profanorum intellegentias* **enuntiari**

5. Allocation of a daemōn:

Apul. *Soc.* 15: Osiris is listed among *daemones*
Expositio 8: *proprium* **δαίμονα**

11.27: *invicti Osiris . . . sacris illustratum*

6. Coming back to Life and Narrating:

Val. Max. *F&D* 1.8.1: **revixisse . . . narrasse**
Macr. *Somn.* 1.1.9: **narraturum** *quam*
reviviscere
Aug. *De civ. D.* 22.28: **reuixisse** *et* **narrasse**
Aug. *De civ. D.* 18.18: *quasi somnia* **narrasse**
Eul. *De Somn. Scip.* 1: **re<v>ixisset . . .
narrasset**

11.16: **renatus**
11.21: **renatos**
11.19: **narratis** . . . *meis . . . pristinis
aerumnis et praesentibus gaudiis*

7. Return to Life / Previous Body:

Macr. *Somn.* 1.1.2: *a quodam* **vitae reddito**
Aug. *De civ. D.* 22.27: *ut . . .* **redirent** *animae*
ad corpora
Aug. *De civ. D.* 18.18: *iterum* **ad se redirent**
Eul. *De Somn. Scip.* 1: **reditu in vitam**

10.29: *quae* **me** *priori meo Lucio* **redderent**
11.2: **redde me** *meo Lucio*

8. Dreaming vs. Resurrection:

Macr. *Somn.* 1.2.5: *quietem Africani nostri*
somniantis
Aug. *De civ. D.* 18.18: *quasi* **somnia** *narrasse*
Eul. *De Somn. Scip.* 1: **sollertis somnii**
cf. also **somniantium philosophorum** . . .
commenta

11.3: *lucidum simulacrum . . . ante me . . .* **visum
est**
11.20: **sollertiam somni**
11.30: *divini* **somnii** *suada maiestas*

9. Recollection before Reincarnation:

Expositio 8: *quamdiu non transierint* **prioris
vitae meminerint**

10.29: **priori** *meo Lucio*
11.6: **memineris** . . . *mihi reliqua* **vitae** . . .
curricula

Bibliography

AAGA 1 = B. L. Hijmans and R. Th. van der Paardt, eds. 1978. *Aspects of Apuleius' "Golden Ass."* Vol. 1. Groningen: Bouma.

AAGA 2 = M. Zimmerman, V. Hunink, Th. D. McCreight, D. van Mal-Maeder, S. Panayotakis, V. Schmidt, and B. Wesseling, eds. 1998. *Aspects of Apuleius' "Golden Ass."* Vol. 2, *Cupid and Psyche*. Groningen: E. Forsten.

AAGA 3 = W. Keulen and U. Egelhaaf-Gaiser, eds. 2012. *Aspects of Apuleius' "Golden Ass."* Vol. 3, *The Isis Book*. Leiden: Brill. https://doi.org/10.1163/9789004224551

Adams, J. N. 1982. *The Latin Sexual Vocabulary*. Baltimore: Johns Hopkins University Press.

Adkins, E. 2022. *Discourse, Knowledge, and Power in Apuleius' "Metamorphoses."* Ann Arbor: University of Michigan Press. https://doi.org/10.3998/mpub.11648449

Allan, R. 2020. "Narrative Immersion: Some Linguistic and Narratological Aspects." In Grethlein, Huitink, and Tagliabue, *Experience, Narrative, and Criticism*, 15–35.

Allan, R., I. de Jong, and C. de Jonge. 2017. "From *Enargeia* to Immersion: The Ancient Roots of a Modern Concept." *Style* 51.1: 34–51. https://doi.org/10.1353/sty.2017.0003

Alpers, K. 1980. "Innere Beziehungen und Kontraste als 'Hermeneutische Zeichen' in den Metamorphosen des Apuleius von Madaura." *WJA* 6: 197–207.

Anderson, G. 1976. *Lucian: Theme and Variation in the Second Sophistic*. Leiden: Brill.

Annas, J. 1981. *An Introduction to Plato's "Republic."* Oxford: Oxford University Press.

Asmis, E. 1995. "Epicurean Poetics." In *Philodemus and Poetry: Poetic Theory and Practice in Lucretius, Philodemus, and Horace*, edited by D. Obbink, 15–34. Oxford: Oxford University Press.

Bailey, C. 1947. *Titi Lucreti Cari "De Rerum Natura" Libri Sex*. Oxford: Oxford University Press.

Bakhtin, M. M. 1981. *The Dialogic Imagination: Four Essays*. Translated by C. Emerson and M. Holquist. Austin: University of Texas Press.

Baldwin, B. 1961. "Lucian as Social Satirist." *CQ* 11.2: 199–208.

Baltes, M., and M.-L. Lakmann, eds. 2004. *Über den Gott des Sokrates*. Darmstadt: Wissenschaftliche Buchgesellschaft.

Barnes, T. D. 1971. *Tertullian: A Historical and Literary Study*. Oxford: Clarendon Press.

Barney, R. 2010. "Platonic Ring-Composition and *Republic* 10." In *Plato's "Republic": A Critical Guide*, edited by Mark McPherran, 32–51. Cambridge: Cambridge University Press. https://doi.org/10.1017/CBO9780511763090

Barnouw, J. 2004. *Odysseus, Hero of Practical Intelligence: Deliberation and Signs in Homer's "Odyssey."* Washington, DC: University Press of America.

Bartsch, S. 1989. *Decoding the Ancient Novel: The Reader and the Role of Description in Heliodorus and Achilles Tatius*. Princeton: Princeton University Press.

Bartsch, S. 2006. *The Mirror of the Self: Sexuality, Self-Knowledge, and the Gaze in the Early Empire*. Chicago: University of Chicago Press.

Bartsch, S. 2007. "'Wait a Moment, Phantasia': Ekphrastic Interference in Seneca and Epictetus." *CP* 102.1: 83–95.

Bartsch, S., and J. Elsner, eds. 2007. "Ekphrasis." Special issue, *CP* 102.1.

Beaujeu, J. 1973. *Apulée, Opuscules Philosophiques ("Du dieu de Socrate," "Platon et sa Doctrine," "Du Monde") et Fragments: Texte établi, traduit et commenté*. Coll. Budé. Paris: Budé.

Beck, R. 2000. "Apuleius the Novelist, Apuleius the Ostian Householder and the Mithraeum of the Seven Spheres: Further Explorations of an Hypothesis of Filippo Coarelli." In *Text and Artifact in the Religions of Mediterranean Antiquity: Essays in Honour of Peter Richardson*, edited by S. G. Wilson and M. Desjardins, 551–67. Waterloo: Wilfrid Laurier University Press.

Beer, B. 2011. "Lucius bei den Phäaken: Zum Nostos-Motiv in Apuleius, *Met*. 11." *Ancient Narrative* 9: 77–98.

Belfiore, E. 1992. *Tragic Pleasures: Aristotle on Plot and Emotion*. Princeton: Princeton University Press.

Beneker, J. 2011. "Plutarch and Saint Basil as Readers of Greek Literature." *Syllecta Classica* 22.1: 95–111.

Benson, G. 2016. "Seeing Demons: Autopsy in Maximus of Tyre's *Oration* 9 and Its Absence in Apuleius' *On the God of Socrates*." *Ramus* 45.1: 102–31. https://doi.org/10.1017/rmu.2016.4

Benson, G. 2019. *Apuleius' Invisible Ass: Encounters with the Unseen in the "Metamorphoses."* Cambridge: Cambridge University Press. https://doi.org/10.1017/9781108602501

Bierl, A. 2018. "Longus' Hyperreality: *Daphnis and Chloe* as a Meta-Text about *Mimesis* and Simulation." In *Re-Wiring the Ancient Novel*. Vol. 1, *Greek Novels*, edited by E. Cueva, S. Harrison, H. Mason, W. Owens, and S. Schwartz, 3–28. Groningen: Barkhuis.

Bitel, A. P. 2000. "*Quis ille Asinus aureus?* The Metamorphoses of Apuleius' Title." *Ancient Narrative* 1: 208–44.

BIBLIOGRAPHY 313

Bloch, R. 2019. *De Pseudo-Luciani Amoribus*. Berlin: de Gruyter.

Booth, W. C. 1988. *The Company We Keep: An Ethics of Fiction*. Berkeley: University of California Press.

Bowersock, G. 1994. *Fiction as History: Nero to Julian*. Berkeley: University of California Press.

Bowie, E. 1994. "The Readership of Greek Novels in the Ancient World." In Tatum, *Search for the Ancient Novel*, 435–59.

Bowie, E. 1996. "The Ancient Readers of the Greek Novels." In *The Novel in the Ancient World*, edited by G. Schmeling, 87–106. Leiden: Brill.

Bowie, E. 2006. "Viewing and Listening on the Novelist's Page." In *Authors, Authority, and Interpreters in the Ancient Novel*, edited by S. Byrne, E. Cueva, and J. Alvares, 60–82. Leiden: Brill.

Bowie, E. 2013. "Milesian Tales." In *The Romance between Greece and the East*, edited by S. Thomson and T. Whitmarsh, 243–57. Cambridge: Cambridge University Press. https://doi.org/10.1017/CBO9781139814690

Bradley, K. 1998. "Contending with Conversion: Reflections on the Reformation of Lucius the Ass." *Phoenix* 52.3: 315–34. https://doi.org/10.2307/1088674

Bradley, K. 2000. "Animalizing the Slave: The Truth of Fiction." *JRS* 90: 110–25. https://doi.org/10.2307/300203

Bradley, K. 2005. "Apuleius and Carthage." *Ancient Narrative* 4: 1–29.

Brancaleone, F., and A. Stramaglia. 2003. "Otri e proverbi in Apuleio, *Met.* 2,32–3,18." In *Studi apuleiani: Note di aggiornamento di L. Graverini*, edited by O. Pecere and A. Stramaglia, 113–17. Cassino: Edizioni dell'Università degli studi di Cassino.

Brandt, P.-Y. 2022. "Contemporary Models of Conversion and Identity Transformation." In Despotis and Löhr, *Religious and Philosophical Conversion*, 17–42.

Braund, S. 1999. "Moments of Love: Lucretius, Apuleius, Monteverdi, Strauss." In *Amor: Roma. Love and Latin Literature*, edited by S. Braund and R. Mayer, 174–98. Cambridge: Cambridge University Press.

Braund, S. 2009. *Seneca: "De Clementia."* Oxford: Oxford University Press. https://doi.org/10.1093/actrade/9780199240364.book.1

Bryson, N. 1994. "Philostratus and the Imaginary Museum." In *Art and Text in Ancient Greek Culture*, edited by S. Goldhill and R. Osbourne, 255–83. Cambridge: Cambridge University Press.

Buffière, F. 1956. *Les mythes d'Homère et la pensée grecque*. Paris: Les Belles Lettres.

Callebat, L. 1968. *Sermo cotidianus dans les "Métamorphoses" d'Apulée*. Caen: Faculté des Lettres de l'Université.

Carver, R. 2007. *The Protean Ass: The "Metamorphoses" of Apuleius from Antiquity to the Renaissance*. Oxford: Oxford University Press. https://doi.org/10.1093/acprof:oso/9780199217861.001.0001

Caston, R. 2014. "The Divided Self: Plautus and Terence on Identity and Impersonation." In *Plautine Trends: Studies in Plautine Comedy and Its Reception*, edited by I.

Perysinakis and E. Karakasis, 43–62. Berlin: De Gruyter. https://doi.org/10.1515/97 83110368925

Cavallo, G. 1996. "Veicoli materiali della letteratura di consume: Maniere di scrivere e maniere di leggere." In *La letteratura di consumo nel mondo Greco-Latino*, edited by O. Pecere and A. Stramaglia, 11–46. Cassino: Università degli studi di Cassino.

Cavallo, G. 1999. "Between *Volumen* and Codex: Reading in the Roman World." In *A History of Reading in the West*, edited by G. Cavallo and R. Chartier, 64–89. Amherst: University of Massachusetts Press.

Cavallo, G. 2006. *Lire à Byzance*. Translated from Italian by P. Odorico and A. Segonds. Paris: Budé.

Chaplin, J. 2000. *Livy's Exemplary History*. Oxford: Oxford University Press.

Clairmont, C. 1951. *Das Parisurteil in der antiken Kunst*. Zürich: N.p.

Clay, D. 1975. "The Tragic and the Comic Poet of the *Symposium*." *Arion* 2.2: 238–61.

Clay, D. 1992. "Plato's First Words." In *Beginnings in Classical Literature*, edited by F. Dunn and T. Cole, 113–30. Cambridge: Cambridge University Press.

Close, A. J. 2008. *A Companion to "Don Quixote."* Woodbridge, UK: Boydell and Brewer.

Coarelli, F. 1989. "Apuleio a Ostia?" *DArch* 7: 27–42.

Collins, J. H. 2011. "Prompts for Participation in Early Philosophical Texts." In *Orality, Literacy, and Performance in the Ancient World*, edited by E. Minchin, 151–82. Leiden: Brill. https://doi.org/10.1163/9789004217751

Collins, J. H. 2015. *Exhortations to Philosophy: The Protreptics of Plato, Isocrates, and Aristotle*. Oxford: Oxford University Press. https://doi.org/10.1093/acprof:oso/9780 199358595.001.0001

Constantini, L. 2018. "The Entertaining Function of Magic and Mystical Silence in Apuleius' *Metamorphoses*." In *Re-Wiring the Ancient Novel*. Vol. 2, *Roman Novels and Other Important Texts*, edited by E. Cueva, S. Harrison, H. Mason, W. Owens, and S. Schwartz, 117–33. Groningen: Barkhuis. https://doi.org/10.2307/j.ctvggx289.31

Constantini, L. 2021. "Apuleius on Divination: Platonic Daimonology and Child-Divination." In *Divination and Knowledge in Greco-Roman Antiquity*, edited by C. Addey, 248–68. London: Routledge. https://doi.org/10.4324/9781315449487

Conte, G. B. 1996. *The Hidden Author: An Interpretation of Petronius' "Satyricon."* Berkeley: University of California Press.

Conticello, B., and B. Andreae. 1974. *Die Skulpturen von Sperlonga*. Berlin: Gebruder Mann.

Copeland, R. 1991. *Rhetoric, Hermeneutics, and Translation in the Middle Ages: Academic Traditions and Vernacular Texts*. Cambridge: Cambridge University Press.

Cotton, A. K. 2014. *Platonic Dialogue and the Education of the Reader*. Oxford: Oxford University Press.

Cueva, E., and S. Byrne, eds. 2014. *A Companion to the Ancient Novel*. Malden, MA: Blackwell. https://doi.org/10.1002/9781118350416

Davies, M. 2023. *The Hero's Life Choice: Studies on Heracles at the Crossroads, the Judge-*

ment of Paris, and their Reception: "Verbalising the Visual and Visualising the Verbal." Leiden: Brill.

D'Alconzo, N. 2021. "Decoding the *Erôtes*: Reception of Achilles Tatius and the Modernity of the Greek Novel." *AJP* 142.3: 461–92. https://doi.org/10.1353/ajp.2021.0015

De Biasi, L. 2000. "Le descrizioni del paesaggio naturale nelle opera di Apuleio: Aspetti litterari." In *Apuleio: Storia del testo e interpretazioni*, edited by G. Magnaldi and G. F. Gianotti, 199–264. Torino: Edizioni dell'Orso.

DeFilippo, J. 1990. "*Curiositas* and the Platonism of Apuleius' *Golden Ass.*" *AJP* 111.4: 471–92.

de Jong, I. 2001. "The Prologue as a Pseudo-Dialogue and the Identity of Its (Main) Speaker." In Kahane and Laird, *Companion to the Prologue of "Metamorphoses,"* 201–12.

de Jonge, C. 2020. "Longinus on Ecstasy: Author, Audience, and Text." In Grethlein, Huitink, and Tagliabue, *Experience, Narrative, and Criticism*, 148–71.

Deniston, J. D. 1954. *The Greek Particles*. Oxford: Clarendon Press.

Denyer, N. 2001. *Plato's "Protagoras."* Cambridge: Cambridge University Press.

Derrida, J. 1972. *La dissemination*. Paris: Seuil.

Despotis, A. 2022. "Philosophical Conversion in Plutarch's *Moralia* and the Cultural Discourses in the Ancient Mediterranean." In Despotis and Löhr, *Religious and Philosophical Conversion*, 203–18.

Despotis, A., and H. Löhr, eds. 2022. *Religious and Philosophical Conversion in the Ancient Mediterranean Traditions*. Leiden: Brill. https://doi.org/10.1163/978900450 1775

DiGiulio, S. 2020. "Gellius' Strategies of Reading (Gellius): Miscellany and the Active Reader in *Noctes Atticae* Book 2." *CP* 115.2: 242–64. https://doi.org/10.1086/708236

Dillon, J. M. 1977. *The Middle Platonists: 80 B.C. to A.D. 220*. Ithaca: Cornell University Press.

Dillon, J. M. 2004. "Dämonologie im frühen Platonismus." In Baltes and Lakmann, *Über den Gott des Sokrates*, 123–41.

Domaradzki, M. 2017. "The Beginnings of Greek Allegoresis." *CW* 110.3: 299–321. https://doi.org/10.1353/clw.2017.0019

Domaradzki, M. 2020. "Antisthenes and *Allegoresis*." In *Early Greek Ethics*, edited by D. Wolfsdorf, 361–79. Oxford: Oxford University Press. https://doi.org/10.1093/oso/97 80198758679.001.0001

Dougherty, C. 2001. *The Raft of Odysseus: The Ethnographic Imagination of Homer's "Odyssey."* Oxford: Oxford University Press.

Dowden, K. 1982. "Psyche on the Rock." *Latomus* 41.2: 336–52.

Dowden, K. 1994. "The Roman Audience of the *Golden Ass*." In Tatum, *Search for the Ancient Novel*, 419–33.

Dowden, K. 1998. "Cupid and Psyche: A Question of the Vision of Apuleius." In *AAGA* 2, 1–22.

Dowden, K. 2001. "Prelogic, Predecessors, and Prohibitions." In Kahane and Laird, *Companion to the Prologue of "Metamorphoses,"* 123–36.

Dowden, K. 2006. "A Tale of Two Texts: Apuleius' *Sermo Milesius* and Plato's *Symposium*." In Keulen, Nauta, and Panayotakis, *Lectiones Scrupulosae*, 42–58.

Drake, G. 1968. "*Candidus*: A Unifying Theme in Apuleius' *Metamorphoses*." *CJ* 64.3: 102–9.

Drews, F. 2006. "Der Sprecherwechsel zwischen Apuleius und Lucius im Prolog der *Metamorphosen*." *Mnemosyne* 59.3: 403–20.

Drews, F. 2012. "*Asinus philosophans*: Allegory's Fate and Isis' Providence in the *Metamorphoses*." In *AAGA* 3, 107–31.

Drews, F. 2015. "A Platonic Reading of the Isis Book." In *GCA* 2015, 517–28.

Drosihn, F. 1871. *Kebētos Pinax*. Leipzig: Teubner.

Dufallo, B. 2013. *The Captor's Image: Greek Culture in Roman Ecphrasis*. New York: Oxford University Press. https://doi.org/10.1093/acprof:oso/9780199735877.001.0001

Duff, T. 1999. *Plutarch's "Lives": Exploring Virtue and Vice*. Oxford: Oxford University Press.

Edmonds, R. G. 2017. "Putting Him on a Pedestal: (Re)collection and the Use of Images in Plato's *Phaedrus*." In *Plato and the Power of Images*, edited by P. Destrée and R. G. Edmonds, 66–81. Leiden: Brill. https://doi.org/10.1163/9789004345010

Edmunds, L. 2010. "The Reception of Horace's *Odes*." In *A Companion to Horace*, edited by G. Davis, 337–66. Malden, MA: Wiley-Blackwell. https://doi.org/10.1002/9781444319187

Egan, R. 2004. "Narcissus Transformed: Rationalized Myth in Plato's *Phaedrus*." In *Metamorphic Reflections: Essays Presented to Ben Hijmans at His 75th Birthday*, edited by M. Zimmerman and R. T. van der Paardt, 143–59. Leuven: Peeters.

Egelhaaf-Gaiser, U. 2012. "The Gleaming Pate of the *Pastophorus*: Masquerade or Embodied Lifestyle?" In *AAGA* 3, 42–72. https://doi.org/10.1163/9789004224551_004

Elsner, J., ed. 1996. *Art and Text in Roman Culture*. Cambridge: Cambridge University Press.

Elsner, J., ed. 2002. "The Verbal and the Visual: Cultures of Ekphrasis in Antiquity." Special issue, *Ramus* 31.

Elsner, J. 2007. *Roman Eyes: Visuality and Subjectivity in Art and Text*. Princeton: Princeton University Press.

Englert, J., and T. Long. 1973. "Functions of Hair in Apuleius' *Metamorphoses*." *CJ* 68.3: 236–39.

Farrell, J. 2004. "Roman Homer." In *The Cambridge Companion to Homer*, edited by R. Fowler, 254–71. Cambridge: Cambridge University Press. https://doi.org/10.1017/CCOL0521813026

Farrell, J. 2012. "Art, Aesthetics, and the Hero in Vergil's *Aeneid*." In *Aesthetic Value in*

Classical Antiquity, edited by I. Sluiter and R. Rosen, 285–313. Leiden: Brill. https://doi.org/10.1163/9789004232822

Ferrari, G. R. F. 1987. *Listening to the Cicadas: A Study of Plato's "Phaedrus."* Cambridge: Cambridge University Press.

Ferrari, G. R. F. 1992. "Platonic Love." In *The Cambridge Companion to Plato*, edited by R. Kraut, 248–76. Cambridge: Cambridge University Press. https://doi.org/10.1017/CCOL0521430186.008

Fick, N. 1987. "L'Isis des *Métamorphoses* d'Apulée." *Revue Belge de Philologie et d'Histoire* 65: 31–51. https://doi.org/10.3406/rbph.1987.3571

Fick, N. 1990. "Die Pantomime des Apuleius (*Met.* X.30–34.3)." In *Theater und Gesellschaft im Imperium Romanum*, edited by J. Bländsdorg, 223–32. Tübingen: Francke.

Fick-Michel, N. 1991. *Art et mystique dans les "Métamorphoses" d'Apulée*. Paris: Annales littéraires de l'Université de Besançon. https://doi.org/10.3406/ista.1991.2511

Finkelberg, M. 2020. "Frame and Frame-Breaking in Plato's Dialogues." In Kaklamanou, Pavlou, and Tsamakis, *Framing the Dialogues*, 27–39.

Finkelpearl, E. 1991. "The Judgment of Lucius: Apuleius' *Metamorphoses* 10.29–34." *CA* 10.2: 221–36.

Finkelpearl, E. 1998. *Metamorphosis of Language in Apuleius: A Study of Allusion in the Novel*. Ann Arbor: University of Michigan. https://doi.org/10.3998/mpub.15689

Finkelpearl, E. 2004. "The Ends of the Metamorphoses (Apuleius *Met.* 11.26.4–11.30)." In *Metamorphic Reflections: Essays Presented to Ben Hijmans at His 75th Birthday*, edited by M. Zimmerman and R. Th. van der Paardt, 319–42. Leuven: Peeters.

Finkelpearl, E. 2007. "Apuleius, the *Onos*, and Rome." In Paschalis et al., *Greek and Roman Novel*, 263–76.

Finkelpearl, E. 2009. "Marsyas the Satyr and Apuleius of Madauros." *Ramus* 38.1: 7–42. https://doi.org/10.1017/S0048671X0000062X

Fish, S. 1967. *Surprised by Sin: The Reader in "Paradise Lost."* New York: St. Martin's Press.

Fish, S. 1970. "Literature in the Reader: Affective Stylistics." *New Literary History* 2.1: 123–62.

Fish, S. 1972. *Self-Consuming Artifacts: The Experience of Seventeenth-Century Literature*. Berkeley: University of California Press.

Fitzgerald, J., and L. White. 1983. *The Tabula of Cebes*. Chico, CA: Scholars Press.

Fitzgerald, W. 2000. *Slavery and the Roman Literary Imagination*. Cambridge: Cambridge University Press. https://doi.org/10.1017/CBO9780511612541

Fletcher, K. F. B. 2023. *The Ass of the Gods: Apuleius' "Golden Ass," the "Onos" Attributed to Lucian, and Graeco-Roman Metamorphosis Literature*. Leiden: Brill. https://doi.org/10.1163/9789004537170

Fletcher, R. 2014. *Apuleius' Platonism: The Impersonation of Philosophy*. Cambridge: Cambridge University Press. https://doi.org/10.1017/CBO9781139179010

Flower, H. I. 1996. *Ancestor Masks and Aristocratic Power in Roman Culture*. Oxford: Clarendon Press.

Ford, A. 2002. *The Origins of Criticism: Literary Culture and Poetic Theory in Classical Greece*. Princeton: Princeton University Press. https://doi.org/10.1515/9781400082 5066

Fortin, E. L. 1981. "Christianity and Hellenism in Basil the Great's Address *Ad adulescentes*." In *Neoplatonism and Early Christian Thought: Essays in Honour of A. H. Armstrong*, edited by H. J. Blumenthal and R. A. Markus, 189–203. London: Variorum.

Fowler, D. 1990. "Narrate and Describe: The Problem of *Ekphrasis*." *JRS* 81: 25–35.

Fowler, D. 2001. "Writing with Style: The Prologue to Apuleius' *Metamorphoses* between *fingierte Mündlichkeit* and Textuality." In Kahane and Laird, *Companion to the Prologue of "Metamorphoses*," 225–30.

Fowler, R. 2016. *Imperial Plato: Albinus, Maximus, Apuleius*. Las Vegas: Parmenides Press.

Fox, M. 2001. "Dionysius, Lucian, and the Prejudice against Rhetoric in History." *JRS* 91: 76–93.

Frangoulidis, S. 1991. "Vergil's Tale of the Trojan Horse in Apuleius' Robber-Tale of Thrasyleon." *Parola del passato* 46: 95–111.

Frangoulidis, S. 2008. *Witches, Isis and Narrative: Approaches to Magic in Apuleius' "Metamorphoses*." Berlin: de Gruyter. https://doi.org/10.1515/9783110210033

Fredouille, J.-C. 1975. *Apulei "Metamorphoseon" Liber XI; Apulée, "Métamorphoses" Livre XI*. Paris: Presses universitaires de France.

Fredouille, J.-C. 1981. *Tertullien: "Contre les Valentiniens," II. Commentaire et index*. Paris: CERF.

Freudenburg, K. 2007. "Leering for the Plot: Visual Curiosity in Apuleius and Others." In Paschalis et al., *Greek and Roman Novel*, 238–62.

Frontisi-Ducroux, F. 1996. "Eros, Desire, and the Gaze." In *Sexuality in Ancient Art: Near East, Egypt, Greece, and Italy*, edited by N. B. Kampen and translated by Nancy Kline, 81–100. Cambridge: Cambridge University Press.

Gaisser, J. H. 2008. *The Fortunes of Apuleius and the "Golden Ass": A Study in Transmission and Reception*. Princeton: Princeton University Press.

Gaisser, J. H. 2014. "How Apuleius Survived: The African Connection." In Lee, Finkelpearl, and Graverini, *Apuleius and Africa*, 52–65.

Galinsky, K. 1972. *The Herakles Theme: The Adaptations of the Hero in Literature from Homer to the Twentieth Century*. Totowa, NJ: Rowman and Littlefield.

GCA 1985 = Hijmans, B. L., R. Th. van der Paardt, V. Schmidt, C. B. J. Settels, B. Wesseling, and R. E. H. Westendorp Boerma. 1985. *Apuleius Madaurensis, "Metamorphoses*." *Book VIII*. Groningen Commentaries on Apuleius. Groningen: E. Forsten.

GCA 1995 = B. L. Hijmans, R. Th. van der Paardt, V. Schmidt, B. Wesseling, and M. Zimmerman. 1995. *Apuleius Madaurensis, "Metamorphoses*." *Book IX*. 1995. Groningen Commentaries on Apuleius. Groningen: E. Forsten.

GCA 2000 = M. Zimmerman. 2000. *Apuleius Madaurensis, "Metamorphoses*." *Book X*. Groningen Commentaries on Apuleius. Groningen: E. Forsten.

GCA 2001 = D. van Mal-Maeder. 2001. *Apuleius Madaurensis, "Metamorphoses." Livre II: Texte, Introduction et Commentaire*. Groningen Commentaries on Apuleius. Groningen: E. Forsten.

GCA 2004 = M. Zimmerman, S. Panayotakis, V. Hunink, W. H. Keulen, S. J. Harrison, Th. D. McCreight, B. Wesseling, and D. van Mal-Maeder. 2004. *Apuleius Madaurensis, "Metamorphoses." Books IV 28–35, V and VI 1–24. The Tale of Cupid and Psyche: Text, Introduction and Commentary*. Groningen Commentaries on Apuleius. Groningen: E. Forsten.

GCA 2007 = W. Keulen. 2007. *Apuleius Madaurensis, "Metamorphoses." Book I: Text, Introduction and Commentary*. Groningen Commentaries on Apuleius. Groningen: E. Forsten.

GCA 2015 = W. Keulen and U. Egelhaaf-Gaiser. 2015. *Apuleius Madaurensis, "Metamorphoses." Book XI: The Isis Book*. Groningen Commentaries on Apuleius. Leiden: Brill.

Germany, R. 2016. *Mimetic Contagion: Art and Artifice in Terence's "Eunuch."* Oxford: Oxford University Press.

Gianotti, G. F. 1986. *'Romanzo' e ideologia: Studi sulle "Metamorfosi" di Apuleio*. Napoli: Liguori.

Gibson, C. 2012. "How (Not) to Learn Rhetoric: Lucian's *Rhetorum Praeceptor* as Rebuttal of a School Exercise." *GRBS* 52.1: 89–110.

Gigante, M. 1984. "Per l'interpretazione del libro di Filodemo *Del buon re secondo Omero*." *La Parola del passato* 217: 285–98.

Glad, C. E. 1995. *Paul and Philodemus: Adaptability in Epicurean and Early Christian Psychology*. Leiden: Brill.

Goldbacher, A. 1872. "Ueber Lucius von Patrae, den dem Lucius zugeschriebenen Λούκιος ἢ Ὄνος und des Apuleius *Metamorphosen*." *Zeitschrift für die österreichischen Gymnasien* 23: 323–41 and 403–21.

Goldhill, S. 1995. *Foucault's Virginity: Ancient Erotic Fiction and the History of Sexuality*. Cambridge: Cambridge University Press. https://doi.org/10.1017/CBO9780511627330

Goldhill, S. 2001. "The Erotic Eye: Visual Stimulation and Cultural Conflict." In *Being Greek under Rome: Cultural Identity, the Second Sophistic and the Development of Empire*, edited by S. Goldhill, 154–94. Cambridge: Cambridge University Press. https://doi.org/10.1017/CBO9780511627323

Gombrich, E. 1977. *Art and Illusion: A Study in the Psychology of Pictorial Representation*. 5th ed. London: Phaidon.

Gow, A. S. F. 1952. *Theocritus*. Cambridge: Cambridge University Press.

Gowers, E. 2001. "Apuleius and Persius." In Kahane and Laird, *Companion to the Prologue of "Metamorphoses,"* 77–87.

Gowers, E. 2012. *Horace: "Satires" Book 1*. Cambridge: Cambridge University Press.

Graver, M. 2016. "Anatomies of Joy: Seneca and the *Gaudium* Tradition." In *Hope, Joy, and Affection in the Classical World*, edited by R. Caston and R. Kaster, 123–42. Oxford: Oxford University Press. https://doi.org/10.1093/acprof:oso/97801902782 98.001.0001

Graverini, L. 2001. "L'incontro di Lucio e Fotide: Stratificazioni intertestuali in Apul. *Met.* II 6–7." *Athenaeum* 89: 425–46.

Graverini, L. 2002. "Corinth, Rome, and Africa: A Cultural Background for the Tale of the Ass." In Paschalis and Frangoulidis, *Space in the Ancient Novel*, 58–77.

Graverini, L. 2010. "Amore, 'dolcezza,' stupore: Romanzo antico e filosofia." In *"Lector, intende, laetaberis": Il romanzo dei Greci e dei Romani*. Atti del Convegno Nazionale di Studi, Torino, 27–28 Aprile 2009, Allesandria, edited by R. Uglione, 57–88. Torino: Editore dell' Orso.

Graverini, L. 2012a. *Literature and Identity in the "Golden Ass" of Apuleius*. Translated by B. T. Lee (= 2007. *Le "Metamorfosi" di Apuleio: Letteratura e identità*. Pisa: Ospedaletto). Columbus: Ohio State University Press. https://doi.org/10.2307/j.ctv17h m7wb

Graverini, L. 2012b. "*Prudentia* and *Providentia*: Book XI in Context." In *AAGA* 3, 86–106.

Graverini, L. 2013. "Come si deve leggere un romanzo: Narratori, personaggi e lettori nelle *Metamorphosi* di Apuleio." In *Collected Studies on the Roman Novel*, edited by M. Carmignani, L. Graverini, and B. T. Lee, 119–39. Córdoba: Editorial Brujas.

Graverini, L., W. Keulen, and A. Barchiesi, eds. 2006. *Il romanzo antico: Forme, testi, problemi*. Roma: Carocci editore.

Graverini, L., and L. Nicolini, eds. 2019. *Apuleio "Metamorfosi."* Vol. 1, *Libri 1–3*. Rome: Fondazione Lorenzo Valla.

Grethlein, J. 2015. "Aesthetic Experiences, Ancient and Modern." *New Literary History* 46.2: 309–33.

Grethlein, J. 2017. *Aesthetic Experiences and Classical Antiquity: The Significance of Form in Narratives and Pictures*. Cambridge: Cambridge University Press. https://doi.org /10.1017/9781108131582

Grethlein, J. 2020. "World and Words: The Limits to *Mimesis* and Immersion in Heliodorus' *Ethiopica*." In Grethlein, Huitink, and Tagliabue, *Experience, Narrative, and Criticism*, 127–47.

Grethlein, J. 2021. *The Ancient Aesthetics of Deception: The Ethics of Enchantment from Gorgias to Heliodorus*. Cambridge: Cambridge University Press. https://doi.org/10 .1017/9781009003513

Grethlein, J., and L. Huitink. 2017. "Homer's Vividness: An Enactive Approach." *JHS* 137: 67–91.

Grethlein, J., L. Huitink, and A. Tagliabue, eds. 2020. *Experience, Narrative, and Criticism in Ancient Greece: Under the Spell of Stories*. Oxford: Oxford University Press. https://doi.org/10.1093/oso/9780198848295.001.0001

Grethlein, J., and M. Squire. 2014. "'Counterfeit in Character but Persuasive in Appear-

ance': Reviewing the *ainigma* of the *Tabula Cebetis*." *CP* 109.4: 285–324. https://doi
.org/10.1086/677858

Grillo, L. 2023. "The Early Reception of Apuleius: An Echo in Tertullian." *CQ* 72.2: 799–
804. https://doi.org/10.1017/S0009838822000532

Grimal, P. 1985. "Apulée, conteur romain." *Vita Latina* 99: 2–10.

Griswold, C. 1986. *Self-Knowledge in Plato's "Phaedrus."* New Haven: Yale University
Press.

Gumbrecht, H. U. 1975. "Konsequenzen der Rezeptionsästhetik oder Literaturewissenschaft als Komunikationssoziologie." *Poetica* 7.3–4: 388–413.

Gumbrecht, H. U. 2004. *Production of Presence: What Meaning Cannot Convey*. Stanford: Stanford University Press.

Gwyn Griffiths, J. 1975. *Apuleius of Madauros: The Isis-Book*. Leiden: Brill.

Habermehl, P. 1996. "*Quaedam divinae mediae potestates*: Demonology in Apuleius' *De
deo Socratis*." In *Groningen Colloquia on the Novel 7*, edited by H. Hofmann and M.
Zimmerman, 117–42. Groningen: E. Forsten.

Habinek, T. 1990. "Lucius' Rite of Passage." *MD* 25: 49–69.

Haffner, M. 2013. "τί ποτε αὕτη ἡ μυθολογία δύναται: Die Macht der Rede in der *Tabula
Cebetis*." *Hermes* 141.1: 65–82.

Hägg, T. 1983. *The Novel in Antiquity*. Berkeley: University of California Press.

Hägg, T. 1994. "Orality, Literacy and the 'Readership' of the Early Greek Novel." In *Contexts of Pre-Novel Narrative: The European Tradition*, edited by R. Eriksen, 47–81.
Berlin: de Gruyter.

Hall, J. 1981. *Lucian's Satire*. New York: Arno Press.

Halliwell, S. 1988. *Plato "Republic" 10*. Warminster: Aris and Phillips.

Halliwell, S. 2002. *The Aesthetics of Mimesis*. Princeton: Princeton University Press.

Halliwell, S. 2007. "The Life-and-Death Journey of the Soul: Interpreting the Myth of Er."
In *The Cambridge Companion to Plato's "Republic,"* edited by G. R. F. Ferrari, 445–73.
Cambridge: Cambridge University Press. https://doi.org/10.1017/CCOL052183
9637

Halliwell, S. 2011. *Between Ecstasy and Truth: Interpretations of Greek Poetics from Homer
to Longinus*. Oxford: Oxford University Press.

Halperin, D. 1986. "Plato and Erotic Reciprocity." *CA* 5.1: 60–80.

Hardie, P. 1988. "Lucretius and the Delusions of Narcissus." *MD* 20/21: 71–89.

Hardie, P. 2002. *Ovid's Poetics of Illusion*. Cambridge: Cambridge University Press.

Harrauer, C. 1973. "Kommentar zum Isisbuch des Apuleius." PhD diss., Universität
Wien.

Harrison, S. J. 1990. "The Speaking Book: The Prologue to Apuleius' *Metamorphoses*."
CQ 40.2: 507–13. https://doi.org/10.1017/s000983880004307x

Harrison, S. J. 1998a. "The Milesian Tales and the Roman Novel." In Hofmann and Zimmerman, *Groningen Colloquia on the Novel*. Vol. 9, 61–73.

Harrison, S. J. 1998b. "Some Epic Structures in *Cupid and Psyche*." In *AAGA* 2, 51–68.

322 BIBLIOGRAPHY

Harrison, S. J. 2000. *Apuleius: A Latin Sophist.* Oxford: Oxford University Press.

Harrison, S. J. 2008. "The Sophist at Play in Court: Apuleius' *Apology* and His Literary Career." In Riess, *Paideia at Play*, 3–15.

Harrison, S. J. 2012. "Interpreting the *anteludia* (Apuleius *Metamorphoses* 11.8)." *Trends in Classics* 4: 377–87.

Harrison, S. J. 2013a. *Framing the Ass: Literary Texture in Apuleius' "Metamorphoses."* New York: Oxford University Press.

Harrison, S. J. 2013b. "Heroic Traces: Theseus and Hercules in Apuleius' *Metamorphoses.*" In *Collected Studies on the Roman Novel*, edited by M. Carmignani, L. Graverini, and B. T. Lee, 141–55. Córdoba: Editorial Brujas.

Harrison, S. J., and M. Winterbottom. 2001. "The Prologue to Apuleius' *Metamorphoses*: Text, Translation, and Textual Commentary." In Kahane and Laird, *Companion to the Prologue of "Metamorphoses,"* 9–16.

Havelock, C. 1995. *The Aphrodite of Knidos and Her Successors: A Historical Review of the Female Nude in Greek Art.* Ann Arbor: University of Michigan Press. https://doi.org/10.3998/mpub.14837

Haynes, M. 2013. "Framing a View of the Unvieweable: Architecture, Aphrodite, and Erotic Looking in the Lucianic *Erōtes.*" *Helios* 40.1–2: 71–95. https://doi.org/10.1353/hel.2013.0010

Heath, J. 1982. "Narration and Nutrition in Apuleius' *Metamorphoses.*" *Ramus* 10.1: 57–77. https://doi.org/10.1017/s0048671x00005208

Heath, J. 1992. *Actaeon, the Unmannerly Intruder: The Myth and Its Meaning in Classical Literature.* Lewiston: Peter Lang.

Heath, M. 2007. Review of *The School of Libanius in Late-Antique Antioch*, by R. Cribiore. *Rhetorical Review* 5.3: 4–9.

Heffernan, J. 1993. *The Museum of Words: The Poetics of Ekphrasis from Homer to Ashberry.* Chicago: University of Chicago Press.

Helm, R. 1910. *Apulei Opera Quae Supersunt. II.2. Florida.* Leipzig: Teubner.

Helm, R. 1927. "Lukianos: Epigramme." *RE* 13: 1725–78.

Helm, R. 1931. *Apulei Opera quae supersunt I: Met. Libri XI.* Leipzig: Teubner.

Helm, R. 1955. "Apuleius' *Apologie*: Ein Meisterwerk der zweiten Sophistik." *Das Altertum* 1: 86–108.

Hercher, R. 1869. "Τῆς Χαρικλείας ἑρμήνευμα τῆς σώφρονος ἐκ φωνῆς Φιλίππου τοῦ φιλοσόφου." *Hermes* 3.3: 382–88.

Herman, D. 2013. *Storytelling and the Sciences of Mind.* Cambridge, MA: MIT Press.

Hermann, F.-G. 2007. "Longus' Imitation: *Mimesis* in the Education of *Daphnis and Chloe.*" In Morgan and Jones, *Philosophical Presences in the Ancient Novel*, 205–30.

Herrero de Jáuregui, M. 2022. "Back to a Classic Debate: Conversion and Salvation in Ancient Mystery Cults?" In Despotis and Löhr, *Religious and Philosophical Conversion*, 407–26.

Hijmans, B. L. 1978. "Significant Names and Their Function in Apuleius' *Metamorphoses.*" In *AAGA 1*, 107–22.

Hijmans, B. L. 1987. "Apuleius: *Philosophus Platonicus.*" *ANRW* 2.31.1: 395–475.

Hillgruber, M. 1994. *Die pseudoplutarchische Schrift "De Homero."* Vol. 1. Stuttgart: Teubner.

Hindermann, J. 2009. "The Elegiac Ass: The Concept of *servitium amoris* in Apuleius' *Metamorphoses.*" *Ramus* 38.1: 75–84. https://doi.org/10.1017/s0048671x00000643

Hindermann, J. 2010. "Does Lucius Really Fail to Learn from Socrates' Fate? Elegiac Themes in Apuleius' *Metamorphoses* (books 1–3)." *CW* 104.1: 77–88.

Hinds, S. 1998. *Allusion and Intertext: Dynamics of Appropriation in Roman Poetry.* Cambridge: Cambridge University Press.

Hodges, V. Forthcoming. "The *Mulier Equitans*: Erotic Choreography and the *Meretrix* in Apuleius' *Metamorphoses.*" In *Materiality in Ancient Narrative*, edited by E. Adkins and E. Cueva. Groningen: Barkhuis.

Hoenig, C. 2018a. *Plato's "Timaeus" and the Latin Tradition.* Cambridge: Cambridge University Press. https://doi.org/10.1017/9781108235211

Hoenig, C. 2018b. Review of *A New Text of Apuleius: The Lost Third Book of the "De Platone,"* by Justin Stover. *CP* 113.2: 227–32.

Hofmann, H., and M. Zimmerman, eds. 1997. *Groningen Colloquia on the Novel* 8. Groningen: E. Forsten.

Hofmann, H., and M. Zimmerman, eds. 1998. *Groningen Colloquia on the Novel* 9. Groningen: E. Forsten.

Höistad, R. 1948. *Cynic Hero and Cynic King: Studies in the Cynic Conception of Man.* Uppsala: B. H. Blackwell.

Holub, R. 2008. "Reception Theory: School of Constance." In *Literary Criticism.* Vol. 3, *From Formalism to Poststructuralism*, edited by R. Selden, 319–46. Cambridge: Cambridge University Press. https://doi.org/10.1017/CHOL9780521300131.013

Holzmeister, A. 2014. "*Ekphrasis* in the Ancient Novel." In Cueva and Byrne, *Companion to the Ancient Novel*, 411–24.

Hooker, W. 1955. "Apuleius' *Cupid and Psyche* as a Platonic Myth." *Bucknell Review* 5.3: 24–38.

Howley, J. 2018. *Aulus Gellius and Roman Reading Culture: Text, Presence, and Imperial Knowledge in the "Noctes Atticae."* Cambridge: Cambridge University Press. https://doi.org/10.1017/9781108186810

Huitink, L. 2019. "*Enargeia*, Enactivism and the Ancient Readerly Imagination." In *Distributed Cognition in Classical Antiquity*, edited by M. Anderson, D. Cairns, and M. Sprevak, 169–89. Edinburgh: Edinburgh University Press.

Huitink, L. 2020. "*Enargeia* and Bodily *Mimesis.*" In Grethlein, Huitink, and Tagliabue, *Experience, Narrative, and Criticism*, 188–209.

Hunink, V. 1997. *Apuleius of Madauros, "Pro se de magia."* Vols. 1 and 2. Amsterdam: J. C. Gieben.

Hunink, V. 2002. "The Date of Apuleius' Metamorphoses." In *Hommages à Carl Deroux.* Vol. 2, *Prose et linguistique, médecine*, edited by Pol Defosse, 224–35. Brussels: Latomus.

Hunink, V. 2004. "Plutarch and Apuleius." In *The Statesman in Plutarch's Works*. Vol. 1, *Plutarch's Statesman and His Aftermath: Political, Philosophical, and Literary Aspects*, edited by L. de Blois, J. Bons, T. Kessels, and D. M. Schenkeveld, 249–60. Leiden: Brill.

Hunink, V. 2006. "The *spurcum additamentum* (Apul. *Met.* 10.21) Once Again." In Keulen, Nauta, and Panayotakis, *Lectiones Scrupulosae*, 266–80.

Hunter, R. L. 1985. *The New Comedy of Greece and Rome*. Cambridge: Cambridge University Press. https://doi.org/10.1017/CBO9780511627361

Hunter, R. L. 1997. "Longus and Plato." In *Der antike Roman und seine mittelalterliche Rezeption*, edited by M. Picone and B. Zimmermann, 15–28. Basel: Birkhäuser.

Hunter, R. L. 2004. *Plato's "Symposium."* Oxford: Oxford University Press.

Hunter, R. L. 2005. "'Philip the Philosopher' on the *Aithiopika* of Heliodorus." In *Metaphor and the Ancient Novel*, edited by S. J. Harrison, M. Paschalis, and S. Frangoulidis, 123–38. Groningen: Barkhuis.

Hunter, R. L. 2006. "Plato's *Symposium* and the Traditions of Ancient Fiction." In *Plato's "Symposium": Issues in Interpretation and Reception*, edited by J. Lesher, D. Nails, and F. Sheffield, 295–312. Washington, DC: Center for Hellenic Studies.

Hunter, R. L. 2008. "Ancient Readers." In Whitmarsh, *Cambridge Companion to the Greek and Roman Novel*, 261–71.

Hunter, R. L. 2009a. *Critical Moments in Classical Literature: Studies in the Ancient View of Literature and Its Uses*. Cambridge: Cambridge University Press. https://doi.org/10.1017/CBO9780511729997

Hunter, R. L. 2009b. "The Curious Incident . . . : *polypragmosynê* and the Ancient Novel." In *Readers and Writers in the Ancient Novel*, edited by M. Paschalis, S. Panayotakis, and G. Schmeling, 51–63. Groningen: Barkhuis.

Hunter, R. L. 2012. *Plato and the Traditions of Ancient Literature: The Silent Stream*. Cambridge: Cambridge University Press. https://doi.org/10.1017/CBO9781139003377

Hunter, R. L. 2014a. *Hesiodic Voices: Studies in the Ancient Reception of Hesiod's "Works and Days."* Cambridge: Cambridge University Press. https://doi.org/10.1017/CBO9781107110816

Hunter, R. L. 2014b. "Horace's Other *Ars Poetica*: *Epistles* 1.2 and Ancient Homeric Criticism." *MD* 72: 19–42.

Hunter, R. L. 2018. *The Measure of Homer: The Ancient Reception of the "Iliad" and the "Odyssey."* Cambridge: Cambridge University Press. https://doi.org/10.1017/9781108604277

Iser, W. 1974. *The Implied Reader: Patterns in Communication in Prose Fiction from Bunyan to Beckett*. Baltimore: Johns Hopkins University Press.

Iser, W. 1978. *The Act of Reading: A Theory of Aesthetic Response*. Baltimore: Johns Hopkins University Press.

Iser, W. 1980. "The Reading Process: A Phenomenological Approach." In Tompkins, *Reader-Response Criticism*, 50–69.

Iser, W. 1989. *Prospecting: From Reader Response to Literary Anthropology.* Baltimore: Johns Hopkins University Press.

Jahn, M. 1997. "Frames, Preferences, and the Reading of Third-Person Narratives: Towards a Cognitive Narratology." *Poetics Today* 18.4: 441–68. https://doi.org/10.23 07/1773182

James, P. 1987. *Unity in Diversity: A Study of Apuleius' "Metamorphoses" with Particular Reference to the Narrator's Art of Transformation and the Metamorphosis Motif in the Tale of Cupid and Psyche.* Hildesheim: Olms-Weidmann.

James, P. 1998. "The Unbearable Lightness of Being: *Levis Amor* in the *Metamorphoses* of Apuleius." In *AAGA* 2, 35–50.

Janson, T. 1964. *Latin Prose Prefaces: Studies in Literary Conventions.* Stockholm: Almqvist och Wiksell.

Janzsó, M. 2017. "*Tabula Cebetis* and Christianity." *Chronica* 17: 37–43.

Jauss, H.-R. 1982a. *Aesthetic Experience and Literary Hermeneutics.* Translated by M. Shaw (=*Ästhetische Erfahrung und literarische Hermeneutik.* München). Minneapolis: University of Minnesota Press.

Jauss, H.-R. 1982b. "Der poetische Text im Horizonwandel der Lektüre (Baudelaire's Gedicht: 'Spleen II')." *Romanistische Zeitschrift für Literaturgeschichte* 4: 228–74.

Johnson, W. A. 2010. *Readers and Reading Culture in the High Roman Empire: A Study of Elite Communities.* Oxford: Oxford University Press. https://doi.org/10.1093/acprof: oso/9780195176407.001.0001

Joly, R. 1963. *Le tableau de Cébès et la philosophie religieuse.* Brussels: Latomus.

Jones, C. P. 1984. "Tarsos in the *Amores* Ascribed to Lucian." *GRBS* 25.2: 177–81.

Jones, C. P. 1986. *Culture and Society in Lucian.* Cambridge, MA: Harvard University Press. https://doi.org/10.4159/harvard.9780674181328

Jones, C. P. *Apuleius: "Apologia," "Florida," "De Deo Socratis."* Cambridge, MA: Harvard University Press.

Jope, J. 2011. "Interpretation and Authenticity of the Lucianic *Erotes*." *Helios* 38.1: 103–20. https://doi.org/10.1353/hel.2011.0004

Kahane, A. 2007. "Disjoining Meaning and Truth: History, Representation, Apuleius' *Metamorphoses* and Neoplatonist Aesthetics." In Morgan and Jones, *Philosophical Presences in the Ancient Novel*, 245–70.

Kahane, A., and A. Laird, eds. 2001. *A Companion to the Prologue of Apuleius' "Metamorphoses."* Oxford: Oxford University Press.

Kaiser, E. 1964. "Odyssee-Szenen als Topoi." *Museum Helveticum* 21: 109–36.

Kaklamanou, E., M. Pavlou, and A. Tsakmakis, eds. 2020. *Framing the Dialogues: How to Read Openings and Closures in Plato.* Leiden: Brill. https://doi.org/10.1163/9789004 443990

Kamen, D., and S. Levin-Richardson. 2015. "Revisiting Roman Sexuality: Agency and the Conceptualization of Penetrated Males." In *Sex in Antiquity: Exploring Gender and Sexuality in the Ancient World*, edited by M. Masterson, N. Rabinowitz, and J. Robson, 449–60. New York: Routledge.

Kelting, E. 2021. "'Characterizing' Lucius: Pythagoreanism and the *Figura* in Apuleius' *Metamorphoses*." *AJP* 142.1: 103–36. https://doi.org/10.1353/ajp.2021.0003

Kennedy, D. 2020. "Metalepsis and Metaphysics." In *Metalepsis: Ancient Texts, New Perspectives*, edited by S. Matzner and G. Trimble, 223–45. Oxford: Oxford University Press. https://doi.org/10.1093/oso/9780198846987.001.0001

Kenney, E. J. 1990a. *Apuleius: Cupid and Psyche*. Cambridge: Cambridge University Press.

Kenney, E. J. 1990b. "Psyche and Her Mysterious Husband." In *Antonine Literature*, edited by D. A. Russell, 175–98. Oxford: Oxford University Press.

Kenney, E. J. 2003. "In the Mill with Slaves: Lucius Looks Back in Gratitude." *TAPhA* 133: 159–92. https://doi.org/10.1353/apa.2003.0007

Kenny, B. 1974. "The Reader's Role in *The Golden Ass*." *Arethusa* 7.2: 187–209.

Ker, J. 2009. "Outside and Inside: Senecan Strategies." In *Writing Politics in Imperial Rome*, edited by W. J. Dominik, J. Garthwaite, and P. A. Roche, 249–71. Leiden: Brill. https://doi.org/10.1163/9789004217133

Kerényi, K. 1927. *Die griechisch-orientalische Romanliteratur in religions-geschichtlicher Beleuchtung*. Tübingen: J. C. B. Mohr.

Keulen, W. 2000. "Significant Names in Apuleius: A 'Good Contriver' and His Rival in the Cheese Trade (*Met.* 1, 5)." Apuleiana Groningana 10. *Mnemosyne* 53.3: 310–21.

Keulen, W. 2003. "Comic Invention and Superstitious Frenzy in Apuleius' *Metamorphoses*: The Figurc of Socrates as an Icon of Satirical Self-Exposure." *AJP* 124.1: 107–35. https://doi.org/10.1353/ajp.2003.0021

Keulen, W. 2004. "Lucius' Kinship Diplomacy: Plutarchan Reflections in an Apuleian Character." In *The Statesman in Plutarch's Works*. Vol. 1, *Plutarch's Statesman and His Aftermath: Political, Philosophical, and Literary Aspects*, edited by L. de Blois, J. Bons, T. Kessels, and D. M. Schenkeveld, 261–74. Leiden: Brill. https://doi.org/10.11 63/9789047413820_023

Keulen, W. 2006. "*Ad amussim congruentia*: Measuring the Intellectual in Apuleius." In Keulen, Nauta, and Panayotakis, *Lectiones Scrupulosae*, 168–202.

Keulen, W. 2007. "*Vocis immutatio*: The Apuleian Prologue and the Pleasures and Pitfalls of Vocal Versatility." In *Seeing Tongues, Hearing Scripts: Orality and Representation in the Ancient Novel*, edited by V. Rimell, 106–37. Groningen: Barkhuis.

Keulen, W. 2009. *Gellius the Satirist: Roman Cultural Authority in "Attic Nights."* Leiden: Brill. https://doi.org/10.1163/ej.9789004169869.i-364

Keulen, W. 2015. "*Lubrico virentis aetatulae*: Lucius as Initiate (*Metamorphoses* Book 11)." In *Characterization in Apuleius' "Metamorphoses": Nine Studies*, edited by S. J. Harrison, 29–55. Newcastle upon Tyne: Cambridge Scholars.

Keulen, W., R. Nauta, and S. Panayotakis, eds. 2006. *Lectiones Scrupulosae: Essays on the Text and Interpretation of Apuleius' "Metamorphoses" in Honour of Maaike Zimmerman*. Groningen: Barkhuis.

Kindt, J. 2012. *Rethinking Greek Religion*. Cambridge: Cambridge University Press. https://doi.org/10.1017/CBO9780511978500

Kirichenko, A. 2007. "Writing like a Clown: Apuleius' Metafiction and Plautus' Metatheater." *GFA* 10: 259–71.

Kirichenko, A. 2008a. "*Asinus Philosophans*: Platonic Philosophy and the Prologue to Apuleius' *Golden Ass*." *Mnemosyne* 61.1: 89–107. https://doi.org/10.1163/156852507x1 69636

Kirichenko, A. 2008b. "Satire, Propaganda, and the Pleasure of Reading: Apuleius' Stories of Curiosity in Context." *HSPh* 104: 339–71.

Kirichenko, A. 2010. *A Comedy of Storytelling: Theatricality and Narrative in Apuleius' "Golden Ass."* Heidelberg: Winter.

Kirichenko, A. 2013. "Mimesis, Metamorphosis, and False Closure in Apuleius' *Golden Ass.*" In *The Door Ajar: False Closure in Greek and Roman Literature and Art*, edited by F. Grewing, B. Acosta-Hughes, and A. Kirichenko, 277–308. Heidelberg: Winter.

König, J. 2007. "Fragmentation and Coherence in Plutarch's *Sympotic Questions.*" In *Ordering Knowledge in the Roman Empire*, edited by J. König and T. Whitmarsh, 43–68. Cambridge: Cambridge University Press. https://doi.org/10.1017/CBO9780 511551062

König, J. 2008. "Body and Text in the Greek and Roman Novels." In Whitmarsh, *Cambridge Companion to the Greek and Roman Novel*, 127–44.

Koning, H. 2010. *Hesiod: The Other Poet*. Leiden: Brill. https://doi.org/10.1163/ej.97890 04186163.i-440

Konstan, D. 2004. "'The Birth of the Reader': Plutarch as a Literary Critic." *Scholia* 13.1: 3–27.

Konstan, D. 2009. "The Active Reader and the Ancient Novel." In *Readers and Writers in the Ancient Novel*, edited by M. Paschalis, S. Panayotakis, and G. Schmeling, 1–17. Groningen: Barkhuis.

Konstan, D. 2010. *Before Forgiveness: The Origins of a Moral Idea*. Cambridge: Cambridge University Press. https://doi.org/10.1017/CBO9780511762857

Konstan, D. 2018. "Comedy and the Athenian Ideal." In *The Hellenistic Reception of Classical Athenian Democracy and Political Thought*, edited by M. Canevaro and B. D. Gray, 109–21. Oxford: Oxford University Press. https://doi.org/10.1093/oso/978019 8748472.001.0001

Kornhardt, H. 1936. "*Exemplum*: Eine bedeutungsgeschichtliche Studie." PhD diss., Göttingen.

Krabbe, J. K. 1989. *The "Metamorphoses" of Apuleius*. New York: Peter Lang.

Krabbe, J. K. 2003. *Lusus Iste: Apuleius' "Metamorphoses."* Washington, DC: University Press of America.

Krieger, M. 1992. *Ekphrasis: The Illusion of the Natural Sign*. Baltimore: Johns Hopkins University Press.

Kukkonen, K. 2013. *Contemporary Comics Storytelling*. Lincoln: University of Nebraska Press.

Kukkonen, K. 2014. "Presence and Prediction: The Embodied Reader's Cascades of Cognition." *Style* 48.3: 367–84. https://www.jstor.org/stable/10.5325/style.48.3.367

Kukkonen, K., and M. Caracciolo. 2014. "What Is the 'Second Generation'?" *Style* 48.3: 261–74. https://www.jstor.org/stable/10.5325/style.48.3.261

Labhardt, A. 1960. "*Curiositas*: Notes sur l'histoire d'un mot et d'une notion." *Museum Helveticum* 17.4: 206–24.

Lada-Richards, I. 2005. "'In the Mirror of the Dance': A Lucianic Metaphor in Its Performative and Ethical Contexts." *Mnemosyne* 58.3: 335–57. https://doi.org/10.1163/1568 525054796854

Laird, A. 1993. "Sounding Out Ecphrasis: Art and Text in Catullus 64." *JRS* 83: 18–30. https://doi.org/10.2307/300976

Laird, A. 1997. "Description and Divinity in Apuleius' *Metamorphoses*." In Hofmann and Zimmerman, *Groningen Colloquia on the Novel* 8, 59–86.

Laird, A. 2001. "Paradox and Transcendence: The Prologue as the End." In Kahane and Laird, *Companion to the Prologue of "Metamorphoses*," 267–81.

Laird, A. 2003. "Fiction as a Discourse of Philosophy in Lucian's *Verae Historiae*." In Panayotakis, Zimmerman, and Keulen, *The Ancient Novel and Beyond*, 115–28.

Lamberton, R. 1986. *Homer the Theologian: Neoplatonist Allegorical Reading and the Growth of the Epic Tradition.* Berkeley: University of California Press.

Lamberton, R., and J. J. Keaney, eds. 1992. *Homer's Ancient Readers: The Hermeneutics of Greek Epic's Earliest Exegetes.* Princeton: Princeton University Press. https://doi.org /10.1515/9780691197678

Lancel, S. 1961. "'Curiositas' et préoccupations spirituelles chez Apulée." *RHR* 160.1: 25–46. https://doi.org/10.3406/rhr.1961.7663

La Penna, A. 1985. "Una novella di Apuleio e l'Iliupersis Virgiliana." *Maia* 37: 145–48.

La Rocca, A. 2005. *Il filosofo e la città: Commento storico ai "Florida" di Apuleio.* Roma: L'Erma.

Lateiner, D. 2001. "Humiliation and Immobility in Apuleius' *Metamorphoses*." *TAPhA* 131.1: 217–55. https://doi.org/10.1353/apa.2001.0013

Lee, B. T. 2005. *Apuleius' "Florida": A Commentary.* Berlin: de Gruyter. https://doi.org /10.1515/9783110894059

Lee, B. T., E. Finkelpearl, and L. Graverini, eds. 2014. *Apuleius and Africa.* London: Routledge. https://doi.org/10.4324/9780203105504

Leigh, M. 2012. "*De brevitate vitae*: Seneca e il mondo romano." In *Letteratura e Civitas: Transizioni dalla Repubblica all'Impero*, edited by M. Citroni, 341–51. Pisa: Edizioni ETS.

Leigh, M. 2013. *From Polypragmōn to Curiosus: Ancient Concepts of Curious and Meddlesome Behaviour.* Oxford: Oxford University Press. https://doi.org/10.1093/acprof:o so/9780199668618.001.0001

Leitao, D. 2012. *The Pregnant Male as Myth and Metaphor in Classical Greek Literature.* Cambridge: Cambridge University Press. https://doi.org/10.1017/CBO978113908 3638

Leo, F. 1905. "Coniectanea." *Hermes* 40.4: 605–8.

BIBLIOGRAPHY   329

Lesky, A. 1941. "Apuleius von Madaura und Lukios von Patrai." *Hermes* 76: 43–74.

Lévi, N. 2014. *La révélation finale à Rome: Cicéron, Ovide, Apulée; Études sur le "Songe de Scipion," "De republica" VI, le discours de Pythagore, "Métamorphoses" XV et la théophanie d'Isis, "Métamorphoses" XI*. Paris: Presses de l'Université Paris-Sorbonne.

Lévi, N. 2018. "*MVLTISCIVS*: la conception apuléienne de la polymathie au miroir de la notion grecque de πολυμαθία." In *Les savoirs d'Apulée*, edited by E. Plantade and D. Vallat, 19–43. Hildesheim: Georg Olms Verlag.

Levine Gera, D. 1995. "Lucian's Choice: *Somnium* 6–16." In *Ethics and Rhetoric: Classical Essays for Donald Russell on His Seventy-fifth Birthday*, edited by D. Innes, H. M. Hine, and C. B. R. Pelling, 237–50. Oxford: Oxford University Press. https://doi.org/10.1093/oso/9780198149620.001.0001

Libby, B. 2011. "Moons, Smoke, and Mirrors in Apuleius' Portrayal of Isis." *AJP* 132.2: 301–22. https://doi.org/10.1353/ajp.2011.0017

Lodge, D. 1984. *Small World: An Academic Romance*. New York: Penguin.

Long, A. A. 1992. "Stoic Readings of Homer." In Lamberton and Keaney, *Homer's Ancient Readers*, 41–66.

Lu Hsu, K. 2020. *The Violent Hero: Heracles in the Greek Imagination*. London: Bloomsbury Academic.

Luzzatto, M. T. 1996. "Dialettica o retorica? La *polytropia* di Odisseo da Antistene a Porfirio." *Elenchos* 17: 275–357.

Lytle, E. 2003. "Apuleius' *Metamorphoses* and the *spurcum additamentum* (10.21)." *CP* 98.4: 349–65. https://doi.org/10.1086/422371

MacDougall, B. 2016. "The Book of Isis and the Myth of Er." *AJP* 137.2: 251–85. https://doi.org/10.1353/ajp.2016.0012

Macleod, M. D. 1967. *Lucian VIII*. Cambridge, MA: Loeb Classical Library.

Magnaldi, G. 2020. *Apulei: Opera philosophica*. Oxford: Oxford University Press. https://doi.org/10.1093/actrade/9780198841418.book.1

Malherbe, A. J. 2013. "Heracles." In *Light from the Gentiles: Hellenistic Philosophy and Early Christianity; Collected Essays, 1959–2012*, edited by C. R. Holladay, J. T. Fitzgerald, J. W. Thompson, and G. E. Sterling, 651–74. Leiden: Brill. https://doi.org/10.1163/9789004256521

Marangoni, C. 1974–75. "Il nome Asinio Marcello e i misteri di Osiride (Apul. *Metam.* XI 27)." *AAPat* 87.3: 333–37.

Marchetti, S. C. 2004. "I precetti paterni e le lezioni dei filosofi: Demea, il padre di Orazio ed altri padri e figli." *MD* 53: 9–63.

Marcovich, M. 1986. "The Isis with Seven Robes." *ZPE* 64: 295–96.

Marincic, M. 2007. "Advertising One's Own Story: Text and Speech in Achilles Tatius' *Leucippe and Clitophon*." In *Seeing Tongues, Hearing Scripts: Orality and Representation in the Ancient Novel*, edited by V. Rimell, 168–200. Groningen: Barkhuis.

Martijn, M. 2022. "Colourful Planets: The Reception of an Astronomical Detail in the Myth of Er." *Mnemosyne* 75.1: 145–68.

Martin, R. H. 1976. *Terence: "Adelphoe."* Cambridge: Cambridge University Press.

Mason, H. J. 1994. "Greek and Latin Versions of the Ass Story." *ANRW* 2.34.2: 1665–1707. https://doi.org/10.1515/9783110851403-018

Massaro, M. 1977. "*Aniles fabellae.*" *SIFC* 49: 104–35.

Mathis, A. G. 2008. "Playing with Elegy: Tales of Lovers in Books 1 and 2 of Apuleius' *Metamorphoses.*" In Riess, *Paideia at Play*, 195–214.

May, R. 2006. *Apuleius and Drama: The Ass on Stage.* Oxford: Oxford University Press. https://doi.org/10.1093/acprof:oso/9780199202928.001.0001

May, R. 2008. "The Metamorphosis of Pantomime: Apuleius' *Judgement of Paris* (*Met.* 10.30–34)." In *New Directions in Ancient Pantomime*, edited by E. Hall and R. Wyles, 338–62. Oxford: Oxford University Press. https://doi.org/10.1093/acprof:oso/97801 99232536.001.0001

May, R. 2013. *Apuleius: "Metamorphoses" or "The Golden Ass." Book 1.* Warminster: Aris and Phillips.

May, R. 2019. "Apuleius' Photis: Comic Slave or Elegiac Mistress?" In *Slaves and Masters in the Ancient Novel*, edited by S. Panayotakis and M. Paschalis, 203–20. Groningen: Barkhuis.

Mayer, R. 1991. "Roman Historical Exempla in Seneca." In *Sénèque et la prose latine*, edited by B. L. Hijmans and P. Grimal, 141–69. Foundation Hardt: Genève.

Mayer, R. 1994. *Horace: "Epistles" Book 1.* Cambridge: Cambridge University Press.

McCarty, W. 1989. "The Shape of the Mirror: Metaphorical Catoptrics." *Arethusa* 22.2: 161–95.

McGlathery, D. B. 1998. "Reversal of Platonic Love in Petronius' *Satyricon.*" In *Rethinking Sexuality: Foucault and Classical Antiquity*, edited by D. H. J. Larmour, P. A. Miller, and C. Platter. 204–27. Princeton: Princeton University Press.

Merkelbach, R. 1962. *Roman und Mysterium in der Antike.* Munich: C. H. Beck.

Michalopoulos, A. 2016. "Homer in Love: Homeric Reception in Propertius and Ovid." In *Homeric Receptions across Generic and Cultural Contexts*, edited by A. Efstathiou and I. Karamanou, 289–302. Berlin: de Gruyter. https://doi.org/10.1515/978311047 9799

Mitchell, W. J. T. 1986. *Iconology: Image, Text, Ideology.* Chicago: University of Chicago Press.

Mitchell, W. J. T. 1994. *Picture Theory: Essays on Verbal and Visual Representation.* Chicago: University of Chicago Press.

Moles, J. 1985. "Cynicism in Horace *Epistles* I." *PLLS* 5: 33–60.

Montiglio, S. 2005. *Wandering in Ancient Greek Culture.* Chicago: University of Chicago Press.

Montiglio, S. 2007. "You Can't Go Home Again: Lucius' Journey in Apuleius' *Metamorphoses* Set against the Background of the *Odyssey.*" *MD* 58: 93–113.

Montiglio, S. 2011. *From Villain to Hero: Odysseus in Ancient Thought.* Ann Arbor: University of Michigan Press. https://doi.org/10.3998/mpub.2802465

BIBLIOGRAPHY 331

Moore, H. 2020. *"Amadis" in English: A Study in the Reading of Romance.* Oxford: Oxford University Press. https://doi.org/10.1093/oso/9780198832423.001.0001

Morales, H. 1996. "The Torturer's Apprentice: Parrhasius and the Limits of Art." In Elsner, *Art and Text in Roman Culture,* 182–209.

Morales, H. 2004. *Vision and Narrative in Achilles Tatius' "Leucippe and Clitophon."* Cambridge: Cambridge University Press.

Moreschini, C. 1968. "Reminiscenze apuleiane nel *De Anima* di Tertulliano?" *Maia* 20: 19–20.

Moreschini, C. 1978. *Apuleio e il Platonismo.* Florence: Olschki.

Moreschini, C. 1989. "Divinazione e demonologia in Plutarcho e Apuleio." *Augustinianum* 89.1: 269–80.

Moreschini, C. 1994. *Il mito di Amore e Psiche in Apuleio: Saggio, testo di Apuleio, traduzione e commento.* Napoli: D'Auria.

Moreschini, C. 2015. *Apuleius and the Metamorphoses of Platonism.* Turnhout: Brepols. https://doi.org/10.1484/m.nutrix-eb.5.108555

Morgan, J. 2001. "The Prologues of the Greek Novels and Apuleius." In Kahane and Laird, *Companion to the Prologue of "Metamorphoses,"* 152–62.

Morgan, J. 2007. "The Representation of Philosophers in Greek Fiction." In Morgan and Jones, *Philosophical Presences in the Ancient Novel,* 23–52.

Morgan, J., and M. Jones, eds. 2007. *Philosophical Presences in the Ancient Novel.* Ancient Narrative Supplementum 10. Groningen: Barkhuis.

Morgan, K. 2012. "Theriomorphism and the Composite Soul in Plato." In *Plato and Myth,* edited by C. Collobert, P. Destrée, and F. J. Gonzalez, 323–42. Leiden: Brill. https://doi.org/10.1163/9789004224360

Münstermann, H. 1995. *Apuleius: Metamorphosen literarischer Vorlagen.* Stuttgart: de Gruyter.

Murgatroyd, P. 2004. "The Ending of Apuleius' *Metamorphoses.*" *CQ* 54.1: 319–21. https://doi.org/10.1093/cq/54.1.319

Murray, M. 2009. *The Poetics of Conversion in Early Modern English Literature: Verse and Change from Donne to Dryden.* Cambridge: Cambridge University Press. https://doi.org/10.1017/CBO9780511770562

Murray, P. 1996. *Plato on Poetry.* Cambridge: Cambridge University Press.

Naldini, M. 1984. *Basilio di Cesarea: Discorso ai Giovani.* Biblioteca Patristica. Florence: Nardini Editore.

Nesselrath, H.-G. 2005. "Von Kebes zu Pseudo-Kebes." In *Die Bildtafel des Kebes: Allegorie des Lebens,* edited by R. Hirsch-Luipold, B. Hirsch, R. Feldmeier, H.-G. Nesselrath, and L. Koch, 3–66. Darmstadt. Wissenschaftliche Buchgesellschaft.

Nethercut, W. R. 1968. "Apuleius' Literary Art: Resonance and Depth in the *Metamorphoses.*" *CJ* 64.3: 110–19.

Nicholson, G. 1999. *Plato's "Phaedrus": The Philosophy of Love.* West Lafayette: Purdue University Press.

Nicolini, L. 2010. "Due Proposte al Testo Delle Metamorfosi di Apuleio (5,28 e 11,23)." *Philologus* 154.1: 149–54.

Nicolini, L. 2012. "In Spite of Isis: Wordplay in *Metamorphoses* XI." In *AAGA* 3, 28–41.

Nightingale, A. 2004. *Spectacles of Truth in Classical Greek Philosophy: Theoria in Its Cultural Context.* Cambridge: Cambridge University Press. https://doi.org/10.1017/CBO9780511482564

Nì Mheallaigh, K. 2007. "Philosophical Framing: The *Phaedran* Setting of *Leucippe and Clitophon.*" In Morgan and Jones, *Philosophical Presences in the Ancient Novel,* 231–44.

Nì Mheallaigh, K. 2009. "Ec[h]oing the Ass-Novel: Reading and Desire in *Onos, Metamorphoses,* and *The Name of the Rose.*" *Ramus* 38.1: 109–22.

Nì Mheallaigh, K. 2014. *Reading Fiction with Lucian: Fakes, Freaks and Hyperreality.* Cambridge: Cambridge University Press. https://doi.org/10.1017/CBO9781139941594

Nock, A. D. 1933. *Conversion: The Old and the New in Religion from Alexander the Great to Augustine of Hippo.* Oxford: Oxford University Press.

Nünlist, R. 2009. *The Ancient Critic at Work: Terms and Concepts of Literary Criticism in Greek Scholia.* Cambridge: Cambridge University Press. https://doi.org/10.1017/CBO9780511575891

Nussbaum, M. 1993. "Poetry and the Passions: Two Stoic Views." In *Passions and Perceptions: Studies in Hellenistic Philosophy of Mind,* edited by J. Brunschwig and M. Nussbaum, 97–149. Cambridge: Cambridge University Press. https://doi.org/10.1017/CBO9780511470325

O'Brien, M. 2002. *Apuleius' Debt to Plato in the "Metamorphoses."* Lewiston: Peter Lang.

O'Brien, M. 2011. *"larvale simulacrum:* Platonic Socrates and the *Persona* of Socrates in Apuleius, *Metamorphoses* 1.1–19." In *Echoing Narratives: Studies of Intertextuality in Greek and Roman Prose Fiction,* edited by K. Doulamis, 123–38. Groningen: Barkhuis.

O'Brien, M., and P. James. 2006. "To Baldly Go: A Last Look at Lucius and His Counter-Humiliation Strategies." In Keulen, Nauta, and Panayotakis, *Lectiones Scrupulosae,* 234–51.

O'Connell, R. J. 1989. *St. Augustine's "Confessions": The Odyssey of Soul.* New York: Fordham University Press.

O'Connell, R. J. 1994. *Soundings in Augustine's Imagination.* New York: Fordham University Press.

O'Connell, R. J. 1996. *Images of Conversion in St. Augustine's "Confessions."* New York: Fordham University Press.

O'Connor, D. 2007. "Rewriting the Poets in Plato's Characters." In *The Cambridge Companion to Plato's "Republic,"* edited by G. R. F. Ferrari, 55–89. Cambridge: Cambridge University Press. https://doi.org/10.1017/CCOL0521839637

Olsen, S. 2012. "Maculate Conception: Sexual Ideology and Creative Authority in Heliodorus' *Aethiopica.*" *AJP* 133.2: 301–22. https://doi.org/10.1353/ajp.2012.0017

BIBLIOGRAPHY 333

O'Sullivan, N. 1992. *Alcidamas, Aristophanes, and the Beginnings of Greek Stylistic Theory*. Stuttgart: F. Steiner.

O'Sullivan, T. 2007. "Walking with Odysseus: The Portico Frame of the Odyssey Landscapes." *AJP* 128.4: 497–532. https://doi.org/10.1353/ajp.2008.0007

O'Sullivan, T. 2016. "Human and Asinine Postures in Apuleius' *Golden Ass*." *CJ* 112.2: 196–216. https://doi.org/10.1353/tcj.2016.0014

Oudendorp, F. 1776. *Apuleii opera omnia I: "Metamorphoseon" libri XI* (editionem paravit D. Ruhnken). Leiden: Van der Eyk et Vygh.

Panayotakis, C. 2001. "Vision and Light in Apuleius' Tale of Psyche and Her Mysterious Husband." *CQ* 51.2: 576–83. https://doi.org/10.1093/cq/51.2.576

Panayotakis, S., M. Zimmerman, and W. Keulen, eds. 2003. *The Ancient Novel and Beyond*. Leiden: Brill. https://doi.org/10.1163/9789047402114

Panayotakis, S. 2016. "Underworld Journeys in Apuleius' *Metamorphoses*." In *Reading the Way to the Netherworld: Education and the Representations of the Beyond in Later Antiquity*, edited by I. Tanaseanu-Döbler, A. Lefteratou, G. Ryser, and K. Stamatopoulos, 234–53. Göttingen: Vandenhoeck and Ruprecht. https://doi.org/10.13109/9783666540301.toc

Paratore, E. 1942. *La Novella in Apuleio*. Palermo: Fratelli Vena.

Paschalis, M. 2002. "Reading Space: A Re-Examination of Apuleian *ekphrasis*." In Paschalis and Frangoulidis, *Space in the Ancient Novel*, 132–42.

Paschalis, M., and S. Frangoulidis, eds. 2002. *Space in the Ancient Novel*. Groningen: Barkhuis.

Paschalis, M., S. Frangoulidis, S. Harrison, and M. Zimmerman, eds. 2007. *The Greek and Roman Novel: Parallel Readings*. Ancient Narrative Supplementum 8. Groningen: Barkhuis.

Pasetti, L. 2005. "*Ille ego*: Il tema doppio e l'ambiguità pronominale." *Lexis* 23: 237–53.

Pasetti, L. 2023. "The Wisdom of the Eagle: A (Middle) Platonic Reading of Apuleius, *Florida* 2." *Bulletin of the Institute of Classical Studies* 66.1: 67–77.

Pellizer, E. 1987. "Reflections, Echoes and Amorous Reciprocity: On Reading the Narcissus Story." In *Interpretations of Greek Mythology*, edited by J. Bremmer, 107–20. London: Routledge.

Penny Small, J. 1997. *Wax Tablets of the Mind: Cognitive Studies of Memory and Literacy in Classical Antiquity*. London: Routledge. https://doi.org/10.4324/9780203441602

Penwill, J. L. 1975. "Slavish Pleasures and Profitless Curiosity: Fall and Redemption in Apuleius' *Metamorphoses*." *Ramus* 4.1: 49–82. https://doi.org/10.1017/s0048671x00004513

Penwill, J. L. 1990. "*Ambages Reciprocae*: Reviewing Apuleius' *Metamorphoses*." *Ramus* 19.1: 1–25. https://doi.org/10.1017/s0048671x00002939

Penwill, J. L. 2009. "On Choosing a Life: Variations on an Epic Theme in Apuleius *Met.* 10 and 11." *Ramus* 38.1: 85–108. https://doi.org/10.1017/S0048671X00000655

Peponi, A.-E. 2012. *Frontiers of Pleasure: Models of Aesthetic Response in Archaic and Classical Greek Thought*. Oxford: Oxford University Press. https://doi.org/10.1093/acprof:oso/9780199798322.001.0001

Perry, B. E. 1926. "An Interpretation of Apuleius' *Metamorphoses*." *TAPhA* 57: 238–60. https://doi.org/10.5406/illiclasstud.41.2.0405

Perry, B. E. 1930. "Chariton and His Romance from a Literary-Historical Point of View." *AJP* 51.2: 93–134. https://doi.org/10.2307/289861

Perry, B. E. 1967. *The Ancient Romances: A Literary-Historical Account of Their Origins.* Berkeley: University of California Press.

Phillips, K. M. 1968. "Perseus and Andromeda." *AJA* 72.1: 1–23. https://doi.org/10.2307/501819

Platt, V. 2011. *Facing the Gods: Epiphany and Representation in Graeco-Roman Art, Literature and Religion.* Cambridge: Cambridge University Press.

Popescu, V. 2014. "Lucian's True Stories: Paradoxography and False Discourse." In *The Ancient Novel and the Frontier of Genre*, edited by M. Futre Pinheiro, G. Schmeling, and E. Cueva, 39–58. Groningen: Barkhuis.

Poulet, G. 1972. "Criticism and the Experience of Interiority." In *The Structuralist Controversy: The Language of Criticism and the Sciences of Man*, edited by R. A. Macksey and E. Donato, 56–72. Baltimore: Johns Hopkins University Press.

Pradeau, J.-F. 1999. *"Alcibiade": Translation and Commentary.* Paris: GF Flammarion.

Pucci, P. 1987. *Odysseus Polutropos: Intertextual Readings in the "Odyssey" and the "Iliad."* Ithaca: Cornell University Press.

Putnam, M. 1998. "Dido's Murals and Virgilian Ekphrasis." *HSPh* 98: 243–75. https://doi.org/10.2307/311344

Rambo, L. R. 1993. *Understanding Religious Conversion.* New Haven: Yale University Press.

Reeves, B. T. 2007. "The Role of the *Ekphrasis* in Plot Development: The Painting of Europa and the Bull in Achilles Tatius' *Leucippe and Clitophon*." *Mnemosyne* 60.1: 87–101. https://doi.org/10.1163/156852507X165856

Regali, M. 1983. *Macrobio, "Commento al Somnium Scipionis," libro I.* Pisa: Giardini.

Reitzenstein, R. 1927. *Die hellenistischen Mysterienreligionen nach ihren Grundgedanken und Wirkungen.* Leipzig: Teubner.

Relihan, J. 1993. *Ancient Menippean Satire.* Baltimore: Johns Hopkins University Press.

Repath, I. 2010. "Plato in Petronius: Petronius *In Platanona*." *CQ* 60.2: 577–95. https://doi.org/10.1017/S0009838810000200

Rhode, E. 1876. *Der griechische Roman und seine Vorläufer.* Bern: Breitkopf.

Rhode, E. 1885. "Zu Apuleius." *RhM* 40: 66–113.

Richardson, N. J. 1981. "The Contest of Homer and Hesiod and Alcidamas' *Mouseion*." *CQ* 31.1: 1–10. https://doi.org/10.1017/S0009838800021029

Richter, D., and W. A. Johnson, eds. 2017. *The Oxford Handbook of the Second Sophistic.* Oxford: Oxford University Press. https://doi.org/10.1093/oxfordhb/9780199837472.001.0001

Riefstahl, H. 1938. *Der Roman des Apuleius.* Frankfurt: Klostermann.

Riess, W. 2008a. "Apuleius *Socrates Africanus*? Apuleius' Defensive Play." In Riess, *Paideia at Play*, 51–74.

BIBLIOGRAPHY   335

Riess, W., ed. 2008b. *Paideia at Play: Learning and Wit in Apuleius*. Groningen: Barkhuis.

Rifaterre, M. 1966. "Describing Poetic Structures: Two Approaches to Baudelaire's *Les Chats*." *Yale French Studies* 36/37: 200–242.

Rist, J. M. 2001. "Plutarch's *Amatorius*: A Commentary on Plato's Theories of Love?" *CQ* 51.2: 557–75. https://doi.org/10.1093/cq/51.2.557

Robert, F. 2012. "La représentation de la pantomime dans les romans grecs et latins: Les exemples de Longus et d'Apulée." *Dialogues d'Histoire Ancienne* 38.1: 87–110. https://doi.org/10.3917/dha.381.0087

Robertson, D. S. 1910. "Lucius of Madaura: A Difficulty in Apuleius." *CQ* 4.4: 221–27.

Robertson, D. S. 1940–1946. *Apulée: Les "Metamorphoses."* Translated by P. Valette. Paris: Budé.

Roller, M. 2018. *Models from the Past in Roman Culture: A World of Exempla*. Cambridge: Cambridge University Press. https://doi.org/10.1017/9781316677353

Rosati, G. P. 2003. "*Quis ille?* Identità e metamorfosi nel romanzo di Apuleio." In *Memoria e identità: La cultura romana construisce la sua imagine*, edited by M. Citroni, 267–95. Firenze: Università degli Studi di Firenze.

Rosen, R. 2004. "Aristophanes' *Frogs* and the *Contest of Homer and Hesiod*." *TAPhA* 134.2: 295–322. https://doi.org/10.1353/apa.2004.0015

Roskam, G. 2014. "Once Again on the Title of Apuleius' *Asinus Aureus*." *Hermes* 142.2: 255–57. https://doi.org/10.25162/hermes-2014-0016

Ryan, M.-L. 2001. *Narrative as Virtual Reality: Immersion and Interactivity in Literature and Electronic Media*. Baltimore: Johns Hopkins University Press.

Ryan, M.-L. 2014. "Story/Worlds/Media: Tuning the Instruments of a Media-Conscious Narratology." In *Storyworlds across Media: Toward a Media-Conscious Narratology*, edited by M.-L. Ryan and J.-N. Thon, 25–49. Lincoln: University of Nebraska Press.

Ryan, M.-L. 2015. *Narrative as Virtual Reality 2: Revisiting Immersion and Interactivity in Literature and Electronic Media*. Baltimore: Johns Hopkins University Press. https://doi.org/10.1353/book.72246

Sabnis, S. 2013. "Donkey Gone to Hell: A *Katabasis* Motif in Apuleius' *Metamorphoses*." In *Intende, Lector—Echoes of Myth, Religion and Ritual in the Ancient Novel*, edited by M. Futre Pinheiro, A. Bierl, and R. Beck, 177–99. Berlin: De Gruyter.

Sandy, G. N. 1972. "Knowledge and Curiosity in Apuleius' *Metamorphoses*." *Latomus* 31.1: 179–83.

Sandy, G. N. 1974. "*Serviles voluptates* in Apuleius' *Metamorphoses*." *Phoenix* 28.2: 234–44. https://doi.org/10.2307/1087421

Sandy, G. N. 1978. "Book 11: Ballast or Anchor?" In *AAGA 1*, 123–41.

Sandy, G. N. 1994. "Apuleius' *Metamorphoses* and the Ancient Novel." *ANRW* 2.34.2: 1511–74.

Sandy, G. N. 1997. *The Greek World of Apuleius: Apuleius and the Second Sophistic*. Leiden: Brill. https://doi.org/10.1163/9789004330320

Sandy, G. N. 2001. "A Neoplatonic Interpretation of Heliodorus' *Ethiopian Story*." In

OPÔRA: La Belle Saison de l'Hellénisme, edited by Alain Billault, 169–78. Paris: Presses de l'Université de Paris-Sorbonne.

Schlam, C. C. 1968. "The Curiosity of *The Golden Ass*." *CJ* 64.3: 120–25.

Schlam, C. C. 1970. "Platonica in the *Metamorphoses* of Apuleius." *TAPhA* 101: 477–87. https://doi.org/10.2307/2936066

Schlam, C. C. 1978. "Sex and Sanctity: The Relationship of Male and Female in the Metamorphoses." In *AAGA 1*, 95–105.

Schlam, C. C. 1984. "Diana and Actaeon: Metamorphoses of a Myth." *CA* 3.1: 82–110. https://doi.org/10.2307/25010808

Schlam, C. C. 1992. *The "Metamorphoses" of Apuleius: On Making an Ass of Oneself*. Chapel Hill: University of North Carolina Press.

Schlam, C. C., and E. Finkelpearl. 2000. "A Review of Scholarship on Apuleius' *Metamorphoses*, 1970–1998." *Lustrum* 42: 7–230.

Schmeling, G. 1974. *Chariton*. New York: Twayne.

Schmeling, G., and S. Montiglio. 2006. "Riding the Waves of Passion: An Exploration of an Image of Appetites in Apuleius' *Metamorphoses*." In Keulen, Nauta, and Panayotakis, *Lectiones Scrupulosae*, 28–41.

Schmitz, T. A. 2017. "Professionals of *Paideia*? The Sophists as Performers." In Richter and Johnson, *The Oxford Handbook of the Second Sophistic*, 169–80.

Schneider, R. 2001. "Toward a Cognitive Theory of Literary Character: The Dynamics of Mental-Model Construction." *Style* 35.4: 607–39.

Scobie, A. 1969. *Aspects of the Ancient Romance and Its Heritage: Essays on Apuleius, Petronius, and the Greek Romances*. Meisenheim am Glan: Anton Hain.

Scobie, A. 1975. *Apuleius: "Metamorphoses" ("Asinus Aureus") I*. Meisenheim am Glan: Anton Hain.

Screech, M. A. 2006. *Rabelais: "Gargantua" and "Pantagruel"*. London: Penguin.

Seddon, K. 2005. *Epictetus' "Handbook" and the "Tablet of Cebes": Guides to Stoic Living*. London: Routledge. https://doi.org/10.4324/9780203357002

Seel, M. 2005. *Aesthetics of Appearing*. Translated by J. Farrell (=2000. *Ästhetik des Erscheinens*. München: Carl Hanser). Stanford: Stanford University Press. https://doi.org/10.1515/9781503619852

Segal, C. 1978. "The Myth Was Saved: Reflections on Homer and the Mythology of Plato's *Republic*." *Hermes* 106.2: 315–36.

Segonds, A.-P., ed. and trans. 1985. *Proclus sur le premier "Alcibiade" de Platon*. Paris: Budé.

Sharrock, A. 1996. "Representing Metamorphosis." In Elsner, *Art and Text in Roman Culture*, 103–30.

Sheffield, F. C. C. 2001. "Alcibiades' Speech: A Satyric Drama." *Greece and Rome* 48.2: 193–209. https://doi.org/10.1093/gr/48.2.193

Sheffield, F. C. C. 2006. *Plato's "Symposium": The Ethics of Desire*. Oxford: Oxford University Press. https://doi.org/10.1093/acprof:oso/9780199286775.003.0001

BIBLIOGRAPHY 337

Shumate, N. 1996. *Crisis and Conversion in Apuleius' "Metamorphoses."* Ann Arbor: University of Michigan Press. https://doi.org/10.3998/mpub.23280

Singleton, N. E. 1977. "Venus in the *Metamorphoses* of Apuleius." PhD diss., Ohio State University.

Slater, N. W. 1997. "Vision, Perception, and Phantasia in the Roman Novel." In *Der antike Roman und seine mittelalterliche Rezeption*, edited by M. Picone and B. Zimmerman, 89–105. Berlin: Birkhäuser Verlag.

Slater, N. W. 1998. "Passion and Petrifaction: The Gaze in Apuleius." *CP* 93.1. 18–48. https://doi.org/10.1086/449372

Slater, N. W. 2001. "The Horizons of Reading." In Kahane and Laird, *Companion to the Prologue of "Metamorphoses,"* 213–24.

Slater, N. W. 2003. "Spectator and Spectacle in Apuleius." In Panayotakis, Zimmerman, and Keulen, *The Ancient Novel and Beyond*, 85–100.

Smith, W. S. 1972. "The Narrative Voice in Apuleius' *Metamorphoses.*" *TAPhA* 103: 513–34. https://doi.org/10.2307/2935991

Smith, W. S. 2012. "An Author Intrudes into 'His' Narrative: Lucius 'Becomes' Apuleius." In *AAGA* 3, 202–19. https://doi.org/10.1163/9789004224551_012

Smith, W. S. 2023. *Religion and Apuleius' "Golden Ass": The Sacred Ass.* London: Routledge. https://doi.org/10.4324/9781003258469

Smith, W., and B. Woods. 2002. "Tale of Aristomenes: Declamation in a Platonic Mode." *Ancient Narrative* 2: 172–93.

Sorabji, R. 1972. *Aristotle on Memory.* London: Duckworth.

Squire, M. 2009. *Image and Text in Graeco-Roman Antiquity.* Cambridge: Cambridge University Press.

Squire, M. 2011. *The Art of the Body: Antiquity and Its Legacy.* Oxford: Oxford University Press.

Squire, M. 2014. "Ekphrasis at the Forge and the Forging of Ekphrasis: The 'Shield of Achilles' in Graeco-Roman Word and Image." *Word and Image* 29.2: 157–91. https://doi.org/10.1080/02666286.2012.663612

Stafford, E. 2012. *Herakles.* London: Routledge. https://doi.org/10.4324/9780203152454

Stahl, W. H. 1952. *Macrobius, "Commentary on the Dream of Scipio."* New York: Columbia University Press.

Stanford, W. B. 1963. *The Ulysses Theme: A Study in the Adaptability of a Traditional Hero.* Oxford: Blackwell.

Steiner, D. 2001. *Images in Mind: Statues in Archaic and Classical Greek Literature and Thought.* Princeton: Princeton University Press. https://doi.org/10.2307/j.ctv141 64b9

Steiner, G. 1969. *The Graphic Analogue from Myth in Greek Romance.* Urbana: University of Illinois Press.

Stephens, S. 1994. "Who Read Ancient Novels?" In Tatum, *Search for the Ancient Novel*, 405–18.

338   BIBLIOGRAPHY

Stierle, K. 1975. *Texts als Handlung: Perspektiven einer systematischen Literaturewissenschaft*. Munich: W. Fink.

Stierle, K. 1980. "The Reading of Fictional Texts." In *The Reader in the Text: Essays on Audience and Interpretation*, edited by S. Suleiman and I. Crosman, 83–105. Princeton: Princeton University Press.

Stinton, T. C. W. 1965. *Euripides and the Judgment of Paris*. Supplementary Paper 11. London: Society for the Promotion of Hellenic Studies.

Stover, J. 2016. *A New Work By Apuleius: The Lost Third Book of the "De Platone."* Oxford: Oxford University Press. https://doi.org/10.1093/actrade/9780198735748.book.1

Stramaglia, A. 2010. "Le Metamorfosi di Apuleio tra iconografia e papiri." In *I papiri del romanzo antico*: Atti del convegno internazionale di studi Firenze, 11–12 giugno 2009, edited by G. Bastianini and A. Casanova, 165–92. Florence: Istituto papirologico Vitelli.

Svendsen, J. T. 1978. "Apuleius' *The Golden Ass*: The Demands on the Reader." *Pacific Coast Philology* 13:101–7. https://doi.org/10.2307/1316370

Swain, S. 2001. "Apuleius Sophista." *Classical Review* 51.2: 269–70. https://doi.org/10.10 93/cr/51.2.269

Tagliabue, A. 2021. "Re-Enactments of the Prologue in Cupid's Palace: An Immersive Reading of Apuleius' Story of *Cupid and Psyche*." *CQ* 71.2: 799–818. https://doi.org /10.1017/S0009838821000926

Tarrant, H. 1985. "Albinus, Nigrinus, Alcinous." *Antichthon* 19: 87–95.

Tarrant, H. 1999. "Shadows of Justice in Apuleius' *Metamorphoses*." *Hermathena* 167: 71–89.

Tatum, J. 1969. "The Tales in Apuleius' *Metamorphoses*." *TAPhA* 100: 487–527.

Tatum, J. 1979. *Apuleius and the "Golden Ass."* Ithaca: Cornell University Press.

Tatum, J., ed. 1994. *The Search for the Ancient Novel*. Baltimore: Johns Hopkins University Press.

Taylor, R. 2008. *The Moral Mirror of Roman Art*. Cambridge: Cambridge University Press.

Thibau, R. 1965. "Les Métamorphoses d'Apulée et la théorie platonicienne de l'Eros." *Studia Philosophica Gandensia* 3: 89–144.

Tilg, S. 2007. "Lucius on Poetics? The Prologue to Apuleius' *Metamorphoses* Reconsidered." *Studi italiani di filologia classica* 5.2: 156–98.

Tilg, S. 2011. "Religious Feasting in Apuleius' *Metamorphoses*: Appetite for Change?" *TAPhA* 141.2: 387–400. https://doi.org/10.1353/apa.2011.0012

Tilg, S. 2012. "Aspects of a Literary Rationale of *Metamorphoses* 11." In *AAGA* 3, 132–55.

Tilg, S. 2013. "Das 'missing link' in der Geschichte des lateinischen Romans: Die *Milesiaka*." *Gymnasium* 120.4: 325–42.

Tilg, S. 2014a. *Apuleius' "Metamorphoses": A Study in Roman Fiction*. Oxford: Oxford University Press. https://doi.org/10.1093/acprof:oso/9780198706830.001.0001

Tilg, S. 2014b. "The Poetics of Old Wives' Tales, or Apuleius and the Philosophical Novel." In Cueva and Byrne, *Companion to the Ancient Novel*, 552–69.

BIBLIOGRAPHY   339

Timotin, A. 2012. *La démonologie platonicienne: Histoire de la notion de daimōn de Platon aux derniers néoplatoniciens.* Leiden: Brill. https://doi.org/10.1163/978900422 4018

Tompkins, J., ed. 1980. *Reader-Response Criticism: From Formalism to Post-Structuralism.* Baltimore: Johns Hopkins University Press.

Too, Y. L. 1996. "Statues, Mirrors, Gods: Controlling Images in Apuleius." In Elsner, *Art and Text in Roman Culture*, 133–52.

Too, Y. L. 2001. "Losing the Author's Voice: Cultural and Personal Identities in the *Metamorphoses* Prologue." In Kahane and Laird, *Companion to the Prologue of "Metamorphoses,"* 177–87.

Toohey, P. 2004. *Melancholy, Love, and Time: Boundaries of the Self in Ancient Literature.* Ann Arbor: University of Michigan Press. https://doi.org/10.3998/mpub.16583

Trapp, M. B. 1990. "Plato's *Phaedrus* in Second-Century Greek Literature." In *Antonine Literature*, edited by D. A. Russell, 141–73. Oxford: Oxford University Press.

Trapp, M. B. 1997a. "On the Tablet of Cebes." In *Aristotle and After*, edited by R. Sorabji, 159–80. London: University of London.

Trapp, M. B., ed. 1997b. *The Philosophical Orations.* Oxford: Oxford University Press.

Trapp, M. B. 2001. "On Tickling the Ears: Apuleius' Prologue and the Anxieties of Philosophers." In Kahane and Laird, *Companion to the Prologue of "Metamorphoses,"* 39–46.

Trapp, M. B. 2007. "What Is This *Philosophia* Anyway?" In Morgan and Jones, *Philosophical Presences in the Ancient Novel*, 1–22.

Trapp, M. B. 2017. "Socrates in Maximus of Tyre." In *Socrates and the Socratic Dialogue*, edited by A. Stavru and C. Moore, 772–86. Leiden: Brill. https://doi.org/10.1163/97 89004341227_038

Uden, J. 2010. "The *Contest of Homer and Hesiod* and the Ambitions of Hadrian." *JHS* 130: 121–35. https://doi.org/10.1017/S0075426910000054

Ulrich, J. P. 2017. "Choose Your Own Adventure: An *Eikōn* of Socrates in the Prologue of Apuleius' *Metamorphoses*." *AJP* 138.4: 707–38. https://doi.org/10.1353/ajp.2017.0036

Ulrich, J. P. 2020. "Hermeneutic Recollections: Apuleius' Use of Platonic Myth in the *Metamorphoses*." *CP* 115.4: 677–704. https://doi.org/10.1086/710995

Ulrich, J. P. 2022. "Eating Up the Plot: 'Ontological Metalepsis' in Apuleius's Tales of Aristomenes and Diophanes." *TAPhA* 152.1: 243–82. https://doi.org/10.1353/apa.20 22.0012

Ulrich, J. P. 2023. "Apuleius and Roman Demonology." In *The Oxford Handbook of Roman Philosophy*, edited by M. Garani, D. Konstan, and G. Reydams-Schils, 87–107. Oxford: Oxford University Press. https://doi.org/10.1093/oxfordhb/978019932 8383.001.0001

Ulrich, J. P. Forthcoming a. "Dionysiac Paintings: The Presence of Visual Art in Longus' *Daphnis and Chloe*." In *Materiality in Ancient Narrative*, edited by E. Adkins and E. Cueva. Groningen: Barkhuis.

Ulrich, J. P. Forthcoming b. "Inverted Allegories of the Underworld: Topography,

Allêgorêsis, and the Ups and Downs of Apuleius' *Metamorphoses*." In *Reading across Divides: Imperial Allegory, Its Cultural Contexts, and Intermedial Entanglements*, edited by J. Grethlein and B. Kruchio. Cambridge: Cambridge University Press.

Ulrich, J. P. Forthcoming c. "Outlined Bodies, Painted Souls: Entrancing and Excluding the Embodied Reader in Petronius' *Pinacotheca* (*Sat.* 83)." In *Ancient Narrative and Reader Response*, edited by C. Caruso, L. Graverini, and J. P. Ulrich. Groningen: Barkhuis.

Usher, M. D. 2002. "Satyr Play in Plato's *Symposium*." *AJP* 123.2: 205–28. https://doi.org /10.1353/ajp.2002.0030

Valgiglio, E. 1975. "Basilio Magno *Ad adulescentes* e Plutarco *De audiendis poetis*." *Rivista di Studi Classici* 23: 67–86.

Van der Paardt, R. Th. 1978. "Various Aspects of Narrative Technique in Apuleius' *Metamorphoses*." In *AAGA 1*, 75–94.

Van der Paardt, R. Th. 1999. "The Unmasked 'I': Apuleius, *Met.* 11.27." In *Oxford Readings in the Roman Novel*, edited by S. J. Harrison, 237–46. Oxford: Oxford University Press.

Van der Paardt, R. Th. 2004. "Four Portraits of Actaeon." In *Metamorphic Reflections: Essays Presented to Ben Hijmans at His 75th Birthday*, edited by M. Zimmerman and R. Th. van der Paardt, 21–39. Leuven: Peeters.

Vander Poppen, R. E. 2008. "A Festival of Laughter: Lucius, Milo, and Isis Playing the Game of *Hospitium*." In Riess, *Paideia at Play*, 157–74.

Van der Stockt, L. 2012. "Plutarch and Apuleius: Laborious Routes to Isis." In *AAGA 3*, 168–82.

van Liefferinge, C. 2012. "Les Sirènes: Du chant mortel à la musique des sphères; Lectures homériques et interprétations platoniciennes." *Revue de l'histoire des religions* 229.4: 479–501.

van Mal-Maeder, D. 1995. "*L'Âne d'Or* ou les metamorphoses d'un récit: Illustration de la subjectivité humaine." In *Groningen Colloquia on the Novel* 6, edited by H. Hofmann, 103–26. Groningen: E. Forsten.

van Mal-Maeder, D. 1997. "*Lector, Intende: Laetaberis*—the Enigma of the Last Book of Apuleius' *Metamorphoses*." In Hofmann and Zimmerman, *Groningen Colloquia on the Novel* 8, 87–118.

Vannini, A. 2018. "Sull'intromissione auctoriale di Apuleio in *Metamorfosi* 11.27." *SIFC* 16.2: 233–50.

Wagner, P., ed. 1996. *Icons—Texts—Iconotexts: Essays on Ekphrasis and Intermediality*. Berlin: De Gruyter.

Walsh, P. G. 1968. "Lucius Madaurensis." In *Phoenix* 22.2: 143–57.

Walsh, P. G. 1970. *The Roman Novel: The "Satyricon" of Petronius and the "Metamorphoses" of Apuleius*. Cambridge: Cambridge University Press.

Walsh, P. G. 1981. "Apuleius and Plutarch." In *Neoplatonism and Early Christian Thought: Essays in Honour of A. H. Armstrong*, edited by H. J. Blumenthal and R. A. Markus, 20–32. London: Variorum.

Watson, G. 1988. *Phantasia in Classical Thought*. Galway: Galway University Press.

Webb, R. 1999. "Ekphrasis Ancient and Modern: The Invention of a Genre." *Word and Image* 15.1: 7–18. https://doi.org/10.1080/02666286.1999.10443970

Webb, R. 2009. *Ekphrasis, Imagination and Persuasion in Ancient Rhetorical Theory and Practice*. London: Ashgate. https://doi.org/10.4324/9781315578996

Webb, R. 2016. "Sight and Insight: Theorizing Vision, Emotion and Imagination in Ancient Rhetoric." In *Sight and the Ancient Senses*, edited by M. Squire, 180–204. London: Routledge. https://doi.org/10.4324/9781315719238

Wesseling, B. 1988. "The Audience of the Ancient Novels." In *Groningen Colloquia on the Novel* 1, edited by H. Hofmann, 69–79. Groningen: E. Forsten.

Westerbrink, A. G. 1978. "Some Parodies in Apuleius' *Metamorphoses*." In *AAGA 1*, 63–73.

Whitmarsh, T. 1998. "The Birth of a Prodigy: Heliodorus and the Genealogy of Hellenism." In *Studies in Heliodorus*, edited by R. L. Hunter, 93–124. Cambridge: Cambridge University Press.

Whitmarsh, T. 2002. "Written on the Body: Ekphrasis, Perception and Deception in Heliodorus' *Aethiopica*." In Elsner, "The Verbal and the Visual: Cultures of Ekphrasis in Antiquity." Special issue, *Ramus* 31, 111–25.

Whitmarsh, T., ed. 2008. *The Cambridge Companion to the Greek and Roman Novel*. Cambridge: Cambridge University Press. https://doi.org/10.1017/CCOL9780521865906

Whitmarsh, T. 2011. *Narrative and Identity in the Ancient Greek Novel: Returning Romance*. Cambridge: Cambridge University Press. https://doi.org/10.1017/CBO9780511975332

Whitmarsh, T. 2013. *Beyond the Second Sophistic: Adventures in Greek Postclassicism*. Berkeley: University of California Press. https://doi.org/10.1525/california/9780520276819.001.0001

Whitmarsh, T. 2020. *Achilles Tatius: "Leucippe and Clitophon," Books 1–2*. Cambridge: Cambridge University Press.

Whitmarsh, T., and S. Bartsch. 2008. "Narrative." In Whitmarsh, *Cambridge Companion to the Greek and Roman Novel*, 237–60.

Wilson, N. G. 1975. *Saint Basil on the Value of Greek Literature*. London: Duckworth.

Winkle, J. 2014. "Necessary Roughness: Plato's *Phaedrus* and Apuleius' *Metamorphoses*." *Ancient Narrative* 11: 93–132.

Winkle, J. 2015. "*Epona Salvatrix?* Isis and the Horse Goddess in Apuleius' *Metamorphoses*." *Ancient Narrative* 12: 1–20.

Winkler, J. J. 1985. *Auctor and Actor: A Narratological Reading of Apuleius' "Golden Ass."* Berkeley: University of California Press.

Wlosok, A. 1969. "Zur Einheit der *Metamorphoseon* des Apuleius." *Philologus* 113.1: 68–84.

Worman, N. 1999. "Odysseus *panourgos*: The Liar's Style in Tragedy and Oratory." *Helios* 26.1: 35–70.

Wowerius, J. 1606. *L. Apuleii opera omnia*. Frobeniano.

Zadorojnyi, A. 2002. "Safe Drugs for the Good Boys: Platonism and Pedagogy in Plutarch's *De audiendis poetis*." In *Sage and Emperor: Plutarch, Greek Intellectuals, and Roman Power in the Time of Trajan (98–117 A.D.)*, edited by P. Stadter and L. Van der Stockt, 297–330. Leuven: Leuven University Press.

Zadorojnyi, A. 2010. "ὥσπερ ἐν ἐσόπτρῳ: The Rhetoric and Philosophy of Plutarch's Mirrors." In *Plutarch's "Lives": Parallelism and Purpose*, edited by Noreen M. Humble, 169–95. Wales: University of Swansea.

Zanker, P. 1995. *Die Maske des Sokrates: Das Bild des Intellektuellen in der antiken Kunst*. Munich: C. H. Beck.

Zeitlin, F. 1994. "Gardens of Desire in Longus's *Daphnis and Chloe*: Nature, Art, and Imitation." In Tatum, *Search for the Ancient Novel*, 148–70.

Zimmerman, M. 2001. "*Quis Ille . . . Lector*: Addressee(s) in the Prologue and Throughout the *Metamorphoses*." In Kahane and Laird, *Companion to the Prologue of "Metamorphoses*," 245–55.

Zimmerman, M. 2002. "On the Road in Apuleius' *Metamorphoses*." In Paschalis and Frangoulidis, *Space in the Ancient Novel*, 78–97.

Zimmerman, M. 2006. "Echoes of Roman Satire in Apuleius' *Metamorphoses*." In *Desultoria Scientia: Genre in Apuleius' "Metamorphoses" and Related Texts*, edited by R. R. Nauta, 87–104. Leuven: Peeters. https://doi.org/10.1093/actrade/9780199277025.book.1

Zimmerman, M., ed. 2012. *Apulei "Metamorphoseon" Libri XI*. Oxford: Oxford University Press. https://doi.org/10.1093/actrade/9780199277025.book.1

Zimmerman-de Graaf, M. 1993. "Narrative Judgement and Reader Response in Apuleius' *Metamorphoses* 10.29–34." In *Groningen Colloquia on the Novel* 5, edited by H. Hofmann, 143–61. Groningen: E. Forsten.

Zunshine, L. 2006. *Why We Read Fiction: Theory of Mind and the Novel*. Columbus: Ohio State University Press. http://dx.doi.org/10.17613/M6Q83J

Index Locorum

ACHILLES TATIUS
Leucippe and Clitophon
  1.1.11: 181n116
  1.6.6: 173, 173n96, 173n94
  1.9.4: 212n41, 215, 228
  1.9.4–5: 201, 201n15, 214

AELIAN
Varia Historia
  4.20: 98n36

AELIUS ARISTIDES
Panathenaicus
  196.10: 212n41

ALCIPHRON
Letters
  3.7: 28n84

ANONYMOUS SEGUERIANUS
  96: 25

APOLLONIUS SOPHISTES
Homeric Lexicon
  114: 103n52

APULEIUS OF MADAURA
Apologia
  3.8: 113
  4: 203, 204
  4.11–13: 203
  7: 171n84

9: 300–301n16
12: 31n93, 230n84
13: 114n77
13–16: 110n70
13.3: 113
13.4: 113
14: 142, 146, 150, 290n122
14.7: 190
15: 115, 172n92
15.4: 224n73
15.4–7: 110
15.6: 113
16: 56n33, 112
16.1: 205
16.6: 112
16.7: 112, 113
16.11: 7, 114
22: 72n82
25.3–4: 7
25.11: 209n32
31.5: 75n94
36.8: 113
39.2: 113
42.21: 166n72
48.5: 113
61.5: 113
63: 202, 245
63–64: 198n4
63.3: 202, 271
63.6: 272
63.7–8: 204
63.9: 292

64: 30n90, 204, 272n73, 292, 293
64.1: 271
64.3–5: 205
64.5: 113, 199, 238
64.8: 202
65.4: 113
74.7: 149n33
76.4: 184n118
85.3: 224–25n73
96.7: 271n71
103: 130, 144–45
103.2: 130n123, 202
103.2–3: 110

Compendiosa Expositio
8: 273, 309, 310

De deo Socratis
1.2: 199
2: 175
6.2: 287, 291
6.4: 291
7: 291
7.1: 291
7.3: 254, 291
9.2: 287
10.1: 287, 288
14.7: 253n21
15.6: 253n21
15.9: 253n21, 270
15.10: 253, 253n69, 270
16: 272
16.3–4: 273
16.5: 278
17: 103, 292n126
17.3: 85
19.5: 106
19.6: 106, 108, 131
20.2: 106
20.4: 106, 131
20.6: 253n21
21.1: 106, 253n21
22.1: 106
23.2: 107, 122
23.4: 107, 122
23.5: 107
24.3–4: 104
24.4: 71

De mundo
17: 171n84

De Platone et eius Dogmate
1.1: 259n39
1.1.5: 280n99
1.3: 34n101
2.22: 194n149

Florida
2: 37n115, 209, 209n31
3: 204n23
3.9: 74n91, 235n100
7: 142n16, 180
7.6: 180
9.24: 74n91
15: 198n4, 204n22
16: 142n16
18: 298n12
18.1–2: 278n89
18.19: 74n91
20: 298n12
22: 72n82
22.3–4: 53n25

Metamorphoses
1: 89, 109, 230
1.1: 9, 33n98, 34–36, 108, 116, 117–18, 121,
    123–24, 140, 244n128, 249, 256, 295, 302,
    307
1.2: 82, 98n37, 108, 121, 126–28, 127n114,
    171n85, 176, 213, 302
1.2–1.4: 126
1.3: 129–30, 224–25n73, 276–77
1.3–1.4: 108
1.4: 132
1.5: 277
1.6: 31, 166n72
1.6–1.9: 171
1.7: 6n15, 194n148
1.8: 194n148
1.12: 72, 80, 171n87
1.13: 172, 233n94
1.16: 79n105
1.18: 172, 176
1.19: 13, 172, 176
1.20: 108, 131, 266n61, 278
1.24: 24–25n73
1.26: 130n124, 133, 224–25n73
2.1: 13, 89, 133–34, 135
2.2: 77, 108n63
2.4: 13, 40, 143, 157–60, 164–66, 166n72,
    176–77, 178, 191n144, 192, 201, 288, 305n36
2.5: 149, 174, 221, 236, 295

INDEX LOCORUM 345

2.6: 221, 221n62, 271
2.7: 179n109, 222–23, 244
2.8: 190, 224, 225, 244
2.9: 13, 201, 226–28, 235, 235n99, 240
2.10: 171n85, 194n148, 228–29, 237
2.11: 242n123
2.12: 62n54, 144, 190, 221, 282
2.16: 149n33
2.17: 32, 179, 194n148, 219, 235, 235n100, 244
2.18: 194n148, 243
2.32: 76
3.19: 76–77, 79n104
3.20: 220
3.21: 174n100, 176, 234n97
3.22: 224n71
3.24: 224n72, 245n131, 305
3.27: 288
4.6: 284
4.13: 194n148
4.13–21: 260–61
4.14: 194n148
4.20: 283–84
4.27: 194n148, 278n93
4.28: 176, 232
4.29: 232
4.31: 166n70
4.32: 231
5.1: 288
5.22: 207, 232, 233–34, 235
5.23: 171n85, 235, 236, 237
5.24: 230, 251n14
5.25: 166n70
5.26: 194n148
5.28: 166n70
5.31: 194n148
6.1: 237
6.11: 237
6.19: 237
6.21: 237
6.24: 194n148
6.30: 192n145, 224n71, 261n47
7.11: 194n148
7.21: 194n148, 229
7.24: 224n72
8.12: 166n72, 194n148
8.16: 192n145, 224n71, 261n47
8.29: 299
9.10: 128n119
9.13: 48n12, 62n53, 74–75, 98n37, 104, 187, 188, 249n8, 255, 271, 293

9.19: 194n148
9.30: 9, 295
9.40: 11, 13n32, 39
9.42: 11–12, 300n14
10.3: 166n70
10.4: 194n148
10.17: 194n148
10.19–22: 260–61
10.20: 194n148
10.20–22: 230n81
10.22: 186, 224n72, 229–30
10.23: 194n148
10.26: 243n127
10.29: 80, 176, 193, 269
10.29–35: 175
10.30: 177–78
10.31: 80, 178–79, 194n148, 218
10.32: 191n144, 194n148, 222, 288
10.33: 69n75, 104, 172n92, 184–87, 188, 189, 204n22
10.34: 177, 189
10.35: 75, 189, 255
11.1: 239, 239n112
11.2: 239, 267n62, 269
11.3: 166n72, 189–90, 240–41, 288–89
11.5: 239, 257
11.6: 124, 269, 271
11.7: 243, 258
11.8: 224n71, 259–63
11.9: 258n38
11.12: 78
11.13: 224n72, 305
11.14: 76, 121, 243–44, 255
11.15: 43, 79, 82, 83, 186, 194n148, 252, 267, 268, 271, 275, 279n94
11.16: 78, 253n20
11.17: 243
11.18: 257n31
11.22: 291
11.23: 194n148, 274–76, 277, 284, 291–92, 307
11.24: 123–24, 191, 192, 193, 194, 194n148, 245, 289, 291
11.24–25: 189
11.25: 27n82, 192–93, 245, 272
11.27: 24, 121, 296, 301–2, 303–4, 304n33
11.28: 194n148
11.30: 27–29, 32, 268, 285, 286, 289–90

346 INDEX LOCORUM

ARISTOPHANES
Frogs
  961–62: 206–7n26
Wasps
  191: 12

ARISTOTLE
Metaphysics
  982b12–13: 125n108
Rhetoric
  3.3.1406b12: 85, 86n1

[ARISTOTLE]
De Mundo
  395a33: 212n41
Problemata
  915b29: 212n41

ATHENAEUS
Deipnosophistae
  12.510c: 73n86
  13.590f–91b: 200n12

AUGUSTINE
Confessions
  8.8: 82n116
  8.12: 45, 54n28, 82n116
  8.12.29: 11
  10.33: 38n117
  10.33.49: 22n65
  10.35.55: 22, 22n65
De civitate Dei
  18.18: 284, 309, 310
  22.28: 282, 310
Epistles
  138.19: 297n9

AULUS GELLIUS
Noctes Atticae
  praef. 12: 7n17
  6.17: 98n38
  10.12.4: 128n117
  10.12.5: 98n38
  10.22: 9
  10.22.24: 9
  11.13: 37–38
  11.13.4: 38
  11.13.5: 38
  11.16: 92n22

  13.25: 29n88
  14.4: 180
  16.8: 8
  16.8.17: 8
  18.4: 38
  18.4.2: 38
  19.9.8: 30n92
  19.9.9: 30n92

BASIL OF CAESAREA
Exhortation to the Young to Read Pagan
    Literature
  4.2: 60, 60n45
  4.8: 66, 66n66
  4.10: 66
  5.55–77: 54n28

CALLISTRATUS
Descriptions
  5.1: 165n66

Carmina Priapea
  31.3: 235n102

CATULLUS
  61.215–24: 148n29

[CEBES]
tabula Cebetis
  3.2: 67
  4.1: 69
  5.2: 67–68
  6: 68
  6.2: 68
  6–9: 68
  12.1: 69
  15: 68n71
  15.2: 68
  19.1: 69

CELSUS
De medicina
  6.4.3: 233n95

CHARITON
Callirhoe
  2.11.2: 148n29

INDEX LOCORUM 347

CICERO
Academica
  2.108: 79n105
De finibus
  5.49: 56, 75, 97, 98, 128
  5.49–50: 56n35
  5.50: 98, 113
De natura Deorum
  1.52–54: 34n101
De officiis
  1.117: 54n28, 81
  1.118: 81
  1.119: 82
De oratore
  1.219: 38n119
De partitione oratoria
  40: 282n101
Epistulae ad Familiares
  5.12.3: 81n113
Hortensius
  6.1: 34n101
Pro Archia
  4.4: 306n40
Timaeus
  23: 287n113
Topica
  37: 288n114

[CLEMENT]
Homilies
  5.26.1: 212n41

CLEMENT OF ALEXANDRIA
Paedagogus
  2.10.110: 54n28, 65
Protrepticus
  4.51: 220n59
  7.76.6: 30n89

COLUMELLA
De re rustica
  1.pr.11: 98n38
  6.37.4: 251n15

CORPUS HIPPOCRATICUM
Internal Affections
  14: 211n35

DEMOCRITUS
  fr. B 299, 6–8 DK: 98n36

DIO CHRYSOSTOM
Orations
  1: 54n28, 65, 68n71
  1.66–83: 54n28
  8.5: 73n89
  10.30–32: 66n68
  13: 17n51
  59: 187n130, 266n59
  59.8: 187n130

DIOGENES LAERTIUS
Vitae Philosophorum
  4.25–26: 99n43
  7.152.9: 212n41

DONATUS
De comoedia
  1: 90, 90n13
  5: 90

FAVONIUS EULOGIUS
Disputatio
  1: 282, 309, 310

[GALEN]
Ad Gaurum quomodo animetur fetus
  6.1.6: 212n41

GORGIAS
  fr. B 11 DK: 206–7n26

GREGORY OF NYSSA
De Beatitudinibus, Oratio VIII
  44.1105.33: 212n41
  44.1272.21: 212n41
Epistles
  19.3: 212n41

HELIODORUS
Aethiopica
  4.8: 140–41
  4.8.4: 155, 155n48

HERACLITUS
Homeric Problems
  79.2–3: 96n33

348   INDEX LOCORUM

HERODOTUS
Histories
  1.8.4: 93n25

HESIOD
Theogony
  199: 239n116
Works and Days
  235: 141–42n15, 148n29
  286–92: 47, 48–49
  289: 53n24
  290–91: 68

HOMER
Odyssey
  1.3: 75n92, 101
  6.128: 255, 255n26
  8.83–86: 30, 256
  8.84–85: 30n92
  8.86: 30n92
  8.493: 265n56
  9.5–10: 96
  12.45–46: 8
  12.158–200: 47
  12.188: 75, 98
  13.119: 75, 255

HORACE
Ars Poetica
  133–34: 148–49n31
  142: 101
Carmina
  1.5.5–6: 148–49n31
  1.33.1–4: 148–49n31
  3.14.26: 174n100
Epistles
  1.2.1–2: 99
  1.2.3–4: 99
  1.2.17–26: 100
  1.2.22: 105n55
  1.2.23–25: 105
  1.2.55: 105
Sermones
  1.4.106: 93–4
  1.4.110: 94n28
  1.4.115: 94
  1.4.128: 94

JUSTIN MARTYR
Apology
  2.11: 54n28

JUVENAL
Satires
  6.533: 28n84

Life of Aesop
  94: 54n28

LIVY
Ab urbe condita
  1.*pr*.10: 94
  1.18.3: 98n38

LONGUS
Daphnis and Chloe
  1.*pr*.3: 125

LUCIAN
Anacharsis
  16: 30n89
Hermotimus
  86: 28n84
How to Write History
  51: 90n12
Imagines
  4: 220n59
Nigrinus
  5: 57
  19: 57–8, 58n39
  37: 58
On Salaried Posts
  42: 28n84
On the Dance
  45: 181n115
  72: 90n12
  81: 215n47
  81.8: 212n41
The Parasite
  10–11: 96n33
  11.1: 96n33
Rhetorum praeceptor
  6: 66n67, 69n72
  25: 65
Symposium
  18: 28n84

INDEX LOCORUM   349

[LUCIAN]
Amores
13: 217, 218, 228
14.1: 217
15: 219, 221
16: 219
17: 220
Onos
45: 12
49.3: 72n85
54: 255n26
56: 224n72

LUCRETIUS
De rerum natura
4.2.11: 167n73

MACROBIUS
Commentary on the Dream of Scipio
1.1.2: 310
1.1.5: 279n94
1.1.9: 278n91, 309, 310
1.2.4–5: 281
1.2.5: 310
1.2.7–8: 279
1.2.8: 22n66, 88n11, 281
1.2.12: 310
Saturnalia
2.7: 300

MARTIAL
Epigrams
2.66.7: 233n95
6.27: 148n29
6.73.6: 235n102

MAXIMUS OF TYRE
Orations
3: 69n75
14: 65, 69n73
14.1: 54n28
15.9: 102
18: 66, 69
18.3: 69
18.5: 69, 70
26.1: 101
40.6: 30n89

NICOLAUS
Progymnasmata
68.12: 25

OVID
Amores
3.1: 54n28
Ars Amatoria
2.123–24: 102n50
Fasti
2.177–86: 261n44
Metamorphoses
3.142: 167, 195
3.158–59: 165
3.348: 148n28, 211
3.418–19: 223
3.421: 223
3.426: 212
5.553: 259n39
5.561: 259n39
15.879: 28n83

PAUSANIAS
Periêgêsis
2.2.3: 73n89

PERSIUS
Satires
5.30–40: 54n28

PETRONIUS
Satyricon
26: 174n100
83–89: 174n97
109.8: 227
109.8–10: 28n84
127.5: 259n39
128.7: 209n33

"PHILIP THE PHILOSOPHER"
383.27–32: 61, 70, 293–94
387.23–24: 70n77

PHILO
De opificio mundi
76.3: 212n41
De somniis
2.206.3: 212n41

On the Sacrifices of Abel and Cain
20–44: 54n28

PHILOSTRATUS
Vita Apollonii
2.30.30: 212n41
6.10: 54n28
6.10.5: 65, 80n111
8.7.399: 212n41

PHOTIUS
Bibliotheca
116: 125
129: 285n105

PINDAR
Nemean Odes
7.14: 86n1

PLATO
Alcibiades 1
103a1: 125n108
132a5–6: 37n115, 209
133a1: 212nn40–41
217b4–5: 209n33
217c7–8: 209n33
Apology
19b4: 250n9, 250n11
23b5: 266
31c3: 266n58
31c5: 250n9
41b: 188n132, 255
41b5–6: 188
Charmides
154c4: 207
154c9: 207
154d3–4: 208
154d4: 226
154e4–5: 226
154e4–6: 208
161b–163c: 93n24
162a1: 93n24
162a2–3: 93n24
Crito
53b–e: 171n87
Gorgias
484c6: 7
484c9: 7
485a5: 7

485a6: 7
486c7: 7
523a1: 7
523a–527e: 250n12
526c4: 250n12
527a5–6: 7
Laws
905b4: 212n41
Phaedo
68c: 266n59
81e: 171n86
81e2: 251
81e5–82b9: 262n49
82b6: 269
82b7: 269
82c: 266n59
82c7: 266n59
115b9–10: 198n3
Phaedrus
227a4: 127
227b9: 127
229c4: 129
229e3: 266, 266n60
229e5–230a1: 115
229e6: 93n24
230a1: 266
230a2: 129
230a3–4: 115n79, 129, 295
230a4: 266
230a5: 266n60
234d1: 206–7n26
237a4: 30
237a5: 30
243b4–7: 29–30
247d: 101n49
248c5–e3: 262n50
248c7–8: 230–31
248e5–6: 269
249c: 224n70
250a6: 206n26
250a6–7: 207
250a7: 221n61
250e1–251a1: 216
250e4: 198
250e5: 220
251a2–7: 234n96
251a5: 207–8, 232
251a6: 201, 225, 232
251a7: 211

INDEX LOCORUM 351

251b1–2: 211
251b6: 211, 224
252e7–253a5: 198n3
254d6–7: 245n131
255b4: 206n26
255c1–e1: 210–11, 256n29
255d2: 224
255d4: 212n41
255d5–6: 90n12, 200
258e–259a: 35n104
259a: 186n121
259a3: 50
259a3–4: 50
259a5: 50, 52n23, 82, 171
259a5–b2: 50
259a7: 58n39
259b8: 206–7n26
260c7: 12
275b3–4: 120
275b5–c1: 120–21, 307
275c1: 307
275d4–e5: 152
276a1–2: 152
276d1–5: 198n3
276d–e: 63n57

Republic
1.328e3–4: 68n71
4.433a8–9: 93
4.443d: 93n24
4.443d1–2: 93n24
7.514a5–6: 13n32
7.516a6–7: 13
7.516a7: 239n112
7.516a9–b1: 239n112
7.518c–d: 17n51
9.581a–b: 266n59
9.586a7–8: 173n94
9.586a–b: 171n86
10.596d9–e1: 150
10.596e1–3: 150
10.599a1: 150, 164
10.603a7–b2: 151
10.603b1: 155n48
10.603b4: 151
10.606b1–2: 93n24
10.607e4–5: 151
10.614b2: 254
10.614b4: 276
10.614b6: 276

10.614b8: 276
10.614c1: 276
10.614c4: 276
10.614d2–3: 276
10.614e3–4: 257n31
10.616e9: 257
10.617a: 101n49
10.617e4–5: 268
10.618b–619b: 268n63
10.619a5–6: 248
10.619b3–6: 247
10.619b7–c8: 248
10.619c2: 248, 265
10.619c4: 265–66
10.619c4–5: 248
10.620a–d: 264
10.620a2: 264
10.620c3–d2: 265
10.620c6–7: 76, 187, 249
10.620d4–5: 266n60
10.621b8–c1: 276

Symposium
180d6–7: 239n116
192b7: 206n26
197e5: 280n99
198b5: 206–7n26
206c1–3: 145–46
208e1–2: 153
208e2–3: 153
208e5–209a1: 153
209c2: 146, 155n48
209c2–3: 153
209d2: 146, 153
210e2–3: 153
211d5: 206n26
212a3–5: 153
215a4–5: 119–20
215a5: 120, 123
215b1: 204n23
215b2: 123
215b3: 120, 123, 208, 286
215c3: 2
215c7: 2
215d5–6: 2, 206–7n26, 208
216a5: 60
216a6–8: 2, 51
216d3: 206n26
217b4–5: 209n33
217c7–8: 209n33

352 INDEX LOCORUM

219c5: 209n34
221a1: 123
221d8: 123
221e2–3: 188
221e3–4: 51, 209
221e4: 189
222a4: 123, 189, 208
222a8: 209n34
223b–d: 287
Theaetetus
155d2–3: 125n108
Timaeus
36a: 287n113

PLAUTUS
Amphitruo
299: 77n101
329: 77n101
441: 90n15
461–62: 31n94
556: 77n101
736: 77n101
986: 77n101
Epidicus
383: 90n15
386–87: 90n15
Menaechmi
902: 96n33
Stichus
199: 92, 112
200: 112

PLINY THE ELDER
Natural Histories
36.20: 242
36.21–22: 220n59

PLINY THE YOUNGER
Epistles
3.1.9: 306n40

PLUTARCH
Advice to the Bride and Groom
141d1: 111
141d1–2: 111
Amatorius
749a3–4: 213n44
765b1–2: 213
765b–f: 213

765d2–3: 214
765f6: 212n41
765f6–7: 201n14
765f9–766a1: 213–14
766b6–7: 213
766b7: 224n70
De gloria Atheniensium
347c1: 180
De Iside et Osiride
352c: 28n84
361e2: 270–71
362e4: 271n70
How to Study Poetry
14f: 58–59
15a: 59
15d: 59n41
15e: 59
15f: 59
16a: 59
Life of Alcibiades
4.4.7: 215n46
On Curiosity
516a–b: 60
516c: 250n11
516c7: 250n11
519c: 74n91
520d: 57n38
520e4–5: 218n54
On Progress in Virtue
77d: 62
79c–d: 63
79f: 63, 67
Platonic Questions
1002a8: 212n41
Quaestiones Convivales
740b8: 281n100
740b5–6: 281n100
740b–c: 281n100
Timoleon
1.1: 90n12, 92n19

[PLUTARCH]
On Homer
6: 207n28

PORPHYRY
In Carmina
3.14.26: 174n100

INDEX LOCORUM 353

QUINTILIAN
Institutio Oratoria
  8.3.62: 140
  9.4.112–13: 8n20
  12.11.15–16: 8n20

[QUINTILIAN]
Declamationes Maiores
  18.2.2: 173n95

SCRIPTORES HISTORIAE AUGUSTAE
Life of Albinus
  11.8: 5n13
  12.12: 5–6, 8

SEMONIDES
  7: 63

SENECA THE ELDER
Controversiae
  4.*pr*.1: 135

SENECA THE YOUNGER
De beneficiis
  2.1: 37n113
  5.1: 37n113
De clementia
  1.1: 36–37, 87, 90n12, 94–95
De constantia
  2.1–2: 97n35
De ira
  2.13.1: 130n122
  2.36.2: 112n72
  3.39.4: 135
Epistles
  20.11: 37n113
  22.10: 37
  31.2: 102n51
  33.5: 37n114
  56.15: 102n51
  59: 96n32
  76.32: 37, 209
  88.5: 97n35
  88.7: 99n39
  88.7–8: 99n39
  108.2: 98n38
  115.3: 37
  123.12: 102n51

Natural Questions
  1.17.4: 111, 148
  3.17: 282n101
On the Brevity of Life
  2.4: 6
  7.1–3: 6
  12.1–4: 6
  12.4: 6
  13: 99n39
  16.3: 6
  19.2–3: 6n16
Thyestes
  757: 37n112

SEXTUS EMPIRICUS
Outlines of Pyrrhonism
  1.45: 173n95

SILIUS ITALICUS
Punica
  15.17: 80n111
  15.18: 80n111, 82n116
  15.18–128: 54n28
  15.22: 81n113

STATIUS
Silvae
  5.2.58–59: 173n95
Thebaid
  12.815: 306n40

STRABO
Geographica
  15.1.59: 277n88

SUETONIUS
Domitian
  18.2: 226–27
Julius Caesar
  49.3: 184n118
Nero
  52: 173n95

TACITUS
Annals
  14.40: 304n29
Histories
  1.1: 173n95
  2.3: 239, 242

TERENCE
Adelphoe
414–16: 91
415: 95n29
417: 91
418: 91
419: 91
Self-Tormentor
76–7: 92

TERTULLIAN
Adversus Valentinianos
14.3–4: 299–300
De praescriptione haereticorum
39: 66n67

THEMISTIUS
Orations
2.11: 54n28

VERGIL
Aeneid
1.495: 223
2.774: 223n66
12.669: 134n135

XENOPHON
Memorabilia
1.3.7: 103n52
2.1.21: 52, 80, 82, 83
2.1.22: 52, 181–84, 190n138, 218
2.1.23: 52–53
2.1.26: 188
2.1.27: 53
2.1.28: 53
2.1.29: 130
2.1.30: 53
Symposium
1: 119, 119n90

Subject Index

Note: Page references in italics indicate illustrations.

Achilles Tatius, 228; *Leucippe and Clitophon* by, 154, 173, 173n93, 181n116, 201, 214–15; Plato and, 212

Actaeon, 21, 167n76, 167n78; being attacked by dogs, *161*; in Byrrhena's atrium, 176–77; *simulacrum* of, 166–67, 169–70, 177–78, 185, 189–95; *sparagmos* of, *177. See also* Diana-Actaeon

active reading, 21, 39–40, 135, 202, 209; in Plutarch, 23n67

Adelphoe (Terence), 90–92

Adversus haereses (Irenaeus), 298

Advice to the Bride and Groom (Plutarch), 111–12

Aelius Aristides, 212

Aemilianus, 89, 112–17, 125, 128, 149n33, 292

Aeneid (Vergil), 223, 298

Aethiopica (Heliodorus), 61; Charicleia in, 140–42, 155–56

agalmata theôn, 30n91, 124, 203, 208, 209, 286–87

agalmatophilia, 171n85, 194, 206; in *Cupid and Psyche*, 236–37; in *Phaedrus*, 198, 200, 202, 216; Photis and, 224, 228, 229, 236–37; Pliny the Elder and, 220n59; in Second Sophistic, 200

ainigma, 70; *eudaimonia* and, 71; *pinax* and, 67, 68; Winkler on, 71

Alcibiades, 9; as *erastês*, 209n33; Socrates and, 2, 3, 5, 8, 20, 30n91, 51, 51n22, 58, 58n39, 60, 88, 89, 120, 123–24, 124n106, 145, 188, 209, 233, 244–45, 290, 293

Alcibiades 1 (Plato), 208, 209, 209n34; Socrates in, 225

Allegory of the Cave, 13, 13n32

allotria, 266, 307; *curiositas* and, 115; New Comedy and, 108

Amatorius (Plutarch), 201, 213–14; *Phaedrus* and, 213

Amor, in *Cupid and Psyche*, 206, 236–37

Amores (pseudo-Lucian), 217; *Cupid and Psyche* and, 237; Photis and, 219n55, 228

amoris parilitas, as *anterôs*, 236

Amphitruo (Plautus), 31, 77n101

Andromeda, 155n50, 164; Perseus and, *156*; Persinna and, 140–41, 141n15, 155

aniles fabulae, 6n14, 8, 230n83, 278n93

anteludia: compared to Myth of Er, 252, 257–58, 263, 265n56; of Isis, 252, 259, 261–62, *262*

anterôs: in *Leucippe and Clitophon*, 215; Photis and, 229; Plato and, 228

Antiochus of Ascalon, 56, 97

Antonius Diogenes, 125

Aphrodite, 73, 181, 181n114, 199–200; *Amores* and, 217; in *Cupid and Psyche*, 231–32; *curiositas* and, 218–19; *ekphrasis* and, 218; in *Ephesiaca*, 154–55; Isis and, 239n116; Maximus of Tyre and, 71; Praxiteles and, 200, 217; *simulacrum* of, 239; in *Symposium* by Plato, 31, 69, 230, 239

355

356 SUBJECT INDEX

Apologia (Apuleius of Madaura), 7, 72, 88, 89, 97; Aemilianus in, 89, 112–17, 125, 128, 149n33, 292; aesthetic and utilitarian viewing in, 202–6; Aristotle in, 130; *daemones* in, 292; *explorare* in, 130, 224n73; *mimesis* in, 142–43, 150, 166; *Phaedrus* and, 205; *simulacrum* in, 208–9, 271; Socrates in, 266; Socrates' "triangulative mirror" in, 109–16; *speculum* in, 150

Apology (Plato), 249–50; Odysseus in, 187–88, 255; Socrates in, 255, 266, 266n58

aporia, 10, 31, 44; Heracles and, 54; in Myth of Er, 249; of Winkler, 10, 15–16

Apuleius of Madaura, 5n13, 6, 6n14; *De Platone* by, 273, 273n77; *Florida* by, 72, 103n54, 198, 209; Graverini on, 303n27; *Madaurensem* problem and, 24, 121, 301–6, 303n27; Milesian tales and, 5; *Punicae Milesiae* by, 33, 298; Socrates and, 6n15. *See also Apologia; specific topics on Metamorphoses*

Archimedes: Cicero and, 134–35; *Katoptrika* of, 112, 113, 114; Piso and, 113

argumenta, in Macrobius, 281

Aristides of Miletus, 118

Aristomenes, 6n15, 89, 277n86; *fabulae* of, 129–33; Socrates and, 172

Aristophanes, 287; *Daedalus* by, 12n30; *Wasps* by, 12

Aristotle, 130, 224n73

Ars Poetica (Horace), 101

Asinius Marcellus, 301, 303, 304, 304n30, 305

askêsis, Stoics and, 63n56

aspritudo, 128, 128n118

Augustine, 18; *Confessions* by, 11, 45, 60; on conversion, 16; on Myth of Er, 282, 284

Aulus Gellius, 7n17, 8–9; on *graphice*, 180; on *intspicere*, 36, 37–38; *Noctes Atticae* by, 7n17, 37–38, 180; Plutarch and, 57n38; on *polypragmosynê*, 92n22

Bartsch, Shadi, 211, 289n118

Basil of Caesarea, 18, 22, 55; *Exhortation to the Young to Read Pagan Literature* by, 59–60, 66

The Bathing Diana, 40, 165, 169, 195, 197, 200

Benson, Geoffrey, 4n9, 286n108

Bildeinsatz, 154–55, 154n47, 157

The Birth of Tragedy (Nietzsche), 255n24

The Blinding of Polyphemus, 163

Booth, W. C., 2n3

Botticelli, Sandro, 137–39

Bryson, Norman, 164

Byrrhena's atrium: Actaeon in, 176–77; Diana-Actaeon and, 40, 181; Diana in, 242; *ekphrasis* of, 150, 169–75, 178; *mimesis* in, 157–75; Photis and, 221, 229; *simulacrum* in, 158, 173; Venus and, 176–77, 181

Callicles, 7, 9

Callisto, 261

calvus mimicus, 27–32

Calypso, 39, 72, 171, 256, 267

captatio benevolentiae, 2, 9

Carmina (Horace), 63

Carroll, Lewis, 136

Cervantes, Miguel de, 138

Charicleia, 140–42, 155–56

Charmides (Plato), 207, 225–26; *Florida* and, 209; Socrates in, 225; *Symposium* by Plato and, 208

Cicero: Archimedes in, 134–35; Caelius in, 80; *De finibus* by, 56, 75, 97, 113; *De officiis* by, 81; Heracles in, 82; Macrobius on, 281; Menander and, 128n116; "mirror of the text" and, 90; *multiscius* and, 98; on Myth of Er, 278, 278n91, 281–82, 281n100; Odysseus in, 97, 134–35; Sirens in, 88, 113; Xenophon and, 81

Circe, 18, 39, 45, 47–48, 48n10; Odysseus and, 103; in Philip the Philosopher, 68–69; in Vergil, 226n74

Clement of Alexandria, 18, 22, 55, 65, 220

Clodius Albinus, 9, 20, 57, 298; *aniles fabulae* and, 8; Septimius Severus and, 5, 6, 7, 8

cognitive narratology, 21–22, 21n62, 25n74

Colotes, 277n88, 281

Compendiosa Expositio, 273, 273n77

Confessions (Augustine), 11, 45, 60

consenescere, 8–9, 8n20

Constance School, 21, 21n61, 25

Conte, Gian Biagio, 24n17, 40n120, 138

Controversiae (Seneca the Elder), 135

conversion, 13–20, 44–47, 45n4, 46n6, 83, 249n6; *Confessions* and, 11; contemporary models of, 17n48; Myth of Er and, 254

conversion to philosophy, 17–18, 17n51, 20–21

Crito (Plato), 171n87

cult of Isis. *See* Isis

SUBJECT INDEX 357

cult of Osiris. *See* Osiris
Cupid and Psyche, 5, 5n12, 30n90, 288; *agalmatophilia* in, 236–37; *Amor* in, 206, 236–37; Aphrodite in, 231–32; *ekphrasis* in, 233, 234; *ekplêxis* in, 233–34, 238; *erastês* in, 232–33; Graverini on, 207; *inspicere* in, 237; *katabasis* in, 237; *lector scrupulosus* in, 235, 238; mytho-mania and, 77; *novacula* in, 233–34, 233n95; *Phaedrus* and, 230–31, 238; Plato and, 230–38; *simulacrum* in, 232; *Venus vulgaris* in, 230; *voluptas* in, 237
curiositas, 6nn15–16, 29, 32, 218–19; *allotria/aliena* and, 115; DeFilippo on, 44n2; Mithras and, 43–44; in Myth of Er, 187, 249, 251, 252; *polypragmôn* and, 92–93, 93n25; *polypragmosynê* and, 93n25, 252n18; *scrupulosus* and, 275
Cynics: Diogenes, 102; Heracles and, 72n82; Odysseus and, 96n34, 102; *polytropia* and, 46n7

daemones, 248, 285–94; in *Apologia*, 292; *katabasis* and, 270–77; *lector scrupulosus* and, 289, 293; in Myth of Er, 253, 285–86; Osiris as, 253, 254, 271, 285; Plato and, 252–53; in *Republic*, 273n75; of Socrates, 89, 131, 287, 292
Daphnis and Chloe (Longus), 67, 125, 174n97
De clementia (Seneca), 36–37, 87, 94–95
De deo Socratis (Apuleius of Madaura), 71, 99, 122, 131, 175, 253–54, 270–73, 278, 287–88; mirror of the *Odyssey* in, 103–9
DeFilippo, Joseph, 44n2
De finibus (Cicero), 56, 75, 97, 113
Delphic maxim, 112; in *Phaedrus*, 114–16, 129, 266; Seneca and, 111; Socrates and, 125, 127, 250, 266
Demosthenes, 12; in Lucian, 65; in Plutarch, 180
De officiis (Cicero), 81
De Platone et eius Dogmate (Apuleius of Madaura), 273, 273n77, 280
De saltatione (Lucian), 181n115, 215n47
Diana: bathing, 169, 195, 197, 200; in Byrrhena's atrium, 242; *ekphrasis* of, 288; Photis and, 221n62, 223n69; *rimabundus* of, 236; *simulacrum* of, 201; striding, 165, 168, 168, 195
Diana-Actaeon, 40–41, 142, 143, 150, 160, 161–62; Byrrhena's atrium and, 40, 181; Venus and, 143n21

Dido, 207n28, 223, 298n12
Dio Chrysostom, 18, 227
Diogenes the Cynic, 102
Diotima, 145–46, 148, 153, 286
Disputatio (Favonius Eulogius), 282
divertissement, 34, 34n101, 35, 117, 279, 292
Divine Institutes (Lactantius), 298n10
Donatus, 90, 90n13
Don Quixote, 40, 136, 138
Dougherty, Carol, 56n35

Edmonds, Radcliffe, 198
"Education of Heracles" (Prodicus), 181, 186n125, 243
Egan, Rory, 211–12
Egelhaaf-Gaiser, Ulrike, 28
ekphrasis, 22, 25n75, 26, 67n69, 139n8, 164, 265; in *Aethiopica*, 141; analeptic, 259, 261; of Aphrodite, 218; of Byrrhena's atrium, 150, 169–75, 178; in *Cupid and Psyche*, 233, 234; of Diana, 288; in Judgment of Paris, 178; *mimesis* and, 139–40, 142, 154; *phantasia* and, 140, 140n10; Photis and, 167–68, 200–201; of *spectaculum*, 184; Venus and, 143n21, 179–80; Winkler on, 186
ekplêxis, 185, 206–10, 207n28, 216, 223; in *Cupid and Psyche*, 233–34, 238; in Photis episode, 210; Plato and, 224
Elsner, Jas, 199–200, 238
enargeia, 25, 25n75, 26; *phantasia* and, 139
Encolpius, 109n67, 126n110, 138, 227
Encomium of Hair (Dio Chrysostom), 227
enkrateia, 57n38, 62
Entwicklungsroman, 14, 14n37, 17, 143n19, 269
Ephesiaca (Xenophon of Ephesus), 154–55, 157
Epicurus, 96n33, 281
Epistles (Horace), 56n36, 88, 99
Erasmus: Rabelais and, 2, 2n2; *Sileni Alcibiadis* by, 2, 3, 123
erastês: Alcibiades and, 209n33; in *Cupid and Psyche*, 232–33; Lucius as, 211, 224–25; in *Phaedrus*, 32, 207, 210–11, 224, 225; Plato and, 224; Socrates on, 211
erômenos: in *Alcibiades 1*, 209, 209n34, 233; in *Charmides*, 207, 208, 226; in *Phaedrus*, 228, 256; Photis as, 211; Psyche as, 232; Socrates and, 210
Erôs, 31, 32; in *Phaedrus*, 152; Socrates and, 120, 132; in *Symposium* by Plato, 64, 153

358 SUBJECT INDEX

eudaimonia, 68; *ainigma* and, 71; Lady Vice and, 188; *paideia* and, 54; *pinax* and, 67
exanclo, 79
exemplum: in *Apologia*, 110; of Horace, 94n28; "mirror of the text" and, 91; in Myth of Er, 252; of Odysseus, 103, 123, 255; in *Odyssey*, 72, 86–87; of Socrates, 106–7, 123, 132
Exhortation to the Young to Read Pagan Literature (Basil of Caesarea), 59–60, 66
exordium: Graverini on, 244; of Roman comedy, 118, 119n88
explorare: in *Apologia*, 130, 224n73; Photis and, 224–25

fabulae, 6n14, 8, 35, 127–28, 128n117, 135; of Aristomenes, 129–33; *logos* and, 132; Macrobius on, 253–54, 281n102; in Myth of Er, 277, 278, 279, 281
farce, 14, 143; Winkler and, 14n35
Favonius Eulogius, 282
Finkelpearl, Ellen, 27nn80–82, 186n126, 223n66, 226n74
Fish, Stanley, 22n64
Fletcher, Richard, 17–18, 17n51, 20–21, 103, 114n78, 120
Florida (Apuleius of Madaura), 72, 103n54, 198; *Charmides* and, 209
the Forms, 13, 198, 199, 202, 224
Fortin, Ernest, 60

Gaisser, Julia Haig, 297
Gargantua (Rabelais), 1–2, 11
gaudium, 32, 96
Georgics (Vergil), 63
Germany, Robert, 22n63, 26n77, 138, 140, 154
Geryon, 76–77
Gombrich, Ernst, 150
Gorgias (Plato), 65n64; Socrates in, 7
Gowers, Emily, 94
grammaticus, 38
graphice, 180
Graverini, Luca, 4n6, 6n14, 7, 10n26, 28, 88, 121n97, 136, 298; on *Cupid and Psyche*, 207; on *exordium*, 244; *lepidus susurrus* and, 35, 35n104; on Macrobius, 280; on *Madaurensem*, 303n27; on *multiscius*, 48n12; on mytho-mania, 138; on *prudentia*, 188
Gregory of Nyssa, 212

Grethlein, Jonas, 5n11, 25n74, 26n79
Grillo, Luca, 298–99, 300, 300n14
Gumbrecht, Hans Ulrich, 23
Gwyn Griffiths, John, 240n117, 261

Habinek, Thomas, 16, 16n46, 46n6
hairesis, in Myth of Er, 248, 252, 258, 265–66, 272
Halliwell, Stephen, 146, 151n40
Harrison, Stephen, 126, 259, 261, 263
Harrauer, Christine, 44
Heliodorus, 69, 155n48; *Aethiopica* by, 61, 140–42, 155–56; Philip the Philosopher and, 70n77, 83
Heracles, 19, 21, 39, 45, 46, 47, 53; *aporia* and, 54; at crossroads, 62–71; Cynics and, 72n82; Mithras and, 130; Odysseus and, 71–83; *pinax* and, 66–67; Second Sophistic and, 49, 66; Socrates and, 82; *voluptas* and, 81, 87
Hercules, 77–78, 186n125; in *Amphitruo*, 77n101; Prodicus on, 81
Hermes: *môly* of, 103n52; Odysseus and, 103, 103n52; *Symposium* by Plato and, 204n23
Hesiod, 18–19, 47n8; "two roads" of, 47, 47n9, 48–49, 54n28, 62, 66, 67, 68, 68n71, 69n72; *Works and Days* by, 48–49, 52–53; Xenophon and, 54
Historia Augusta, 5, 6n14, 298
Homer, 8, 8n19, 19, 47n8; Horace and, 99–101; *Iliad* by, 187; as *multiscius*, 75n94; Myth of Er and, 248, 249; Socrates and, 150–51. See also *Odyssey*
Horace: *Ars poetica* by, 101; *Carmina* by, 63; *Epistles* by, 56n36, 88, 99; *exemplum* of, 94n28; Homer and, 99–101; Hunter on, 88; *inspicere* and, 103; Odysseus and, 56n36, 100, 102–3; Philodemus and, 100n45; *sapientia* and, 100, 100n45; *Sermones* by, 93–94, 100, 111
Hostius Quadra, 111, 228; Narcissus and, 211
How to Study Poetry (Plutarch), 58–59, 62
Hunter, Richard, 2n2, 65, 75, 99; on Horace, 88; on Sirens, 8n19, 48n11

Iliad (Homer), 187
Imagines (Lucian), 220
immersion, 25n74, 26n79, 139n6
Incredible Wonders beyond Thule (Antonius Diogenes), 125, 185n120

SUBJECT INDEX   359

inspicere, 33, 35–36, 37n114; in *Cupid and Psyche,* 237; Horace and, 103; *lector scrupulosus* and, 33–34; "mirror of the text" and, 91; New Comedy and, 118–19; *speculum* and, 117; Terence and, 101

introspicere, 36–38

Iser, Wolfgang, 21n61, 24

Isis: *anteludia* of, 252, 259, 261–62, *262;* Aphrodite/Venus and, 239, 239n116; cloak of, 241n120; conversion to, 13; Judgment of Paris and, 288; *katabasis* and, 253; Lady Virtue and, 238; Photis and, 240–44, 289n117; *simulacrum* of, 194

Isis book, 14, 14n34, 15n39, 41–42, 175, 289n118, 295; *lector scrupulosus* in, 270; Myth of Er and, 256–58, 268–71, 277–85; paradigms of lives in, 255–69; Plato and, 238–94; reader-response theory in, 247–94

Isocrates, in Lucian, 65n63

James, Paula, 28

Jauss, Hans Robert, 21n61, 22, 23, 24, 296

Judgment of Paris, 40, 73, 80, 181n115, 186–87; *ekphrasis* in, 178; Isis and, 288; Venus in, 142–43, 180–81, *182, 183,* 288

Justin Martyr, 18, 55

Kahane, Ahuvia, 178

Kakia, 81, 96n32, 111, 181

katabasis: in *Cupid and Psyche,* 237; *daemones* and, 270–77; Isis and, 253; Mithras and, 268; in Myth of Er, 274, 276, 283, 285; *pastophorus* and, 307; Plato and, 254; of Socrates, 274

Katoptrika (Archimedes), 112, 113, 114

Keulen, Wytse, 36, 118, 120

Kirichenko, Alexander, 9n23, 10n26, 186n126

Koning, Hugo, 49

Krabbe, Judith, 77

Lactantius, 298n10

Lady Vice, 45, 47, 52, 53; in "Education of Heracles," 181; *eudaimonia* and, 188; Prodicus and, 80, 130, 188, 218; in *Somnium* by Lucian, 64; *topos* of, 72–73; Venus and, 80, 218, 288

Lady Virtue, 19, 45, 52–53, 54; Heracles and, 64; Isis and, 238; Seneca and, 96; vs. *Venus vulgaris,* 190

Lamberton, Robert, 61n52

Lanuvium Actaeon, 160–61, *161*

lector scrupulosus, 9, 19–20, 30, 33–39, 159, 197, 202; in *Cupid and Psyche,* 235, 238; *daemones* and, 289, 293; in Isis book, 270; Winkler on, 12, 122–23

Leigh, Matthew, 6n15, 92

lepidus susurrus, 34, 35, 35n104

Leucippe and Clitophon (Achilles Tatius), 154, 173, 173n93, 181n116, 201; and the *Phaedrus* and, 214–15

Levine Gera, Deborah, 64, 64nn61–62

Life of Albinus, 5

Life of Alcibiades (Plutarch), 215n46

Livius Andronicus, 96

Livy, 94, 94n28

locus amoenus, 30n89, 35, 50, 132, 172, 172n88; of *Phaedrus,* 256

locus classicus, 90–91, 113, 148n31, 155; of *Phaedrus,* 127; of *Symposium* by Plato, 8

Lodge, David, 137–39

logos: fabula and, 132; in *Gorgias,* 7; *mimesis* and, 152; in Myth of Er, 281n100; in *Phaedrus,* 120, 152; of Socrates, 132, 152

[Longinus], 140

Longus, 67, 125

Lucian, 215n47; *Imagines* by, 220; *Nigrinus* by, 56–58; Odysseus in, 62, 86; *Rhetorum praeceptor* by, 64–65; Socrates and, 65n63; *Somnium* by, 64, 65

Lucius. *See specific topics on Metamorphoses*

Lucretius, 166–67

ludicra litteraria, 5, 6

MacDougall, Byron, 257

Macrobius, 8, 279–81, 279n94, 280n95; on Cicero, 281; on *fabulae,* 253–54, 281n102; on Myth of Er, 282–83; Plato and, 280n99

Madaurensem problem, 24, 121, 301–6; Graverini on, 303n27

Marsyas, 2

matrona, 27, 186, 230, 260–61; in *Onos,* 224n72

Maximus of Tyre, 18, 30n89; Heracles in, 71; Odysseus in, 101–2; *Oration 14* by, 65; *Oration 18* by, 66; *Phaedrus* and, 113; on Socrates, 69–70, 69n75

Mayer, Roland, 100

Memorabilia (Xenophon), 80–81; Socrates in, 51–52

Menaechmi (Plautus), 96n33

Menander, 12n30, 280; *argumenta* of, 281; Cicero and, 128n116

Metamorphoses (Apuleius of Madaura). *See specific topics*

Milesian tales, 118n84; by Apuleius of Madaura, 5, 5n13; *paideia* in, 4; Septimius Severus on, 33

Milo, 32, 130n124, 133, 197, 221. *See also* Photis

mimesis, 24; in *Apologia*, 142–43, 150, 166; in Byrrhena's atrium, 157–75; *ekphrasis* and, 139–40, 142, 154; *logos* and, 152; mythomania and, 136, 170; Plato and, 145–46, 152–53, 156, 160–61, 164, 217, 257; in *Republic*, 139, 150–51, 150n38, 151n40, 155n48; *speculum* and, 146–49

Mirror of the *Odyssey*, in *de deo Socratis* (Apuleius of Madaura), 103–9

"mirror of the text," 36n110, 37, 40, 90–103

Mithras, 46, 73, 76, 186, 253, 253n20, 279n94; on *curiositas*, 43–44; Heracles and, 78–79, 82, 130; on *katabasis*, 268

Moles, John, 101

Montiglio, Silvia, 55–56

multiscientia, 74, 75; of Odysseus, 187

multiscius: Cicero on, 98; Graverini on, 48n12; Homer as, 75n94; Sirens and, 75

Münstermann, Hans, 133n132

Murray, Molly, 16, 16n47

Myth of Er, 247–49, 248n3; Augustine on, 282, 284; Cicero on, 278, 278n91, 281–82, 281n100; compared with *anteludia*, 252, 257–58, 263, 265n56; conversion and, 254; *curiositas* in, 187, 251, 252; *daemones* in, 253, 285–86; *exemplum* in, 252; *fabulae* in, 277, 278, 279, 281; *hairesis* in, 248, 252, 258, 265–66, 272; Isis book and, 256–58, 268–71, 277–85; *katabasis* in, 274, 276, 283, 285; *logos* in, 281n100; Macrobius on, 282–83; Odysseus in, 41–42, 105, 265–66, 267–68; *Odyssey* and, 254; Plutarch on, 281–82; *polypragmosynê* in, 48n14; Sirens in, 258–59, 258n38; Socrates in, 292; transformations in, 264, *264*

mytho-mania, 40, 175; Conte on, 24n71, 138; in *Cupid and Psyche*, 77; of Encolpius, 169; Graverini on, 138; with *matrona*, 186n125; *mimesis* and, 136, 170; Plato and, 41

Narcissus: Hostius Quadra and, 211; Ovid on, 166n72, 215, 223; Plato and, 201n16; Socrates and, 148n28, 172–73

Natural Histories (Pliny the Elder), 128n117

Natural Questions (Seneca the Younger), 111, 228

Nero, 36, 36n109, 87, 96n30

Nestor, 106

New Comedy, 90, 90n14, 92n20; *allotria* and, 108; *inspicere* and, 118–19; *polypragmôn* in, 92, 93, 94, 107; Socrates and, 112

Nicolini, Lara, 121n97, 305n35

Nietzsche, Friedrich, 255n24

Nigrinus (Lucian), 56–58

Nock, Arthur Darby, 16, 17–18, 17n51

Noctes Atticae (Aulus Gellius), 7n17, 37–38, 180

non obumbrato vel obtecto calvitio, 28, 29, 30, 32

novacula, 233–34, 233n95

O'Brien, Maeve, 28, 171n87

occupatus, 6–7, 6n15

Odusia (Livius Andronicus), 96

Odysseus, 18, 19, 20–21, 30n92, 39, 46n7; in *Apology* by Plato, 187–88, 255; Cicero on, 97, 134–35; Circe and, 103; Cynics and, 96n34, 102; Epicurus and, 96n33; as *exemplum*, 103, 123, 255; Heracles and, 71–83; Hermes and, 103n52; Horace on, 56n36, 100, 102–3; Lucian on, 62, 86; Maximus of Tyre on, 101–2; *multiscientia* of, 187; in Myth of Er, 41–42, 105, 249–50, 265–66, 267–68; Ovid on, 102; Piso on, 56n35, 75, 97, 98; Plutarch on, 62, 86; as *polypragmôn*, 48, 48n12, 102; *polytropia* and, 105n55; *polytropos* and, 101, 105; *prudentia* and, 104, 105; in *Republic*, 250, 268; Second Sophistic and, 46–47, 55–62; Seneca on, 102; Sirens and, 45, 45n5, 47–48, 48n10, 49, 50–51, 50n20, 57–58, 60, 71–72, 75; Socrates and, 133n132, 187–88, 255–56, 267; Stoics on, 46n7, 97, 97n35; *topos* of, 56, 57; *voluptas* and, 105

Odyssey (Homer), 40, 45, 47; *Apologia* and, 89; *exemplum* in, 72, 86–87; Horace and, 88; as mirror in *De deo Socratis*, 103–9; *multiscius* in, 74n91; Myth of Er and, 254; Theagenes of Rhegium and, 56n31

Olsen, Sarah, 141, 155

SUBJECT INDEX   361

On Anger (Seneca the Younger), 135
On Curiosity (De curiositate) (Plutarch),
    57n38, 60, 218n54; polypragmosynê in,
    74n91
Onos (pseudo-Lucian), 12, 12n31, 13n32, 14n38,
    72–73; matrona in, 224n72
On Progress in Virtue (Plutarch), 62–64
On the Brevity of Life (Seneca), 6
Oration 14 (Maximus of Tyre), 65
Oration 18 (Maximus of Tyre), 66
Origen, 18
Orpheus, 263
Osiris, 14, 123–24, 249, 252, 301–2, 304; as dae-
    môn, 253, 254, 271, 285; pastophorus of, 285,
    301
Ovid, 212; on Actaeon, 167, 194–95; on Narcis-
    sus, 166n72, 215, 223; on Odysseus, 102;
    Sirens of, 259n39

paideia: eudaimonia and, 54; in Milesian
    tales, 4
Palinode, 24, 27, 29–32, 199, 210, 256, 307
Pamphile, 82, 149, 174n100, 175, 221, 234n97
pastophorus, 268, 302, 303, 304; katabasis and,
    307; of Osiris, 285, 301
Paul, St., 44–45
Penwill, J. L., 73
Perry, Ben Edwin, 15n39, 20, 231
Perseus, 155–57, 207n28; Andromeda and, 156
Persinna, Andromeda and, 140–41, 141n15, 155
Petronius, 109n67, 126n110, 138, 174n97, 227,
    280
Phaedo (Plato): metempsychosis in, 251, 262,
    269; Socrates in, 198n3, 251, 262, 269
Phaedran coloring, 132–33; of Aristomenes'
    tale, 172; of Cupid and Psyche, 230–31, 238;
    of Leucippe and Clitophon, 214–15; in Sec-
    ond Sophistic, 30n89, 200–201
Phaedrus (Plato), 57, 115n80; agalmatophilia
    in, 198, 200, 202, 216; Amatorius and, 213;
    Apologia and, 205; Cupid and Psyche and,
    230–31; Delphic maxim in, 129, 266; erastês
    in, 32, 207, 210–11, 224, 225; erôs in, 152;
    locus amoenus of, 256; logos in, 120, 152;
    Maximus of Tyre and, 113; mirror in, 154;
    Plutarch and, 215–16; Second Sophistic and,
    197–98; Sirens in, 48; Socrates in, 24, 27,
    29–32, 106, 115, 120–21, 127, 251, 261, 262–63,
    266n60, 269, 307; as Sôkratikoi logoi, 49–50

phantasia, 139n9; ekphrasis and, 140, 140n10;
    enargeia and, 139
[Philip the Philosopher], 61, 61n51, 62n53, 70;
    Circe in, 68–69; Heliodorus and, 70n77, 83
Philodemus, 100n45
Philo of Alexandria, 18, 55
philosophia, 7–8
philosophus Platonicus, 3, 89, 115, 160, 277–78,
    294, 297
Philostratus, 65
Photis, 32, 197, 206, 211; agalmatophilia and,
    216, 224, 228, 229, 236–37; Amores and,
    219n55; amoris parilitas of, 236; anterôs and,
    229; Byrrhena's atrium and, 221, 229; Diana
    and, 221n62, 223n69; ekphrasis and, 167–68,
    200–201; ekplêxis and, 210; hair of, 228,
    234–35, 235n99; Isis and, 240–44, 289n117;
    Platonic coloring of, 41, 221–30, 256; pronus
    and, 229; sex appeal of, 221n62; simulacrum
    and, 240; as Venus Anadyomene, 26–27;
    Venus and, 179; Venus pendula and, 222n63;
    Venus Pudica and, 244; Venus vulgaris and,
    222
pinax: ainigma and, 67, 68; eudaimonia and,
    67; Heracles and, 66–67
Piso, 99; Archimedes and, 113; Odysseus and,
    56n35, 75, 97, 98; Seneca and, 99n39
Plato: Aelius Aristides and, 212; Allegory of
    the Cave of, 13, 13n32; anterôs of, 228; in
    Cupid and Psyche, 230–38; daemones and,
    252–53; ekplêxis in, 224; erastês of, 224; in
    Isis book, 238–94; katabasis and, 254;
    Lucian on, 65; Macrobius on, 280n99;
    mimesis and, 145–46, 152–53, 156, 160–61,
    164, 217, 257; mytho-mania and, 41; Narcis-
    sus and, 201n16; on posture, 171; Second
    Sophistic and, 206–21. See also specific
    works
Plautus, 34n101; Amphitruo by, 31, 77n101;
    Menaechmi by, 96n33; Stichus by, 92
pleonasm, 29, 29n88, 30, 31
Pliny the Elder, 128n117, 180, 220; agalmato-
    philia and, 220n59; Venus of, 242
Pliny the Younger, 306n40
Plutarch of Boetia, 18, 22, 58n40, 121, 302;
    active reading in, 23n67; Advice to the Bride
    and Groom by, 111–12; Amatorius by, 201,
    213–14; Basil of Caesarea and, 66; on
    Colotes, 277n88; Demosthenes in, 180; How

362 SUBJECT INDEX

Plutarch of Boetia (*continued*)
to *Study Poetry* by, 58–59, 62; *Life of Alcibiades* by, 215n46; on Myth of Er, 281–82; Odysseus in, 62, 86; *Phaedrus* in, 215–16; Plato and, 212; *On Progress in Virtue* by, 62–64; *Symposium* by Plato and, 213. *See also On Curiosity*
polypragmôn: *curiositas* and, 92–93, 93n25; "mirror of the text" and, 92, 92n22; in New Comedy, 92, 93, 94, 107; Odysseus as, 48, 48n12, 102; Socrates as, 93n25, 131, 250
polypragmosynê: Aulus Gellius on, 92n22; *curiositas* and, 93n25, 252n18; in *On Curiosity*, 74n91; in Myth of Er, 48n14; of Socrates, 250
polytropia: Cynics and, 46n7; Odysseus and, 105n55
polytropos, 46–47, 46n7; Odysseus and, 101, 105
Praxiteles, Aphrodite/Venus of, 200, 217, 242
Prodicus, 47, 49, 54, 66, 69; "Education of Heracles" by, 181, 186n125, 243; Heracles and, 82; on Hercules, 81; Lady Vice and, 80, 130, 188, 218; in *Memorabilia*, 52
pronus, 166, 167, 170–71, 171n185; Photis and, 229
prudentia, 72, 74, 89; Graverini on, 188; Odysseus and, 104, 105; as self-control, 173–74; Socrates and, 104, 255
pseudo-Cebes, 18
pseudo-Clement, 212
pseudo-Lucian, 198, 237. *See also Amores; Onos*
Psyche. *See Cupid and Psyche*
The Punishment of Dirce, 161, 162

Quintilian, 8n20, 140

Rabelais, 2n2, 3–4, 3n4, 9, 59, 198, 277; *Gargantua* by, 1–2, 11; Sirens and, 48; *voluptas* and, 36–37
reader-response movement/theory, 10, 22n64, 24, 286–87; of Constance School, 21, 21n61, 25; *Erwartungshorizont* and, 23; in Isis book, 247–94; Second Sophistic and, 22, 51–52, 187; in *Symposium* by Plato, 154, 208n30
reformatio, 305–6
Republic (Plato), 41–42; *daemones* in, 273n75;

Hesiod's "two roads" in, 68n71; Macrobius on, 253; *mimesis* in, 139, 146, 150–51, 150n38, 151n40, 155n48; Odysseus in, 250, 268; Socrates in, 93, 150–51, 155n48, 276–77; *speculum* in, 154. *See also* Myth of Er
Rhetorum praeceptor (Lucian), 64–65
rimabundus, 174–75, 174n100; of Diana, 236
Roman comedy, 33, 33n97, 88, 90–92, 92n21, 99, 117–18, 149; *exordium* of, 118, 119n88; generic markers of, 118; Winkler on, 119n88
Roman Eyes (Elsner), 199–200, 199n8

sapientia, 72, 89; Horace and, 100, 100n45; of Socrates, 104, 255
Satyricon (Petronius), 109n67, 126n110, 174n97, 227
Schlam, Carl, 167
scrupulosus, 11; *curiositas* and, 275
Second Sophistic, 18, 19, 22, 39, 44, 53–54; *agalmatophilia* in, 200; Heracles in, 49, 66; imperial period and, 55–62; Odysseus in, 46–47, 55–62; *Phaedrus* in, 197–98; Plato and, 206–21; reader-response movement/theory and, 51–52, 187; Socrates and, 250n11; *Symposium* by Plato and, 197–98. *See also specific topics*
Self-Tormenter (Terence), 92
Seneca the Elder, 135
Seneca the Younger, 6nn15–16, 135; *On the Brevity of Life* by, 6; *De clementia* by, 36–37, 87, 94–95; *inspicere* in, 36–37, 37n114; Lady Virtue in, 96; *Natural Questions* by, 111, 228; Odysseus in, 102; *philosophia* of, 7–8; Piso and, 99n39; Stoics and, 102; *voluptas* in, 95
Septimius Severus, 253, 297–98; *aniles fabulae* and, 8; Clodius Albinus and, 5, 6, 7, 8; *consenecscere* and, 9; on Milesian tales, 33
Sermones (Horace), 93–94, 100, 111
serviles voluptates, 81, 251n15, 295
Sextus of Chaeronea, 108, 121, 302
Shumate, Nancy, 17
Sileni Alcibiadis (Erasmus), 2, 3, 123
Silius Italicus, 18
simulacra deorum, 42, 153n43, 203–4; Socrates and, 124
simulacrum: of Actaeon, 166–67, 169–70, 177–78, 185, 189–95; of Aphrodite/Venus, 239; in *Apologia*, 208–9, 271; of Byrrhena's atrium, 158, 173; in *Cupid and Psyche*, 232; of Diana,

201; of Diana-Actaeon, 40–41; *inspicere* and, 124–25; of Isis, 194; Isis book and, 240; meaning of, 166n72; *mimesis* and, 143; Photis and, 240; *voluptas* and, 144, 194

Sirens, 8n19, 18, 38; Cicero on, 88, 113; *multiscius* and, 75; in Myth of Er, 258–59, 258n38; Odysseus and, 45, 45n5, 47–48, 48n10, 49, 50–51, 50n20, 57–58, 60, 71–72, 75; of Ovid, 259n39; in *Phaedrus*, 57, 171; Rabelais and, 48; in *Symposium* by Plato, 57

Slater, Niall, 135, 158–59

Small World (Lodge), 137–39

Socrates, 19; in *Alcibiades 1*, 225; Alcibiades and, 2, 3, 5, 8, 20, 30n91, 51, 51n22, 58, 58n39, 60, 88, 89, 120, 123–24, 124n106, 145, 188, 209, 233, 244–45, 290, 293; *anteludia* and, 267; in *Apology*, 255, 266, 266n58; Apuleius of Madaura and, 6n15; Aristomenes and, 172; in *Charmides*, 225; in *Crito*, 171n87; *daemones* of, 89, 131, 287, 292; Delphic maxim and, 125, 127, 250, 266; on *erastês*, 211; *Erôs* and, 120, 132; *exemplum* of, 106–7, 123, 132; in *Gorgias*, 7; Heracles and, 82; Homer and, 150–51; *katabasis* and, 274; *logos* of, 132, 152; Maximus of Tyre on, 69–70, 69n75; in *Memorabilia*, 51–52; in Myth of Er, 292; Narcissus and, 148n28, 172–73; New Comedy and, 112; Nietzsche on, 255n24; Odysseus and, 133n132, 187–88, 255–56, 267; Palinode of, 199, 210, 256, 307; as pauper, 122; in *Phaedo*, 198n3, 251, 262, 269; in *Phaedrus*, 24, 27, 29–32, 106, 115, 120–21, 127, 251, 261, 262–63, 266n60, 269, 307; as *polypragmôn*, 93n25, 131, 250; *polypragmosynê* of, 250; *prudentia* in, 104, 255; in *Republic*, 93, 155n48, 276–77; *sapientia* of, 104, 255; Second Sophistic and, 250n11; *simulacra deorum* and, 124; surface-level looking and, 126–36; in *Symposium* by Plato, 2, 5, 8, 20, 51, 58, 58n39, 60, 69, 86, 123, 124, 189, 286–87; in *Theaetetus*, 125n108; "triangulative mirror" of, 109–16

Sôkratikoi logoi, 49

Somnium (Lucian), 64, 65

Sophocles, 12n30

sparagmos: of Actaeon, 177; *ekphrasis* and, 143–44; of Orpheus, 263

spectaculum, 175, 178, 181, 193; *ekphrasis* of, 184

speculum: in *Apologia*, 110, 111, 150; *inspicere*

and, 117; *mimesis* and, 146–49; "mirror of the text" and, 90, 91; Odysseus as, 86; in Terence, 111, 117

Sperlonga, 161; *The Blinding* of *Polyphemus* at, 163; statues of, 164

sphragis, 24, 302–3, 302n23, 304n30

Stichus (Plautus), 92

Stinton, T. C. W., 181

Stoics, 99; *askêsis* and, 63n56; Odysseus and, 46n7, 97, 97n35; Seneca and, 102

Stover, Justin, 273

The Striding Diana, 165, 168, 195

Suetonius, 226–27

Sulpicius Apollonaris, 38

Symposium (Plato), 3; Aphrodite in, 31, 69, 230, 239; *Charmides* (Plato) and, 208; Diotima in, 145–46, 148, 153, 286; *Erôs* in, 64, 153; Hermes in, 204n23; Plutarch and, 213; reader-response movement/theory in, 154, 208n30; in Second Sophistic, 197–98; Sirens in, 48; Socrates in, 2, 5, 8, 20, 51, 58, 58n39, 60, 69, 86, 123, 124, 189, 286–87; *Sôkratikoi logoi*, 49–50

Symposium (Xenophon), 119, 119n90

Synesius of Cyrene, 227

tabula Cebetis, 66–71, 66n67, 67n69, 69n72, 83

Tacitus, 239

Terence: *Adelphoe* by, 90–92; *inspicere* and, 101; Livy and, 94, 94n28; Seneca and, 95; *speculum* and, 111, 117; *topos* of, 94

Tertullian, 298–300, 300n14

Theagenes of Rhegium, 56n31

Theaetetus (Plato), 125n108

Themistius, 18

Titus Castricius, 38

Too, Yun Lee, 148, 204, 204n23, 290n122

topos: of Lady Vice, 72–73; of Odysseus, 56, 57; of Second Sophistic, 65, 67; of Terence, 94

track of life metaphor, 271, 271n71

Trapp, Michael, 35, 35n103, 117–18

"Typhonic choice," 108n61, 115n80, 129–32, 134, 266–67, 266n61, 295

utilitas, 20, 22

Vannini, Angelo, 304nn29–30

Venus, 110n70; of Botticelli, 137–39; Byrrhena's atrium and, 176–77, 181; in *Cupid and*

364 SUBJECT INDEX

Venus (*continued*)
Psyche, 232; Diana-Actaeon and, 143n21; *ekphrasis* of, 143n21, 179–80; hair of, 228; Isis and, 239; in Judgment of Paris, 142–43, 180–81, *182*, *183*, 288; Lady Vice and, 80, 218, 288; Photis and, 179; of Pliny the Elder, 242; of Praxiteles, 242; seductions of, 175–89; *simulacrum* of, 40
Venus Anadyomene, 26–27
Venus pendula, 222n63
Venus Pudica, 32, 200, 201; Photis and, 244
Venus vulgaris, 175, 186; *Cupid and Psyche* and, 230; Lady Virtue and, 190; Photis and, 222
Vergil: *Aeneid* by, 298; Circe in, 226n74; *Georgics* by, 63; Ovid and, 223; *Phaedrus* and, 223n66
Vita Apollonii (Philostratus), 65
voluptas, 20, 22, 35, 85; in *Cupid and Psyche*, 237; Heracles and, 81, 87; Odysseus and, 105; Rabelais and, 36–37; Seneca and, 95
Vorlage, 14, 14n38

Wasps (Aristophanes), 12
Whitmarsh, Tim, 139–41, 289n118
Winkle, Jeffrey, 129
Winkler, J. J., 4, 4n6, 28–29, 44, 305, 305n36; on *ainigma*, 71; *aporia* of, 10, 15–16; on conversion, 15; on *ekphrasis*, 186; on farce, 14n35; on *lector scrupulosus*, 12, 122–23; on *Madaurensem* problem, 302–3; on Roman comedy, 119n88
Works and Days (Hesiod), 48–49, 52–53

Xenophon: Cicero and, 81; Hesiod and, 54; *Kakia* of, 81, 96n32, 181; *Memorabilia* by, 51–52, 80–81; *pronus* and, 171; *Symposium* by, 119, 119n90; Venus in, 181–82
Xenophon of Ephesus, 154–55, 157

Zadorojnyi, Alexei, 86–87
Zahn, Wilhelm, 181n114, *182*
Zimmerman, Maaike, 34n99, 36, 65–66, 72, 184